Paperback ISBN:978-1-990675-03-4
Hardcover ISBN: 978-1-990675-08-9

# Contents

# The Reaper Incarnate

### A Reaped Novella

# Copyright

*Copyright © 2021 C.A. Rene & R.E. Bond*

# Dedication

This one is for Lisa.
Thanks for creating the perfect opportunity for
the best tasting Peanut Butter and Jelly sandwich.

# Prologue

"That's right, baby," he moans as he shoves my head onto his miniscule dick. "Take all of it."
Not a difficult task if I'm being honest.

"I want to go home and fuck my wife knowing your mouth was just there." He sounds like a fucking idiot, and I bet his wife thinks so, too.

I release his needle dick with a pop and raise my head to look him in the face.

"Or you can go home and rape your stepdaughter again?"

His eyes widen and his mouth drops in shock. He begins to push my head away as he stutters, but it's hard to move in a small Honda Fit.

"Who are you?" he chokes out when I sit back in the passenger seat.

"I'll give you three guesses." I smile wide, showcasing my bright white teeth.

"I don't know…" He shakes his head.

"You lose," I sing-song.

I pull the gun from my purse at my feet and press it to his forehead.

"No, wait…" I watch as his small, flaccid dick spouts with piss.

"Gross." I screw up my face and pull the trigger.

The back of his head explodes all over the driver's side window, and I feel blood splatter across my face. I smear my fingers through it, then suck them into my mouth. Nothing tastes better than the blood of a predator.

I reach behind his concave head and press my finger into the blood and brain matter mixture on the window.

*Reaped.*

# Chapter One

## Selene

The overhead streetlight casts a dim yellow aura around me as I lean against the pole, waiting for him. I've tracked him for the past two weeks and the bastard has become predictable.

I'm standing outside of his favorite tavern—he hits this one up on Mondays and Fridays—and he'll stagger out in about ten minutes, looking for a taxi. I settled on this place for our *meeting* because the alleyway beside it is perfect for a clandestine hook up.

"See you next week, Charles." His voice grates on my nerves and when he laughs, I fantasize about cutting it out of his throat.

He stands beside me and peers up then down the street, looking for the bright yellow paint of a cab. I can feel the moment his eyes land on me because my skin crawls and I feel an uncontrollable urge to pop them out of his head.

"Have you been waiting long?" he slurs, and I curl my hands into fists.

"About ten minutes." I keep my voice level and sweet.

I swing my gaze to meet his and feel the bile creep up my throat at his appreciative perusal. His highlighted blond hair sways in the breeze and his green eyes crinkle with mirth. Those full lips pull up into a handsome smirk. He kind of looks like a Ken doll.

"I haven't seen you here before." He stumbles, then rights himself.

"I've seen you," I say seductively, and slowly flutter my lashes.

"Is that so?" He two-steps excitedly.

"Oh yes," I nod. "I think you are one of the most handsome men I've seen."

"No!" He *pffts* with his mouth and waves me off.

"Mm-hmm." I nod again.

"Well, I'm here now." He holds his hands out and stumbles. "Question is, what are you going to do with me?"

See? Predictable cunt.

"Hmm." I tap my chin, pretending to be deep in thought. "How about we go down that pathway and get acquainted?"

"The alley?" His eyes widen with excitement.

"Why not?" I shrug.

He motions for me to lead the way and I grin, knowing I have him right where I want him. I step into the alley and the little light from the streetlamp completely dissipates. It's pitch black and I can smell urine, making me gag.

All it takes him is three steps, and he has my face pressed against the brick. I roll my eyes and pretend to panic.

"Hey!" I call out. "Take it easy."

"You're an easy little bitch," he growls, and the stench of whiskey on his breath floods my nostrils. "I usually like them fighting."

"I know." I say as I rear my head back and crack him in the nose.

He falls back against the adjacent wall, clutching his nose, and roaring. I stalk toward him and kick him swiftly in the balls, grinning when he falls to his knees.

His nose is running with blood and dripping off his chin. His hands are cupping his sac as he sways and cries, and I bend at the waist to meet him eye to eye.

"You've been naughty." I wag my finger at him. "Very naughty."

He begins to moan and plead with me to leave him alone.

"Can't do that." I straighten. "Remember all those campus girls that begged for the same thing? You didn't show them mercy."

"Who are you?" Spit flies from his mouth, and blood runs between his teeth.

"You all ask the exact same questions and expect an answer," I tsk. "What does it matter? You'll be dead soon."

The fucker throws his head back and laughs at my revelation. "Dead?"

"Yeah." I pull the knife out of its holster on my hip and point it at his face.

The smile falls from his mouth and his eyes darken with anger. I watch as he lifts one of his hands toward me and I swing the blade, cutting across the flesh at his wrist. The blood spurts and rapidly flows from the open arteries, hitting the pavement in large splatters.

His other hand grabs his wrist and I laugh as the blood oozes out around his fingers. He looks up at me with shock lining his features and leans over to puke at my feet. Lovely.

I knee him in the forehead, and he falls back against the wall, his arms flying to his sides. Like taking candy from a fucking baby.

I bend down and grab his uncut wrist, slowly running the knife's edge over the skin, watching as it splits apart. He moans and tries to sit up, but I've given him a few good cracks on the head, not to mention how drunk he is.

The blood pools around his hand and his body begins to twitch as death enters his limbs. I pull my finger through the crimson fluid and draw a scythe onto the ground. Then I rise, wipe the blood off the blade with his shirt, and tuck it back in the holster.

I leave the alley, whistling softly and planning my next hit.

# Chapter Two

## Selene

The worst thing about my life revolving around my work is that I'm always fucking hungry. Whether it be my next victim, or food, it's all the same. I shut down the darknet chat on my laptop and try to calm myself. So many motherfuckers on there looking for women and children to abuse and they are all falling into my traps.

I watch the world go by out the window of my small apartment, shoveling my burger into my mouth as if it's my last meal. Ketchup oozes out and drips onto my plate, and I absently swipe it up with my finger and suck it clean.

I close my eyes and smile at the memory of my last kill, his blood covered skin giving me the same feeling as a bright Christmas tree would for a child. I can't tell you how many people I've wiped from the face of the earth, getting vengeance for those who were victimized by those worthless pieces of shit.

I am no fucking saint, but someone has to right the wrongs of those who have no remorse for their actions. Hell, I don't give a shit if they feel remorse or not. There is no forgiveness when it comes to the predators of this world. Nothing pisses me off more than a man who thinks he has the right to touch a woman or a child, just because they smile in their direction or give them a boner, just for looking good.

Everyone knows there's a vigilante running around town, slaying those who prey upon the innocent or vulnerable. I find my kills on the darknet, searching for the sick fucks who answer to my ass of wanting torture, and then let them lead me to all their friends. Obviously, no one knows it's me, because I don't want the praise or jail time that comes along with it.

I just want those to pay who can't keep their dicks and hands to themselves.

I've been posing as a prostitute for years now, and the amount of devils in disguise are disgusting. I always find the irony in using sex as a weapon to draw them in. Kind of feels like karma and a good way to get revenge.

I make them all suffer, but the ones I stalk who have put their vulgar dicks near a child? Well, I can be a little dramatic with their exits sometimes.

It can take weeks of learning their patterns, and I enjoy the hunt just as much as the kill.

My heart rate spikes with excitement at the thought of my next job. He is a typical rich asshole who thinks his shit doesn't stink, but he has so many skeletons in his closet that I just know he must suffer in the worst way. He loves kids a little too much, and women are never the same after being with him. He is sadistic, and he gets off on their pain and tears.

I've been watching him for the last week or two, seeing the most fucked up deals take place, and I hunger to carve him to pieces with my knife. I can see his clean canvas in my mind, becoming mixed with blood and slashes as he cries for mercy. I can't wait to hear that sick fucker beg.

I'd bathe in his blood for those lost at his hands.

I finish my burger and drop the plate in the sink, wandering into my bedroom to find my notebook. I keep tabs on everyone I'm hunting, burning the papers when I'm done.

I glance over my notes, memorizing as much as I can. He meets with his friends every Wednesday at the bar on Main Street, usually trying to lure some poor woman into his grasp. He has lunch at the Chinese takeout downtown every Thursday and Friday while he meets another person who just happens to be on my list, who is ironically the guy who's sold him children previously. The last kid was an eight-year-old boy.

I scowl and drop my notebook, running my fingers through my long blonde hair and pull sharply to feel the burn. I can't lose control of my emotions, no matter how angry my findings make me.

I should have a plan before spraying brain matter and blood everywhere. If I slash him to pieces too quickly, he won't suffer, and this man needs to suffer badly.

He has a son who I assume is as bad as he is, but I haven't set my eyes on him just yet.

Daddy dearest ought to go first, then his child trafficking friend is next. I'll get around to the rich asshole son after that.

I'd already put myself in the rich asshole senior's path, making sure he noticed me. I bumped into him as he was leaving the Chinese place the other day, pretending to apologize dramatically while reining in my need to gut him right there in the street.

I'm crazy, not stupid.

I made sure to wear the smallest amount of clothing possible, allowing him to steady me from the collision as his eyes took me in. He was interested, which made everything so much easier for the next time I confronted him. He was going to think he'd hit the fucking jackpot when I just happen to be at the Chinese place for lunch before he arrives, and I'll let him pay for my food because it's the least the asshole can do.

Men always think you owe them after they've done something nice for you, because they're fucking pigs. They only hold the door open for you so they can check your ass out as you leave, and they can be so self-righteous that they think they're doing you a favor for letting you choke on their pathetic dicks as if it were a gift just for you.

He'll be the one choking when I cut his dick off and shove it down his throat for choking the last woman he had to death.

# Chapter Three

## Selene

"Order up for Selene!" the guy behind the counter yells. I head to the front of the restaurant and take the bag containing my chicken chow mein, smiling at the guy.

"Selene." I hear his voice and goosebumps break out along my skin. "That's a lovely name."

I look up into the piece of shit's nearly black eyes and put on my prettiest smile. "My mother named me after the Greek goddess of the moon."

"Here you are, Henry, same as always." He's handed his lunch.

"I will pay for Selene's today as well, Tyler," Henry says with a smile my way. Look at that, all these asshole predators are so fucking predictable.

"Oh, no!" I throw my hand to my exposed cleavage, watching as his eyes follow. "You don't have to do that, sir."

His eyes shine with appreciation at my calling him sir, and I feel the bile scorching up my fucking throat.

"It's the least I can do for nearly mowing you down last week." He winks.

I giggle, making sure my tits bounce, and watching as his eyes latch on to their movements. He hands a credit card to Tyler and leans his hip on the counter. He looks sharp for a man in his late fifties, a tailored suit, expensive leather shoes, and what looks to be an authentic gold tie clip.

His salt and pepper hair is combed back over his head to hide his balding crown and his face is clean shaven. He's handsome and to the unsuspecting woman, I would assume he's alluring, but to me he's a bag of shit and I can hardly stand the fucking stench.

"Are you bringing that back to your office to eat?" He asks as he takes the receipt and thanks Tyler.

"Oh, I don't have an office." I look up at him through my dramatic, false lashes. "My job is a bit … well … unconventional."

We step out onto the street, and he gives me a slow once over, his eyes devouring me from my feet up. He knows exactly what I mean by unconventional.

He reaches into his inside blazer pocket and hands me a business card. Henry Walton. C.C.R.E. Import and Export services.

"Call me to discuss business sometime." His fingers brush along my arm and I plaster a smile on my face. *Don't kill the cunt on the street*, I pray to myself.

"I will, Henry." I watch as he steps to a black Rolls Royce and gives me a final look over his shoulder.

Henry doesn't have a single fucking clue what he just got himself into.

I lift the hood of my ankle length black trench and stand across the street from Henry's mansion. Tonight, there's a drop off from the piece of shit human trafficker and I wanted to be here to watch as much as I can.

I hear heavy metal music blare as a sleek black Dodge Challenger comes veering from up the street. I hide farther behind the large oak and watch as the wrought-iron gates open. The car stops just inside, and two guys step out. I can't really distinguish the features, but they look like fucking assholes.

Both have black bandanas on their heads and are dressed in dark clothing, with leather jackets covering their frames. They lean against the car, and one sparks a joint, taking a deep toke before handing it to the other.

This is who Henry associates with? A bunch of fucking street kids? They are a direct contrast to the businessman image he is trying to portray, and the only thing I can think of is that he hired some goons for the exchange that's about to go down.

They smoke their joint with minimal interaction and a few minutes later; I see a large cargo van pull up to the gates. It's black with blacked-out windows and the license plates are missing. Not fucking suspicious at all.

The gangsters straighten up when the van rolls through the gates and they follow behind it on foot, reaching for their pieces tucked into the backs of their jeans.

They get farther away and out of my line of sight, and I huff against the tree in frustration. If I want to know more, I will have to get closer, and to get closer means I have to fuck the old man.

Guess it's time to set up a business meeting with the fucker.

I flip the thick, expensive looking business card between my fingers and sigh. It's so fucking hard keeping up with a charade, but I took on this work so I will see it to the end.

I dial the number for his cell phone and gag when he picks up.

"Walton here."

"Henry?" I make myself sound innocent and confused. "Sorry, may I speak with Henry?"

"Selene?" His voice lowers, and I can hear the fucking undercurrents of satisfaction in it.

"Yes, it's me," I giggle.

"I'm happy you called. What can I do for you?" Why does he make that sound so fucking slimy?

"I ... ah ... wanted to discuss business?" I saturate my tone with uncertainty.

"You called the right place. Where shall we have this discussion?"

"I usually have them in my client's car—"

"I'll meet you at the corner of Elmer and Delia," he cuts me off. "Same car as earlier."

Before I can even open my mouth to confirm, I hear the dial tone in my ear and growl at his confident manner. I can't wait to see him scared and begging me for mercy.

I make the choice to dress in my appropriate business attire and I straighten out my long wavy blonde hair, letting it hang loose down my back. I line my big baby blues in kohl, making them pop even more, and then I brush some blush onto my freckled cheeks, giving my pale skin some color.

I squeeze my girls into a leather crop top, grinning when their fullness nearly pops me in the chin, and then I pair it with a leather mini, the bottoms of my ass cheeks peeking out. My best fucking business suit.

I finish it off with a pair of thigh high heels because, duh, Pretty Woman, and pull my trench over the top. I give myself a once over in the mirror and chuckle at my appearance. Thank God for the genes that make me look at least five years younger than my twenty-five. I know Mr. Walton likes them young.

I'm ready to get this shit started and I can feel my skin crawling with the need for blood.

# Chapter Four

## Selene

My heels clack on the pavement as I make my way toward the Rolls Royce, the driver exiting the vehicle to open the back door for me and give us privacy.

I murmur a polite thank you as I ease myself inside, finding myself beside a beaming Henry Walton.

He wastes no time handing me a champagne glass, his fingers brushing against mine slightly.

"Selene, I'm so glad you called," he says with a toothy grin, eyeing my trench coat with annoyance.

I bite back a scoff and slip the apparently offending piece of clothing off my shoulders, pretending to admire the interior of the car.

"What a beautiful car you have. It's so roomy."

He licks his lips as his eyes roam my barely covered body, resting on my tits with no shame.

"I do enjoy beautiful things. Can we jump straight into business talk?" he asks, his voice sending unwanted shivers down my spine that he misreads as pleasure.

Typical sleazebag thinking he's making me cream in my panties with the temptation. My coochie is as dry as a nun's, thanks to him.

I bat my lashes at him and tuck a loose piece of my blonde hair behind my ear to act shy. Men like Henry feel powerful for dominating the quiet girls and turning them into freaks in the sheets.

"Of course, Mr. Walton. What would you like to know?"

He boldly places his hand on my thigh, his eyes darkening.

"How about you suck me off and we'll talk after that? Kind of like a try before you buy?" Is he for real?

I giggle, biting my lip as I peer over at him.

"Show me what goods I'm working with then, and I'll see if I can impress you," I say coyly, a deep chuckle coming from him as he reaches for his belt.

"Curious little thing, aren't you? How long have you been at the job? I haven't seen you before, and I think I'd remember a pretty face like yours."

He pulls his dick free, and I lick my lips when I know he's watching. He's a decent size, but I bet he has no fucking idea how to use it. They rarely do, which is why they prey on those who are too innocent to know the difference. It gives them an ego boost to make someone cry.

"Oh wow, Mr. Walton, I don't think I'll be able to take it all. I'm still pretty new at this, so you might have to guide me," I gasp, putting a hand over my mouth for dramatics.

I know how to take dick, but it does wonders for his ego.

He smirks, encouraging me to slide closer to him.

"I'll show you just how I like it. So, this time is free?" he asks, waiting for me to get onto my knees on the seat and his eyes drift over me to stare at my ass in the air. I can't wait to bleed the dick-bag out.

I nod, trying to look nervous as I lean down, stretching my mouth to accommodate him. He lets me slide my mouth up and down his length a few times before his fingers thread through my silky straight hair, tightening to the point of pain as I expected him to.

"Open that pretty mouth all the way for me. Yes, that's it," he murmurs, before slamming my head down firmly, causing me to choke.

He keeps moving my head how he wants me, not giving a shit that I'm choking on saliva and his stupid dick.

"You like that, you little whore? You like choking on my fucking cock?" he growls, tightening his fist in my hair even more until he's relentlessly fucking himself with my face.

My eyes water, and my stomach lurches as he reaches past me and slaps my ass hard, showing me the monster he hides away, as he keeps speaking down to me like shit.

"I bet you've taken a lot of dicks, you filthy slut. You'd be nothing without men like me helping you pay your way in society. Do you think of all that cum you take whenever you pay a bill? When you eat your lunch? Girls like you need men like me, because it's the only way someone could ever want you."

I choke some more, his hand coming down hard on my ass again. I let him belittle me until he holds my face down and grunts his release. He lets me choke on his dick and cum for a moment before removing his grip and allowing me to sit back. I wipe the moisture from under my eyes and catch my breath, running my tongue over my lips and giving him a sweet smile.

"Thank you, Mr. Walton," I force out, knowing it's the right thing to say as his eyes light up while he absently fixes his pants. He looks thoughtful for a moment before replying.

"I think this will be an exceptionally good investment. It's been a long time since I've come across a woman with manners and who acknowledges what I give her. I'm taking you to my house to clean up," then he grabs his phone and sends a text, the driver instantly climbing in behind the wheel.

This is not part of my plan, but I'm not going to say no to being invited into his house. I have to scope it out eventually, so it just makes my work a little easier without having to be so sneaky.

We don't speak the entire drive, but he won't shut the fuck up once when we arrive, enjoying show off all his money and possessions. He takes my arm and guides me up the front steps, leading me into the main room that houses the most pompous works of art I've ever seen.

Most are paintings of himself, but there are a few of himself and whom I would assume is his son the farther into the house we go. It just makes me want to kill him even more, no one should be that far up their own ass.

We walk through multiple rooms and hallways, and I try hard to remember as much as I can. I need to map the place out on paper when I get home so I can add to my plan of attack.

Once in the bathroom, he points to the sink and a small cupboard.

"Everything you need should be in there. I'll be in my office. One of the staff will show you where to go when you're done." Then he turns and leaves me alone, like the stupid idiot that he is.

I quickly clean my face and rinse my mouth out with some mouthwash, glaring at the painting above the toilet of him naked. That's a little weird.

I take my time as I wander back throgh the house, adding to my mental map and wishing I had my knife on me to get it over with, but too many people know I'm with him, so I have no choice but to wait.

My heels seem to echo through the house on the marble floors, and I slow when I get to the kitchen, finding his son drinking a bottle of water, his throat working as he swallows. He's only in a pair of shorts. My eyes linger on his tattoo covered abs before I look up at his face.

He works out, that's for sure.

He finally glances over at me, his eyes widening in surprise at the company before his nostrils flare and his eyes narrow.

"Who the fuck are you?" he growls, reminding me that this Ab God is just a junior version of his asshole daddy. I can practically smell the money and arrogance on him.

I give him a bright smile, clasping my hands together in front of me and drawing his attention right to my tits as the leather pulls tighter across them, pushing them further together.

"I'm sorry, I'm a little lost. Do you know where Mr. Walton's office is? He told me to find him when I was finished in the bathroom," I ask softly, his gaze snapping back to mine. He takes me in for a second before rolling his eyes.

"Henry's office is back down the hallway and up the stairs. It's on the left," he grunts, turning and stalking out of the room.

"I'm Selene," I blurt out, making him pause in the doorway. He peers over his shoulder at me, pity underlining his features before he snaps out of it and snorts.

"Good for you. I don't give a fuck." Then he leaves me standing there without a backwards glance.

His ass is all right, too.

I make my way in the direction he told me to go, but someone steps in front of me and blocks my path.

"Mr. Walton had to take a business call and has asked me to show you out."

No apology, nothing. Typical rich asshole moves.

I give him a smile and nod.

"I completely understand. I'd hate to be in his way. Please tell him thank you for the hospitality he gave me." I beam, wanting to puke at my own voice. I hate my job sometimes because I am not the type to be sweet, let alone grateful.

He nods, motioning behind me to get me to walk, making sure to stay by my side until we reach the door. I'm hoping he'll at least call me a cab, but the moment I am out the door, it is shut right behind me, and I'm on my own.

I roll my eyes and walk down the driveway, heading toward home.

His son's car speeds past me, and I snort, not at all surprised that Walton Junior doesn't offer me a ride.

Zander Walton is a daddy's boy, and I can't wait to get to work on him, too.

It's going to be such a shame to waste something that looks so good. I can't lie.

# Chapter Five

## *Zander*

My father and the dirty fucking prostitutes he brings to our house. I am about to fucking lose my shit. I pull the car out of the garage and speed down the driveway. It's not until I've hit the bottom that I see the girl walking alone. Should I wait here and pick her up?

Fuck it, she made her choice with him and now she can fucking walk in it.

I pull out onto the street and press the Bluetooth button on my wheel.

"Call Blaze."

"Calling Blaze." I've set my spoken voice to an Australian female who sounds as hot as fucking sin, and I've named her Jocelyn.

"'Sup?" Blaze's deep voice fills my 'Vette.

"We need to make a move on this bastard because I am fucking losing it," I snarl.

"Bro, hold it down. You need to breathe. It's coming and soon. Do not fuck our plans up or else I will kill you as well."

That's Blaze. We've been friends from middle school, but the guy wouldn't bat an eye if he had to kill me.

"Yeah." I scrub a hand down my face and try to relax.

"Come over and do some lines," he says and hangs up.

I was doing well until he brought one into the house. Was it fucking necessary? Did it need to be so blatant in my face so soon after my mother's death?

I pull a U-turn, burning my tires, and head back toward Blaze's. I need a fucking night to relax and not think of all the shit that's weighing me the fuck down.

When I pull into his driveway, I can hear the music blaring and a line of other cars parked. Looks like a party, and I'm ready to lose myself in coke and pussy.

I walk into the house to see girls dancing on the tables with their tits out and random couples making out in darkened corners. Fuck yes.

"Zan!" I hear Blaze call out, and I turn into the kitchen.

He has his table set up with a buffet of drug choices and a girl is kneeling in front of him, sucking his dick, his piercing glinting in the kitchen lights.

"When you said a few lines, I thought you meant a few lines, not this shit." I grin and bump fists with him.

"Sit down, bro." He points to a bitch to the right. "Fill Stacey's mouth with something."

"My name is Tracy." She rolls her eyes but comes forward, anyway.

I pull out a chair and grin when she kneels in front of me and undoes my pants. Blaze has the best fucking parties.

"Take one," he says as he chucks me a bag of pills.

I open the bag and pop one in my mouth, swallowing it dry, and then I'm feeling lips wrap around my dick. This is what life is supposed to be like.

"All your dicks are being sucked and mine is lonely sitting on my balls."

I open my eyes at Santos' voice and grin when I see the bastard leaning against the fridge with a beer to his mouth. He's crazy and loves to watch anything bleed. I really do mean anything.

Blaze groans and I look over at him with his head tipped back and his mouth open wide. He's a scary-looking motherfucker with that angry scar down his face and standing close to six and a half feet. None of us get in his way because he's fucking mean and, like I said before, he doesn't care who he has to kill.

This is just what I needed to get my mind off my father and the girl with the big blue eyes. Just thinking about her tits has me coming down Stacey's throat.

"Yes, Stacey," I groan, and she slaps my thigh.

"My name is fucking Tracy," she retorts as she wipes my cum from her lip.

What the fuck ever.

"Zan!" Santos calls out. "Tuck your little white dick away and come check something out."

"Fuck you." I grin and get up from my seat.

Whatever pill Blaze gave me is working fast, and the room begins to haze around the edges. I grab a beer from the fridge and follow Santos into the billiards room. There on one of the tables is a girl hogtied and Darius is plowing into her from behind.

"Holy fuck." I chuckle.

"She consented." Santos laughs and pulls out his switchblade. "I want to watch her bleed a bit. What do you think?"

He gets that wicked look in his eye, and I know I'm in for a show.

I shrug and watch as he sets his beer down on the table and stands to the side of the chick. The noises she's making sounds like enjoyment, so I lean against the wall and take a swig of my beer.

Santos runs the blunt side of his blade along her back, underneath her hogtied limbs, and then runs it down between her ass cheeks. Santos has an unhealthy obsession with blood, and he loves to see it run from his victims or his sexual partners. It makes no fucking difference.

Darius doesn't slow his thrusts, even though Santos's blade comes close to his dick.

"Look at her pussy, Zan," Santos says as the tip of the blade presses against her asshole. "Isn't she pink and pretty?"

Darius slams in one more time and groans his release. The girl shudders and her screams are muffled by the gag in her mouth. Darius pulls out and grabs Santos' beer, downing its contents in one fucking go.

"What's up, Zan?" He grins as his fucking dick flops around, still wet from the girl's pussy.

"Nothin' man, looks like you guys got this party started early." I grin at him.

"That's sweet pussy." He thumbs over his shoulder.

I watch as Santos drops his pants and lines himself up to the girl's entrance, his knife resting on her lower back. He eases himself inside and scoops up his knife. I know what comes next and I'm not much of a fan. I push off the wall just as Santos' knife cuts into the girl's lower back and Darius is right back there, both dipping into her blood with their fingers as the girl screams.

Not my thing.

I leave the room and stumble toward the back porch, my vision blurring. This is the fucking life, not having to watch flesh exchanges and crying bitches in your own front yard. That shit isn't fun on any day.

# Chapter Six

## Selene

I finally get home and curse when I pull off my thigh highs, blisters raw on my feet. The fucking asshole. No Ubers were around that area and I just decided to say fuck it and walk home. The worst mistake.

At least something good came from the fucking bullshit. I got a tour of the cunt's house, and now I have to make a complete plan. This isn't like any of my usual victims. Henry Walton is a big fucking fish, and I can't trap him in a car to blow his brains out. It just won't work.

I have to plan this out to a T and also consider every fucking alternative that can happen. I am also working on a short time crunch because the asshole's next shipment of girls is coming up, and I need to somehow kill him, then save those females.

I was kind of hoping to see some evidence of where he keeps them in the house, but that was just wishful thinking. I knew this shit wasn't going to be easy, and I knew frying a big fish like Henry would be fucking difficult.

Admittedly, I didn't think the pervy fucker would have such a hot fucking son and if this situation were completely different, he'd be exactly my type. The second I saw him, I knew I would climb that fucker like a tree. But just the thought of him being anything like daddy dearest sours the sentiment instantly.

I start my shower and wait for this cheap ass apartment to spew out the hot water. My savings are beginning to run out and I know I need to wrap this up as soon as possible.

I peel out of the leather outfit and step into the hot water. I still can't get the sight of Henry's son out of my mind, the way his throat worked when swallowing the water, or his abs glistening with sweat, and that voice, all gruff and angry.

The hot water cascades over my body and I lift my foot to press into the tub's edge. It's been a while since I've even cared about my own needs, always about the men I must kill, and never getting myself off.

My fingers skim down over my large breasts, giving my nipple a tweak on the way, and down my soft belly to settle over my mound. My heart rate kicks up and I run my fingers through my folds. I moan, tipping my head back and feeling the water rush over my face, the feeling refreshing.

I circle my clit and think of Henry's son, those dark angry eyes, and rough voice. I feel myself grow wet and slide two fingers inside, working myself exactly how I like it.

My other hand comes up and tugs at my nipple, sending tingles straight to my pussy. I can't erase his face from my brain and it's perplexing to be masturbating to a sick son of a bitch, but I can't stop myself now.

My thumb hits my clit as my fingers dance inside of me, brushing that spot I know will send me over the edge quickly.

I can feel my wetness coating my hand and I rub myself back and forth, my lower belly beginning to tighten. I wish I were riding his dick and I wish his father were watching it all happen. Then, when I was done, I would slice both of their throats and bathe in their blood.

That thought has me tumbling over the edge as visions of Henry gripping his throat and his son screaming for mercy floods my senses.

My pussy contracts around my fingers and my release continues as I envision the warm water as their blood spraying over my face.

That is a first. I have never gotten off to a victim and the fantasy of their deaths, but I may make it a fucking routine now.

I finish up in the shower and pad my way over to the papers scattered on my desk. Thank god I'm fucking relaxed after that shower because looking at this shit shows me just how much work I have.

Time to get this fucking show on the road.

# Chapter Seven

## Selene

I pull an all-nighter, mapping out the obnoxiously large mansion and marking as many things as I can remember about the layout. Every door I walked through, every stupid painting, everything.

I mutter to myself as my feet throb from the walk home, cursing out the rude cunt for the millionth time for not bringing me home. I don't want him knowing where I live, but he could have dropped me a lot fucking closer to home instead of expecting me to walk.

I flick through some papers I'd scribbled on recently, double checking his movements and actions I'd noticed through the week. I add that his son obviously lives at home, which is annoying as fuck, but not a complete issue. If I'm lucky, I can get the pair of the rich cunts in one go, I just have to play it smart.

I stash everything away before grabbing my shoes and calling an Uber, wandering outside to wait for it on the curb.

My day is planned out well.

I'll have breakfast at the diner in town to wake my ass up properly. I need to buy a new dress for my next meet with Henry, and then the local bar is calling my name. I really need a fucking stiff drink.

I indulge a little too much on breakfast, knowing it'll hurt the bank, but I'm fucking starving, so it's worth it. Especially when they bring out my plate, that's piled high with eggs, bacon, and toast. The coffee is a gift from the gods, too.

I take my time eating, scoping out the other customers and keeping my ears open for anything interesting. It is amazing how many people talk about shit that they shouldn't, making my life a hell of a lot easier.

Now that I feel slightly human again, I walk the short distance across the street to the dress store, browsing through the stunning dresses until my eyes land on a tight, thigh high black dress. It's dipped low in the back, and the moment I try it on, I know it's the one.

It makes my tits look fucking amazing, and once I add some heels to the outfit, my legs will look fucking stunning, too.

I guess all I need now is a drink.

I wander farther down the street to the bar, surveying the room as I sit on a stool and order a drink. I'm aware of the drunken sleazebag beside me, but I blatantly ignore him and sip my whiskey, scanning the room again before turning my attention back to my drink.

"Hey, you look lonely, dollface," Sleazebag slurs, almost falling off his bar stool as he leans closer. The smell of whiskey and cigarettes is sickeningly strong on his breath, and I fight the urge to gag.

"I'm talking to you, you stuck-up bitch!" he growls when I continue to ignore him, my eyes finally sliding to his as I cock my head a fraction.

"I was hoping you'd get the picture and take a hike," I say sweetly, his bloodshot eyes narrowing.

"Fucking slut!" he spits out, staggering to his feet to try and tower over me. If I were going to run away from the asshole, his breath would have done it, not his height. He is barely five and a half feet tall.

He jabs his fat finger into my chest, stumbling slightly as he belches in my face.

"You think you're too good for me?" he demands, and I let out a light laugh.

"I know for a fucking fact that I am. Like I said, take a hike, asshole."

I brace myself as he throws himself at me, almost knocking me off balance, but a hand comes out of nowhere and grabs the back of the guy's shirt, hauling him back sharply. Before the drunken dick-bag can react, a fist hits his face just before the side of his head is slammed down onto the bar.

My eyes flick over to my defender, and I'm surprised as fuck to see the rich asshole's son standing there, holding the guy down by the back of the neck as he struggles.

"Hank, the fuck have I told you about attacking women who don't want your shriveled-up dick? Apologize. Now," he demands, surprising me further. I was unaware the prick even knew the word apologize.

The man stutters, rambling on about some random crap, but Zander growls loudly, slamming him down again.

"Hank, I'm not fucking around."

"Sorry, Miss," the man who's apparently named Hank blurts out, stumbling away the moment he's let go. Cowardly piece of shit.

Zander's eyes skim over me before his lips kick up into a cruel smirk.

"You're the paid whore that Henry brought home yesterday."

I quirk an eyebrow, grabbing my drink and downing it before replying.

"I haven't taken any money from Mr. Walton, so the name calling is a little unnecessary if you ask me," I say dryly, but he snorts and leans against the bar, not taking his eyes off me.

"No one was asking you."

I turn my attention back to the bar, flagging the bartender down to pour me another drink, but Zander's eyes are burning a hole in the side of my head, so I struggle to keep my no fucks given attitude in place. All I can think about is him bending me over the fucking bar and plowing himself into my pussy. Spectators be damned.

When I don't give him another glance, he crosses his arms and speaks again, his voice rough.

"Are you honestly sitting here alone? Let me guess, you're looking for your next client?"

I down most of my fresh drink and shrug.

"I wanted a drink, so I'm having one. Why do you care? I can handle myself," I say curtly, as annoyance takes over his features.

"I don't give a fuck what happens to you. I was just calling you out for being stupid. This place is probably teeming with herpes, so have at it," he grits out, his fingers twitching by his side as he uncrosses his arms.

"Makes all the sense that you're here. Anyway, I was thirsty, and I have things to do, so I'd better be on my way. Please tell Henry I said hello, sir," I answer smoothly, standing and turning to leave, but his voice stops me.

"Don't call me 'sir', I'm not my father and I'm sure as shit not middle-aged. I'm Zander," he grunts out, and I'm not sure who is more surprised, me or him.

I give him a soft smile, reaching out to touch his arm lightly on my way past him.

"Well, Zander, please tell your father I said hello," Then I walk out, making sure to sway my hips as I go.

I feel his burning gaze on me until I close the door behind me.

# Chapter Eight

## Zander

"Fuuuuck, who's the walking wet dream?" Santos asks as I join the guys in the back at a booth. I was pretty sure the horny bastard had unlimited cum and stamina, because he literally blew his load down some slut's throat out in the side alley when we arrived.

I still can't believe I fucking helped that dumb slut Selene, let alone actually gave her my name. The fuck was wrong with me?

I shake the thoughts of her out of my head, giving Santos a bored glance.

"She's nobody, just some paid whore Henry brought home yesterday," I reply, taking a drink from Darius, who smirks at me.

"Paid whore, huh? Get her digits from your dad so I can throw some dough her way. I want her trussed up in my bed pronto. She has the perfect pale skin to mark with my ropes."

"You'd really stick your dick in something that Henry's banging? Dude, c'mon. Have a little bit of dignity," I scoff, but Santos laughs like a fucking hyena, his gaze jumping between me and Darius.

"I'd sure as shit fuck her. She's hot as sin, and I bet she screams real pretty against my blade. You honestly wouldn't tap that? You should hit her up and see if you can get a family deal going on since Henry's boning her, but then tell her we're all cousins, so we get a discount too."

I have no idea how to handle him some days.

"So what if she's hot? I don't want to fuck her," I snort, but Darius grins and nudges Santos.

"I say we fuck her. Wanna tag team?" Jesus fucking Christ.

Blaze watches them silently as they plot their next sexcapade, but he finally looks up at me and smirks cruelly, the scar stretching on his face slightly with the motion.

"Just get her number and let them have her, since you don't want her. Besides, if they scare her enough, you won't have to worry about seeing her in your house again. The best way to get a bitch to never come back is to let Santos' crazy ass near them."

The man has a point, but something nags inside me, making me scowl. I don't want them to scare her to death, but the thought of never having her in the house again sucks.

There's something strange about her, and I'm a curious kind of guy. The guys were right, too. I did want to fuck her, but there is no way in hell that I'd let my dick go anywhere near a cunt my dad has been in.

Wait, what if she ends up being my stepmom? I can't handle that idea at all. Apart from being pissed at Henry for moving on so fast, I don't want Selene under my dad's firm hand.

He's messed me up, so fuck knows what he'd do to her.

He'd break her, and I don't think she has any idea on what she's messing with.

"Earth to Zander! Where the fuck did you go, asshole? You in wet pussy land with your pin dick again?" Darius exclaims as he snaps his fingers in my face, drawing me back to the conversation. I hadn't meant to zone out like that.

Santos grins, practically bouncing in his seat.

"So, you gonna let us play with her? You sure you don't wanna play with her cunt before I get my hands on it? Can't promise I won't break her," he says with glee, high-fiving Darius as I sigh and motion toward them with my hand.

"Just don't break her too quickly, all right? I wanna figure out if she's just sex to Henry, or if he's got his eyes on her a little closer to home. She claims she's never received money from him. I don't like the idea of some bitch becoming my new mommy when the cunt looks younger than me," I grumble, causing Darius to groan and rub his dick through his pants with no shame. He's a lower level of crazy compared to Santos, but the fucker is still twisted.

"I'm gonna get her to call me daddy while she's bouncing on my dick. Fuck, I bet it would be hot as fuck coming from those lips when she's breathless. Santos, we gotta make her call us daddy."

"If the cunt's speaking, she's not screaming. I don't give a fuck what she calls you, but she's gonna be screaming and bleeding for me," Santos smirks, not hiding his excitement as it flashes in his eyes.

I hope you're ready, Selene.

My boys are coming for you.

# Chapter Nine

## Selene

Ican't believe that piece of shit Walton Jr. was at the fucking bar. I didn't see that coming, and now I'm going to have to add watching him on the list.

Zander. I knew his name before today, of course, having stalked the fuck out of his father, but there weren't any recent pictures of him I could find online, and he and his father didn't seem to like to be around each other, save for when they're trading in meat.

I get inside my little apartment and throw the dress onto my threadbare couch, walking straight for my bottle of whiskey. Now I have to play the waiting game. If Henry wants me, he has my number, and it needs to be him that wants me. Then all of this can really take off.

I need to release the pent-up anger I have for Zander and his peekaboo act today; I think a late-night shift at my unconventional fucking job sounds nice. I pull out a thick manilla envelope from under my couch cushions and open it up.

Inside is a compilation of hits I need to get through this year and as thick as it is now, it was once twice as large. I've been a busy fucking girl.

I hold up the first paper and grin. Looks like I'll be paying a certain gynecologist a visit.

This man, Dr. Carl Ignis, likes to touch women inappropriately and then rapes them for good measure. A few women have come forward, but it's always been shut down due to no evidence and Dr. Ignis being an upstanding citizen with a family at home.

Dr. Ignis is a piece of shit, and I can't wait to get my hands bloody.

I dress in a pair of black skinny jeans and a white crop top, pairing it with my trench. Carl likes to peruse the few blocks that's known for young prostitutes and seedy drug deals. It's Friday, so let's see if Carl comes out to play.

I'm fucking walking around in these fucking boots again, but I can't help how much I enjoy the connection to Pretty Woman, and I'll gladly take the pain. A few of the girls I know call out to me and a few others screw up their faces. There's no in-between.

"Have any of you seen the gyno yet?" I ask a few standing under a streetlamp.

"Dr. Ignis hasn't come by yet," his regular giggles. Sorry, bitch, the cunt is mine tonight.

About two hours pass and I have ignored about four different guys, then I see him. He drives a white Range Rover and slows down when he sees his regular girl. Can't have that.

I walk right up to his passenger window as he's lowering it.

"I want you," I tell him, leaning forward into the window.

"Really?" His shit brown eyes shine bright and eager.

"Yes. I've been waiting for hours." I let my pouty mouth curl up into a slow smile. "Don't keep me waiting any longer."

His tongue snakes out and runs along his thin lips as he combs his fingers through his thinning blond hair.

"Get in," he says, and I smile wider.

Got you, bitch.

"Dr. Ignis," his regular calls out. "Will you be back later?"

"He won't be back later." I close the door and lean out of the window. "Find a new regular."

Carl chuckles from beside me, thinking a pair of whores are fighting over him, but in reality, I'm telling her he isn't coming back because he'll soon be choking on his own blood.

He takes us to a deserted mall parking lot and parks the vehicle, looking over at me expectantly.

"Tell me what you want." I grin at him and lower my lashes.

"How much will this cost me?" He runs his finger over his fish thin lips. "And are you old enough to be doing this?"

"Tonight's on me, and would it matter?"

"No." He shakes his head. "It wouldn't matter."

I know, Carl. You just want pussy, no matter the age.

"Undo your pants and let me get acquainted with you."

He does as I ask and when he pulls out his thin noodle dick, I try my best not to laugh. No wonder he turns to prostitutes and unwilling patients. The man's got nothing down below. He's even hard, clearly not impressive.

"Oh!" I say excitedly. "Look at this cock. I can't wait to have it choking me."

He grins and leans back farther in his seat. Stupid fucker. I'll be lucky if the fucking thing reaches my throat. I've slurped ramen thicker than him.

I lean forward and wrap my small hand around him, choking back a laugh as my fingers meet. I spit down onto his head and begin to jack him off. There's no way I'm sucking him off without a condom because this fucker likes to stick his little friend into just about anything.

"Is this how you like it?" I ask him.

"Oh yeah," he groans.

"Would you rather I go slower, faster, or if I was saying no?"

"Huh?" He's only half paying attention.

"Yeah." I lift my head up and stop my movements. "Do you prefer me unwilling? Isn't that what you do with the girls you rape in your office?"

His eyes widen and then his eyebrows crash together in immediate anger.

"What the fuck did you say?" he growls.

There he is.

"I said," I tighten my hold around his toothpick dick, "don't you like sticking this itty, bitty cock into unwilling participants?"

He grabs a fistful of my hair, bringing my face away from his dick, and I swing my fist into his nose. He's not expecting it, and the spray of blood lands all over my face.

"What the fuck?" he yells, releasing my hair and grabbing his nose with both hands.

"Dr. Ignis has been a naughty boy," I tsk and pull my knife from my pocket, switching open the blade. "Let's play a game. I'll ask you questions and for every wrong answer I get to stab you."

"You're a fucking lunatic!" he screams and reaches for the door handle.

"Wrong answer," I sing-song and stab him in his side.

"Stop!" he pants, gripping his side.

"How many girls have you raped?"

"Fuck you!" he spits, and I wiggle in my seat with excitement.

"Another one!" I squeal and stab him in his thigh. His scream of agony washes over me and I moan at the sound.

"Stop." His words are a bit slower. "You will be going away for a long time."

"How many girls did you threaten after raping them?" I point the tip of my blade at him.

He watches it warily and reaches his hand once again for the door handle.

"Stop it." His bloody fingers slip on the metal.

"You're not going to be truthful, huh?" I snicker. "Looks like I'm wasting a perfectly good night."

Before he can say anything else, I stab the knife through his throat, and watch as he tries to get a grip on it, choking through his blood.

"When you get to Hell, Dr. Ignis, warn the devil I'm coming." I pull out the knife and coat my hand in the blood.

I press my blood-soaked finger to his forehead and hum as I draw the Reaper's scythe.

# Chapter Ten

## Selene

J'm blow drying my hair and basking in the aftermath of my latest bloodbath when my phone rings. It's one in the morning and I can't imagine who the fuck would be calling me right now. It's not like I have friends.

I hold up the phone screen and smile when I see Henry Walton's name.

"Hello?" I pick up, making sure I sound breathless.

"Selene." His voice is low and commanding.

"Yes, sir?" I coat my words in innocence and grin when he catches his breath.

"I want to see you."

"Now?" I act surprised.

"Yes, I'm sending you a car to bring you here. What's your address?" Fucking bossy asshole.

"I'll meet them at the same spot as last time." No way will he ever get my address.

"You have twenty minutes." Then he hangs up.

Sounds like a grumpy someone needs a good cock banging and I need to pretend I'm fucking enjoying it.

I head into my bedroom and pull out a short jersey dress, then pile my hair on top of my head. Time to look a little younger and tempt Walton into doing naughty things to me. I need to gain his trust so that I can find out where he keeps his shipments and how often he gets them.

I walk to the same corner as our last pick up and sure enough, the same Rolls Royce is there idling on the side. As soon as the driver sees me, he gets out and opens the back door.

"Hi." I smile at him and get a stern nod in return.

Looks like he could deal with a good cock banging, too.

I get comfortable in the back seat and stifle a yawn into my hand. I was looking forward to a good sleep after gutting Carl, and now I need to act like a good little whore. I doubt Henry wants a sleepy one.

We pull through a set of familiar gates and the driver stops in front of the front door. I wait for my door to be opened and by the time I step out, Henry is waiting. Eager much?

"Hello, Selene." His voice makes me want to puke in his mouth.

"Hello, sir." I smile through my nausea as his mouth pulls back into a wide smile.

He holds out his arm, ushering me inside, and I step through the threshold. Is Zander here tonight? I look around the foyer, hoping to see his scowling face. For what reason, I don't have the slightest clue. Maybe I want him to see me about to fuck his father.

"Would you like some wine?" Henry asks.

"No, I want to suck your cock again." I don't have all night and I really want to get back home to sleep.

He chokes on my answer and quickly regains his composure. "Good answer."

I bet it is, Dickface Walton.

He leads me into an office and slams the door behind us. He really is fucking eager.

"Get up on my desk and spread your legs. I want your pussy in my mouth," he demands, and I do just as he asks.

I will never say no to having my fucking pussy eaten out. That's fucking blasphemy. I spread my legs and show the old bastard that I forgot to put on a pair of panties.

"Oh fuck," he groans and kneels in front of me.

"Please make me come, sir."

He growls and grabs my thighs in each hand before he buries his head into my pussy. Henry is a fucking douchebag, but the fucker can eat a pussy. He's not shy of the asshole and shows my rear hole some love, too. I thread my fingers through his hair and pull it tighter. I'm craving this release.

As soon as I feel that telltale tightening, I begin to rub my clit along his nose, and he fucks me with his tongue.

"Fuck yes, sir," I moan.

I tip my head back and groan through my release, stuffing his head in tighter. I hope the fucker dies of suffocation.

He comes up and I watch as he licks his wet lips, my juices all over his chin.

"You missed some," I say as I lean forward, running my finger along his chin, and sucking it into my mouth. "Mmm."

"Get down and lean over the desk," his gruff voice orders me. Looks like I'm getting a dick down.

"Yes, sir."

I hop down and turn around, slowly leaning over. I hear the crinkle of a condom wrapper and then he's flipping my skirt up and slamming inside of me. Thankfully, I am wet because he is rough and fast. I moan when the tip of his cock hits a certain spot inside of me and I begin to imagine it's Zander fucking me, not his father.

His fingers dig into my hips and his balls slap against my clit, making me begin to tighten again. Fuck, he really does know how to work this cock and the more I think about Zander's abs, I'm rushing toward a second orgasm.

"You like this cock. Don't you, you fucking whore?" Here we go. "Take it like the dirty piece of shit you are. How many cocks have been in your cunt today?"

"Only yours, sir." I moan as he becomes rougher.

"You lying, dirty bitch," he snarls and grabs my hair, yanking my head back. "How much cum have you swallowed today?"

I moan as I clench around his dick and my eyes close as I come, seeing visions of Zander fucking me hard.

"You filthy whore." He slaps my ass hard. "Tight pussy whore."

He groans and slams inside of me one final time, coming finally, then he pulls out quickly and I turn to watch him chuck the condom into the wastebasket, landing beside a few others. Gross.

"Could I get that drink now?" I ask him.

He nods and pulls his pants up, giving me an evil grin. "Worked you up to a thirst, huh?"

"Oh, yes." I nod. Get the fuck out of the room.

He's striding out a few moments later, and I quickly look at my surroundings. There's not much I can do since he has a camera in the upper right corner. Sick perv probably makes videos of all the women he brings in here.

There's a painting of an older man sitting over the mantle of the fireplace and it's sitting slightly askew, like maybe it's moved often. Henry walks back in and sees me looking at the painting.

"That's my father." He hands me the water. "He started our business from nothing."

Just a couple of girls back then, I bet.

"He's handsome." I look at him. "I see where you get it from."

"The car is waiting for you out front," he tells me.

Thank God.

"Thank you." I nod and follow him to the front door.

"I'll call you again, Selene." He grasps my chin in his hand.

"Goodnight, sir." His eyes flash, and then he nods, stalking back inside.

I can't wait to go home and relive this. Only with his son is his place.

# Chapter Eleven

## *Zander*

I can smell her.

She has somehow taken over my massive fucking house with her scent, and the moment my dick stirs I demand it go back down.

I can't let her get to me. No way in fucking hell. She's just a prostitute, for fuck's sake, nothing special.

My dick disagrees, though, like the treacherous bastard that it is.

I make my way through the kitchen and up to my room, becoming angrier as more of her scent consumes me. She is fucking everywhere.

I grab the back of my shirt in my hand and pull it over my head, throwing it on the floor as I make my way toward my bathroom to shower. I kick my pants off, along with my boxers, before reaching for the taps and turning the water to scalding hot.

Maybe burning my balls off will set me straight.

I climb under the spray and close my eyes, trying to remove the pretty blue-eyed hooker from my thoughts.

Fuck, now I'm hard.

I consider my options for a second, then grasp my throbbing dick in my hand, stroking it firmly a few times before resting my forearm against the shower wall, leaning my forehead against it.

I pump my fist faster, a small groan leaving me at the building pleasure. I don't have to wait long once I picture Selene on her knees, her eyes staring up at me as she swallows my dick deep, her wavy blond hair

51

wrapped firmly around my fist.

Heat tingles down my spine as my balls tighten, causing me to grunt and slow my hand as hot cum jets from my dick and hits the shower wall.

I stand there for a moment, not moving, needing to steady myself from the intensity of it. I swear I haven't cum that hard in my fucking life.

I finally rinse the evidence of my weak moment from the wall before rinsing my body and turning the water off, stepping out to grab a towel. I'm not expecting Blaze to be leaning against the sink with his arms crossed and his signature scowl on his face. I didn't even hear him come in.

"Well, that was fucking disgusting," he comments, but the ghost of a smile tugs at his lips.

I wrap the towel around my waist and snort, frowning at him with annoyance.

"You didn't have to watch, asshole. I'm in my fucking bathroom. It's not like I did it in the kitchen."

Seriously, I can't even jack off in my own fucking bathroom any more without someone complaining?

His eyebrow quirks up, amusement filling his eyes. Well, it's as close to amusement as it gets. Blaze is way too serious all the time.

"She's getting to you more than you let on, Zander."

"Who?" I grumble, moving into my room with him hot on my heels.

"The whore your dad's fucking," he grunts as if I'm stupid.

I stare at him for a moment before grabbing some boxers and quickly pulling them on.

"I haven't thought about the cunt. Why would she be getting to me?" I bite out, but he smirks, cocking his head at me.

"You said Selene when you nutted. That's her name, isn't it?"

Fuck.

I go to speak, but he rolls his eyes and cuts me off.

"I think it's a dumb idea, but fuck her and get her out of your system or something. You need to get to her before Darius and Santos do, or there's going to be nothing left for you to stick your dick in. Fuck her, then let them have her. I meant what I said earlier, man. You won't have to see her again once those two get their hands on her. Fuck her, then get your head in the game."

"She's just a paid slut that Henry likes to blow in. She's nothing more than a cum bucket, so it's not like she's messing me up. My head's in the game, I promise," I grit out, not liking this conversation in the slightest.

He scoffs, giving me a dirty look. If looks could kill, I'd be six feet under right now.

"That's the problem, Zander. The other two are always running loose and fucking shit up, but you're more level-headed. You've been off with the fucking fairies all afternoon, and now you're in here jerking on your dick to that cunt?" he snaps.

"My head's fucking fine, Blaze. You have nothing to worry about," I argue, but he just glares at me, his voice low.

"No? I was in your room when you got home and you didn't even notice, let alone when I walked into the bathroom. Like I said, go and fill her cunt up with your cum, then get your ass into gear before you end up fucking hurt or dead. Anyone could have been in the house tonight instead of me, and you weren't observant enough to even notice. Is her pussy really worth your fucking life?" he snarks, turning and stalking from the room, leaving me standing there like a fucking idiot.

Bad thing is, I am starting to want a piece of that pussy and I can't seem to shake it off.

I let Blaze go, not wanting to deal with his fucking drama any longer. I climb into bed and grab my phone, scrolling through my contacts until I find her name.

I shouldn't have taken her number from Dad's phone, but it's for Santos and Darius, not me. Well, it's not supposed to be for me, but my fingers twitch with the temptation to send her a text.

Instead, I copy the contact details and send them to Santos, turning my phone off for the night and rolling over to sleep before I can regret my decision.

Too late.

# Chapter Twelve

## Selene

My phone beeps as a text comes through, and I frown at the unknown number. I'm a little surprised when I open it to discover it's one of Zander's friends. He literally said hello and that his name is Santos, Zander's hot friend.

Fucking wacko.

I finish my morning coffee before replying, not sure why he's even texting me to begin with. I don't have to wonder for long after asking him what he wants. He wants to do some business with me.

Well, with my pussy.

I can't tell him no, because it will fuck up my cover, but I don't want to get involved with them. The farther away I stay, the better, because the moment Henry Walton is dead and cold, I'm going for his son.

I can't have people seeing me around them too much.

I groan when he sends another text after a while, an address showing up on the screen with a time. He's having a party apparently, and he wants my pussy to keep his dick company.

Just wonderful.

There's no way out of this without causing questions, so I thank him for the invite and say I'll think about it. It could be a good idea to get closer to Zander and his father, so I know I have to go. Luckily, I have a few hours to get ready.

I have a shower and shave everything, before climbing out to blow dry my hair. I decide to straighten it before applying my make-up, giving my eyes a smoky effect to make them pop.

Then I grab the black dress I bought the other day and hesitate before putting it on. I originally bought it to lure Henry a little more, but I want to see Zander's expression when he sees me in it for some fucked up reason. The guy is taking over all my fucking brain cells, and it's driving me mental.

I slip on some strappy black heels, showing off my lean calf muscles and long legs, my ass nearly sticking out the bottom of the dress as I turn in front of the mirror to see my handy work. I have to admit; I look good.

I'd fuck myself.

Glancing at my phone to check the time, I realize I'm already late, so I call an Uber and find my purse before wandering down to the street for my ride.

I know I'm at the right house when the driver pulls up on the curb and I can hear music thumping from inside as people spill out of the side door, drinking and smoking.

I swing my legs out the door, only to have a shadow fall over me.

My eyes dart up and I find myself staring at an angry dude with a scar down his face, his scowl giving him a mean look. It's kind of hot in a scary way.

"He seriously invited you?" He asks as if he can't believe it, my eyes narrowing in defense.

"Santos did, yeah. Why?"

Something crosses his dark eyes before his lip twitches, as if fighting a smile.

"Oh, did he now? Hope you're ready then, because this is going to be the worst day of your fucking life. I can't believe that fucker actually invited you. This is hilarious," he grunts, not seeming like it's as funny as he says.

He steps aside and lets me out of the Uber, but when I turn to speak to him again, he's already halfway toward the booming house party. I'm not surprised, really, he's a bit of a dick.

I make my way up to the house, letting myself inside and almost get bowled over by Zander, who looks murderous.

"He seriously fucking invited you?" he demands as if I'm lying, causing me to take a small step back in surprise. I regain my ground and take a step almost against him, my pussy pulsing as his scent hits my nose and my chest brushes against his firm body.

"Where's Santos? Why do you care?" I ask, his eyes boring into mine with hate.

"He's in the back room. I told that fucker not to invite you," he spits, confusion and annoyance washing through me. I want to punch him in the face, but then I'll feel obligated to kiss it better. Not today, motherfucker.

I cross my arms, causing my chest to pop out and draw his attention.

"What's the big deal? I'm working, so…"

"So you're just here to make a quick buck? Or are you here to suss me out some more?" He demands, towering over me until my back is pressed against the door.

Fuck, he's onto me.

"Zander, I'm not here to be a bother to you. Santos invited me, so I said I'd show up. That's it. Why would I need to suss you out?" I laugh lightly, kicking myself for putting myself in the spotlight so much. He is getting suspicious.

"You don't think I know what you're doing? Worming your way into my rich dad's pocket like you are? You trying to get to know me so you can try some of that step-mommy bullshit with me?" He argues, but his hands absently hang by my side, his fingers lightly brushing against the thin fabric of my dress. My heart rate spikes as his eyes darken, but he gets hold of himself as I clear my throat and push him back a step.

"I'm not a gold digger, and I sure as shit am not looking for a husband, if that's what you're implying. It's strictly business, that's it. I'm too young to be your fucking mommy anyway," I say defensively, his features cooling slightly.

"How old are you?"

"Twenty-five. I'd prefer to earn my money on my knees than let someone just pay for my shit. Don't act like you know me, asshole, because you fucking don't," I murmur before slipping away from him. I startle as I walk into the back room and instantly get shoved lightly against a wall.

The guy looks certifiably crazy, but he is hot as fuck. He presses himself against me, his tongue tracing his lips as he watches me with a smirk.

"Hey, Selene, right?"

"Santos?" I ask with a small smile, his eyes shining at me, knowing his name.

"That's me. I was going to get you to blow me while I do lines with the guys, but I don't particularly want them to see you enjoying me so much. You know, because they'll get jealous."

I don't even get a word out before his lips are on my neck, a gasp leaving me as his teeth bite firmly into my soft skin. I'm starting to second guess my decision to show up. He looks ready to fuck me and kill me at the same time, and I have no idea how to handle that.

I press my palms against his stomach to push him back, but I hesitate as I feel the solid abs beneath the shirt. My fingers trace the grooves of his muscles, and he chuckles in my ear.

"You like what you feel? Wait until I get you naked. You'll be screaming for me," he practically whispers in my ear, sending tingles down my spine.

Someone grabs my hand and gently tugs me aside, causing Santos to scowl.

"Darius, fuck off. She's mine right now."

Darius rolls his eyes but smiles at me, his voice as smooth as silk as he tucks my hair behind my ear.

"I'm Darius, and you're fucking hot. Do you allow, let's say, multiple people in a business transaction?" he asks as if we were swapping pantry goods, my mouth going dry for some reason. Both guys are hot as hell, but there is something off about them, too. I just can't place what it is.

I give him a coy smile, fluttering my lashes at him.

"I don't know what you're talking about. I just wanted to come to the party since I had a night off."

He chuckles, his eyes lighting up, knowing I'm full of complete shit.

"How about you join me and Santos upstairs and we will show you how to fucking party, then?"

When I don't answer him instantly, he swoops down and kisses the living shit out of me, and I can't hold back the moan as he sandwiches me between him and Santos, who groans and rubs the hard bulge in his pants against my ass.

"Fuck, man. Throw her over your shoulder and let's get this started."

Someone screams from the other room, and Zander runs into the back room like his ass is on fire.

"Get everyone out, now. Antony's guys just fucking showed up!" he shouts, Darius moving back from me instantly and pulling a gun out of the back of his pants, while Santos is already demanding people to fuck off out the back door. They scatter, because that fucker is one crazy son of a bitch. Half his words are coming out in Spanish, and he's waving his own gun around like a crackhead at the local gas station.

A gunshot rings out through the house, and Scarface storms in with a semi-automatic rifle and rage all over his face. Something tells me the fucker is never happy. Even if he has his dick buried in the best pussy in the world, the cunt will still glare at them.

"Fuck me, this bitch is still here? Fine, fuck. Can you shoot?" he asks me, offering me a handgun without waiting for my answer. I much prefer my knife, but you don't bring a knife to a gunfight, so it will have to do.

Zander's glaring at his friend like he's crazy, when the actual crazy friend is jumping up and down while laughing.

"Fuck yeah, all bets are off since he's brought this shit to my house, motherfuckers," he laughs, his eyes darting around between them all as if he needs permission to let loose.

Darius glances at Scarface, who grunts, motioning to the door.

"Yeah man, it's your house. Go crazy."

Santos lets out a hyena laugh, making *pew, pew* noises as he darts down the hallway, causing Darius to chuckle before following him, glancing over his shoulder to wink at me.

"I'll finish this, then get back to finishing you. Deal?"

I giggle, hating the sound that leaves my mouth, but he flashes me a bright smile and goes to help his friend, leaving me with the angry dude and Zander, who looks just as pissed.

He eyes my weapon and snorts.

"Do you even know how to use that thing?"

"Of course I do. I'm a prostitute in this shithole. I'd be stupid not to know how to defend myself," I snap, hating it when men assume I'm defenseless and need saving all the goddamn time.

Before he can stop me, I stalk after Santos and Darius, my eyes landing on a heavily tattooed guy in the kitchen. He grins at me, cracking his knuckles.

"Just what I fucking wanted, a portable cum dump. The guys will like you. Put the gun down and come here. I won't hurt you, unlike these assholes," he croons, and I can't stop the fucking eye roll.

Is he for real right now?

I lift my gun and cock my head.

"Why do guys think I'm worried about getting hurt when I'm usually the biggest monster in the room?" I question, confusion flashing in his eyes before I smirk and pull the trigger, his nose splattering as blood sprays from the wound. He drops like a sack of shit, but a deep groan comes from him, telling me he's alive.

I silently dart across the room and slit his throat with my knife, creeping through the room and toward another door, flinging it open to find another guy that has somehow managed to get his arm around Santos' neck.

The door opening distracts him enough for Santos to break free, but the fucker keeps getting in my way as I follow the guy with my gun. After a few seconds, I scowl.

"Fuck's sake, asshole. Duck!" I shout, Santos turning instantly, his eyes going wide for a second before he drops to the ground and out of my way.

I grab my knife again and throw it across the room, the blade lodging in the guy's forehead just as Darius joins us, his face and chest covered in blood.

The room goes quiet as the guy drops to the floor, and I tsk as I walk over to him and put my foot on his head, yanking my blade out.

"What an idiot. I even warned him I was going to get him because I told you to duck. Are all men so fucking stupid?" I ask, turning to face them to see them both staring at me, mouths open.

Santos has a raging boner, but I'm not surprised. Crazy, remember?

Zander and the other asshole jog in as we hear car tires screaming away from the house, and Darius points at me as if it were all my fault.

"She did it."

"She saved my ass. Now I'm horny as fuck, and I'm about to start humping the couch cushions. Fuck, my dick is seriously fucking hard right now. Did you see that, Darius? She got him smack bang in the forehead!" Santos exclaims, not hesitating to wrap his arms around my waist and spin me around, kissing me hard. Death seems to make me horny too, so I moan into his mouth and don't fight him off, despite the audience.

I'm yanked back hard, and Zander glares at Santos as if he has the right to.

"We have shit to clean up, and you are not going to leave it with us while you fuck her in victory. Get to work. Blaze, run her home," Zander orders, but Scarface scoffs.

"I'm not taking her anywhere. She can't fucking leave after what just happened. Are you stupid?"

My back stiffens as anger rolls through me.

"You can't keep me here, jackass. I killed two people, so why would I say anything?!" I shout, but his angry eyes land on mine and he sneers.

"Because no bitch knows how to kill a guy like that, let alone without remorse. You haven't even blinked at it, so you're not just some hooker slut from the city, you're trained to fucking kill."

Oh, fuck.

# Chapter Thirteen

## Zander

"J don't give a shit if she's trained. That just makes me wanna fuck her even more. Seriously, she threw a fucking knife at him from across the room and got a bullseye! Please let me keep her, she's perfect!" Santos begs, grinding my gears a fraction.

I've never known the fucker to be so fucking obsessed with a chick before, but since she saved him in a bloodied way, he wants her right or wrong.

Blaze shakes his head, glaring at our friend.

"The fuck is wrong with you? Other than the obvious. She might be a fucking spy for all we know. We can't have her fucking up our plans!" He hisses.

I watch Blaze for a moment before sighing, rubbing my temples with frustration.

"She's right, you know? We can't keep her locked up here."

"Says fucking who? I thought you would have loved the opportunity to be locked up with her, Zan. Go get her out of your system while you can," Blaze snaps, causing Santos' eyes to dart to him with a frown.

"Hey! I get her! She distracted that dude until I broke free, then she—"

"I'm aware she saved you and killed the guy with a knife. We've been going over this for nearly an hour, dick head. Zander wants her, so let him have her," Blaze grunts, all eyes going to me with confusion.

I count to three in my head, needing to compose myself before speaking.

"She stays tonight, then we take her home tomorrow and suss out her house, all right? No one fucks her until we know who she fucking is and who she works for. Got it?" I say calmly, making Santos scowl and throw complaints at me in the process, but Blaze gives me a nod, agreeing with me. I can always rely on him to side with me.

I have to admit, though, I'm surprised that Selene got involved in any of it and didn't run the moment she could. If I thought she consumed all my thoughts before, she sure as fuck did now.

Who the fuck is she?

"I don't want her to go. I like her! She obviously likes me if she'll kill a guy for me!" Santos continues to argue, draining some of my willpower.

"We talk to her tomorrow about it all, all right? Tonight she stays until we can get some information out of her. You and Darius stay here. Blaze and I will go and see what we can find out," I mutter, both of them groaning at me.

They'd end up fucking her if we let them go and interrogate her without supervision.

I head back out to the back room where we left Darius in charge of the little imp and find them in a heated argument.

"I am not fucking staying here!" she screams and lifts her gun to me as we walk in.

"Whoa." I raise my hands. "Chill. We have a few questions about what just went down."

"I saved your useless fucking lives," she sneers. "I should've fucking ran when I had the chance instead."

Okay, so she's pissed and understandably. But I need to know why the fuck a weapon trained hooker is fucking my father.

"She's pissed," Darius echoes my thoughts and grabs his cock through his jeans. "Fuck, I really like her pissed."

"Same," Santos pipes up behind me. "Baby, we really like you pissed."

She rolls her eyes, but I see a ghost of a smile hover around her lips.

"Listen, I like to suck and fuck cock," she shrugs. "But men tend to think a female deserves to be beaten or raped instead. All of what you saw was self-taught."

Nope, not buying it.

"Look, it's late as fuck. We're gonna clean up and crash." I look into her ocean blue eyes. "Please stay here so we can talk in the morning."

"Do I have a fucking choice?" she retorts.

"Nope," Blaze growls, and she deflates.

"I sleep with my knife and I'm taking this gun." She lowers her arm in defeat.

"Fine," Blaze nods. "You stay with Zander, though." His hand lands on my shoulder and I groan.

"Fine," she shrugs, unaffected by the thought of sleeping in a room with me.

I mean, why would she be affected? She's swallowing and fucking dick every day.

"Lucky cunt," Santos growls, and Darius shoots me a dirty look.

I lead her to a bedroom on the lower floor while the guys head upstairs.

"How will the interrogation start?" Her husky voice hits my back as we enter the room. "Orgasm deprivation? Knife play? Waterboarding?"

"The fuck?" I turn on her.

"I like most of those things, except waterboarding, but I can hold my breath for a long ass time," she grins. "What's first?"

"First you can shower in there." I point to the bathroom, and I open a drawer with some of my clothes. I have clothes at each of the guys' houses.

"Then you will sit in there while I wash this blood off me." I throw a t-shirt and a pair of boxers at her.

"Whatever," she huffs and turns on her heel into the washroom.

Is that blood on her thigh? I tip my head back on a groan and pray for my dick to deflate. I feel like I'm sixteen all over again.

I hear the shower start and then her voice floats out. She's fucking singing in the shower while washing blood off of herself, and she sounds like a dying cat.

What fucking gets me though is how she's so cool through all of this? Fuck it, the best way to corner someone is while they're naked, and I can get some images together for my spank bank.

I open the bathroom door and cringe when her voice gets louder. Is she singing Adele? Dear fucking god, she's singing Adele.

"I think you've broken every window in the fucking house," I growl, fighting hard to hold in my laugh.

"What's that?" She pokes her head out around the glass door. "Are you offering to wash my back?"

Fuck yes, I am. I may be suspicious of the hooker, but I'm a fucking man, too. I drop my pants and whip off my shirt before climbing in behind her and shutting the door. I know I should be wary of her, but I'm thinking with my fucking dick.

"No hidden knives in here, right?" I ask her and nearly shoot my load on her back when she grins over her shoulder.

She has a full back piece done, and it's a detailed Grim Reaper. All black, blues, and purples swirling together and the gray of his scythe shines like it's actually catching the light's reflection. The art is so fucking detailed and beautiful. I look a little closer and notice it's not a male reaper but a female, one with strands of blonde hair blowing from under its hood.

"You'd be missing your balls if I did have a knife," she interrupts my gawking and looks down at my cock, then back up at my face. "Look who's bigger than Daddy."

That should turn me off, right? I shouldn't be harder because of it, and I shouldn't be basking in the praise that implies she's fucking my father.

"Unless you're going to put that mouth to good use, I suggest keeping it closed." I reach for the shampoo and my cock brushes her ass.

She tenses and then arches her back to press into me harder. I run my finger down her spine and revel in the moans that my touch brings out of her.

"You want my cock, Selene?" I ask. "After you just had Daddy dearest? I could smell you in my fucking house last night."

"Yes," she breathes. "I fucked your daddy last night. He even ate me out like a champ. The real question is, can you erase him? Are you better than him?"

Her words have me burning with anger and lust. I yank her around and lift her into my arms. This bitch has no idea what she just got herself into.

# Chapter Fourteen

## Selene

Zander's grip on my ass cheeks is bruising as he stalks out of the washroom, uncaring of the water being dropped everywhere. He throws me on the bed and in the next second, he's hovering over me. His eyes are a mixture of green and brown, and right now they're looking at me in a silent challenge.

His upper body is completely tattooed and his legs each have a few here and there. His muscles flex as he holds himself above me, and I grin at the scowl on his face. So much like Daddy, indeed.

"After I fuck you," his hand curls around my chin painfully, "you no longer fuck my father."

"Are you asking me to quit my job?" I smirk.

"What?"

"I'm a prostitute." I roll my eyes. "And Daddy is a good client."

He rolls off me and sits at the edge of the bed. "Why are you fucking my father and how is it you can slam a blade into someone's head from across the room?"

"I fuck your father because he pays well." I sit up. "How close are you to him?"

"I hate him." His admission shocks me.

"Why?"

He looks at me over his shoulder and narrows his eyes.

"He killed my mother, and he likes to abuse women." His brow

67

raises. "He likes to rape women."

Huh. The shithead is telling me everything I already know, but why? And a better question yet, what's his place in all of it?

"And you?" I lay back down, unashamed of my nakedness. "Do you help Daddy with all of that?"

"Me? I'm going to kill him," he snarls, and grabs a pair of pants. "And if you happen to be there when I do, I'll kill you, too."

I want to tell him that I have the same plan, that I want to watch his fucking father die with his blood on my hands, and I want to help all the women he's enslaved. But I can't be sure he's telling me the truth.

I already knew about Henry killing his wife because I was there watching as he wrapped his hands around her throat and then threw her in the pool.

It was the final nail in the coffin, and I made my decision to move forward on the plan to make Henry's death a long, sufferable one.

Zander opens the bedroom door and slams it shut behind him. I have to find a way out of here tonight and I need to get away from this group of guys that both infuriate me and fucking have me dripping wet with only a few words.

I get out of the bed and pull my dress back on, then Zander's shirt over it. I slip the knife and gun back into my trench pockets and toss it on the bed.

I look behind me to the window that faces the street. Do they really believe I wouldn't try to slip out? Or is that what they're hoping for?

I get up, pull on my trench, and thumb both the knife and gun in my pockets. Fuck it, I have never done what I've been told and I sure as fuck am not going to start now.

I pull the window up and look out with a laugh. It's about a five-foot drop and I decide to hold my heels in my arms until after the jump. I can't afford a broken ankle right now.

I swing my leg over and then the other, sitting on the windowsill. I feel a twinge of guilt but swallow that fucker down quick; I don't owe these assholes a single thing, and I still don't know whose side they're on.

I hop out the window and land to the ground with a grunt. I slip on my heels and just walk myself away.

I got plans and there's no way in hell I'll be derailed by four hot men and their questionable loyalties.

# Chapter Fifteen

## Zander

"You let her get away?!" Darius yells into my empty bedroom.

"Nope," I say as I unlock my phone's screen.

"She's not here, asshole." Santos spreads his arms and turns on the spot.

"I know," I nod.

"He let my future wife get away." Santos sinks to the bed. "I had visions of Bonnie and Clyde."

"Will you shut up?" I snap at him.

"Where is she?" Blaze asks from over my shoulder.

"Three blocks down and just got in a vehicle," I answer him.

"What the fuck? You put a tracker on her phone?" Darius' grin takes over his whole face.

"Yeah." I smirk back at him. "Just before I got in the shower with her."

His grin immediately falls, and Santos jumps to his feet with a snarl, but Blaze grunts at me.

"Let's go follow this bitch and find out what she's all about," Blaze says, then stalks toward the door.

"You two stay here," I point to Santos and Darius.

They each give me an eye roll, but know it's the smart thing to do since the Diablos attacked us. It's been a while since they had the nerve to roll up on us, and I think it has everything to do with my father. Maybe he's switching crews since our last argument.

We hop in Blaze's Camaro, and death-metal assaults my ears.

"I don't know how you listen to this shit," I say as I turn it down.

"Helps me concentrate," he replies.

I guide him to where the dot is moving on my screen and my heart kicks up in speed. It's been a while since I've been on the hunt and I have to admit, it's one of my favorite things to do. I used to be so fucking good at it, but then I realized I was hunting down girls for my father to rape and ship off as sex slaves.

"Just up here." I point to an apartment complex. "This is where she lives?"

Saying it's run down would be an understatement. The place has windows boarded and homeless sleeping out front. The bushes have begun to take over the walkway and started to grow their way up to the front door, which is hanging on by one hinge.

"Was that a rat?" Blaze asks as we see something the size of a cat scurry out.

"You stay with the car," I tell him because this car would be screaming to be stolen here. "I'll head in and see what's up."

I pull out my gun and hold it in my right hand as I get out of the car and make my way up the walkway. I enter the building and choke on a gag, covering my nose with my sleeve. It stinks of urine and maybe a rotting body somewhere.

The dot told me she was in the far-right corner of the building, and I am cursing myself for following her here. I could very well die from the stench alone. She can't possibly be living here, and if she is, then she's not charging her clients near enough.

I walk down a short corridor and watch how each apartment becomes more and more decrepit. Doors hang off hinges, showing rotting furniture and what could be bloodstains on the floors. I get to the last one and the door is completely missing. The door jamb destroyed like someone kicked it down.

I creep inside and look around at the total destruction of the place. The couch is ripped apart and missing its cushions, there are dishes smashed all over the floor, and what looks to be a girl's barbie house is completely destroyed.

"I noticed the tracker when I got into the cab." Her voice hits my back and I turn to see her standing in the kitchen area, flipping her knife in the air. "Smart."

"What is this place?" I ask as I holster my gun.

"I grew up here." She nods to the Barbie house. "That was mine. My sister worked overtime for two weeks just so she could afford that for Christmas."

Alarm bells begin to ring, but I step toward her, eager to hear more about her. I want to know why someone so beautiful and obviously tough ended up where she is.

"Our mother was a junkie and practically lived on the street. She only came back here when she remembered she had to eat. My sister Jan was six years older than me and by fourteen she had to drop out of school to raise me." She slams the knife's blade down into the counter. "That was the beginning of the end."

"What happened?" I ask, completely entranced.

"She got a few jobs, and I would stay with the neighbors while she was out. Things were good until my mother started coming back around. She would beg Jan for money and when that wasn't enough, she began to pimp her daughters. I was ten years old when I had my first client."

The bile rushes up my fucking throat and I swallow several times to keep it from spewing.

"My sister had it worse. She was attractive and clearly becoming a curvy woman. The men loved her, and my mother was making a killing. This went on for a few years and once I hit fifteen, my sister promised we were leaving. She had found an apartment for us, and we were leaving the next night."

Her face hardens, and she pulls the knife out of the counter and walks up to me.

"She left for work that night and I never saw her again. I hit the streets at fifteen and spoke to people, took some self-defense classes, and took up knife throwing classes. I found out a few months later that the word on the street was that my mother sold her to a man, a businessman who liked to deal in the flesh of young children."

My mouth goes dry, and my limbs begin to tingle. I know where this is going.

"I confronted my mother, and she fucking confessed to it, said my sister got her one thousand dollars. She was proud of herself and before she could finish her praise, I stabbed my knife through her eye. Right there on that couch, then I destroyed the place, and left, never to look back. But now I have a problem, Zander." Her chest hits mine, and she stands toe to toe with me. "You're poking your nose in my business and I can't have you fuck up my plans."

"Was it my father?" I ask her, my eyes never leaving her big blues.

"He ended up with her and I can only imagine she had the same fate as your mother because otherwise she'd have come back to me by now."

"You want to kill my father," I nod, "looks like our plans match."

Her eyes narrow, and she brings the point of her knife to my throat. I know she could kill me easily, but I'm trusting the information I can provide would deter her.

"You're The Reaper Incarnate. Explains the tattoo on your back." I swallow and my skin presses farther into the blade. "We can help you."

"How?" she growls. "How the fuck can I trust the son of that monster?"

"Because I'm a monster, too. And he needs to die for what he's done to my mother."

"I saw Darius and Santos at the last exchange. If we have the same plans, why are you helping him *export*?"

"It's all a ruse so we can get more information, and we always try to free as many as we can. Only problem is, I think he's onto us and he's the one that sent the Diablos last night. We needed another way in, and I think you can help us with that."

I brush the hair out of her face and stare at her big blue eyes.

"Will you help us?" I ask her.

# Chapter Sixteen

## Selene

"Will you help us?" Zander asks.

Will I? This has been my solo mission for so long and I'm having a hard time wanting to give it over to anyone else. Especially to the son of the man I plan on torturing for a while.

"I can see you fucking struggling to decide." He grabs my wrist that's holding the knife. "I don't expect you to trust me and I sure as fuck don't expect you to tell us the whole plan. But let us prove ourselves."

He needs an insider, and I need information that he could provide. I drop the knife back to my side with a sigh.

"I need to know the shipments in advance, and I need to know the process after the exchange," I tell him.

"I need you to worm your way into my father's bed and keep his attention. I want to know who calls him all hours of the night and where he goes at two or three in the morning." He counters.

"Probably prostitutes." I hold out my arms and gesture to myself.

"No," he shakes his head. "My father has his own whores. Which brings me back to how you got involved with him."

"Let's get out of here," I tell him and stride ahead of him out of the apartment that smells of piss and rot. "And you will never step foot where I live."

I turn on him, causing him to stop short and curse.

"If you try to track me again." I stand toe to toe with him. "I will cut your dick off and fuck you with it."

"I don't think that's physically possible ..." he begins, but I raise my brow at his protest. "All right, no more trackers."

I exit the building as rats scurry down the steps and see Blaze sitting in the vehicle. It's a fucking two-seater and I stop, looking back at Zander.

"Are you walking?" I smirk. "This neighborhood is a bit rough."

"Shut the fuck up." He grins back and steps around me.

He opens the door and sits in the seat, patting his lap. "Come sit on Daddy."

"I already sat on your daddy's face a few nights ago." I cross my arms.

Blaze barks out a deep thunderous laugh that shocks both me and Zander.

"Fuck, she's good," he continues to grin.

"Will you just get in here?" Zander growls.

I roll my eyes and sit on his lap. "Where are we going?"

"Back to the house. We have some questions for you," Blaze says as he pulls out onto the street.

Yeah, I got questions too, fuckers.

"Fuck yes!" Santos yells as we come in the door. "You got her!"

"You got me, fuckers." I turn and face Zander and Blaze, taking my knife out of my pocket and flipping it in my hand.

"Do we tie her down?" Darius asks, and I raise both eyebrows at Zander.

I turn around quickly and fling my knife, watching as it sails toward Darius' head. It nicks his cheek before continuing past and slamming into the plastered wall.

"I fucking dare you to try, bitch," I snarl.

Darius touches his cheek and looks at the blood on his hand with shock.

"I think I just came," Santos groans and drops down onto the couch.

Darius looks back at me and a crazy grin stretches across his face.

"We're gonna be the next Bonnie and Clyde," Santos moans.

He turns and pulls the knife out of the wall, tossing it back at me. I catch it and put it back in my trench pocket.

"We need to talk," Zander states and flings his arm over my shoulders.

I shrug off his arm and sit between Darius and Santos on the couch. I reach up and swipe the drop of blood gathering on Darius' cheek, popping my finger in my mouth. Zander gives me a pissed off look and Blaze looks just plain pissed off as they sit across from us.

"Selene here is the Reaper Incarnate," Zander tells the guys, and the room falls deathly silent.

"No," Santos is the first to speak. "That's a dude. They found his latest victim in the alley yesterday and he was double her size."

I don't bother to fucking convince him otherwise, because I really don't care what anyone thinks.

"You're sitting beside the girl that took down the guy in the alley," Zander nods.

"I need to fuck that pussy so bad right now," Santos says into my ear, causing my pussy to throb at his words. My panties are fucking soaked.

"I may have to take you up on that offer," I say as I turn my head and our lips brush.

He's quick to grab the back of my neck and haul me up onto his lap. His lips crash into mine and his cock hardens between us. We're a moaning and writhing mess when I hear someone cursing.

"Can you separate the horny fucking teenagers?" Blaze growls. "We need to sort this shit out."

He's right, I know that, but Santos' dick is perfectly pressing against my panties underneath my dress, and I give it one more slow grind.

"I'm fucking you after this," he says once our mouths separate. I can't complain about that idea.

He lifts me effortlessly, turning me to face the others but pulling my back against his front, keeping a firm grip on me as if I'm his personal possession. That should make me angry as fuck, because I don't belong to anyone, but my head tilts back to rest on his shoulder and my nipples tighten instead.

Jesus fucking Christ, I hate girls who swoon over that kind of alpha bullshit, but here I am leaning into him with my pussy creaming for him.

Zander eyes us with irritation as he fills the guys in on our conversation from earlier, but Blaze flat out glares at me the whole time as if picturing his hands around my throat, choking the life out of me. I shiver, and Santos nips my neck hard, his warm breath teasing my skin as he whispers in my ear.

"Did you want me to fuck you to death right here? Because if you keep projecting your horny mood like that, you're going the right way about it," he warns, my breath hitching at the threat. I turn my head to reply, but Zander's voice cuts through the air sharply, stopping our banter.

"If you two can't focus on the conversation, I'll make you sit your ass on Blaze's lap. You want to know what we know, so do us all a favor and pay attention. I'm not going to fucking repeat myself."

Santos flips him the bird and runs a hand down my stomach, moving lower until he's cupping my pussy firmly.

"Don't tell me what to do with her. She's fucking mine. Besides, you only don't want me to fuck her right in front of you because you'll be the one getting distracted," he exclaims, letting out a snarl as Blaze stands and grabs my bicep, yanking me down beside him before I can even argue. He glares at me some more, his voice rough and full of venom.

"You can be a whore later. Right now, we need you to fucking focus. I'm doing you a favor. Santos will likely bleed you out in all his excitement."

I lean closer, brushing my lips against his cheek.

"God, I fucking hope so." Then I drag the flat of my tongue up his cheek, giving him a wink. The best way to get to Blaze is to pretend I like him. Grumpy piece of shit.

He wipes his damp cheek with a scowl, but he doesn't say anything else as Zander draws our attention.

"Anyway, as I was fucking saying, we have years' worth of shit against Henry. We have easily saved over one hundred girls, but so many more have been sold and lost. Like I said before, Selene, he's catching on to us, so we want to get this shit burned to the ground as soon as we can, before too many more girls get hurt. We have a shipment this week, so we need you to work on getting closer to him to try and distract him a little. I need to do some snooping in his office, but he's always in there when he's home. Do us a favor and try to occupy him elsewhere in the house. I have a feeling he's setting us up with the shipment, so I need to find out what the fuck he's planning. After the attack, I don't trust the bastard to play fair anymore," he explains, glancing at Darius, who grunts.

"What if he fucking hurts her? We've all seen what the asshole is like with women. He could kill her."

"Like you're any better. Between you and Santos, do you have any idea how much damage you have done to all the sluts you've stuck your dicks in? Never mind, Selene can handle herself," Zander replies, his eyes sliding to mine as if challenging me to argue. I shrug, throwing a leg over Blaze's lap, ignoring the warning growl.

"I'll kill that fucker before he gets one over me, don't you worry about that, money bags."

"I'm worried that you will kill him. There's a reason he's still alive, idiot. He has a lot of reach in the underground because he spends so much money on skin, and he's helped move bodies for a long fucking time now. We need the intel on who else is involved, but we also need to play it smart, so we don't get a big fat hit on our heads, too. The only thing getting stabbed is your cunt with his dick, got it?" Zander snaps, my eyes narrowing as I shove myself up from the seat.

"Roger that, dick breath. Santos, care to join me? I feel like laying down and screaming for a while," I retort, Zander's eye twitching as Santos wastes no time throwing me over his shoulder with a psychotic laugh.

"I've got you, babe. Where do you want it? Wait, don't answer that. You don't get a say, anyway. Darius, you coming?"

Darius stands, his tongue sweeping over his lips as a dark smirk takes over his face.

"Not yet, but I will be."

If they kept talking like that, I'm going to come in my panties before they even get their dicks out to play. If I'm able to walk tomorrow, I'm going to be highly disappointed.

# Chapter Seventeen

## Selene

**S**antos stalks up the hallway, laughing as I punch his firm ass cheek.

"I can walk, you know?" I growl, but Darius snorts from close behind us.

"Not for long, you little hellcat. Just shut up and take it."

"Keep that kind of talk up, and I'll cum before we even get to where we're going," I coo, letting out a breathy moan as Santos' large hand cracks against my butt sharply.

"You don't know what you're in for by taunting us, you cheeky wench."

We enter a room and I'm thrown down on a bed, my body bouncing slightly from the impact. Santos yanks Zander's shirt off me, and I move to sit up, but he presses a hand against my shoulder, pinning me down as he pulls a knife from his pocket, his eyes twinkling with craziness and desire.

"Don't fucking move," he warns before grabbing the material of the dress and slicing down the front of it with the blade, ripping it completely open to expose my bra and panties.

"Hey! That was fucking expensive!" I snap, but he raises an eyebrow, gliding the blunt end of the cool blade from my throat to my stomach.

"I'll get you a new one. I wasn't kidding when I said you don't get a say, this is our show, not yours," he states in a dark voice, my skin shivering as he slips the blade under the material of my panties, giving it a slight tug to tear it as well.

He doesn't give me time to argue before slamming his lips down on mine, tossing his blade aside to fist my hair tightly. I moan, arching my body up to try and grind against him, but he keeps his body away from my touch, proving he's in charge.

The sound of clothes dropping to the floor catches my attention, and I gasp as Santos slips his hand between my legs, slicking his fingers with my creamy juices before shoving two fingers inside me roughly without warning.

I groan loudly into his mouth, my hands gripping his shoulders as if to push him away, but I dig my nails in to keep him close. A feral growl rips from him at my approval as he moves his face back to stare down at me, his fingers moving faster and deeper.

Fingers wrap around my wrists and pull my hands away from Santos, a deep chuckle coming from Darius as he pulls my arms back above my head. I glance up to see him butt-naked, a thick rope clasped between his teeth.

For a moment I tense, not wanting to give them the ability to trap me, but I relax slightly as Santos runs his nose down my throat, nipping at my skin.

"We're going to fuck you so hard that the only words you'll be able to remember are our names. Heads up, you don't get a safe word," he murmurs against my soft skin, a breathy moan leaving me.

They are scrambling my fucking brain already. Allowing them to tie me up is a stupid move, but I am beyond caring at this point.

The rough rope wraps around my wrists, and Darius grins down at me once I'm secured to the headboard and I give it a test tug. It isn't going to come loose any time soon.

"You won't get out of that until I let you, but it's cute that you tried. Don't struggle, or you'll get some wicked rope burn," he warns, vanishing from my sight for a second, but I soon feel rope on my ankles as he ties my feet to the foot of the bed, spread out for their taking.

"Do you really believe I'll run off in the middle of sex?" I scoff with amusement, but Darius just stands beside the bed, continuing to grin.

"Not sure yet, but I've tied you down for two reasons. Nothing gets my dick harder than seeing my ropes restraining someone, and Santos is likely to make you jump all over the place the moment his face is between your sinful legs."

I don't have to wonder why for very long, because Santos scoots his body down the bed and nips my clit almost painfully, causing my hips to lift slightly from the bed as a shriek of surprise leaves me. He smirks up at me as I strain my neck to glare down at him, and his tongue darts out to lick right up my slit.

I drop my head back to the pillow with a groan.

"Selene, keep your fucking eyes on Santos, or you'll be punished," Darius threatens, and I do my best to keep my eyes on the wicked man between my legs as he licks and sucks at my pussy like a man starved.

My body's a shaking mess, and I drop my head back slightly without thinking, a sharp sting piercing my side.

I whip my head up to see Santos' blade against my skin, a wicked glint in his eye as he digs the blade in slightly as I glare at him.

A drop of blood trickles down my side, and he pulls back to watch it. His breath fans across my damp folds and I whimper at the loss of contact, but my pussy clenches as he leans over me, keeping his eyes on mine, and he runs his tongue across the small amount of blood.

I pull against the ropes and growl, hating not having my hands free.

"Untie me so I can touch you," I demand, but he smirks, cocking his head to the side as he sits back.

"Why the fuck would I do that when I'm having so much fun watching you squirm?" he asks, but Darius blocks my sight from him as he sits his bare ass on my chest, fisting his hard length and running the tip across my lips.

"You talk too much. Open wide, Reaper," he orders, making me scowl for a moment at the use of my name before doing as he asks.

He's not gentle as his fingers tangle in my hair to tug me over his dick more, a groan leaving him as I take him deep, despite the awkward angle.

"That's better. Choke on my dick," he mutters, lifting himself a fraction to force himself deeper.

I choke, a sadistic grin taking over his face as he pushes down my throat even more, forcing saliva to slip from my lips and down my chin. I've spent my life chasing down guys like this, letting them treat me like dirt until I get the last laugh, but something tells me these guys won't humiliate me. Hurt me, maybe, but not humiliate me.

"Fuck, you love choking on it, don't you? Darius, she's wet as fuck," Santos groans almost as if in pain, bending down to suck on my clit, going back to stroking his fingers in and out of my now drenched pussy.

He finds that magic spot inside me and sucks harder on my bundle of nerves, causing my body to lock up as my orgasm rips through me. I swear my eyes roll into my fucking head as he keeps the same pace.

# Chapter Eighteen

## Zander

I walk into the bedroom just as Selene comes, her body writhing under Darius, who's fucking her mouth like a madman. I have to admit; she doesn't scare easily. He's being rough as fuck, and I almost cum in my fucking boxers at the sight.

Santos sits back with a grin, licking his lips before wiping his mouth with the back of his hand.

Selene's eyes flutter as she glances over at me in her orgasmic haze, a small smile tugging at her lips as Darius climbs off her.

"You coming to join us, money bags? Plenty of room," she giggles, causing my dick to jerk to life. I am supposed to get her the fuck away from them, but she looks fucking stunning laid out on the bed at their mercy.

I can't even form words, but Santos goes ahead and snaps me out of it.

"If you're going to stand there like a little bitch, at least open your mouth and swallow my load like one."

I glare at him, but Selene tugs against her restraints, watching me with pleading blue eyes. She wants me, and my dick is one hundred percent on board with that plan, but I'm not going to take her with these two fuckers. I want her in my bed, screaming my fucking name, not theirs.

I pull all my willpower together and take a step back, giving them a dirty look.

"Nope. Have a good night," I bite out, stalking from the room before I can change my mind.

Blaze raises an eyebrow as I enter the kitchen, amusement hidden deep inside.

"Something wrong, brother?" he questions, and I grit my teeth with annoyance.

"I'm fucking fine."

I don't know why I snapped at the others, and now I'm taking my mood out on Blaze. Fuck, I do know. I have a thing for the hooker who's fucking my piece of shit father.

"You should've hauled her out of there if you want her so bad," Blaze says, ignoring my attitude.

"Am I that fucked up?" I ask him as I sit at the table. "I want the whore my father is using as a cum dumpster."

"Yeah," he shrugs. "But being fucked up is our thing. Just tell her you get her next."

"What?" I chuckle at him. "We're all just going to have her, like a big happy sharing family?"

"Don't bring me into this bullshit," he snarls. "I don't want the dirty whore."

"All right, my bad," I chuckle and back out of the kitchen. "Let's get a hold of Mack and find out when he's setting up his meat delivery to my father."

"Yeah, we'll call him after I get some sleep."

Blaze runs cold until he's triggered, and then the mean fucker is scalding fucking hot. Don't fuck with what's his or he will blast a bullet into your brain in a matter of seconds. He's guarded and doesn't trust easily, and having Selene in on our plans is most likely starting to trigger him.

He doesn't trust her, and I don't blame him. We don't know her, but I saw her inside that fucking apartment. She showed me a piece of herself, and I believed every word she said. I really do believe her mother sold her sister and I also believe my father ended up owning her. I want to find out more, and the only way I can do that is if Selene can distract my father.

My father keeps everything locked up in that office and it's well secured with video surveillance. But I can drop the feed and loop it for ten minutes. All I'll need is ten fucking minutes, because I know exactly where to look.

I just need her help.

# Selene

Having him watch me as I came all over Santos' face made my orgasm that much better. I fucking want him to come back and join in with us because the more dicks, the better. I feel a quick swipe of the blade against my inner thigh and then my blood once again rolling toward the bed.

I growl as I look down and see Darius coating his finger in the blood while Santos licks it off the tip of the blade. Then Darius slips that bloody finger inside me, and I whimper at the sweet intrusion.

"Start fucking her," Santos says as he gets up and comes to the head of the bed. "Now it's time to choke on my cock, Reaper."

I grin at him and snap my teeth at his tip.

"Don't get crazy," he grins right back. "I'll fuck you with my knife instead."

Darius presses his cock to my entrance, and I gasp as he begins to stretch me wide. He takes his time for the first few inches, and I lift my head to get a better look. It's when he looks up at me with a crazy laugh that I begin to fucking worry.

He slams home and I scream through the pleasurable pain.

"Keep that mouth open wide," Santos chuckles, and his cock thrusts into my mouth, hitting the back of my throat. "Gag all over my cock."

I do. I gag all over his cock and his sinister laugh sounds when saliva drips down my chin. Darius picks up the pace between my legs, making me meet Santos' thrusts and forcing him farther down my throat.

Then Santos crams himself in farther and my throat constricts around his length as I struggle to fucking breathe.

"Fuck yes," Darius groans. "She's tightening up. Keep that throat filled."

I pull against my binds as I attempt to dislodge Santos from my airway, and my wrists sting with the burn from the harsh rope.

"Told ya not to fight against those." Darius slams in one more time and I feel his hot cum shoot inside of me.

Santos pulls out in time with Darius, and I suck in air, choking as my tight chest begins to loosen.

"You crazy motherfuckers," I growl at them, and Santos is once again between my legs.

"I want to taste my boy inside of you." That's the only warning I get as his mouth begins sucking at my pussy hole.

"Fuck!" I exclaim as his tongue slides inside of me, licking me thoroughly.

It's fucking turning me on that he's sucking and licking his friend's cum from inside of me, and I feel myself coiling tighter again.

He gets up and lines himself up at my entrance, thrusting into me with a powerful plunge. My pussy clamps down on him and I scream as he grabs my waist and fucks me into oblivion. I crest the high of my orgasm and fall over the edge, screaming things completely unintelligible. I don't give a fuck though because I am having an out-of-body experience.

Santos bottoms out inside me a few moments later, groaning through his release, and I feel Darius undoing the restraints on my wrists.

I'm out of it, completely fucking destroyed, and the last thing I remember is someone washing my pussy with a warm cloth.

# Chapter Nineteen

## Zander

When I finally wake up, it's late afternoon and I growl that I've missed half the day. I get out of bed and shower, finally pounding one out to the image of her blue eyes as she came.

I get to the kitchen and almost cum again when I smell the coffee and bacon. I walk in and find Selene at the stove with just my t-shirt on, her long tanned legs on display as she cooks the bacon.

Darius chuckles when he sees me gawking.

"She's a fucking sex maniac," he tells me as Selene turns to look at me.

"Good morning." Her voice is so fucking sexy and husky.

"Morning," I mumble and head for the coffee machine.

I don't want to look at her standing there looking satisfied in my shirt when I attributed nothing to that state, and the sight of the small cuts on her neck has me boiling inside. Santos really laid into her, and Darius too, if the rope burns around her wrists, means anything.

"Your daddy has called and summoned me to your big ole house," she says, her words laced heavy with sarcasm. "Bet he misses this pussy."

"He'd be fucking stupid not to," Darius chuckles and gets up to leave the kitchen.

The anger that comes over me at her words is fucking swift, and I grab her blonde hair in my hand and haul her over to face me.

87

"Do you think I need to hear about some whore fucking my father?" I snarl into her face, my spit hitting her cheeks.

"Why are you so pissed if I'm just a whore?" She's calm, unaffected by my violent outburst. Like she knows she can take me on.

The thought has me rock hard in my pants and I drag her in closer, pressing into her stomach.

"Because you've ridden almost every dick but mine." I'm shocked at my admission.

"All you have to do is ask," she purrs up at me and I release my hold on her hair.

"Whatever." I turn my back and take a few deep breaths. "What time are you going there?"

"Same time as before. Midnight," she answers and begins to hum as she cooks.

I can't be in this room with her right now while she's looking thoroughly fucked, because my cock has ideas, and I can't seem to get a grip on my sanity with her around.

"Get dressed and let's plan this shit out," I grumble.

"I have no clothes because your psycho friend decided it would be fucking fun to cut them off me."

Fucking Santos.

"I'll grab you some pants." I'm out of the kitchen and the air feels clearer, not so cloyed with her scent.

It's no better seeing her in my shirt and pants as she moans over bacon, sucking the grease off her fingertips. All of us—even Blaze—are squirming in our fucking seats and refusing to look away. She eats like she's perpetually stoned, enjoying every fucking morsel.

"I need to fill your mouth again," Darius groans, and I watch as he grabs onto his cock.

"Same," Santos moans.

"Fuck off," Blaze growls and slams his fist onto the table. "These women, these *children*, need our help and instead of making a plan, you're lusting after a fucking hooker."

The room falls silent, and I can feel the tension thicken.

"That's not very nice, scary man," Selene says, popping her fingers out of her mouth. "I have my plan and I've had it for a long fucking time."

"So have we," I tell her. "But if we're going to work together, we need those plans to mesh."

"All right." She drops the bacon to her plate. "I am going to your father's place tonight. I plan on letting him do dirty nasty things to me and that's where you come in. Get in that office and check behind the painting of his father."

It's like being hit by a fucking freight train. I've been looking for his vault for years and I narrowed it down to his office. I just didn't know where inside.

"How do you know that?" I ask.

"The last time I was there, he fucked me in the office, and I saw the painting. It was slightly off center, which could happen, but it was the dust free bottom right corner that really caught my eye. Like someone keeps touching it on that exact spot, several times a day."

Fuck, she's good. I can feel my impression of her shifting in this exact moment and it's fucking shocking. Sure, I knew she could maim, fucking kill, and I knew she used her pussy as a weapon as well, but she was also fucking smart.

She just shaved off all the time it would take me to find the fucking vault in his office. I wouldn't even need the full ten minutes now.

My heart begins to race with excitement and before I can even fucking stop it, I'm launching myself around the table and crashing my mouth into hers. She tastes of salty bacon and something else entirely unique to her.

My tongue pushes itself into her mouth and she's moaning, clutching at the front of my shirt. I hear the clearing of a throat and finally snap out of my stupor, instantly pulling away from her mouth.

"Well…" She runs a finger across her swollen red lips. "Three down."

"That's all you'll get," Blaze says, his voice dark and mean.

"Sure," she shrugs and starts back into her bacon. "So, good plan?"

"Yes." I sit back in my chair.

"Cool." She sticks out her hand. "Someone pay me for the dress that Slasher over here destroyed. I need to impress big-dicked daddy."

And she's back to her-fucking-self.

# Chapter Twenty

## Selene

Santos handed me a credit card and told me there's no limit. Motherfucker has shit for brains because I just bought myself a new wardrobe and enough alcohol to drown myself, and then some. I bought Louboutin's too because why not? Daddy Henry needs to be impressed.

I stand at the mirror, checking myself out at every angle, and decide I'm a hot bitch. This tight black tube dress is clinging to every curve, making my tits pop and my ass ripe. I'm sure Henry will love all the easy access to my best parts.

I get a text from Zander, telling me everything is in place, and now I just need to wait for Henry to tell me where to meet his driver. About twenty minutes later, Henry sends me a text to meet the driver in the same location as last time.

I get to the Rolls Royce and it's the same driver, only this time the fucker is a bit more eyesy. He keeps looking at me through the rearview mirror and it's making me want to shoot the fucker in the back of the head.

We finally pull up to the house and when he comes around to open my door, he has the audacity to ask for my number. But being the good hooker that I am, I give him the local pizza joint's number by my house and blow him a kiss for good measure.

Henry meets me just inside the door and his eyes rake over me appreciatively.

"Good week?" The piece of shit asks.

"Yes," I smile at him. "I expect to be paid tonight for the last time as well." I wink at him.

"Yes, of course," he nods and heads for the office.

"Wait," I call out to him. "Can we go somewhere else?"

I keep to the script that Zander and I rehearsed.

"Pardon?" He quirks his brow.

"This is such a big house." I widen my eyes. "Do you blame me for wanting to see it?"

He relaxes and throws me a smile. "What would you like to see?"

"I have a thing for cars, and I've always wanted to be fucked on the hood of a classic."

He tips his head back and laughs. "What makes you think I have any classics?"

"Any car over a hundred grand will do." I flutter my lashes, and he laughs again.

"I will admit, it sounds intriguing." He takes my hand and leads me away from the office. I know the layout and I grin to myself when we head for the garage.

According to Zander, it's soundproofed and the farthest point in the house from the office.

The second we step into the garage; my breath leaves me in a rush. There are about ten cars in here, and each one of them is at least a hundred grand.

"Wow," I say, and for the first time tonight, I'm not acting.

"Pick your poison," he offers and gives me a wink.

It's fucking unfortunate that Henry is a slimy motherfucker that's into raping girls and if he doesn't end up killing them, he sells them to the highest bidder, because this piece of shit is handsome.

I walk over to a red Corvette and run my hands along the hood.

"That's one of my son's," he says.

"Oh?" I look over my shoulder at him. "Think he'll mind?"

I begin to pull up the hem of my skirt, planting my feet apart, and bend over to rest my elbows on the hood, my ass out and waiting for him.

He comes up behind me, running his hands along my ass cheeks, and then up my back to settle against my neck.

"All these cuts and bruises." His voice is quiet.

"Some clients get a little rough." I shrug and look back at him.

"And you allow that?" he asks, sounding curious.

"If the pay is right."

His hand brushes along the top of my head and before I know it, he slams my face down onto the hard, cold surface of the hood. I grunt at the impact and count to ten to stop myself from attacking him back. I need him to believe I'm nothing more than a helpless whore. But it's fucking hard.

"Now we can really have fun." His chuckle is dark and foreboding.

I hear his belt come undone and I stay completely still under his firm hand. I could easily get out of this and kill the fucker with my bare hands, but I'm sadistic and, like my sex just as sadistic.

He releases my head and I lift it to look behind me, only to have his belt slipped over my head and around my neck. This is a little disconcerting, especially knowing he likes to strangle and kill girls.

The belt tightens and breathing becomes difficult. I feel his fingers brush my core and I can't help as it clenches in anticipation. Greedy little bitch.

He rips my thong off, and I hiss at the sting, his laugh grinding my fucking nerves.

But my pussy is wet, like I said, sadistic.

I hear the crinkle of a condom wrapper, and the belt tightens again as he lines himself up. I may die here tonight, but at least my pussy will be thoroughly beaten.

I plant my hands and brace myself for what I know will be a rough fucking ride. He doesn't let me down as he props my knee to the hood and roughly plunges inside me. My mouth falls open at the intrusion as my pussy grips his length.

"Fuck," he groans as he pulls on the belt and slides all the way out.

When he slams back in, my hands jerk off the hood and I strain against the belt, choking for a split second until I get my hands back under me. The heightened sensation of being choked and fucked hard has me climbing toward my release.

Just as I'm about to fucking crash over the edge, I hear his voice.

"This looks interesting."

Motherfucker. This just *got* interesting. Henry's thrusts falter as his son's voice echoes around us.

"Did it have to be on my car?" He sounds slightly amused.

The belt around my neck loosens and I greedily suck in a lung full of air.

"Don't stop on my account," Zander purrs out as he goes to the driver's side door and leans against the top. "She's not your usual."

Henry is still inside of me, and I can feel his cock twitch, but he still hasn't said anything. I give Zander a look that says, *what the fuck are you doing?*

Henry begins to slowly pump back into me, and I moan as Zander keeps his eyes on my face. It's fucking hot because I'm between a father and son. Henry slams into me, and I gasp as he tightens the belt back around my throat.

Zander reaches out and brushes the hair from my face.

"How is her cock sucking?" he asks his father.

At his words, my stomach tightens, and I moan as I feel myself cresting again.

"She's good," Henry grunts behind me, and I can't help but grin at Zander. His daddy thinks I suck cock well.

He sees my smug look and his eyes narrow as he begins to undo the button and zipper on his pants. Is he going to join in?

The belt tightens and Henry's voice drifts from behind me.

"Be a good little whore and suck his dick, too."

Zander has his cock in his hand, and I can't help but wonder if the two of them have done this before. I open my mouth and run my tongue along his tip, tasting him.

Then Zander grabs my hair and forces my head back to stick his cock in my mouth. The belt tightens to hold me in place as Zander brutally fucks my mouth and breathing is not an option.

"Dirty fucking whore." Henry's hand slaps down on my ass. "You'd choke on any cock, wouldn't you?"

I can feel the tears slip down my cheeks from lack of oxygen and my pussy is leaking just as much from Henry's punishing rhythm. He slaps down on my ass again and I groan around Zander's cock in my mouth.

Zander pulls out of my mouth, giving me just enough time to take a breath. And then he's plowing back in. The ferociousness from both father and son has me tumbling over the edge, my vision blacking out.

"She's so fucking tight around my cock." Henry slams in once more and releases inside of me.

"Her mouth is like heaven," Zander moans and shoots his load down my throat.

The belt comes off my neck and I fall forward onto the hood of the car, still swallowing down Zander's bitter cum. I hear them both doing up their pants and then a large wad of bills lands beside my face.

"She's expensive," Zander whistles.

"I owed her for another night. Mind walking her out? I need to get work done." I lean up in time to watch Henry walk away and back into the house.

I grab up the bills and whistle to myself when I see at least five thousand dollars.

"Did you get it?" I ask him.

"Yeah." He heads to the driver's side door. "We need to leave before he notices it missing."

I'm sore between my legs after my night with Santos and Darius, and now Henry. So, walking to the passenger side is difficult.

But I just had a Daddy and Son sandwich. The fucking pain is worth it.

# Chapter Twenty-One

## Zander

Holy fucking shit. Pretty sure that was the best head I'd ever had in my goddamn life. If Selene wasn't already consuming my senses, she sure as fuck is now.

I glance over at her as we pull up in the driveway at Santos' place, noticing her staring out the window blankly.

"Were we too rough with you?" I ask as I kill the engine and unbuckle my belt, but she snorts and glares at me with complete defiance in her stunning blue eyes, almost taking my breath away.

"That was nothing. I can take more than a belt and a rich dude sandwich. Pretty sure I'd scare Santos if I let loose completely," she huffs, causing my lips to kick up into a smirk.

I startle her slightly as I grab her chin roughly and kiss her hard, sitting back after a second to stare into her eyes.

"Next time, it's going to be my dick in your cunt, not Henry's. I'm going to fuck you so hard that all memories of that asshole will be erased from your fucking head, and my dick's all you can think about," I say in a low voice, her body shivering at my words.

We climb from the car and head towards the house, nearly getting bowled over by Santos and Darius, who seemed to think they'd never see her again.

"You're back! How was the old dude's dick? Actually, don't answer that or I'll go over there and gut him for touching you," Santos scowls, hauling her against him roughly and hugging her so tight that she chokes slightly.

"Santos, I need air," she manages to get out, making him laugh as he steps back and ruffles her wavy blonde hair, much to her annoyance.

"No, you don't. You held your breath longer than that when Darius's dick was jammed down your throat. So, you two were successful?" he asked, his gaze bouncing between us.

"Took two seconds. Selene knew where the safe was hidden," I smirk, but she just shoots me a fake sweet smile, fluttering her long lashes at me.

"Thank fuck, or you would have missed out on dumping your load in me."

Blaze looks at me as if I was slacking on the job, but Darius grins.

"You got to tap that, huh? If it were possible after what we did to her, and then Henry, I'd say you definitely have a pin dick and no cunt skills whatsoever," he teases, but Selene just can't help herself as she rubs against me, her voice sultry.

"Oh, he just shut me up while Daddy dearest filled my cunt. You taste good, Zander," she breathes, standing on tiptoe to lick me up the side of my face. She is lucky I don't get Santos to hold her down while I fuck her. Sore pussy be damned.

Blaze manages to look surprised, but Santos cackles with laughter, his psychotic hooting bouncing off the walls.

"You joined in with Henry? You sick fuck, I love you. I say, you and I fuck her senseless, and I accidentally slip one in you, just to see how freaky you get!" He laughs, sitting on the couch and motioning for Selene to join him.

My body becomes cold as she moves away from me and lowers herself onto Santos' lap, snuggling against his chest.

"It's not even that freaky. It's not like he rubbed balls with his dad," she sighs, bored with the conversation.

"Did you even get what you went there for?" Blaze snaps, anger and irritation seeping out of him in waves.

He stalks towards me and snatches the papers that poke out from my pocket, running his eyes over them without waiting for my answer.

Darius rolls his eyes and plonks his ass down beside Santos, pulling Selene's feet onto his lap and absently massaging them.

"Anything weird stick out to you? Assassination plans or some shit?” he asks, tilting his chin at me to answer him. I shrug, feeling Blaze's annoyance from beside me without turning my head.

“I glanced over things quickly. I didn't read in detail.”

“That's because you were too busy dicking daddy's whore,” Blaze grunts, not taking his eyes off the paperwork.

Santos scowls, and I really think he's about to go kill Henry and fuck up our plans, but Selene stands and moves up to Blaze, dipping her fingers below the elastic on his sweats and leaning forward with a coy smile.

“Sounds like someone's jealous. You want some release, grumpy? I'll even give you a freebie because I'm a good buddy like that.”

His hand darts up, his fingers spanning around her pretty neck as he squeezes firmly, swatting her other hand away from his pants.

“Do not fucking touch me,” he grits out, but she's not even fucking fazed as her eyes fill with some form of crazy lust, my dick jerking slightly.

“If you're going to choke me, at least do it from behind. I bet you're a savage in bed. Can you tear the pussy up, Blaze?” she breathes, causing Santos and Darius to groan.

Blaze glares at her for a split second before shoving her back and slamming the papers against my chest.

“You go over this shit. I'm leaving. Control your bitch before I have to,” he spits before stalking from the house and slamming the door behind him.

Selene pouts, and I can't help myself as I wrap her hair around my fist and tug her flush with my front, dipping down to suck her pouty lip between my teeth. She stares at me with heated eyes, but I chuckle and nip her sharply before letting her go.

“You need to sleep. I'll give these papers a once over and we can talk about it in the morning. It's late, and you've had a workout today.”

Santos goes to stand, but I put my hand out, stopping his escape.

“You two, on the other hand can sit here with me and leave her the fuck alone. Her pussy won't vanish overnight, so let her rest.”

“Fucking seriously?” Santos snaps, but Darius rolls his eyes, not bothering to move.

“Santos, let her sleep. We can fuck her cunt in half tomorrow.”

Always the problem solver.

Santos perks up at that idea, letting Selene head to bed without argument.

I am actually surprised when she doesn't argue, but I can tell she's sore. She's been walking funny ever since we got back to my place.

Once she is out of the room, I hand the papers to Darius to glance over, and I sit beside them to look over things.

All I know is my father sure as shit has caught onto us, because one of the papers is a letter from some cunt, letting him know he'd accepted the job and it is none other than the leader of the Diablos, Antonio.

Now that we know who the fuck is on our asses, it's time to start planning on how to burn Henry's kingdom to the fucking ground.

## Selene

I usually would have beat Zander's balls for dismissing me to bed, but I can't lie, my coochie hurts and I am tired as fuck. I'll let them find the information that we need, then hopefully by the time I wake up, we can get a plan into order.

I feel the bed dip, just a slight movement behind me as I lie in bed. I instinctively feel for my knife under the pillow and quickly turn, straddling the person to pin them to the mattress with my knife against their throat.

Santos' eyes fill with desire as he thrusts up against me, his voice rough from sleep.

"Wow, you like to get into it early, huh, baby? All right, but just a quickie or we'll get in trouble from the cock blocking assholes," he grins like the crazy fucker he is, and I press the blade more firmly against his skin as I lean down to speak in his ear.

"That depends. Do I get to tie you up this time?" I whisper, his dick jerking from under me.

"Maybe later, kitten. Right now, I need you to get on your back and spread those legs for me. Keep the knife out though, I like it," he purrs, sliding his hand up my waist and along my smooth skin. A quickie couldn't hurt.

I pull the knife back and climb off him, giggling as he rolls me onto my stomach and pins my arms against my back, holding my knife between his teeth with a chuckle. He tugs my panties down my legs and lifts my ass in the air, dropping my knife onto the bed so he can open a condom without letting my hands go with the other.

He slams into me, causing me to scream into the pillows as my pussy adjusts to the sudden intrusion, his fist going to my hair to yank my face away from the pillow clouds.

"Scream my name. Let's see if we can both come before they kick the door down," he growls, and my pussy clenches in excitement at that idea. I arch my back as I feel the cool handle of my blade press against my clit, and I moan loudly as he starts rubbing it against my sensitive bundle of nerves while pounding into me.

He slows, bringing his free hand around in front of my face and running his thumb along my lips.

"Suck it," he demands, a groan of satisfaction coming from him as I draw it into the wet heat of my mouth and roll my tongue around it until he pulls it away from me.

He runs his hand down my spine, hooking his wet thumb into my ass and picking up the pace again, the blade handle moving faster.

"Fuck, fuck, fuck, I'm going to come!" I blurt out, and he presses his thumb deeper into my ass, causing me to explode. White light flashes behind my eyelids as I scream, his thrusts becoming erratic as he tosses the knife aside and grabs hold of my waist, rutting into me so hard that my orgasmic stars get fucking stars.

The door slams open and bounces off the wall just as Santos comes hard, shoving into me as deeply as possible with a grunt. He drops beside me, his eyes lighting up as he stares at my naked body.

"Fuck, that's so hot," he exclaims, causing me to look over my shoulder to see bloodied handprints on my waist. I frown in confusion, but Santos laughs like a psycho, holding his bloodied hand in front of himself.

"Well shit, maybe I held the knife a little too tightly. Whoops! You look hot as fuck with my blood on you, Selene. Pretty sure it's going to make me come again."

Blaze is in the doorway, the rage on his face slipping slightly as he stares right at my pussy that's still in the air. I wiggle my ass, snapping him out of it as I giggle.

"You want a go? Might make you smile for once in your fucking life, angry man," I taunt, not at all surprised when he sneers at me and gets hold of his wandering thoughts.

"Santos, get down to the kitchen and help Zander. You were supposed to leave her to sleep, not come in here and have play time," he grumbles, his eyes narrowing on me as I roll onto my back and spread my legs, running a hand down my mound to tease my clit.

"You sure you don't want to start your day with a smile? I think it would be good for you."

He barks at Santos to hurry the fuck up before storming off, leaving Santos with me unsupervised. I waggle my eyebrows at him, but he groans and rolls off the bed, putting distance between us as he throws the condom in the bin by the bathroom door.

"You heard the grumpy bastard. Playtime is over. We will get back to this later, you little minx. I'm going to get Darius to tie you up again, and I'm going to choke you with my dick until you pass the fuck out. Hopefully Zander will want to come play too. Then we could fill all three holes at once. Fuck, I'm getting hard again just thinking about it. I'm going to do some work before Zander stalks up here and shouts like a jealous idiot. Maybe blow him again before we get into this plan, might relax him a little," he jokes before leaving the room to give me some peace.

I wince as I sit up, making my way into the bathroom to wash up, having to rummage through the drawers for something fresh to wear.

Pretty sure Zander's eyes nearly fall out of his head when he sees me wander into the kitchen in his clothes again.

Blaze huffs as if I'm the reason nothing's getting done, but Zander finally snaps out of his staring and clears his throat, motioning to Darius.

"You and Santos are scoping out one of Henry's shipments today. Blaze is talking to some contacts about the assholes Henry sent after us, and I have to get our security bumped up in case of another attack. Selene, you—"

"I'm busy," I cut in, all their eyes swinging at me.

"Pardon?" Zander snorts. "Doing what exactly? Thought you wanted to fucking help?"

"I do, but Daddy Walton isn't my only client that I have to deal with. I have another piece of shit to take out today, but then I can be back here tonight if you need me," I explain, giving them a half shrug. Blaze looks ready to kill me, but Zander seems almost relieved.

"All right, you handle that, and we will handle this shit. Let us know if you need backup," he offers, earning a snort from me.

"There's more chance of you needing to call me for backup, money bags, but thanks for the offer."

Santos grins at me like I'm the best thing he's ever seen, and Darius chuckles, handing me a coffee with a wink.

"I'll need help to get off this afternoon, so I'll definitely be calling you in for backup."

I can't even be mad, because hello, coffee?

I sip it with a groan, all four sets of eyes watching me with the same intensity as if I'd taken my fucking clothes off and shaken my tits at them. I quirk an eyebrow at Darius, biting my lip before speaking softly.

"How many freebies do you think you're getting, exactly?"

"You're not even a real hooker," he pouts, his eyes lighting up as I move towards him and kiss his cheek.

"The money doesn't hurt, though. My funds will run out eventually and I'll have to move on again," I reply, Santos' head whipping around to glare at me.

"What the fuck are you talking about? You're not going anywhere, you're fucking mine, Selene. If you leave, I'll fucking drag you back by your hair!" he snaps, and I struggle not to giggle as his eye twitches.

"You can only kill so many assholes before moving on. I don't want to get caught, and my list of people is practically worldwide. Doling out punishments is hard work, but someone's gotta do it," I shrug, but his eyes are blazing as he grabs my bicep, sloshing my coffee over the brim of the cup.

"You're. Not. Leaving. Me."

Darius doesn't look happy with me either, but he gets between us and manages to get Santos to release his hold on me.

"C'mon, we all have shit to do today. We can get on with our shit, and she'll meet us back here later. Won't you, Selene?" he says firmly, waiting for me to nod before letting his friend go. Santos scowls and stalks off with Darius behind him, slamming the front door as he leaves, but Blaze just snorts.

"Knew your pussy was going to cause fucking problems. Do us a favor and get this shit done so you can fuck off. I'll see you later, Zan," he grunts and takes off too, leaving Zander and me alone. Zander rubs his temples before looking my way with conflict in his gaze.

"I really wish you two would get along," he mutters with irritation.

Why the fuck does he care if we get along or not? Didn't I just say I was leaving? Maybe he's not the brightest crayon in the fucking box?

"Hey, all he's gotta do is bend me over this kitchen table and I'll be his best friend. He's the one with the issue, not me. I'm going to go and get ready for my date. I want to go dress shopping with the money Henry gave me," I grin, but he rolls his eyes and thrusts his credit card at me.

"Save your money. Take this and buy a new outfit. Don't wreck it while you're annihilating old rich assholes today. I want to tear it from you myself when you get back here," he says in a low voice.

My coochie clenches in anticipation with that plan, so I smirk and kiss his cheek, making sure to brush my body against his.

"Sounds good, Zan. I'll see you later." Then I call an Uber and head off home to get some of my plans together for the day.

# Chapter Twenty-Two

## Selene

Zander is going to come down his fucking leg when he sees this dress on me. It is bright red, strapless, and it practically stays up with willpower and prayers. It is tight as fuck, and I love how good my ass looks in it.

My next victim, Harold Aster, is in his early sixties. He'd done well to cover his tracks, but not well enough to hide from me. He'd made the mistake of joking about it with an old friend of his, who just so happened to be a previously chatty client I'd dealt with nearly three months ago. The old cunt hadn't shut his mouth about it, so it was easy to start digging once I'd started.

Harold has been married three times, has seven daughters and two sons between all those wives, and he'd pimped the majority of them out to his rich asshole friends from the moment they all reached the ripe age of thirteen. To make matters worse, one of the wives even knows about it and takes a cut from the profit.

One of the daughters committed suicide at the age of seventeen, one of them has a bunch of mental health issues including anorexia, and one of the sons despises all forms of affection and is basically a robot. The sad thing about the son is he would probably end up on my list one day, because his anger issues towards women are pretty fucking strong.

His mother is the one who knows what's going on, and he hates her for it.

Not that I blame him.

I make my way towards the limousine that's parked down a side alley, and I open the back door myself, not noticing any driver around. The moment I slip inside, my senses go on alert as I find Harold and who I assume is the driver, sitting there waiting for me.

Harold smiles at me like a creep, his eyes raking over my figure.

"You are a beauty. I hope you don't mind that my friend watches."

Fuck. Looks like I'm just fucking and not killing today.

I paste on a charming smile, letting out an annoying giggle.

"Oh, that's perfectly fine! Anything extra will cost, though."

The driver fumbles in his pocket and pulls out a wad of bills, practically throwing them at me.

"Can I touch you? Is that enough?"

Pretty sure he's a fucking virgin, because no man throws that much money at a woman just to touch them while looking that fucking nervous. I flutter my lashes at him, biting my lip and parting my legs to tease him.

"You can have a ride too, if you want? If Mr. Aster doesn't mind, that is," I answer in a breathy voice, and Harold's smile becomes dark.

"Of course I don't mind. How about you get out of that dress and show us what we're working with," he asks, and I oblige, like the good little paid whore that I am. I slip from the dress but leave the silver strappy heels on, sliding my foot up Harold's leg.

"Well? Do you like what you see, Mr. Aster?"

The driver looks ready to fucking combust at the sight of my tits, let alone my pussy being on display. Who needs underwear, right?

Harold hauls me onto his lap, smelling my neck like a weirdo.

"You smell divine. Put a condom on me," he orders, shuffling his pants down awkwardly without moving me from his lap. I accept the condom and lean back, placing it over the head and slowly rolling it down his shaft while biting my lip.

He was already groaning, so I knew it wouldn't take him long once I actually start fucking him. But things don't always go as planned.

The driver suddenly grabs both my arms and holds them tightly behind my back, chuckling in my ear.

"You don't think I know who you fucking are? You killed my dad, you little slut. Found his car burned to a crisp outside of town, his body in the back and your reaper mark left in the fucking dirt," he murmurs, and for the first time in a while, I was a little thrown at that surprise. That asshole didn't have kids, and I have no idea how that connects to Harold.

Harold grins, pinching my nipples hard.

"The thing about rich pricks like myself is that we know other rich pricks. You're the talk of the town, Reaper. It's time that you paid for your sins," he growls, shoving a finger inside me roughly.

If he really thinks he can rape me as punishment, he has another think coming. I was a pro at detaching myself from my body when it came to sex after all this time, so I'd just have to wait it out.

His driver kept my arms pinned as Harold did a shitty job at punishing me with his fingers, but I'm suddenly pulled backwards and slammed down onto the seat, my face pushing into the luxury fabric and my legs are held down to stop any of my fancy ninja moves. The driver is pretty good at the hold he has on my arms still, but he'd lose focus and give me a window to escape soon. They always did.

Nails dig into my legs as the weight lands on my back, and I take my chance to yank an arm free and swing my elbow back. There's a grunt before a fist hits me in the eye, pinning my head painfully to the seat.

"You little fucking whore! Just for that, I'm going to fuck your ass hard without lube. No teeth in my seats or I'll slit your fucking throat," Harold grits out as he scrambles to keep my arms restrained. I know this isn't going to be pleasant, so I try to relax my body to avoid too much damage happening, but the door's yanked open and I hear a gurgling sound, one I know well as a throat being slit.

"I have money! I'll give you what you want, but don't hurt me!" Harold cries, letting go of me as he pleads for his life. I realize I should be panicking too, but I peer over my shoulder and a sense of calm washes through me.

Santos looks savage as he climbs into the car and shuts us inside, grabbing Harold by the neck and slamming him down onto the seat beside me as I sit up a fraction.

"I don't give a fuck about your filthy money. No one touches my fucking baby girl!" He seethes, not hesitating before digging his blade into Harold's throat, hacking it open so that blood spills all over the place. Between the driver and Harold, there's blood everywhere, and it's not until their bodies stop moving that Santos' eyes flick to me, a mix of emotions in there that twists my stomach slightly.

"You're mine," he states clearly, his hand twitching as he grips the knife firmly still. I reach for him, uncurling his fingers from the weapon and tugging him towards me. But it's a tight fit with the two dead assholes slumped on the seat with us.

"Yeah, Santos. I'm your girl," I whisper, a pained groan coming from him before his lips crash against mine and he fucking consumes me. His hands roam my skin, and a grunt leaves him as I reach for his belt and free his dick from his pants.

I shuffle back, making room for him between my legs, and his eyes darken at the sight of my back pressed against the dead dudes, their blood still drying on my skin.

He wastes no time as he hooks his arms under the back of my knees and lifts them, slamming into me forcefully and without mercy. I scream, the delicious pain licking at my fucking soul as he rearranges my insides.

I throw my head back as he slides a hand between us to rub my clit.

I fall apart from under him, with god and the dead dudes as my witness, and I can't help myself as I grab Santos' throat in my hand and drag him down to kiss me. It's rough, it's dirty, and I fucking love it.

His thrusts become short and sharp until he pulls out and comes on my tits, a devilish smirk on his face as he swirls his thumb through the wetness on my chest before pushing it against my lips.

I suck his thumb into my mouth, staring into his eyes as I move my tongue across his skin, and for a second I'm content. Santos is my kind of crazy, and I want to let him loose on my goddamn soul. His darkness fills me so easily, but it brings me to fucking life, too.

"Fuck, it should be illegal to be that hot," he murmurs, pulling his thumb free and drawing a wet path down my stomach until he reaches my clit again, circling it a few times before pushing two fingers inside me.

I arch up, chasing his touch as I feel more blood drip down my shoulder to mix with the cum on my chest.

His eyes remain on me as he brings me closer to release again, but just before my climax can push me over the edge, his voice hits my ears.

"Don't fucking come yet."

"I can't—"

"Fucking hold it!" he snaps, fucking my pussy with his fingers harder until I'm not even breathing anymore, trying to hold my release back. His voice is low, but his eyes are alight with desire.

"Come for me," he murmurs.

Don't have to fucking tell me twice.

I come hard, my pussy gripping his fingers as it constricts in waves, wetness gushing as he keeps finger fucking me through my screams. English words aren't even a capability at this point, it's just jumbled crap.

"Good girl," he praises, slowing his hand and leaning forward to bite my lip sharply, drawing blood. He sucks it into his mouth, running his tongue over the small cut with a groan.

"Where have you been all my fucking life? You're made for me," he whispers, more to himself than me, moving back and grabbing the back of his shirt to pull it over his head. He wipes the wetness from between my legs before cleaning my chest like it's his favorite thing to do. He might be a crazy son of a bitch, but deep down he gives a shit, and I love that I bring that out of him.

"So, now what? We can't leave this mess here," I chuckle as I observe the bloodied mess behind me. He smirks, waggling his eyebrows.

"Easy. I'll drive it out of here and we will deal with it. I'll call Darius to help."

His take charge attitude only makes me horny again, so I lick my lips and give him a coy smile.

"How about we do that again, only this time, you spank me while you choke me?"

He manhandles me until I'm straddling him, grabbing my throat hard to speak against my lips.

"Only if you ride me like a fucking porn star first, baby girl."

Best fucking plan, ever.

## Zander

"God fucking damn! You guys really made a mess!" Darius hoots with laughter, but my eyes widen as I notice Santos and Selene wandering into the room behind Darius, their bodies covered in blood. Selene has Darius' shirt on, and Santos is only in his pants.

"The fuck happened?" I demand, but Santos winks at me, hooking his arm around Selene's neck to tug her against him.

"Nothing we can't handle."

"That's not what I fucking asked," I growl, but Darius grins, waving his hands around with enthusiasm.

"These crazy fuckers killed two people and fucked on their dead bodies! I'm a little upset that no one thought to call me to join in, but I'll let that shit slide since Selene's going to blow me because I said please," he exclaims, my eyes narrowing on the dress in Selene's hand.

"Is that your dress? I told you to fucking keep it safe."

She quirks an eyebrow at me like a brat, holding it out to me.

"I kept it safe. Might need a wash, though. Fuck knows what's on it now," she replies, heading straight for the fridge to grab a beer. Blaze won't take his eyes off her the moment he joins us, and the scowl only deepens when Selene sits on Darius' lap and opens her legs, staring back at Blaze as Darius' hand wanders down to her swollen cunt. Santos must have really given it to her.

Jealousy surges through me, but I torture myself longer as I watch Darius touch her, his teeth dragging along her neck as she closes her eyes.

Just as he dips a finger inside her, Blaze slams a fist down on the table.

"For fuck's sake, she's not crack. How hard is it to leave her the fuck alone?!" he snarls, but Darius' lip kicks up into a taunting smirk, pushing his finger into her sinful pussy further.

"C'mon, I'll hold her legs apart while you work out some of that anger, if you want? You really gotta get laid, bro. You're starting to get wrinkles from all that scowling you do."

I bite back a chuckle, moving over to them and hauling Selene to her feet.

"Go and shower, then meet back down here so we can talk, all right?"

"We can talk first," she argues, but I run my fingers through her hair and tug her head back to stare up at me.

"We can't, because I'm going to fuck you if you don't go and wash up and put some pants on. Take Santos, he needs a shower too," I offer, stopping the argument easily.

She grins, crooking her finger at Santos.

"Come on, baby cakes. You and I are going for playtime in the shower."

I asked for that, honestly.

Why the fuck didn't I offer to help wash her?

Santos tosses her over his shoulder and carries her up the hallway with a sharp spank on her ass, and Darius follows them with his eyes. He turns to me when they're out of sight, pouting again. He was just as whipped as that other crazy fucker.

"Can I go too? Please?"

"Since you asked so nicely, I guess—" I managed to get out before he tears up the hallway as if I'd change my mind.

"You know we won't see them for hours now, right?" Blaze snarks, sitting in the chair and snatching the beer Selene had left behind, downing it with annoyance. Darius wasn't kidding, Blaze needed to get laid pronto, before he self-combusts with rage.

I shrug, pretending I didn't give a shit, but in reality, I was craving to join them.

Darius and Santos are on a different kink level than I am, but there is something about Selene that makes me forget all about that shit, because if she has pleasure written all over her face from things they're doing to her, I'd nearly be down for anything.

Blaze was wrong.

Selene is like fucking crack, and she has the power to turn me into a junkie for life.

# Chapter Twenty-Three

## Selene

I watch as Darius starts the shower, his back muscles flexing as he adjusts the temperature, and his shirt rides up to show the beginnings of a large tribal tattoo. I bite my lip to hold in a moan and hear Santos' chuckle beside me.

"You're looking at him like a piece of meat."

"He has one chunk of meat I'm most interested in." I shrug. "But my fucking pussy is dicked-out right now and I'm not sure what the fuck you guys want from me."

"Your ass is good though, no?" Darius asks as he looks over his shoulder.

"And that pretty little mouth," Santos chimes in.

Fuck. I may be exhausted, but the thought of being alone right now is a bit depressing. I'm tired of being alone. Since my sister disappeared and I killed my mother, I've only ever been alone.

"Let's see if you can earn it," I wink at them and strip off the shirt.

My skin is itchy from the dried blood and cum, but defiling those bodies was the best thing I've done in a while. It's time to celebrate.

I step into the warm spray of water and watch as Santos hops out of his pants to quickly join me. Darius leans back against the counter and crosses his arms over his chest.

"Are you coming in?" I ask as I dip my hair back under the spray.

"I'm a big man, Selene." His voice takes on a mischievous tone. "And you two are bloodied. When you're nice and clean, I'm fucking that tight asshole."

Well then, I better get a fucking move on.

I quickly clean my hair and body; all the while Santos has his hands on my tits or his fingers in my pussy. Then I move aside for his turn. I get out and Darius wraps me up in a plush towel, then kisses me softly.

"That's the sweetest thing you're getting," he warns before his lips curl up against mine. "After this, it's all debauchery."

"I'm done!" Santos turns off the water and jumps out of the shower.

His wet body plows into mine from behind and I'm sandwiched between them. All the hard, bulging muscles touching my soft curves.

Darius' big hands land on my shoulders and he gently pushes me down to my knees.

"I'll take what you promised me now," he grins.

I go to my knees and Santos rips the towel off me.

"I'll hold her head steady," he chuckles as his fingers grip my strands.

Darius has his pants down and cock out in a flash, it's hard and angry looking.

"Open wide," he says as he presses the wide mushroom head to my mouth.

I do as I'm told and moan as soon as his taste invades my mouth. His salty flavor rushes over my tongue and I slurp around the head of his cock. My tongue pays extra attention to the rough ridge under the head, and I feel his legs relax as a rough groan leaves his mouth.

"Feels good, huh?" Santos asks him as his fingertips massage my scalp.

"Fuck yes," Darius replies.

"Are we done with the sweet shit?" Santos growls. "Can I fuck you with her face now?"

Darius grunts and I clench my eyes shut, knowing exactly what's coming. Santos digs into my scalp and forcefully begins thrusting my face into Darius' dick.

"Holy fuck," Darius groans. "You sure do know how to suck dick, Santos."

"You already knew that."

Huh? What?

My confusion leaves me unprepared for when Santos shoves my face right into Darius' pelvis, his cock slamming down my throat. I gag and my hands push against Darius' thighs, trying to create some space.

Santos pulls my head back and I have about two seconds to inhale before I'm shoved right back against Darius again. I'm fucking furious at being manhandled like this, and my anger takes on a new level when Santos pulls me back.

I forcefully throw my head back and slam it into Santos's dick. He drops behind me like a sack of potatoes, cursing me colorfully. Then I jab my fist into Darius' lower belly and glare when he pitches forward on a harsh exhale.

"You motherfuckers," I seethe as I get to my feet. "I'm down for rough play. I fucking like it, but do not—and I mean do not—force it on me."

I get to my feet, shoving Darius back, and kicking Santos in the chest.

"You're lucky I'm not fucking gutting you," I growl and stomp out of the bathroom into my room. "I may be a whore, but I am not your fucking property to do as you please!" I yell at them.

I throw on yet another pair of Zander's boxers and a t-shirt and make my way back to the kitchen. Zander and Blaze are having what looks to be an intense conversation and I stop in the doorway.

Blaze sees me first and rolls his eyes, the scar tugging his features a bit to the side. "Over so soon?"

"Your men may or may not be suffering in the washroom." I shrug and walk in further. "Had to teach them a fucking lesson in consent."

"Whores require consent?" Blaze narrows his eyes.

"Blaze…," Zander grits out in warning.

"Especially whores," I shrug and plop my ass on the chair beside him. "Money is our contract. Your boys were getting it for free and took advantage."

"Selene!" I hear Darius call from the hallway.

"Fuck." Zander presses his fingers to his forehead. "Here we go."

Darius storms into the kitchen naked, his face red, and his cock still hard and angry.

"Yes?" I raise my brow at him.

"We've done worse!" he exclaims. "What the fuck was all that?"

"With my permission." I hold my finger up.

Santos comes around the corner and props up against the wall, still gripping his junk. "The fuck was that?"

"What did you do?" Zander looks at them with boredom.

"They bruised my esophagus with Darius' dick and forced me to choke against his pubes." I give them a pointed look.

Santos begins to look sheepish, but Darius' face only boils hotter.

"That's all part of a good cock sucking," he retorts.

"Oh, yeah?" I lean my face on my hand, elbow resting on the table. "Show me what you mean."

"What?" Zander and Darius ask at the same time.

"I don't know what you mean by saying a bruised esophagus and pube choking are all part of a good cock sucking." I point from him to Santos. "So show me."

"Oh, for fuck's sake," Blaze mutters and stands. "You are all so fucked up." Then he's storming out of the kitchen.

I'm going to wear him down, eventually.

Santos begins to yank down his sweatpants, and Darius rolls his eyes. "You really want me to suck his dick?"

"Yeah," I nod. "And choke on it."

Darius shrugs like this is no big deal and drops to his knees, throwing me a wink over his shoulder. "Take notes."

I press my lips together to stop myself from laughing and watch as Darius grips Santos' cock in his big hand, giving it a few lazy pumps.

My pussy clenches and I turn to see Zander's eyes on me. I look away from him and back to Darius just as he begins to fucking swallow Santos' cock. I mean fucking swallow all the way down his throat, his nose nestled deep in pubes, and his hand massaging the balls.

This isn't his first rodeo, and the thought has me standing slowly. I may be fucking sore, but my pussy is dripping as I watch them. Santos has his head tossed back against the wall and his hands in Darius' hair as he moans loudly.

Then Darius does indeed begin to choke on Santos' dick, gagging loudly. The moan escapes my mouth before I can stop it and Zander's hands encircle my waist, dragging me towards where he's sitting.

"You like that, baby?" he whispers, and I nod, my eyes still glued to Darius.

Zander pulls his boxers down my legs and adjusts me to straddle his waist. His finger slides through my pussy and he groans at how wet I am.

"Guys," he looks at Darius and Santos. "Don't fucking stop. She's loving this."

They don't bother to answer him, too lost in their own moment, and I begin to grind down onto Zander's fingers.

"You want me inside you, baby?" he whispers in my ear. "Fucking you while Darius sucks Santos' cock?"

"Yes," I moan and watch as Zander pulls his cock from his pants.

He lifts me by the waist and slowly impales me along his wide cock. I begin to grind on Zander while Darius' sucking noises fill the room.

"Fuck!" I exclaim as my pussy squeezes Zander's length.

I begin to ride him faster. My pussy's sucking sounds fucking rivaling Darius'.

"Oh fuck no," I hear Darius growl just before I'm lifted off of

Zander's lap. "We worked hard for this. There's no way you're giving it to this asshole."

Zander leisurely continues to pump his glistening cock and grins.

"All of us," I pant in Darius' arms. "Bedroom, now."

Darius heads there, his long strides eating up the space in no time, and I hear the others following close behind. I have never had three guys at once; I haven't even had double penetration, but I'm more turned on by the idea than I am apprehensive.

Darius falls back on the bed, keeping me straddled on top, and motions towards the side table.

"Get the lube and condoms."

"No need for lube," Santos murmurs.

I hear the slide of the drawer and the crinkle of condom wrappers, but I can't look because Darius has his tongue down my throat. I can taste the musky flavor of Santos in his mouth and moan while my hips search out his cock.

I feel him slide a condom on and he wastes no time sliding deep inside me.

"Fuck." I pull away from his mouth.

I feel a sharp sting on my ass cheek and whip my head around in time to see Zander rubbing his hand against a brand-new cut courtesy of Santos and wiping it down the length of his cock. That's a fucking first, blood as lube. Then Santos has his hand wiping my blood from the cut to my asshole.

I clasp my ass cheeks together at the sticky feeling.

"No, no baby girl." Zander says from behind me. "This one is mine."

The bed dips to our left and I turn away from Zander in time to see Santos' cock bob in my face. I open my mouth, and he pushes inside, this time giving me time to adjust to his size. At the same time, I feel Zander's wide cock slowly begin to stretch open my puckered hole, the burn immediate, but the slippery texture of the blood making the intrusion easier.

As soon as his head breaches the tight muscle, he pushes himself in, and I'm moaning around Santos' cock.

"Fuck," Santos groans. "Make her do that again."

Darius pulls out, then slams back in, Zander pulls out, then slams back in, and their rhythm makes me a whimpering mess around Santos's cock.

"Fuck." His fingers curl into my hair. "I'm going to come down that pretty throat."

No sooner than his words leave his mouth, he does just that. The salty, musky taste of him invading my mouth. I swallow him down and suck him softly as he pulls out from between my soft lips. He falls over onto his back on the bed and watches as Darius wraps his hand around my neck, pulling me in for a deep kiss.

It's like he's licking Santos's taste right out of my mouth, and the thought of him swallowing Santos's dick has me almost blacking out as my orgasm bowls me over.

"So… tight…," Darius grunts up into me and groans his release.

He keeps himself lodged inside of me as Zander continues to punish my asshole.

"She's so tight," he agrees, and his thrusts become sloppy and erratic. "So tight."

Then he thrusts in once more, spilling himself deep in me, and his fingers leaving bruises on my hips.

I fall forward on top of Darius and immediately pass out.

# Chapter Twenty-Four

## Zander

I have Darius and Santos with me for the drop, the three of us having been summoned by my piece of shit father. He's never liked Blaze, and I always get a thrill of satisfaction when he cringes at his scar.

Blaze is home babysitting our newest obsession. Selene is highly unpredictable, and I can't have her seducing her way into things, so that leaves Blaze, who is unaffected by her charms, to keep her occupied.

Tonight the shipment is coming by Mack himself, and this only ever happens when he has something special aboard. Special as in kids. That's right, kids, young too, like ages ranging from five to sixteen. Those shipments are my father's favorite, since he gets a large price tag for them.

"I fucking hate doing this." Darius kicks at a stone at his feet.

"I need to see how many are on this shipment," I explain. "We have to figure out how to get them out of here in three days."

My father has an export container docking in three days to send his shipment overseas into Morocco.

"Yeah." Darius scrubs his hand down his face. "I know."

Santos wets up the spliff in his hand and sparks the end, the cloying scent of marijuana attacking our sense of smell. It's a must for us to get a little stoned for these drop offs. It helps us pack away the emotions and just gather the information needed to help the helpless.

We pass the spliff between us until there's nothing left, and Santos crushes it under his boot. The sun has long since gone down and the moon illuminates the trees and bushes lining this estate's driveway. When my mother was killed, or like my father likes to say, had a terrible accident, I barely stayed in this house. Her angry spirit haunts the place and my fucking nightmares.

"He's here," Santos says quietly.

We all turn our heads and watch as an eighteen-wheeler pulls into the driveway, carrying a large cargo container behind it. It slowly moves up the driveway as Santos and Darius move to my flanks. I need to get this shit done and get the fuck back home to a pussy I am now addicted to. Oh, and an asshole too, apparently.

We watch as Mack parks and hops down from the driver's seat. He's a fat cunt and I cringe as I watch his knees take the fucking impact of his obesity.

"Boys!" His rough voice calls out. The fucker smokes two packs of cigarettes a day and he fucking sounds like it. "I have the goods tonight!"

His hands rub together, and I fist mine at my sides. I want to smash my knuckles into his fat, ruddy face and watch as he spits out teeth from the force.

"Let's get it done," Darius calls out. "I got a juicy cunt waiting for me at home."

"Hold your horses." Mack comes to stand in front of us and it's at that moment I hear a low cry of a child inside the container.

My teeth crack from grinding them so fucking hard.

"Hear that?" Mack grins, his front teeth brown and his bottom teeth missing. "Those children are pristine. I haven't even had my way with any of them."

"Let's get it done," Santos growls, repeating Darius' sentiment, all while flipping his knife in his hand.

Mack, like the stupid fucking idiot he is, doesn't heed his warning and throws his head back with a cackle.

"I remember being young like you boys. Life was grand, me and my boys would run the town, and fuck every girl." His fat pink tongue dabs at his bottom lip. "Oh man, those were the days."

I bet he raped all the girls because I can't imagine anyone wanting this piece of shit. I pull out the pieces of rolled up papers from my inside jacket pocket and read over the details.

"Twenty-four women, six young men, five young boys, and seven young girls, correct?" I ask him.

"Nice haul, huh?" he chuckles.

"What a thing to be proud of." I make sure the sarcasm is heavy in my voice.

"Listen, kid." He reaches into his jacket pocket and pulls out a pack of smokes. "This will be your company when your father is done. You better start to enjoy it and enjoy the money that comes with it."

I watch as his short stubby fingers places a cigarette between those swollen bluish-red lips and lights the tip. His first inhale takes in a quarter of the smoke, and he exhales directly into my face. My first instinct is to reach forward, but luckily Darius throws his arm across my chest.

"Easy, bro." His voice is low. "Now's not the time."

He's right, we need to get this done because the hit my father has out on us could be anywhere and us being out in the open for too long could cost us our fucking lives. My father wouldn't have the Diablos anywhere near his shipment, but that doesn't mean they aren't waiting for when we're finished here.

I nod at Santos, and he opens the passenger side door of the car and pulls out a briefcase. The fucker is filled with enough money to feed a small country, and it's painful to watch it being handed over to this dirty cunt.

"Thanks, boys." His toothless grin has me choking back a gag. "Let's begin the offloading."

He opens the back, and we peer inside at the bodies huddled together, all with burlap bags over their heads, and not much clothing on. Some were even barefoot, and even though I smoked that joint, I still wanted to rip Mack's fucking head off.

I watch as Darius begins to line them up and Santos guides each of them inside the house, then down to the basement like all the other times we've been through this. I stand out here with the biggest piece of shit and keep an eye on our surroundings.

The fucker lights what must be the tenth smoke in ten minutes and begins another fucking story about how he was in college. I don't fucking give a shit and I can't wait until I am able to slide my knife through his throat.

"Then your father thought it would be a good idea to become partners, and we then became millionaires by the age of twenty-three..." *Blah, blah, blah.*

I give the front of the house a quick perimeter scan and nearly jump out of my skin when I watch a familiar form, completely decked out in black, and a hood up over her head, rush around the side of the house.

What the fuck is Selene doing here? And where the fuck is Blaze?

# Selene

Every man is fucking predictable, even the ones that swear up and down that they don't want you, and I just proved that point tonight. Blaze is indeed blazing hot under that deep umber skin and prominent pinkish-white scar, and he is on the verge of giving in to me.

I know exactly what the guys are up to tonight because I have filthy Mack's itinerary for the next few months, and I know tonight is the biggest shipment of underage children this year. Even if I wanted to, I can't miss this opportunity, and I needed to get out from under Blaze's thumb. So, I had two options: kill the fucker or get him riled up and leave the room.

Option one would've gotten me in hot water with the others, so I went with option two, and as per usual, Blaze stormed from the room. I hadn't even gotten to sinking my fingers in my exposed pussy yet, just a few swipes through my folds.

I Ubered to a few blocks from the Walton mansion and walked the rest of the way on foot. That's when I stumbled upon a car with two shady looking fuckers sitting outside the gates. They looked way too similar to the guys that rushed Blaze's house the night of the party and I couldn't take the chance that they would try something on my boys.

Yeah, I fucking said it, my boys.

I approached the open passenger side window and leaned in seductively. Before the guy could say a fucking thing, I had my gun to his head and his brains exploding on both me and the driver.

After that, it was easy to get the second guy talking since his face was coated in his buddy's blood. They were the Diablos, and on a stake-out mission to collect info for some Antonio dude. Once I had that, I blew his forehead open wide and, for the fun of it, drew my scythe into the brain matter clotting along the dash.

Hopefully, that sends a clear enough message to this Antonio.

Now, as I make my way up the driveway, I spot Zander standing with the disgusting sloth, Mack. He looks like he's fucking vibrating with anger, and I can feel the tension even from over fifty feet away. Mack looks completely engrossed with his own conversation and neither notice as I pass behind the rows of trees approaching the side of the house.

I made sure to be completely covered in black so that I would blend better and not catch the eyes of onlookers. Another good thing about coming here tonight? Henry Walton turns off all surveillance during a drop off, so there is absolutely zero evidence if he's ever investigated.

Lucky me, not so lucky, Mr. Walton.

I see Santos and Darius ushering the women and children inside, so I slip by them and down the side of the house. I see the door obscured by climbing vines and slam my fist through the small window. I know this narrow doorway is an old servant's entrance and that this side of the house is rarely used.

I slip inside and look around the empty mudroom, the dark shadows concealing me well. I know exactly where Henry is and getting there will be no problem, but getting by those other three pains in my ass will be the hard part.

This mudroom leads to a smaller kitchen that's long been abandoned. It looks like it was used by the servants to cook and eat in. Pretentious assholes. I step out of the kitchen and I'm immediately inside a small living room. There's a door straight ahead leading to a corridor and back into the front of the mansion and a door to my right that leads to an old wine cellar.

I turn to the right and unlock the bolt, cringing when it scrapes loudly, and open the door. I hear the shuffle of feet and a few murmured voices telling me that they are indeed keeping the fresh meat in the cellar. I know beyond the cellar is a small office and then a stairwell leading up to the main kitchen in the house.

In that small office, I will find Henry, taking accounts of what he's receiving. I can hear both Darius and Santos below, mumbling about something, and leading the line into the cellar. If they even catch the smallest glimpse of me, I know they'll recognize me, and to be fucking honest, I would be pissed if they didn't.

Knowing they're there, I sit at the top of the stairs and wait it out. I hear a few muffled sobs and some not so muffled children's cries, breaking my fucking heart. Soon, I tell myself. Soon, I will have them all safe. They just have to endure this next step, and if they've survived this long, I know they're strong enough to keep going.

I'm sitting on that cold concrete stair for at least a half hour when I hear Zander call out from the other stairway.

"Darius, Santos. Let's go, we got shit to discuss."

"Make sure you're back here when the export is ready!" Henry calls out to him.

Export.

Like they are fucking cattle.

I can't wait until I get that motherfucker alone and show him just what I think about his import/export business. I hear the door upstairs close, and I continue to sit on the fucking stairs for another fifteen minutes.

# Chapter Twenty-Five

## Zander

"I saw Selene go into the house," I tell Darius and Santos as we stand outside in the driveway.

"That's fucking impossible," Santos huffs. "Blaze wouldn't take his fucking eyes off her."

"Unless she killed him," Darius offers and gets an excited look in his eye. It's the same one he gets whenever he thinks about our girl.

"Call him," Santos says as he begins to light another spliff.

"No need," I hear Blaze's distinct growl from behind us.

I turn and cross my arms over my chest. "Bro, why did you let her come here?"

"Let her?" There's a wild look in his eye. Something I haven't seen in a long time. "The bitch got the jump on me."

"She's inside," I nod towards the house. "How the fuck are we getting her out?"

"We?" Blaze's lip curls up in anger, his scar pulling at his left eye. "I'm dealing with her tonight. You three go on back to the house."

I sigh, knowing nothing is going to stand in his way now he's set his mind to it.

I give him a nod, motioning for the other two to follow me as Blaze scowls and stalks into the house, and I hope to God he doesn't fucking kill her. She pushes all of his buttons, so I'm not surprised he's starting to snap.

125

We climb into the car, and I start the engine, glancing over at Darius.

"You think he's going to kill her?"

Santos hoots in the back, slapping his knee for dramatics.

"As if. Our girl would win that fight easy with her fucking eyes shut. I kind of want to stick around and watch it happen. She's always horny after a kill, and my dick gets rock hard seeing her covered in their blood."

"You're disgusting," I mutter, mentally cursing my dick as it jumps behind my zipper at the image that's now in my head.

We drive down the driveway and I do a second take when I notice a car parked by the gates. The guys spot it too, and just as Santos pulls his gun out to prepare for it to rain bullets between the two cars, I spot the blood splatter all over the windshield.

"What the fuck?" Darius murmurs from the back, waiting for me to pull over before carefully climbing from the car to inspect the situation.

Santos lets out a low whistle as he walks around the car, peeking in the window to see the mayhem inside.

"Diablos?" Darius questions, raising an eyebrow as Santos opens the door to get a closer look. They were practically unrecognizable, but I recognized one from the night they went through the fucking house and attacked us.

"Who the fuck…" I mumble before my eyes zeroed in on the dash to see the scythe drawn into the bloodied brain matter. "Selene did this."

Santos groans, rubbing his dick through his pants, but Darius frowns.

"You sure?"

"Yep. She left her reaper mark." I nod, motioning to the symbol.

"Well fuck, we agreed to keep her, yeah? Because I'm not letting her go. Starting to think she's crazier than I am. I'm impressed." Santos grins, slamming the door and moving around to me. Selene and Santos are dangerous together, but the fuckers are perfect for each other.

I roll my eyes and jerk my chin towards our car.

"C'mon, let's get out of here and wait for our girl and the angry asshole to get home."

I can't wait for her to get her psycho ass home so I can get her under me again.

# Selene

The basement becomes still, and I can hear a few sniffles here and there, but for the most part everything has died down. I can hear papers shuffling now and then, telling me Henry is still in his office and that suits me just fucking fine.

I head down the stairs and cut a quick left at the bottom, entering a room designed for pleasure or torture, depending on the person's perspective. This is Henry's pleasure room, and it's his sex slaves' torture room.

I look around and fucking almost lose it when I see swings and chains all over, blood still along their surfaces. Then I hear a whimper and see about twenty people and children crammed into a cage that's no more than eight feet across and ten in length.

I hold my finger to my mouth, praying they listen, and slowly creep towards them. A woman comes forward, a child clutched to her thigh, and reaches her hand out.

"We just want to go home," she whispers.

"I know," I nod. "I'm here to help. I just need you to be very quiet. Okay?"

She nods.

"Can you pass it along to everyone? To please stay calm and quiet?" I ask her and she nods once again, then disappears through the throng.

I back away and look along the adjacent wall, seeing a ton of floggers, whips, and just about every sexual torture device you can think of. Even big ass strap on dongs.

The guy is a fucking parasite, and I can't wait to give him a taste of what he's been dishing out for decades.

I walk back to the cage bond the woman stands there wide eyed and shaking. "Everyone is going to be quiet," she whispers.

"Perfect," I nod and notice a huge padlock on the door. I look around and find a huge set of keys sitting on the table. This fucking guy is just so sure of himself.

I grab the keys and unlock the gate. "I need you all to go back up the way you came. Wait for me on the far left of the front gates. Stay together and I will be out when I'm done. Understood?"

She nods and murmurs the instructions to the rest.

"Be very quiet," I remind them as they begin to shuffle out in a single file.

I watch as they head up the stairs, back out the way they came, and then I go back inside the torture room, lifting myself up to the table, waiting for Henry.

He doesn't keep me waiting long at all. I bet the fucker wanted to come in here and begin his torture, and I thank the fucking stars everyone was quick and efficient.

He strides in and stops suddenly when he sees me lounging on the table.

"Selene?" His brows crash together, and his eyes shift quickly to the cage.

When he sees it empty, his eyes snap back to mine. "What the fuck did you do?"

"No, Henry," I tsk as I hop off the table. "What the fuck have you done?"

His face turns beet red, and he bares his teeth as he storms towards me. I whip my gun out of my pocket and point it right between his fucking eyes.

"Now, now," I grin at him. "Take it easy. Let's have a little chat."

"Where is my fucking shipment?" he snarls as he stares down the barrel of my gun.

"Where is my fucking sister?" I exclaim, and his eyes widen at my very first show of emotion. "Don't push me Henry, I want you to die, and it would be so fucking easy to squeeze this trigger and watch your head explode."

His hands slowly begin to rise, like the dumb fucker just figured out I'm fucking serious, and I roll my eyes.

"What sister, Selene?" His voice becomes eerily calm, like he's trying to soothe me.

"Her name was Jan." I narrow my gaze on him. "Sold by a meth addict woman for a thousand dollars."

"Look, I have my ledger out on my desk." He points behind him towards the office. "I'll help you, but I need you to bring everyone back."

"Wrong answer!" I sing-song and aim the gun at his knee, pulling the trigger.

Even with the silencer on, the popping noise seems to reverberate around the room, like an echo. Then Henry's screams of pain join in, and I begin to sway with the melody.

"You crazy fucking bitch!" he screams as he holds the wound on his knee, blood oozing out between his fingers.

"Now you're beginning to get the right answers!" I giggle maniacally and prance on the spot. "Shall I reward you, Henry?"

He's moaning with pain, and when his eyes finally meet mine, I see the look of resignation in them. Like the fucker knows I'm here to kill him and that this was my plan all along.

"Get up on the table, Henry." My voice sounds as sweet as fucking sugar.

He shakes his head and let's it drop to his chest. "No."

"Oh, no!" I exclaim. "That was another wrong answer!"

I cock the gun and his head snaps up quickly, "No! Wait!" But I've already put pressure on the trigger and there's no turning back.

The bullet slams into his shoulder and he falls back onto the concrete floor. He begins to writhe on the ground, and I begin to twist a lock of hair around my finger while I wait for him to fucking stop screaming.

"Henry," I chastise. "I need you up on the table, please." Sweet as fucking pie.

He slowly rises to his feet, his hand clutching the wound on his shoulder and putting no weight on his shot knee.

"I need a doctor," he pants as he hops to the table, and I come up behind him to shove him forward.

He hits the table with a grunt, and shouts when his knee feels the impact. Must hurt like a fucking bitch.

I hold the gun to his head, and he stills when he feels the cold metal.

"Stay on your stomach and remove your pants," I speak low and slow.

"What?" he mumbles, and I press the gun harder into his skull.

"Okay!"

He does as I say and struggles to remove his pants, his moans of pain making me laugh.

"Underwear too, Henry." I slap his ass. "Be a good little whore."

I see his shoulders begin to shake and I choke back a laugh at the thought of him crying. I can just imagine how many women and children he had in this very same predicament, crying just the same, and on this table, no less. The thought is validating, and I feel almost vindicated.

Almost.

He pulls off his underwear, and I hear a quiet sob escape his chest. They all cry in the end. Once they realize they can't beg their way out of it, they cry for mercy. I have yet to show any of my targets mercy.

I round the top of the table and drag my gun across his head with me. Once I reach the other side, I see his eyes are tightly shut, and he has tears coursing down his cheeks.

*Boo-hoo, little bitch.*

"Henry," I say sweetly. "What's your favorite piece here on the board?"

His eyes open wide, and he looks up at me. "No, don't."

"No? Don't?" I mock him. "Why would you purchase these if you don't like them yourself?"

His sobs become harder, and I cackle as I watch him.

"I like this." I reach my hand out and brush my fingers along the large black silicone strap on.

He just shakes his head as I pull it off the board.

"No," he grits out and begins to lift himself off the table.

"Not a good idea, Henry," I tsk as I slam the handle of the gun into his temple, effectively knocking him out.

I walk down to the foot of the table and drag his body down until he's bent over in an easily accessible position. Again, the feeling of sweet revenge courses through me and I chuckle as I strap the foot long dong onto my body.

A foot long.

Twelve fucking inches of pain and this is what he loved to serve up to his victims. Well, I'm about to find out what it's like to have a swinging cock and plunge it into a tight hole. Every man's desire.

I pull apart his ass cheeks and line myself up, which is a lot harder to do when you're this well hung. The fucking thing swings all over the damn place and when you think you're about to hit the bullseye, you tap a sac instead.

Finally, I hit his tiny pink puckered hole and begin to push forward. It's tough to do because it's just so small and this fucking dong has the girth of a fucking eggplant. But I'm nothing if not a go-getter and I keep at it. I breach the tight circle of muscle and then it's the home stretch. See what I did there? Stretch?

I begin to laugh as I watch his asshole *stretch* and then I slam in all the fucking way. He comes back to consciousness with a scream, and I pull out a bit only to slam right the fuck back in. He's trying to kick, but he has one injured knee and movement is just about impossible without a lot of pain. Plus, I can imagine he's losing a lot of blood, and now adding his asshole to the list of wounds only increases that.

I can hear the drips of blood hitting the floor and I can't tell if it's coming from his knee or his asshole. I've literally ripped him a new one.

His body slumps forward again, the pain having him lose consciousness, and I figure my torture session is done for the day. It's really unfortunate that Henry couldn't take a good pegging, he sure was good at giving it himself. I pull out of him, remove the strap on, and let it hit the ground with a thud. Blood sprinkles out with the impact.

*Ouch.*

I pull him the rest of the way off the table and watch as his body hits the concrete with a sickening crack. I stand still, watching to see if his chest still moves with his breaths, and curse when it moves slightly. This fucker is still alive.

I pull my knife out of my pocket and crouch down over his body, cutting open his shirt to expose his muscular torso. Same build as Zander.

I dig my knife into his unmarred skin and begin carving my sigil, the reaper's scythe. I want everyone to know Reaper Incarnate was here.

"What the fuck is going on?" I hear a familiar angry voice behind me.

Just great, the fucker found me.

# Chapter Twenty-Six

## Selene

"Blaze," I call out to him. "I'm a little busy. Can you come back in fifteen?"

I hear his heavy combat boots hit the concrete floor with each step.

Thud.

Thud.

He's taking his time making his way over to me, like maybe my erratic behavior is scaring him, and I can't help but feel a bit of excitement about that thought.

"This was your end game." His voice is gruff, but the anger is dissipating.

"He killed my sister," I say quietly. "There's a ledger, probably in his office, that has all the names of the people he's ever... acquired. Her name has to be in it."

"Is he dead?" He slowly crouches beside me.

"Almost."

He looks at what I'm carving into his chest. "You really are the fucking Reaper Incarnate."

"I said I was."

He grabs a hold of my chin and forces me to look away from the bleeding scythe. "Finish him off."

"Will Zander hate me?" My voice sounds small and the most

vulnerable it's been since my sister disappeared.

"No, just disappointed he didn't get to do it himself."

I look back down at Henry and watch as his eyes crack open. The breath rattles in his chest and he opens his mouth to speak, but I don't give him the fucking chance as I slam my knife down into his throat.

The blood sprays up and lands on my face, hitting Blaze's too. I watch as his eyes darken and rove all over my face, taking in the blood.

"You look like a warrior." It's the nicest I've heard him speak. "You *are* a fucking warrior."

Then his mouth is on mine, and I can taste the metallic flavor of Henry's blood mixed with Blaze. It sets me off, and I push him to his ass and straddle his waist. The buildup between us has been rising towards this very moment and it's threatening to blow, taking down everything around us.

I want his hands on my skin and his cock in my pussy. I'm nearly soaked all the way through my pants just thinking about it.

"Don't do this with me, only to fucking pull back later," I snarl into his mouth, then lick at the scar that starts at his top lip and ends at his temple. "Because I will fucking kill you."

He pulls away and looks into my eyes, his dark skin blooming with a red undertone. "I think you know as well as I do that this is what was always going to happen."

His plush mouth is back on mine and I'm grinding down onto him, desperately wanting him inside me. I stand up abruptly and begin to pull my leggings down, noticing they are saturated in Henry's blood. My skin has a sheen of red and it makes me feel more wanton, greedy for Blaze's cock.

He's in just as much of a rush as he stands in a flurry, discarding his clothes. Then he's standing in front of me, gloriously naked, and scars riddling his entire body.

He sees me looking at them and shrugs. "We all have a story to tell."

I get to his cock, and it stands proudly, a piece of metal gleaming at its tip. I look down to the dong on the floor and back to his cock, comparing the size and swallowing in anticipation or fucking fear. There's not much of a difference and I want it inside me, even though I'm fucking scared of it going inside me.

"Get on all fours," he demands, and I look down at the puddle of blood slowly pooling across the floor. "Go on." He nods at it.

Should be fucking disgusting, right? It should make me dry up like the Sahara desert, right? Well, not this bitch. I'm practically coming as I kneel down in Henry's still warm blood, and plop forward on my hands, his blood splattering on my chest. It's still warm, and it pools around my hands while I stare into Henry's dead eyes.

I feel Blaze kneel behind me and his fingers search out my core.

"Fuck, you're so wet."

I push back against him and hear his dark chuckle.

"Do you think this little pussy can take my cock?" he asks as he sinks two fingers deep inside me.

The coarse feeling of his fingers against my soft insides feels rough and so fucking amazing, I continue to ride his fingers, feeling my wetness coating my thighs. I want more.

His thumb hits my clit and I moan loudly at the contact. "Fuck, Blaze. Don't stop."

He chuckles and presses his fingers in farther, rubbing furiously against my bundle of nerves. I hang my head and pant, my orgasm building.

"Look into his face when you come," Blaze demands. "Show him just how much you've conquered."

I scream and look into Henry's face as I come hard around Blaze's fingers, my pussy convulsing quickly. I barely have time to come down when I feel his wide cock begin to push its way inside me. My pussy is slick, and the greedy bitch moves to accommodate him, sucking him inside.

"Fuck." It's his turn to curse.

I snort and begin to push back against him, his cock spreading me in the most delicious way. Finally, after what feels like ages, he bottoms out inside me, and I moan at the feeling of being filled past the brim.

"So wet, my little whore," he moans deeply.

Little whore. Fuck, he makes that sound so hot. He pulls out and begins to push back in, his piercing scraping along my walls. The feeling of it gliding over that certain spot inside me has me cresting quickly, and I can feel my lower belly gathering heat.

"Can I come inside you?" he asks, and I want to moan at the

thought of it.

"Yes," I pant and scream out when he picks up the pace.

My core coils so tight, I curl my fingers in the thick blood, and scream Blaze's name when it snaps, a flood of sensation washing over my whole body. I'm squeezing him tightly inside me, making it hard for him to move, and he lightly grinds into me until I'm coming back down.

"Ready?" he whispers as he curls over my body, his bloody hand curling into my hair.

Ready for what?

He rears back up, and I look over my shoulder, watching as he grins at me. The fucker is gorgeous. I'm busy watching his face in awe, unprepared when I'm almost slammed forward into Henry's face at Blaze's new punishing rhythm.

He's pounding into me, chasing his orgasm, and eliciting noises from my pussy I've never heard before. His fingers dig into my hips and I'm a whimpering mess as he uses me roughly. He slams in one final time, groaning as I feel him jerk inside of me, and I try desperately to catch my fucking breath.

"I'm now a crack pussy addict like the rest of those dumb fuckers," he growls as he pulls out. "I get it now. This pussy is fucking crack."

"I knew it was just a matter of time," I grin and get to my feet.

I have Henry's blood all over me and it's hard to fucking get my clothes back on.

Fuck! I suddenly remember I have people waiting outside for me.

"Fuck!" I try jumping into my pants.

"What?" Blaze asks, as he tries pulling his shirt down.

"I have people waiting for me." I grab up my trench and pull my knife out of Henry's throat.

"I had them pile into a cargo van I asked a friend to bring by. There was one girl who was adamant about staying until you got back up. I didn't want them in the fucking cold."

I fly forward and wrap my arms around him as he tentatively wraps his around my waist.

"Thank you," I mumble into his chest. "Thank you for being here."

"I would've been down here sooner if I didn't have to help them," he grumbles, back to his grumpy self.

"Then you would've walked in on me fucking Henry up the ass." I pull away and grin up at him.

As much as he tries, he can't stop the smile that widens his mouth, and I'm almost shocked as he belts out a laugh.

"Kinda wish I did see it, though," he says through the laughter. "Let's grab that ledger, and I'll get Santos and Darius back here to clean him up." He nods at Henry.

"Can you get upstairs to the people waiting for me?" I widen my eyes at him, trying to emulate the innocence of my blue eyes give me. "Make sure they're not freaking out and I'll grab the ledger?"

His calloused fingers clasp my chin, and he hauls me into his body, his lips crash down on mine. I moan into his kiss, the abrasive feeling I lock away as being uniquely Blaze, and my fingers snare into his shirt, pulling him in even closer. His plush mouth at odds with the rough way he kisses has me ready to rip his clothes off again. How did we go this long without tearing into each other?

"You want to look through that ledger for your sister, right?" he asks, his lips brushing against mine with each word.

"Yes." My voice breaks at the very same moment my heart does. I give myself the two seconds to feel it, pressing my forehead to Blaze's, and grieving for everything I'm about to lose. Two seconds and then I'm hauling up my big girl panties and pulling back to look into his eyes.

"I get it," he growls and yanks my head back by my hair. "You need your space. I'll take care of the people upstairs and then I'll meet you at home. But Selene," his voice holds something dark and dangerous in its depths. "If you're not home and naked in my bed in one hour, I will have to hunt for you." Then his face lights up with a manic grin, the scar pulling against his mouth and eye. "I'm a good hunter."

I know my grin matches his as I reply, "Are we going to run a train? All five of us?" I turn and point at Henry's wall of sin. "I want to be the caboose."

He rolls his eyes and tugs on my hair again before releasing me. "Santos and Darius wouldn't complain. Save your train rides for them."

He kisses me one final time, hard and quick, and then he's climbing the stairs, easily taking three at a time with his long, beautiful legs. I knew he'd give in eventually the grumpy fucker; too bad he chose now to do it.

I rush into Henry's office and squeal when I see the open grey ledger sitting there on his desk. I imagine he was adding up his newest tally. I quickly shut the thick tome, some of the pages yellowed with time, and hold it to my chest.

*Janelle, I'm going to find you.*

# Chapter Twenty-Seven

## Blaze

My knives are spread out on the bed, my clothes shoved into a knapsack, and my Glock sitting on top. I run my finger along my lip, stopping when I feel that hard ridge of skin, and gritting my teeth to force back the memories it tries to unearth. I can't think about that now. I have less than forty minutes before I embark.

"Going somewhere?" Zander's voice hits my back.

"Someone's got to go find our girl." Just those words alone have my stomach swirling in anticipation.

"What?" I can hear the panic in his voice at the prospect of losing Selene and it takes every ounce of my will to not slam my fist into his whining mouth. "Where is she?"

"I wouldn't have to hunt her if I knew, would I?"

"You let her get away." The accusation in his voice annoying the fuck out of me.

"You better not be talking about my little bloodthirsty angel." Santos crashes into the room and I groan as Darius joins not too far behind him.

"She's gone?" Darius practically wails, his eyes wide as if I'd told them she was dead. Santos' eyes fill with panic and confusion, not used to giving a fuck about any bitch. I had to get her back not just for my sake, but for his too, or he'd drive us mental with his moping.

"Why the fuck would she leave us? She can't just be gone!" he exclaims, his voice lethal but full of pain. Darius nudges him, promise in his tone.

"We will drag her ass back and punish her, right? She doesn't get to come into our lives like a fucking tornado, just to walk away. Fuck that."

"Do we put out an amber alert? Fuck, I need tracking dogs and a big net," Santos says in a rush. "She can't run if I throw a big net over her and hoist her over my shoulder."

"She's not a fish," Zander deadpans.

"She's slippery like one!" Santos bites back, making Darius snigger beside him.

"Listen!" I scream over their frantic protests. "She was always going to search for her sister, we knew that. What I knew and what you three should've known is that she would do it alone. She's been alone for most of her life. Why would she rely on anyone now?"

That quiets them down and they stand there in contemplation.

"What do we do now?" Zander asks. "I knew I should've taken the risk of losing my dick by adding another tracker."

"You have an amazing tracker." I grin at him and finally his mouth turns up.

"When do we leave?" Santos perks up and rubs his hands together.

"No." Zander holds out his hand and cuts him off. "Blaze will find her and bring her back."

"He'll kill her." Darius points at me.

"Not if she behaves."

"He's going to kill her. Our hell cat would never behave." Darius' nostrils flare.

"He won't kill her," Zander says slowly. "He's had a taste of her."

Darius and Santos look at me stunned and then they simultaneously begin hooting like a pair of fucking pigeons. I roll my eyes and pack up my knives. I have twenty minutes now. The anticipation coils and I can feel my senses already beginning to open up, everything sharpening as my body prepares. It's been too long since I've hunted. The training I endured as a child has laid dormant for far too long, and now I can barely hold it back.

"I can see it in your face," Zander murmurs as he comes to stand beside me. "Are you going to be able to handle this? Is there a risk you'll lose yourself?"

He has every right to ask that because he was the only one to witness me losing my grip on reality. Just once and it was a very long time ago. I can taste his fear for Selene and that pisses me off, doesn't he know she can handle herself by now? Even if I do let my hunter out to play.

"It'll be fine," I grunt, and stuff my knives into my bag. "I have sixteen minutes and then the time I gave her is up. I need to eat and get on the road."

"Bring her back here so I can give her ass a good lashing," Santos grins as he flicks his knife.

"Clothing optional." Darius' smile is wide.

I give a brusque nod and push past them, sliding my bag onto my shoulder. I grab an apple off the table and a bottle of water out of the fridge. I will need to put something in my belly before I lose all thoughts on necessities. I continue on to the front door and turn the handle to open it.

"Blaze," Zander calls out, halting me in my tracks. "Keep us in the loop."

Not a fucking chance.

<h1 style="text-align:center">Zander</h1>

"This is a bad idea, I can feel it," Darius moans as his ass hits the couch. "They'll kill each other."

"Let's bet on it." Santos snaps his fingers. "I'm betting Selene is back here in one piece without a scratch on her."

I want to tell them to stop acting stupid and shut the fuck up, but I can't. I can't because I have no idea what's going to go down between them. They haven't seen Blaze lose himself and can't know what Selene may be facing when he finally catches up with her. I pray I'm wrong and that Selene can somehow coax him back. She was able to win him over, after all.

"Then we'll put our own scratches on her." Darius' eyes light up, and I know they've effectively moved on from worried to horny.

I quietly escape from their animated conversation about tying her up and cutting her open, slipping into my room, and shutting the door.

I pull my phone out of my back pocket and pull up Selene's contact. I hit dial and hold the phone to my ear, my foot tapping against the carpet impatiently. After nine rings, a generic voicemail comes on, and I groan. Once the beep sounds, I clear my throat.

"Hey," I sound like a fucking pussy. "Thought you'd be home by now. Call me."

There, maybe she'll think we're not onto her and call me back. Or maybe I'm a fucking loser for thinking that because that female is fucking smart, and she'll see right through me. Should I send a text message too? No! Fuck, when did I grow a fucking vagina? I stare down at my phone, willing it to ring, and hear her voice laughing through the speaker, threats spewing from her mouth. Nothing.

Fuck it, I've clearly already lost my balls. What's the harm in one text? I send her a short text asking for a phone call when she gets the chance, like the little bitch I am, but when the phone stays silent, I throw it on the bed and stalk back out to the main room. Darius and Santos are still talking about what they'll do to punish Selene, and I curse as my cock swells in my pants. She really does take those punishments like a fucking champ.

I lean against the wall, staring at the front door, and thinking about where Blaze might be right now and if he has any idea of where Selene is. How long before he's back with her thrown over his shoulder and cursing him? How long until she's back under me where she fucking belongs?

## Santos

I've never felt like this before. My heart is twisting painfully as confusion takes hold.

Did she really leave us? I don't want to believe it, but something deep down tells me she's gone.

No one ever matches my crazy, but Selene slots in perfectly beside me, not batting an eye at my openness in the bedroom with Darius. We always mess around because it feels good. Why would we deny ourselves of that?

She's fucking perfect, and I'm never letting her go.

Darius grabs the back of my neck firmly in his hand and tugs my face around to look him in the eye, his swimming with mixed emotions.

"Stop it. She didn't leave to hurt us. She did it for her sister. You heard Blaze," he murmurs in a low voice, trying to draw me out of my own emotions. If anyone can, it's him. He's been my anchor for so fucking long that I know I can't function properly without him now.

"Doesn't mean I'm not fucking hurting," I rasp out, letting him see my pain. He always sees me.

He rests his forehead on mine, knowing his closeness calms me down.

"I know, I hurt too. Blaze will bring her back, then we can get her between us and remind her who she belongs to."

I close my eyes and focus on my breathing, not wanting to get out of control. If I think about it for too long, I'll lose my fucking mind, then anyone within a ten-mile radius of me is in trouble. I'll burn the town down to find her if I have to, and Darius knows it.

"What if he can't find her?" I finally ask, not surprised by his response.

"Then we set some fires and smoke her out. She's good at hiding, but we're good at finding. Between Blaze hunting her down and the people we know, someone will spot her at some point. Now, pull yourself together and box the crazy away. Let it out to play later if we need it," he orders, waiting for me to nod before he ruffles my hair and sits back.

For everyone's sake, I hope Blaze finds her because if he doesn't? I won't be able to keep my shit together for long.

## Darius

Can't lie, I'm worried. Santos won't contain his emotions for more than a day or two. Then we're all fucked. We won't be able to contain him once he goes on a rampage, and I hate to think of how much damage he'll cause.

I love seeing him mesh with his crazy when he's passionate about something, but usually it's just his excitement to cause blood and mayhem. His feelings for Selene are so strong that I know he'll destroy himself without her.

"I'm going to punish her so bad when I get my hands around her throat," Santos confirms, nodding briskly as if agreeing with himself. His hands tighten on his lap as he thinks, his brow creasing in the process.

"I'll bend her over my lap and hold her still while you spank her," I reply, his eyes flashing to mine with a small grin.

"I'm going to do more than spank her. She won't be able to sit for a month once my dick leaves her tight body. I want her to choke on your dick so bad that she passes the fuck out."

"Don't you remember what happened last time we tried that? She head-butted your junk and punched me in the guts," I snort, his eyes flashing almost cruelly.

"Can't swing at us if she's knocked the fuck out. If she can swing, you're not far enough down her throat," he chuckles, leaning back to rest his head on his arms. "I'll bind her wrists behind her back, just in case."

"Do you think she'll let us use blood as lube again? Fuck, my cock got so hard last time," I growl, my cock twitching in my pants.

"She'll damn well do as she's told, or I'll gag her. Well, she'll be gagging on your cock anyway, so how can she complain?" he asks seriously.

He has a point.

Zander's glaring at the door, half paying attention to our conversation while deep in thought. Our fucking group dynamic has fallen to pieces from Selene, tearing it down, and we were crumbling without her now.

She's become the air we breathe, and there's no option about not bringing her back home. The pain will eventually turn into anger, and anger will fuel the fire inside us until we explode and let chaos reign.

She has no idea what she's done by leaving us instead of bringing us along to help, but she'll sure as fuck find out when we catch up to her.

# Epilogue

## Selene

My phone pings with a message from Zander and I lock away the slight twinge of guilt with the rest of my feelings. I don't have time to miss them, and I don't have enough space inside of me for feelings. I am finally on the right path to my sister and those four men won't fuck this up, or else my pretty knife will be through their throats and my bloody scythe on their foreheads.

I sink back into my seat and watch the New York scenery pass me by through the bus window. I found a few entries in the ledger for the year my sister was taken that could match her description, and both were sold to a MC gang in Nevada. I like the thought of heading into a large compound filled with big burly bikers and gunning it down for my sister. I will raze all of Nevada to the ground if it means I find her, and I'll enjoy every fucking minute.

Can I find a blimp to fly over the state afterward with a large *Reaped* painted on the side?

Hunting The Reaper
REAPED BOOK ONE

# Copyright

# Dedication

To everyone who read our novella in the
Violent Tendencies Anthology and loved it, this is for you.

# Prologue

## Selene

"You have two options," I take a step closer into his body, enjoying when it begins to tremble, "you tell me what I want to know, or we play a game."

His eyes widen and his mouth falls open as I slowly pop the buttons on his long-sleeved plaid shirt with my knife. "A game?"

I stop my descent with the blade and giggle. "Did you pick a game?" Excitement courses through me. "I love games."

"No, I…" he chokes on a sob as the tip of my knife presses into his skin. "I don't know a Janelle or a Jan."

I feel a bead of sweat begin to slide down the side of my face and I step back with a huff; the Nevada heat is dry. I've been here a month and I still haven't gotten used to it. One good thing about Nevada? So many twisted souls who need to be wiped out. I was meant to come here, and I was meant to clean it in the only way I know how.

"I believe you." I nod and grin when I see him visibly relax.

I found this gem the same way I've found many before him, on the darknet. I put out an ad for a realistic rape fantasy and this is who responded. After one week of investigation, I found out that Earl Jr. here likes to stalk young women and then rape the ones who live alone. If my sister was sold to a sex ring or as a sex slave like so many of Henry Walton's victims were, then I needed to follow the crumbs of perverts, and trust me, they all run in the same circles. I'm getting closer.

151

I watch as Earl tries to squirm, but he doesn't get too far, not when I have all his limbs tied, spread eagle between two large trees and his pants have been long cut off. You see, I met him at a bar and when I saw him slip a little powder in my drink—he thought he was being slick—I switched glasses when the football game on the screen stole his attention. I guess he doesn't just like to play at rape; he wants the real thing. After that, I could've convinced him his nana was a horse and he would have believed me. He even helped me pull out the ropes from the trunk of my car and didn't say a word as I began to tie him up. Four hours later though, he's sobering up and thank fuck because I am starving.

"Are you going to let me go?" His voice shakes. Little pussy.

"Not just yet." I shake my head and continue to cut open his shirt. "How about you tell me about some of your friends who like the same things?"

He's quick to toss out three names and even where I can find them, awfully helpful, this one. I'm partially listening to him throw his pervert friends under the bus as I clean my nails with my knife. I wonder how my guys are doing. No. I give myself a shake and continue to listen to this asshole's confession. Did he say gang rape?

Zander is probably cursing himself for not adding another tracker. Darius and Santos are most likely ready to burn their town down looking for me, and Blaze is probably out for blood. He's going to want to watch me bleed and not in the way Santos does, more like watching me bleed in the dying way.

"Shut up, Earl," I huff and roll my eyes. "You're giving me a headache."

I throw my blade and it slips through his throat, embedding it to the hilt. He's wide eyed and choking on his blood as I stroll back to stand in front of him. Finally, his eyes lose focus and then all life leaves his body as his greasy head falls forward. I pull out my blade and wipe the blood off onto my trench. Killing rapists and pedophiles is such a fucking messy business.

I rip his shirt further apart and stand transfixed, watching his blood run down his chest and stomach in a steady stream. When the blood flow slows and begins to thicken in the heat, I run my finger along its surface, grinning at the velvety feel. My finger moves of its own accord, drawing the scythe in perfect detail, and then moving beneath it, one word large and prominent.

*Reaped.*

*Earl had to die…*

# Chapter One

## Selene

I'm being followed.

Tingles sporadically race up the back of my skull and down to the nape of my neck, but I never react or look around. That's just giving away the fact that I know someone's watching me. It's like those horror movies you watch when the killer is stalking the little female and he's watching her. She's constantly looking around like a flighty little bird.

*That bitch ain't me, honey.*

I'm fucking excited and I'm hoping I can lead them down a darkened path, only to slice their throat open. I've gathered enough enemies and narrowing down who it might be would be difficult, so I'll wait until they grow a pair to approach me. Until then, I hope they enjoy the show I'm about to give them.

Earl was nice enough to guide me to a few of his friends and I now have a date with a man named Mr. Haynes. Mr. Haynes gives me the same vibe as Mr. Walton did, and that makes me even more excited. I feel like I'm finally getting somewhere, and I'll soon learn what transpired with Jan. I'm patient when the time calls for it and right now, I have patience in abundance.

"Ain't it dark wrapped up in that tarp, Earl?" I sing. *The Chicks* could honestly tell the future.

I've sharpened my blade and put it away in its custom-made holster strapped around my waist, then I tie up my trench. There are those pesky tingles again, making me giggle, and anticipation glides over my skin. I love being the apple of someone's eye, and I love carving out those fucking eyes when they piss me off. They always do.

I think of the four men who haven't pissed me off to that point yet and quickly bury it down. I can't lose focus. No one is as important as my sister. She's the whole reason why I started this, and if there's even the slightest chance I can save her, I won't falter. No matter how much I miss the burn of Darius' rope and the sting of Santos' blade.

*Stop, Selene.* I chastise myself, thinking of them will do nothing to help me with what I need to accomplish. These are foreign feelings for me and getting close to those guys may have been my biggest mistake, especially if they've fucked with my concentration.

I pull my long, thick blonde hair into a high pony and check my face in the mirror. I'm going for the young look tonight because any man who prefers the prefix Mister and nails prostitutes is usually looking to hit the young ones. It's an assumption, but it's one that's never been wrong, and I have done this… often. I'm wearing a dress with a plunging neckline, the hem sitting at mid-thigh, and my signature thigh-high boots, but I have it all wrapped tightly under my trench. Prefix Misters usually like their women proper in the streets but sluts in the sheets. Another assumption I've never gotten wrong.

I'm hoping I won't need to fuck Mr. Haynes tonight because I haven't had anyone since Blaze. I close my eyes when the memory of him and me fucking in Henry's blood assaults my vision and I let out a small whimper. The way he fucked me and looked at me with reverence in his eyes, he called me a warrior. I let out a shaky breath and try to clear my mind. Even Grumpy needs to take a backseat. I hate that we only had one single moment and then I disappeared; I wanted more. *I want more.*

I shake off the lingering thoughts of my dark, brooding guy with the angry scar on his face and bring myself back to the present. It's time to face the task at hand. My new phone vibrates in my pocket, and a grin crawls across my face. This one's also punctual, like all prefix Misters. I open the old-style flip phone—that's all I need as a burner—and drop my voice a few octaves, letting the huskiness come through.

"Right on time."

"Hello, miss Selene," he rasps. "I gather you are ready?"

"Of course, Mr. Haynes."

I can practically hear him purr at my use of 'Mister'. "Be outside the coffee shop in five minutes." He hangs up before I can answer, and I breathe out my frustration. I can already imagine his skin covered in drying blood and my scythe carved through it.

I press my blood-red lips together and pucker them in my reflection, my favorite fucking color. Then I'm out the door of my tiny new apartment and on the street, walking to the coffee shop where I met Mr. Haynes earlier today. His schedule was harder to track down because he wasn't someone who kept it routine. But I did notice him liking this coffee shop a little too much, especially the few waitresses inside. So, I staked it out—naturally—until he finally showed up today.

I chuckle to myself at the memory as I walk down the street. He was coming out of his car, and I hurried to rush outside, knocking into him. My coffee hit his chest and the anger in his eyes almost awakened mine until he gave me a slow perusal. It's always the same. A pair of hot tits and long legs have their charm; I had him eating out of my hand in record time. When he offered to drop me off at work, I told him I don't start until well into the night hours, and at no particular spot. He caught on, and his eyes shone with excitement. Hook, line, and sinker motherfucker.

I stand outside of the coffee shop, its interior lights off, and the closed sign hanging in the door. I check my reflection in the darkened windows and feel those tendrils of watching eyes skim along the back of my neck. They're here and they're watching me. I try to check out the street behind me in the reflection, but there's nothing. I like that. It means they're good at what they do and it only amps up my excitement more. Hopefully, I give them an eyeful tonight.

A sleek black Lincoln Town Car pulls up behind me and I turn slowly, dropping my eyes to the ground, looking meek and shy. You can't let men like Mr. Walton and Mr. Haynes see the intelligence in a woman's eyes. Their small balls will curl up into their bellies, and they'll avoid you like the plague. They'll even go as far as to ensure you stay away from their wives and daughters, too, because that intelligent affliction just might be contagious.

I slowly walk to the car, and a driver jumps out, rounding the tail end. He opens the back door for me, and I give a little giggle, acting like my brain is made of stuffing. I slide inside and come face to face with Haynes himself. He's not attractive—at all—and I flutter my eyelashes to stop my eyes from rolling. He's in a velvet robe. Did the fucker really not want to get dressed?

"You look divine." He leans over and grasps a lock of my hair between his fingers. "You smell like a meadow of wildflowers."

*I want to smell like your fucking blood, you cunt.* "It's a new perfume." I give him a small smile. "I'm glad you like it."

"Now, Selene." He leans back in his seat and his robe starts to fall open. *Here we go.* "What exactly must we do to create this fortunate coupling?" The fuck is he trying to say?

"I need your signature… in blood." It's out of my mouth before I can stop it, and I curse my intelligent affliction. I giggle into my hand, and he smiles, shaking his head as if I were a silly toddler. Probably exactly his type, really. "You tell me what you would like, and I'll give you the price."

"I want your mouth on my cock and then your pussy milking me dry." Well, straight to the point.

"Fifteen hundred dollars." His eyes widen at the number, and I curse myself for not doubling it. His chest hair alone could act as a sweater.

"That's quite a large number for a young prostitute." Hook.

"I started young; I have experience." Line.

*Come on, you furry ape, take the fucking bait.*

"How young?" His smile grows sinister. Sinker.

"Twelve," I whisper, like it's a secret meant for only the two of us. "I never turned back."

"Deal." He throws open the robe and shows me his cock. If I thought his chest was bad, his cock looks like it's wearing a pair of furry earmuffs. I can't help but think I will die of suffocation, and I'll never see my guys again.

"Look at all this," I coo. He thinks I'm praising his cock when I'm really trying to figure out how to Hoover without dying of pube inhalation.

I kneel on the seat and bend forward, grabbing his cock. I push downward, trying to get the pubic hair to obey, and place my mouth on the tip. One lick. That's all it takes. Just one lick and the fucker's cum hits my lips and chin. Easy work, really, I can't complain.

"Mm," I say as I scoop it off and wipe it into his fluffy cock's mane.

"Sorry about that." He grins as I sit up, still wiping remnants of him off my chin. "Would you care to come by my humble abode for the finale?"

This guy is further off his rocker than I am, and that means he's practically under it. "Oh yes, please." I nod my head furiously, watching as his flaccid dick gets swallowed up by his pubic hair, and I swallow down the urge to heave.

The car pulls away from the curb and I remember there's another person in the front seat. I look up into the rear-view mirror and see he has his mouth turned up into a grin, probably finding this whole thing fucking amusing. Well, I'm glad someone is.

His 'humble abode' is a fucking castle. No, seriously, he built himself a castle and told me he likes to speak like royalty, expecting his *subjects* to treat him as such. I'll fucking admit it. I want to be Queen. His house staff bow to him as he walks by, and his maids hurry ahead to prepare the 'bed chamber'.

He has paintings of himself everywhere, much like Henry, but oh so fucking different. Where Henry Walton liked self-portraits showing his body, Haynes likes his to show his crown and scepter, I'm not kidding. I want a painting, but of me, obviously.

I follow him and his train of maids upstairs and we enter a large room. There's a bed that must be bigger than a king-size and a fireplace, then more portraits.

"Do you like it?" he asks me, watching my face closely.

"Fuck, yes," I breathe and I'm not even lying. I'm trying to figure out if I'd be able to Dyson his cock for the rest of my life, just to be Queen.

His face brightens and his smile becomes reminiscent of the Cheshire Cat. "Let's begin." He drops his robe and I watch as his cock slowly pushes through the maze of fur. I drop my trench and startle when a young woman appears out of nowhere. She looks maybe eighteen at most and she's pretty. Her hair is a sleek chestnut brown, and her skin is like rich terra cotta, reminding me of Santos. She picks up my trench and goes back into the shadowed corner, still watching. I kind of like an audience. "That's an interesting belt," he points to my sheath.

It does resemble a belt with the knife handle looking like the buckle. "Thank you." I smile and give him a shy look. "Should we lie down?"

He hurries to the bed and climbs on, crawling up on all fours. I bite down on my tongue to hold in the gasp when I see his ass looking like a Chewbacca. How the fuck do I end up in these situations? I really wish I could tell Santos all about it because he would appreciate this the most. Haynes flops onto his back on the bed and waits for me to join him, licking his lips with excitement. *This one's for you, Jan.*

I crawl up his body and I'm astonished at the hair on this man. It really is amazing. Like a Neanderthal or something. I straddle his waist and lean down over him, grinding into his cock.

"Oh, yes," he begins to tremble, "put me inside you."

"In a minute," I tease and sit up, rolling my hips forward. "You have really pretty maids." I look over my shoulder at the corner.

"Would you like her to join?" he asks.

"Do they do that? Is that why they're here?" I fall forward and press my mouth to his ear. "Are they sex slaves?"

"They're whatever I want them to be," he answers smugly. "That's what I paid for."

Paid for. I really am on the right track. I lean back up and continue to grind down on him, listening to his grunts of pleasure. "I like them and all, but I want it to be just you and me. Is that okay?" I lower my lashes.

"Out!" he screams through the room, and I startle, watching three girls scurry past.

I pull my dress up around my waist, making sure he's watching, and pull my panties to the side. I glide along his dick, not at all wet, and trying not to giggle when his powder puff tickles my lady bits.

"If I wanted a sex... ah… maid," I grab his chin and force his eyes back to mine, "how could I find one?"

"I know a guy." He throws me his skeevy grin. "I can take you to meet him."

"Oh! Really?" I clasp my hands and squeal, "What's his name?"

I have two more names on my list and I'm hoping this sex slave seller is one of them. Haynes gives me a weird look and I bite into my lip, trying to look coy. I don't want him catching on to me so fast. I drag my fingers down my tongue and reach between us to grasp his cock, gliding my fist along it.

"Oh!" he moans and tips his head back.

I pump him harder and lean over, licking along his mouth. "Name?"

"John Dempster!" he screams as he comes all over my fist.

"Oh, no!" I gasp. "Did I ruin the finale, my king?"

His eyes shine with appreciation at my choice of words and his hands reach up, giving my tits a squeeze. "I think you earned every damn bit of that money, Miss Selene. When can we do this again?"

I roll off him and wipe his cum into his blanket, making an exasperated sigh. "I'm awfully busy."

"How about I give you double what you asked for and see you again tomorrow night?" He rolls off the bed and opens his bedside table, pulling out a large wad of cash. He starts counting out the bills and barely puts a dent in the roll, tossing me three thousand dollars.

I grab the money and tuck it into my bra, making a big show of squeezing them. He comes to stand in front of me and looks down into my face. Fuck, he really is hairy. It's going to feel like I'm putting down a dog, seriously. I wrap a hand around the hilt of my knife and run my finger down his chest.

"I really wish we could do this again, King Haynes." I put a sugar sweet tone in my voice. "But alas, that's simply not meant to be, Milord." This is so much fun, I really am tempted to keep him.

"I beg your pardon?" He looks at me, confused.

I pull out the knife and stand, pulling Haynes into a hug. "You're just not my type," I whisper as I sink the knife into the back of his neck. I watch him sink to the floor and wipe my blade off onto the blanket. I slide it back inside the holster and run to that bedside table. I deserve every fucking cent in there after what I just endured with Toto the dog.

I open the drawer and find three giant wads of cash, grabbing them up in my hands. I rush to my trench and drop them inside the pocket, then pull it on over my shoulders. I walk back over to Haynes and crouch over his trembling body. "Not yet dead, sire?" I say in a dodgy English accent. I dip my finger into the blood seeping around his head and begin to draw my scythe on his forehead. It's the only hairless part of him.

I stand and wipe my finger off on his bed, giving him a small curtsy. "Happy dyin', Milord." I turn on my heel and open the bedroom door. I step out and startle when I find the same girl leaning against the wall.

"I wouldn't go in there for a while. He's a sticky mess." I screw up my face and motion to my groin. She snorts and gives me a nod. I start in the same way I came and stop when I hear her voice.

"I heard him say John Dempster."

I look at her over my shoulder and give a quick nod.

"He's the one who sold me to him." She thumbs to the closed bedroom door. "That John man is a lunatic."

"Is he?" My heart hammers with excitement. "What's your name?"

"Cara." Her mouth dips down in the corners. "It's been a while since anyone has called me that, though."

"Where are you from?"

"Around." She shrugs.

"Do you have a family to go back to?" I ask her and she looks at me, confused.

"They're the ones who sold me to John."

"Listen, I suggest you get the hell out of here." I toss her one of the wads. "He's dead, anyway."

Then I carry on to the front door, leaving her gasp behind me. Next up, John Dempster.

# Blaze

I watch her get into that same fucking Lincoln Town Car and I bet the same piece of shit from earlier today is in there, too. She's back to her old tactics of fucking dangerous men to find out information about her sister. She wouldn't have had to do that if she had just asked us to help, and we would have because she had every one of us wrapped around her finger.

The car doesn't move for a while, and I fight every urge to walk up to it and shoot aimlessly inside. The possibility of killing Selene is the only thing stopping me, but fuck, that bitch still manages to piss me off. After about ten minutes, the car pulls away from the curb and I trail a couple of cars behind it. Nevada is boring and luckily, I get to follow the little Reaper Incarnate for some entertainment. After watching her string up that other guy and cutting him, it's been dull. Now at least something is happening.

My fingertips drum against the steering wheel and my mind begins to skip, I'm so close to losing myself. I want to grab her every time I see her and drag her home, and it takes a lot to convince myself not to. I know she'll only run again and then she'll truly be lost to us.

They pull onto a dirt road, and I follow them until I see a fucking castle rising up in the distance. Where the fuck are we? I slow down and let the car get out of sight, fearing they'll see the kick up of dust from my tires. After a few minutes, I slowly crawl towards the castle, and stop when I see Selene getting out of the car. She's looking up at the stone structure in awe and I don't blame her, so am I.

I see another dirt road off to my right. I turn down it, and it finally leads me to two wooden structures. I don't see anyone around, and I throw the car into park, getting out to stretch my legs. I hear animal sounds in one of the structures and walk up to the large double doors, opening them slowly. I peer inside and see horses, beautiful dark Arabians by the looks of them. I step in and shut the door, walking from stall to stall, petting the ones who are curious. This guy owns a castle and has horses. He's bat shit crazy. Sounds like a male version of Selene, if I'm being honest. Maybe I should buy her a horse for when she comes home. If I don't end up killing her, that is.

I step out of the stable and walk along a stone path, passing a fountain with a statue of a man, the water flowing from his penis like piss. This place is fucking weird. The path takes me to the castle, but I end up behind it and I find a garden of exotic looking flowers. I bend to smell a bush of ombre roses when I hear voices coming up ahead. I dive behind the bush and sit still, not moving a muscle.

"John Dempster will be coming by in a week." The man sounds nasally. "We need to make sure the basement is clear."

"How many for the auction this time?" another man asks.

"I think ten, and this time we have some virgins."

"Man," the second man whines. "I love the virgins."

Selene is here because she found something in Henry's ledger about her sister and right now, I am hearing about another piece of shit who deals in skin. I wonder if her sister is here. I wait as they speak some more about John Dempster, and I know he will be Selene's next target. The breadcrumbs she's following are leading her to a den of rabid animals and she's lucky I found her when I did.

When the voices fade, I slowly stand and look around. I run to the stone wall and follow it back around to the front of the castle; the Town Car is still sitting where they left it. I go to push off the wall when I hear the front door open, and Selene's voice rises.

"I need an Uber to this castle place!" She's yelling down at the screen of her phone. I roll my eyes and pull up the Uber app on my phone. Ordering one to come here as she punches her fingers into the screen with frustration.

She's so beautifully deranged and she owns her crazy like a

fucking armor. I give her a quick scan from head to toe to make sure she's okay. Is that blood on her face? Did she kill the guy? My cock swells rapidly and I think of the one time I had her, in a pool of Henry Walton's blood.

Nothing will ever compare to her screaming my name while covered in blood.

# Chapter Two

## Santos

Red hot anger and confusion burn inside my chest the moment Zander hangs up the phone after Blaze's recent update. His hazel eyes can't hide the fear he's feeling. Is she screwing those fucking bastards for information again? If she'd asked before she ran off, I would have ripped them out of their houses and tortured the information out of them for her.

Zander's eyeing me with underlining worry from the other couch, but Darius doesn't hesitate to speak his mind from beside me. There's a reason he's my best friend. That fucker can read me like a book, and he gets me.

"San, breathe. She's all right, Blaze will bring her home soon. Look at me," he says calmly, his voice turning firm. "*Look* at me."

I tilt my face towards him, my voice gruff. "He found her, so he should've tossed her in the car and been on his way back by now. What the fuck is he waiting for?"

"Have you *met* Selene? We can't handle her like that to bring her home. We have to entice her with good dick game and the promise of vigilante justice," Darius grins, not calming my mood in the slightest. I push back from the couch to stand, angrily flipping the small coffee table to try to ease my inner turmoil.

I can't figure out how to express what I'm feeling, and that's always a dangerous combination when added to my anger. It's been a long time since I've snapped and lost control, but the guys know how devastating I can be on my destructive path once I start.

"This isn't the time to be fucking funny!" I bark, considering climbing in my car to go and get my girl myself. She belongs under my body, so I'll be sure that's where she ends up.

Darius stands slowly, putting his hands in front of him to show he's not going to crash tackle me to the ground.

"I'm not joking. I want her to come home too, but we have to do it the right way. Letting Blaze track her and bring her home his way is the only way it will work. If we go and force her hand, she'll take off again and won't come back when she's done. She's safe, you heard Blaze," he says slowly, not flinching when I turn to glare at him, flexing my fingers until they crack. "Hit me if it will make you feel better."

It isn't the first time he's offered to take my hits, knowing it's the only way I will feel in control of my body again. I've always done the same for him, too. He braces as I dive at him, slamming my fists into his ribs and abs until he stumbles back onto the couch, not fighting back, simply being my personal punching bag.

His eyes flash to Zander in warning, telling me the other asshole wants to stop me. He could try, but no one can stand in my way without ending up under my bloodied fist, too. Hit after hit, the anger releasing from my knuckles until he lets out a grunt of discomfort, snapping me out of it when I realize I'm starting to cause real damage. I jerk back from him, seeing the pain in his eyes as he tries to bury it from me.

I let out a loud shout of frustration, stalking through the house and into my room, slamming the door so hard it almost flies off its hinges. I drop to the bed, tossing my pillows aside as I catch a whiff of Selene's perfume. Her scent is lingering everywhere, and it both relieves and angers me at the same time.

My eyes burn as tears threaten, setting me off all over again. I don't cry, that's not my thing. I shove the contents of my bedside table, a growl rising from my throat in annoyance. Nothing is making these feelings go away. I need my little psychopath to come home and soothe my demons before they take root inside me, growing out of control. I hate that I hurt Darius, but he is my only outlet to the misery and rage within.

My door creaks, alerting me I have company, but I don't need to glance over my shoulder to see who it is. I know it's Darius. No matter what I do to him, he's always there to make sure I'm okay, even if he's not himself.

The door shuts with a quiet click, and soft footsteps reach my ears until they go silent, the mattress behind me dipping right before a hard body presses against my back and a muscular arm wraps around my middle. He doesn't speak, he simply holds me to attempt to put my heart and soul back together. Too bad I sold my soul to the Devil a long time ago.

"Fuck off," I grumble, but there's no heat in my words, and he knows it. I tense as his lips brush the back of my neck, his warm breath fanning across my skin.

"No. You need me," he claims, shuffling closer if it were possible, then he's shoving a leg between mine. I both love and hate it when he gets like this, because I feel guilty for hitting him, but I also crave the comfort he gives.

"Did I break anything?" I finally ask, relaxing my body as best I can.

"Probably. I got plenty of ribs though, don't worry about it," he answers, making me scowl.

"I can't fucking hurt you to regain control. That's bullshit."

"Why? Better me than you who's hurting. Besides, it's not like you don't let me use you when I'm pissed off." He chuckles, his breath catching slightly as his ribs must be hurting.

"Why is it better that you hurt? Usually when you're mad, we get laid to burn the energy," I say sharply, wishing he'd stop defending my shitty behavior.

"Roll over and I'll blow you then, if you think it will help," he murmurs as his hand trails down my front, but I grab his wrist to stop his movements. I miss Selene, and he must sense my emotions because he moves to roll me onto my back, peering down at me.

"She'll come home, and when she does, we'll make her scream for forgiveness for days on end. Until then, shut it all out. Rein in that anger and hold its leash tight. What you're feeling is normal. Stop fighting it."

"Normal? How the fuck is it normal?" I force out through my teeth, letting his wrist go as he spreads his fingers out across my lower stomach.

"You're heartbroken. Nothing unusual. She's not gone forever, she's just not here right now. Focus on that, all right? Our girl's coming home," he promises, staring into my eyes to show me the truth in their blue depths. I nod, closing my eyes for a second to get a grip on myself, then I meet his gaze again.

"I don't like these feelings. They hurt and make me feel weird," I admit, a small smile tugging at his lips.

"It's meant to hurt. It's your heart. We're all feeling the same. We're only hiding it better. I bet Zander is in bed having a cry wank as we speak."

"Can you cry wank me?" I grin lightly, his eyes filling with amusement.

"How is that possible? You're meant to sit in the corner and cry, using your own tears as lube. Don't you know how a cry wank works, idiot?"

"I do. You blow me until you're gagging, then I can use your tears as lube to finish myself off," I answer, my grin widening. I'm a dick, always will be.

We have no issues taking the edge off for each other, so he knows how I like it.

He raises an eyebrow, his fingers trailing lower down my stomach until they slip below the waistband of my pants.

"Get your jeans off then, but you won't need to finish yourself off. I know what I'm doing."

I reach for my button, flicking it open and dragging the zipper down, shoving the material down my legs and kicking them over the edge of the bed. Darius tugs my boxers down enough to grasp my cock in his palm, stroking it a few times until it's rock hard. I never have to guide him. He always knows exactly what I need, even before I do.

He shuffles down the bed, straddling my lower legs and leaning forward to suck the head of my cock between his lips. I groan, absently running my fingers through his light brown hair. Images of Selene flash in my mind, and I squeeze my eyes shut as I pretend it's her blowing me. I must have mumbled her name, because Darius stops to peer up at me, his eyes full of understanding as I meet them with my own.

"Use me. Imagine I'm Selene, fuck my face," he says openly, not giving a shit that I'm not with him at the moment. I nod, dropping my head back and fisting his hair tighter, starting to thrust up into his mouth until he gags.

His fingers bite into my thighs, just like hers would, and I can't hold back as I thrust harder, not caring that my best friend is struggling to breathe. I'm probably bruising his throat, but I don't think of that as I zone out and fuck his face as requested, pouring all my anger and hurt into it.

The sound of my heavy breathing and his gags are all I hear. It's not until my balls tighten and cum shoots from my dick down his warm throat that I release my hold and let him breathe properly.

He drops down beside me, coughing a few times as he tries to catch his breath.

"Better?" he pants, always needing approval. Then again, I'm the same.

"Better." I nod, my weary body finally relaxing enough to shut my mind off for a while. He waits for me to roll over and face away from him before he shuffles against my back to resume our previous position, and before long I'm passing the fuck out, dreaming of our Reaper Queen and pretending everything's okay again for a second.

## *Selene*

Nighttime is lonely. I've gotten so used to having the guys around me that I've forgotten what it feels like to sleep alone. I haven't slept well since leaving, and I'm starting to think I won't again.

I pry my tired eyes open, knowing it's too early to be awake, but also knowing my time of rest is over. In my dreams, I was riding Zander's face, my fingers gripped tight into his highlighted pretty boy hair, as the other three watched through hooded eyes. The moment Blaze stalked towards me and fisted my hair, I woke up.

I swing my legs out of bed and make my way to the kitchen, needing coffee. I have a long day ahead of me. I grab my notebook as I sit to drink my coffee, tapping my finger on John's name. The piece of shit is a dead man walking, but I have to take my time with him, needing all the information inside his head.

If anyone knows where my sister is, it will be him, and I have a feeling I'm going to have a lot of fun pulling it out of him. Men like him don't speak willingly, always trying to bury their secrets as deep as possible. Luckily for me, I can be extremely persuasive.

The best thing about slimy pieces of shit like John? Their dicks are more important than anything else, so threatening their manhood is always a good place to start when digging for information.

I drain my coffee, having a quick shower and getting dressed for the day, not wanting to waste any time. I need to stalk John a little and see what I'm working with.

Luck is on my side, because when I stop for lunch hours later, my eyes catch on an article in the newspaper. Turns out, Mr. John Dempster is an upstanding citizen in the area, if the article about him is anything to go by. The picture gives me a clear shot of his face, his friendly smile covering up the slimy bastard behind the mask.

He has made a hefty donation to install a small park for kids to play in, alongside a youth center for troubled teens, probably so he can track down problematic young girls to groom, then he can snatch them. They are opening the park tomorrow, causing me to smirk. Perfect place to discreetly watch him and suss him out.

I flick through the rest of the paper, not finding anything else interesting, but right as I'm about to stand and leave, the man himself strolls through the door and sits at a table close by. He's in an expensive-looking suit, a slate gray color and it has a sort of shine to it, like silk. His hair is slicked back over his head and the dark brown color glistens under the lights. That's a lot of gel. He's tall but not as tall as my guys, and where they're wide, he looks leaner.

I tug my shirt down slightly, making the girls look a little perkier, then I stand and make my way over to his table. No better time than the present, right?

"Excuse me? Mr. Dempster?" I say in a breathy voice, his annoyed gaze clashing with mine before his brown eyes light up with interest at me.

"Yes? Can I help you?" He smiles, not hiding the fact that he's staring at my tits. Men are such disgusting creatures, I swear.

"I saw you in the paper. I think it's admirable how you're wanting to help the youth in the area. I wish there'd been more men like you around when I was a little girl," I coo, twirling a piece of my blonde hair around my finger. His eyes drop down my body before watching my face, a chuckle leaving him.

"You don't look all that old. You look like you're doing okay." He grins, motioning for me to sit in the chair opposite him. "Please, join me."

"I just ate, but I'd love to stay for a coffee. I'm surprised you're here alone. No woman should ever let her man dine alone, especially not one as handsome as you." I beam, sliding into the chair and fluttering my lashes at him. He is eating it up, just like they always do. You'd think they'd be more careful, but they always think with their dicks first, never their fucking brains.

"I don't have a lady in my life, but I'm not dining alone, am I?" he teases.

"You're single? No way! How does an amazing man like yourself stay single? I bet all the women throw themselves at you! What made you want to help the youth?" I ask.

His voice changes slightly, telling me he's full of shit. "I've seen so many young people, generally girls, who have nowhere safe to go. They don't have access to a hot meal or even a hot shower, so I wanted to provide them with that. A lot of them thrive with help, so I'm hoping to increase their employment options as they get older, by assisting them with resumes and even the option to have a tutor after school. I'm even going to offer a counselor to those struggling. What good is money if you can't use it to help people?" He smiles, and it's almost believable.

I'll bet money on the fact that he is using the counselor bit to con girls into shit, preying on them while they're weak and vulnerable.

I bat my lashes, letting out a light giggle. "You're amazing! I saw you're opening the park tomorrow?"

"Yes, it's going to be a wonderful day with lots of people attending. There will be lunch provided so people can enjoy the day while the kids play. Will you be coming?"

His eyes darken as I give him a coy smile, biting my lip slightly. "I'll definitely be coming, sir. What time should I be there?"

"Ten in the morning. I'll be there. It finishes at three that afternoon, but you can celebrate with me afterwards, if you wish?" he offers, pulling a business card from his jacket and handing it to me. "If you can't make it and want to talk more about this another time, here's my card. Call me and we can do this again."

I slip the card into my bra, giving him a beaming smile. "Thank you, Mr. Dempster. I'll be in touch. Oh no, is that the time? I really must get going. I'll have to pass on the coffee, but you enjoy your lunch."

"Have a good afternoon, miss?" he murmurs, question in his gaze.

"My name's Candy. In and out of work hours," I say sweetly, heat flaring in his dark eyes.

There's always a girl named Candy on every street corner and every strip club, so I leave him with that little idea and part ways, heading back towards where I'm staying with a big smile on my face.

Not long now, and I'll be spilling blood.

# Chapter Three

## Selene

The number of young children here makes me feel anxious. This is the biggest trap I have ever witnessed, and it's reminding me of a croc with its jaws open, waiting for his prey. There is a large board propped up in the middle of the park with the names of all the group homes present. I've counted twenty-six. Twenty-six group homes and most of them filled to capacity. All the children are running through the park, and the wolves drool and wait.

There's a refreshment table, and another table loaded down with treats. The best way to buy a child's trust is by giving them all the things they crave. Treats, toys, attention, and love. The sad thing is they are too young to realize when they're being groomed. I look around at the adults, seeing mostly men and a few women. These are the people who are entrusted with these children's safety and yet money really speaks volumes. If there are enough zeroes at the end of a number, then they can be convinced to turn the other cheek and offer those children up as collateral.

This situation hits close to home for me because of what my mother did to my sister. Janelle was beautiful and so fucking smart, with a bright future in front of her. She had a heart many times too big and even though our crackhead mother treated us like dirt; she kept giving her multiple chances to change. When our mother began bringing men to our apartment, she bought a lock for our bedroom door, and made sure no one could get to me. Even when they would stand outside it and I would shake with fear, Jan always made me feel safe.

Until I wasn't.

I was ten years old when we heard our piece of shit mother offer up one of her virginal daughters as payment for crack, and I had my first taste of what a man was like. My screams must've shaken the very walls of that apartment building, but no one came to help me. Jan was getting her own form of punishment when she was forced to watch it. I was the luckier one in the end. Most of the men our mother brought home wanted Jan, and she was happy enough to offer herself as long as I was left alone. I was such a timid and scared child, I would hide in the closet until it was over, and never once thought of killing our bitch mother. The whole situation became our new normal, and I slowly saw my sister die inside.

It took years and a lot of saving and hiding money on my sister's part, and we finally had enough to move out. I was fifteen years old and already knew my way around a man, having been subjected to them multiple times since I was ten. Those are the breaks of being young and developed. Men like them young, and they like them supple, not minding anything about consent.

A month after I turned fifteen, Jan had an apartment lined up for us, and we were supposed to move in the next week, but she went missing two days later. At first, I thought she left me there alone and maybe moved to the apartment by herself. So, I went to the building and asked the front desk. They hadn't seen her. I went to her work and asked for her there; they gave me the same answer.

I knew something bad happened to her. I went to the police, and they gave a quick shrug of their shoulders. Jan was twenty-one, and they knew our mother well. They were convinced she had had enough and left. But I knew better. She loved me, and she wanted to keep me safe. It was at fifteen years old. I learned the police didn't really care about the poor and even they preferred money. I did my own investigation, and it was scary as fuck.

I would follow my mother's crack dealers back to wherever they came from and question them. I was raped during those interrogations and beaten bloody sometimes, but I never gave up. I soon started taking free self-defense classes at the local community center and I was a natural, a fast learner. It didn't take long for me to become a confident young woman and I went back to those dealers, doling out a beating of my own. Mind you, thinking back on it, these were strung out and starving crackheads, and it was easy enough to overpower them.

I bought a knife with my savings from my part-time job and took up knife throwing classes. I excelled even further in that, and knives became an obsession for me. I also found out, the more you hang out with the crackheads, the more information you can get. Those zombie fuckers will tell you anything if you dangle some drugs at them, and I learned a lot. I learned that my mother somehow found herself in the back of a Rolls Royce and speaking to a man about her two young daughters, daughters she had been pimping for cash. He offered to take them off her hands and wondered what price she'd be willing to take. The bitch said he could only take one, and she wanted a heaping one thousand dollars.

That wasn't because she thought her daughter was worthless. No, to my mother that was a lot of fucking money, and her brain cells were far too obliterated from crack. He agreed, willing to wait it out for the second daughter, knowing eventually my mother would need money, and patience was something Henry Walton had in spades. His mistake is not banking on the hatred a child can develop for the people who are supposed to care for them, and how easily they can be swayed. I was swayed by anger and hatred, my mind consumed with my missing sister, and when I found out my mother sold her to a businessman, I threw my knife into her eye.

I watched her scream and die, laughing when she cried for help. I cried the same words for years and no one came for me, so it was fitting no one came for her. Once the bitch was dead, I took back my knife, and I trashed the whole apartment, making it look like a drug deal gone wrong. I never fucking looked back.

"Candy?"

I look down at the table full of it and turn to look at the man who must be blind if he's standing here looking for it. I come face to face with John and nearly burst out laughing when I realize I told him my name was Candy.

"John." I plaster a large smile on my face. "This is wonderful." I look around the park, then back at him. He's wearing another expensive suit and today his hair is less like a helmet, blowing in the hot Nevada breeze.

"The children are all so happy." He watches a pair of girls spin around and fall to the grass, laughing. "I honestly believe their innocence can be inhaled."

What the fuck is this cunt talking about? I smile and nod because what the fuck do I say to that bullshit? He wants to inhale a child's innocence. Who the fuck says that?

"Come with me." He holds out his arm. "Let's watch the children enjoy this."

I want to add on 'while they still can' but I keep my mouth shut. I need him eating out of my hand and it won't be as easy as giving him a blowjob or riding his dick. He's smart, and he's careful. He's no wannabe king. I need him to believe I admire him and feed his ego a bit, then I can sink my claws in with a little tumble in the sack.

We watch the children, but I feel that I'm being watched as well. The back of my neck crackles like lightning and I move it from side to side to alleviate the feeling. Whoever's watching me is still a fucking coward, and it's only building up the disdain inside me the longer they wait to jump. I'm game either way. A little build up never hurt anybody, and I can't wait until I use their face like a cutting board.

"Candy?" *Oh, fuck me, this name is ridiculous.*

"Sorry." I give John a smile. "I got lost in thought. It must be all the innocence inhaling." I wave my hand around my head.

He chuckles and leads me back to the refreshment table. "Would you like some punch?"

I notice that's the only drink not sealed, and I shake my head. "I would love water." I grab a bottle.

He grabs one too and stares at me while I take a drink. "You're beautiful, Candy. You remind me of someone."

I swallow down the water and look him in the eye. "I think I have one of those faces because I hear that a lot." How the fuck do I look familiar to this prick? I start to get those tingles again and I can't help but be suspicious. Does John have an idea of who I am? I take a deep breath; I'm probably just overreacting.

He looks at his watch and around the park. People are starting to load the children back into vans and small buses and the sun is lowering as evening approaches.

"Dinner?" He smiles at me.

"Sounds great." I nod and follow him to his car. I didn't wear my trench today, but I do have on my belt and if he tries anything, I'll cut his fucking throat.

He drives a BMW, and it looks pricey as fuck. I mean, why wouldn't it be? Dealing in the skin trade is a lucrative business. I sit inside and fold my hands in my lap, fingers brushing the hilt of my knife. He gets in and gives me a large smile.

"Do you like pasta?"

*Who the fuck doesn't, you dumb shit?*

# *Blaze*

John Dempster, a well-known philanthropist in Nevada, is sitting at a table with my fucking girl. People here adore him. He has plaques with his name on them around the city, and yet he sells children and teenagers right under their noses. He has a foreign exchange program where he sends budding young boys and girls, giving them international experiences, and it succeeds because they are all orphans or wards of the state. He controls Nevada's growing population of unwanted children, and the people congratulate him for it.

Right now, the dumb shit is feeding my girl food from his plate, and Selene is gobbling it up. I know she likes to eat; I've seen the way she moans over bacon, but this is too fucking far. Why hasn't she killed him yet? I didn't think she actually dated any of the others and the sex was only ever a means to an end, so what's happening here? My body vibrates in rage, and I try to remember what Zander begged me on the phone. *Don't hurt our heart, Blaze. Without her, we'll all go back to being dead inside.*

I lower my chin to my chest and breathe in deeply, holding it until my lungs strain. When I release it, I raise my head and watch as Selene takes a sip of wine. She really is beautiful, and I can see her appeal, but that's not what I saw in her. I saw a warrior, someone who's been through hell, and made it out with the scars to prove it. I touch the scar on my face. I know it's the truth because I'm the same. She and I are made up of the cruelty of others and the strength of retribution. It's why I tried for so long to deny her. I knew if I ever gave in, it would be explosive, and I would never be able to let her go.

Hence why I'm here watching her giggle at another man. The rage boils but I have it tempered and even though murder is rampant in my mind, I can control it. She's mine and no matter how far she runs, I will always find her. I don't claim ownership of much in life because I know everything can be taken away. I know first-hand how easy it is to have something you cherish ripped from your hands and the difficulty in trying to move on.

My birth parents were killed in a house fire, and I was found a few days later roaming the nearby woods in pajamas, only two years old. The state couldn't locate my next of kin, so I was put in foster care. By the time I was thirteen, I had been in ten foster homes, and I was entering my eleventh, the final home. That makes it sound sweet, right? I found my place and with a loving family who sheltered me until I became of age. That's not how it went at all.

I was put in a home with Anne and Tom Banks. They were an elderly couple, and they had decided to open their home to children in need. I wasn't the only child they had and when I got there; I knew something was wrong. The children were too quiet and a few of them had that deadened look in their eyes. After a week, the children told me that sometimes a kid will leave and never come back. I was fearful that the Banks were killing them, and I couldn't let it go. I began to investigate, and I found paperwork in Tom's office regarding the sale of children to a Mr. Henry Walton.

That was the day he found me, and he beat me to within an inch of my life, cutting a slice into my face with a machete. Then, he told me he was not only proud of me for surviving but also for finding that information to begin with, and that's when my training began. You see, Tom was a retired marine, and he used tactics of torture to toughen me up. Waterboarding was an everyday activity and slicing me with knives was a punishment I received whenever I made a noise. In the beginning, I made a lot of noises and that's why my body is riddled with scars, but in the end, I was quiet. I can thank Tom for one thing, he did teach me how to endure pain and block it out whenever I need to.

I run my finger along the tough ridge of my scar at my lip and watch as Selene's eyes roll into the back of her head as she eats a mouthful of pasta. John is staring at her with a gaping mouth, and I would bet a stiff cock. My knuckles whiten as I grip the steering wheel and once again repeat Zander's words to calm myself down.

The pain rips through my chest, but I don't make a sound. Tom Banks would be proud. Too bad he's rotting in the grave I made for him, and I did have some decency. I made sure his wife was with him, too.

# Chapter Four

## Zander

I want to be angry at Selene for multiple reasons. One, she killed my father. I'm not upset about the bastard dying, but after all the planning, I wasn't the one to bleed the piece of shit out. Two, she left without saying goodbye. I never would have gotten in the way of finding her sister, but I would have liked to know what was going on. She sucks at communication, always has. Finally, I'm angry that I'm not angry at her for all the above.

Our girl's never going to be a team player, I understand that, but fuck! I miss her. Knowing Blaze has her back is the only thing stopping me from hunting her down myself. I want to help her. I wish she'd let us, but she won't. This is something she wants to do alone.

Santos yells something from the gym, causing my teeth to grind. He's our biggest issue in this whole mess. He's unstable as fuck. I already have to worry about Blaze's mental health. I don't want to be worried about Santos too.

Luckily, Darius is doing his best at keeping the asshole under control, but I know he'll eventually snap if we're not careful. He's never cared for anyone like this before, so her leaving has destroyed him.

I hope she hurries up and finds answers, because I want her ass home pronto and her cunt sliding up and down my dick. If I have to jerk off much longer, my fucking arm's going to fall off. Nothing's better than Selene's tight body wrapped around mine. Nothing.

Santos stalks into the room, not glancing my way as he snatches a bottle of water from the fridge and chugs it down, water spilling down his chin and sweaty chest in the process. I'm sure as fuck not going to tell him he's making a mess while in this mood.

His muscles are taut, and I can almost hear the monsters in his head whispering to him, begging him to explode and go after what's his. Love can be powerful, and I think that's why a lot of men don't like having women in the higher ranks of gangs and businesses. Women are beautiful, sexy, *and tempting*. They're literally their own personal fucking weapon and can bring even the biggest asshole to his knees.

Selene is proof of that; she holds all the power, and she doesn't even know it.

I'm relieved that we no longer have to run around for Henry, but now I have no idea what to do with myself. Santos leaves the room, apparently going back to beat Darius on the mat again, having more energy to burn. Blaze might be the best trained weapon we have, but Santos is the one no one ever sees coming.

He's crazy, acts like he doesn't give a shit about anything or anyone, so when he focuses on a target to protect his own? Yeah, it's some scary shit.

I sigh, rubbing my temples with my fingers to clear an ache that isn't there, but it's coming. There's no such thing as a quiet time in our lives, so we need to wait for something to go wrong like it always does.

One of the guys will snap, Blaze will lose sight of Selene, Selene will find the answers she seeks then not want to come back. Anything can happen.

Well, except the last one, because if I have to drag that woman home by the hair and bang her until I'm all she knows, I fucking will. I'm uneasy about this John guy, though, can't lie.

Selene makes a habit of fucking and killing, never getting too personal or close. So why the hell is she trailing after him like a lost puppy? I couldn't believe it when Blaze informed us she's hanging off the asshole still, acting like his arm candy. I'm surprised I've tolerated him touching her this long.

What if she's finally lost her fucking marbles and actually likes the cunt? If she doesn't hurry the fuck up and kill him, Blaze will rip him apart. That's the funny thing about Blaze. He's either emotionless or so overbearing, it's almost concerning.

He always protects us, throwing himself in front of danger without hesitation, but what lengths will he go to for her? I don't think he's even told us he loves us, and we're his family, but that blonde bombshell is embedded in his heart, causing it to tug-o-war between right and wrong.

He's stuck between wanting to let her seek revenge because she's earned that right and dragging her back to do it for her because that's in his nature. He won't risk something happening to her; so, if anything looks dodgy? She'll find out real quick that she hasn't been alone at all.

I bet she tries to stab us. In all honesty, I have a feeling she won't be grateful to see any of our faces any time soon.

# Selene

I love how stupid men can be. John has practically told me his entire routine while giving me his life story over dinner. Most of it is complete bullshit, but the little details are real. His voice changes a fraction when he lies, and I've picked up that he repeats a lot of things that are bullshit.

His favorite places to go to eat? Real.

His trips to see his dying aunt? Bullshit.

Most people wouldn't pick up on it, but I can. So, I keep milking it for all it's worth.

"Do you choose to go to the same place to eat regularly, or do you like to change it up with those other places you like? I love that Thai place that's close to the department store." I smile sweetly, batting my lashes and sipping my coffee.

"I go almost every day to the diner for lunch, but I like to change it up for dinner a lot. I try to come here often, because it's the best pasta I've ever come across, but I also really like that pizza place downtown when I want something more casual," he explains, eyeing me as I open my mouth wide to shove a forkful of food in. I bet the fucker eats pizza with a fork and leaves the crust behind.

I finish chewing before replying, tilting my head slightly.

"You go to the diner for lunch every day? You love the food that much?"

He chuckles, sipping his champagne in thought, before replying.

"It's the most central place to go, and I like eating where people see me. It proves I like helping the smaller businesses in the area and I don't see myself as any better than the rest of the community. People want one of their own to lead, and one day I hope that will be me."

Why do all the rich fuckers have an agenda for world domination? Every single one of them seems to be into child porn, slavery, and they always think the rest of the world is supposed to kiss their shoes and lick off the dirt.

The only one I'd met who didn't seem to give a shit was Zander. Fuck, I miss him.

"Candy? Are you all right?"

I jolt back to reality, giving John a bright smile.

"Of course! Sorry, I got lost in thought. You'd make a fantastic leader for the community. You care, you have good morals, and you're modest. You want to make this a safe place for people, and I admire the effort you put into everything. We are all lucky to have you. I'll be sure to vote for you if you ever run in any part of the government," I answer, adding as much sugar as possible to my words. Goes to show money doesn't buy everything, because all rich fuckers also need constant praise and approval like children.

"That's lovely of you to say. Thank you. I hope others see it the same way as you do. Do you work tomorrow?" he murmurs. He wants me to talk about my fucking work to see if I'm into selling my pussy.

I force a shy smile, glancing away from him. "I was supposed to work tonight, but I took the night off so I could see you."

"Not many places are open around here late at night," he observes, running his gaze over me as I finish eating.

"I don't have set hours. It's a little unconventional, but it pays my bills," I say and lift my shoulder in a half shrug.

"Dancer?"

"Escort," I correct lightly, watching his eyes fill with interest. His foot brushes against mine under the table, and I look up to give him a small smile. "Don't worry, this meal isn't on the clock."

"I feel terrible for keeping you all evening. Are you sure you don't mind spending more time with me tonight?" he asks in a low voice, and I know exactly what he's asking. He wants me on my back, and he's hoping it's free.

Nothing gives a rich dude an ego boost like bagging a free escort. They think it's because they're so powerful and irresistible that we fall over our feet for them. How cute.

"I was hoping you'd want the night to continue after dinner." I giggle, licking my lips and pulling a groan out of him. He snaps his fingers, wanting the cheque. Typical. I wanted fucking desert.

The moment he pays, he's on his feet, offering me his arm to lead me out to his fancy car. He opens the passenger door and motions for me to sit inside.

We don't speak a lot on the drive to his home; the trees passing by as the sun sets behind them. I mentally remind myself not to kill him. I need more information, but my fingers twitch with the familiar sense of chaos. It isn't often I fuck any of the monsters I come across without ending them afterwards. For the first time, guilt eats away at me.

It never bothers me to fuck any of them while I know my guys are at home missing me, because I shake it off and put it down to business. Killing them helps too. I have no reason to feel guilty, but it still bothers me. I'm about to climb onto this rich fucker when it should be Santos, or even Blaze.

They have to let me go, and I have to stop fucking thinking about them. I am not made for happy endings.

I'm surprised when we pull up at a two-story house in a quiet suburban area, my eyes trailing over the flower beds and manicured lawn.

As if sensing my confusion, John chuckles and takes my hand the moment he opens my door. "Not what you expected?"

"Not at all, but I think it's lovely." I smile, letting him lead me up the path and into the house. It's a lot fancier on the inside, and staff are running around cleaning as we walk through. It seems the cunt wants to look like an everyday person on the outside but refuses to let go of his over privileged lifestyle on the inside.

"Would you like some champagne?" he offers, but I shake my head.

"No thank you, the one with dinner was plenty. It's really beautiful here," I state, wanting to make it all about him so he'll keep talking about himself. They never realize just how much they give away because their lack of being humble gets in the way.

"Do you like art? I have a lot in the master bedroom." Real smooth, asshole.

"I do! I think there's something else I'd like to see in there too." I giggle, his eyes darkening.

"Is that right?"

"Yes. You want to show me the way?" I ask, biting my lip and taking a step towards him. He leads the way, his legs eating up the distance between the main room and his bedroom, not wasting any time as he shuts the door and grins.

"What did you want to see then?"

"Your cock is a good place to start," I reply in a husky voice, his fingers flying to the button on his black slacks. He kicks them off, moving towards me as he unbuttons his shirt.

"I want you to ride me," he growls, but I tsk and put a finger up to stop him.

"How about you sit on the bed and let me blow you? I've been thinking about it ever since I saw you this morning," I murmur, fighting the urge to roll my eyes as he drops his boxers down his legs and sits on the bed like a good boy.

He's a decent size, and he trims his bush, which is a pleasant surprise. I wish he'd had words with Sir Haynes, leader of the tangled suffocation bush. Men always expect us to be properly presentable, but then they refuse to make the effort themselves. Fucking cunts.

I drop to my knees, crawling towards him and licking my lips. "Wow, what a treat! If I'd have known you were hiding that, I wouldn't have made it through your speech at the park!"

He starts to lose his composure slightly, and the moment he fists my hair, I know he's going to let some of the real monster out. He pushes my face down until I gag, a low growl leaving him as he holds me there for a second before yanking me back. The bastard is lucky I don't punch him in the balls while I'm down here.

I relax my jaw, allowing him to guide me how he wants me until he pulls me back in time to come all over my face with zero warning. My eye burns as cum splashes in it before I get the chance to shut them. Motherfucker!

I drop back, panting and needing a minute as I stand and try not to stab him for being a dick.

"May I use your washroom?" I say sweetly, imagining his blood spurting all over the surrounding bedding.

"Across the hall," he mumbles, not giving me another glance as I excuse myself to clean up. I'll have to wash my fucking make-up off, or it's going to end up running down my fucking face, anyway.

I flush my eye out as best as possible, trying to scrub it off with my hands. I find a cloth in the cupboard under the sink which helps get the rest of it off, and by the time I wander back into the bedroom, John's snoring on his back, his soft cock still exposed.

I didn't even have to fuck him, nice.

I call for an Uber and leave the house, waiting on the side of the road, the familiar tingle running down my spine as I feel eyes on me. My stalker is good, I'll give them that.

# Chapter Five

## *Blaze*

Selene leaves his house looking less than sated and I can't help but grin. When I fucked her, she could barely stand afterward, and right now she looks ready to tear into the concrete with her heels. John Dempster either has erectile difficulties or my girl knows who she belongs to. Maybe when she eyes a new dick, she sees one of ours.

I let her leave and don't bother following her back to her tiny ass apartment. I know where to find her, anyway; what I really want to do is watch our new friend John. What he doesn't know is whomever Selene befriends, I do too, and I feel sorry for any motherfucker I have in my sights. I slouch down in my seat and blow some air on my coffee to cool it down. Time to see who visits John when everyone else is in a slumber.

It's a few hours later and I watch as a pickup truck pulls up. It has one of those trailers you attach to the hitch behind it. I see horses transported in those, but I know this time there aren't any fucking horses. Those air holes are to keep the skin suits breathing, because that's all they really are now, an empty shell of what they once were. Something inside me ignites when I realize Selene is braving a dangerous road and if this was her plan all along, I might just kill her.

These aren't the type of people you infiltrate on your own, no matter how trained you are, and they're successful because they can sniff out the rats. No matter how often she uses her pussy and tries to claim that as her business, they will eventually catch on. She's lucky I'm here with her and she'll show me her appreciation for it soon. If I decide to keep her alive for it. I'm fucking pissed at her, and I still don't know if keeping her breathing will be beneficial for us. Look how much she's fucked with Santos and Zander. Zander hides it better, but Santos has gone off the deep end. Not that he wasn't straddling it before she showed up.

The license plate on the pickup says Kansas and I huff, knowing this is not limited to being just local. These are big time players, and I would go as far to assume bigger than Walton ever was.

John Dempster's house is modest, but I wonder what his basement looks like and just how far it extends. Or maybe he has a shed in the backyard for when his *shipments* arrive, a holding place, and seemingly unobscured. I want nothing more than to sneak onto the property and find out for myself, but the whole place is littered with cameras.

The downfall of Dempster's need to look normal and blend easily is that his house has neighbors, close ones. Both houses beside him have no cameras, and I bet if I get into one of their backyards, I'll be able to get a better picture of what's around his house. I wait for the men to exit the pickup truck and when John opens the door to let them in, I quickly get out of the car. I jog up the neighbor's driveway to his right and I hear quiet crying coming from inside the trailer. Just as I thought.

I hop over the small fence leading to the backyard and breathe out a sigh of relief when the fence is only six feet tall. I can see over at my six-and-a-half-foot height. John does indeed have a structure in his backyard made of cinderblocks, and I know that's not a typical shed. So, is this what they do, line the people up and walk them inside? That can't be it, and the more I try to look, the more I see that the structure has no fucking door. There's a secret entrance somewhere. I bet it's a tunnel from the basement, and I bet that structure is fucking soundproofed. How do the neighbors not question a doorless structure?

I hear noises from the front of the house, so I creep back towards the driveway and crouch down to listen.

"I'll open the garage, but I need this to be quicker than last time." This must be John. "No fucking around."

Two guys answer in a monotone, 'Yes, boss' and I hear the truck being backed into the garage. Is the entrance to the secret tunnel there?

I want to lift my head and look over the fence, but I don't want to risk getting caught. I still haven't found out enough information. I'd have to kill everyone and that would leave Selene without answers, ensuring she stayed here longer. We are all coming to the end of our patience with her being away, and I'm supposed to be helping to speed this mission up, not slow it down. But I do crave a little bloodshed.

I hear hinges creak and metal banging off metal, but I can't decipher what's being opened and closed. I hear children crying softly and now and then the crack of skin on skin, followed by a whimper. It takes about fifteen minutes, and then the night falls back into silence. A few minutes after that, I hear the hinges creak again and the booming of doors shutting in the still of the night. The sound of the truck starting and pulling out of the garage fills the air, the engine loud until it disappears down the road. Without much more to learn, I head back to my car and watch John's house a little longer, curious about what happens next.

It's a good thing I don't sleep much.

Craving coffee and some of Selene's bacon, I scroll through my phone. I send a quick text to Zander that I have some info, promising to call later, and then hear the motor of the garage door opening. I slouch down and watch as John pulls out of the garage in his BMW, closing it quickly before he speeds down the street. He can't be leaving for too long, considering the company he has, and my stomach burns with jealousy as I imagine him possibly picking up my girl for breakfast.

I look at the dash and snort when it says six a.m. knowing fully well that she's not up yet. I've learned her routine and I know she'll be asleep for at least another two hours, then she's off playing P.I. I settle in, knowing the business as I do, and wait for the buyer to show up today. Nobody wants to sit on product, regardless of what the business is. You're not making money if it's chilling in your possession. One hour later, John returns with another van in tow, and this time, when the door opens, I freeze. It can't fucking be, but I know my eyes aren't deceiving me, and I know well enough, because this man has been in my life since I was thirteen. Mack Delaney.

He was Henry Walton's 'mover' meaning he picked up the imports and exported them. He moved skin, and he did it for Tom Banks as well. My first run in with Mack was when I was thirteen years old, and I got to watch as he loaded up two of my foster siblings into a van much the same as he's driving now. Motherfucker.

The fat fuck lights up what will be his first of many smokes and laughs with John, his gaped-tooth mouth on full display. Is his name on

Selene's list as well? My blood runs cold at the thought of her trying to coax information out of him and knowing he enjoys killing women, then fucking their corpses.

No, I can't let her deal with him on her own and that means I will have to step in before that point.

# Selene

I tried to make plans with John Dweebster today, but he's busy, apparently. I really don't like the sound of that and it's eating at my brain. I should go by his house and pop in unannounced like a crazy woman. No one would ever disagree with that statement. The only thing stopping me is that I know nothing yet. I'm taking it slow with him, draining him bit by bit, and when I finally confirm the last name on my list, I will fucking gut him.

I look down at my notebook and chew on the end of my pencil. Earl gave me the name Delaney and I know that's a last name. It's common enough and when I searched for it in the Nevada directory, thirty-two options came up. I could go through all thirty-two and cross them out one by one, but even I know this Delaney may be from out of state. I need to work over John some more and make him trust me. I want him to believe since I'm in the sex industry that maybe I have the potential to help him out. I only have to nudge him gently. If I push too hard too soon, he'll get spooked.

Since I have all this time on my hands today, I decide to take a tour of the area I'm living in and try to hear what the word is on the street. I know some of the best information is found on street corners or in darkened allies and I am no stranger to either one. I pull on my trench—knowing I will die of the heat—because it's my security blanket and fasten my 'belt' around my waist.

It's nine in the morning, and the sun is already blasting hot, sweat already forming on the back of my neck. I've been through worse, and dealing with a little heat is no big deal. I start for the coffee shop I frequent every morning, loving the dark roast and sometimes pairing it with a side of pastry. Sometimes sitting there; you hear things as well. People love gossiping over coffee.

The bell dings as I step in and the girl behind the counter waves, already so accustomed to my morning visits. I smile and head for the counter, smiling wider when she puts my order in front of me.

"I knew you'd be by." She grins and gives me a quick once over.

"Thank you, Wendy." I smile.

I pay her and head to my usual table in the center of the room, watching as the place fills up around me. I sip my coffee and open the paper in front of me, gasping when I see none other than King Haynes himself. His smiling face mocks me as I quickly read the article.

*Eugene Haynes was found slain in his home last night and word is one of his house attendants is under suspicion.*

House attendant? Do they mean his sex maids? I think back to that girl I found in the hallway and my heart squeezes. I hope she got out. I quickly skim over the rest and find no other useful information, slapping the paper closed in frustration.

"Mr. Haynes was killed in his own home." My ears pick up the conversation behind me. It sounds like two older men, and I also hear the rustle of a newspaper.

"I heard," the other grunts. "He was an odd one, living up there in a damn castle."

"He had all those maids and such," the first carries on. "Maybe he was mistreating them."

"I wouldn't doubt it."

I like that narrative floating around because I know he didn't get the traditional form of justice, but at least his name can be sullied, and those girls can claim self-defense. I get up out of my seat, taking my pastry to go, and dumping my now chilled coffee in the trash. I walk out to the sidewalk and look up and down the street.

I know a small farmer's market is to my right and I could probably start there for gossip. Or I could go to the left where the strip of bars is, knowing it's early, and still willing to bet they'll all have patrons. Left it is.

Farmer's Markets are for non-GMO moms and organic food humpers. Not that I disagree with that, I never had the choice when I was growing up, instant anything was my only option. Besides, I know how to converse with drunks better than trophy wives.

My first bar has a few men on the stools, and I find a booth ordering a greasy breakfast. I love a greasy pub meal. I dig into my dippy eggs and crispy bacon, my moans attracting all sorts of stares, but fuck them, this shit is amazing. A waitress comes by and refills my coffee, chuckling at my appreciative display. I watch the TV and the news channel is running the story on Haynes.

"Did you know him?" I ask the girl, and she shrugs.

"His rich blood was never in here."

"Do you think he was actually killed by his maid?" I ask with a snort.

She gives me a once over and deems me no threat. "There were rumors about him," she whispers.

"Let me guess." I tap my chin. "He danced in the rain naked and sacrificed babies."

She chuckles and shakes her head. "More like those girls he had up there," she looks around, "weren't … you know … employed."

"Really?" I sit up. *Bingo*. "What else?"

"We've been having a lot of young women going missing here," she clears her throat, "from the night jobs." Prostitution.

"Go on."

"I knew a few of them and they were regulars in here every night, looking for business. Then they stopped showing up."

"Huh." I sit back.

"Are you … um … a night worker?"
"Yes," I reply without hesitation. "So thank you for the heads up."
She nods and continues back to the bar, looking over at me now and then. Once my breakfast is done, I get up and toss her down a couple hundred dollars. Her info was good, and Haynes is paying for it.

It's six bars later and a throbbing head when I finally get back to my apartment; I write down everything I was told. Most of the information is the same, girls going missing, and relief that Haynes is dead. You're welcome y'all, I grin to myself. But it's the last thing I write that sends chills down my spine.

*The number of children reported as runaways from group homes across Nevada is rising, except no one genuinely believes they've run away.*

I need to speed up this situation with John and I need to do it soon. I don't want any more children or young women falling prey to him or Delaney.

# Chapter Six

## Selene

oans fill my ears as I make my way past the dark allies in the middle of the night. The night strip well and truly underway. A lot of the prostitutes do business in dark corners or out in the open, not giving a fuck to who sees them.

I am glad my targets always seem to be rich; it means I get to do business in the back of flashy cars with tinted windows, giving me a fraction of privacy. Then again, I'm grateful for the privacy so no one sees me stab them afterwards, not because it hides my naked body. I don't give a shit about that.

I can sense eyes on me, and even though I know people are glancing at me, I know it's my stalker. I thought they would've made themselves known by now, but they haven't even left a hint of their existence, other than the burning sensation on my skin from their eyes.

"How much for a ride, sugar?"

I slow my steps and glance up at the young man who's running his eyes over me with appreciation, relief rolling through me to see he isn't an old shriveled up fossil. I know it's work, but if I have to endure one more limp noodle-dicked, old cunt this week, chances are high I'm going to sew my fucking flaps together and call it a day.

I cock my head to the side, giving him a small smile. "That depends on the kind of ride you want. Aren't you a little young and a little too pretty to be paying for sex? I doubt you struggle to reel the girls in."

"Aren't you a little too pretty and a little too sweet to be standing out here like a cracked-out whore?" he throws back without hesitation, making me grin.

"Touché. So, what did you want? Need a blowie to put a pep in your step?"

He snorts, stepping closer but not grabbing at me like I anticipated. Apparently, some men aren't complete pigs.

"I can get a blowie anywhere, babe. A decent lay is another thing, though. So, how much does it cost to rock your world?" he asks with a smirk, and I have to bite back a laugh that almost leaves me. They always think they're rocking my world, but in reality, I get a shitty lay and no orgasm, while they're left panting and satisfied.

"Three grand, and it's yours."

"Two and a half," he drawls, earning a laugh that flies from my lips.

"This isn't a fucking auction, asshole. Take it or leave it."

"How about three grand, but if I make you dizzy from a pile of orgasms, it's two and a half?" he barters, his lip lifting into a nasty smirk.

"You talk a lot of game, Mister?"

"You don't really need my name, do you?" he asks swiftly, telling me the fuckbag is probably engaged or married. He's too nice for his own good.

"Not particularly. My clients usually like me screaming their names. I personally don't give a shit if I know it or not, though. So, where did you want to do this?" I ask, his eyes drifting over towards the brick wall by the dumpster. Lovely.

"No car?" I half joke. His eyes light up in the dark with the reflection of the streetlamp.

"Nope. You one of the fancy girls who are grossed out by fucking outside in the open?" he teases, making me roll my eyes. Why the fuck is this bastard joking around like we're old friends? I should gut him, just to prove I'm in charge here.

I take his hand, tugging him towards the wall and concealing us in the shadows.

"Sue me, I like to be comfortable when I'm working. I have no problem fucking outside, though. Drop them," I exclaim, motioning to his pants as if I have somewhere to be. Technically, I'm supposed to be sussing out the corner by the old railroad tracks where one of the recent missing prostitutes had been last seen—so the whispers told me—but I can't exactly turn the guy away. For all I know, this guy could be the freak taking them; I need to get close to anyone who goes out of their way to ask me for business.

I wish the bastard would pick me; he can make my job a hell of a lot easier if he hands himself over on a silver fucking platter.

The guy chuckles, unbuttoning his pants and pushing them down his legs, raising an eyebrow in challenge. "Well? You next, Blondie."

Pet names now? *Argh. Yuck.* I change my mind. He's a pig too.

I'm only wearing a tight emerald skirt and a lacy shirt that probably has less material than a bra, so I roll the skirt up over my waist and tug my tiny thong down my legs, stepping out of it with a grin.

"So, how do you want to *blow my mind*?" I sass, knowing I'm about to be let down as usual. The moment he pulls his boxers down, I have to hold back a groan of appreciation. There's rarely a time that I admire a cock, but he's clearly blessed. No lie.

He takes my elbow and pushes my front gently into the wall, the cool brick work causing my nipples to pebble against the material.

"Am I on a time limit?" he purrs in my ear, a light laugh leaving me.

"Never needed one. Why? You think you're good enough to be charged hourly? I highly doubt I'll have to give you that kind of rate. Go ahead and surprise me, though."

His hand rests on my waist, squeezing slightly as he fists himself with his other hand. He's gliding a condom along his length, and guides it closer to my pussy, teasing me and confusing the hell out of me. Why the fuck is he teasing me?

"Do you have rules?" he asks randomly, making me snap.

"Would you shut the fuck up and fuck me? You're not paying me to talk," I hiss, gasping in surprise as he slaps his cock against my pussy, biting my shoulder firmly but not painfully.

"I don't want to hurt you, *sue me*," he mocks, rubbing himself in my juices before slowly pushing inside.

"You talk too much," I grit out, but I can't hold back the breathy moan that surfaces as he grinds into me at a surprisingly good angle.

"You'll be the one making too much noise in a minute, babe," he practically whispers, holding my waist with both hands and thrusting firmly into me, alternating between grinds and thrusts until I feel the familiar tingle.

"No fucking way," I mutter, disbelief coursing through me. This fucker is going to pull a goddamn orgasm from me. They never manage to do that, mainly because they don't give a shit about me feeling good. They pay me to make *them* feel good. Most don't know how to find my g-spot even if I give them a fucking map.

One of his hands leaves my waist and snakes around my front, his fingers lightly but quickly strumming across my clit until my legs shake and my pussy clamps around his cock, a scream leaving my lips in response.

He fucks me harder, his teeth grazing my neck as a growl erupts from him. "Again." For real? This guy is weird as fuck. Does he really want to pay me to make me feel good? I'm not going to say no.

My bare stomach is starting to get chaffed up from the bricks, but the bite of pain is needed to make it not so nice. I don't do nice sex, ever, especially from a client. Zander's face flashes in my mind, and I squeeze my eyes shut and focus on the burn from the bricks, the guy behind me working hard to pull another climax from me.

The second one isn't as powerful as the first, but it still causes my legs to shake, and he absently puts an arm around my middle to stop me from falling on my ass, the sting of the rash on my stomach becomes a welcomed distraction. He's lasted longer than my other clients, but he's also a lot younger than most, so he probably has good stamina trained in him. His lips trail down my neck, and I fight the urge to pull away. I don't want nice.

"I need to come," he grunts, making me snort.

"Then come."

He buries deep and comes, resting his forehead on the back of my head as he catches his breath. I hate that it's nice, which is stupid. I've spent years wishing my clients had some fucking respect, but now that I've found one who treats me properly, guilt swarms inside me for enjoying it.

I imagine Santos' tired chuckle after we finish, and we joke about something. Darius' banter as he jokes with us. Zander's sweet words that wouldn't seem so sweet to anyone else but were exactly what I'd need to hear at the time. Blaze's intense eyes as he watches me come apart.

What I just did is supposed to be work, so why the fuck do I hate myself for it?

The guy steps back, tosses his condom aside, and fixes his pants, surprising me ever more as he bends over to snatch my panties from the ground, leaning down and offering me to put my feet into them. I silently do, and the moment his eyes trail up my body, they latch onto the bloodied scrapes on my stomach.

"Fuck, I hurt you!" he barks before I can shrug him off, his gentle hands grabbing my waist as his thumbs move up and down my hips while he inspects the damage.

"It's fine," I mumble, but he fixes my skirt properly and takes my hand, tugging me down the street. "Where are we going?" I demand, wondering if maybe he is the kidnapping bastard after all, but we stop by a random building as he ushers me closer, pulling the shirt over his head and turning a tap that's attached to the exterior.

I eye him warily as he soaks some water into the shirt, turning to me and asking permission with his gaze. When I don't speak, he steps closer and squats in front of me, cringing as he dabs at the bloodied cuts on my skin, expecting me to flinch.

I've been hurt by experts, so a bit of brick rash isn't going to bother me.

"You don't need to do that," I grumble, but he snorts and glances up at me.

"Like fuck. I didn't mean to mark you like that. I didn't even think…"

"I said it's fucking fine!" I snap, confusion shining in his eyes as I step back, needing to get away from him.

The guilt weighing on my shoulders is making me angry, and I clench my fist, letting my nails bite into my palms to draw me out of it. It isn't working though, and more images of my guys flash through my mind.

They aren't my guys, for fuck's sake!

The guy touches my arm, and I pull it from his grip like it's a snake.

"Don't fucking touch me. Get the fuck out of my face," I warn, and surprisingly, he steps back.

"I just…"

"Fuck off. We're done here," I grind out through my teeth, turning to leave, but he darts around me, halting my escape. I go to yell at him, but

I stop as he grabs a stack of bills from his pocket, offering them to me.

"Here."

I snatch them, ignoring how his eyes watch me with worry. I don't want his pity or whatever the fuck he's feeling. "Thanks."

"My name's—"

"I don't give a fuck. Get out of my way before I gut you like a fucking fish," I snarl, and thankfully, he moves aside and lets me leave, guilt nipping at my heels the entire way home. Out of all the men who've ever left their scent on my body, his was the one I wanted to scrub off the quickest in the shower.

I'm fucked up. It's official.

## Darius

My body aches like a motherfucker. Santos really got me good last time. If being on the receiving end of his fists is the way to keep him contained, I'll fucking do it daily, and I pretty much have been. If he loses it now? We'll all be screwed. I don't want to be cleaning up after him if he goes off and massacres a bunch of people, looking for an escape from his pain.

I can't fault him, though; I'm not handling Selene being gone well, either. The one reason I'm happy to be Santos' punching bag is because I deserve it. How did we let her sneak off and run like that? Losing her is killing us all slowly, and even though Zander seems all right, it will be slowly eating away at him she's left us behind.

I am getting worried about Blaze. We can't risk him losing himself on the road, but he'd been right to go alone. We'd only slow him down when he's hunting, but I hate he has to do it on his own. I can't worry too much about him, though. I have to leave that for Zander. I have enough on my plate while I watch Santos lose his shit. He's currently beating his fists into the boxing bag without gloves on, his knuckles already split and bleeding all over the material, but the stubborn fucker won't stop. I tried to stop him ten minutes ago, but he nearly knocked me out with a crack to my jaw, then went back to wailing on the bag as if I'd never interrupted him.

I get comfortable in a chair in the corner, tossing him a towel to clean his fists with once he's dead on his feet, panting as he drops onto the floor in front of me. He wipes the fabric over his face to mop up the sweat, then he presses it against his busted knuckles, the blood soaking into the light blue material.

"You know not to get in my way, fuckface," he growls, but there's no heat in his words. He's worn himself out, so for that I'm grateful.

"I know. I'm sorry I give a shit about you, asshole." I snort, his eyes lifting to mine and showing me the emotions consuming him. He's hurting, more than I've ever seen, but for once it isn't a pain I can take away by killing or torturing some bastard.

I never thought a woman could worm her way into his heart, let alone all our hearts, and her silence is deafening. If she fucking called every day to say she was all right and missed us, maybe Santos wouldn't be so devastated. Maybe my heart wouldn't be breaking as I watch my best friend create a void between us that's slowly becoming an ocean wide.

"I want to go and get her, man. We have to," he says softly, but he knows it's no use. We have to play this smart, not with force. I sigh and stand from my chair, dropping to the floor beside him and sitting cross-legged.

"We're all hurting without her, but she'll hate us if we drag her back home, demanding she do as she's told," I explain for the hundredth fucking time, but his lip lifts in a snarl, his eyes flashing with anger.

"I don't care if she hates me, as long as she hates me here."

"You do care if she hates you, so shut the fuck up. If she looks at you with disgust or hate, it will eat you alive. I promise we'll get her to come home, but we need to make sure she's dealt with her demons first. We have to let her go so she'll come back," I say through my teeth, hating the taste the words leave in my mouth. "I don't care if you have to lay into me every fucking day to release your emotions."

"D, you can't be my punching bag forever. You don't deserve any of my anger," he grunts, but I clap his sweaty shoulder with my hand, making him hold my gaze.

"Watch me. I fucking love you, you stupid prick. I'm here in any way you need me to get through this, and I'll be right here when our girl comes home to help you remind her where she belongs."

"Tag team?"

"I'll even let you take charge of me too," I promise, a sudden calmness swirling in his eyes as he finally gives me a soft smile.

"Is that your way of asking me to fuck you? Just gotta ask, bro. I'll plow your ass like a field," he teases, a chuckle leaving me.

"You wish, fuckface. Go shower. I want to go get burgers and turn in early for the night. We can call Blaze bright and early and make his day. I bet that fucker is missing us, don't you think?"

"No doubt," he grins, getting to his feet and helping me stand. "Thanks, bro."

"You know I've got you," I reply lightly, knowing he needs to hear that I'm not going anywhere. Selene is getting spanked hard for abandoning us. My hand is already itching to feel the crack against her skin.

# Chapter Seven

## Blaze

Did she really disappear down a fucking alley with a guy? I know he's not a target because I've been watching her and he's the one who approached her this time. What the fuck is she doing? I know what she's supposed to be doing, and this is not it. She's been gathering information on the missing children and prostitutes, and in doing so, has had to walk these streets late at night. But never has she disappeared down a fucking alley. I swear I'm going to kill the bitch.

I get out of the car and jog across the street, ignoring the hoots from a few girls at the corner. I stand at the mouth of the alley and hear voices bleeding out, making my jaw tighten. What the fuck are they talking about and why the fuck did they need to go down an alley to do it?

I step inside and press myself against the brick wall. My nose is immediately assaulted by the smell of sex. I can hear them, and I am stunned into place, my mouth drying. I know her lifestyle and I know the things she does to get the information she needs, but this is different. He wasn't a target and right now he's a client, in the middle of a filthy alley. Like she couldn't wait to take him to a car or his place. It had to be done here with the fucking rat shit.

I want to rip his dick off and force it down her throat. That's how fucking angry I am. My whole body is shaking, and my teeth are clattering together as if it's the middle of winter, only it's stiflingly hot here in Nevada. My vision blurs around the edges, and I can feel the thumps of my rapid heartbeat pulsing around my skull.

I step up beside a dumpster and listen to every moan, even when she cries out with her release. I crouch down and try to breathe as she comes again, my hand curving around the knife at my waist. Yeah, she clearly wants to die. She just handed over a piece of herself that belongs to the guys and me.

I hear them talking and I hear the rustle of clothing. The noises registering but my thoughts overpowering all the rest. I can feel myself slipping and I know of only one way to bring myself back. She better pray I get my head together or else I will be shipping her heart back home to Santos. He'll want a fucking piece of it after this. I hear her voice growing louder and my brows crash together at the sound. Is he forcing her to do something?

Then they appear in front of me, briskly walking out of the alley, and hooking an immediate right. I hate what's happening, but I can't stop the smile that curves over my face. I'm going to finally hunt.

I give them a minute to pull ahead and then I fly out of the alley, following the bob of my girl's blonde head. They stop and I watch as he pulls his shirt off, wetting it with the spout that's connected to the brick building. What the fuck is he washing? Again, the pulses start, and I can't control the step I take forward. It's getting harder and harder to keep myself together. The sound of her snapping at him is the only thing that stops me from carving them into pieces, right here on the fucking street.

I watch as she rushes off and the pretty boy stands there, looking like he just lost his puppy. Well, he's about to meet a full-grown dog. I stalk forward, grabbing him by the hair, and taking him down the next alley. He tries to fight me, but the only way he's getting away is if his scalp detaches from his fucking skull.

"What are you doing?" he snaps. "Who are you?"

I throw his puny body into the wall and bend down to look into his eyes. "You were just fucking my girl."

"The prostitute?" He looks incredulous, and I smack him hard across the face.

"Her name is Selene, and she wasn't yours to touch."

"Look man," he holds up his hands, his skin growing paler by the minute, "she didn't tell me she was taken."

"I know." I smile, feeling giddy inside. "She'll be punished for that, too."

I grab his small neck in my large hand and squeeze, watching as his eyes begin to bulge. He claws at my wrist with his stubby fingers, but it's not going to do a damn thing. I let go of him and when he bends over to suck in a choking breath, his throat meets my knife. The tip slips right in and when he tries to come back up; I hold his head down with my other hand. I force him down until my knife's serrated tip pokes out of the back of his neck and I can hear the gurgles of his blood choking him.

I pull out my blade and watch as he falls to the ground, his small body shaking on the asphalt. I crouch down beside him and swipe my finger through the blood on my knife. I begin to draw on his chest as his eyes lose life and stand up to look down at my handy work. It looks close enough. I drew her scythe and then the word *reaped* beneath it. She might as well have killed him herself; it was all her fucking fault, anyway.

I wipe the rest of the blood off onto the dead guy's wet shirt and stride out of the alleyway. No one pays me any mind and if they saw me go in there with someone and now leave on my own, they don't say anything about it. Maybe that's how it is around here. People see these things all the time, and it's normal. I don't care either way.

I head back to my car and start it up, heading back towards Selene's. I need to make sure her ass is home and not out sucking another asshole's dick tonight. I check out my hands as I drive and exhale in relief. I'm no longer on the cusp. That kill ensures Selene will live another night.

I pull up to her decrepit apartment building and shake my head at the sight; she is attracted to danger. I climb out and head around to the side of the building, jumping up to grab the fire escape ladder. I haul it down and quickly climb up, peering into other apartments on my way. There are a few crackheads and a couple of families in this building, an eccentric group. I get to the sixth floor and stand in front of her window, the yellowing lace blowing in the breeze. She leaves her window open most of the night and the only thing separating her from anyone is a screen.

I know she can take care of herself, but I can't help but think she's begging for trouble, anything to give her the high I know she gets from a fight or a kill. Just like me. I hear her shower running and I pull out the screen, like I've done so many other times. I step inside her living room and head straight for the bathroom; I want to drag her out by her wet head. As I reach for the door, the sound of a dying animal hits my ears. Did she bring a cat in there? Just as I'm convinced that she's killing cats, I decipher words through the awful noise and chuckle when I realize she's singing. Damn, that's awful.

I step back and go into her bedroom; the light begins to flicker. It's a cheap ass place and I snarl when I see a blow-up mattress on the floor. I'm pissed at her, but I don't want her living in these conditions. I find her suitcase on the floor and lift the top with my boot, her awful singing still filling the surrounding space. I bend down and unzip a compartment, finding all her panties. I scoop them all out and toss them on the bed, pulling my knife from my waist.

I may not be killing her tonight, but I will leave her a message and hopefully she gets the meaning of it. I pick up each one, bringing it to my nose. I do miss her.

# Selene

Singing in the shower has always been a stress reliever for me, and I know I have the voice of an angel. I take an extra-long shower this time, scraping the guy from my skin, and leaving long welts in places. The water runs cold long before I'm finished, and I don't care. I will freeze to death before stepping out and taking the chance of still having his scent on me.

As soon as I wrap my body in a towel, I get the feeling I'm not alone, and I can swear I hear movement from the other room. I open the bathroom door slowly and look out into the apartment. It's a small place and I can see nearly every angle from where I'm standing. Nothing is in the apartment, but my bedroom door is closed, and I never close it, not even when I'm sleeping. I creep out and take quiet steps towards the room, cursing under my breath when I realize my knife belt is in there. I was in such a rush to scrub him off me I didn't take it into the bathroom. I always have it with me. I slowly turn the handle and shove the door open quickly, hoping to startle anyone who may be inside. The door bangs off the drywall and sinks inside, creating a hole I know my deposit will cover.

The room is empty, but what I find sends a chill down my spine. Someone was definitely here. I step towards my bed, picking up a pair of panties, and gasping when I see what's been done. There's a large cut through the crotch and when I look to my bed, every one of my panties is scattered there. I lift each one and see they all have the same cut, my heart pounding furiously. This stalking shit has gone on long enough and now I need it to end. I quickly change into a tracksuit, without underwear, and step back out into the main room.

I check the door and it's still locked tight from the inside, which leaves the fire escape. I stride over to the window and find it open wide; the curtains sucked outside. The screen is sitting neatly outside, leaning against the brick like it was left for me to find. Almost as if they are warning me of the potential danger of using this window. They could've come into the bathroom and gutted me while I showered, but they didn't. I was ripe for the taking, and still they chose to leave me a warning instead.

This was either an extremely sick person or someone I know, and honestly, that means they could very well be both. If they thought they could scare me, they're so completely wrong and don't know me at all. I get dressed and throw on my trench, strapping my belt around my waist. I thought my night was over, but I guess it's not. I should thank the fucker for pulling me out of my funk.

I pop the screen back inside the window track and close the window, locking it tight. It'll never be opened again unless I'm sitting in front of it and watching for someone to try me. I know most people would move at this point, scared and feeling like their space was invaded. I'm a little happy that one, I can now go panty shopping, and two, my stalker has upped the ante. It was about time they grew into their balls.

I walk back to the front door and stop in the middle of the room, holding my nose in the air. A scent so familiar hits my nose and I breathe deeply. I know it. I just don't know where it's from. I commit it to memory this time and promise myself I won't forget it. The next time I smell it, my knife will be cutting into their flesh.

"You're back," the waitress says, as I walk into the bar I was in earlier this week.

"I am." I grin at her and sit on a stool. "Whiskey please, on the rocks."

"You got it." She begins to fill up a tumbler with ice. "How was your night?"

I know she's wondering about if I've come across trouble in my night job.

"Pretty uneventful." I nod, as she hands me the glass and I take a large gulp.

The burn skates its way down my throat and warms my belly. I needed this.

"I have to warn you to be extra careful." She leans over the counter, staring into my eyes. "A regular hasn't shown up tonight and she's here every night."

"Does it happen to many of the girls who frequent here?" I raise a brow and sip my drink.

"Yes." She swallows thickly and looks around.

"Why do you think that is?" Another sip and I begin to look around at the faces.

"I don't know." She shrugs. "We are a popular spot."

"Looks like it." I nod.

"I just feel terrible because our boss is just beside himself with the connection," she tuts and begins to wash some glasses.

"Yeah, I can see how that would affect business." I tap my glass for a refill.

She fills my glass nearly to the brim and gives me a wink. "On the house tonight, unless you're a fish."

I laugh and gulp down almost half the glass, watching as her eyes widen. "I'll pay, trust me."

We both chuckle and the door chimes as someone walks in. I turn to see a young woman, her hair a thick mass of tight purple curls and her skin a beautiful ebony. My breath gets lodged in my throat when she throws the waitress a smile. She's so damn gorgeous.

"That's Aniyah."

"What's your name?" I tear my eyes off the girl and look at the waitress.

"Colleen." She smiles, her blue eyes twinkling. "Yours?"

"Selene."

"Is Aniyah in the same profession as I am?" I laugh when Colleen rolls her eyes.

"Yes, she is very sought after."

"I can see why." I toss another look at her over my shoulder.

"She's sweet, but I wish she would stay away from here. It's not safe," she murmurs, looking worried as she dries the tumblers.

"Have you told her to be careful?"

"Yeah, but she's the boss' favorite," she huffs.

"His favorite?" I quirk a brow.

"Yeah, you know, for hire?" She rolls her eyes.

"Oh, he frequents the ladies of the night as well," I snort, and she chuckles.

"He'd like you too," she nods. "He likes the tougher ones and you're certainly tough."

I can't help but wonder if the boss of this place is somehow a player in the women going missing. It would be a good front, having a bar that supports the women, and supposedly keeps them safe. Actually, it would be a brilliant idea.

"What's your boss' name?" I ask with a grin. "In case I want to offer my services."

She lets out a cackling laugh and I join in, taking another long gulp of my drink.

She stops laughing and wipes the corners of her eyes. "John Dempster."

"Pardon?" I lean over the bar; I couldn't have heard that right.

"John Dempster."

# Chapter Eight

## Zander

"She fucking what?" Santos barks, his fists tightening on his lap until his knuckles crack. Darius managed to calm him down once today, but by the look of this conversation, he'll have to do it again before the day is over.

"I said she was working a client who wasn't a target. He was young, and the bastard was nice as fuck to her," Blaze growls through the phone, my eyes darting to Darius, who snorts.

"Oh, that rat bastard was nice to her? She must have been terrified," he deadpans, and Santos scowls at his sarcasm. Selene is in deep shit when she gets home because Santos has completely passed the in-love phase and has nose-dived straight into possessive beast mode.

"He was all over her. I nearly stormed over to them and slit his throat when he made her come," Blaze continues, causing me to frown.

"Are you sure it was a client? She's not dating him, is she?" I ask, Santos instantly standing and almost knocking the table over as his leg swipes it.

"I'm going to fucking kill that piece of shit!"

"They exchanged money. She took off real fast though, so I have no idea what was going on. I bled that fucker dry in the street, so he won't be touching her again," Blaze snarls, relaxing Santos instantly, but worry seeps into my bones as Blaze rants about the entire thing.

He's losing it, just like I was worried about when the big prick left to go hunt her alone. He's not the type to go off on a rampage like that, so knowing he's left a body in the street is concerning.

"Do you need us to come to you, brother? You sound like you need it," I say carefully, knowing he can go off like a bomb when pushed. He chuckles, his voice appearing steady, but I can imagine his hands fisting in his lap as he fights for control.

"I'm fine. I can fucking handle the bitch perfectly fine on my own. If she gets too out of control, I'll cut her to pieces," he says through his teeth, a sigh leaving me as I rub my temples with my fingers. I swear I've had a constant headache since she left.

"That's what I'm worried about," I mutter, but he's not listening. He's too busy giving Santos all the fucking gory details about the nice dude he left bleeding. I should be relieved he killed the cunt before he could sway our girl into seeing him again, but I'm not. I'm too worried about what it means to Blaze.

When he finally hangs up, Santos pins me with his eyes, not hiding the crazy inside them.

"I think it's a good time to go after her. She's fucking people for the sake of it now, Zan. What if she's setting up a life for herself there? That's not the first person she's fucked and hasn't killed, she…"

"I'm aware, but the answer's still no. You heard Blaze, give him more time and he'll call us if he needs help," I answer, keeping my voice stern. I don't feel like being punched in the face repeatedly today, so I hope my tone is right.

As if sensing my wariness, Darius takes Santos' hand and tugs him back down onto the couch beside him, not letting his hand go.

"Remember what I said? She's coming home, so breathe. Blaze has her, and he's killing all those pieces of shit who fuck with what's ours, all right?"

I hope he doesn't kill anyone else, not because I give a fuck about those people, but because Blaze will slowly become the monster he hides below the surface, and nothing will bring him back from that.

Santos, surprisingly lets out a steady breath and nods, squeezing Darius' hand in response, not using his words. We sit in silence for a while, until Santos excuses himself and heads to his room, quietly shutting the door behind him.

I look up at Darius and sigh. "He seems better."

"Only today. Tomorrow, he'll probably be losing his shit again. I don't know how much longer I can hold the fucker back, Zan," he warns, genuine concern filling his eyes.

"Won't be long now, and we'll have our girl home," I promise, his throat bobbing as he swallows hard.

"I miss her."

"I miss her too, man."

## Selene

I nearly spit my coffee as I watch the news over breakfast at the diner.

A body was found early this morning in an alley, my fucking reaper mark left on them in blood. I know I'm a little crazy, but I'm fairly sure I'd remember murdering someone before bed. I think. Am I losing it enough to forget killing some piece of shit?

Confusion pools in my stomach, my coffee tasting sour as I catch a glimpse of the body. It's covered by a blanket as the cops try to do their job. But that leg? Quite sure it's what had helped pin me to the wall and fucked the hell out of me last night. I left him there, staring after me. I know I didn't kill him.

"More coffee?"

I jolt as I realize the waitress is standing beside me, and I quickly plaster on a bright smile.

"Yes, please. Sorry, I zoned out for a second there. If that doesn't state I need a refill, nothing does," I joke, her lips quirking into a grin.

"I'm not a morning person myself, I get it. I'll be right back with your breakfast."

I thank her as she walks away, but my eyes catch on an image of a young woman on the TV. Left widowed after her husband—the nice guy—was murdered.

I knew that cunt was a fucking fraud.

The waitress returns with my breakfast, and I moan as I shovel a piece of bacon in my mouth, sucking my greasy fingers in after it. The waitress gives me an amused glance, but she leaves me to it, pretending she can't hear my orgasms while I eat.

Another lady looks at me with disgust, but I simply lick my fingers clean and give her a wink. "The food's fucking good, am I right? Remember to tip your waitress."

She scowls, turning away from me and letting me enjoy my

breakfast without her judgement. Not that I give a fuck. Would Darius have eaten bacon out of my coochie?

I pause at the mental image, my panties dampening as I close my eyes and a low groan leaves me.

*Wait, stop that.*

My eyes fly open and land on the woman who was scowling a second ago, and I make sure to stuff more bacon in my mouth like a savage, getting grease all over me. Anything to stop the images of Darius burning into me any longer.

I focus on my eggs next, using my toast to mop up some yolk as it drizzles onto my plate.

"Good morning, Candy."

I startle for the second fucking time this morning, finding John standing beside my table. I quickly wipe my mouth with a napkin, giving him a bright smile.

"Mr. Dempster! It's lovely to see you! Please, join me!" I exclaim gleefully, when in reality I want to carve the fucker's eyes out of his skull and play Beer Pong with them.

He slides into the seat opposite mine, giving me an apologetic smile.

"I'm sorry I've been busy. I was hoping we could catch up again soon," he states, watching me as I practically lick my plate clean.

"I know you're a terribly busy man, sir. Whenever you can fit me into your schedule, I can be there," I beam, finishing my coffee so I can give him my full attention. He seems pleased with my statement, and he leans across the table to take my hand. He's lucky I wiped them on the napkin, or he'd get a handful of grease.

"I really enjoyed the other night. I'd love to do it again sometime," he murmurs, and I have to fight a scowl. I have to act like it has been a dream, so I flutter my lashes instead.

"I'd love to come over again. I really enjoy your company."

He gives me a look of approval, his eyes shining with desire.

"I'll be sure to get hold of you again this week, then. Be careful when you're working, please. There've been a lot of people going missing late at night, and I'd hate for something to happen to you," he bullshits me, making me fake horror as I press my hand to my chest.

"I know, it's dreadful. Those poor people."

He turns the subject around to talk about himself, but I prefer that. He goes on about all his accomplishments, his new painting, and how successful the youth center and park are.

By the time we part ways, he promises to call within a day or two, and then he's gone. I know I need more information on John Dempster and his bar, but also about his preference for us ladies of the night.

I stand outside the bar and look up at the sign, "Good Times" it reads, and I try not to snort. *I bet it is, John.* I head inside and see Colleen behind the bar, sidling up on what's becoming my regular stool. Her dirty blonde hair is up in a messy bun on her head and her large chest is threatening to spill out of her top.

"Selene," she nods, and I thank God I gave her my real name. That way, if she and John ever happen to speak about me, he won't connect that I'm the same person he's been seeing.

"Colleen," I grin. "The usual, please."

She hands me my whiskey on the rocks and lets out a huff. "There's so much death around here lately."

"I saw a few things on the news." I nod. "Looks like cops will be swarming the place soon."

"Yeah," she puffs out her breath. "A few of the girls are worried about that."

"I would be more worried about getting snatched or killed." I shrug. "Cops are easy enough to deal with. You're not dead."

"True."

"Has Aniyah been by tonight?" I ask, trying to sound nonchalant.

"Yes," she gives me a small smile. "She's fine."

"Do you expect her to be back tonight?"

"Yes," she grins. "Are you in need of her services?"

"Something like that."

"Stick around for a few hours and you'll catch her." She heads off down the bar to pour a drink for another patron.

It's exactly two hours later when Aniyah shows up, her bright purple curls prominent in the darkened room. Tonight, she has on a silver tube top and a short leather skirt, her long legs gleaming. She really is so beautiful.

I get up off my stool and walk towards her, her brown eyes landing on me, and a small smile curving on her perfectly cupid bow lips.

"My name is—"

"Selene," she cuts me off, her smile growing wider. "Like the Greek Goddess of the Moon."

Her voice is like a melody, and I can feel myself softening, growing aroused by her words. "Yeah," my voice is husky and soft. I can see what makes John so infatuated with her. I want her, too.

"You're new around here." She steps in closer and fingers the lapel on my trench coat. "I know I would remember that face."

Her scent washes over me and I can't help the moan that escapes my mouth. I've never had such a strong reaction to a woman before.

"I did want to speak to you about a client." I shake my head to clear the fog. "Could we sit down somewhere private?"

"You're taking time out of my night." Her hand lands on her hip. "It'll cost you."

"Sounds good." I nod.

I follow her to a booth in the far corner of the bar and slide in across from her. She fiddles with the napkin holder and watches me from under her lashes.

"I heard you are close with the owner of the bar," I begin, straight to the point.

"John?" Her nose crinkles at his name. "He's just a client who asks to spend time with me. We don't fuck."

"Oh." My brows crash together in confusion. "What do you guys do?"

"We talk," she shrugs. "Sometimes he orders take out and we binge Netflix."

This is fucking strange.

"So, he has never tried anything?" I ask her.

"Nope," she shakes her head. "He's gay."

*No, the fuck he's not.* I rest my chin on my hand and try to figure out why he would tell her he's gay when he's clearly not.

"All the girls know he's gay," she chuckles. "He just hangs out with us some nights and pays us like a regular client. It gives us a break."

"All the girls that come by here?"

"Yeah." She leans forward. "I really think he's trying to protect us from whoever it is that's making the girls disappear."

Then it hits me like a ton of bricks. A gay man would make a girl feel completely comfortable, and her trust would be gained so easily. It must be John who's snatching them up.

# Chapter Nine

## *Blaze*

**G**ood Times.

I glare at the sign illuminated above the brick structure Selene just entered. Good Times, my fucking ass, this place is sucking up what little patience I have, and if she doesn't hurry up and get her shit together, it'll be her fault when the bodies begin to drop. I can't keep this up for too much longer and if she doesn't take my threat in her apartment seriously, I may have to slit her flesh next.

The place looks popular with many patrons flocking in and out, but I can't help but notice the number of prostitutes that frequent. I know they're prostitutes because I have been watching this strip and I never forget a face. I don't understand why they all congregate at this bar, and I know there must be a connection for Selene to be here, but what is it?

I pull up my hoodie and yank it down low over my face. It's a risk I'll be seen, but I need to know the connection so I can speed this bitch along. We've been here too long, and the boys back home are losing their shit. If I fail at bringing her home, I'll probably have to kill them to retain my peace of mind.

I jog across the street and open the door to the bar, stepping into the bustling space. The music is booming from a jukebox and the lighting is dull; the darkness working in my favor. I sit at a booth in the front of the bar, sliding all the way into the wall, and I wait. I don't know where Selene is, but I'm sure she'll appear and, in the meantime, I'll listen to the surrounding people.

"What can I getcha, sir?"

I look up and see a waitress standing with a hand on her hip, her face trying to see under my hood. Her face is plain, too thin lips, and a hooked nose. Not interesting at all.

"Soda water," I reply and avert my face. I hate nosy bitches.

"You came to the bar for soda water?" she chuckles.

"I came to the bar to get out of the house," I snap.

"Gotcha." She taps her fingers on the table. "I'll get your drink, then."

She comes back and slides the glass across the table, the collected sweat on the outside wetting my hand. "On the house, sir," she huffs. "You let me know when you want a real drink."

I ignore her and she walks away with a tut, her attitude grating on my last frayed nerve. If I decide to start a fucking slaughter, she's first, then Selene. I rest back against the back of the booth and open my ears, letting the sounds assault my ear drums. As much as Tom Banks was abusive, he was also useful, and he taught me how to zero in on noises, drowning out others. I hear John's name and zero in on that conversation.

It's a woman with a beautiful voice and I wonder if she sings.

"John?" she pauses. "He's just a client who asks to spend time with me. We don't fuck."

Then I hear the next voice, knowing it's my girl, and my hand tightens around the glass. Of course, she's digging for information, and it bothers me how blatant she is about it. I listen in on their conversation and when I hear John is gay; I let out a snort. No, he fucking isn't, I've seen the way he looks at my woman, and there's nothing gay about it.

I wonder if Selene is piecing everything together as well as I am, knowing John owns this bar, and that he's capturing prostitutes on the promise he would rather suck dick than eat a pussy.

She better hope she is because I can't keep up this guise for long. I want to kill John and Mack, then drag her ass home and watch the guys punish her. Santos will be the most interesting. I take a drink and swallow it down, knowing that's not how this situation will go down. Selene wants to find her sister and I have a feeling Mack would know where she is, probably having transported her himself.

I finish my drink, and keeping my hood low, I stand to leave the bar. I've heard all I need and now I have to update the guys. I know our girl is tough, but I don't want her taking on John alone. He's a big fucking fish. I don't think I could take him on alone, either.

"Leaving so soon?" the waitress purrs from behind the bar as I walk by. She does nothing for me and so I ignore her, throwing open the door with more force than necessary.

I need to figure out a plan before calling the guys. This needs to be handled perfectly.

## Selene

The entrance to the bar bangs open and I snap my head around to catch the back end of a tall, well-built man leaving the joint. His stature looks familiar and my pussy clenches at the sight. Once the door shuts, I shake my head and pull myself back into my conversation with Aniyah.

"I really wouldn't mind striking up the same deal with this guy." I lean in. "It's getting dangerous around here and spending time with a safe man like that sounds great."

"It is," she smiles. "I can introduce you."

"Can you?" I make sure the excitement is clear on my face.

"He's busy this whole week, but he's asked me to meet him here next Tuesday."

That's eight days. I know I'm due to hear from him in a few days, but he only promised a phone call. Eight days gives me a good amount of time to come up with a plan, and I can't think of any other way than to surprise him with a visit one night, outing myself and him at the same time.

"That would be amazing, really." She has no idea just how much.

I throw down five hundred on the table—double what she asked for—and stand. Her eyes widen and she gives me a once over, stuffing the bills into her bra.

"Let me know if you ever want to hang out again." She winks, and I can feel the wetness rush between my legs.

"I'll know where to find you." I bite into my lip and force myself to walk away. If I stay there with her, I'll be on my knees in no time, and working her pussy with my tongue.

I stride to the bar, trying to push back my wanton thoughts of Aniyah, and sit on my stool. I've drank too little or not enough. Either way, I'm ordering another, and I'll use it to drown my thoughts of pussy.

Colleen pours me a glass without my having to ask and I smile in thanks.

"We just had a weird customer." She puts the bottle of whiskey back. "I've never seen him before, and he ordered a soda water."

"Ew," I screw up my face. "That shit's like drinking no cellphone service."

She cackles loudly and nods. "Yeah, he wouldn't show his face, but he was big and ominous."

"That's the one I saw stomping out of here." I take a sip. "Did he say anything?"

"Nothing of importance."

"We'll have to keep an eye out." I gulp down my drink and toss some money on the counter. "I need to sleep off this hangover." I say as I stand. "I'll see you tomorrow."

"Be careful on your way home." She looks nervously at the door.

I nod and pull my trench's collar up around my neck. I wish someone would try to nab me. It's the surest way to find out what's going on, where my sister is, and satisfy my need to kill.

# Chapter Ten

## Selene

It's my third night in a row at the bar and I have yet to see the stranger again. Colleen says he hasn't been back either and no one else has gone missing. Aniyah has been here each night and every time I see her, my body becomes more responsive. I don't know what it is about the woman with the bright purple hair, but I fucking want her, and I can't stop thinking about it.

I'm sitting on my regular stool, my eye on the door, and in walks Aniyah with a handsome man on her arm. She's wearing a purple off the shoulder top and a dark blue pair of skinny jeans. He's tall—not as tall as Blaze—maybe about Zander's height of six feet-two inches and his body is lean. Nothing like my guys. He's got a swimmer's body, trim, and he's dressed in a pinstripe suit, pinstripe. None of my guys would wear that. I groan internally and try once again to push them out of my mind.

I watch as Aniyah leads him to the booth we were in yesterday and his black hair gleams unnaturally under the table lighting. It's such a contrast to his alabaster skin and I wonder if it's dyed.

"Colleen," I call out and she comes to stand in front of me. "Who is that with Aniyah?"

"Don't know him."

"Does that hair look natural to you?" I ask and she snickers.

"Girl, let the man live. Maybe he has grays."

"Or maybe he's changing his appearance?" I shoot her a look.

"Oh," she breathes.

"You know Aniyah," I begin. "How would she feel if I joined them?"

"I've seen the way she's been looking at you," she grins. "I'd say it'll be welcomed and by them both."

"Could you send their table a tray of Wet Pussy shots?" I ask her with a grin. "Might as well make it known what I expect."

She throws her head back and cackles, "I don't know how I ever got through the nights without you here, Selene." Then she heads off down the bar to make the shots.

Ten minutes later, I follow Colleen as she carries the tray to the table, setting it down between Aniyah and the stranger.

"Selene wanted to send you guys some shots," she murmurs, and Aniyah looks up at me with a smile.

"They're Wet Pussy shots," I tell them. "Colleen sure is shy to say it, but not as much to make it."

Colleen chuckles and walks away with a blush spreading up her neck and face.

"Join us, my Moon Goddess," Aniyah purrs, sliding over in her seat to make space.

I sit beside her and give the guy across from us another closer look. He's clean shaven, and he has the most striking pale blue eyes, making him look even paler.

"Ah yes, Selene." He smiles and his pale pink lips flatten, showing straight, white teeth. "Moon Goddess. Very nice name."

"Thank you." I nod. I stare into his eyes, unable to look away. His lashes look so unnaturally long and black. "I didn't mean to interrupt your night," I look at Aniyah, "I just couldn't seem to stay away."

Her dark eyes brighten, and she leans into me, pulling a piece of my hair with her fingers. "I'm glad."

I know I'm not imagining her interest in me, and this pull we have is getting harder to ignore.

"Will you be joining us tonight, Selene?" Stranger cuts in. *Oh right, fuck, I forgot about the Addams Family.*

"I don't know," I smirk at him. "Can you afford that, Mr.?"

"Angelo Gomez," he replies, and I almost spit out my Wet Pussy. His name is Gomez? Like the fucking Addams family. This must be fake, right?

"Okay, Mr. Gomez—"

"Angelo is fine," he cuts me off, and I exhale with relief. I don't think I'd be able to call him Gomez with a straight face. "Money is never an issue."

I beam at him, showing all my teeth, and Aniyah links her fingers through mine. She leans in and presses her mouth to my ear. "I have been waiting for this."

I turn my head and brush my mouth against hers. "You have no idea."

I see Gomez Addams across the table lean in to watch us closely, and I groan when Aniyah's tongue flicks against my lower lip. I wind my hand around her neck and haul her in, devouring her mouth with mine. Katy Perry was completely accurate. She tastes just like cherry Chapstick, and I don't think I can stop. She moans into my mouth, her tongue meeting mine, thrust for thrust.

A throat clears and I almost growl at the fucker sitting across from us. How dare he interrupt?

"Is this a regular thing?" he asks as we pull apart.

"No," Aniyah answers, breathlessly, "but I've been wanting her."

"I can see that." He squirms in his seat, and I would bet my last Wet Pussy he's adjusting his cock in his pants.

I take my shot just as Aniyah leans over the table. "My pussy's wet and I want to eat hers. When can we get out of here?" I choke on the liquid, and Aniyah rubs my back while looking at Angelo.

"Yeah, okay," he swallows thickly, looking at us with excitement in his eyes.

*Same, dude.*

He has a motel room on the ground floor, and I can see my shitty ass building a few blocks over. I hope he actually has enough money for this because it's going to be pricey. I take off my trench coat and hang it over the red velvet chair, then carefully unsnap my belt. I carefully remove it and place it over my jacket, hiding the fact that it's a knife.

"Would you two like a drink?" Angelo asks, and I watch Aniyah strut across the room.

She stands in front of me, her purple curls glistening, and her eyes alight with passion. "No," she snaps, sounding impatient, and slams her mouth to mine.

I match her ferocity and one hand grabs onto her hair while the other snakes up her shirt. Her skin is so soft and we both moan at the contact. My fingers brush along the underside of her bra and she breaks our kiss to toss her shirt over her head. I do the same and then we're right back at each other. Our teeth clash and our bodies collide, the heat from her skin warming mine.

I've made out with girls before. I've even fucked them for money, but it's never been like this. No real feelings and never the overwhelming need to taste them. Pussy has never been something I sought after; right now, I would kill to taste hers. I unclasp her bra and break our kiss to pull it off her body. Her breasts bounce with the motion, and I can feel the fluid between my legs. I bend forward and take a brown nipple into my mouth, whimpering at the taste of her skin.

"Get on the bed," I hear her bark at Angelo as I make my way down her taut stomach and begin to unlatch her jeans.

She helps me pull them down, taking her panties with them, and as soon as I smell her arousal, my eyes sink back into my head. This can't be natural; she smells too fucking good. I drop to my knees and grab her thigh, hauling her leg over my shoulder. Her pussy spreads open, and I spread it more with my fingers. She's fucking dripping wet, and I waste no time sucking it all into my mouth, reveling in her scream.

"Yes," she begins to grind against my face, "fuck my pussy with your tongue." I hear Angelo on the bed removing his clothes and then Aniyah has her hands gripping my hair, the force ripping out a few strands.

I sink my tongue deep inside her and use my nose to rub against her clit. Her hands pull on my hair to bring me closer and I replace my tongue with two fingers, sucking her clit between my teeth.

"Oh fuck, Moon girl," she moans. "That's it."

I can feel her juices along my chin and cheeks, but I don't stop. I want to swallow every drop from her. I pump my fingers faster and nip down on her clit, her pussy walls clenching around.

"I'm coming!" she screams out. "Fuck, Selene."

"Jesus," I hear Angelo from the bed, the slap of his cock loud in the room.

She comes with a gush of wetness that trickles over my cheeks and into my hair, some dripping to the floor.

"Holy shit," she moans as I continue to lap it up.

I finally release her, and she stumbles a bit, her eyes glazed over and satisfied. I stand and wipe my face into my shirt, looking over at Angelo. I startle when I see the stark white of his pubic hair, everything suddenly making sense. His pale skin and dyed hair, he's an albino. Fuck, this is a first, it really is. I have never had an albino. His cock is large, and he has a Jacob's Ladder running down the underside, exciting me even more.

I can't wait to bounce on that.

I scramble out of my clothes as Aniyah crawls up his body, her long purple nails scraping his pale skin and sucking his cock down her throat. She really is the fucking equivalent to a Hoover, and I have nothing on her skills. I'm fucking jealous because I want her mouth on me, not Angelo. She releases his cock with a pop and looks at me over her shoulder.

"Get over here."

I've never moved so fast in my life, and I watch as Aniyah rolls off the bed, my stomach instantly dropping with disappointment.

"Suck his cock," she demands, and I eagerly do so, wanting to taste her on his skin. There's a lingering taste of cherries, and I moan around him, causing him to jerk in my mouth. The bumps of his piercings knock against my teeth, and I admit, I can't wait to have them inside me.

Blaze's pierced tip was amazing, so I can only imagine what this will feel like. My stomach begins to sour with the thought of Blaze, and guilt begins to bubble inside me until I feel my ass cheeks being spread. I continue to stroke Angelo's cock, my palm bumping over the piercings, and look over my shoulder at Aniyah. She gives me a quick wink and then her face disappears between my legs, her purple hair the only thing I see.

When her tongue sinks into my pussy, I gasp, and my hand pauses on Angelo's dick. He makes up for my lack of movement by pumping up into my palm and I lose myself in the feel of Aniyah nipping and sucking on my pussy lips. I hear a high pitch whine and shock myself when I realize it's coming from me. She sinks two fingers inside me, and I am almost embarrassed by the noises my pussy makes as she fucks me with them.

Once she has a good rhythm going, I lean back down and take Angelo's cock into my mouth. Paying extra attention to that rough ridge under the head. He begins to pant and jerk in my mouth and I'm on the edge as Aniyah works my pussy. Then I feel her flattened tongue glide along my asshole, and I gasp around Angelo, choking when he pushes upward.

Aniyah chuckles behind me and continues lashing her tongue against my rear hole, then pushing it inside. The feel of her spreading me with her tongue and fucking me with her hands has me falling over the edge, my pussy clamping down on her hard. I black out and scream her name, stars exploding behind my eyes. When I come around, I have tears soaking my cheeks from the intensity and my body is trembling.

I'm fucking keeping her.

# Blaze

I won't lie, it was hot watching my girl eat out another and then vice versa. I heard her scream from my parked car in front of the motel room. The part that disturbed me was her sucking that asshole's dick and then watching as her pussy sank down over it, all those piercings making her eyes roll back in her head.

Now, the Albino fucker must die, only this time Selene will be getting a bolder message. She clearly isn't fucking getting the picture.

The two girls leave together, sharing an Uber, and I wait a few minutes while the guy stays on the bed, unable to move or even wash his dick. Fucking gross. When I see his chest moving in a slower rhythm, I know he's fallen asleep, and I also know the dumb fuck didn't get up to lock the door. It's like it's all meant to be, and this is what I'm supposed to be doing.

I let myself into his room and the snores are reverberating off the walls, the sounds akin to a chainsaw. The smell of sex is so fucking thick in here and it makes my cock harden, despite the circumstances. I miss her and it's supposed to be my dick she's riding.

I walk up to the top of the bed and look down into his face. I hate that he's sleeping here, sated by my girl's pussy, and enjoying the aftermath like he owns it. Too bad he'll never get it again, or any other pussy for that matter.

When his mouth opens again on another Earth-shaking snore, I slam one of my hunting knives down inside of it, stopping only when it sinks into the mattress under his head. His eyes snap open and he begins to tremble. He's now a quadriplegic. I stroll down to the middle of the bed and stop adjacent to his flaccid cock and stare at it as it lays against his thigh. Selene really seemed to love those piercings. Maybe I will get that for her. I'm the only one out of us four who could take that pain, anyway.

His body continues to jerk, and I grab his limp dick, studying the piercings closer. I can get this for her. I pull out my phone and snap a picture. I'll need to show the piercer exactly what I want. Then I grab the other knife strapped to my waist and slip it through the base of his cock. It easily cuts through the flesh, leaving behind a clean bleeding stump. I walk back up and see his eyes are closing. He's on the brink of death. I pull my other knife out of his throat and wipe it on the bed, then replace it back in the holder. He'll be dead within a few minutes. At least he was fucked well before he died.

I use the bloody end of his cock in my hand and draw her scythe. Santos is going to love this.

I pull up to her apartment building and see she has the lights on. Maybe she brought her new friend home. I yank on the fire escape and listen as it drops with a clatter, uncaring if she hears it above. Maybe it's time she finds out I'm here.

I climb up quickly; the metal shaking beneath me, and the sound rattling inside my head. I reach her apartment and look inside the window, not bothering to hide, and not worried about her killing me. I don't see her anywhere, but I do see an opened bottle of wine and a few glasses. They probably moved to the bedroom. I pull on the window and chuckle when I find it locked. I pull out my knife and run it between the trim and the glass, popping the old-style lock without issue.

I yank up the pane of glass and step inside, hearing giggling coming from her bedroom. I pull out the Ziplock bag with the severed cock and open it, emptying the contents on her small kitchen counter. She won't miss it. Then I take a seat on her sofa, so sick of sitting in my car, and rest my head on the back of it. This place smells like her and it toys with my senses. My cock hardens and I undo my pants just as I hear breathless moans coming from the bedroom.

I grab my swelling cock in my hand and give it a hard squeeze, a drop of cum dripping from the tip. I smear it around the head and begin a punishing rhythm. I hate masturbating, but the bitch has driven me to it. I feel my balls tighten just as Selene screams out to her god, or the bitch between her legs, and I cum all over her small table in front of her couch.

I shake off any lingering drops onto the floor and tuck myself away. I head back for the window, deciding to close it this time, and ensure she doesn't screw it shut. I skip back down the steep metal stairs, my mind once again clear, and my need to release sated.

It was a productive night.

# Chapter Eleven

## Santos

I can't wait to drag my fucking blade across Selene's perfect skin, carving my mark into her flesh to warn others away. Every time Blaze updates us about her, my blood boils, and a primal need to claim her in front of every other man breaks through to the surface, dragging me back to my angry pit of violence.

She's blurring the lines between work and pleasure, and I don't fucking like it one bit. Half the people she's been with lately are giving her pleasure, pleasure they have no right to give her. She belongs to us, no one else.

Darius' fingers tighten on my knee, drawing me back to the conversation and away from my violent thoughts, and I can't help but appreciate how attentive he is to my emotions. He always knows exactly what to do or say to me.

"So, she's got a new friend?" Zander states calmly, and he's lucky I don't punch him in the face for how in control of his emotions he's been since she left. I don't like her having a new friend, which means having ties in different places, and the only tie she needs is to us.

Blaze scoffs, his voice blunt as usual. "If you wanna call a whore that, then sure. After what I saw and heard last night, I'd say they're a little closer than that."

I sit up straighter, glaring at the phone that's sitting on the coffee table in front of us.

"Wait, you think they're becoming involved or something? She can't fucking love that bitch, she…" I am going to fucking kill some cunt.

I don't give a fuck if it has a set of tits, I'll still kill it.

"I didn't say they're falling in love, dick head. I'm just stating that they're close. Wine glasses on the table and giggling from the bedroom are usually a good sign that the girls were off the clock and winding down after a hard day of dick," he grunts, confusion pulsing through me.

"Wait, you got that close to where she's staying, and you didn't snatch her up and throw her in the car? What the fuck, Blaze?!" I bark, literally hearing his eyes roll through the phone.

"Close? I sat on her couch and hung out for a while."

"She just let you hang out and didn't try to gut you?"

"I never said she knew I was there," he answers, and Zander cracks a smirk.

"She's going to kill you when she realizes you've been inside her house. You know that, right?" he asks, but Blaze laughs, not sounding amused.

"The cunt can try, but I'm close to killing her with my bare hands if she doesn't shut her fucking legs."

"Santos," Darius says quietly under his breath, warning me to calm down. My fists bend tightly into balls, and I'm this close to shoving my feet in my shoes and strapping some ammo to a vest. If she wants me to come and get her, I'll be coming in hot and fucking fast.

I relax my hands, ignoring how Zander's eyeing me like I'm a wounded dog. He knows if anyone gets too close right now, I'll fucking bite a chunk out of them, so he's not wrong to stay back.

I let out a breath, turning my attention to the phone. "Anything else to report? What's that John fucker doing? Is he still trying to fuck her? Can I help you blow his fucking brains across the pavement yet?" I growl, calming a fraction as Darius agrees.

"Yeah, need us to come gun anyone down yet?"

"Stay fucking put or I'll be the one gunning you fuckers down. She's not done with him apparently, or he'd already be dead as a Dodo. I left her a gift, so hopefully it encourages her to wrap up her bullshit and get her ass home," Blaze says casually, Zander groaning in response.

Blaze gives interesting gifts, that's for sure.

"What did you do?" Zander demands, making me chuckle, the weight on my chest lightening at knowing Blaze is on my side. That girl is ours, and it's about time she fucking knows it.

"I possibly helped some albino fuck dismantle his sex stick. Since Selene loved it so goddamn much, I left it for her as a memento," he replies smoothly, a smile of victory in his tone. I hoot with laughter at the image I get, despite the fact he said our girl enjoyed it.

"You freaky fucker! Did you leave her a floppy dildo?!"

"I did. I hope she shoves it up her ass and fucks herself silly, too," he grunts, seeming distracted. As much as I wish to be the one who causes bloody mayhem and drags her home, I'll be more than happy for Blaze to go ape-shit and fuck everyone up. That fucker is a beast when let loose.

"So, what do we do about this chick she's spending time with? Can we kill her?" I grin, and Darius chuckles from beside me.

"Down, boy."

"Please!" I beg, making Zander and Blaze both snort. They should just appreciate the fact that I'm asking and not diving straight into my own agenda. It's still in the cards.

"You're a dick," Blaze mutters, causing my grin to widen.

"How? You wanna lick me, big boy? Do I excite you like a big peen? It's a new kink, but I'll try to lie still while you run your tongue over me. Oh! Want me to bring some maple syrup? How about whipped cream in a can?" I offer, curses spilling from him before he hangs up, apparently sick of my bullshit.

Darius raises an eyebrow, his voice low. "You know, one of these days, that big bastard's going to take you up on your stupid offers, just to spite you," he warns, making me laugh.

"I've never come across something I haven't liked. Other than that time, I tried to put my knife blade first into my butt. I don't recommend trying that at all," I scowl, remembering the tiny cut being a major problem all week. I was terrified of pooping for days.

Zander stands, giving me a level look. "Trust me, no one was hoping to try that, you fucking psycho."

"What are you going to do to Selene when we get her back, Zan?" I ask, not giving a fuck if he thinks I'm crazy. Crazy people don't know they're crazy, and I know I am. Therefore, I'm not crazy.

"It's probably easier to tell you what I'm not going to do to that bombshell when I get her under me again," he shrugs, but I see it in his eyes before he can hide it. He's hurting more than he's letting on, just like I know he is.

# Zander

The gunshots sound like heaven as I raise my gun, firing at the targets down the range. We are all worked up and anxious, so I decided it was best to let out some of our moods before we ended up killing someone for real.

Santos dragged a pile of weapons along, and so far, he's probably used more bullets than our enemies fucking own. He's re-enacting some of our shoot outs, a small smile quirking my lips up as he loudly and dramatically screams *pew-pew* through the range, dodging and weaving imaginary bullets in the process.

Darius seems more relaxed as he fires a few rounds, hitting his targets with ease, then glancing over to check on Santos regularly. We needed this more than I thought, and I'm so glad I forced them into coming. Not that Santos needs an excuse to shoot at shit, because that fucker was out the door and getting in the car before I even finished my sentence about the afternoon plans.

It feels weird without Blaze and Selene here, and I force myself to think about something else as the familiar pit settles in my stomach. Our family is fractured, and I'm hurting for all my brothers. We need to work a job or something to keep us busy, but I have no idea what to do.

There are a few people on my shit list, but I need a clearer head to handle those. Nothing major, just rapists and skin sellers, but I can't afford for us to make mistakes if we aren't using our heads right. Santos will gun down half the fucking neighborhood once he starts, and even though Darius is usually well put together with his emotions, he's slowly snapping too.

Between containing Santos' demons as well as his own broken heart, the cracks are starting to show, and I'm worried about what he'll do if given the chance.

I can't have them running loose around the streets, or we'll have a massacre, and I can't clean that up alone while they wage war on the town.

"Take that, you pissy pants, motherfucker!" Santos screams, catching my attention as he literally dives forward to duck and roll, holding his gun out and firing three shots at his target. That is practically one big fucking hole now.

"Why is he a pissy pants?" I snort, a sadistic smirk taking over his sweaty face.

"Well, he's a pissy pants now that I'm done with him. One glance my way, and his dick was whizzing right down his leg and warming his socks! Don't distract me!" He laughs manically, suddenly dropping to the ground and dramatically clutching his chest. "I've been hit! You fuckbag! You got me hit!"

Darius is laughing loudly, and I simply roll my eyes.

"I'll fucking shoot you myself in a second, drama queen. There are plenty of distractions out in the real world, so I'm just helping you prepare." I shrug.

"Lies!" He exclaims, aiming his gun my way playfully to fake shoot me, his eyes going wide as he accidentally taps on the trigger and sends a bullet whizzing right past my fucking head. "Oopsie daisy!"

"Santos!" I snap, but he's on his feet and darting behind Darius, using him as a human shield.

"Sorry!" He grins, moving to fake shoot me again, but he jerks back as I shoot at their feet lazily.

"I'm this close to cutting off your fucking balls," I promise, holding my thumb and pointer finger apart the tiniest amount, and Darius can't help but join in with the fun.

"As long as he touches your balls, right, San?"

"Ooh, Daddy Zander wants my balls?" Santos says and fakes a groan, my stomach twisting at his words. If anyone gets to call me Daddy, it's my blonde, psychotic sex kitten.

*Just get your ass home, Selene.*

Darius and Santos are wrestling, thankfully without guns in their hands, and I sigh as I lean back against the wall. I need Blaze home too, before I drown in childish bullshit from the other two. We have a balance, and this separation is fucking with it.

# Selene

My muscles hurt in every way and it's so fucking delicious. I stretch out and hear a soft purr beside me, smiling when I realize my new obsession stayed the night.

"Are you smiling at me?" Her voice is like liquid sex. "I can feel it." She presses her full tits into mine and drapes an arm over my waist.

"I am." I chuckle and bury my face into her curls. "Do you want some coffee?"

"Sure, in like twenty minutes, let me sleep more," she husks out, and I can feel myself growing wet at her tone.

I slip out of bed and throw on a robe, quietly stepping out of the room. I walk across the hall to the bathroom and relieve myself. I'm sore down there too and I moan when I think about why. Aniyah used a few toys on me, and I can honestly say she looks sexy as fuck with a strap on. I walk out to the kitchen and rub the sleep from my eyes, opening the fridge for the water to start the coffee. I have one of those old school percolators and the smell that fills the apartment when it's on is divine.

The scent of coffee permeates my fog addled brain and I moan into the open tin. *Fuck, that's so good.* I take out a few scoops and set up the machine, turning to look across the room. My eyes zoom in on an object sitting on my counter and the spots of blood around it, something glinting in the light along its length. I'm instantly awake and my stomach threatens to push its bile up my throat.

I take a single step and dry heave into the room, recognizing what's laying on the counter. There's no way; it can't be. Only, I know it is. I know those piercings, and even though the skin is now gray, I know it was once an unnatural white. My heart stutters in my chest when I look back to my bedroom. Aniyah can't see this. I grab a bag from under my sink with some disinfectant wipes. I slip the bag over my hand and grab the appendage, sealing it inside the plastic. I tie it and throw it into my garbage, gagging at the soft feel of the flesh. I wipe down the blood and spray air freshener into the room, cursing at the nerve someone has.

The bedroom door opens a few minutes later and I exhale with relief that she wanted to sleep in. How the hell would I explain that I have a psycho stalker? And that they're accelerating by killing the men I've slept with. My stomach drops when I look at Aniyah. Will they kill her next?

"Oh my," she groans, coming into the kitchen. "That smell is amazing."

I know she won't let me crowd her and if I even suggest she not going anywhere without me, she'll cuss me out. Last night when I told her I wanted to keep her, she laughed and said that this was just fun, and one day we'll go our separate ways. It broke my heart, but she's right, this isn't a forever thing. So how do I tell her to watch her back and to stay away from me?

I nod at her statement and grab her a mug, filling it with the black elixir. I watch as she sips and moans at the taste, my pussy clenching with want. I push it down and ready myself to pull away. I need to make sure she stays alive. She strolls to my couch and sits down as I fill half my cup with creamer.

"What the fuck?" she murmurs, and I freeze, looking up at her. What else is there? "Did you have a client over last night?"

"I don't bring clients here," I tell her as I walk over to see what she's inspecting.

"That tells a different story." She smirks and points at the table.

I look down and my stomach flips once more. Cum. There's cum all over my small coffee table and a lot of it. It's drying but still thick globs dotting the surface. I look at the window and see it's shut. The front door is also shut and locked.

"It looks fresh too, unless…" she sniffs at it. "Nope, that's definitely cum." When she looks up at me, she must see the confusion and anger. "Someone was in here without your knowledge." She stands and looks around. "Do you think whoever is taking the girls is following us?"

"I don't know," I whisper, my voice shaking with anger. "We should get you home." I don't want her here any longer. This person might just catch on to how important she is to me, and she could be the next one with my scythe on her body.

It's clear now that someone is killing the men I sleep with, and I can't stop the image of Santos sliding through my brain. It can't be them; they don't know where I am, and they can't track me. I don't have the same phone; I don't use credit cards, and I didn't leave the ledger behind. My Reaper symbol and the mutilated bodies tell another story, though.

I shake my head and let those thoughts go. I just miss them and maybe a piece of me is hoping they found me. I think that's why I'm clinging to Aniyah and looking for some sort of attachment. Even though

I went through most of my life without any, I miss the few attachments I had, and I can't seem to purge my mind of them.

Aniyah sits unperturbed by the drying bodily fluids in front of her and finishes off her coffee. I guess the sight of cum wouldn't make her squeamish, since that's a huge part of our jobs. Still, seeing her undisturbed about someone being in here and following us is pissing me off. I want her to be fearful so she will watch herself better. I can't be there to protect her all the time.

She pulls out her phone and stares at the screen. "My ride's here." She stands. "Will I see you at the bar later?"

"Yeah." I nod as she leans in to kiss me.

She grabs her purse and saunters out my door, her ass swinging seductively from side to side. How can I keep her safe when even her walk screams *come fuck me*? I throw myself back down onto the couch, staring at the cum, and fisting my hands. I don't know if I locked the window or door, and with the rush I was in last night to have Aniyah's pussy in my mouth, it's possible I didn't. I'm acting stupid and not myself here, my emotions running the show. I changed the moment I gave myself over to the guys and now I only have myself to blame as I look to fill the void that leaving them behind has caused.

I turn on the small tube TV I have in the corner, and I only have three free channels to surf through. One shopping channel, one kid's channel, and one local news. I turn to the local news and take a sip of coffee, spewing it across the cum table when I see the image on the screen. There's a one million dollar reward out for anyone who can locate the Reaper Killer. A close up of Angelo's pale white skin is on the screen with my scythe drawn into it with blood.

Someone is trying to get my attention.

# Chapter Twelve

## *Blaze*

Selene has been subdued the last few days and, I must admit, kind of boring. Not that I want her fucking random people, but I do miss her stabby ways. She's been walking up and down the strip, speaking to hookers, and watching the clients who come to pick them up. She hasn't hung out at the bar and only pops in and out, probably assuring her friends she's alive and well, for now.

I haven't been back inside her apartment because I know she's probably been more vigilant, but I did see her buy a new bolt lock and a window bar from the local hardware store. I can still work my way around a window bar if need be. All in all, things have been quiet and we're both waiting patiently for John to come back around. He's been busy clearing out the shipment I watched him receive the other night, and last night was his last *export*. I feel bad that I couldn't help those people, but I had to stay the course; just as Zander likes to say, we can only do our best.

I'm waiting for the moment he contacts my girl because I know he will, and I think tonight is the night. I saw the way he watched her, and I can't imagine him putting it off longer than necessary. The sun begins to set, and it's about the regular time Selene begins her patrol, only she's not coming out. I look up at her apartment and see the lights are on, and everything looks quiet, but why hasn't she made her way down yet?

I'm about to get out and investigate when I see the BMW pull up to the curb. The windows are tinted, but I know John's car well enough. I slide down in my seat and watch as a few moments later, Selene slinks out of the door. I'm shocked she had him pick her up here. It's fucking dangerous and reckless for him to know where she lives. What's she planning?

"Candy!" he exclaims as he gets out of the car and rounds the front to embrace her.

"Candy?" I mumble with disgust. The fuck kind of stripper name is that?

She's whispering something in his ear and smiling when he kisses her cheek enthusiastically. She's wearing a long black cocktail dress, strapless, and a slit that nears her fucking hip. I growl when I see it flap gently in the wind. He opens her door and before she slides inside, her eyes land on my car. It's the first time in a long time that my heart beats excitedly and I can't tell if it's because she might have seen me or that I'm looking into her eyes for the first time in so long.

She disappears into the car, and I instantly miss her eyes on me. The loneliness I've tried to ignore swelling up larger than ever. The car pulls away and I wait a few beats before I pull out a few cars behind them. They were both dressed up, and that means they're going somewhere classy. Selene is not a classy female, but maybe *Candy* is. I shudder at the name and instantly recoil. It's disgusting and I can't believe she chose that over her gorgeous name's meaning.

Just as I thought, I watch as the BMW pulls in front of a theater, and they both get out, Selene's eyes landing on my car again as I drive by. She's noticed my vehicle and now I need to decide my next move. Do I keep it and let her know I am indeed following her, or do I rent another and throw her off my scent? It also boils down to safety. Do I risk a knife in my throat or not?

I pull into a parking lot a few buildings down and haul out my phone, dialing Zander.

"What's happened?" He picks up, sounding frantic.

I roll my eyes and shake my head. "You sound like a little pussy."

"Yeah," he exhales. "I know. Things are getting out of hand over here and I need something."

"She's met up with John again, finally."

"Are you ready to take him down? When do you want us to come?" Again, he frantically throws out questions.

"I'm waiting to get a good idea on the next shipment, and I think that's the information Selene is looking for, too," I explain.

I hate having to constantly tell him each move I make, but if I don't keep him up to speed, they'll show up and Santos will blow all our covers.

"I can't believe Mack is dropping off for John, too. What are the fucking chances of that?"

"It's fucking luck if you ask me," I growl. "Now I can finally kill that fat, toothless fuck."

Zander grunts his agreement into the phone, knowing I've more right to kill that bitch than any other.

"I think she saw me," I say quietly, and Zander sucks in a breath. "Or she's noticing the car."

"Fuck," he groans. "Do you think she'll run again?"

"Hell no," I scoff. "I think she'll try to kill me."

"Even if she knows it's you?" He sounds shocked.

"Even more so," I chuckle. "I left her gifts like a fucking cat leaving bird heads around. She'll gut me without thought."

"She's so fucking disturbed. It's so fucking hot," he moans, and I roll my eyes, even though I agree.

"I'll call with an update in the morning." I hang up before he can pry more info out of me and scrub my hand through the scruff on my chin.

I pull up the theater on my phone and find out it's playing two Broadway Productions tonight. One that is nearly over and another that's starting in ten minutes. The duration is two hours. I pull out of the parking lot and head over to John's place. It's an assumption, but I do believe he'll bring her back there, especially after seeing her place and knowing his tastes.

I drive by the bar and see the woman Selene was with a few nights ago. She's leaning against the brick and speaking to two men. She looks uncomfortable, and I consider it for all of two seconds before I pull a U-turn and pull up to the curb.

"Are you free?" I call out to her, and she stares at me, probably the scar on my face putting her off. Then she looks to the two guys who were crowding her space and steps around them.

"Sure, Sugar." She walks up to the car, her purple hair looking even brighter under the streetlamp. She leans into the open window and swallows nervously. "What were you looking for?"

"Nothing actually." I shrug. "You looked uncomfortable with them crowding your space, thought I'd see if you needed help."

She looks back at the guys over her shoulder as they leer at her upturned ass. "I was uncomfortable." She looks back into my face. "But you also look like you might murder me."

"Only if you annoy the fuck out of me from here to wherever you want me to drop you off." It's the truth.

She laughs suddenly and the sound shocks both her and I. "Okay, grumpy. Thanks for the ride."

My heart thumps against my ribcage at her calling me grumpy. That's what Selene used to call me in the beginning, too. I pull away from the curb as the other two guys call out. Both pissed off, I took their entertainment.

"Aren't you afraid to be doing this job right now? With all the shit going on?" I ask her. "And where am I dropping you off?"

"It's scary, but I don't have a choice." She points ahead. "See those apartment buildings? My friend lives there. I think I'll pay her a visit."

She's talking about Selene and even though I know she's not home, I can't tell her that. I drive to the apartment building and park in front, looking at her expectantly. I hate talking to people and I'm already regretting picking her up because she's not moving. The things I do for Selene.

"Is there a way I can repay you?" Her voice turns raspy, and my dick begins to swell. Maybe it's because I miss my girl and I know this one sitting beside me had a taste of her. She looks down at my lap and whistles. "He's a big boy." Her hand reaches out, and I latch onto the wrist, squeezing her bones together. She whimpers and the noise has me hard as a fucking rock.

"I don't need your payment," I grit out.

"I wanted to regardless of if you did anything for me. I think you're intriguing."

No one has ever called me that. The ugly scar down my face has always scared people, and in all honesty, I like it that way. I press her hand down on top of my dick and she gasps as she grabs it through my track pants.

"Tell me what you want," she whispers, her eyes still rounded at her hand gripping my cock.

"I want you to choke on it."

She grins and pulls me out, literally purring when she sees the piercing through the top. "I wish I could have this inside me." I ignore her words because I couldn't imagine ever being inside another woman again. Selene's pussy is it for me. But I don't mind her choking on it. She flicks the piercing with her tongue, and I grunt, the sensation snaking down into my balls.

She begins a steady bobbing rhythm on my cock and it's kind of boring. It only makes me miss my crazy ass bitch more. I fist her purple curls in my hand and shove her down on my cock, her gags making my balls tighten. I savagely continue to shove her down and bring her up, her hands finding purchase on my thighs. I close my eyes and imagine it's my girl, her throat constricting as I punish her esophagus. Her nails dig into the skin of my thighs, and I moan through the sting.

With one final rough thrust, I empty myself down her throat, and she swallows rapidly. I finally release her head, and she snaps up, anger clear in her eyes. She's panting, trying to catch her breath, and I give her a slow, taunting smile. She fucking asked for it. I unlock the car doors; the sound resounding in the small space and wait for her to get the fuck out.

"You're crazy," she breathes, and I raise a brow. I just want her out of my car. She served her fucking purpose.

She turns on a growl and throws open the door, stepping out onto the sidewalk. Then she slams it hard behind her and I can't help the chuckle that works its way up my chest. She's a fireball too, and I can see why Selene is so intrigued.

# Selene

John's annoying me tonight. Everything right down to his voice is grating on all my nerves, and when he suggests we head back to his place, I have to force myself to smile and seem keen on the idea. In reality, I'm imagining all the ways I can end him when I have no use for him anymore.

He makes small talk the entire fucking drive, talking about the theater and giving me no choice but to swoon at his bullshit. I'm already uneasy after knowing some cunt came all over my coffee table then left the albino fucker's severed dick behind, but I spotted the same car a few times tonight when I felt someone's eyes on me, and that's causing my good mood to sway towards murderous.

I hope to God John 'Dumpster' just wants a blow job and passes the fuck out like last time, because I want to barricade myself in my apartment and get my shit together. I need to be prepared in case that bastard breaks in again. I might spend the evening sharpening my knives and getting ready to go all Edward Scissor-Hands on the prick.

I need to kill someone, but I have to be extra fucking careful since there's a copycat lurking around. My thoughts stray to Santos again, confusion swirling in my brain. It's definitely something he'd do to fuck with my head, but he would have shown himself by now, wanting me to know it was him.

I miss that crazy psycho. And I miss the hell out of his devil dick and sharp blade. No one fucks like my guys.

Well, Aniyah fucks like a dream, I guess.

The car slows and I convince myself to relax, not wanting John to pick up on my mood. He'll ask questions, and if he thinks something is weird even for a second, he'll catch on that something isn't right. I can't fucking risk it.

He steps from the car and offers his hand, waiting for me to take it so he can help me step out. Knowing it's an act makes my blood boil.

How many girls did he make swoon before abusing their fucking trust? How many young women or children looked to him for safety, just to be used and broken? Fuck, I have to get hold of myself before I beat the piece of shit to a pulp and use him as compost in his own fucking garden.

"You look good enough to eat," John murmurs as we wander

inside, my heels clicking on the shiny floors.

"I hope so," I giggle, fluttering my lashes and putting my placid mask back in place.

He leads me up to his room, not even offering me a drink this time, before shutting the door and pressing me against it, his lips trailing down my neck with a groan.

"You smell delicious. I've hardly been able to keep my hands to myself all evening," he says against my skin, and I wish I could slam my knee into his balls.

If my stalker is killing off the men I fuck, why haven't they hacked this cunt to pieces? Surely, they've seen us together a few times. Do they have their eyes on him too? Do they know something about the missing women I don't? I wish they'd come out of fucking hiding so I can decide if they're useful, or just another stab for my blade.

I'll stab them for sure for the fucking gifts they've left me, but their willingness to help would determine where and how deep I'll stab them.

I fake a moan as John's fingers run across my pussy from the outside of my clothes, and just before he can dip his fingers under the fabric, his phone rings loudly from his pocket.

He scowls, glancing at the screen before his face becomes serious.

"Sorry, Candy. I need to take this. One of the girls will show you out." Then he opens the door and leaves me standing there, my prayers answered.

I head back down to the front door, not bothering to snoop even though it's the perfect opportunity. I want my bed and a quiet night.

I order an Uber and wait on the side of the road, only having to wait a few minutes. I stare out the window the entire way home, my eyes zoning in on the car that has been following me today. The windows are too tinted to see through, but I can feel their eyes on me as I step out of the Uber.

The moment I step towards my apartment, the stalker car pulls away from the curb, making me frown. Were they making sure I got home safely, or making sure I'm home alone to come back while I'm sleeping and gut me? Fucker can try.

I make my way up to my door, halting, when I notice Aniyah waiting in front of it. After the day I've had, the last thing I feel like doing is making chit chat over wine. Why the fuck didn't she call before showing up?

Her eyes dart to mine as I approach, and I hate how her face lights up. She doesn't want me, but here she is, acting like I mean something to her after a long shitty day on the job.

"Hey, babe. I—"

"What are you doing here?" I cut in bluntly, her smile dropping as I nudge past her to unlock my door. Petty, I know, but she has no right fucking with my head like this.

She follows me inside without an invitation, causing my teeth to grind.

"I wanted to see you. Is that a crime?" she asks lightly with a laugh, but it's forced, so I know she's picked up on my mood. Why is she still here then?

I drop my keys on the table and grab a bottle of whiskey from the shelf, not bothering with a glass as I drink straight from the bottle before answering.

"You should have called. Why'd you just show up?" I grunt, usually not caring about being a bitch, but something nags at me this time. I need her gone, mainly because of that psychopathic stalker on the loose, but also because I want to be alone.

I need to center myself again, then take on the next day's challenges with a clear head. I might even hunt down a piece of shit to let out some of my thirst for blood that I have to keep under control.

Aniyah watches me closely, her jaw clenching as she finally looks away.

"I had a shitty night and thought I could stop by to forget about it. Everyone was a dick to me, and now you're being one, too."

"You're the one in my apartment. I didn't track you down. I can't fucking afford you tonight anyway," I throw back, knowing it's a cheap shot.

Anger fills her eyes for a moment before she spins on her heels and heads towards the door, speaking over the shoulder I had my teeth in last night.

"Sorry, I should have checked your fucking budget first. Fuck you."

The door slams behind her, and I drop my head back against the wall and gulp down a healthy amount of whiskey. I hope my stalker breaks in again because I'm ready to make some fucker bleed. I don't give a fuck if it's in my own fucking kitchen, either.

# Chapter Thirteen

## Darius

I jerk my gaze down the bar when I hear a loud smash, not surprised to see Santos brawling with some drunken idiot. He's been trying to pick a fight with someone for hours, and it seems someone finally snapped at his antagonizing.

Zander raises an eyebrow as he joins me, watching our psycho buddy beat the shit out of the guy. "I fucking told you this was a dumb idea," he grunts, making me shrug.

"He's got some steam to let loose. He's fine."

"Fine? Dude, he's going to murder that asshole with his fucking bare hands. Get over there and break it up," he growls, turning his attention to me. He's never been the type to tolerate our bullshit, but he's worse without our girl around.

I sigh, draining my glass and standing. "Give him a few more minutes. It would be nice to get home and not get the hell kicked out of me for one night."

"If we need to lock him up…"

I glare at him, wanting to punch him in the face for even suggesting we lock Santos up. He's crazy, but he isn't a fucking animal.

I must look like I'm ready to strangle him, because he puts his hands out in front of himself.

"I'm joking, but go and contain him before some cunt calls the cops. The last thing we need is that idiot getting arrested and trying to murder a bunch of them."

I roll my eyes at his dramatics as I move towards the fight, letting out a whistle to draw Santos' attention. He glances up, his drunken gaze connecting with mine. "C'mon, brother. Wrap this up and let's get home."

"Five more minutes?" he whines, waiting for me to nod before grabbing the guy by the front of the shirt and wailing into him again. The bartender gives me a filthy look, and I narrow my eyes on him.

"The fuck are you looking at?" I demand, his eyes widening a fraction.

"Your buddy needs to go. I can't have people fighting in my bar," he insists, jumping as I slam my palm down on the bar.

"My boy just needs a minute, then we'll be gone. Can't you see he's stressed?" I bite out, glancing at Santos, who's practically laughing like a hyena suddenly.

"Take that, ye scallywag! Victory is mine!" he declares, causing a smirk to tug at my lips. He really means the world to me, the funny fucker.

The bartender glares at me, so I flip him the bird. "Yeah, yeah. I'm getting him."

I walk up to Santos, who gives me a big grin. "Did you see that, D? I fucking got him good!" he beams, dropping an arm over my shoulders to give me some of his weight. He's beyond drunk, and he's lucky Blaze isn't around to stab him. That grumpy bastard hates it when either of us gets annoyingly drunk like this.

I slide an arm around his waist, giving him more support. "How the fuck can you fight when you can hardly walk?"

"Just like how I manage to dick someone down when I'm drunk. Superpowers and whiskey!" he exclaims. Zander shakes his head and chuckles as he walks up to us.

Santos suddenly yanks back, almost stumbling over like a rag doll. "Hey! Take a fucking photo, asswipe!" he barks at the bartender, staggering towards the bar.

"Dammit, Darius," Zander growls, but I motion towards the bartender and shrug.

"What? I said to that fucker we were going. It's not my fault he looked at Santos."

Santos bickers with the dickhead for a while, before grabbing a bar stool and smashing it against the bar, sending pieces of wood flying.

"Avast ye! Ye lily-livered sea bass!"

"What the fuck did he just say?" Zander snorts.

"He said pay attention, then insulted him. It's like the polite version of a cunt, I guess," I reply, sensing his eyes landing on me.

"You actually understand that gibberish?"

"Gibberish? It's pirate," I gasp, acting offended and earning an eye roll. I'd die for Zander, but our relationship is different to the one Santos and I share.

"Does ye want to dance the hempen jig?!"

Zander glances at me and waits, making me sigh. Pirate isn't that hard to interpret, compared to all the other shit Santos says on the regular.

"He threatened to hang him."

"Where the fuck do you two learn this shit?" he scoffs, a laugh leaving me.

"Google. We get bored sometimes."

Santos manages to scramble onto the bar, holding a broken bar stool leg in his grip as he waves it at the bartender, who doesn't seem to know what to do.

"En garde! Shark bait!" he screams, and I interpret as he goes.

"You can figure out en garde, and shark bait basically means he's gonna die."

Zander is snickering as we watch our brother, and it's the most fun we've had in ages, I swear. Just when I think he's calming down, he throws his make-shift sword, knocking bottles off the shelf in the process. "I'll make ye walk the plank!"

"Get him out of here. They're going to call the cops," Zander laughs as Santos snatches a bottle of whiskey and starts chugging it. I finally move up to the bar and grab him by the legs, tugging him back and managing to catch him before he breaks his neck.

"You're three sheets to the wind, matey," I chuckle, starting to drag him towards the door before he gets any more ideas on his attack. I try to wrestle the whiskey out of his hands, but he fights me on it.

"Hands off me booty!" he slurs, laughter bubbling up before I can stop it.

"I'll put my hands on your booty whenever I want."

"Wait! We can't go yet. I have to blow the man down!" he argues, but he gets nowhere as Zander takes up his other side to help me.

"Why do you need to do that?" Zander grins. "Because dead men tell no tales?"

Santos stops fighting me and stares at him, his eyes going wide. "I didn't know you spoke pirate too!"

By the time we manage to get him into the car and get the whiskey away from him, our stomachs are hurting from laughing so hard. Santos falls into the back seat, cursing as he smacks his head on the car door. "Son of a biscuit eater!"

I'm laughing so fucking hard I swear I'm going to piss my pants, and Zander's fighting to contain his too as he slides into the driver's seat. I sit in the back with Santos, helping him sit up straighter so I can buckle him in.

"You're lucky Blaze isn't here, because he would have fucking stabbed you tonight," I inform him, making him snort.

"He loves me! Why would that asshole stab me?"

Zander starts the car, peering over his shoulder at Santos with a smirk. "Because Blaze is daddy."

"Well, he can suck on my cackle fruit," he mumbles, and I hoot with laughter.

"Your chicken eggs?"

"Shit, that's not right," he mutters to himself, trying to remember the right term.

The drive home is full of him complaining that he didn't get to kill anyone, and it takes both Zander and me to carry the drunk bastard up to his room. Zander brings a bucket in to sit beside the bed, then leaves me to undress Santos and tuck him in, saying goodnight and knowing I'll be sleeping in here with him.

I strip down to my boxers, then manage to pull Santos' shirt over his head before reaching for his belt, making a low chuckle leave him as he lies on his back with his eyes shut.

"You're not even going to buy me dinner first?"

"I think we're past that, don't you?" I tease, unbuckling the belt and loosening his pants to tug them down his legs. I help him into bed properly once he's in nothing but his boxers, and I'm surprised when his hand darts out to grab the back of my neck, dragging me down to kiss him.

His hand lets go once he knows I won't pull back, and he slides it down my bare back, pulling my body closer. He's way too drunk to get hard, I know that much, but as his tongue glides against mine, something calms in my chest.

It's been hard without Selene, and our emotions are all over the place without her, but this? This is what we need. The comfort that only we can bring to each other. I know Santos will never leave me, but he hasn't let me wander far from his sight since she left us, probably worried that maybe I'll abandon him too.

Santos is a crazy bastard, but he gives his everything to those he loves.

I groan as his hand slips into the back of my boxers and his palm squeezes my butt cheek, his leg going over mine to keep me close.

When I finally pull back, we're both panting, and Santos' eyes appear calm for the first time in days. He needs me to calm his demons, and I'll always do that for him.

"I love you, D," he murmurs, his eyes flicking between mine. He needs to feel wanted, and I'll gladly give him that.

I curl against him, nuzzling into his neck and running my hand over his abs.

"Love you too, San. Get some sleep. I'll be here when you wake up," I promise, knowing it's the right thing to say, because within seconds his breathing evens out and he is asleep.

# Zander

I wake up to the sound of retching, knowing Santos' big night is back to bite him in the ass. I lie in bed for a while before moving. Darius will be looking after him, and I'm not needed.

It's weird not having Blaze around to maintain control, and I miss that grumpy prick something fierce, but I must admit, it was funny watching Santos last night. I have no idea how Darius keeps up with him, but they're two peas in a pod and I can't imagine them being without each other.

I chuckle as I think back to Santos on the bar, waving his fake sword around. That fucker is crazy, and as much as he drives Blaze and I mental regularly, I wouldn't have him any other way.

I finally climb from the bed and pad down the hallway, peeking into the bathroom to find Santos sitting in front of the toilet with his head in it, while Darius sits back and runs a hand up and down his spine.

Santos violently heaves, and I wince at knowing how his stomach will feel later if he's heaving like that for long.

I step inside and lean against the wall, meeting Darius' gaze as he notices me. "Morning. How's the Captain this morning?"

Santos throws up again, a groan of pain leaving him. "Pretty sure Davy Jones' locker is awaiting me," he manages to get out, making me smirk.

"Learned your lesson, then?"

"Fuck no," he mumbles and leans back, getting comfortable between Darius' legs and pressing his back against his chest to close his eyes.

"So, what's on the agenda for today?" I ask, managing not to snicker when Santos replies.

"Death."

Darius absently presses a kiss to his shoulder, and it takes a second for me to process it. They share a bond between them that's different from what they share with Blaze and me.

They've never labeled what they are, just going with what feels right and having each other's backs.

"Day at home then?" I offer, and Santos nods, wincing with the movement.

"Yeah. Maybe in a few hours we can put a movie on or something. We can just hang out," he answers, shivering slightly from the cold.

"How about you two get off the cold floor and get dressed? Actually, scratch that. Get Santos in the shower. He smells like stale whiskey," I retort, causing Santos to groan and lean forward to throw up again.

Darius manages to get him to his feet, stepping into the shower with him to help hold him up. These two are pros at writing themselves off, so I leave them to it and head into the kitchen, knowing everyone will be needing some fucking coffee.

# Selene

I haven't heard from Aniyah in a few days and to be honest, that's a good thing. This is what I wanted, right? To push her away and keep her safe. I've been staying away from the bar because I haven't wanted to see her and spent the last few nights on the other side of town speaking to a group of girls. Girls are going missing all over Nevada and the news outlets haven't been reporting it. What's a few missing hookers, anyway?

I can see the fear in their faces and it's wrenching my heart right out of my chest. They have no other choice but to come out here every night and face their demons, their fears having to be pushed to the back burner. How else will they survive when this is all they've ever known?

"Have you felt anything weird about a certain client?" I question one girl who looks no older than eighteen. "Maybe he was new around here?"

"They're all new," another girl chimes in. "They come here to get away from their wives, gamble some money, and fuck a few whores."

"I hear you," I nod. "Listen to your instincts, we have them more than others, and don't get in a car with anyone looking suss." I can't warn them anymore and if they at least know something weird is going down, maybe it'll make them more cautious.

"There was one rich motherfucker the other night. He said he was having a party," a girl with long, bleached blonde hair says as she strides up to me. She looks a bit like me. "He said he wanted me to come and offered me ten grand."

Another girl whistles, and I raise a brow. "Why didn't you go?"

"Because ten grand is way too much for just a simple party. I knew I was either getting gang raped or snatched. No one should have to entice a hooker with a large number. Most of the time, they're trying to fight our prices down." She's not wrong.

"That's smart," I smile at her. I know many girls who would've run for that money without a single thought.

"Just because we sell our pussies doesn't mean we're dumb," she retorts and gives me a once-over. My trench is done up and my hair is in a messy bun on top of my head. Looking at me, I guess it wouldn't look like I work the same damn job she does.

"Don't I know it, sweetheart." I step closer to her. "I think we're smarter because of it."

Her eyes widen with my admission, and I turn away from her, no longer wanting to carry on the conversation. I walk down the street, my strides wide, and scan all the cars on the side of the road. I haven't seen the black sedan with the dark tinted windows in a few days, but that doesn't mean I'm not being followed. I can still sense it and I can't shake the feeling this person knows where I came from.

I was hoping for a while it was one of my boys, that they cared enough to follow me here, and wanted to keep me safe while I searched for my sister. I no longer think it's them. They would've shown themselves by now for sure. Especially seeing as someone dumped a fucking sausage on my counter.

Fifteen minutes later and I'm standing in front of Good Times. I haven't been here for a few days and right now I'm longing for the few friends I've made here. My life has been a slideshow of loneliness and the guys showed me what it was like to have someone. Now I crave it.

I step through the doors and see it's a bit livelier than usual, the music a few notches louder. I go to my stool and find a female sitting in it, twirling her red hair around her finger.

"You're in her seat." Colleen appears, telling the girl I'm staring at.

She turns to look at me with a look of disgust until she takes in my appearance. I don't look like a sugar Candy sweetheart today, I'm in all black, and my makeup is dark. I watch her swallow visibly, then slide off the stool, hurrying to the other end of the bar.

I sit on my stool and a whiskey on the rocks slides in front of me. "Been a while," Colleen tsks and I look up at her.

"Just busy." I shrug. "I was checking in."

"I know," she leans on the bar, "it's just been boring here without you."

I gulp down the amber liquid and welcome the familiar burn as it skates down my throat. I haven't looked around the bar for purple curls yet and I don't know why, I've clearly become a pussy.

"How's Aniyah been?" I look into Colleen's eyes.

"She hasn't been with you?" I watch as worry saturates her features, and my heart begins to pound.

"No." I straighten. "Why the fuck would you think she was with me?"

"I saw you two leave together and you've both been MIA these last few days…" she trails off, horror filling her eyes. "No."

"She was at my apartment a few days ago, but I haven't seen her since then." I stand abruptly and the stool tips over behind me. I remember Aniyah telling me about a date she had scheduled with John and my mouth instantly goes dry.

Why would he take her now? It's makes no fucking sense. I run out of the bar, and I hear Colleen calling out to me, but I can't waste any more time. I run down the sidewalk and toward my building, praying that she'll be there. What if the person who was stalking me decided to snatch her? What if I find a body part of hers in my house? My heart feels like it's pushing up through my throat and I'm taken back to when I first lost Jan.

I rush inside and when I get to my floor, my heart sinks further when I don't find her waiting there. I throw open my apartment door and stalk inside. I look through each room and when it turns up empty, I'm both relieved and scared. I pull out my burner phone and fire a text off to John. I think it's time for him and me to really get together. I really hate that I didn't take the opportunity to snoop when I had the chance, but I can't do anything about it now.

He messages me back, sounding smug that I'm so eager to see him, but says for me to come by his place. This is it, my chance to really find out what I can about John and hopefully find Aniyah in the process. I can only hope she's off sulking somewhere about our last exchange, but I know she's not. She was only interested in sex with me, and she wouldn't be sulking. She's pissed.

I pull on a bright pink sweater and a light blue jean skirt, pulling my hair back into a high ponytail. I make sure to strap my belt around my waist and then I call an Uber to pick me up. It's time to get the answers I've been pussyfooting around for and if I have to spill John's guts on the floor tonight, so fucking be it.

I step to the curb just as the Uber pulls up and my eyes focus over the top of the car, landing on an all-black sedan idling across the street. I can't see the driver, but for some reason I want them to know I see them, and I want them to follow me. Even if it's my stalker, I want at least one person to know where I am, and that makes me feel like maybe I'm not so alone.

When John's house comes into view, I feel a cold chill slip down the nape of my neck, and I sense an evil I've never felt any other time I've been here. Something's different or fuck, maybe I'm just different, but tonight changes everything. There's no more Miss Nice Selene. I get out of the car and hear another idling not too far behind, causing me to pause. That tingle on my neck is strong and I know without looking just what car is sitting down the street.

I walk up the driveway and notice the garage door is only halfway shut, like the motor got stuck or something is blocking the sensor. I can see the BMW's bumper in there and I brush it off as I step up to the porch. I ring the doorbell and John appears a few seconds later in an unbuttoned dress shirt and gray slacks.

"I was surprised when I got your message—"

"Cut the shit, John," I cut him off and step into the house, slamming the door behind me. His brows raise at my tone and use of language. "You're going to fuck me and you're going to do it now."

I fist his sweater and haul him in, watching as his eyes darken with lust. He licks his lips and grins as he grabs my hair in his hand, yanking my head back forcefully. There you are, you little prick.

"I really like this side of you, Candy," he growls before sucking on the skin of my neck. "This makes me want to do things to you I shouldn't."

"Nothing's off the table, John." I fist his hair in my hand and yank him off my neck. "Just stop toying with me. It makes you sound like a fucking pussy."

His growl is the only warning I get before I'm forcefully turned around and shoved into the wall, his hand gripping the back of my neck. Here we go. He flips up my skirt and slaps my ass, hard. I moan at the contact and Blaze is here, clear in my mind. I can get through this if I imagine it's him. His rough hands slapping down on my tender flesh and scruffy chin digging into my neck.

My hand slides down the wall and lands on a door handle. I press down on the lever since I'm supposed to be scoping the place out, and the door opens into the garage. I see the BMW and a large steel trapdoor on the floor before John reaches out, pulling it shut.

"Sorry," I whisper, and he goes right back to slapping my ass. Worst shit ever. I can't even imagine Blaze because he would be so much better than this.

I wonder what's under that trapdoor. Nothing good ever sits beneath a trapdoor, and I have a feeling that's where I need to go look. John latches onto my thong and rips it off my body, the fabric burning my skin with the force. I hiss through the sting, and he chuckles, giving me another slap on the ass. I can't wait until he's bleeding out and then I will slap the shit out of his fucking ass. He jams a finger up inside me and I bite my tongue to hold in my snarl. I can get through this and then I'm going to use my pussy power to make him tell me what's in that garage.

I feel the tip of his cock press against my barely wet pussy when his phone rings.

"Do not answer that." I sound more aggressive than I mean to.

"I…" I can hear him debating inside his pea brain and roll my eyes.

"I can come back tomorrow," I huff and yank down my skirt. I turn to look at him and he's stuffing himself back in his pants.

"Yes." He begins to pull his phone out. "Thank you, Candy."

I pull out my phone, seemingly to call an Uber, and step outside. I'm happy his cock never got the chance to sink into me. I step down onto the driveway and look at the garage door. A smile creeps along my mouth. I forgot this thing was left halfway open. I bend down and look inside, seeing the door still shut to the house. I crawl under the door and stand up inside, making my way to the trapdoor.

I run my foot across the gleaming metal and tap it lightly. It sounds solid and what other reason would this be here but for a nefarious one? Who has a trapdoor in their house to store anything but skin? This must be where he keeps the people he *traps,* and this must be where Aniyah is. I bend to get a better look and see a large industrial latch with a large industrial padlock. *Fuck.*

It's a newer one that has a rotary set of four numbers on the front. Four numbers from zero to nine and I don't have the slightest clue what they could be. I can't break it open because that would be too noisy and sitting here trying to figure out a combination of numbers is impossible. I let out a small groan and lean back against his fucking car, the license plate digging into my back. I turn to move away from it when the numbers literally flash in my vision.

8818.

It can't be. Would he be so fucking stupid? I grab the padlock in my hand and rotate the numbers to match the license plate. I take a deep breath and pull it, watching as the bar pops open at the top. I fucking love how stupid some criminals can be. It really works in my favor. I pull open the door and look down at a steep descending staircase. I rest the heavy door against the garage wall and begin my way down. It's dark save for the square of light coming from the doorway. I step to the bottom of the stairs and look ahead into a blackened abyss. There's no light at the other end.

I hear hinges creak above me and look up quickly, startled by the noise. Standing at the opening is John, and his smile is wide. "This saves me a lot of trouble, Candy. I'm glad you found your own way down there."

"What is this place, John?" I ask, no longer acting like the sweet little prostitute.

He smiles maniacally and closes the door. "Have fun in the dark, Candy."

If he wants me to scream, then he is barking up the wrong bitch. I pull my phone out and see there's no reception, not that I need any. I have no one to call. The little light from the screen is what I really want, and I shine it ahead of me. I see another set of stairs about twenty feet away and head towards them. Where else can I go? The floor is concrete, as are the walls and ceiling, all fortified and tough. It would have to be to withstand being underground. I get to the stairs and see another door above. I hope that one's unlocked because, if not, I'll end up dying down here.

I begin to climb the stairs, closing my phone and popping it back in my pocket. I get to the door and give it a shove, thankful when it opens. I pop my head out and groan when I see what's in front of me.

# Chapter Fourteen

## *Blaze*

She went into that garage and never came back out. I don't know what she found in there, but I can bet she's trapped, either of her own making or by John. Now I'm at a loss for how to proceed. Do I head in there and possibly fuck everything up for her? Or do I watch everything closely and follow like the dog I am right now? I feel like a watchdog, and I just want to sink my teeth into some perverted flesh and watch them bleed out.

A few hours later and still no movement from the house, so I call up the boys. I think it's time we crash her party. Selene doesn't seem to be getting any further in her search, and I haven't seen her come out of this damn house. I can see the sun beginning to set and I have a bad feeling. I pull out my phone and call Zander.

"Blaze." He always picks up the phone sounding anxious. I bet those two idiots are driving him mental.

"Pack your bags and get your asses here. I'm sending you the address and I'll need you on the red eye."

"Santos!" he screams into the phone, and I fist my hand. "We're going to get our girl!"

"Finally! I already packed our bags when she took off, let's gooooo!" I hear his voice in the background.

"He sounds a bit off," I remark.

"You don't understand how bad we need to do this." Zander sounds tired.

"Sleep on the plane and hurry the fuck up." I hang up the phone and send them John's address. Now I wait.

I hear an engine coming up the street and sit up in my seat. It's Delaney's van and when he pulls into the driveway, my heart nearly falls out of my ass. He's here for a pickup and my fucking girl is in there. I can't take them both on and make sure the girls are kept safe. I don't even know how to get to them. I look at the dash and huff. Still another half an hour until they arrive. They've landed, but driving here will take time.

We have some time because I know they won't load the girls until well into the night, and then they'll have to wait until the street grows quiet. Time moves slowly and so do my fucking friends; they should be here by now. Who the fuck is driving? Darius? He's the fucking grandpa out of us behind the wheel. Santos is never allowed to drive because he thinks it's funny to 'nudge' people out of the way with his bumper.

The BMW is pulled out of the garage and the van backs into the space, readying for a pickup. I slam my fist to the wheel, knowing there's not much I can do, and I just pray that John will divulge all he knows as he stares down the edge of my blade. I try to get a good look inside the garage, but it's no use, and it fuels my anger even more. Wouldn't Selene put up a fight? Unless she's wanting to be loaded up like cattle.

It takes all of ten minutes this time and the van is once again leaving the driveway, the windows black. It's impossible to tell if she's in there. I slam my fist into the steering wheel a couple more times and hold on to the guilt I'm feeling for letting this happen. I'll need it to gut our new friend John.

Five minutes later, Zander pulls up and drives by the house slowly, pulling up to park behind me. I stay in the driver's seat and watch as they all get out. Zander looks tired, but his eyes are filled with fury. Darius looks cautious and his body is tight with tension. Then there's Santos. He's hopping out of the damn vehicle like he's about to watch the circus, his smile stretching wide across his face. Crazy fucker.

I open the door and step out, cracking my stiff neck. Zander approaches cautiously and lays a hand on my shoulder.

"Brother," he squeezes. "How are you doing?"

"No slips," I assure him. "Until now."

I can feel the rage swooping in and I'm about to lose myself to it. He sees the moment I vibrate and turns to the guys.

"Let's get inside and bleed this fucker out."

Santos hoots and pulls out a blade, checking the sharpness of the edge. Darius is rubbing his hands together, all too excited to cause some mayhem. So the fuck am I.

"I don't know if she's still in there. Mack was by earlier for a pickup," I tell them.

"But that little pussy bitch is still inside, right?" Santos grins. "The one who's been dating our girl?"

"Yeah," I nod.

"Then let's go find out where she is." Zander starts for the driveway, the rest of us following behind.

I let him lead because I'd rather protect my brother's backs. They need me, and I would never let anything happen to them. Zander rings the doorbell while Santos smooths down his shirt, like he's meeting the fucking president. I stand up beside them and the four of us have the fucking porch crowded. John would be smart not to open the door, not that anything would stop us.

He is a dumb fuck, it seems, since the door opens, and his eyes widen as he looks between us.

"Can I help you?" His voice cracks.

"We are Girl Guides, and we have a bag of cookies for you to buy," Santos cuts in and causes the other two to snicker.

I push through them and then I'm shoving John back, my anger now fully in control.

"You have something that belongs to me and I'm gonna need it back." My spit flies on his face. Like most people, he takes in the scar on my face, and swallows thickly in fear.

"I think you're mistaken; I have nothing here." He is fucking shaking under my grip.

The guys enter the house after me, kicking the door shut behind them.

"Let's go to the garage," I say and watch as his eyes widen.

I shove him hard, and his hand shakes as he reaches for the door handle.

"What's in the garage?" I hear Santos ask behind me. "Better not be my sex kitten."

I watch as John walks over to the large steel trapdoor in the center of the garage and breathes out a large breath. "Open it," I demand.

He puts the combination into the lock and then he's hefting the large door, revealing a narrow staircase. We all stand around and peer down at the pitch black.

"Let's go." I grab John's collar and shove him forward.

Zander pulls out his phone and turns on the flashlight app, illuminating the steps. There's about ten of them and then nothing but a tunnel. It makes me angry thinking Selene is down there or was down there. John takes a shaky step down into the hole, stretching his hand out to the wall for stability.

"They're not here," he says quietly, and I crack my teeth together.

"Where are they?" I demand, stepping down behind him.

"With their buyer by now."

"Well, you're going to show me where you keep them, regardless." I shove him, and he stumbles down the last few stairs.

We hit the ground and I growl as we walk in darkness to another set of stairs. It smells like a horse stable. Of course, the girls weren't cared for while here, and the smell is evidence enough. He starts up the next set of stairs and opens the door above our heads.

"Oh fuck, it stinks." Darius covers his nose.

It has a strong scent of urine, and even I crinkle my nose at the scent. I shove John upward and into what I know is the small structure that's located in his backyard. We all come up behind him and look into a room that has a few chairs. There are a few buckets in the corners that I gather are filled with piss.

"See, nothing here." He holds out his arms and Darius springs forward, smacking him in the face like the bitch he is.

"Where is Selene?" he screams.

"I don't know who that is." John begins to shake as we all crowd around him.

"Tall blonde with nice tits," Santos elaborates, and Zander snorts.

"Candy?" John asks, and I punch him in the gut.

"She is sweet as candy, but only when she's sleeping," Zander snickers.

"Where are the girls?" I ask John and shove him down into a chair.

"I sold them." He licks his lips and Zander pulls out a gun. "Okay." He holds up his hands. "I can tell you to whom."

"You better make it fast. That girl is really special," Zander growls.

"To an MC in northern Nevada. They call themselves *Dientes Afilados*."

"Sharp Teeth?" Santos mutters and looks unconvinced.

"Yes, they are in McDermitt." John nods profusely. "I will give you a cut of what I made if you'll just let me go back to the house."

"How do you know Mack Delaney?" I ask him and his eyebrows shoot up.

"Him and I met through mutual business partners."

"Enough talking, time for blood." Darius steps forward and Santos follows with his blade.

## Santos

If I don't reel myself in a little, I'm going to kill this fucker too fast. I need the cunt to suffer for putting his hands on our girl, even if she allowed it.

Darius grins as he moves around behind the guy, giving me an amused glance. "What do you think, brother? Should we start cutting off the body parts that touched our girl?"

I laugh, the loud sound bouncing off the solid walls and causing John to startle.

"I think that's a fucking excellent plan. Hey, John. How many times did you touch my fucking queen?" I ask as I circle him, a whimpering sound spilling from him as he opens his mouth to speak.

"I didn't know she had a boyfriend! She came to me. I didn't chase her!" he insists, letting out a girly scream as Darius grabs his biceps from behind and shoves him down into a chair.

"I haven't even fucking started yet! Why're you squealing like a little piggy?" I exclaim, not looking away as someone dangles a rope in front of me. I take it, wrapping it around John's legs and the chair, making sure he can't kick me before I squat in front of him, inspecting my knife.

I know Darius will keep his top half in the chair, so I take my merry fucking time. I check my teeth in the reflection, suddenly jerking forward to stab the blade right into the top of John's thigh.

He screams bloody murder, but there's no use. He built this place to block out the screams and cries of all the women he takes, so no one will be coming to save him from us.

"Where are your balls, dude? My girl doesn't even bat an eye when a blade's sliding through her soft skin. Man up a little, would you?" I tsk, eyeing him like a shark. There are so many things I want to do to this piece of shit, but I need to draw it out and make sure he doesn't die until we want him to.

I snatch his arm and hold his wrist firmly, feeling the bones shift under the pressure. Not enough to break, but enough to cause discomfort.

"Eenie, meenie, miney, mo," I laugh maniacally as I point to each finger on his hand before stopping at mo, forcing his palm down on the arm of the chair with a sadistic grin. "Yo, one of you boys wanna give me a lighter?"

John's eyes go wide, but Zander approaches me instantly, holding his lighter out and flicking the gas, sparking the flame to life. He knows what I'm up to. They've all seen my party tricks many times.

Blaze silently pulls a blade from his pocket and holds it over the flame, earning a big smile of approval from me.

"You're turning me on, brother."

"I'll turn you off in a second with my fist," he says flatly, apparently not in the mood. Nothing new there.

I shrug, not bothered by his asshole behavior.

"You're going to brand me?" John gasps, but Darius smacks him in the back of the head sharply.

"No talking unless spoken to," he orders, my dick twitching at his tone.

I grip John's hand harder against the arm of the chair, giving the asshole a wide grin.

"I'll talk to you, Johnny boy. The answer is no. I won't waste time branding you."

Relief swims in his eyes, but he screams as my knife slams down on his finger, severing it completely. "I need to cauterize the wound though, so you don't go bleeding out on me. Playtime with Santos is fun, right?"

His screaming is music to my ears, the sound vibrating through me and calming the demons in me a little. He isn't going to live after touching my girl, and he sure as fuck isn't going to die quickly.

Blaze hands the hot blade to me, a content sigh leaving me as I press it against the bleeding stub, the smell of burning flesh filling my nose. Just as John starts to pass out from the pain, Darius tuts and shakes him awake.

"Hey! Wake up, fuckbag! You're a terrible fucking host!" he barks.

John jolts and screams again, making me groan.

"I really wish you didn't have to suffer, John. Trust me. But I can't let you escape your sins so easily. You should be grateful it's us who gets to kill you. If Selene had, you'd be mutilated in ways you can't even begin to imagine. You know the Reaper Incarnate?" I whisper in his ear as I stand and move behind him.

"She—"

"Our girl is a woman of many talents. She can turn you into a pile of jelly in seconds, right? You should see what she can do with a blade. It's hotter than anything she would have done to your dick. My baby's a silent assassin, and you would have been at the top of her list," I chuckle, fisting his hair and yanking his head back to expose his throat. As tempting as it is to slide the sharp point of my blade across it, I restrain myself and release him, enjoying the scare tactic more than I should.

We repeat the finger process until I've removed four, leaving just his thumb on that hand. "Did you ever press that thumb against my girl's clit and make her feel good?"

His head is drooping, and Zander scruffs his hair and yanks him back to look up at me.

"Answer him!"

"No," he slurs, blinking rapidly to try and stay awake.

I prowl closer, rubbing my dick through my pants as I watch the fear leap into his eyes. I wish my baby were here so we could fuck on John's body when we were done. It would have been almost poetic, I think.

"So, you *didn't* treat her right?" I demand, stabbing the blade into his unharmed thigh.

The sounds leaving him aren't enough, and I motion to Blaze with a smirk. "Come on, brother. I know you want to play too."

The monster inside him is rearing to be released. I can see it a mile away. It's a mirror of my own, after all.

# Chapter Fifteen

## *Blaze*

Come on, brother. I know you want to play too." Santos' words rip through my ears and lights something dark and dangerous deep inside.

It's been lonely without them and even though they make me want to bury them on a daily basis, they're my brothers. I wouldn't be where I am without them, and I will never be able to make it on my own. They keep me grounded and, at times like this, let me release the beast.

When I step forward, Santos begins to grin maniacally, and he knows this is where things start to get really messy.

"I grew up in a place that treated children and young adults as cattle. Bought and bartered like prized meat, auctioned when the features were exceptionally good." I bend down into his groggy face. "I don't like what you're a part of and for that, I have to make an example out of you."

I pull the small hatchet I have from the belt around my waist and spin it in my hand. "The Vikings had amazing torture techniques and the devil I was placed with growing up loved to demonstrate some of them. The one I was most interested in, unfortunately, I never got to see in real life. But I want to give it a try, nonetheless. You'll probably die before the good part, but at least me and my brothers can enjoy it."

Santos hoots, and Darius has a wide smile, his teeth looking large and ominous. Zander gets a certain excited look in his eyes. And I know they will remember this for the rest of their lives.

"Get him on his knees and I'll remove the shirt."

Santos and Darius jump to my command, grabbing John. They put him on his knees, and he begins to weakly plead for his life. He sounds like a fucking infant and that pisses me off. He sure acted like a grown man when he was trapping women. I grab my knife and cut the shirt down the center of his back, watching as it falls open and hangs from his arms. I can hear him begin to sob and the sound is like a dying animal, one I need to put out of its misery.

I remember every detail about what I read about this technique and my blood pumps with the chance to use it. I take my sharpened knife and slice through the skin on his back, digging down past the muscle. The blood pours out and over my hands, making the procedure messy. You're never prepared for the mess because the blood isn't depicted in any photos and it's a fucking hindrance. The slippery feel of it and then the twitching of muscles while the participant screams. It's not easy to be precise this way, and it takes away from some of its beauty.

"Fuck, that's pretty," Santos coos.

It is pretty, I agree. I begin to rip the muscle from his ribs and John slumps over, hitting the chair in front of him. He lasted longer than I thought, and I don't know if he's dead or on the brink, but it doesn't matter. I want to leave a beautiful masterpiece for any of his partners who may come looking for him. Something to remember him by and a silent threat that will follow them around.

I grab my hatchet and start chopping into the ribs, breaking them open one by one. I hear Zander heave from behind me and roll my eyes. He was always the weaker one when it came to torture. He prefers his kills to be quick.

Once the ribs are cut, I begin to pry them open, pulling them outward and revealing the lungs. Beautifully red and delicate, the tissue is like the thinnest sponge. I run my fingers along the soft surface and smile as it flutters beneath my touch. The human body is an amazing thing, and the intelligence of each organ is astounding. I grip each lung in my hands and lift them out carefully, placing them over the ribs. They look like soft, red wings.

"That's beautiful," Darius whispers with awe.

We all stand in a line and stare down at the masterpiece before us, almost reverently. My hands drip with blood, my clothes are saturated with it, and my head is once again cleared.

"What is this?" Santos asks.

"The Blood Eagle."

## *Selene*

The van tips as it rounds a sharp turn and I plummet into a few of the girls.

"Son of a bitch!" I scream and bang on the van's door.

"Just sit down, Selene." Aniyah says from the corner. She looks sick, or hungry, or fucking both. Most of these girls do.

I heard the name of the driver when John carted us out like cattle, Delaney. The last name on my list and even though I'm not where I want to be, I'm closer than ever to the answers I seek. I even gave John a quick kiss goodbye on the cheek, promising I would be back, and telling him to be prepared. He laughed it off, not knowing who I am, but he will soon enough, and I will reap his soul for the Devil himself.

I sit down beside Aniyah, and she drops her head to my shoulder, her breaths coming out labored. She had been held inside that room for four days with a bucket to piss in and another to drink filthy water out of. She's starving and dehydrated. She told me John must've drugged her because the last thing she remembered was sitting and watching a movie with him. Then she woke up in the room with four other girls. One of which is the same prostitute who tried to convince me she was too smart to be caught. I haven't said I told you so to her, but there's still time.

"Did you know John was the man snatching up the women?" Aniyah asks quietly. She's asked me this three times now, and it's beginning to worry me that she's not retaining any information.

"Yes," I tell her and run my hand over her limp curls. "That's why when I found out you were missing, I went to him to find you."

"Thank you," she whispers, and I know it's only a matter of time until she's asking me the same questions all over again.

"Where are we going?" one of the girls whimpers, and I tamper down the need to snap at her. Like be strong, stand up for yourself, and be prepared to fight.

"Doesn't matter." I finger my belt. "Once I get the chance, I'm gutting them all."

The smooth ride turns bumpy, and I can tell we're on gravel. A dirt road in the middle of nowhere sounds like a death sentence. The only thing stopping me from breaking loose is the fact that I know we're too valuable to be killed. The van stops and a few girls gasp in fear while I stand to face the door. I will be the first person they see and if they try anything, the fucking last as well.

The doors open to show Delaney and his gap-toothed smile, his obese gut hanging out of his shirt. He's sweating profusely in the Nevada heat and his milky yellow eyes look like the fucker might have jaundice. I look beyond him and see another van idling, two mean looking fuckers standing to the side with their arms crossed over their chests. Beyond them, it's a desert wasteland, and the heat waves off the sand.

"Let's go ladies, off to your forever homes." Delaney reaches in to grab my wrist, but I snap my leg out and kick him in the face, probably freeing his gums of a few more rotting teeth. "Fuck!" he screams as he tries to sit up, looking like a beached whale, and grabbing his mouth.

I jump down from the van and suddenly the two big, tattooed, muscled men pull out guns, training them on my face. I could throw my knife and kill one, but then that other one would shoot me for sure. I need to protect the girls.

"We won't hurt you," one calls out and takes a step forward. I swear that's what every fucking serial killer ever says. I should know, I am one.

"Who are you?" I call out, giving Delaney another good kick in the head when he finally sits up, and I laugh when he's flat out once again.

"*Dientes Afilados*!" one calls out. "Do you know who we are?"

"No, I don't speak French," I huff with my hands on my hips.

They begin to chuckle, and the same one motions to the van behind me. "We paid for all of them. I promise no one will get harmed. Can you please get into the van?" He motions to the vehicle behind him where I see a cooler. "We have some fruit in there and water." My parched throat clenches at the mention of water, and I know I can't deprive them of that.

I go back to the van, giving Delaney another shot to the gut, and I can hear the guys still chuckling behind me. I grab the few girls who can walk and help them down from the van, watching closely as they approach the guys. They keep to their word and hand them each a bottle of water. I hoist Aniyah up and wrap her hand around my neck, putting her down gently.

One of the guys approaches us slowly, his gun down by his side, and his hand reaching out to us. "Can I help you? What's wrong with her?"

"They weren't fed or given clean water. I'm sure she's sick," I snap and he wraps his arm around Aniyah's waist.

"Okay, we'll make sure she's okay." He gives me a tight nod. "I'll need you in the back while she comes up front with us. We'll drop her off at Medical."

"Medical? Like a hospital?" I question.

"No, we have a doctor on site. You'll all get checked out, eventually."

I don't like the sound of it, but I don't have any other choice and Aniyah needs the help. I give him a nod and hop up into the back of yet another van to be carted off to yet another place unknown. The girls are shoving mango in their mouths and gulping water, but I refuse to let my guard down. Yes, this feels better than John's holding facility and then Delaney's van, but we're still being treated like purchased property.

I can't tell how long we're in the van for, I've lost all sense of time, and I can't even decipher how many days it's been since I was taken. The van stops and when the back doors open, it's dusk. I let everyone else out before me and I see one of the guys standing at the door.

"Where's my friend?" I ask him, and he jerks his chin behind me. I turn to see the other guy holding Aniyah and taking her into a building. "What're your names?"

He raises his brow. "I'm Bank, and he's Coin."

"I see what you did there, like Coin in the Bank. Is Coin in you often?"

He lets out a startled cackle and shakes his head, a blush running along his cheeks.

"Don't worry," I shrug. "Two of my guys like to fool around too, and it gets me hot to watch."

"*Two* of your guys?" His grin stays firmly on his face.

"Yes, I have four."

He shuts the van's doors behind me and leads me to the building the other girls disappeared into. "Where are they then? How'd you wind up on the market?"

"I left them behind." I try to sound nonchalant as my heart breaks over the words. "I need to find my sister; she was stolen many years ago."

"What's her name?"

"Janelle." I look at him, hoping to see recognition at the name.

"Nope," he shakes his head. "I don't know a Janelle around here." He sees my shoulders slump with his answer. "Sorry."

I follow him inside and see that it's a small building with multiple bedrooms. "You'll stay here until Digs comes by," he tells me.

"Digs?"

"That's our Doc. We call him Digs because he digs out bullets on the regular," he chuckles, and I decide I like the sound.

"Oh, yeah," I nod. "That makes all the sense. Where are we?"

"You're in McDermitt. It's an old, abandoned town in North Nevada. We run the MC here called *Dientes Afilados*. Spanish for Sharp Teeth."

"Why Sharp Teeth?" I scrunch my nose at the name.

"We like to bite." He snaps at me playfully and I growl. "You'll fit in here. I hope they don't move you."

"Listen, *garçon*." He snorts at me. "I don't care how I was purchased, but you guys need to get a refund, because as soon as I can, I'm getting all of us out."

"We don't hold anyone hostage," he growls. "You'll find many of the girls we help from those skin bags want to stay."

He shows me to a room and points to a shower. I groan at the sight, and he chuckles as he walks out the way we came in, the distinct sound of a bolt locking reaching my ears. We may be in fancier dwellings, but we're still fucking prisoners. Not for long. I walk into the bathroom and when I see girly bath products, I squeal like a stuck pig. I strip out of my filthy clothes and start the shower.

I step out and feel like a brand-new woman, my skin smelling like papaya. I grab the terry robe from the back of the door and grab my belt from the floor, not caring about the rest. I head to the small closet and find a few white t-shirts with a few sweatshirt dress things. I get dressed in one of those and wrap my belt back around my waist, tying my long blonde hair up into a messy bun.

I find the communal kitchen and the girls are there stuffing their faces with more fruit. I sit down and decide to join in because I need the strength that comes with food and water.

"What is this place?" a girl asks. I didn't bother with names because I won't know them well beyond setting them free.

"A motorcycle club called Sharp Dentures," I shrug.

"Are they a bunch of old guys running the joint?" another asks.

"Don't care," I shrug. "I'm getting out, so whoever wants to come is more than welcome."

"I wanna check it out first," one says and the rest murmur in agreement.

"Sure," I nod, finishing off my food.

I get up and walk over to the barn style door, laughing when I see it's made of wood. The lock I heard earlier was probably a slab of wood settling across, like you would find at a barn. I take my knife out of the holster and stab it through the slat, feeling it sink into the wooden slab. I begin to lift it straight up and once I feel it give away; I push the door open. It's now pitch-black outside, but I can hear loud metal music blaring from a large compound to my right. Some MC this is. No one felt the need to guard a bunch of females, and that's their fucking problem, not mine.

I yank my knife back out and start for the building. I saw them take Aniyah. If she's hurt any worse than when I last saw her, I will be blowing this place into fucking pieces. I open the door and find a young guy sitting on a chair in a leather vest.

"Hey!" He stands and I'm already across the room, slamming the butt end of my knife into his forehead. He slumps to the ground, and I roll my eyes. Too fucking easy.

It's one large room with curtains sectioning off areas and I stand in the center. Three of them are closed with the curtains. The first one has a guy with a nasty wound on his chest, the second one has another guy who's mumbling in his sleep, and the third is a female, but not Aniyah. Looks like the party compound is getting a fucking surprise.

I stride back outside and start to walk across the compound when I hear tires squealing at the front gate.

# Santos

Zander speeds along the dirt driveway, slamming down on the brakes and causing a cloud of dust to form around us. I'm not even thinking about the consequences of showing up at an MC club house unannounced. All I can focus on is the blonde bombshell in front of us.

She looks like a fucking deer caught in the headlights, as she fucking should.

Zander grabs Blaze's arm tightly before he can lunge at her, but I shove open my door and slam it behind me, not taking my eyes off her as I stalk towards her.

"Santos?" Selene squeaks out, all the usual signs of bravery gone. She knows she fucked up by abandoning us, and I'm caught between wanting to kill her and fuck her. Or kill her while I fuck her. I'm not too sure yet.

"No, it's Father fucking Christmas," I grit out sarcastically. "You really thought you could outrun me? Outrun all fucking four of us?"

She looks ready to run in the opposite direction, smart girl, but she hesitates for too long, and my hand is wrapped around her slim throat and squeezing firmly before she can comprehend what's happening.

"You fucking left me!" I shout, squeezing harder until she squeaks out. "I'm sorry."

My grip loosens a fraction, just before I swoop down and claim her mouth with mine, my emotions running rampant inside me. I kiss her like she's the air I need to breathe, then I remember I'm pissed as fuck at her and fist her hair with my free hand, yanking her back to force her eyes up to mine.

"I could fucking kill you, Selene. Do you have any idea how fucked up we've been without you? How insane it drove me to not be with you while knowing you were putting yourself in danger like this?" I demand, her eyebrows shooting up in surprise.

"You knew where I was?" she pants quietly, appearing ready to knock me back and escape, but she doesn't. I snarl, towering over her, and I know I must look beyond murderous because she actually shrinks back the smallest amount.

"Of course we fucking did. Blaze has been following you since the moment you left. We will follow you to the depths of fucking Hell and back, baby. You should have known there'd be no escaping us."

I growl as she's pulled away from me, but I calm as Darius yanks her to his chest and kisses the living shit out of her, needing to feel her body against his to prove she's all right.

She smells fruity, and my dick swells as I think of all the ways I'm going to punish her for hurting me. She's lucky I don't shove granola bars up her ass and turn her into the world's prettiest vending machine.

"I'm going to fucking kill you," Darius murmurs against her lips, a breathy moan coming from her in response.

"You can try, asshole."

Zander and Blaze finally join us, and she turns her attention to the big angry bastard as he glares at her silently. "So, you were my stalker?"

He grunts, his lip lifting in a sneer. "You should have known it was me. I left you enough fucking hints. You know better than to keep your fucking windows unlocked, too. Are you stupid?"

"Apparently," she says softly, her eyes flickering over him. "You really came for me?"

His sneer drops a fraction, but he holds his ground pretty well. "Of course, I did. You don't get to fuck me like you did and then bail. That's not how this shit works. Do you know how many opportunities I had to kill you? Your attention to detail is slacking," he barks, some of her cocky attitude returning as she snorts.

"Did you really have to leave a severed dick on my counter and your cum on my fucking coffee table? I assume that was your work of art, you fucking heathen."

He suddenly smirks darkly, stepping closer until he's looking down at her like she is his prey.

"I was getting pissed at watching you let those cunts touch you. What can I say? I was hoping you'd get the fucking hint and shut your fucking legs for five minutes," he answers, her eyes narrowing.

"It's none of your business what I do with my pussy, and I'm going to gut you for leaving your man spunk all over my fucking house," she seethes, but he grabs her by the throat and hauls her onto her tiptoes, getting in her face.

"Matter of fact, that pussy's ours, Selene. You never should have given us the deed to it if you never wanted it to be that way. Did you have fun fucking with us? Was it a way to kill time and get to Henry? Was that it?"

"No! I just want to find my fucking sister!" she screams suddenly, anger pulsing through me. I manage to shove Blaze back, shrugging off Darius as he reaches for me.

"You didn't think we'd help you? I'd do anything for you, for fuck's sake! I'd have dropped everything at home to follow you, helping you day and night until we found her!" I spit, her eyes softening. Her emotions are fucking her up too, and I hope it fucking hurts.

"I couldn't drag you guys along. I needed—"

"Why the fuck not? What if something had gone wrong and you ended up dead? You might as well have aimed the gun at us and pulled the trigger yourself. We're nothing without you, baby. Fucking nothing," I force out.

She's suddenly kissing me, and I bite her lip sharply, a metallic tang spreading over my tongue as I dip it into her mouth. She moans, her fingernails digging into my back as she keeps me close, the demons in me wanting to be let out to punish her.

"Let's finish this at home," Zander grunts, snapping Selene out of our make-out session. She jerks back, pure rage written all over her face.

"I'm not going fucking anywhere, asshole. This is a lead, and I need to stick it out. Besides, I need to help these women get out if these MC fuckers aren't good on their word," she spits, causing Zander's jaw to clench. We all want to get her ass home and punish her, but dragging her away and wrecking her chance at finding her sister would cause us more grief than we'd like. We can punish her later.

Darius nods, dropping an arm around her shoulders to show he's on her side, the kiss ass.

"You think these guys are cool? You've spoken to them?" he asks, her body relaxing at his understanding tone.

"Yeah. They're apparently saving the women. It might be bullshit, but I want to make sure the women are safe before I leave. I have a friend here I want to find," she answers, making Blaze snort.

"The purple-headed whore who tickles your clit?" he asks flatly, and Selene looks like she's seconds away from using his face as a punching bag.

"She's my friend, and she was a mess when we were being transported here. The men are giving her medical help, apparently, so I want to make sure they fucking are. You're about to cop a fist to the face, grumpy," she hisses, but he simply glares back at her.

"Excellent. Because you're about to cop my fist right up your cunt."

Zander rolls his eyes at their banter, while Darius and I grin with amusement. I wish I could be there the next time Blaze gets her hot little body under him, because I bet they'll put on a fucking show.

"Are we checking shit out, or what? I'm bored," I declare, moving towards the sound of the music. I do love a good party.

## Darius

Selene chases after Santos, bitching him out about just wandering into an MC's hangout, leaving us to trail behind them. Blaze takes up the rear, keeping his eyes peeled as Zander and I talk.

"Do you think these guys are legit?" I ask, hearing him scoff.

"Legit? No. They might be trying to help women, but I doubt there's not a catch. Is she seriously about to just walk right through the door?" he growls, a smirk tugging at my lips as she grabs the door handle and flings it open, snarking at Santos as he walks so close to her that he almost knocks her over. He isn't going to let her out of his sight ever again. I hope she knows that.

People are glancing our way, but Selene stalks right over to one of them and starts talking, her hands moving around with angry motions. I assume the dude's going to haul her ass back to the other women, but a booming laugh leaves him as he grins.

His eyes move up to us as we approach, and he raises an eyebrow in question. "You think wandering in here is a smart move, my friend?"

"My girl's worth the bullets. I ain't *your* shit," Zander growls, his fingers twitching, ready for a fight. The guy chuckles, eyeing Blaze for a moment before motioning to Selene.

"She mentioned you four to my boy when she got here. I'm Coin." He offers his hand and I give it a dirty look, but Zander steps forward, moving into the leader role he seems to end up with.

"Zander. This is Darius, Santos, and the guy behind me is Blaze. You like buying skin?" he asks bluntly, Coin giving him an amused smile.

"We'd prefer the term, freeing. The girls we end up with are usually in terrible condition, so we feed them, hydrate them, and get them back on their feet."

"Then you fucking keep them by the look of things," Santos snaps, his sharp eyes moving around the room at the few women. Coin laughs, leaning back on his heels to cross his arms.

"None of them are here by force. A lot choose to stick around, others leave once they're healthy enough. May I ask why the fuck you're all here? I'm surprised you didn't take off, blondie," he states as he turns his attention to Selene, her lips lifting in a sneer.

"My friend. Where is she?"

"She's being treated. You can see her tomorrow when she's rested. You don't seem like a girl who'd allow herself to be snatched and sold," he observes, her eyebrow lifting a fraction.

"I was investigating the missing women. I'm looking for answers about my sister who went missing when I was a teenager. I have a hunch you fuckers might know something about that."

He shrugs, looking thoughtful for a moment before replying. "Your best bet at finding out information on any of the girls we've been in contact with would be Papi Loco. He's not here right now though, so stick around and grab a beer or something. No threatening my brothers, all right? I'm looking at you, shifty eyes," he grins, cocking his head at Santos, who puffs out his chest.

"I only bring out my weapons if I need to," he exclaims, making me snort.

"No, you don't."

He flips me the bird, turning his attention to Selene as Coin walks off, trusting us to behave for some stupid reason. His casual approach to us is grating on my nerves a little.

Zander and Blaze grumble something about checking the bar out, giving me a look to tell me we better be good. Fat chance.

Santos backs Selene up until her ass is pressed against my front, my hands dropping instantly to her waist. He leans down, his voice low and full of promise.

"You're in so much trouble, babe. You won't be able to sit down once we're through with you."

She shivers, trying to stand her ground but failing, her body responding to his voice by pressing back into me further.

"Do your worst, fuckface."

There are people everywhere, but a dark corner isn't hard to find. I tug her back as Santos follows, his eyes burning into her with the threat of violence. The moment my back hits the wall, my teeth and lips are on her neck, sucking and biting my way across her skin and breathing her in.

Santos doesn't give a shit if anyone sees us or not as he shoves his hand up her skirt, not wasting time as he pushes his fingers inside her roughly. She moans loudly, the music drowning it out as he pumps his arm at a punishing pace.

Every time he gets her close, he pulls back, starting all over again until she's growling.

"Let me come, you piece of shit," she snaps, a crazy laugh spilling from his lips as he hauls her forward, tugging her further into the room. The lighting isn't the best. Lucky for her, otherwise everyone in the entire room will be seeing her getting nailed in a second. I see him fiddle with the front of his sweatpants and grin.

"You don't fucking deserve to," he bites out, hiking her thigh up around his waist, appearing to be dirty dancing against her, but I know differently from the way Selene's body reacts. She gasps, her back arching into me as a low chuckle vibrates from my chest.

"Did you miss us, baby? Did you think about us when you had someone else's dick inside you?" I ask roughly. She curses, nodding her head as Santos grinds his dick into her pussy, her butt pressing back against my groin.

I slip a hand up her skirt and pull her panties aside, running my fingers through her juices and along Santos' length as it moves in and out of her, gathering the wetness to slide it up her crack. She gasps as I press a finger against her tight hole, easing it inside her slowly while sinking my teeth into her shoulder.

"All we've done since you left is think about all the ways we could fucking punish you for leaving us. Do you understand why we're pissed?" I growl, biting her sharply again when she doesn't answer.

"I should have told you guys, I get it," she snarls, but she grinds her body between us, telling us she's not even mad.

I add a second finger, stretching her more as I unzip my jeans and pull my dick free, sliding it between her legs. Santos pulls out, pulling her forwards to kiss, while not hesitating to reach between her legs for my dick, helping to guide it into her dripping pussy.

She moans into his mouth, her walls clamping around me as I grind into her, wanting to get my dick as wet as possible. I wanted to punish her, but I didn't particularly want to tear her ass up in the literal sense.

The people and sounds around us fade as I finally slide into her ass, a groan leaving me as Santos pushes inside her pussy again. We grind into her, building her up just to withhold her release.

"Please," she grits out, but we ignore her and chase our own releases, not giving into her pleading. I come first, biting into her neck so hard I draw blood, and the second I pull out of her and fix my pants, Santos backs her into the wall again and fucks her hard, not giving a shit if he gets caught.

Selene starts cursing, her body tense as it gets ready to explode, but Santos slams in hard, filling her pussy with his cum and pulling out, fisting her hair to make her focus on him.

"A few weeks of fucking you without letting you finish is looking mighty appealing, babe. Stay with Darius. I need a drink." Then he releases his hold on her and fixes his pants, stalking off in the direction of the bar without another word.

Selene's fuming, her fists balling at her sides as she glares at his retreating back. I lean against the wall, running my eyes over her as if to make sure she really is here.

"You hurt us. You fucking broke Santos," I say, her eyes swinging my way as if she forgot I'm here. She goes to swing at me, but I catch her wrist firmly, tugging her closer. "You fucking broke him, Selene. I was by his side every second of the fucking day, getting my ass beat so he could let out some of his demons instead of going after you and massacring everyone in the process. He's been blind drunk, he's cried, he's screamed until his lungs gave out, and I took the brunt of his emotions because I'd do anything to stop his hurting. I'd do the same for you, so why the fuck didn't you just ask us to come with you? I thought we were a team?" I ask, confusion flickering in her pretty eyes.

"I'm not your problem. I'm not worth your life, D," she replies softly, only just loud enough for me to hear over the surrounding racket. I snort, releasing her and shaking my head.

"You're not a problem, baby. You're a part of us, and it's about time you realize just how much you mean to us. You're not a possession. You're not a mountain we conquered. You're a part of our fucking family, and you ripped us apart when you left. If Santos is only withholding orgasms from you for a while, you got off lightly in my eyes," I state, stepping forward to grip her chin gently. "You're not a lone wolf anymore. Fucking face that fact, so we can all move on and find your fucking sister together."

She wants to argue. I can see it on her face, but she finally wraps her arms around my waist and presses her cheek to my chest, surprising me slightly.

"I missed you too," is all she says, but it's as close to an apology as I'll get, so I put my arms around her and hold her tightly, simply happy to have her back.

# Chapter Sixteen

## Zander

"I think they're fucking each other," I state as I slug back half the fucking beer in my hand.

"And she fucking called *me* a heathen," Blaze grumbles over his neat scotch. For a nasty looking brute, he sure likes a fancy man's drink.

"How much do you want to bet they fill both her holes with cum and leave her hanging?"

Finally, a small smirk settles over his lips, yanking on the white skin of his scar. "How about we join in on that?"

He's never one to play around like this and I can feel something settle in my chest with his admission. Blaze has fallen just as hard for her as the rest of us. I never thought I would see the day that he let himself give in to anyone outside of the four of us. His upbringing ensured that he would never trust anyone wholly and the things he endured sealed his heart in cement until her. Luckily, we all feel the same way and us sharing her keeps us together.

"I'm down." I nod, gulping down the rest of my beer.

We turn and watch as Selene separates herself from Darius and walks towards a group of girls. They smile at her, but I can see the wariness in their eyes. They point her down a hallway and I snort.

"Bet she has a lot of cleaning up to do. Think of how much build up we have." I grin at Blaze.

"I can't wait to fill it right the fuck back up. You take her pussy;

I'm shoving my cock in her ass," he growls, throwing back his drink.

I cringe at the thought of Blaze's dick forcing its way into her tight asshole. I hope she has life insurance. Another beer is placed in front of me and another drink is in front of Blaze. Santos appears, squeezing between us, and looks completely sated.

"How was it?" I ask, and he shoots me a grin.

"Like sticking my dick in a fruit cup, wet and sweet."

"What the fuck?" Blaze growls.

"She smells like fruit." Santos shrugs. "And she was fucking dripping wet."

"Did she come?"

Santos laughs maniacally and shakes his head. "Not gonna happen. You lot better not let her either. We need to band together for this."

Blaze and I nod, a ghost of a smile on his scary face. "Did you find out anything about this place when your dick wasn't stuck in a fruit cup?" Blaze growls.

"Let's call her pussy a fruit cup forever." Santos snaps his fingers. "And yes," he nods, "I was speaking to the bartender—his name is Licker—get it? Like liquor, but it's L-I-C-K-E-R."

"Yes," I roll my eyes, "go on."

"Clever fuckers here," he chuckles. "Anyway, they call themselves *Dientes Afilados*—that means Sharp Teeth—and they've been around for a long time. They may not like to sell skin, but they sell just about everything else. Drugs and weapons being their most profitable."

"Licker told you all this in one sitting?" I raise my brow.

"I think Licker had his tongue in some liquor." He shrugs, and I groan at his stupid joke. "So the Pres. is a guy named Papi Loco and he's an old son of a bitch. As mean as a bull, he likes killing, and he likes to leave body parts as gifts to people who wrong him. His Vice Pres. is named Loquito and is also his son. Just as crazy and unhinged. But really, they sound like my kind of people. Licker warned me that they are bat shit but love their people."

"Sounds like you'd fit in here," Blaze grunts.

"Don't worry, you sexy ass fucker," Santos bats his eyelashes at him, "I will never leave you. I only recognize one *Papi* around here."

I choke on my beer as Santos blows him a fucking kiss and walks back over to Darius.

"Some days I swear that fucker is suicidal," Blaze says, unperturbed by Santos' antics.

"I hope us being here doesn't set Papi fuckface off. I'm not prepared for a shootout. I couldn't bring my machine gun on the flight."

Blaze gives me a little snort and I relax, seeing him finally let that dark part of him recede. I saw the moment he released it. He was ripping John's ribs apart and now I want to gag again, just thinking of it.

"Looks like she cleared the dumpster," Blaze snarks, and I look over to find Selene exiting a corridor.

"Too bad for her. Today is garbage day," I retort.

"My cum ain't garbage," Blaze sneers.

"It is if you're calling her pussy a dumpster."

"Touché." He nods and downs his drink. "Let's give our little reaper a scare."

"Does she have her knife on her?" I give her a once over.

"Yep," Blaze nods. "She thinks that belt hides it."

I stare at the belt, trying to see the knife, and Blaze flicks my ear. "You're as dumb as nails, you know that?"

"Fuck you. I hope she stabs you first." I stalk towards Selene.

The moment she sees me, her eyes widen, and then widen further when she sees Blaze behind me.

"No," she shakes her head. "Not you two. I will kill someone tonight if you try that same shit."

I grab her by the throat and yank her into me, pressing my mouth to hers. "You don't get a fucking say any longer, Reaper. You take whatever the fuck we give you and you smile while it's happening." I flick my tongue against her bottom lip, and she snaps at it, making me laugh.

"Are you gonna dance with me, grumpy?" she asks Blaze over my shoulder, not the slightest bit worried about my hand around her throat.

"The only dancing you'll be doing is over this cock," he retorts.

"I remember our last dance," she moans and licks her lips. "I can't wait for an encore."

My cock swells painfully and I need to rip it out of my pants, then sink it into her. I've never gone this long without sex, and that gives me another reason to be pissed off at her. How dare she give me something I will never be able to find anywhere else? I turn us around and shove her back into Blaze's chest, my hand still wrapped around her throat. The bitch doesn't flinch. If anything, she looks like she's ready to combust, and I can't let that happen. I made my boy a promise.

I lean over her shoulder and whisper in Blaze's ear, "Avoid the clit."

He gives me a brusque nod as I lean back down and look at Selene, her eyes hooded.

"Are you two going to kiss?" Her voice is breathy.

"Wrong duo," I growl. "But don't worry, we'll soon remind you who we are."

"So, show me," she says as she yanks her skirt up around her waist.

I sandwich her tight between us and look around the room, expecting other men to have their eyes on my woman. But all I see are naked girls, some dancing and others fucking, just like we're planning to do. I fucking like it here.

I step back and undo my belt, my cock straining to be set free. Blaze reaches down and rips her thong clear off her body, holding it up to his nose. "Smells like cum."

"I was filled like an eclair." She makes a grab for the scrap of fabric. "What the fuck do you expect?"

"I've always been partial to the Boston Cream," I say as I hitch her leg over my hip and begin to rub my cock through her already soaking pussy.

"Yes, Zander. Fuck, Boston Cream me." She begins to shake, her body begging for a release, and I pull away.

"Did you think I was going first?"

"What?" She looks up at me with lust and confusion.

# Blaze

My cock is out in my hand and the metal through the tip glints. I reach between her legs and grab her arousal, feeling her shudder between Zan and I. I grab an ass cheek and spread her wide, lining myself up. I feel her tense as soon as my head touches her puckered hole, and she begins to shake her head.

"No Blaze," she begs, and I grow even harder. "You won't fit."

"Let's find out." I lean into her ear while pushing against her tight hole. "Take a deep breath."

"No." she continues to shake her head, but her pleas fall on deaf ears. I won't be taking any mercy on her, or her dumpster.

My head breaches her ass, but it's so fucking tight, and I do fear I'm going to cause some damage. She's whining as her head falls back on my chest, her own chest heaving, and sweat forming on her temples.

"Does it hurt?" Zander asks as he reaches between them and slowly begins to push into her.

"Yes," she moans. "So fucking good."

I grab the back of her head and shove her forward into Zander, the impact of her forehead to his chest jarring them both. Zander bottoms out inside of her, but his chest rumbles with laughter as I use this new angle to plummet my length all the way in. She screams into his chest, and I'm not bothered if it's in pleasure or pain at this point. I yank her head back up and begin thrusting in time with Zander, our cocks rubbing together through the thin layer separating us.

She reaches down to rub her clit, but Zander grabs her hand up and winds it around his head. He chuckles at what I imagine being a scowl on our reaper's face. I look down to watch myself disappear inside her, grinning when I see some blood; knowing her scream was one of pain. I continue plowing into her, Zander doing the same from the front, and when I feel her tighten, we both still.

"No," she growls, grabbing Zander's chin. "Do not fucking think about it."

As soon as she's relaxed again and she lets out a groan, I slam it back home. I chase my release and it feels so fucking good to finally be inside of her again. I can see Zander doing the same and we both thrust one final time, spilling ourselves into her. I feel her clench around us, trying to work herself over, and grinding into us. But it's no use when we both abruptly pull out and I spread her open to watch my cum mixed with her blood seep out.

She yanks her skirt down and shoves Zander out of the way, stalking off back to the bathroom. We're both tucking ourselves in when I hear a whistle behind me. I turn and find two bikers, mean as fuck looking. They're staring us down and I don't break eye contact as I shove my cock back in my pants.

"That's your woman?" One of them juts his chin towards Selene.

"Something like that," I grunt at the same time Zander says, "Yes."

"What are you guys doing here?" he asks, and we walk over to them.

"Chasing down skin sellers and trying to locate her sister who went missing a long time ago," I answer him.

"Skin sellers, huh? We're doing the same thing. We have an axe to grind, too." I take a good look at them and begin to see the resemblance.

"Kho." The one talking nods at us. "This is my twin brother, Khaine."

Zander snorts beside me, and I look back and forth between them. "Are you for real? Your names are cocaine?"

"Kho and Khaine." Khaine shrugs and grins. "It is now, anyway."

"What's with the names in this place?" Zander chuckles.

"Pres. lives up to his name, but he's given us all a chance to start over and shed who we were before," Kho explains. "We were picked up by a skin seller when we were fourteen and *Papi L* saved us. Now we're in charge of distribution."

"Of cocaine." I take a wild fucking guess.

"Yes!" they exclaim together.

"I feel like we're in Wonderland," I tell Zander and laughter rips from his mouth.

"I fucking love it here," he says as tears build up in his eyes with the force of his laugh.

I feel a sharp slap on my ass and turn, my fist lifted. Selene stands there with her brow raised, taunting me, and grinning when I lower it.

"You made my ass bleed, you fucking animal!" she yells, and I snort.

I wrap my arm around her shoulder and haul her in beside me. "I'm gonna do it again later."

The guys in front of us are smiling and laughing as Selene looks between them. "Who the fuck are you?"

She always sounds like she owns wherever the fuck she's standing, lacking any respect for the people who actually own it, and I can't help that my cock swells with pride.

"This is Kho and Khaine," Zander says, his voice still holding a bit of humor.

"Great," she nods. "Can you guys make the pain in my ass disappear?"

They both grab their stomachs and laugh, finding the little reaper under my arm amusing. Little do they know, she'd have no problem bleeding them out here, and in front of an audience. And I'm rock fucking solid again.

"Do either of you know a girl named Jan? Or Janelle?" she asks, and they both crinkle their brows in thought.

"No." They shake their heads together, looking very much like Tweedle Dee and Dum. "Who is she?"

"My sister." Selene's shoulders slump. "She was taken and sold when I was younger."

The one named Khaine stares into her face, studying her features, and when I growl, he gives me a lazy grin. "Boss tries to keep track of who's passed through here so you can talk to him when he's back."

"When will that be?" Selene huffs.

"Tomorrow morning." Kho nods. "I'll have Sunshine make up a room for you. I'm assuming one is good?"

"Yes," Zander says when I say, "No."

"C'mon," Selene coos. "We'll play hide the pickles."

I roll my eyes at her remark as everyone else laughs.

"Sunshine!" Khaine calls out and an older lady with a scowl that could rival my own comes over. Sunshine, my fucking ass. "Can you set these guys up with a room for the night?"

Sunshine has frizzy, bleached hair that stands up in all directions, the damaged strands no longer smooth. Her face is wrinkled, and she has deep creases around her mouth from smoking too fucking much. Her saggy tits are forced into a push-up bra, and they rival her face for wrinkles. I shudder when I'm done with my once over.

"Who the fuck are they?" Her voice sounds like she smokes a pack of cigarettes a day. "How do we know they won't gut us in the middle of the night?"

"Because I just got double-dicked down, twice," Selene growls at her. "I'm fucking tired. The only blood spilling will belong to my men for not letting me come."

*Her men.* I hate how I love the sound of that so much. The two women stare each other down and Santos comes up to us with Darius in tow.

"Kho and Khaine!" Santos exclaims, and I roll my eyes. Of course he's met them.

"San!" they exclaim right back, bumping his fist with their own.

When Selene tosses him a questioning glare, Santos shrugs, "I met them earlier when I was grabbing a drink. Licker introduced us."

Sunshine grumbles a bit more but motions for us to follow her. She takes us down the corridor that Selene disappeared into for the bathroom and then up a set of stairs. The second floor is a labyrinth of interconnecting corridors, all of them lined with doors.

"This one is a guest room," she says as she opens the door. Inside is a king-size bed, thankfully, and a couch as well. Then she shuts it behind us, leaving quickly.

"A ray of sunshine indeed," Zander remarks.

"Do you think we'll get names here?" Santos' eyes light up.

"Yeah," I grunt. "You two will be Don and Key." I swing my finger between him and Darius.

They both hoot and start laughing, "Was that a joke, Daddy?" Santos exclaims, and I storm away from them into the adjoining bathroom. I refuse to engage.

When I finish up and step back out, it's like a fucking preschool classroom. Everyone is bickering.

"One of you is getting between my legs and licking me clean. I refuse to sleep without coming." Selene stomps her foot.

"Should've thought of that before you ran off," Zander growls.

"Fine!" She crawls up the bed, her ass and pussy on full display under her skirt. "I'll do it myself." She reaches between her legs as we all stand in a line at the foot of the bed, watching as she begins to play with her clit.

Just as she really begins to pant and her pussy is glistening with arousal, Darius jumps on the bed. He grabs both her hands as Santos holds her feet, wrapping a belt around her two wrists, and straps her to the bedpost.

"Not tonight, Reaper," Santos says, kissing her foot as she kicks it out.

"Undo this right now." She struggles against the bonds.

Zan, Santos, and Darius climb up on the bed, ignoring her demands as I fall onto the couch.

"Fuck, I'm beat," I groan, and everyone chuckles. All save for the little reaper who is doling out death threats.

# Chapter Seventeen

## Santos

The click of a gun has my eyes springing open, the sun peeking through the crack in the curtains and reflecting off the weapon in question. I squint, my tired eyes adjusting and zoning in on the man standing beside the bed.

I don't even hesitate before throwing myself out of bed and slamming my shoulder into the guy, landing on top of him as we hit the ground. The commotion wakes the others up, but I don't look their way as I wrestle the gun from the prick and crack my elbow against his jaw, his head snapping to the side with a psychotic laugh.

"You're a fucking wild one!" he cackles before throwing his weight up and managing to buck me off, scrambling to his knees, and pulling another gun from nowhere. He aims it at my face, a cocky smirk stretching across his lips. "What now, asshole?"

I grin, confusing him a fraction. "I'm not the real threat in the room."

One of the guys must have untied Selene while we were rolling around on the fucking floor, because she moves up behind him silently and wraps one of the belts tightly around his neck to yank him back sharply, a choked sound leaving the guy in surprise.

My girl has balls of steel, because she stands over him and shoves a foot down on his chest hard the moment he lands on his back, glaring down the barrel of his gun without flinching.

"You think you can touch one of my guys and live to fucking tell the tale?" she snaps, her eyes filling with heat. Hell fucking no. I get to my feet and stand beside her, growling at him like an animal.

He quirks an eyebrow at me before turning his attention back to Selene, his voice amused. "It's been a while since a woman got that rough with me. You want to play, kitty cat?"

I snarl and lift my gun to shoot his stupid face, but Selene elbows me in the ribs hard, causing me to drop the gun into her waiting hand.

"The deal was we wouldn't fucking threaten any of Coin's brothers, dumbass," she says swiftly, narrowing her eyes when I wave my hands in the asshole's direction.

"Excuse the fuck out of me then, because when someone's pointing their gun in my face, I don't usually stick to a moral code of respect. I also never agreed to his request," I spit, relaxing as Darius moves in beside me and rests his hand on my hip, squeezing firmly to draw my attention off the smug bastard on the ground at our girl's feet.

He laughs, the sound loud in the small room.

"You're friends with Coin? Why didn't you fucking say so! His brothers are my brothers! Or *piñatas*, depending on the situation. Right now, you could be either, so you want to tell me who the fuck you are and why the fuck you're sleeping in my clubhouse?"

"Not particularly," Selene deadpans, not removing her foot from him. "How about you tell us who the fuck you are?"

"I guess I'll play your little game since you asked so nicely, *Mamacita*." He winks.

Selene's foot moves up towards his throat, pressing down. "I'm not a little mama, asshole."

"Give me twenty minutes of your time and you will be," he wheezes as she applies more pressure, and lucky for him, Darius grabs my arm to yank me back before I can beat the shit out of him.

Zander's standing close to me too, so I know they're hoping I don't get us all shot at. They'll want to beat the prick too, so they can fuck off if they don't think I'm going to kill him.

"Name!" Selene snaps, sick of his bullshit like we are.

He rolls his eyes and waits until she removes her foot a little before speaking.

"I'm Loquito."

"I could have told you that," I growl, but he ignores me and keeps his eyes on Selene as she assesses the situation. She finally steps back, allowing him to get to his feet.

"You're the VP?" she asks, her eyes lighting up with hope. "Is Papi Loco back too?"

His eyes narrow at her questions, but Zander steps forward and offers his hand like the good boy he is. So I step back to sit on the bed, grabbing my jeans off the floor.

"I'm Zander. Coin told us to stick around because Papi Loco might be able to help us with a problem."

Loquito doesn't look convinced, but he holds a hand out to shake. "What kind of problem?"

"A missing woman problem," Selene states firmly, giving me a dirty look as she watches me quietly pull my knife from the pocket of my jeans. "Hey, *estúpido*. Stand down unless directed otherwise."

I grumble as I step into my pants, shoving the knife into my pocket again. "You're no fun."

"Oh, I'm sorry. Am I not giving out a happy vibe this morning?" she hisses, causing my dick to twitch behind my zipper.

"Baby, you're giving my dick a happy vibe. Tone down the flirting. We have company," I grin, chuckling as she flips me the bird. Loquito is watching us closely, his eyes darting back to me every so often. He doesn't like me? Well, good, because I don't like him either.

I roll my eyes as Zander starts spilling his guts about why we're here, Selene glaring at me regularly as I keep giving Loquito dirty looks. The moment he turns his back, I'm going to put a bullet in him.

As if knowing my evil plans, Darius sits on the bed and hauls me back, dropping an arm over my middle to get comfortable.

"What's up with you?" he whispers, my eyes dropping to him as he sinks his teeth into my bare peck, pulling a growl from me.

"I don't like being woken up with a gun in my face. Sue me for being sensitive about the matter."

"You are being a little extra for someone who got laid last night," he teases, and I can't fight the grin as it spreads across my face.

"I'd hate to know how pissy she's going to be today. I might fuck her again after lunch and not let her get off," I murmur. Darius is hooting with laughter and drawing attention to us. Blaze is sitting on the couch with a gun in his hand, playing guard dog as usual, but Zander, Selene, and

Loquito all glance over at us with a frown.

I laugh too, only making Selene's annoyance stronger. "What the fuck is so funny?"

"Nothing, babe. Go back to your conversation," Darius chuckles, but she stomps over and smacks me in the back of the head.

"Hey! What was that for?!" I bark, but she leans in close so that her breath fans over my lips.

"You know exactly what that's for, you bastard," she growls, her fist landing against my ribs as I grab her waist and haul her on top of me. I bite her neck sharply, but before I can taunt her some more, Zander snatches her arm and tugs her away from me.

"For fuck's sake. Fuck around later, you two. We have shit to deal with. Loquito was about to show us where to go for breakfast."

Loquito barks out a laugh, his eyes bright and alert as if he's just shoved his face into a bag of cocaine and inhaled the hell out of it.

"Was I now?"

"Yes. You need to tell us about where Papi Loco is," Selene retorts, looking back at me with a scowl. "I'm sure you two can get along over breakfast. You guys are so similar, it's scary."

I snort, glaring at Loquito as I get to my feet, snatching my shirt up and pulling it over my head.

"I'm not sitting near this cunt. Not even for you."

## Darius

I eye Santos as we all sit at the table, one of the women scurrying around and bringing us plates of food. Loquito keeps smirking at him, causing anger to pulse through him in waves, and I won't be surprised if he snaps and lunges over the table at him.

Selene's usual moaning draws my attention as she licks bacon grease from her fingers, Blaze and Zander staring at her like hawks. I don't blame them; our girl makes food feel like a sexual experience.

"So, you want to speak to my dad?" Loquito finally asks, Selene snapping her head his way.

"Yes. Coin claims he'd be the man to speak with," she confirms, surprisingly forgetting about her food as she continues to watch him. You know she's seriously in thought when the food stops being shoveled into her mouth as if she were a Hungry Hippo game. My girl's far from a hippo, but you know what I mean.

"This girl must be important. Where are you guys from?" he questions. "I haven't seen you around, and I think I'd remember you."

Santos' fork bends in his grip, and Blaze snatches it from beside him, slamming it down on the table.

"Act civilized for once in your fucking life, you crazy prick."

Santos' lip lifts in a sneer, but Loquito grins.

"He's fine. We're all a little crazy around here. Besides, I'd stab myself too if I were him. I'm assuming the sexy lady at the table is his woman?" he taunts, and I dig my fingers into Santos' thigh to give him something to focus on. Thankfully, they ignore his jab.

He growls under his breath, but he grabs a buttered roll from the table and shoves it into his mouth like a savage, chewing loudly and earning a dark glare from Blaze.

"Anyway. Tell me about the chick you're looking for. Who is she?" Loquito continues as if Santos isn't about to murder him with the butter knife he's currently eyeing while he chews.

"She's my sister. She was taken a long time ago. I assumed she was dead, but the more I looked, the more I discovered hints that she wasn't. I've basically spent my entire life searching for her," Selene says firmly, but I hear the emotion in her tone that she's trying to hide.

Zander drops an arm over her shoulders, appearing casual, but we know it's to give her comfort discreetly. Loquito's eyes dart over to Santos, seeming surprised that he isn't flipping out. When he doesn't rip his shirt off and Hulk smash the table, Loquito slides his eyes back to Selene and cocks his head.

"And you think Papi Loco had something to do with that?"

I can see her eyes blazing with annoyance, and I know she doesn't trust these MC cunts at all, so I quickly speak to stop the argument before it starts.

"No. We think maybe she's come through in one of the shipments you've helped save. Why do you save them, anyway?" I quiz, his eyes narrowing to slits.

"Why the fuck wouldn't we? We're crazy, not heartless. No woman should be taken and sold like cattle. Most of those women end up beaten and raped until their bodies give out."

"So, you guys don't have strip clubs and hookers?" Santos snaps.

"We do, but they're all employed the old-fashioned way. All the women who get on their back or knees are here because they choose to be. No one's forcing their hand. That's not how we roll," he snorts, looking back at Selene with a softer expression. "If your sister came through here, Dad would know for sure."

"So, where the fuck is he?" Selene grumbles, causing a breath of annoyance to leave Blaze. Loquito isn't bothered, though, and he snatches a buttery roll and takes a bite, grinning at Santos to agitate him some more.

"I left earlier than him. He'll be here soon though, don't stress. If any of you guys need some company, the girls..."

A knife whizzes past his head, slamming into the wall behind him, and he raises an eyebrow at Selene, who's fuming. "Oh, it's like that, is it, *Tormenta Pequeña*?" he teases, but his eyes turn serious as Blaze growls a warning.

When Zander's arm tightens around Selene a little more, Loquito nods.

"Respect. Apologies. I didn't realize you were all spoken for."

"I'm still not sorry for throwing the knife," Selene grunts and shovels bacon into her mouth as if she never stopped.

His eyes light up with amusement, a chuckle leaving him as he leans back in his chair.

"I'd be disappointed if you were."

Selene's right. It's scary how alike this dude is to Santos. From the way he holds himself and speaks, right down to some of his looks. Those crazy eyes? Mirror image of my boy's.

# Selene

There's something about Loquito that doesn't sit right with me. The fucker is shifty, and he makes me want to see how many holes I can poke into him within a minute. I suck the bacon grease off my fingers and moan at the salty goodness. My pussy throbs, threatening to combust over pig meat. So fucking good, though.

Blaze clears his throat and I roll my eyes, knowing it's directed at me without even looking at the fucker.

"I don't like your shifty eyes," I point at Loquito, and he laughs heartily, "and you're clearly a few screws short of a box."

He keeps the smile firmly on his face as he leans on the table. "It's one thing to talk to me like that, I really don't give a shit about how people see me, but do not think you can speak to my father like that. And another word of advice? Don't speak to Henny."

"Henny?"

"That's my pop's old lady." Loquito nods as he scratches his head with the barrel of his gun.

"Why can't we speak to some old woman?" Santos snarls. "We have the best pussy around. We don't want an old one."

"She ain't old, man," Loquito laughs. "That's just what we call our women. She's young, but she's feisty and she won't think twice about clawing your eyes out."

"Whatever," I shrug. "I'm not here for Hen or whoever."

"You're trained. Loqi has the eye." He taps the gun off his temple.

"Loqi?" I snort. "Yes, I'm trained."

"But why?" He stares at me with real curiosity. "Why did you become the Reaper Incarnate?"

The tables fall into an immediate hush, and I see Santos tense in my peripheral.

"Sorry, what?" I crinkle my nose in confusion.

He leans back and chuckles, looking relaxed despite the large men around the table looking ready to pounce on him. "Henry Walton used to provide us with some girls, boys, anything really, and then we heard he was carved up like a Christmas ham. A Reaper's mark left on his body like so many of his associates before him. Not that we'd miss the fuck. Then Mack Delaney let us know he could pull up the slack with this new guy John down here in Nevada. So, we agreed, hunting down skin trades in our own state is easier, and we were up for the challenge."

"Only you didn't succeed," Santos snarks.

"Nope, someone got to John before us, made a real mess too, but no reaper mark on his body. Not like the other bodies found around Vegas."

John is dead? I look at each one of my guys and realize that would've been the only way they found me. I'm fucking pissed that I can't live up to the promise I made to Dempster, but I'm glad it led them to me.

The table stays quiet, and I curse myself for being such a fucking celebrity. It's hard being famous. "Not *all* the Vegas ones were me," I say, and he hoots again as I give Blaze a dark look. I still can't believe the asshole posed as the Reaper Incarnate, the fucking nerve.

"You still haven't answered my question." He leans in again and I see the sharp intelligence in his eyes.

"I know." I lean in as well. "I don't need to explain myself to anyone, *Loqi.*"

"Perc and Vico have a theory," he grins. "They think you were raised by skin traders, being prostituted out and then you snapped. But I just saw your Reaper tattoo this morning and pieced it together."

"Perc and Vico?" Zander snorts. "Pill pushers?"

"Fucking Wonderland," Blaze retorts.

"I raised myself." I shrug and leave it at that.

"I love a mystery." He winks at me.

"Loqi!" We all turn and see Kho and Khaine striding into the dining hall. "Papi is twenty minutes out."

Loqi gets up from the table and taps his knuckles on the wooden top. "I'll let him know you want to speak to him."

I give him a nod and then watch as he walks out of the room with a slow steady swagger, the walk so fucking familiar to me.

"That guy is a fucking noodle dick," Santos snarls, and I turn to look at him.

"Noodle dick?" I grin. "How do you know that? You feel it while you were tussling?"

"Nope," he smirks right back at me, the sexy fucker. "I didn't feel a damn thing, that's why, noodle dick."

Darius snorts as he's drinking and begins to choke as Zander pats his back.

"Bunch of fucking clowns," Blaze mutters, but I can see the slight ghost of a smile on his face.

I don't know why I ever thought leaving them was a good idea. They were made for me, and each in their own way. I finally found a family after Jan, and I almost destroyed it with my denial. I thought I would never find anyone on the same frequency as me and instead I found four. It will take nothing short of an apocalypse to separate us now.

# Chapter Eighteen

## Selene

’m wound so fucking tight and I know if I could just get off, I would feel so much better. I could do it myself, but it’s the damn principle. I have four guys with big ass dicks that should be doing it for me. On top of that, I’m punishing myself just as much as they are. I shouldn’t have run from them. I can’t keep blaming shit on my mommy issues or the fact that my life wasn’t rainbows and roses. I should’ve trusted them.

I’m lying on the bed in the room we’re staying in, waiting for my large breakfast to digest, and trying to forget about the pulsing in my cunt.

“A lot can be accomplished in twenty minutes,” Darius murmurs as he starts to crawl up my body.

I jam my knee up and into his balls, twisting to watch him howl in pain. “I’m not in the mood for more of your games.” I sit up. “I’ve gathered a liking for pussy recently. Maybe I can find a suitable replacement for four limp dicks.”

“Watch it, Reaper,” Blaze growls from his perch on the couch. “Nothing about me is limp. I’ll make you swallow those words.”

Santos is standing over Darius, rubbing his buzzed head but smirking as he continues to moan. “So, you want some clubhouse whore? Their pussies are used like a merry-go-round.”

“I wonder what they name their club whores,” Zander snickers.

“I would name mine *Puss in Boots*,” I say proudly, and all the guys laugh, including Blaze.

I give them all a dirty look and head to the door. "Maybe it'll be a set of twins, Puss and Boots."

They all laugh riotously behind me, and I grab the handle in my hand. Just as I'm about to turn it, I feel a warm body at my back.

"Take your hand off the door, Reaper." Blaze's hand grabs my hair and yanks my head back. "Or don't. Either way, I'm ready to fucking punish you."

"About time, asshole," I growl just before his mouth lands on mine in a punishing kiss.

He drags us both backward towards the bed just as Zander hits my front and begins to lift my shirt. "Naughty, Reaper," he mutters just as his mouth latches around my nipple. The sensation shoots straight down to my sopping wet pussy, making it clench with need.

"If one of you doesn't make me come, I'm stabbing every fucker in this fucking compound," I snarl, and Blaze chuckles as his mouth moves down my neck.

Blaze moves from behind me and shoves me down on the bed, my back bouncing off the plush mattress. I look up and find Darius standing over my head, his cock in his hand. He wears a sly smirk, and I can't help the one I give in response.

"Kiss and make it better," he says as he drags me toward him, making my head hang off the side.

I open my mouth wide and laugh when he hesitates. "Come on, let Mama kiss your boo-boo."

Darius' eyes roll back into his head as I take him into my mouth. My head is at the perfect angle for him to fuck my throat. I feel my pants being pulled off my legs and when I feel the brutality of the mouth between them, I know it's Blaze. I moan around Darius' cock, and he hisses.

"Keep that up, Blaze," he grunts as he tears into my throat.

I feel a set of lips running along my stomach, and judging by how gentle they are, it must be Zander. I begin to feel the tightening in my lower belly, and I grind into Blaze's mouth, trying desperately to find the friction. My pussy clamps and then his mouth is gone, my orgasm ebbing away again. Darius continues fucking my throat and I hear him chuckle when I growl in frustration. He's going to wish he didn't do that.

I relax my throat, and he pushes in further, then I clamp my teeth into his sensitive skin. Not hard enough to draw blood, but hard enough to hurt.

"Fuck!" he squeals, the pitch so high, making me grin around his cock. "Stop!" He tries to pull back, but my teeth are pulling on his velvety skin.

The guys all stop touching me and I continue keeping my teeth clamped to Darius' dick.

"No more," Darius says with panic in his voice. "Get her off."

"How do we do that?" Santos asks. "She'll take your boy with her, Bobbitt style."

"No!" Darius grits out and I chuckle around his softened cock. "Make her fucking come."

"So, we're just going to give in to her now?" Blaze grunts. "You're giving her back all her power because she's lovingly biting your cock?"

"Oh yeah, asshole?" Darius snaps back. "Let's switch spots."

"I'll do it," Santos offers, and I feel him move between my legs. "But it'll be my way, sweetheart."

My heart rate accelerates, and I can feel it thumping at my ribcage. His way means pain and blood. His way means I'm going to come harder than I have in a long time, probably since the last time he cut me open and used my own blood to defile me. His mouth attacks my clit and my own widens in a soundless scream. Darius' cock is released, to his relief. I lean up on my elbows, staring down at Santos as he devours me, and my legs begin to shake. I need this.

"I almost lost it," I can hear Darius sniffle.

"They could sew it back," Zander says absently as he moves closer to where Santos is making a dessert out of my ass and pussy. "Tell me how she tastes."

Santos leans up and I growl at Zander for making him stop, reaching out to fist his shirt. I drag him into me just as I feel the sting on my inner thigh.

"I'm about to add some seasoning," Santos chuckles.

I release Zander, who continues to crawl up onto the bed and begins to suck on my neck, but my eyes stay trained on Santos' fingers as he coats them in blood. Then he's pressing them into my pussy and pulling strange noises from inside me. He pumps them a few times and then pulls them out, smearing through the blood once more. This time, his mouth lands on my clit and those bloodied fingers slip into my ass.

Stars fucking explode, my pussy clamps so fucking tight, and I get a strange sensation throughout my lower belly. I can't stop as it plows over me, and I feel the rush of wetness between my legs. It runs down between my ass cheeks and along the fingers still lodged in my ass. A scream is trapped in my throat, and I can't seem to take in a breath. I collapse to the bed just as I feel Santos lining his cock up to my entrance.

My head is once again pulled down over the side and now it's Blaze standing there, his cock in his hand. His other hand wraps around my extended throat and he bends down into my face.

"You bite my dick, Reaper." His voice making me gasp just as Santos plows inside. "I will cut this fucking throat."

I believe him, nothing Blaze says should be taken lightly, and he always speaks the truth. I can feel Santos grabbing the slice on my thigh as he spreads my legs wider and fucking slams into me over and over. Then Blaze's wide cock is shoving into my mouth and down my throat, hitting deeper with each one of Santos' thrusts. I gag around him and struggle to breathe, the tears slipping from my eyes and dripping from my temples. Then a mouth latches to my clit as Santos is pumping into me and at first, I think it's Darius because of the proximity to Santos' dick, until I hear Zander.

"That does add seasoning." Zander moans and dives back down.

"Come on over here," I hear Santos say. "I've got a place you can put that."

I know he's talking to Darius, and I'm relieved when Blaze comes down my throat, meaning I can watch what's about to happen. Blaze slips out and crawls onto the bed at my side, biting down on my nipple. I lift my head in time to watch Darius step behind Santos and push him forward, making him bend. I gasp when Darius coats his fingers through my blood, then reaches behind Santos, prepping him with it.

"Oh fuck," I moan as I feel myself tighten again.

"You're fucking right, Reaper," Blaze chuckles. "You like watching that?"

I nod as I stare into Santos' face, seeing the moment Darius breaches him, and the mixture of pleasure and pain has me clenching again.

"I'm gonna come again," I pant and fall back to the bed.

I can feel the erratic rhythm of Santos inside me and know it has everything to do with Darius being inside *him*. The thought pushes me over the edge just as I feel Zander nudging my mouth open. I open on a scream as my pussy clamps around Santos, but the sound is cut off as I'm stuffed with Zander's cock.

## Santos

Holy fucking shit. This is way better than I thought it would be.

I plow into our girl harder as Darius pushes himself to the hilt in my ass, almost causing me to blow my fucking load instantly. No wonder Selene loves this shit.

I have no choice but to slow down for a moment, not wanting it to end so damn fast, but Darius is driving my senses into overload as he keeps a steady pace, my body clenching around him with every stroke. Fairly sure I died because nothing has ever felt so good before, and I'm definitely in Heaven. Better make the most of it, because the moment God realizes I'm at his big shiny gates, he's going to throw my ass back down to hell where I belong.

*Look out, Satan, I'm on my way.*

Darius grips my hip, kneading my flesh with his large hand, and lets out a guttural groan I've never heard before, drawing a similar sound out of Selene. I don't realize I've stopped moving until Darius swats my ass sharply, reaching around to grab my throat firmly.

"Move, or I'll have to fuck you so hard, I'll be fucking you into her too," he warns, my lips kicking up into a smirk.

"Don't threaten me with a good time. Are you trying to make me bust already?" I tease, but his eyes darken as I peer over my shoulder, his voice low.

"You asked for it."

I hardly have time to brace myself with Selene's hips before Darius picks up the pace, fucking me with so much force that he throws my body forward into Selene, a gasp leaving her in surprise.

Zander chuckles while pulling his dick out of her mouth, then dives to claim her lips with his, swallowing her sounds as Darius continues to rail into me hard and fast, my balls becoming tight as he repetitively keeps hitting the right spot, and Selene's pussy gripping my dick like a vice.

I glance down to see the blood mixed with Selene's juices, my dick getting even harder if that's possible, and my fingers are digging into her slender waist so hard that I know for a fact it will bruise. I love seeing my marks all over her pretty skin, and I can't help but pull one of her legs up higher to bite her calf muscle firmly, watching her reaction.

No girl has ever reacted like Selene does, and knowing she's willing to take everything I've got to give makes my dick hard every time I think about it. I know I can always rely on Darius to make me feel good, but having Selene too? I'm the luckiest asshole alive.

I manage to get some sort of control over myself and start thrusting of my own accord, clenching my teeth, and trying hard to hold off on my release as Darius reaches around to cup my balls, rolling them firmly in his hand with a small bite of pain, causing my breath to become short and sharp.

"You don't get to come until she does," Darius orders, making me growl.

"Then maybe stop making it feel so fucking good, holy fuck," I hiss as he slows down to deep, slow strokes, giving me a second to recover. Blaze snorts but keeps his eyes on Selene as Zander kneels over her face, giving me a grin.

"I need lube."

Darius slows almost to a stop, most likely giving him the same look that I am. Zander isn't usually one to play our type of games, but the look in his eyes says otherwise.

"You want me to make some lube for you?" I ask darkly, groaning when he nods.

"Yep. I want to slide my dick between these beautiful tits," he answers. No sooner are the words out of his mouth, he's jumping almost right off the fucking bed, and Selene lets out a tired giggle.

"Stick your asshole in my face and expect me to lick it, big boy. You're lucky it wasn't a finger," she snickers.

"*You're* lucky it wasn't a finger," he snaps, giving me a look to hurry the fuck up. I quickly place another cut on her thigh close to the first one and squeeze around it, drawing more blood from below the surface as I rub my hands in it. I reach out to run one hand down the center of Selene's chest, leaving the sticky blood behind for Zander to use.

I press my hands on her stomach lightly, mesmerized by how pretty the bloodied prints look against her skin. She's mine. Ours. She was fucking made for us, and I must have done something good in a past life to deserve her.

Zander pushes her tits together, sliding between them with a groan and he watches himself fuck them slowly.

He's gritting his teeth and suddenly inhaling sharply. "Selene."

"It's just a tongue, you big baby," she mumbles, making a choking sound as he leans back to attempt to suffocate her with his balls.

"Fuck!" he barks and falls forward so far that if my dick weren't buried in our girl, it would have ended up down the back of his throat. "She stuck her finger in my ass!"

"I'm going to stick my dick in you in a minute if you come any closer," I chuckle. Annoyance takes over his face as he leans back to glare at me.

"Try it, fuckface."

"That's Captain fuckface to you, peasant," I throw back, groaning as Darius slaps my ass harder than last time.

"Would you both shut the fuck up? It's just a finger, Zan. Lean back and let her blow your mind," he exclaims, thrusting firmly into me and making me hiss out a breath. My ass is getting tender, but I don't want him to stop. My boy knows I like it when it hurts.

I start fucking Selene like it's the last time I'll get to feel the warmth of her pussy, a strangled scream coming from her as she's muffled by Zander's balls, my fingers snaking between us to rub her clit furiously, pulling an orgasm from her out of nowhere.

The moment her body clenches around mine, Darius grips the back of my neck and fucks into me as deep as he can go, pushing me over the edge. I come so fucking hard that black spots dance in front of my eyes, and my body jerks as Darius keeps going without breaking pace.

"Jesus fucking Christ, man. Stop!" I force out as my fingers fist the bedding below us, my body pulsing even more as his dick draws out my release until I'm a pile of fucking jelly. He ignores me for a few more seconds before growling and burying deep, going still as he sinks his load inside me.

Selene's a panting mess, and she must be tired after that, because she leaves Zander's ass alone.

Once Darius and I collapse, Zander grins and moves so he can flip her onto her knees, having no choice but to hold her up as her arms and legs shake. I raise an eyebrow as I watch him cup her pussy, catching my cum and dragging it up to her ass, not hesitating before sliding his dick into the hilt.

It doesn't take him long to finish, and Selene's a sobbing mess by the time we all sprawl out to catch our breaths. Next time, I'm shoving my dick in Darius and giving that man the ride of his life. Holy fuck.

## *Darius*

I have no idea why Santos decided today was the day he wanted me to fuck him, but I wasn't going to fight him on it. I've always wondered what his ass would feel like around my dick, and it didn't disappoint.

Selene's curled up between Daddy Blaze and Zander, Blaze murmuring threats into her ear and making her swoon like the pain junkie she is, while Santos happily snuggles into me, a light laugh leaving him as I drop an arm over his sweaty stomach.

"Fuck, D. My ass is pulsing like you're still inside me."

"Feel good?" I mumble with a smile, his abs tensing as my fingers move over the ridges, my dick stirring at knowing he enjoyed that as much as I did. I'm surprised it has any life left after that bomb-ass sex.

I don't think before grabbing his chin firmly and tilting his face up, dropping a lazy kiss on his lips and biting firmly into the plump flesh, a desperate groan leaving him instantly. One of his hands trails up my bare chest, his hand resting against my throat and tightening the smallest amount.

I hear Selene mumble something about us making her pussy wake up again, but I keep my attention on Santos, knowing he needs a second for me to center him. We shared a lot more than just sex, and I know it's the start of something more.

I'll need more than blow jobs from him from now on because holy fuck, that was hot.

He pulls back and peers down at me, a cheeky grin on his face.

"You do know your ass is mine next time, right? I'm going to fuck you so hard I'll come in your throat."

"God, I hope so," I grin back, but Blaze gives us a dirty look as he props himself up on his elbow.

"If you two don't shut the fuck up, I'll fuck the pair of you so hard, you'll both snap into two pieces."

"Ooh, Daddy Blaze is mad," I chuckle, but Santos lets out a loud groan.

"You'd make it hurt so good, too. Spread my cheeks and spit in my ass first, though, okay? I like to work up to the burn."

Blaze snarls and grabs a pillow, hitting Santos firmly in the face, but he just cackles in response. "A naked pillow fight? You naughty boy! How'd you know that was one of my kinks?"

"Would you fuckers knock it off?" Selene grumbles, her face presses into Zander's neck as she tries to snuggle into him more to escape our banter. Zander pulls her on top of him, wrapping his arms around her and not giving a shit that our cum is probably leaking out of her and onto his skin.

"Yeah, guys. Shut up so we can nap," he states, his fingers drawing patterns on her bare back and capturing my attention. Her skin is covered in dried blood, and the moment my dick springs to life, Blaze attacks me with the pillow, too.

"No more playtime, you fucking heathen. Give it a rest already before one of us dies from a fucking heart attack," he snaps, but I snatch the pillow and give him a smirk.

"You don't think that hot little pussy is worth dying over? Dude, totally fucking worth it. Wanna go again, Selene?"

She moans, reaching a hand out to rest on Santos' chest.

"I can't move."

"You don't have to move, baby. I'll do all the work," I half joke, knowing if she says yes, I'll take her again. Santos mumbles his agreement, but he doesn't move either, giving me a nice big ego boost. It takes a lot to tire him out, and I seem to have succeeded. It's like unlocking an achievement on the Xbox. I'm cool as fuck.

I reach over Santos to run my hand over Selene's ass, but Zander slaps me away with a grunt.

"Leave her alone. She needs to rest, and we should probably feed her before she's hangry."

"I'll fucking feed her this monster cock in a second," Santos mumbles, but he's half asleep on the pillow. I laugh, poking him in the ribs with my finger.

"You're going to force feed her daddy's dick? Kind of you."

"Don't fuck with me. You know I should really have a license for this weapon of cunt destruction," he chuckles, peeking at me and winking.

Well, I'm pretty sure it's a wink. Hard to tell when half his face is in the pillow.

"Sure you do. Better get that sorted right away before someone arrests you," I deadpan, his eyes closing as he smirks.

"The only fucker alive who I'll let cuff me is right here, thank you," he murmurs as he falls asleep, and Blaze rolls his eyes at me as I grin. I'd be totally down for that.

## *Zander*

I didn't realize how badly I needed a nap until I woke up hours later to find Blaze snoring beside me. Everyone else is missing. I sit up and rub my eyes, glancing around the room to find the bathroom door open and laughter coming from inside.

I swing my legs out of bed and pad towards it, pushing the door open more to step inside. I find Selene sandwiched between Santos and Darius in the shower as they wash the blood and cum from her skin. I lift the toilet seat and take a piss, glancing over my shoulder to sneak a peek at Selene. She is fucking stunning.

She raises an eyebrow when she catches me staring, her body arching into Santos as he dips down to suck a nipple into his mouth.

"If you piss on the floor, I'll rub your fucking nose in it. Do you want to come and join us?"

"I'm not a bad dog," I scowl. "And I think I've played with you three enough for a few hours." I can't believe I used her blood as titty lube. The way Santos and Darius play has always made me scrunch my nose up. It's not my thing, but fuck, I was horny as hell watching them at work earlier. I knew I'd pussy out if I didn't just jump straight into it; I asked Santos to cut her for me before I could think about it any longer.

It felt kind of weird, the blood being warm and sticky unlike the lube I usually use, but my dick was more than happy to jump right into it, even with the sneaky wench prodding and licking at my ass. Won't lie, kind of felt good. I really have to stop spending so much time with Santos. His crazy must be rubbing off on me.

"You saying you've had enough of me, Zan?" she pouts, making me snort.

"No. If you want me to fuck you, I'll fuck you, but those two clowns can go find something else to do. There's only so much crazy I can handle in a day, and I'm at capacity."

I finish my piss and lean back against the sink, crossing my arms to watch them. Selene winces as Darius' fingers slip between her legs, her body tender from the pounding it took earlier, but she still leans into his touch like she can't get enough. No matter how bad it hurts, she won't run because our little hellcat craves the pain.

Surprisingly though, Darius doesn't shove his fingers inside her like I thought he would. He simply moves his fingers across her skin, washing away the evidence of our fun. Santos does the same with her breasts, grumbling about having to wash away his mark from her skin.

Big softies.

Blaze finally stumbles in, barks at everyone to hurry the fuck up, then he climbs in the shower the moment it's vacated. Grumpy piece of shit.

I don't bother to speak as I step into the shower too, ignoring the death glare from him.

"What the fuck are you doing?" he demands as he scrubs soap all over his chest.

"I smell and look like a fucking crime scene. We share a girlfriend. I'm pretty sure we can share a fucking shower without grabbing each other's dicks. You're not my type anyway," I reply, his face twisting into a scary smile.

"You're exactly my type. I do love having little bitches on my dick."

He scares me so much more when he's making jokes. Freaky asshole.

# Chapter Nineteen

## Selene

I slip on my boots and pull the brush through my hair a few times. "I'm starving," I moan. "I'm about to become a cannibal. Darius gave me a taste for human flesh."

He grabs his junk through his pants and pales. "We never speak of that again."

I throw my head back and cackle as Santos snickers. "She almost made a lifelike dildo out of you."

Darius continues to growl as I open the door. "Let Blaze and Zander suck each other off. I can't wait anymore. I'm starving."

"Papi Loco should be back by now," Santos says as he and Darius follow me out the door. "But we should wait for Blaze and Zander before we talk to him."

"Agreed." Darius nods as his arm lands around my shoulders, hauling me into his body. "You wouldn't *really* hurt my love stick. Right, baby?"

"In a heartbeat," I tell him. "You put it anywhere near another girl and I'll have it off and down your throat. You ever hold back orgasms from me again. I'll cut it off and shove it up your ass."

"Babe…" he sputters as Santos hoots.

"I wouldn't laugh, dipshit," I sneer at Santos. "You'll be chewing on your balls if you ever torture me like that again."

He swallows hard and nods. "Got it. But keep in mind, I will bleed you dry if you ever decide to run from me again."

"Deal." I smirk and we continue on our way to the front.

The place is filled more than it was earlier and way more than the night before. Looks like the full club is back home, and I look around at the unfamiliar faces.

"Reaper!" I hear Loqi call out and I turn toward the sound with a groan. "Hungry?"

"He knows the magic word!" Darius says, and I snort.

Perc and Vico are sitting with Loqi, and I gather they are his men, while the others are Papi's. Just an observation but I would put money on it, but not my next meal because I'm about to kill someone if I don't get fed soon. The three of us approach their table and when Loqi raises his hand, three chairs are added. I sit in the one directly across from him while Santos sits on my right and Darius on my left.

"Where are the other two?" Loqi asks with a grin.

"Showering my blood off themselves," I lean across as his smile grows larger, "together."

He tips his head back and his black curly hair flops with it as he laughs. "I think you should stay here with us. What do you need so badly in New York?"

Santos' fist hits the table, and he bares his teeth with a growl. He sounds like a fucking Pitbull. "Watch it."

Loqi's hands go up, but the smile on his face grows. He likes fucking with my boys and pushing their buttons; I need to be the one that puts a stop to it. He places both hands on the table and leans forward, seemingly to say something to me, but I don't give him the chance. I grab his wrist and my knife is embedded into the wood between his fingers, nicking his skin along the way. Perc and Vico stand as do Darius and Santos, but Loqi raises his other hand, halting his men's movements.

"Listen Loqi," I get right up into his face, "I've been respectful, and my boys have been taking your shit in stride, but it stops now. Don't fucking push me any fucking further because I don't give a fuck who your daddy is. I'll gladly die after sawing your fucking head off."

He pauses and takes a good look in my eyes, his widening a fraction with what he sees. I know I'm unhinged and now he does too.

"I hear you," he nods slowly, "loud and clear."

I sit back in my chair, taking my knife with me, and with my eyes still trained on him, I lick his blood from my blade. Actually, maybe unhinged doesn't cover it, but I don't think I need to reiterate a single thing. He's got the picture now. So do his men, by the apprehensive look in their eyes. Finally, a girl gets the respect she deserves.

"Now, did you say food? Because I wouldn't lie about that either."

"Yes." He stands up from his chair. "Out back, we have a grill going. Hamburgers, dogs, and shrimp." We get up and follow him out the back door. "Grab a beer." He points to a cooler. Darius and Santos do just that, but I want to keep my wits about me.

We grab some burgers and hotdogs, and then we follow Loqi to an empty picnic bench. I'm surprised his boys let him leave with us without them, but he looks at ease. I guess he should since the twenty plus men outside wouldn't hesitate to shoot our heads off.

"My dad's just resting right now. It was a long ride, and he's old as fuck," Loqi says as he takes a swig of his beer. "Soon he'll need me to take over."

"Watch your mouth," an older biker says from the table to our left. He's a mean motherfucker with a patch over his eye, and a long gray beard to match his long gray hair. "Papi would still bend you over his knee, boy."

"Yeah, yeah," Loqi waves him off, "that's Hook."

Santos chokes on his beer and stands up abruptly. "Do you speak pirate?" he calls out and when Hook gives him an odd look, Darius hauls him back down to his seat.

"Have you lost it completely?" Darius chuckles and Santos glowers at the old man.

"Fucking scallywag," he mutters and gulps down his beer.

I begin to laugh and Loqi joins in just as Blaze and Zander wander outside, clearly looking for us. I watch as they're ushered over for food and when their plates are full, I raise my hand. They make their way over and sit down, digging into their food.

"Did you have a nice shower together?" Loqi asks sweetly, and Blaze chokes on his food.

"It was nice, thank you," Zander says before he bites into his burger. I snort and Blaze cuts me a look of death. Sexy motherfucker.

"Where's the old man we need to talk to?" Blaze asks around a mouth of meat.

"See?" Loqi calls out to Hook. "They haven't even met him, and they know he's an old man."

"Probably from the shit you're spewing," Hook retorts.

"Papi is resting, apparently," I answer, doubt lacing my words.

I watch as a couple of guys begin throwing knives. The target is on the side of the building they threw me into when we got here. I watch closely and snort when one completely misses the target.

"They're going to kill someone," I jut my chin toward them.

"Those are our prospects." Loqi smiles wide. "Maybe they need someone to show them how it's done." I know what he's insinuating, and I ignore him while I bite into my burger.

"Scout and Chance!" Loqi calls out. "We have a treat for you today."

"Are those real names?" Zander asks, looking shocked.

"Nope, those are the names we give every prospect. We take two at a time and when we recruit them, Papi changes their name."

"I see." Zander nods as Chance and Scout approach.

"Guys, I have a real treat for you today." Loqi rubs his hands together.

"No, you don't." I shake my head.

"Oh, come on, one shot at the target. Unless you're afraid you'll miss it?" Loqi sneers, and I know what he's doing, trying to call me out like I'm an insecure man.

I bite the bait anyway. "Fine, but you're the target." I stand up and pull my knife from the belt around my waist.

"What?" He gets a mischievous look in his eye. "You want to kill me?"

"Yes," I deadpan and then point to the bowl of tomatoes and onions. "But I'll settle for throwing a knife at the vegetable on your head." He lifts a brow and I chuckle. "Unless you're scared."

A few of the guys sitting at the tables laugh and Santos snorts, "I wouldn't mind seeing that hilt sticking out of an eye socket."

My guys laugh at that and Loqi stands from his seat. "Fine." He walks over to the table with the bowl of veggies and grabs an onion.

"*Oh, come on,*" I mimic him. "Grab the tomato, make it lifelike."

Again, snickers circle the lot, and I can see a light blush stain his cheeks. I fucking bask in his embarrassment. He stands in front of the target with the tomato on his head and a taunting grin.

"Okay, Reaper—" he's cut off by the whir of my knife as it flies through the air, into the tomato, and slams into the center of the target, the tomato completely splattered on the wood like blood. Loqi hasn't moved, and the lot falls completely quiet.

"Chance," I say without looking at either of the prospects. "Grab me my knife."

One prospect runs to the knife embedded in the wood as Loqi finally blinks free of his shock. The lot begins to pick up, but I now have the attention of a few older men. Their curiosities make my stomach tighten; this is what I wanted to avoid. I don't want any interest lingering on me, because once I find out what happened to Jan, I'm out of here. I won't be taking on any Reaper jobs for any of them because that's what I'm expecting with their interest.

"Who trained you?" he asks.

"You wouldn't know him if I told you, but I mostly trained myself. Long hours practicing and daydreaming about my blade sinking into the people I wanted to kill."

"It's going to be hard to let such an asset go," he murmurs, and it's honestly something I suspected would happen as soon as they found out who I was.

"I'm not your asset."

"But you could be." He nods as he guides me back to the table. "We need help. Skin trafficking here is at an all-time high, and assholes keep encroaching on our turf, selling their product." He looks to my guys for backup, but each one of their faces stays blank. They would never agree to something without me.

"Look," I say as I lean on the table with both hands. "The skin trade is on the rise everywhere. I'm needed back home." The prospect comes back and hands me my knife, the blade red with tomato juice. "I wouldn't mind helping you guys if you actually helped me as well. Which you haven't yet. I was picked up like cattle and dragged into this compound. From the second I asked for my sister, you've been putting me off from talking to the one man who can apparently help me. Bad business."

He lets out an exasperated breath and scrubs his hand down his face. "What if we don't know where your sister is? What if she never came through here?"

"Then I'll be on my way to follow other leads. But I need to find out either way."

"What about if we paid you well for your services?" He begins grasping at straws.

"We don't need money," Money-bags Zander retorts and when a few of us snicker, he raises a brow. "What? We don't."

"You heard him." I thumb at Zander. "We don't do this for profit, we do it to save people. If we made money from saving skin, then that would make us no better than the cunts who sell it."

The place falls quiet again, and Loqi scratches at his head. "My sister was taken as well," he begins, and I sit down for what will be his final sell. "She was twelve, and we searched everywhere for her, but we failed. We never found her."

"How long ago was that?" I ask him.

"Seven years."

"With all due respect," I lean across the table. "Mine has been missing a lot longer than that. I need to find my sister, my flesh and blood, before I help anyone else find theirs. Now, I'm sure you understand, seeing as your own sister is missing."

"Okay, I hear you," he exhales and stands. "Let's go talk to Papi and figure this all out."

"Thank you." I nod and stand to follow him. I feel the guys at my back, and I feel safe with them being so close. I chastise myself again for attempting to do this without them.

We're led through the main room. They had the party in last night and Darius whistles when we see the mess. "Is that a used condom?" He points to what is definitely a condom, used or not, laying across a couch cushion.

"Yeah." Loqi chuckles. "Never sit on those couches. The old men had them before us and they've been cum soaked for years."

"Charming," I mutter, and Zander laughs as his arm snakes around my neck.

"Like you were earlier," he whispers in my ear.

"Watch it," I warn him, but I can't keep the smile off my face. "Or I'll start talking about your daddy's big dick." He drops his arm with a grumble and Loqi turns to give us a questioning look. "I fucked his daddy first," I explain with a wink. He gives me an answering chuckle and continues to lead us down a narrow hallway.

"Stop telling people you fucked my dad," Zander mutters.

"Next time you talk shit, I'll tell them you both fucked me together."

Santos roars behind me, and Darius joins in. "You just did, baby," Darius says between chuckles.

"I guess I did." I wink again as Loqi looks between me and Zander. "I was the ham in that fat, juicy club sandwich."

"Oh my god," Zander moans and covers his eyes with his hand. "Stop talking."

"Tons of mayo in that sandwich," Blaze pipes up, and I look back at him in shock. He rarely joins in our fun, but I can see he likes torturing Zander.

"On both buns," I snicker, and we both chuckle.

"Fuck you both," Zander moans and motions to Loqi to continue. "Let's get this over with."

"You're fucking freaky up there in New York," he whistles. "I wouldn't mind a ham sandwich with Henny if dad would let it." He shakes his head and leads us to a set of couches. "Chill here, I'll call him and see if he's done with his … uh … meeting."

"I'm not sitting on any of your couches." I shake my head, and he laughs.

"No one is allowed back here, much less get a chance to fuck on them. Papi would slit throats." Loqi motions for us to sit. "I'll be back." He disappears behind a door that has a large golden plaque reading, 'Vice President.'

We sit and Darius gets a naughty look on his face as he pulls me onto his lap. "Let's see if he can slit five throats, though." My knees land on either side of his thighs and I ground down onto his hard cock.

Arms come around my waist and I'm lifted off, then settled on another lap. I turn to look over my shoulder and find a dark set of brown eyes looking at me, irritated. "Sorry, Daddy." I lean in and kiss the scar on the side of Blaze's face. "You know my weakness is cock."

His hand locks around my throat and I'm hauled back against his shoulder. "I do know that, but ours will be the only cocks you'll have for the rest of your life, hooker. Understand? No more albinos or other hookers."

"Aniyah!" I exclaim and sit up in his lap.

"Yeah, that bitch," he grumbles.

"No!" I swat at his chest. "I'm supposed to find out about Aniyah today too. I'm a terrible friend. I got cock-stracted."

"Cock *what*?" Zander asks.

"Distracted by cock," I moan. "We need to find out where Aniyah is."

"Fuck her," Blaze grumbles, and I swat him again. "She doesn't join us."

"She wouldn't want to." I roll my eyes. "But I still need to make sure she's okay."

Finally, Loqi comes out of his office, and I stand to face him. "Where's Aniyah?"

He cocks his head and looks confused.

"One of the girls I was snatched with, she was really sick when we got here, but I haven't seen her yet."

"Oh, the girl with the purple hair?"

"Yes!" I nod.

"She's back and in Medical, she had an overnight stay at the clinic, she was pretty dehydrated. But she's okay now."

My shoulders deflate and I feel immense relief. "Thank you."

"No problem, we're not monsters." He grins and leads us to a door with an identical plaque to the one on his, only this one says 'President'. "He's ready for you now." Loqi opens the door, and we find who I would assume is Papi standing between a set of bare legs. The chick is engulfed by his size as she sits in front of him on the table. Even from the back, he's large and wide, stacked with muscle. "Man," Loqi whines. "You said you were done."

"We are done," Papi answers. His voice is so deep, and he has a bit of a Mexican accent. "I'm just saying bye to my woman."

His *woman* swats him on the arm, and I see her small delicate hand. It's adorned with rings.

"Shut up," she says, and the sound of her voice has my brows crashing together. Then I see her head pop out from the side of his body and I'm stunned in place. Pale blonde hair, bordering on white, pale white skin, and a dusting of freckles meet the hair line. My finger touches the few I have on my nose and remember I used to call them fairy kisses. Jan told me they were fairy kisses.

"Hey." Her voice calls out to us, and my feet are stuck solid to the ground. I can't move. Her eyes are a dark shade of blue, looking nearly black, and she still has a ring in her left nostril. "I'll just get out of your hair." She smiles, her plush mouth widening with the motion and her straight, white teeth fucking sparkling. Papi doesn't let her move, and she giggles while she swats his chest.

"Wait, a minute …" Blaze says as we all listen to her giggle, and then his eyes land on mine.

I nod. "Jan," I say loud and clear into the room, and I hear her gasp. Her face appears again, and she pushes Papi aside. Everyone is watching as she hops off the table and stands in front of me. She's trembling and her hands land on her cheeks.

"It can't be." Her voice shakes as much as her body.

"I was told you were taken and possibly sold as a sex slave," I can hear the disdain in my own voice, "but clearly that wasn't the case. You built yourself a nice life here, humping the president of a biker gang, no less."

"Selene?"

"Were you hit over the head or something when they grabbed you? You sound slow now," I snap. "Of course, it's Selene, the sister you left behind."

"I didn't leave you behind." She steps forward. "I couldn't ever do that to you."

My hand snaps to the handle of my blade. "Don't come any closer or I'll fucking gut you."

"What?" Her eyes round and I hear a gun getting cocked in my direction. "No, Papi." She puts her hand out. "Put it away." He listens to her and then she continues, "I was sold to a man named Henry Walton by our mother. She was apparently offering him sexual favors for drugs and when he came by our apartment, we were there. He wanted you, but I refused and offered myself instead."

"So, you left me with her?" I snarl and watch as fat tears roll down her cheeks.

"Yes," she moans. "I thought I could break free and come back for you. But I couldn't and before I knew it, I was on my way to Nevada.

I was sold around, and it was years before I was rescued by Papi and his MC." She looks at him fondly and then back to me. "I told him about my little sister, and he helped me come back to New York to find you. But when I went back to the apartment, it was empty, trashed, and blood was all over the couch."

"That's where I threw a knife into our mother's head," I growl, and her eyes widen.

"I was told the place was robbed and everyone inside was killed," she continues to cry, but it does nothing to soothe my anger. She was okay here and living her life while I struggled on my own. She was having the time of her life fucking the president of the MC while I was killing men, looking for her. While I risked my life, time and time again, she was safe here in Nevada.

I turn my back on her and stride out of the room. I can't even look at her right now.

"Wait! Selene!" She chases me into the hallway. "Please, I was told you were dead!"

"I was told you were probably dead too!" I scream and my voice echoes throughout the small space. I can see my guys standing behind her and then Papi and Loqi behind them, watching us and knowing not to interfere. "I was told this entire mission of finding you would be a waste of my time! But I did it anyway!" I take a deep breath, "Because if there was even the slightest chance that you were alive, I was willing to risk my life to find you!"

She drops to her knees and places her hands in a prayer position. "Please forgive me for not trying harder."

I turn my back on her and everyone else. I don't want to be here. I storm off back the way we came, and I hear Zander's voice behind me.

"I'll take care of her."

## Santos

I'm staring at the man they call Papi, and I can't seem to focus on anything else. I barely notice when Selene takes off with the biker bitch hot on her heels, or when Zander declares he'll take care of her. Everything else fades away as pain mixed with hope fills my chest.

No one seems to realize my silence, not that I'm surprised. Blaze lets out an impatient growl, giving us the side eye. "I'll go find them and make sure she doesn't kill the cunt."

"Watch your mouth, boy," Papi warns with a vicious growl, his attention on Blaze, allowing me more time to process my thoughts. I study him and Loqi while Blaze argues with the old bastard, the two of them nose to nose, until Papi pulls a gun out and aims it at Blaze's head.

Blaze grins manically, but Loqi is the one who steps between them.

"Papi, stand down. Let him chase his girl."

"Why should I give a fuck about his whore?" Papi grits out, the grin slipping from Blaze's face, but Loqi continues.

"Why should they care about your girl? Just let the fucker go chase her down and we can all talk later. Now's obviously not a good time."

After a second of grumbling, Papi flicks his wrist towards the door, dismissing Blaze like a dog, and Blaze instantly takes the chance to leave and make sure Zander has everything under control. I hope he does, or we could end up in a rain of bullets trying to fight our way out if Selene snaps like I think she might.

Darius finally notices my silence, glancing over and brushing his hand across mine.

"Hey, you good?"

I keep staring at Papi until I can't take it any longer.

"Papi?" My voice is barely there, but the bastard looks at me with a scowl as if I yelled it.

"What? I have better things to do than stand around here jerking each other off," he barks, my eyes darting to Loqi for a second, his eyes a mirror of mine. I turn back to Papi, my voice stronger.

"Dad."

Darius curses under his breath, Loqi's eyebrows basically fly

325

off his fucking face with how high they go, and Papi stares at me with confusion. His eyes flicker between Loqi and me, his brow creasing as he thinks.

"There's no way."

"I was a fucking kid when you left. Why the fuck did you leave?" I grit out, resentment filling my veins like poison. I am allowed to feel resentful, and it doesn't seem like he's all that happy to see me either.

Loqi is tense like me, and the moment Papi moves closer to inspect me more, I step back with a sneer. I always wondered what had happened to the man who abandoned me, but I guess it's easy to see why he did. He obviously had another family and another fucking son to raise.

"Santos?" he finally murmurs, my heart cracking a fraction before I can block it out. Would I have turned out a different man if he'd stuck around? I eye Loqi and hold back a snort. Obviously not. Loqi has a lot of similarities to me, particularly his violent streak and his smart mouth.

"San?" Darius says softly, taking my hand and giving it a squeeze. "You wanna go?"

I am stuck between wanting to hug Papi and kill the bastard. Papi's eyes drop to our hands, but I don't pull back. If he has a problem with it, I'll gun him down where he fucking stands, not giving a shit about the consequences.

"My boy!" Papi exclaims, a big grin taking over his face as he suddenly embraces me in a hug, weakening the walls I've built around my heart even more. I stand there stunned for a moment, before my arm goes around him and I hug him back, not letting Darius go.

Loqi is frozen like stone, confusion filling his gaze as he watches us, and I have no idea what he's thinking. Something weird tugs inside me as I realize I have a brother. A brother I want to murder every time his eyes run over my baby girl. Blood doesn't make him family, not yet. Selene comes first in every aspect.

"Look at you! So grown up!" Papi states happily as he steps back, glancing at Loqi with excitement. "Loqi! This is your brother, Santos!"

"We've met," he grunts, still not jumping on board with the family reunion. I don't blame him; I don't particularly give two shits about him right now, either. Papi inspects Darius next, noticing my hand tightening around him at his scrutiny.

"The fuck's this?" he asks, disgust rolling off him. Darius goes to speak, but I cut him off bluntly, my voice sharp.

"Touch him and I'll kill you. He's mine."

The ghost of a smile plays on Darius' lips, and Papi snorts.

"You can try, boy. Thought you were with the crazy chick? Real men don't like a dick in their ass."

"Real men love whoever the fuck they want," I grit out, his eyes filling with amusement as I continue. "They're both mine."

"I see. How's your Ma?"

"None of your business," I bark, his eyes narrowing.

"Don't use that fucking tone with me. I was just asking."

"Well, don't. How about we talk about Jan? Or the fact that you never came back for me?" I demand, his face scrunching as if in pain.

"Your ma made it clear that I was to stay away from you after I left. She didn't want some good-for-nothing asshole near her kid. If I was leaving, she didn't want me to come back. Henny is none of your business either," he mutters, making me snort.

"We came here expecting to find *Henny* hurt or dead. Is she really here of her own free will? Is this saving women mission some bullshit front to get away with other shit? I don't believe that you found it in your heart to save women after you abandoned yours."

He snarls and gets in my space, anger pulsing through him in waves.

"Watch it. You don't get to disrespect me in my fucking territory. You've seen the women around here, and they're fucking fine. I might be the biggest bastard alive in your eyes, but I'm not. I do what I can to help those women because they don't deserve to have their lives stripped away by a heavy hand. They don't deserve to be scared and used until they have nothing left. I'll kill any man in cold blood, but never a fucking woman," he spits, his teeth grinding at my accusation.

I know he's right, and at the end of the day I honestly have no idea who the man in front of me is, but that's on him for leaving me.

# *Darius*

Santos is going to explode and massacre everyone soon; I can sense it. Watching his stand-off with his father isn't something I had scheduled on the fucking calendar this month, that's for sure.

Loqi looks just as fucked up as Santos right now. Not that I blame him. This conversation took a turn that none of us expected, and now all I care about is making sure we get out alive and Santos doesn't start stabbing anyone. Killing the Pres. might not be a good idea, just saying.

I tug Santos back a step, allowing him more room to breathe. He doesn't cope well with being backed into a corner, believe it or not. He's tense, and I want to kiss the tightness from his jaw before he breaks a tooth, but I don't think now is a good time to show him affection. I don't feel like a punch in the guts.

"Nice piece of ass you got. Where'd you find her?" Papi smirks, knowing he's pushing buttons. I'll kill him before I let Santos do it, because that split decision would haunt him for the rest of his life.

"She's not a piece of ass," I bite out, Papi raising an eyebrow as he turns to me.

"Oh, you speak. Was starting to think you were mute." Asshole.

My hand rests lightly on Santos' lower back to calm him, my fingers creeping up under his shirt a little to soothe him. I hate not knowing what's going on inside his head right now, but either way, he's either murderous or hurting. I don't like that.

"This shit between you two has nothing to do with me, but our girl does. Don't disrespect her," I answer, focusing on the feel of Santos' skin under my fingertips. He can talk shit about me all he likes, but not Selene.

I turn to Loqi with a scowl. "You honestly knew nothing about this?"

"I didn't know he fucking existed," Loqi glares back, causing Santos to tense even more. Great, now I've made it worse.

Santos laughs dryly, shaking his head slightly as the bitterness leaks into his tone.

"Why am I not surprised? Of course, you never mentioned me. I was the kid you didn't want. Were you having an affair behind Ma's back? Knocked some bitch up and figured that kid meant more to you? He looks like he's my age, which means you were with Ma when he was created."

"It's not like that," Papi growls, but I'm quite sure he's full of shit by the way Loqi flinches. It's not obvious, but I see the slight jerk of his hand. This conversation is going nowhere good, that's obvious.

"Then why the fuck didn't either of us know about the other? Why did you keep us a fucking dirty little secret?" Santos hisses, but he leans back against my touch, my fingers pressing more firmly into his skin.

"It's my dick, I'll stick it where I want," Papi smirks cruelly, confirming he was full of shit a second ago. He cheated on Santos' mother, and he doesn't give a shit about the outcome.

Santos' fists clench by his side, and I reach up to grab his jaw in my hand, forcing him to look at me. He looks ready to punch me, but it wouldn't be the first time.

"He's not worth it," I say gently, his jaw loosening a little as his eyes soften. He stares at me for what seems like hours before taking my hand from his chin and holding it again, centering himself like I'd hoped he would.

Papi scoffs, giving me a dirty look. "You're a pair of filthy cunts. You like poking shit up his ass with your pin dick?"

"No need to sound threatened. Baby daddies who abandon their kids aren't my type," I throw back, hating that he's trying to make what we have sound like a pile of trash. I hope that Zander and Blaze are having a better time dealing with our little firecracker, and I hope none of this shit ends in a bloodbath.

# *Zander*

Selene storms into our room and I follow close behind, shutting the door. She strides into the bathroom and slams the door behind her when I hear a frantic knock on the door. I know who it is, and I wait a few moments before I open the door a fraction.

"Please, can I talk to her?" Jan asks. Her face is blotchy red and swollen, but there's no mistaking that she and Selene are sisters.

I look over my shoulder and groan, "She's really angry and I can't be responsible if she throws a knife at your head."

She nods emphatically, and I let her in just as the shower starts. She looks at the door and then back at me. I shrug. "You can wait here until she's done."

"Okay." She sits on the small chair in the corner. "Tell me what she's like."

"She's fucking crazy." I shake my head, and she laughs.

"She always was."

"She's a killing machine, and she's known as the Reaper Incarnate."

"I've heard of that vigilante, but they say it's a man," she whispers, shockingly.

"I assure you she's a woman," I grin, and she cringes.

"I made her into that."

"No," I feel my irritation begin to rise, "she made herself strong, and she did it *for* you. Don't you dare take credit for what she's become."

"I wasn't taking credit—" she begins, but she's cut off by the sound of my girl singing her heart out in the shower. "Dear god, it's gotten worse," she says as she looks towards the bathroom. "It was bad when she was a kid, but that sound is atrocious."

"Yeah, she can't sing worth a shit," I chuckle.

"I have a friend named Sandra, and she was taken the same time I was. She likes to sing too, especially when she gets to drinking." She smiles fondly. "It reminded me of Selene."

Blaze opens the door then and strides inside, slamming it behind him.

"How could you give up on her?" he snaps, and it sets off another round of crying.

"You don't understand. I thought it was the end. I had no family, and I was young," she sobs.

"Selene was young too when she began chasing down drug dealers to find information on her sister." Blaze takes a menacing step toward her. "When she picked up a knife and began to learn how to use it to defend herself," another step and he's towering over her, "when she started to sell her body to track down the men who took her sister away."

The water shuts off in the shower and Blaze continues to glare down at a sobbing Jan. She's definitely a lot softer than Selene. Selene would've had her knife in his balls already.

"I just want the chance to talk to her," Jan sniffs.

"I'll let it happen if that's what she wants, but you better understand you don't deserve it," he bends down until they are eye to eye, "you don't deserve her."

His words are harsh, but I agree with every single one of them, and it's Blaze's nature to be cruelly honest.

"I know," Jan whispers.

"If you hurt her any more than you already have, please keep in mind that I'm a hunter, and I will enjoy the fuck out of hunting you down."

She nods, and I haul Blaze back as the bathroom door opens. Selene sees us first and even though a naughty grin coats her sexy lips, her eyes are sad.

"Are you two here to make me feel better?" she husks out, and my cock is ramrod hard.

"No." I swallow thickly and give her a slow once over. "Jan is here and wants to talk." I step out of the way and reveal her sister.

"My name is Henny now," she says as she stands. "I couldn't stand being Jan anymore."

"Felt guilty, did you?" Selene states as she drops her towel and begins to dress.

Blaze curses under his breath and I stand transfixed. I can't get enough of her.

"Yes," she nods. "I thought I failed you when I found out you were dead, and I hated myself. I hated Janelle."

Henny gasps when she sees the tattoo that takes up Selene's entire back, a menacing-looking Reaper, and its large scythe that stretches from shoulder to shoulder. Selene sits on the bed and flips her knife back and forth, making me nervous about the other woman in the room. If she kills the president's old lady, we might as well kill ourselves, too.

"I knew that my greatest wish was to find you alive," Selene says. "But it was also my greatest fear." She turns to look at her sister. "Because that would mean you left me behind to suffer with *her*." She must be talking about her mother.

"Not purposely."

"I know that, too. That's why I always convinced myself that if you were alive, you were being held against your will. So, imagine my shock when I find you giggling in the arms of a biker like you didn't just wipe your past out and me along with it."

Fuck. That hit me in the chest and I'm not even the one who forgot her.

"I would've never wiped you out if I thought you were alive." Henny tentatively sits beside her on the bed. "There was so much blood, Selly."

*Selly? Oh, hell no, our girl ain't no Selly.*

"The fuck did you just call her?" Blaze growls, and I mentally give him props. "That's fucking disrespectful. She's a fucking warrior. Call her by her proper name, *Henny.*"

I remind myself to buy the scary fucker a drink later because everything he's saying is honestly how I'm feeling.

"I'm sorry." Henny drops her head. "It's all I can say at this point."

"Thank you," Selene says as she stands and pulls on a shirt, the Reaper slowly getting covered. "I can thank you at least, because if you did continue to look for me, you would've found me easily." She turns to look at her sister and a slow, evil grin slides along her mouth. "And I wouldn't be who I am today."

Henny stays quiet, and the room falls silent around us.

"You can head on back to your man now," Selene tells her.

"You hate me," Henny says as she stands.

"No, you're my sister. I'll always love you." Selene opens the door. "I just need some space and time. I just need you out of my face, really." Henny walks out slowly, and Selene slams the door at her back. "Can you believe this shit?"

Blaze and I look at each other, then back at her, both of us waiting for the bomb to slowly tick down to zero. But it doesn't happen. She puts her belt back on and slips the knife inside, then looks at us expectantly.

"Where's Santos and Darius?"

"We chased after you," Blaze answers and she tsks.

"If that Papi Crazy motherfucker hurt my babies, this place is burning to the fucking ground, and it can take its precious *Henny* with it." Okay, so she's still mad and that ticking bomb may just explode if there's even the tiniest scratch on either Santos or Darius.

She yanks open the door and once again she's off with Blaze and me following her.

"How often are we going to have to chase this one down?" he growls.

"Forever, my man." I clap his shoulder.

## *Blaze*

-

Forever is a long fucking time.

I stare at her back as she strides down the hallway; her damp blonde hair swinging behind her, and her head held so fucking high and proud. Yeah, I guess I could do it forever, for her. I don't know when that happened, my willingness to chase this one woman, and my need to claim her, but it happened and now she's stuck with me. I don't even care that she wants the other three too. It makes my life easier, actually, because the four of us weren't ever going to split up.

Now we have a fifth and she's never splitting from us again. She completes us. I know I sound like a wet pussy, but it's true. Selene was made for us. I look over at Zander and the fucker has the same look in his eyes. We're all fucking crazy about the girl, and it makes me feel good, but also a bit apprehensive.

I was raised to believe that nothing good stays, eventually good feelings; people; and places disappear; and all that remains are the bad. So, I can't help but worry about the things that could happen. What if she falls out with one of us? Does she then fall out with all of us? What if one of the guys decides they're ready to move on? What happens to the rest of us? What if Darius and Santos decide they'd rather just be together? Will she leave all of us?

We step inside the main room and Selene looks around; her shoulders are tense. I can feel myself gearing up for a fight and I check that I still have my knife on my belt.

"Selene?"

I turn at the sound of a female's voice and groan when I see it's the hooker bitch.

"Aniyah!" Selene exclaims and rushes to her friend. Friends sound too casual after they've eaten each other dry, but whatever. "How are you?"

"They really took good care of me," she smiles, but I can see she's still weak. She looks over at me and her eyes widen in recognition. "You know him?" She points to me, and Selene looks over her shoulder.

"Yeah, he's one of my guys." She turns back to Aniyah just as I run my thumb along my throat. Zander chokes on a laugh as Aniyah pales. "Why?"

"I thought he looked familiar," she visibly swallows. "Never mind."

"There's someone else with a large scar running down the side of his face in Nevada?" Selene stands with her hand on her hip. "Looking as angry as this asshole?" She thumbs over her shoulder.

"I was stalking you for a while," I stare at Aniyah as I speak, "maybe she saw me then."

"Must be it." Aniyah looks away, but Selene continues to flick her gaze between us.

"If I find out you two fucked, I'll circumcise you both." She walks over to me and stands on her toes, bringing her mouth closer to my ear. "Twice." I shudder at the mental image and know she fucking means it. Which means if Aniyah is gonna speak, I'll need to shut her up, and permanently.

"That must be it." She shakes her head. "My mind is all over the place at the moment."

Selene walks back to Aniyah and settles on the couch beside her, leaning in close to speak.

"You fuck her?" Zander asks.

"She sucked my dick," I shrug, and Zander laughs.

"You're getting cut a few inches."

"No, I'm not." I look at him. "If that bitch talks, I'll cut out her tongue."

Zander chuckles as he heads to the bar and I follow behind him, making sure to make eye contact with the little hooker one last time. I hope the look in my eye conveys my murderous intent if she is even thinking of talking.

"Licker," Zander hits the bar, "we need two glasses of your best Scotch."

"Coming up!" Licker nods.

"I do like it here," Zander muses as he leans his back to the bar.

"I don't," I grumble. "It's too fucking hot all the time, and here in this compound, people are deranged."

"Do you even know your friends?" he asks me.

"I'm used to you fuckers, and Selene? She's mine," I shrug. "It's different."

"Do you love her?" Zander asks quietly. We watch as both she and Aniyah get up to walk outside.

I watch her closely, the way her body moves, and the energy she puts off. A confident but psychotic attitude that's begging any motherfucker to test her.

"Yeah," I watch her until she disappears. "I think that's what this feeling is."

"Like you would do anything for her?" he muses.

"Like I will kill her if she fucks this all up," I correct him and he laughs. "Do you love her?"

"Yeah," he nods. "No question."

"So, like, do we tell her? And then what? Get married or something?" I screw up my face at the prospect.

"We should tell her, but getting married is a little weird, no?" he raises a brow at me. "Can you imagine it? 'Hey priest! Can you hurry up with the vows? All of us need to get out of here and fill every one of her available holes.'"

I choke on my Scotch and roll my eyes at him. Accurate though.

Both of our heads snap up when we hear a loud crash and Santos' yelling.

"What the fuck was that?" Zander slams down his glass.

"Came from down that hallway." I point ahead and it's the one with Papi Loco's office.

"You have your knife?" he asks as he checks the gun in his holster.

"Yeah."

"Let's go." He darts forward and I hang back to look for Selene.

I don't know where the fuck she went, and I can't waste time looking for her. I chase after Zander and hope she doesn't castrate me for it later.

# Chapter Twenty

## Selene

Aniyah still looks a little pale, and I can see her struggling to focus. I know she was really sick, but I'm still worried about her.

"Are you sure you're feeling fine?"

"Yeah, it's just so loud in here." She gives me an apologetic smile. "I'm not used to this many people."

"I know what you mean." I nod and look around the room. "They're like one big family."

"I like it, but it'll take some time to get used to."

"Are you planning on staying?" I stare wide eyed at her.

"I'm thinking I might," she exhales. "There's nothing in Nevada for me now." She looks sad. I know she's thinking about her fake friendship with John.

"Colleen will miss you," I tell her with a nudge of my shoulder.

"On your way back," she grabs my hand, "could you pop in and tell her I'm doing good?"

"Yeah, I will."

She wipes her hand over her brow, and I begin to worry all over again. "Do you want to go outside for a breather?"

"Yeah," she nods. "That'll be nice."

We head outside, and I can feel the heat from Zander and Blaze's watchful eyes. I know a part of them will always be afraid that I'll run again, but they'll get over it eventually because I've learned my lesson. I need them.

"So, those are your guys?" Aniyah asks as we sit at one of the picnic tables in the lot.

"Yeah, that's two of them," I grin. "We're a hot fucking mess, but shit, I think I love them."

"Whoa." Her eyes become saucers. "Four?"

"Yep." I grin and I must look like a maniac. "All fucking four of them."

"Did you find anything out about your sister?"

My heart sinks with the thought of Jan—*Henny*—and I scrub my hand down my face. "She's here."

"Really?"

"Yep, she's the president's old lady," I chuckle at the fucking irony of it all. "She was here the whole time."

"I'm glad you found her." She smiles and pats my hand.

"I'm not so sure I am," I admit. "I was looking for an enslaved woman or a body."

"Then you must be happy she's alive and happy!" she exclaims.

"That just means she abandoned me, doesn't it?"

"Oh," she breathes with the realization and the air around us hangs heavy with silence.

"I don't know what to do now," I admit and stare down at my fingers.

"You forgive, Selene." She leans across the table. "You must forgive. If not for her, then do it for yourself."

"She didn't even try to look for me." I slam my fist on the table. "If I were truly dead, where would I be buried? Who were the witnesses? Cops must have reports, right?"

She nods along, agreeing with all my points. "Yes. All of that is true. But was she the type," she taps her head, "to think of all that during a stressful moment?"

"If you're asking if she is smart, I would say yes, extremely. She's fucking the top old dog here, smart as a whistle."

Aniyah tips her head back and those purple curls bounce as she cackles. "I guess she is, huh?" she says as she wipes the tears from her eyes. "But listen," she continues after she calms down. "Not everyone is as resourceful as you are. You are street smart, and you have investigation skills a detective would die for. That doesn't mean she's like that."

"I know but—"

"Did you also consider what she went through before getting here?" she cuts me off. "She was also taken, right? And I would assume, abused in every way imaginable. Maybe she still had a victim's mentality and not yet a survivor's one. Maybe, when she heard you were dead, she couldn't see any other option, anyway."

Her words dig into my stomach and settle next to my blackened soul. I never did consider what she went through before landing here with the *Dientes Afilados*. I was just thinking of myself and my pain.

"Thank you," I whisper as images assault me of what I've seen and heard happening to young ladies and children. It happened to my sister and instead of being happy she survived; I could only think of myself.

"Forgive her," Aniyah stresses. "She's your only family."

I lay my forehead on the table and take a deep breath; Aniyah's fingers smooth over my strands. I will forgive. I think I already have, but I just need time to stop being so fucking angry. If I hadn't spoken to Aniyah, it would've lasted a lot longer than this.

"Hey," her voice breaks me out of my thoughts, and I lift my head. "That guy has been out there watching us the whole time." I look to where she's pointing, and my breath gets lodged in my throat.

"I know him." I stand and stare back at the man casually standing against a familiar Rolls Royce.

"Like a *good* know him?" Aniyah stands and asks cautiously.

"He's not a threat," I wave her off. "Sit here and I'll be right back."

"Okay," she sounds unsure but sits back down.

I walk toward the front gate and notice he's across the street, just watching like a fucking creeper. I stop in front of the prospect guarding the gate and point to the guy.

"Did you not find that weird?" I raise a brow. "Which one are you?"

"Chance," he says and then shrugs. "He asked for you, but told me to wait until you were done with your conversation."

"Open the gate."

"Are you sure?" he looks around. "You shouldn't go out there alone."

"Don't make me ram my fucking foot up your ass while I yank my knife out of your skull," I growl.

"Fine." He shakes his head and opens the gate.

I stroll across the street, shielding my eyes from the early evening sun and stopping a few feet in front of him.

"Mr. Walton's driver," I chuckle. "What the hell are you doing all the way down here in Nevada?"

"I work for Zander now," he smirks. "The new Mr. Walton."

The way he says that makes my stomach feel like it's filled with crawling cockroaches. Zander *is* the new Mr. Walton.

"The prospect told me you wanted to speak to me. What's up?"

"Mario's has a bomb pineapple and sausage pizza that I can never get enough of. It's all I've lived off for practically two years." He's smirking, but I don't fucking get what he's saying.

"Nice." I nod slowly. Maybe he has developmental issues?

"You gave me their number when I asked for yours," he explains, his smirk still firmly in place.

It feels like ages ago when that happened, and I can't control the bark of laughter that escapes my mouth. "Sorry," I shrug. "I had my hands full with the first Mr. Walton."

"And now with the second, right?" he winks.

The words are meant to be funny, something to snicker at, but something is telling me he didn't mean it as any joke, more like a snide comment.

"Fucking right." I nod, but it's tight and my smile is strained. Something is off. "You came all the way here to pick us up?" I raise a brow.

"I came to deliver something he asked for." He shakes his head and opens the back door. "And I was told not to bring it on a plane."

Oh, that sounds legit, but something is still off. "And you asked for me because?"

"I saw you sitting there, and it was easier than making some kid run around looking for Zander." Again, sounds legit.

"Hand it over then." I hold out my hand.

"Not that easy," he chuckles. "I can't let this be seen. I couldn't get on a fucking plane. Understand?"

So, it's illegal. My instinct is telling me to back away and go get Zander, but my pride is saying I could handle this douche.

"Get in and I'll sit in the front like I'm taking you somewhere," he says. "Then I'll hand it over and you'll get out."

"Fine." I get into the backseat, and he shuts the door, climbing into the driver's seat.

"Reach under the seat," he tells me, keeping his eyes on me, reminding me of all the times he drove me to Henry.

I do what he says, but I can't feel anything. "There's nothing here," I snark.

"Farther back," he says, and I bend down farther, trying to see under the seat. "Mack is so excited to see you."

"What?" Before I can lift my head, something hard slams into the back of it and the world goes dark.

# Santos

I'm two seconds away from beating Papi to a pulp. If it weren't for Darius gripping the back of my shirt in his fist, I probably would have dived at the fucker already. I'm not fucking gay; I just know what I have with Darius makes me feel good. What's so wrong with that? I bet the piece of shit just needs a big dick up his ass to loosen him up a little. Prick.

"Obviously, your mother failed at raising you. No son under my roof would accept any man's touch," Papi spits, giving Loqi a dark look. "Right?"

Loqi snorts, not seeming bothered by my fucking guys, and that's the only reason I haven't punched his lights out. Papi, on the other hand is about to lose some teeth.

I take an angry step forward, but a chick with purple curls runs in looking panicked, her eyes seeking mine out as if I'd do shit for her. I don't know who the fuck she is, and I don't want any other woman to think they're worthy of my attention.

Before I can shout at her to fuck off, she stops in front of me and speaks.

"Selene just got in someone's fucking car and left."

Anger and pain course through me as I stare down at the purple-headed cunt, my heart aching. What if Selene has run again? Had her sister caused her to flee?

"Who the fuck are you? And what the fuck do you mean by that?" I snap, not meaning to take my mood out on her, but needing to vent it somewhere before I kill someone. I won't cope if Selene runs from us again.

"I'm Selene's friend, Aniyah, and she said you are all her guys. She just got in the car with this guy, and they left. He was waiting at the gate for her, and she went out to him," she answers, making Darius frown.

"Why the fuck would she go outside the gate alone?"

"Selene said she knew him. He had a flashy car, and they seemed to be relaxed. I haven't seen him before though," she states, as if that's fucking helpful.

I grab a nearby chair and throw it hard across the room, smashing empty beer bottles off the desk in the process. Footsteps pound towards us, and I get ready to face down with the piece of shit bikers, but Zander and Blaze run in with wide eyes.

"What the fuck?" Zander growls when he realizes it's me having a tantrum, as he'll call it. I go to throw a fist at Papi to remove some of my pent-up anger, but Loqi's hand darts out of nowhere and grabs my wrist, standing between us with a stern look. "Don't."

"You want to fucking fight me?" I snap, but his lip quirks up into a playful smirk.

"Not today. Trust me, don't do this here."

Aniyah steps back from me, not wanting to get hurt in the crossfire.

"Should I have stopped her?"

"Has all that purple shit in your hair fried your brain? Of course, you should have!" I yell, wanting to strangle the life out of her. I can't believe she let her get in a random car and drive off. I've lost her again.

Before I can say fuck it and punch Loqi in his stupid face, Darius fists my hair and tugs my face around to look at him.

"She didn't leave you."

"You don't fucking know that!"

He goes to speak, but I slam my fist into his jaw, making him stumble back a step. He doesn't seem fazed; he simply moves in front of me again with determination.

"Babe, whatever happened, she didn't run again. I just know," he murmurs, my anger becoming distracted by him calling me babe. My body tingles at the sound, and I can't help but run my fingers across his jaw where I'd hit him.

"How do you know that?" I ask, sounding desperate but not giving a shit. If there's any chance that she has run, I'll be devastated and I'll probably kill her when I catch her again.

"The fuck are you talking about? Where's Selene?" Blaze asks in a low voice, Zander's eyes on us in question.

I give Aniyah a dark look while answering. "Selene got in some fucker's car and left. She told Aniyah she knew them."

It's silent for a second, other than Papi's chuckling. He's finding everything so fucking funny.

"You let her fucking go?" Blaze demands, his eyes on Aniyah with the promise of violence.

## Darius

Aniyah cowers from Blaze as he glares at her, his hands flinching by his sides as he gets ready to kill her. Zander steps between them, his eyes on her.

"Did you get a good look at them? Did she mention who it was?"

"No, she just said she knew them. The windows on the car were tinted. I'm sorry," she breathes as if he's saved her. If Blaze wants her dead, he'll bowl Zander out of the way in the process. Once Blaze loses it, that's the end of it.

I know Selene wouldn't leave us here. She's made it clear she understands what would happen if she did. I'm worried about her, but I'm just as worried about Santos. I can't handle him beating my ass daily again to burn down his pain.

He looks defeated as his eyes remain on me, looking at me as if I have the answer to everything. I don't, but satisfaction rolls through me at knowing the power I hold over him. I'm his anchor, and I always have been.

I have no idea where Selene is or where she's going, but it can't be good if she didn't think about telling us first. If she's just going to be gone ten minutes, she still would have told us.

Zander and Blaze are grilling Aniyah about the car, Santos is still staring at me with a broken heart, and Papi is grinning as if it's the best day of his life.

"Guess you boys were just a piece of ass to her after all." I'm going to kill him.

Santos jerks out of his staring contest with my face, swinging around to punch the bastard, but I haul him back and wrap my arms around him, wheezing as his fist jabs me in the ribs firmly.

"Let me go!"

I don't. I hold him tight enough to make sure he stays in one piece, my voice quiet.

"I can't lose you. Stop."

He goes limp in my arms, his forehead dropping to mine as his eyes fill with agony.

"I can't lose her again."

"We haven't. She's our girl, so let's go get her," I reply, a sudden calm washing through him.

"Right now?"

"Right now. Let's go."

Papi scowls, stepping in front of the open doorway. "You're not leaving yet. We have shit to discuss."

Santos takes my hand, surprising me as he remains calm. "We have nothing to talk about, Papi. Get the fuck out of my way."

I have no idea what the old bastard sees in Santos' eyes, but after a second his features soften, and he steps out of the way.

The four of us leave the office, and I glance back to find Loqi watching us go.

"See you soon," he states casually, making Santos snort.

"Don't fucking count on it."

I know we'll see them again, because even if Santos is pissed today, he'll be curious and demanding answers tomorrow. He's spent his entire life chasing the ghost of his father, so I know it's not the end of their conversation. Not by a long shot.

We head back to our room and gather up anything of ours, not wasting time as we head out to our car and climb in. Blaze slams the door and starts the engine, a dark grin taking over his face.

"Let's go get our girl."

If anyone's hurt her, there will be hell to pay. No one fucks with our family.

Fucking no one.

# Epilogue

## Selene

I'm being moved as the ground underneath me swerves, my body rolls and hits metal. I open my eyes, but it's dark. I have cloth stuffed in my mouth, and my hands are tied behind my back. I've learned how to get out of being tied up a long fucking time ago. I bend my body back and work my hands lower until they slip over my feet. I turn onto my back and reach for my belt, feeling my knife still tucked into it. Thank God I got this made.

I pull out the knife and carefully cut away at the thin rope. What a dumb fuck this asshole is! I get my hands free and pull the cloth out of my mouth. I could work the knife into the trunk's lock and open it, but where would the fun be in that? No, I think I'll just stay here and wait to see where the fuck he's taking me. I slip my knife back into the belt and slip my hands under my head, feeling the bump there with a wince. That fucker is dead when I get out of here. I rest on my hands and begin to whistle. I begin with the tune *She'll be coming 'round the mountain when she comes* and when I decide I like it, I put that shit on loop.

"I'll be stabbing some motherfuckers when I get out," I sing. "I'll be stabbing some dirty cunts when I get out. Stabbing motherfuckers, I'll be stabbing motherfuckers, I'll be stabbing dirty cunts when I get out. I'll be cutting off some dicks when I get out, I'll be cutting off some dicks when I get out. Cutting off some dicks, I'll be cutting off some dicks, I'll be cutting off some dicks when I get out."

The car lurches to a stop and I huff in annoyance. I was just getting to the good part. The rage begins to settle in, and I feel the energy course through my muscles. He must've thought he got one over on me, that he's a big strong man, and he accomplished tying me up and throwing me in a trunk, all while I was passed the fuck out. Big man. I begin to whistle again and when the trunk pops, I can hear his footsteps crunching over gravel. I whistle louder and then the crunching stops, making me grin.

"Oh, come on, big man," I taunt. "You got me in here … now, come get me out."

He's hesitating, so not completely stupid, and then his foot kicks open the trunk. I continue to lie there and when his head comes into view, I grab his hair. I haul myself up and slam my head into his nose, laughing as he screams. I jump out of the trunk and I'm laser focused as I grab my knife out of my belt. He doesn't see me as he's bent forward and gripping his nose. I grab his hair and lift him up, stabbing my knife through his left eye. Dropping him once he's dead.

I hear the cock of a gun and I finally lift my head to see four assholes standing in front of me, all of them with guns out.

"Oh, come on, guys." I prop my bloodied hand on my hip. "I already got enough holes for everyone. I don't need anymore."

"She doesn't recognize us, boys," I hear a familiar voice from behind the wall of bastards.

They split apart and out walks the nasty fat piece of shit that transported me and the girls the day before. Only this time, his face is bruised and his mouth missing a few blackened stubs.

"Delaney," I growl.

"Drop the knife," he sneers and chuckles when I do as he asks. I'm not stupid. You don't bring a knife to a gunfight. "You remember the Diablos, right? You killed a few top ranks in their crew."

"Couldn't have been top of shit if they were that easily killed." I shrug and he laughs, his gaping mouth on full display. *Fuck, he's gross.*

"I don't think they agree," he thumbs to the assholes over his shoulder. "Luckily for you, they want to kill your boys more than you, and so do I." He motions for them to grab me, and I laugh when all four of them step forward.

"What? You think I can't handle four men at the same time?" Their steps falter, and I laugh maniacally. "All right, all right. Let's go." I walk forward towards an SUV. "But I ain't sitting with fatty."

They open the backend of the SUV and I roll my eyes. "Tie her up," the walrus calls out, and I grin.

They grab my arms behind my back and tie my wrists, much like the driver dude did. Fuck, I never even got his name.

"Where are we going?" I ask, sounding bored, and hopping up into the back.

"To New York," Fatty answers as they slam the door shut.

At least we'll be back on home turf, and I know Blaze will figure this out. He'll know how to find me.

And when he does, he and I will make it rain red.

# Claiming The Reaper

REAPED BOOK TWO

# Copyright

# Dedication

To our readers, new and old, we thank you for taking this journey
with us one final time.

# Prologue

## Selene

I've always hated the zoo. I would watch all the animals pacing along the cage, eyeing the people watching them, and in my mind, they were waiting for a weak point to escape. They looked depressed, and some of the more aggressive ones always looked ready to strike.

That's me right now.

I'm a red-assed orangutan, pacing the length of this room, just waiting to toss shit at the next person to come near me. Then I will beat my fists on my chest, showing them who's boss, just before I sink my teeth into their jugular.

I'm *that* red-assed orangutan.

I don't know how long I've been here, but it's had to have been days, and my patience is running out. If my guys don't get here soon, I'll get myself out of here, hunt *them* down and toss some shit their way, too. It can't take this long to find me. What the fuck are they doing? Playing hide the pickles without me?

They better fucking not be. There aren't enough holes. They need me.

The door creaks open, and I watch as heavy boots clunk down the stairs, one slow step at a time. Must be fat-assed Mack Delaney.

*I wish I'd taken a shit.*

The chains around my wrists clank as I cross my arms over my chest, waiting for his huffing, sweating self to reach the bottom. Yeah, they learned their lesson the hard way when I got out of their ropes, *twice*. Now I'm chained, and I'm trying to figure out how I'm going to take these home with me when I get out, Darius would squeal with delight.

"Hello, Reaper." Mack's toothless mouth grins when he finds me waiting for him.

"Hello, Gingivitis." I grin back, and his face falls.

"You have a smart mouth, you dumb whore," he retorts, and I look at him with confusion.

"Which one is it?" I toss my hands up. "Am I smart, or am I dumb?"

"You're a whore," he spits.

"I know," I nod, "and you're toothless. Are you asking for an hour of my time? I'll *bite*—since you can't—I'm a little intrigued. I'd let you have me sit on your face, just to find out what it would be like to have my clit gummed."

"Jesus," he mutters, and shows me a pair of scissors. "I need a lock of your hair."

"You're barking up the wrong orangutan if you think you're getting anywhere near me with those."

"The wrong *what*?"

"I'm a caged beast, Gummy Bear!" I clap my hands, making the chains clink together. "I will rip you to shreds if you get any closer."

"Don't make me call a few guys down to help restrain you." His smirk is sinister. "They may have their way with you after."

"Oh, cute," I snort. "You think a man threatening to rape me will make me compliant?" I snicker. "Call them down, it's been a while," I grab my pussy through my pants, "I could deal with a dick or two."

He curses and turns on his heel, heading back up the stairs. "Let's see how you feel when you've missed a few meals."

"It'll feel like my crack-whore mother forgot to buy groceries, gummy worm," I yell at his retreating back. "Been there, done that."

A few hours later, and I would kill for a glass of water. I've been cushioned, babied, *spoiled*. I drop my head back against the cement wall of the basement and growl in frustration. I've softened up, and I can't let it continue. As soon as I'm out of here, it's back to training. I got some Diablos to take down.

The door opens, and another pair of boots come down the stairs. He's holding a tray, and I see a tall sweating glass of cold water sitting on it. Okay, after this meal, I'll begin training.

"Boss says we need some hair first," the asshole in front of me says.

"Since it's been a while, I can offer my coochie or my head." I throw him a grin. "And if you pick between my legs, you'll have to pay the toll."

"Just a bit from your head, whore." He rolls his eyes, and I snort.

"You're boring." I wave for him to come closer. "Why does he need the hair?"

"To send to your pretty boys," he says as he snips a lock off.

"They are pretty, huh?"

He puts the tray down in front of me and I attack the water like a dried-out raisin. They put bread and butter on the tray, but I've eaten way worse, so I dig in. It's about fifteen minutes later when I feel my mouth dry out and things around me begin to grow foggy. The door opens again, and I hear the boots on the stairs, but I can barely lift my head.

"We're moving you, blondie," someone says as they tip me over a shoulder.

"I'm going to set my orangutan on you," I mumble.

"The fuck did she just say?" I hear someone snicker, and then everything goes black.

# Chapter One

## *Zander*

We're back in New York after Blaze followed Selene's trail. We don't have much but someone has been leaving us nuggets of information along the way, wanting us to follow. We left Nevada and the *Dientes Afilados* assured us that if we needed them, they'd be there.

Santos has been quiet, understandably. He's found his long-lost father and a new brother in the few days we were there, telling me we're all just tangled in fate's big-ass, sticky web. How else could you explain the coincidences? Darius has been silent but strong, watching Santos for any signs of a temper flare. None of us are completely finished with Nevada, not with Santos *and* Selene both finding family there.

With Selene missing again, the air around us is crackling with a dark energy. Not the same as the first time. We were depressed and missing her, but this time, knowing she's been taken, we're on the cusp of something fucking explosive. Santos has been too quiet, too still. Darius has been thrumming, his body practically vibrating. Blaze looks sinister and excited, and I'm coiled tight, waiting to unleash.

The crumbs have led us back to our turf, and that can only mean one thing, Los Diablos. As we slowly drive through the streets, we see more of their presence, like they thought it would be a good idea to move into our town while we were gone. Big fucking mistake.

Blaze growls when he sees a drug deal go down, and I'm next when I see the block has more prostitutes than ever. We cleaned this place up, made it respectable, and ran drugs on the down-low, not being blatant about it. But this is just sloppy.

"Someone is dying today," I snap.

I'm greeted with crickets. Usually I'd get a hoot from Santos, a chuckle from Darius, but instead it's an eerie silence. We've never been in this space before. Not where we're all in the same frame of mind, we're usually pretty even keeled. Santos and Darius are psycho, Blaze is dangerous, and I'm handsome. I mean *level-headed*. But we are balanced. Right now we're tipped to one side, and that scares even me.

We pull up to Blaze's house—now our compound—and as we wait for the gates to open, I see something attached in the center.

"What is that?" But before my sentence is even out, Blaze is already striding up to the object and ripping it off the metal bar.

"We need to check the cameras," Darius murmurs, and I give him a nod.

Blaze gets back in the car and tosses a plastic Ziplock bag into my lap. I hold it up, but it looks like a piece of paper inside.

"What is it?" Santos croaks, his voice shocking me. It's the first he's spoken since leaving the MC's compound in Nevada.

"Not sure." I shake my head as we pull up to the front of the house. "Let's get inside and take a look."

Once we file into the house, everything feels solemn, and the silence just keeps adding to the emptiness we're all feeling. We sit at the table, Blaze kicking out his long-ass legs, Darius straddling his chair, and Santos drumming his tattooed fingers along the tabletop. I open the plastic baggy, pull out the paper, and unfold it, out falls a long flaxen lock of hair.

"Is that…?" Santos leans forward and snatches the hair from off the table, immediately bringing it to his nose. He's up and out of his chair, the wooden legs scraping along the floor. "It's Selene's."

"What does the note say?" Blaze interjects.

I throw the paper to the center of the table, my jaw clenching and my stomach twisting with a fiery rage. I can't even speak right now and reading it to them would be impossible. Darius snatches it up, much to Blaze's irritation, and begins to read.

*"There once was a Little Reaper, her hair so blonde and fair, she loved causing mayhem without a single care. But now she's a prisoner with her hands shackled tight, spreading her legs without much of a fight. Leave town before morning's light, or she'll be dead by the end of*

*tomorrow night.*"

"Poetic," Blaze snarls. "Doesn't sound like *Los Diablos.*"

"Not unless they're working with someone," I grunt.

The kitchen falls quiet, and then I watch as Santos' face begins to light up, the spark coming back to his eye. "Does this mean war?"

"I guess so," I shrug.

"You hear that, San?" Darius stands and holds out his fist. "Looks like we're getting the machine guns and Kevlar."

Santos smashes his fist to Darius' and hoots … *finally.* "Who the fuck are these guys? Telling us to leave our town."

"A bunch of fucking idiots." Even Blaze is grinning, the scary fucker.

"We need to find out where she is first." I scratch my chin.

"On it." Blaze stands and heads to the back room, where we have our surveillance.

"Should we call in a favor with *Dientes Afilados*?" I ask Santos.

His nose crinkles, and then he chuckles. "Your pronunciation is like a white boy ordering Taco Bell."

"I am a white boy," I huff.

"You're lucky you're cute." Santos ruffles my hair. "Let's see what Blaze comes back with, then we'll decide if I think it's worth it to call my asshole father."

Asshole father indeed. Santos may be a fucking handful and he may be the most chaotic person I know, but I can honestly say, thank fuck, he wasn't raised by *Papi Loco*. The name really says it all.

"Let's go try on our vests and see how many weapons we can strap to our bodies," Darius says, leading an excited Santos out of the room.

We really are a bunch of psychos if the prospect of blood and war excites us.

# Blaze

I stretch out in the chair, waiting for the computer to boot up, and clenching my fist. She better not have let anything happen to herself; I will kill her if she did. She doesn't get to make me question what the fuck my heart is doing and then disappear again. I'm sick to death of tracking her down, and I'm not going to want to do this for the rest of my fucking life.

*But I will if I have to.*

There, I admit it. I would do just about anything for the annoying woman with the blonde hair and filthy mouth. She fixed something inside of me I didn't even realize was broken. I roll my fucking eyes at my own-damn-self and wait for the computer screen to boot up.

I have a camera at the front door, at the front of the gates, and the backyard. Another quality I acquired from my abusive foster father—paranoia. Well, it's coming in clutch now. The screens boot up, and I zoom in on the one at the gate. My cameras aren't the blatant ones you see in most homes. I have stealth cameras hiding in areas as small as a screw hole. Again, paranoia.

I shuffle through hours of footage and finally stop when I see a large red pickup truck park outside of the gates. Two guys approach, their faces covered and the plastic baggy in their possession. They look around, probably trying to spot a camera, and then proceed to tape it to the gate. They were here four hours ago.

I can't tell who the fuck they are or who the fuck they work for because they were smart enough to hide that, but not completely intelligent. I zoom in on the truck and right smack there in the center is the license plate. *Bingo.*

I write it down and head back out to the kitchen, finding Zander sitting alone nursing a beer. He looks up at me, his eyes sad but hopeful. Fuck's sake, we're all goners.

"Did you get anything?"

"Yeah." I put the paper down in front of him. "I need you to find out what you can on that."

My expertise is hunting and watching, Zander's is tech, and the other two like shooting things. Zander jumps up quickly, rushing into his room, no doubt to do geeky tech shit while jerking off. This woman has us all kinds of fucked up.

I grab my own beer out of the fridge and sit at the table, taking down half of it in one swig. I hear Santos' excited voice from somewhere in the house, followed by Darius' laughter. I was a little worried when he became sullen after leaving the compound. Finding his biological father like that must've been a hard blow, and then to learn he's a cunt, even worse.

"Got something." Zander skids back into the kitchen, his socks making him glide across the floor. "Reginald James."

"Who the fuck is that?" I snort and finish my beer.

"Don't have a fucking clue, but I got an address to where the license plate is registered to."

"Sounds good." I stand and nod. "Round up the idiots, and let's pay *Reginald* a visit."

"Santos! Darius!" Zander bellows as he rushes back out of the kitchen. "We got something!"

The sound of thundering hooves hits the floorboards and my whole second story sounds like it's going to split down the center. Bunch of fucking pansies.

"Did you find her?" Santos yells.

"No, but we found who dropped her hair off, though," Zander calls back.

"Let's kill them!" Darius adds in.

*Fucking pussy-whipped assholes.*

I grab my keys and rush for the front door, my heart beating with the prospect of a lead. I make it to the front stoop when I hear Zander call out to me.

"Bro!" he snickers. "You may want to get some shoes on."

I look down at my sock-clad feet and let out an exaggerated exhale, "Yeah."

*Pussy-whipped asshole.*

# Santos

My mood has perked up slightly at Zander and Blaze finding a lead on Selene. I'll bring my little demon home one way or another, but I hope I get to shred an army of people to do it. I'm numb but unhinged at the same time, trying to block out my feelings while letting it slip into my mind enough to drive my murderous thoughts.

Finding the man who helped create me is pulling me in two different directions. Relief at finally finding him, but also anger. He abandoned me, raised his other fucking son as if I didn't matter, and left me to fend for myself.

I am giving myself whiplash as I replay that moment in my head, the one where I met eyes with Papi Loco and reality smacked me in the face with full force. Loqi seemed just as surprised as I'd been, but I doubt the prick was having an internal war with his demons like I am.

I sense Darius' concern before it has even happened, always so attuned to my emotions, knowing when I'm quiet, something is wrong. My boys always have my back, but Darius has my fucking heart and soul in his hands.

Now that Blaze has his shoes on, we all pile into the car to chase down whoever this Reginald fucker is. Selene's face flashing through my mind and causing me to temporarily forget about Papi. She's all I care about right now.

Blaze drives while Zander sits in the passenger seat, leaving Darius and I in the back, pretending they can't hear Darius as he speaks to me. "You good?"

I'm not fucking good, not by a long shot, but I shrug and try to keep calm.

"Yeah. I just want our girl home where we can chain her up in the basement. No one's going to get the opportunity to snatch her again."

He grunts in agreement, not hesitating to thread his fingers through mine to give my hand a firm squeeze. "We'll get her back. If we're lucky, she's already ripped half their limbs off and is casually leaning against the door, whistling while waiting for us to arrive. She's fine."

I smile at that, knowing he's probably right. No one gets to restrain Selene and live to tell the tale. Well, other than us in the bedroom, if we ask real nice. *Great, now my dick's getting hard.*

Darius raises an eyebrow, glancing at my groin with amusement.

"At least you're in a better mood. I don't like it when you're quiet. It's scary."

"Keep looking at it like that, and we'll both be scaring Zan and Daddy Blaze," I joke, annoyance flashing in Blaze's eyes in the rear-view mirror.

"Don't even think about it, you crazy piece of shit," he growls, his eyes narrowing as Darius surprisingly runs his fingers through my hair and yanks hard, his face close to mine.

"Sounds like fun, San." He's fucking with Blaze, but I sense he's trying to keep me occupied while my mind is in a better place. I hate sinking into that dark pit I've been spending so much time in lately, knowing my silence and fury will eventually turn to violence and lashing out. Darius is always the one to take the brunt of it.

I chuckle, wrapping my fingers around his throat and forcing him back, his fingers slipping from my hair. "As much as I agree with you, a bullet in my ass isn't on my plans for the day."

"You calling my dick small or deadly?" he says with a fake gasp, making me snort.

"There's nothing small about your dick and you know it. I was referring to a real bullet. Daddy Blaze looks mad, and I don't want to push him until we have our girl back to protect me."

Zander smothers a laugh, while Blaze flicks his eyes from the mirror to the road with a grunt. "Try me, you little shits. See what happens." Grumpy bastard.

Darius relaxes back into his seat, but his eyes remain on me, his hand resting lazily on my thigh. It soothes me to know he's always so close, and the banter we've been having keeps my mind from wandering.

His fingers flex against my thigh, my dick stirring from the simple touch. I've been hornier than usual lately, probably because we had Selene in our grasp again, but the more Darius looks after me, the more I want to bend him over and nail his ass. He knows it, too, because he gives me a cheeky smirk before turning his attention out the window.

# Darius

It's risky to push Blaze, but it makes Santos smile, so I continued to tease him. I'm staring out the window, but I can sense Santos' eyes burning into the side of my head. Sex and violence are Santos' language, so until the violence comes, I'll distract him with sex. Well, I'm not about to fuck him in the backseat, not with Blaze's hand twitching on the steering wheel, his gun close by.

I suck in a breath as Santos grabs my hand resting on his thigh, dragging it farther north until his solid bulge is under my palm, my gaze snapping over to his. He smirks, raising an eyebrow in a playful challenge.

Living life on the edge is one thing, but living life on the edge of Blaze's gun? No thanks.

When I don't move, Santos rolls his eyes and grips my wrist firmly, lifting his hips a fraction to force his dick against my hand, more than happy to risk Blaze murdering us. Zander grins from the front seat, finding amusement in our impending doom, keeping his mouth shut to avoid the drama for as long as possible. He doesn't give a fuck if he sees us doing anything. He's cool like that, but Blaze would blow a fucking fuse. Probably because he isn't getting laid until Selene's back home with us.

I squeeze Santos through his pants firmly, forcing a quiet growl to leave him. I'll play along if he wants, but we aren't going to get off while Blaze is here. That much I know. He's only torturing the pair of us.

Blaze slams on the brakes, spinning to glare at us with all the anger he can muster—which is a lot—ignoring a car as its horn blares behind us. "If you two don't leave each other alone, I'll make Zander sit between you. Clear?"

I grin, giving Zander a wink. "Hear that, Zan? You're invited to the party too. I'll even let you top instead of bottom," I tease, his eyes filling with amusement.

"I'm flattered, honestly. But if you think I'd be anything other than the top, you're delusional."

"Don't fucking encourage them!" Blaze barks, turning his annoyance at his best friend. "If you start acting like those two, I can't be held responsible for my actions! I need at least one of you to not be thinking with your dicks all the time!"

All three of us laugh, but Santos pushes me off his dick and takes my hand in his, the gesture so normal it's almost strange. Santos can give me whiplash sometimes with his moods. Sometimes he's stupidly horny, other times he's angry, but the playful, softer side of him is one of my favorites. It's good to see him relax.

"So, what are we doing with this Reginald cunt when we get our hands on him? If you won't let us fuck, at least let us have a play-by-play of the murdering we will do. That way, I still get to come in my pants," Santos drawls as Blaze starts driving again. Zander turns in his seat, glancing at the grip Santos currently has on my hand, understanding taking over his face. Santos needs to focus on something to keep his temper in check.

"Maybe we can torture information out of him?"

"What if the vehicle was stolen, and this has nothing to do with him?" Santos frowns, making Zander raise an eyebrow.

"Do you give a shit?"

"Not particularly. I'm killing him for having such a shitty name to begin with. Did his parents hate him? Who the fuck looks at a cute screaming little baby and decides he looks like a Reginald? Angry parents with an unwanted pregnancy, that's who," he scoffs.

"Like Santos is any better? You were named after the sacred image of saints," Blaze deadpans. "What the fuck is sacred or saint-like about you?"

"My big-ass dick is pretty sacred. Makes Selene scream out to God, anyway," he throws back without hesitation, glancing at me to back him up. "You think it's pretty good too, right, babe?"

Vulnerability flashes in his eyes behind the mask he tries hard to keep in place, earning a wink from me. "You know it, *amante*."

Blaze mutters about killing us, but Santos grins at me like a kid in a candy shop. His demons soothed for another few minutes. I don't give a shit if it makes me sound dick whipped. I'll call him my lover every damn day if he keeps looking at me like I fix everything for him.

# Chapter Two

## Selene

My mouth is like sandpaper, and my throat feels swollen shut, completely dried out. I have to force my eyes open because they're crusted shut, and when I look around, I see I'm in another basement. This one is dank and musty, and the smell is making my stomach twist.

*Fuck, I'm starving.*

My head feels heavy as I lay it back against the cement wall behind me, the cool surface seeping through my skull. Maybe I shouldn't have threatened Gum Disease with my orangutan. maybe he thought I was going off the rails, or possessed.

Once my head clears, I sit up and lift my hands. I'm still chained. This basement is smaller, and it's filled with damp boxes. I'm fucking breathing mold.

Where the fuck are my guys? I would've found *them* by now. They can't think I disappeared on my own again, right? They're smarter than that, right? I drop my head with a groan. I actually don't know the fucking answer to that, because all we've done together is fuck and kill people. But I mean, they've survived this long, and Blaze did track me down to Nevada.

I begin to relax just as the door opens and two sets of boots hit the wooden stairs.

"Is she awake?" one asks, and I close my eyes.

"Doesn't look like it."

369

"Do you think Mack gave her too much?"

"I don't care," the second one has a bit of an accent, maybe South American. "I need to get home to my *abuela*. She likes to pray the rosary together."

"Man," the first laughs. "You're gonna have to skip the Jesus humping today. This is our mission until Mack and the guys get back."

"What if her guys show up? Reggie, I'm not willing to die for this shit," the first whines. "Let's just kill the chick and leave."

I let out a groan and hear them shuffle back, a bunch of pussies.

"Water," I croak, putting on a show.

A water bottle is rolled across the floor, bouncing off my feet. I pick it up and open it in record time, guzzling down the cool liquid like a nun on a priest's cock. I choke on the liquid as my swollen throat has problems getting it down and I sputter; the water going everywhere.

Both guys look young, but they're dressed like they grabbed their clothes in the dark, and have greasy, dirty hair.

"She looks possessed," Jesus Boy exclaims.

Huh. Maybe I could really work that. I'm chained and I can't lure them with my pussy, so possession it is. I need to get out of here and it looks like I'll have to do it myself. Then I'm killing my guys.

"Fuck," I stare up at him wide-eyed, still choking on the fucking water. "You called him."

"What?" The fucking pussy grabs the crucifix around his neck. "Are you insane?"

"She's fucking with you," the first one laughs. He'll be a harder nut to crack, but I only need to crack one.

"I have something inside of me," I make my voice creepy as fuck. "Deep inside, and he's mean."

"What?" The kid holds out the crucifix. "What's inside of you?"

I close my eyes, making sure the whites show as my eyelids flutter, making the religious fuck gasp. "He's big and hairy all over." I open my eyes up and look at him. "He has a bright red ass and walks on all fours."

"What the fuck?" the first guy bends over laughing. "A red ass?"

"Don't laugh. My abuela says demons can come in any appearance. It would explain how she can kill like she does."

Finally, the first guy eases up and looks at me, wondering if I do indeed have a red-assed, furry demon inside of me who helps me kill people. Are these two on drugs?

"Nah," he laughs again and pushes the guy wearing the crucifix, who's still staring at me in fear. "Don't be a pussy."

"I think we should uncuff her and set her free. Maybe she won't kill us."

"Don't even take the keys out of your pocket." Bingo. "Mack will kill us even if she doesn't."

"I'll get out of here." The second guy is shaking his head, those brown eyes wide in fear. "Jesus will protect me."

I cross my arms over my chest; the chains clanking as I continue to listen to them bicker, and then when it turns a bit more physical, I roll my eyes. So fucking predictable.

I watch as they argue over my sanity, shoving each other back and forth, and when the little God-fearing cunt shoves his buddy a little too close to me, I wrap my shackle chain around his neck. He struggles but I hold tight, all the while smiling at the kid who's praying about his father up in Heaven, or something like that.

When the guy passes out in my arms, I release him, and his unconscious body hits the ground. "Keys." I hold out my hand, and they're thrown at me, landing at my feet.

I unlock the cuffs around my wrists, snickering when the guy starts panicking, looking around for a place to run.

"I could've sworn you said to kill me," I say as the metal hits the cement floor.

With the second key on the ring, I unlock the padlock holding the chains to the industrial loop drilled into the wall, and then swing them up over my shoulder.

I turn and look at the trembling guy again as he clutches his cross around his neck. "Boo, bitch," I say, and he startles just before taking off in a run up the stairs.

"Hey!" I hear a few voices upstairs shout. "Where the fuck you going?"

More people to terrorize. *Goody.*

I sling the shackles over my shoulder, and begin to whistle *Twinkle, Twinkle, Little Star* while I stomp up the stairs. "Bloody, bloody little shits, gonna scream while I saw off dicks. Breaking necks makes me high, but circumcision is fun, I can't deny. Bloody, bloody little shits, gonna scream while I saw off dicks."

I think I missed my fucking calling as a recording artist. The door is open at the top of the stairs. Thanks to the little Christian boy who ran out of here with shit in his pants, *praise the lord.*

"Reggie," a gruff voice calls from another room. "What happened to Pepe?"

I follow the sound and find two other guys sitting on a couch, watching TV, and smoking a joint.

"I told him I was a demon, and the little fucker pissed himself. You think his piss would be considered holy water? You know, because he's a Bible fucker?"

"What the fuck?" The guy who's watching TV, jumps to his feet, while the one smoking a joint, struggles to get up.

I swing out the heavy metal shackles, catching the guy standing hard in the face. He drops like a sack of potatoes just as his buddy finally gets his ass off the couch. He looks at me through squinted eyes, swaying back and forth on his feet.

"How'd you get out?"

"I'm like Houdini." I give him a wink. "Wanna play a game?"

"No." He pulls a familiar-looking knife out of his back pocket, and I gasp.

"You have my baby?" My belt has been feeling so empty without it, and the last I saw it was sticking out of Henry's chauffeur's eye.

"It is nice." He advances on me. "It's mine now."

"No can do," I shake my head with a tsk, "that knife chose me, like Harry Potter."

"Put those things down." He points the knife at the shackles over my shoulder as he advances.

"Sounds good," I say when he's less than a foot in front of me. I drop them to the floor, and still grip them in my hand.

He lunges for me at the same moment I swing the large metal chains, catching him at the ankles. He cries out and drops to his knees.

"Those ankles are sensitive as fuck, huh?" I snicker as I grab my knife and flip it in my hand. "Toes too," I say, just as he gets his feet back under him. I drop the shackles down onto his socked toes.

Once again, he's screaming on his knees, and I begin to hum along. His friend groans from his spot on the floor and rolls over onto his hands and knees, slowly working his way up to his feet.

*This is so much fun.*

My giddy feeling is cut short when the guy does stand and swings a gun around to my face. His whole left side is swollen and bleeding, and he's looking really mad.

"Back downstairs," he growls.

So, they've been ordered not to kill me, even fucking better.

"Let's play a game," I grin at him. "Your friend wouldn't play with me." I point to the guy still moaning on the floor, crying about broken toes.

"Let's play Doctor," he sneers. "I fill you up with some holes."

"Yes!" I nod. "Doctor is fun. I'll be the brain surgeon."

"Get the fuck downstairs," he grinds out, and I shake my head with a snicker.

"Fine," I roll my eyes. "I'll go first." I grip my knife and swing my wrist quickly, throwing it with expert precision.

The sharp blade sinks into his eye, making him drop the gun, and his mouth gaping open. But not a single sound comes out as he crumples to the floor.

"I think I won that round," I say to the sobbing baby on the floor. "Are you my next patient?"

"No," he blubbers out as he begins to crawl backward. "I'm not even a part of Los Diablos. I just came here to buy some weed."

"Is that right?" I crouch down. "How'd you get my pretty knife? Hmm?"

"Carlos gave it to me." He points to my first patient.

"I see." I nod and stand.

He deflates with relief, his head hanging, and his brown shaggy hair slipping over his forehead. None of them are innocent. They all partake in kidnapping girls to sell. I'm not about to let a single one of them live, and I'm eager to send a message back to Delaney.

*I'm going to need a lot of blood, though.*

"Is this Delaney's house?" I ask my second patient.

"No, this is Reggie's house." The guy passed out in the basement.

I walk over to the dead guy on the floor and yank my knife out of his eye, the sound like music to my ears. I wipe the blade off onto his shirt and stand just in time to see the other fucker trying to make a run for it with broken toes.

"And here I was thinking I'd go easy on you. Not all patients end in death," I call out to him as he disappears around the corner. I walk past my shackles, reminding myself to come back for them, and watch as his shaggy hair disappears into another room.

"I'm tired and don't have the energy to play hide and seek, come out so we can do your much needed open-heart surgery," I giggle, the sound manic. I may be tired and weak, but the prospect of gutting someone always perks me up.

I walk into a kitchen. There are open takeout containers everywhere, flies and beer cans scattered. It smells like fucking death and in the center of the room is my patient number two holding a large butcher knife.

"Oh, you want to play butcher instead?" I cock my head to the side. "Do you even know how to fillet a human?"

"Don't come any closer." He hobbles back a few steps.

"The best place to get meat is off the ass," I slap my own, "like a rump roast." My mouth salivates at the prospect of roast anything.

"Stop talking." He's trembling, like one of those little Taco Bell dogs, and his eyes are just as buggy.

"How very *Silence of the Lambs* of you," I snicker. "But looking at you right now, you'd make a poor Hannibal Lector, not me, though. Did you want to try your own brain?"

"No." His voice is high-pitched, filled with fear, and I can't deny I'm inhaling it like a fresh breeze.

"Fine, open-heart surgery it is." I throw my knife and it slams in to the hilt, moving through his shirt and skin like butter.

The knife he's holding crashes to the tiled floor, and he wraps his hand around the hilt of mine, shock registering on his face. His hand tightens, and he pulls the knife from his chest, a strangled wheeze coming from his throat. He drops to his knees as his shirt blooms quickly with blood.

"Dang it!" I stomp my foot. "That's two patients in one day.

Doctors have such a tough job."

He falls forward, his face making a sickening sound as it connects with the floor, and my knife still gripped in his hand. I stride forward and yank it back, cleaning his blood off onto his shirt. I walk back to the room where I left my shackles just as I hear slow measured steps coming up from the basement.

*Reggie.* I clap with excitement.

I stand by the semi-open door and wait, my stomach bubbling with excitement over our cat-and-mouse game. *I love games.* His hand appears first, shoving open the door, and then his foot hits the floor as he pokes his head out. I grab onto his hair quickly, wrapping my arm around his windpipe and pressing my knife to his throat.

"Reggie!" I squeal. "Caught ya! You don't make a good mouse."

"Let go of me." He struggles a bit until I press in deeper with the knife.

"Why am I here? What was Delaney's plan for bringing me here?"

"Fuck you," he snarls, not at all afraid of dying like the others. He must think he still has a chance out of this, and I kind of want him to think he does, too. I love when the cat chases the mouse.

I shove him away from me and slip my knife back into my belt as he stumbles into the room with my first patient, his blood still pooling out of his eye socket. I hear him curse as I come in behind him, making him jump back and narrow his eyes.

"Are they all dead?" *I like him.*

"Nope," I shake my head. "Your little Christian friend ran out." I point to the front door. His eyes skate to the door, his mind trying to work out how he himself can run as well, and the excitement builds. "Shall I close my eyes and count to ten?"

His throat works hard on a swallow, and I watch his Adam's apple move slowly under the thin skin. I'm hoping he takes me up on my offer. I loved Hide and Seek as a child, and the last time I played it was around nine years old with Jan. Just the thought of her has my chest aching, but I can't let the thought of her mess up my fun right now. She's safe, and I'm in the middle of the most fun I've had in ages.

I close my eyes, making sure one stays cracked open, exactly how I did it as a kid. Then I begin to count, my mouth curling upwards as Reggie squirms. I get to three and the fucker bolts, making me squeal in delight. I scoop my shackles off the floor and give chase, both of our feet cracking against the hardwood.

"Ready or not! Here I come!"

"You said you'd count to ten!" he yells over his shoulder, his hand reaching for the door handle.

"I lied!" I exclaim as I throw the cuff end of my shackle, hitting him on the back of the head.

He stumbles, his left shoulder hitting the wall beside the door, and his hand coming up between us. He's panting, his skin is pale, and the defeat in his eyes is palpable. He knows he's about to die.

"They won't leave you alone after this. You will be a target forever," he tells me as he breathes heavily against the wall.

"Not forever," I smirk. "Only until I kill them all."

His eyes darken, the irises threatening violence, and my excitement ramps. Then he comes at me, a growl slipping from between his lips, and his hands wrap around my throat, but only because I let him. His fingers tighten, his teeth are bared, and when I choke out a laugh, his eyebrows crash in the center.

I slip my knife out from my belt and stab him in the stomach, reveling in the feeling of his warm blood coating my hand. Shock registers in his features and then his hands loosen as he falls back against the wall.

"Unfortunately," I grip the handle of my knife and yank it back out, "your death needs to be the messiest. I have a mural to paint."

He begins to cough, blood splattering out of his mouth and landing on my face. "You won't get away with it."

"Sure, I will." I slap his cheek, leaving behind a bloody handprint. "I'm the motherfucking Reaper Incarnate."

I slash my blade across his throat, giggling when his blood spurts out, and his body slinks down to the floor. I slip my blade back into my belt and crouch down in front of him, scooping his blood into my hand.

I begin to paint out what's become my very own branding: a bloody scythe. The dripping blood is a bonus. I get to the end and stare at it, knowing it needs one final touch. So, I scoop up more of Reggie's cooling blood and get to work. Just as I'm finishing, I hear gunshots outside in the driveway, and groan as I rush through the final word.

*Welcome to Hell, you've been reaped.*

I wipe off my hands on Reggie's shirt and take a deep breath as I swing open the front door.

# *Blaze*

We start pulling out all the dead bodies from the car that pulled up to Reginald's house, and just like we thought, Los Diablos. I wanted more than one to interrogate, but Santos got fucking trigger happy. At least the kid in the trunk of my car will do. He's in there now, sobbing and praying to Jesus to save him. Dumb piece of shit.

Once we have the bodies piled together, Zander starts taking a video, and Darius whips out his dick to piss on the mound.

"Are you fucking serious?" I snarl at him, and he tosses me a wink.

"I can't hold it; I'll get a UTI."

"Is that when your dick starts to make cheese?" Santos asks, and I watch Zander gag.

"That's syphilis, you dumb asshole," he says between retches.

"I can't wait until the day I can kill you three and live the rest of my days in peace," I snarl as I stride for the front door.

"He could never," Darius snickers. "The fucker would be bored out of his mind."

*He's not wrong.*

I reach the door and before I can grab the handle; it swings open, revealing the one thing my heart beats for. She's standing there, covered in blood, chains draped over her shoulder, and a shit-eating smirk on her face.

The organ in my chest races, and before I can even form thought, I have her wrapped up in my arms, bloody chains, and all.

"Miss me, Daddy?" she purrs, and my dick solidifies instantly.

"Yeah, baby." I smother my face into her hair. "I really fucking did."

"What took you guys so long?" she mumbles into my chest, her body finally relaxing.

"It's only been twenty-nine hours." I tell her, "we came as fast as we could."

"That's it?" She pulls back and looks at me. "It felt so much longer."

"Is that my baby girl?" Santos calls, and I pull away just in time for him to barrel into her, lifting her up into his arms. "Did you kill everyone in here?" he asks as he looks around her into the house.

"Yeah," she giggles as she snuggles into his neck. "Except for one, he ran out on me." Her pout is exaggerated as she sticks her bottom lip out, and maybe a little adorable.

"We caught a kid running out earlier," I say as I fold my arms over my chest and lean against the door frame. "He's in the trunk, praying."

"That's him!" Her eyes light up.

"We're going to play with him later," Santos coos into her ear, and she giggles.

"I love games. I've been playing them all day."

I look around her into the house and see carnage everywhere. "Looks like it."

"Give her to me." Darius shoves me aside and grabs Selene out of Santos' grip. "Baby, do you have chains?" I can hear the excitement in his voice.

"Not just chains!" She squeals, "shackles!"

The groan that comes from Darius' mouth is guttural and primal, and I can't help but admit this woman is perfect for each of us. Zander is next. He steps up into the house, slow and steady, and watches as she excitedly shows Darius how the shackles fit over her wrist, then gives him keys on a ring. He's patient for his turn to claim her.

Finally, her ocean blue eyes lock onto him, and she wiggles out of Darius' hold, running to Zander. He wraps her up into a tight grip, his face also burying into her hair.

"I love you," he says, and the rest of us pause, the air suddenly thick.

We haven't said that yet, not to her anyway.

She pulls back from him and looks up into his face. "Really?"

"Yeah," he nods. "I needed you to know that because you keep disappearing on me."

"Does that mean you'll be making love to me now?" Her face falls.

"Hell no," Zander grins. "Let's get you home so I can fuck you sore."

I look at both Darius and Santos, seeing their expressions and trying hard not to laugh in their faces. Both looked pissed that Zander chose to be the first one to say it. But I'm buying my time. I won't mind being last because I'll be the most memorable.

They start walking to the car, Selene swinging her shackles as the boys follow behind. I take one more peek inside the house and see she's painted a large scythe with blood, with a sweet message underneath.

*That's my girl.*

# Zander

Selene's wedged between Darius and Santos in the backseat as we head toward home, her sinful smile causing my heart to tug in my chest. I've been unsure whether to confess my love for her, but watching her being reunited with the guys had sealed the deal. She's the only woman for me, and there's no point in putting it off.

I'll never forgive myself if something happens to her, and she doesn't know how much she means to me.

"Bad Santos!" she scolds, her laughter peeling through the car as I glance back to see Santos hauling her into his lap, not hesitating to bury his face between her tits to motorboat them. Darius is watching them with a big grin, happy to have them both back to normal.

We all know Santos' mood has been affecting Darius too, so seeing him relaxed makes me relax. If he doesn't pick up any concern, then we have nothing to worry about. Santos is all right.

"You like me bad, my bloody queen," Santos mumbles from her chest, leaning back while keeping his hands firmly on her waist to stop any escape plan she may concoct. Blaze is fuming in the driver's seat, probably upset to be left out of the titty party Santos is currently having with our girl.

"So true. You know what else I like? Orgasms. You have any of those stashed away for me when we get home? Apparently, being kidnapped and murdering a bunch of people makes me stupidly horny," Selene says with a moan, making me snort.

"You're just figuring that out now? You're soaking wet panties didn't give it away as you played with those bastards?"

She goes to speak, but Santos grabs her throat and yanks her against his chest, devouring her in a kiss that causes a groan to fill the car. I can't tell you which one of us makes the noise, but I don't give a shit.

She's lucky I didn't haul her into the front seat and make her ride me.

She peers over her shoulder at me with a devilish grin, grinding down on Santos' lap and making him groan. "Pretty sure my flaps are chaffed from them. I did a lot of running around playing games today."

"Wait until we get home. Your flaps will be chaffed by the time I'm done with your cunt," Santos growls, his eyes darting to Darius seriously. "At least my dick will be nice and wet to slide right into Darius." Jesus Christ.

Selene moans her approval at the idea, but her eyes never leave me. "You'll kiss it better, won't you, Zan?"

"That depends," I snort. "If your cunt's dripping with cum, Darius can kiss it better instead."

"Can you guys talk about something else? Ever?" Blaze demands, his angry eyes moving to the rear-view mirror to glare at them in the back. "We get it, you're horny little rabbits."

"Don't act like you can't wait to bury your monster cock inside me too," Selene coos, finally taking her eyes off me. "I've been looking forward to going to pound town with you."

Blaze's hands tighten on the wheel, but his eyes soften a fraction, not being able to tell her no. "You'll be the death of me."

"Excellent. Because I have a feeling you'll be the death of my pussy. I'm so wet right now, Daddy," she smirks, licking her lips, a surprised shriek leaving her as Darius suddenly grabs her and tugs her into his lap, kissing the shit out of her like a man starved. Santos pouts, watching as Selene doesn't even put up a fight.

"How come you don't fight him on it? I had to wrangle you like a wild animal to get you in my lap."

"You like the chase," she giggles as she pulls back from Darius slightly, her eyes sparkling with amusement. "It's foreplay."

Blaze looks mad at the banter, but his lip kicks up into a tiny smirk as he keeps his eyes on the road, seeming glad to have us all back together. My best friend is a grumpy bastard when he wants to be, but we are family. Our happiness makes him happy.

"If you come sit back on my lap, I'll make you come," Santos exclaims, causing Selene to jerk her attention away from Darius, who was kissing her neck.

"Promise?"

"I'd never joke about orgasms. Come here," he orders, making Blaze curse as Selene moves across the backseat to do as she's told. First time for everything.

"You are not fucking while I'm driving!" Blaze barks, but Santos chuckles darkly, shoving his hand down the front of Selene's pants, a gasp of surprise leaving her as his fingers press inside her.

"I wasn't going to fuck her. Not unless she begs me."

"I'm begging," Selene pants as she grinds down on his hand, making me laugh. Santos growls, leaning forward to bite her bottom lip sharply.

"You get what you're given until we get home. Got it?"

"Daddy! Santos is being mean!" she huffs, and Blaze can't stop the grin that forms on his face.

"What was that? You want us to give you more orgasm torture and not let you come?"

She clamps her lips shut, giving Santos a dirty look, daring him to hold out on her. He moves his fingers in and out of her, her scent filling the car and causing my dick to harden behind my zipper. Darius leans back to watch the show, chewing on his lip as Santos works to get our girl closer to release.

Sure, I wish I were the one to get her off, but seeing her come apart on Santos' lap is almost as good. Whatever he's doing to her is working, because her head drops back, and her eyes flutter closed. Her muscles tighten and her hands dig into Santos' shoulders, a hiss leaving him at the twinge of pain she gifts him.

"Oh my God!" she screams suddenly, her eyes flying open as Santos fists her hair firmly.

"Look at me!" he snaps, some of his control vanishing. I knew it wouldn't take long.

He doesn't slow down, and she doesn't stop screaming for God. My face scrunching as I suddenly hear something like an echo. I listen closely, not understanding what it is until Selene finally becomes quiet, and Santos lets her forehead fall to his, whispering sweet promises that probably involve blood and violence.

*"Please, God! Save us from these devils!"*

Blaze glances at me with a frown as he drives into our driveway and kills the engine. "What the fuck was that?" He snaps as he gets out of the car.

*"Please, God!"*

Darius sniggers as he opens the door to climb out. "Seems our Bible buddy thinks he's having a prayer session with our girl. Do you think God heard you, baby?"

Santos cackles as he helps Selene adjust her pants before they climb out, too. Even Blaze is finding amusement in the situation. I scramble out just in time to see Blaze open the trunk, revealing the babbling idiot we've locked in there.

His eyes blink against the light, but they find Selene and his eyes widen. "God heard us? He saved you from the Devil? Your demons are gone?"

She grins, leaning down to peer at him closely. "I am the fucking Devil. My demons are my friends."

"Why were you praying then?!" he exclaims, seeming ready to piss his pants as she giggles like the maniac she is.

"Praying? I was coming. Hard, might I add. My baby sure knows how to send me to Heaven."

Santos bats his lashes at her like the lovesick fool he is, ignoring the guy as he starts praying again. "Speaking of Heaven. Let's leave Blaze and Zander to lock this fucker up while we go and fuck our souls into each other's bodies."

"What if we don't have souls?" she questions as Darius and Santos start guiding her toward the house, pretending like they can't hear Blaze and me cussing them out for ditching us.

"There will be orgasms there. Who gives a shit?" he whoops like an idiot, eyeing the shackles she's dragging alongside them. He better make it fast, because the moment Blaze and I are done tying this dude up, we'll be in there to join the party, and I want her on my dick one way or another.

# Santos

Selene is taking too long to walk, so I grab the back of her thighs and hold her against my chest, making out with her like crazy as Darius fists my shirt and drags us through the house with Selene's shackles in hand, guiding me since I can't fucking see. We need to slow down to make sure Selene gets off multiple times, but the selfish part of me doesn't give a shit right now. I just want to be buried inside her and fill her with my cum.

Darius kicks the bedroom door shut behind us and drops the shackles, prying her from my arms, not hesitating to yank her shirt over her head.

"Wait! I need a fucking shower," she states, making him shrug.

"All righty then."

I grin, knowing what he's going to do before she does. He strips her bare and throws her over his shoulder, ignoring her protesting and cursing, carrying her to the bathroom and turning the shower on. I get naked, not wanting to wait for her to be done, my eyes lingering on Darius as he places her on her feet and yanks his clothes off, too.

"You're not joining me," she snaps, crossing her arms as Darius guides her under the hot spray. I roll my eyes, ignoring her as Darius and I climb in with her. She goes to tell us to get out, but I shove her back against the wall, plastering my body to hers and kissing the words right out of her mouth. She slaps at my arm, trying to remain angry at our intrusion, but not wanting me to stop.

She bites my lip hard, drawing blood before sucking it into her mouth as her nails dig into my back. I feel like a teenager again, almost coming down my fucking leg as her body rubs against mine.

Rough hands run across my back as Darius sandwiches me between them, his lips moving across my shoulder lightly to remind me he's there, too. I don't stop what I'm doing, but I reach around until my hand rests on his hip, giving it a squeeze.

Being between them is something I thought about regularly, both of them completing me in ways I didn't know was possible. I realize I'm crazy and irrational, but they love me for it, and they help center me when it's needed.

I lift Selene against the wall, sliding inside her where I belong, her low groan telling me it's what she needed too. I fuck her hard, my butt bumping back against Darius' solid length as he lets me take what I need from her. My mind drifts to the disgust in Papi's eyes when he found out I let Darius touch me. The way he made what we have seem like trash. The fact that he never thought to tell his other son about me, not expecting his two lives to collide like they have.

Anger burns inside me the more I think about it, until I realize I've zoned out as someone is trying to yank me back from Selene.

*Selene?* Fuck.

"Santos, snap the fuck out of it!" Darius shouts, managing to get between us and put Selene on her feet, her eyes wide as she peers at me over his shoulder. What the fuck happened?

As if sensing my thoughts, Darius grabs the back of my neck in a tight grip, his voice low. "You good, man?" My breathing's rapid, and confusion fills me as I try to look at her, but he stays in front of me so my attention can't waver. "You're back with us now?"

I shake my head, trying to control myself as I try to piece together what happened. I can't hurt Selene. It's impossible, and even if I do, no one can stop me. Making her bleed and bruise is something she craves, soaking in the violence we create from pleasure. So why is Darius stopping me?

Once my breathing calms, Darius releases my neck and takes a small step back, turning the water off as he goes. "It's like you were possessed, babe. You weren't hearing or seeing anything. What were you thinking about? You almost fucked Selene through the damn wall." That's nothing new. I always fuck her hard.

My eyes seek her out, seeing her reddened skin, finger shaped bruises on her thighs and a streak of blood in her light hair. "The fuck?" I mumble, noticing a blood streak on the shower wall. Selene can handle anything. We fuck with no restraint all the time, but this is different. I don't like not knowing what's happening.

Did I smash her head into the wall? That's a little rough, even for me. If she's bleeding, I want to know what I did. I hate being in the dark with my own actions.

I must look completely crazed because Selene's eyes track my face with concern. I climb out of the shower, putting my fist through the wall on my way out.

"Santos! Get back here!" Darius growls, but I keep going, needing to break something. Papi isn't allowed to live in my head rent-free and mess with me. I don't give a fuck about him, that's what I tell myself, but a small part of me is fucked up from finally finding him.

"You want to put some clothes on?" Zander teases as I almost run him down in the hallway, his eyes narrowing when I slam him back with my hands, needing him out of my way. I need the gym, the punching bag being a better alternative to the walls.

Footsteps follow me, stopping to linger in the gym's doorway as I stalk over to the heavy bag and start throwing my fists at it, my dick swinging and slapping my thighs. They've seen me naked plenty, so I don't give a fuck. I need to release the rage before I use it on one of the guys.

I feel Blaze's thunderous gaze before he even speaks. "What the fuck is wrong now?"

I don't look up, but I sense Selene enter the room, her scent surrounding me, breaking through some of the anger. It's stupid to let a man I hardly remember have so much control over my emotions, but knowing he ran off to raise his other son? Choosing him over me? Yeah, it isn't good for my mood.

"Leave him alone. He just needs a minute," Selene demands, my eyes darting across the room to hers. She approaches me, not being afraid of my fists like any other woman would be, resting her hand on my hip as I continue to throw punch after punch, making sure to stay back enough to avoid getting clipped with my elbow.

She doesn't stop me, doesn't tell me how to feel. She simply lets me know she's there, waiting for when I'm done purging my demons.

"San, you're all right," Darius says confidently, trying to make me believe it. I'm not, though, I never blackout in a fit of rage like that. I'm pissed I can't remember my actions, but even more pissed for the reason behind them.

"I'm not fucking fine," I growl, swinging my arm as hard as possible, my knuckles cracking on impact as the bag swings.

"Come back to the bedroom. You'll burn your mood out on Selene and me," he answers, making me scowl.

"No."

"What the fuck happened?!" Blaze barks, sick of being kept in the dark. I turn my attention away from the bag, trying to relax as Selene's arm goes around my waist.

"I don't fucking know. That's the problem!"

Darius cringes, "we were messing around in the shower. He was banging Selene and zoned out. She's fine, but we were trying to snap him out of it."

"Did I smash your head into the wall or something?" I ask Selene, making her chuckle.

"No. You can't hurt me, silly."

"There's blood in your hair. I'm not worried about hurting you, you're as psychotic as I am," I chuckle dryly. "I'd just be really mad if I made you bleed and didn't remember it."

"It's your blood. You had your face in my hair and were biting the hell out of your lip," she murmurs as she lifts up on tip-toe, licking my lip, making me frown. I lift my hand to touch it, feeling the sting from a nasty cut. I groan as she leans forward again and gently sucks it into her mouth, tasting my blood without taking her eyes off mine.

She gives me a cheeky smile as she steps back, fisting my dick and giving it a few long strokes. "Now, can you come back to my room so we can finish what we started? You were fucking me so hard I almost saw stars. I'd like to finish. What made you mad, anyway?"

"Papi," I grunt. "I remembered how he spoke about Darius and me, then started thinking of Loqi and lost my shit a little."

Selene watches me with confusion, but Darius snorts. "I don't give a shit what he thinks."

"Excuse me? Why would you listen to that dumbass piece of shit?" Selene demands, her eyes rounding in surprise as I sigh.

"He's my Papi. The one who left me as a kid."

# Darius

Selene kicks us out of Santos' room, wanting to talk to him in private. I've never known him to have blackouts like that, and I hate not being in there with him. Blaze and Zander are quiet as I wander into the kitchen, dressed and needing a beer.

I plonk down on the couch, sighing before taking a long drink to center myself.

"He blacked-out?" Zander mumbles, sitting down to watch me.

"He was banging her, then went harder, zoning out in the process. Selene's fine, as you could see, but she was worried about him when he didn't respond to either of us. His dad's really fucking him up. I could kill him," I scowl, glancing at Blaze, who looks ready to march back into the bedroom and haul Selene out. "Leave him alone, Blaze. He needs a moment."

"What if he's fucking lost complete control? For real? It's never good when Santos loses it. You know that since you're usually his fucking punching bag," he grits out.

"Selene isn't some flimsy bitch we dragged in from a party. She can protect herself and doesn't need us to hover. She's worried about him, not scared of him. Jesus," I spit. "Let her have a heart to heart with him. He obviously has a lot on his chest he needs to vent, and he can catch her up on everything she missed. Papi was a real dick about me being with Santos, but we also didn't expect to run into him, either. His mind's spinning, and Selene will shake it out of him. How's the bible basher?" I ask, changing the subject. Blaze gives me a filthy look, telling me he knows I did it on purpose, but he answers my question.

"He's tied up and ready to be interrogated later. I was hoping to nail our girl first."

"They won't be long," I shrug, hearing a moan from the other end of the hallway, making me chuckle. "Well, they won't be too long. She's obviously fucking him better."

"Is that a good idea after what just happened?" Zander asks, and I shrug again.

"Let them fuck their demons out of each other, then you two can nail her as a welcome home gift."

"What about you?" Zander says with a raised eyebrow, but I'm not worried about missing out. I have all the time in the world to fuck her.

"I won't die without her pussy for another day, I promise. You two feel free to tag-team her while I stay with San. I don't want him alone right now. There's a fifty-fifty percent chance of him running off to massacre his old man and half the MC, so I'll keep an eye on him."

"You're good to him."

"Of course I am. He's mine," I answer, meaning every word. I'd be missing a part of myself without that crazy bastard. If he ran off on a suicide mission, then we'll all go to war to bring his ass back home.

# Chapter Three

## *Blaze*

There's something snapping into place as the three of us sit here in silence. I've always known about the connection Santos and Darius feel, and yet, hearing the confirmation and having Selene solidify it, is making me see things I didn't before. I used to be so afraid of a woman coming between us, weaseling in, and tearing us apart. As much as she's weaseled her way into all of our hearts, she's also healed us in places we didn't even realize were broken.

"I think we should go question the altar boy," I grunt, as I stand. "You want to join us?" I ask Darius, who looks deep in thought.

"Nah," he shakes his head. "I'm good here."

"Let's get this done," Zander yawns, exhaustion finally hitting him.

We head to the basement door and Zan grabs my shoulder. "Do you remember Santos telling us anything about his family or how he grew up?"

"Very little," I shrug. "His mother struggled to raise him and worked a lot. He practically raised himself on the streets."

"I remember when we first met him and Darius. Do you remember?"

"How could I forget?" I roll my eyes. "They both almost received a bullet between their eyes."

Santos and Darius were at a Los Diablos house party that Zander and I had crashed. They were there looking for a few missing girls, and Zan and I were there to get info for Henry. A fight broke out and just in true Santos' form, he went around shooting the place up, with Darius at his back. When they found us in an office pulling files, I had my gun pressed to Santos' forehead, and it was downhill from there. We found the girls they were looking for and they decided to join our cause.

We never questioned how easily we blended, never thought too long about the chemistry we had as friends, and not until a few moments ago did I truly believe in fate. We were all meant to walk this life together, causing mayhem.

We head down into the basement, our nostalgic moment over, and find the little altar boy trembling in his binds.

"I can't believe he's a Diablo." Zander kicks his foot and chuckles when the kid whimpers. "Do they not have standards?"

"Let's ask him," I say as I grab a chair, straddling it to face the kid. "Take the gag out of his mouth."

Zander yanks the dirty cloth out, tossing it on the floor as the kid begins to choke. "I'm … a … new … recruit," he forces out between coughs.

"What made you want to join a gang, kid?" Zander asks as he crouches in front of him, "shouldn't you be studying to be a priest or something?"

"Just because I'm a devout Catholic doesn't mean I don't need the money." He spits out, "and I'm not a kid. I'm twenty-three years old."

"Under-developed then," Zander lines his words with pity, and I can't hold in the snicker.

"Why Los Diablos?" I ask.

"They approached me at church. They saw my grandma was frail and old, and asked me if I wanted to make extra cash."

"Diablos are recruiting at churches now?" Zander gives me a shocked look.

"Praise be to God," I mumble.

"Amen," the guy says from the floor.

"What's your name?" Zander asks.

"Joey, but everyone calls me Pepe. Look, I'm all my grandma has, and if I don't get home soon, she'll worry."

"Should have thought of that before joining a dangerous gang, *Pepe*," I tsk.

"Sometimes choices are limited for guys like me," he mumbles.

"Guys like us," Zander corrects him. "We all have issues, but it doesn't mean we have to sacrifice ourselves to survive."

"What is it you guys do? You're with that woman, right? I could feel the evil coming off her." He looks sincere, but I don't like anyone talking shit about my girl.

So, I slap him across the face, hard. The impact busts open his bottom lip and blood begins to run down his chin.

"I think you should reword that."

"She killed everyone in the house!" he exclaims.

"Did you miss the part where she was kidnapped? Or how about *shackled* to a fucking wall?" Zander grits out, his fists shaking. He wants to hit him, too.

"They told me she killed people, innocent lives. She's the Reaper Incarnate." He leans in as if telling us a secret.

"We know who she is." I roll my eyes. "Tell us," I hold out my hand, "what is it you know about the Reaper Incarnate?"

"She kills businessmen around the city because she hates men."

"He's not too far off," Zander chuckles.

"She kills men who take advantage of women and children, all of whom have bought and sold people for a long time," I inform him.

"Like slaves?"

"Exactly like slaves." I nod. "Los Diablos and Mack Delaney are right now head of that trade here in New York, and you just signed yourself over to them. How would Jesus feel about that?" I widen my eyes.

"What would Jesus do?" Zander says, working hard to hide his smirk.

"Jesus would try to enlighten them about their ways and then pray for their souls," Pepe says.

"Well, there you have it," Zander claps his hands. "All the answers will be found in Jesus."

"All praises be to Jesus Christ." Pepe's chin hits his chest.

"We're going to help Jesus." I clap my hands. "Let's make the Diablos see the errors in their ways."

"Amen!" Pepe exclaims.

"I have an idea," Zander looks at me with a twinkle in his eye, "we can't let them know we're cleansing them of evil."

"No," I agree. "They would fight it."

"Exactly," Zander continues. "Let's instead infiltrate them and bless them from within." He holds out his arms.

"Yes!" Pepe nods emphatically. "Like a soldier for Christ!"

Zander begins to untie him and gives him a stern look. "We need you to be our soldier, Pepe. Can you handle it?"

"They can never know who you're really working for," I add. "Which is Jesus," I tag on.

"I can keep the secret in the name of the Lord." Pepe nods solemnly and then crosses himself. "I am a faithful soldier."

"Perfect." I stand. "And if you fuck up, Pepe," his eyes shoot up to mine, "I will crucify you, much like Jesus himself."

He swallows thickly and nods as Zander covers a chuckle into his hand. "I won't let you down."

"Try to infiltrate where they're going to be on the next pickup. They will have women and children," Zander tells him. "Then you come and tell us so we can save them."

"I will." He nods quickly. "You can count on me."

We walk him upstairs and to the front door, just as Selene screams out for Jesus, making Pepe sign himself.

"Peace be with you," Zander snickers as he opens the front door.

"And also with you." Pepe nods and hurries out.

"Do you think this will work?" Zander laughs as he shuts the door.

"Yeah," I grin, "it'll work fucking beautifully."

# Selene

I leave Santos snoring in bed, and head out to look for the rest of my boys. I honestly don't know how I let the similarities between Santos and Loqi sail over my head. They were way too similar for me not to notice, but I was so consumed with Jan that it didn't fully sink in. Papi Loco is in for a world of pain when we meet again, and we will because I have shit to settle with my sister.

I find Darius asleep on the couch, his chest moving slowly, and his fingers twitching. I kiss his forehead and cover him with a blanket. From the moment Zander professed his love for me, I've been thinking nonstop about my feelings for them in return.

Santos and I were cut from the same cloth and sewn together with the same parental issues. No wonder we fit the way we do. Then there's Darius, whose heart is five times too big and sees the good in us, no matter how unhinged we become. I brush my fingers through his hair and head into the kitchen to find Blaze making bacon. My big grizzly bear, who has a hardened crust, is just a soft gooey teddy bear underneath.

"I thought you might be hungry," he mumbles as he begins to put the strips on a plate.

"I am." I hurry to sit at the table, yanking Santos' shirt down below my ass. I'm not wearing panties and my sore little flower will not be happy if she's smashed into the chair.

He puts a full plate of bacon in front of me and a steaming cup of hot chocolate. I haven't had hot chocolate since I was a kid. I stare down into the mug, and he clears his throat.

"I figured coffee would keep you up and you probably need your rest." He looks bashfully grumpy, and it makes my heart squeeze in my chest.

"Thank you, Daddy."

His dark brown eyes flare with heat, and my pussy clenches with anticipation. I haven't had him inside of me since Henry's basement. He may have joined us in Nevada, but I know that's not his thing. Blaze won't always want to share me like Santos and Darius do.

With his eyes still on me, I begin biting into the crispy meat, the salty flavor making me moan, and I suck my fingers clean after each piece. Once my plate is nearly empty, and my hot chocolate done, Blaze leans on the table.

"Can I ask you a few questions about how you were taken?"

"I was wondering when you would," I grin at him. "Where the others are all action. You like to analyze everything."

He sits on the chair in front of me and grabs my foot up into his lap, his deft fingers kneading into my aching flesh.

"I was stupid," I begin, not liking to admit it. "I recognized Henry's old driver and hopped in his fucking car."

"That was stupid, but," he shrugs, "an honest mistake."

"He knocks me out and tosses me in the fucking trunk." My fist hits the tabletop, my rage coming back full force. "I kill him and find these punks standing around with Delaney."

"We know him as Mack," he tells me. "He and Henry worked closely."

"Well, he's going to be working closely with my fists as I knock his gums down his throat." I snarl, "anyway, I ended up back here in New York in a basement, and it really felt like days."

He nods, the scar on his face pulling with his grimace. "I thought maybe you had run again."

"I thought you guys might have given up on me." I smile and grab his hand in mine. "This is new for the both of us."

"Yeah." He brings my hand to his mouth, brushing his lips back and forth over the skin. Goosebumps rise along my arms, and he grins, knowing his effect on me.

I'm suddenly overtaken by a yawn, my mouth gaping open and my body stiffening. When I finally open my eyes again, he's grinning at me, and I can't help but notice how handsome he is.

"Let's get you to bed." He stands and hauls me up. I jump up into his arms and wrap my legs around his waist.

"Are you coming too?"

His big hands land on my bare ass and he groans into my neck, his cock straining between us.

"No." He licks my neck. "You need rest, but I'll be there to wake you up."

"I need another shower," I moan.

His fingers swipe into my pussy, and he growls, "Am I touching Santos' cum?"

"And mine," I snicker.

He sinks two of his large fingers inside of me, pumping in and out as he takes me back to what's become my bedroom, the one Zander tried to lock me in so long ago. I giggle when I remember jumping out of the window and discovering his tracking app.

"Any reason you're laughing while I finger fuck you?" Blaze snarls.

I grab his face between my hands and kiss him, my tongue dragging over the hard ridge of his scar. "I remembered the first time I was here."

He pulls his fingers out of me, gripping my ass once again, and leaving it wet with mine and Santos' release. "I was so pissed off with having you here." He kicks open my room door.

"Only because you wanted me so bad," I tease him, and he graces me with another one of his rare smiles.

"Maybe, brat." He drops me on the bed. "Now go shower and then sleep."

"Yes, Daddy," I say to his retreating back, and then laugh when he grumbles down the hall.

*I can't wait to fuck the grump right out of his ballsac.*

# Zander

I finish my shower and find myself heading to Selene's room, missing her filthy mouth and warm, tight body. I step into her bedroom and my ears are once again assaulted by the sound of her singing. Is she making up her own words to Twinkle, Twinkle Little Star? I snort as she sings about cutting off dicks, and fall onto her bed, resting my arms behind my head.

There's a new atmosphere in this house. We're all more relaxed, and it feels lighter. I wish it could stay this way forever, all of us here, fucking our girl whenever we want, and not give a fuck about what's going happening on the outside. But that's just not what we signed up for. The four of us banded together years ago in an agreement to take down the industry that took something from each of us. We're reaching the end of our goals, but it's still a way away.

The water shuts off and I hear the blow dryer start, snickering when I think about her washing Santos off of her, only to have me on her next. This will be the story of her life; she'll forever walk funny with a sore pussy. The door opens, and she steps out of it, completely naked, and my cock tents inside my boxers.

"Every time I see your cock, I'm reminded of the fact that you took your daddy's dick and said, '*hold my beer.*'"

"Is this gonna be a forever thing?" I groan into my hands. "You talking about my dead father's dick?"

"It's not every day a girl can say she fucked a dude and his daddy." She prowls toward me. "Now take those off and fuck my ass."

"Jesus," I moan, and quickly shed my boxers.

"No more praying," she holds up her hand, "I've had enough of Jesus today."

She grabs the lube out of her side table and crawls over my body. I lie transfixed as she squirts some into her hand, coating my cock and then her ass.

"You really want me to fuck your ass?" I breathe, my dick jumping with the prospect.

"No, Baby Walton," she rolls her eyes, "I was hoping Daddy Walton would come back and do it for you."

I snarl and lift her up, finding her tight asshole. I line myself up and slam her down on me. The squeeze is so fucking tight and when she screams out; I jerk inside of her, making her cry out again.

"That hurt, asshole." She slaps my chest.

"That's what you get for constantly bringing up my father," I grit through my teeth.

She begins to grind into me, a sly smirk on her face, and I sense something coming before she even has to say it.

"Did you think rough sex was gonna teach me a lesson? Wrong thought you, Yoda."

I chuckle as I grab her hips, pumping up inside of her, knowing I won't last long. I've missed her, I'm afraid to lose her, and I fucking told her I loved her. She must see something in my eyes because she falls forward, her mouth brushing against mine.

"You love me, Baby Walton?"

"Yes," no hesitation.

Her ass clenches around my cock, making me see stars.

"I love you, too." Her words are spoken so softly, but they slip down past my ribcage and wrap around my heart.

I thrust up into her a few more times, and we both come at the same time, her head tossing back as she cries out. She falls down beside me and wraps her arm around my waist.

"You're the second person I've said that to, ever."

"The first?" I begin to feel the burn of jealousy low in my stomach.

"Jan," she says softly, and I pull her in closer.

"We'll figure this all out and get you back with your sister. You both need each other." I kiss her head. "Now sleep."

"Can you tell me a story?"

I chuckle at her request, my fingers skimming lazily along her back. "What story?"

"The one about John Dempster's death. I want every detail."

I groan and cover my face with my hand, "I am really not the one to tell you that. Maybe Blaze, fuck, even Santos. They were the ones who enjoyed it the most."

"But you're here now and I want to hear it."

So, I tell her because that's what my woman wants. I go over every disgusting detail, even gagging at the gorier parts. But it's all worth it to see her face light up with glee, even though her eyes are drooping with tiredness.

Just as I gag my way through John's lungs being lifted from his body, I hear her soft snores and breathe out a sigh of relief. I gather her closer to my body and close my eyes, finally feeling at peace enough to sleep.

# Santos

I awaken to find an arm tightly wrapped around my waist, prickly stubble pressing against my shoulder blade as I go to move. I can sense Selene isn't in the room with me like she was when I fell asleep after banging her brains out, but I don't mind. I'm just happy to wake up to someone.

Being alone in my own head is dangerous lately because my emotions seem to be controlling me a lot more than usual, but something simmers it all down when Darius or Selene are close.

"D?" I mumble, rolling over to face Darius, his eyes cracking open as a soft smile takes over his face. The bastard is making me too soft, but I wouldn't change a thing.

"You better this morning?" he asks, snuggling closer to me and playfully biting my pec. We have shit to do today, so as much as my dick likes the idea of choking him while he swallows my cum, I know it can't happen. After my night with Selene, I'm not sure I have anything left in my damn ballsac, anyway.

"Yeah. I don't think there's any anger left. Selene fucked it right out of my body," I grin, grabbing his wrist as his fingers brush against my dick. "Not this morning, you sex fiend."

"Why not? It's still early," he groans, but he rolls away from me, knowing I'm right. I usually am.

"The others will already be awake, so we might as well get this show on the road. I need a hot shower and a strong coffee," I grumble, rolling out of bed and wandering toward the door, making Darius chuckle.

"You want pants?"

"Not particularly," I reply on my way out, bee-lining to the kitchen to make a coffee. Zander's sitting at the counter, looking ready to bust in his pants as he hand-feeds Selene toast and bacon, her tongue poking out to lick the grease off his fingers in a way that shouldn't look so damn erotic, but it does.

"I've got something better you can suck on," I wink, leaning back against the counter to wait for the coffee to brew.

She raises an eyebrow, sounding offended. "What's better than bacon? I'll tell you right now, nothing is."

"How about bacon wrapped around my dick? I'll even let you

lick the grease from my sack," I offer, Zander giving me a dirty look for ruining his moment with her. Tough shit. If I can lure her away with a bacon covered dick and a greasy ballsac, he isn't doing a good enough job.

"Good morning. Why don't you put pants on? You're ruining my view," Zander grumbles, eyeing my dick like it's the Devil.

"Keep looking at it like that, and you'll have to deal with it," I throw back, my dick hardening slightly as it joins the conversation. Zander's eyes widen before he darts his gaze away, making me grin in victory. He's so easy to rile up.

Darius wanders in, smirking at me but keeping silent, knowing I'm pissing people off, but having one hell of a good time doing it. I should dunk my balls into Blaze's coffee. Might be a tad hot though, and I'm pretty attached to my balls.

As if on cue, Blaze wanders in freshly showered, his scowl hitting me immediately as he catches an eyeful of my junk. "The fuck is wrong with you?"

"You want the book or the dot points version?" I ask seriously, the other three sniggering while Blaze continues to look at me like I pissed in his cereal. I might do that, too.

"I wrote the fucking book about what's wrong with you. I just wanted to know what I was adding to it this morning," he barks. "Now, go cover up your dick before you lose it."

"Wait, you want my dick? Why didn't you say so? Come here, Daddy Blaze. Let me give you some loving!" I exclaim gleefully as I move toward him, risking my manhood as I dart around to climb on his back like a monkey, my dick and balls pressing into his back.

"Santos!" Blaze bellows, trying to shake me off, but I'm like a leech once I have a good grip. I laugh loudly over his cursing, holding on for dear life as he twists his big body to try and throw me off.

"Yee-fucking-haw!"

"You little fucking shit! You're dead!" Blaze shouts, failing to get me to let go, resorting to slapping at me. His hand cracks again my butt, and I let out a fake as fuck groan.

"Harder, Daddy."

"Get him the fuck off me!" Blaze demands, glaring at Darius, who's smothering his laughter, walking over to help with the situation.

"San, let him go."

"Not until he promises to finish what he started. All this yelling and spanking is making me horny," I smirk, almost losing my grip as Blaze twists again while I'm distracted.

"You filthy cunt! Get your boner off me!" Blaze is basically screaming the house down like a woman terrified of a mouse, but I know my life depends on me doing as I'm told.

"Okay! Stop moving and I'll get down!" I chuckle, waiting for him to stop before grinding my dick against his back before jumping down. He turns on me, his fists clenched and ready for murder, but Selene darts in front of me, giving me her back before lifting her shirt and blinding him with her tits.

He halts his attack, staring at them like a beacon in a storm, suddenly snapping out of it to glare at her. "That's a dirty trick."

She fixes her shirt, much to everyone's annoyance, giving me a wink. "No one hurts my baby boy."

"Your *baby boy* is the biggest dick!" Blaze snaps, making her grin.

"We're talking about big dicks now? Have you seen what monster you have in your pants, Daddy?"

"I can't fucking deal with you," he grumbles, but his lips lift into a smile, giving him away. He's been finding more humor in things lately, something else we can give Selene credit for. Then again, seeing the big grumpy cunt smile is just as scary as his anger sometimes.

She stands on tip-toes and kisses his cheek, heading over to the coffee machine to grab my coffee and handing it to me. "Here you go. Drink that to keep your damn mouth shut for five minutes."

"You really know how to turn me on, baby girl," I chuckle, taking it and sipping the liquid gold without complaint.

They discuss Pepe and Mack, wondering where to go next with our plans, and I stay silent like a good boy until my coffee cup is empty. Then I make the most annoying noise I can think of, drawing their attention before shaking my hips to cause my dick to slap against my hips, cackling as Blaze's murderous eyes meet mine.

I dart up the hallway as he goes to stand, shutting myself in the bathroom for my shower before I push my luck any further, hearing Selene and Darius laughing loudly as Blaze snaps at them for finding it funny.

# Darius

After our interesting morning with Santos being back to his usual self, we tidy up after breakfast. I'm surprised when there's a knock at the door and I find Pepe on the doorstep, Blaze stepping in beside me to glare at him. "The fuck do you want?"

Pepe swallows, his Adam's apple bobbing as he glances between us with concern.

"Um, you wanted me to let you know about any shipments?"

"So, you thought you'd just stop by for a coffee to talk about it?" Blaze growls, making the man step back and mutter a prayer to Jesus before he nods.

"I didn't want to waste time."

"You're wasting time now. Fucking talk!" Blaze barks, grabbing the front of his shirt and dragging him inside, shutting the door behind him. I lean back against the wall and cross my arms, eyeing the shaking idiot with amusement. We don't make a habit of letting people into the house, but Blaze obviously wants to play games, which is fine by me. Before the guy can open his mouth, Santos wanders out from his shower, halting when he realizes we have company.

"What's Pipi doing here?"

"It's Pepe," the dumbass states, making Santos grin wide. At least he could take his stupid mood out on this guy instead of Blaze.

"That's what I said! Come here and talk to San. I don't bite! You have gossip for me? I looooove gossip!" He exclaims with excitement, scaring Pepe as he marches over to him and drops an arm around his shoulders, pulling his gun out of the back of his pants and pressing it against Pepe's temple. "Now, speak. Before you and Jesus have an early meet and greet."

Pepe isn't far off pissing his pants, but Santos is having a blast, so I let him have his fun. Selene's grinning from her place beside Zander, loving every second of it, but not wanting to disrupt him by joining in. *Yet.*

"I'll talk! It's why I'm here! There's a shipment being delivered today!" he blurts out, his eyes widen as Santos presses the gun harder against his skin.

"And?"

"It's got a handful of women and about ten teenagers. The youngest is twelve, and they're supposed to be getting some more soon. It's happening at one of our warehouses," he chokes out, his eyes not leaving Santos until I step closer with a low chuckle, dropping an arm around Santos' shoulders to tug him back a step.

"C'mon, babe. Give him a second to think. It's a bit hard to do if you blow his brains out."

"Might give the wall an artistic vibe," Santos grumbles, but does as he's told, moving the gun away from Pepe's face to lean against me. "Maybe we can make him bleed just a little? I need more lube."

"If you think you're using this cunt's blood in my ass, you have another think coming, dick face," I scowl, Pepe's eyes becoming as wide as saucers.

"You're gay?"

I frown, turning to eye him with annoyance. "I'm not gay. I just like his dick in my ass sometimes. Why? You wanna come play trains with us?"

"No! Jesus, please help heal the minds of these men! The Devil has taken them, but it's not too late! Take them in your loving arms and forgive them for all they've done. Teach them the right path to Heaven!" he exclaims to the ceiling, making me snort. Jesus couldn't save us if he tried. We've been soldiers for the Devil for too damn long, and we like it.

Santos flashes Selene a dark grin. "What would Jesus do if he knew I came in your cunt, then Darius licked it clean?"

"With the volume you call to him, I'm pretty sure Jesus knows," Zander deadpans, eyeing Pepe as the idiot babbles prayers under his breath, praying to let us into Heaven. The guy's lucky we find it so amusing, or Selene would have slit his throat by now.

Santos has a glint in his eye, telling me he's not done being a dick yet. "Hold him still."

Pepe goes to move, but I grab his arms tight and press against his back, having no idea what Santos wants, but letting him do it, anyway. The moment Santos drops his pants, I almost choke on my own damn tongue. I've seen way too much of that dick this morning, and not enough of it going inside me.

"What are you doing?!" Pepe practically screams, fear filling the air at not knowing what's happening. Hell, I have no idea either, but I am here for it.

Selene moans, eyeing Santos as he gets naked, but Blaze drops an arm around her waist, trying to look casual as he makes sure she doesn't jump on Santos and fuck him in front of our guest. That might be a little rude.

Santos is smiling so damn hard his face is going to crack soon, and I love every second of it.

"Jesus is lying to you, Pipi. My dick is so good it's in the Bible. He gifted me with this love weapon, and he wants me to use it. Come on, touch it. Let it fuck the straight right out of you."

"No! Keep that Devil dick away from me!" Pepe begs, trying to get out of my grip but having no chance. "Jesus says being gay is a sin!"

"It's sinfully delicious! Why do you think people scream to God when it's in them?" Santos asks as he steps closer, letting his dick rub against the poor man's leg. "Feel that? That's the gay soaking into you. Give it a minute. You'll be shitting rainbows by the time I'm done."

Zander's chuckling as he watches the show, and Selene looks ready to murder Pepe for letting Santos' dick anywhere near him, matching the pissed off glare Blaze is throwing our way. He should be grateful Santos had found someone new to taunt with his dick.

Pepe is hysterical, and Santos finally laughs as he steps back, pulling his pants back on. "You're funny, Pipi. I like you. Now, give the big, grumpy fucker over there the address for your secret warehouse so we can go and save those women and kids. They need to find Jesus and be saved from the Devil, remember?"

The moment I let him go, Pepe darts across the room to Blaze as if he'll save him from our gayness, firing out the address before taking off like his ass in on fire, leaving Blaze to glare at us. "Was that necessary?"

"Yes," Santos and I both chuckle, ending up in a fit of laughter the others soon join in with.

# Chapter Four

## Zander

It doesn't take us long to find the warehouse, and once Blaze and I check it out, we know it's going to be easy. There's only a handful of men guarding the place, and from what we can tell, there aren't many inside.

"Come on, let's go play *'put the knife in the idiot'* so we can get out of here. I'll drive the van," Selene offers, making Blaze and I both snort. There's no way in Hell she's driving. She's not a bad driver, but she'll forget what we are supposed to be doing and probably stop at the diner on the way out for some lunch.

"I'm driving," Blaze answers bluntly, ignoring the glare she throws at him.

"I wanna go play that game," Santos smirks, "but I'll use bullets."

She pats his arm affectionately and smiles. "Yes. You're really good at that game. Tell you what. If you kill more people than me, I'll let you shackle me to the bed and have your wicked way with me when we get home."

His eyes widen as he rubs his hands together. "What if you win?"

"I'll shackle you to the bed while you watch D fuck me," she teases, a growl leaving him as he grabs her waist, jerking her firmly against him.

"You make it sound like a bad thing. I'm more than happy to watch you two fuck each other. For the record, I'm going to win, and I'm bringing my knife.”

“Promise?” she moans, Blaze cutting the conversation off with a groan.

“Shut the fuck up, both of you. Are we being stealthy or…?”

“No chance in Hell,” Santos says. “Look out, fuckers! Pew, pew!” Santos shouts at the top of his lungs as he starts running into the open like the idiot he is, making Selene and Darius chase after him, yipping and screaming random crap as they go.

Blaze glances at me with a sigh, the sound of gunfire filling the air around us. “You know, they really get on my nerves some days.”

“Haven’t noticed,” I chuckle, following him as he runs after the others, dodging bullets as they shoot in our direction.

Blaze takes out the guys by the door who Selene seems to be chatting with, her angry eyes meeting us over her shoulder. “I was playing games with them!”

“We’re here to kill them, not play with them!” Blaze barks, making me laugh as Selene shrugs.

“Same fucking shit.”

We clear the outside fast, heading inside to find Santos massacring two guys across the room, laughing, and boasting loudly to Selene that he’s winning. She lets out a huff as she joins him, stabbing her knife into one of the men’s necks and tearing it open, the blood splashing over her arms and face.

“Zan!” Blaze snaps, drawing my attention to the guy who’s sneaking up on me. I shoot him between the eyes, surprise on his face as he drops to the ground, making me snort.

“As if you didn’t see that coming, idiot.”

Blaze and I work our way through the room, taking out anyone who tries to sneak up on the others, but we don’t expect Santos to drop to the ground on top of one of the bodies, humping them with a loud groan. “How do you like that, dick head?! Thought you could shoot at my baby girl and get away with it?!”

Blaze groans, seeing way too much of Santos’ weird behavior for one day. I can’t stop grinning as Selene smiles at him, loving his show of affection. He’s crazy, but he loves her with all his heart. We can see it.

Darius laughs as he shoots at someone else, the body dropping to the ground. “Hey, San. This guy looked at our girl too!”

Santos is on his feet and across the room in seconds, dropping to his knees and unzipping his pants, showing us his dick for the hundredth time today. Anyone would think he's proud of it. He rubs his balls on the man's forehead, slapping him with his dick. "Taste the rainbow, asshole! Here's your tea bag, minus the cup!" he cackles, finding way too much enjoyment out of rubbing his junk on someone else's face.

"Santos! Get my dick off him!" Selene snaps, clenching her fists around her knife as she dodges some guy who tries to grab her out from nowhere. I roll my eyes and shoot him, wishing they were staying focused, but knowing that ship has sailed.

"Your dick? You already have one!" he answers, halting her as confusion fills her eyes.

"Where?"

Like the idiot he is, Santos heads over to her and pushes her to her knees, ignoring her growling as he suddenly slaps his dick against her forehead. Shock fills her face for a moment as she stares at him, anger taking over as he speaks again. "There! Now you're a dick head!"

"You're fucking dead, *estupido*!" she screams, jumping to her feet to chase him, his cackling sounding over the bullets still firing around the room.

I gun down anyone who goes near them, giving them a flat look as they continue to play tag. "Knock it off!"

"Bite me!" Selene snaps, swiping her knife at Santos, who just jumps out of the way in time, his laughter bouncing around the room.

"That's right, baby girl. Come get me!" he notices a bullet whizzing by his head and glares at the man who fired it. "Oh, yeah. Gun fight. My bad."

I smack my palm against my forehead as he continues to run away from Selene while shooting at the threat, and he's two seconds away from Blaze, putting a bullet in him instead.

Fucking children.

# Blaze

Finally, everyone is dead, and I find the shipping container in the back with the victims inside. What should've been an in and out easy infiltration turned into a fucking circus show. It took all my fucking willpower not to shoot both Selene and Santos dead along with the rest. Zander is looking amused, his mouth in a permanent upswing, and I have to admit it's better than the slump he'd been in since finding out his father was a filthy cunt a few years ago.

"I know they piss you off," he snickers as we guide the women and children to the waiting van, "but this is the best we've been. I know it feels chaotic, but it's an organized chaos. Santos isn't flying off the rails. Darius isn't taking brutal beatings, and I see your sneaking smiles, too."

We walk by said group only to find Darius once again pissing on the pile of bodies, Santos yelling at Selene about winning their bet, and Selene making the motion of jacking off her knife and rolling her eyes while Santos yells. I snort at the scene, and Zander nudges his shoulder against mine.

"See?" He looks back at them affectionately. "We're like a proper family now."

"Whatever," I growl, even though I begrudgingly agree.

"You need to get laid," he huffs. "What are you waiting for? Candles and rose petals?"

"I was supposed to fuck her this morning, but Pepe fuckface showed up and we ended up here."

"That's your problem," he squeezes my shoulder. "You need Selene's magic pussy."

"Yes, he does," she purrs as she comes up behind me, wrapping her arms around my waist. "Just a little Mommy and Daddy time together."

I snort before I can stop it, and Zander falls into a fit of laughter.

"What's funny?" Santos comes up and wraps his arms around both Selene and I. "Are we having a group meeting?"

"Will you get your hands off me?" I growl as Santos' wandering hands find my chest.

"I'm hungry," Selene whines at my back, her hands heading south while Santos' rub over my chest.

"Ask Daddy nicely and maybe he'll take us for burgers," Santos adds.

I shrug out of both of their holds, shoving Zander into my vacated spot, and watching his eyes widen as they do to him what they were doing to me. I snort again and then chuckle as he looks down, finding Selene rubbing him through his pants.

"I'm so glad Baby Walton got Daddy Walton's genes." Selene coos, and I really lose my shit. My laughter rings out in barking waves, and as soon as I'm done, the warehouse is eerily silent.

All four of them are looking at me in shock, but Selene is the first to laugh. "Daddy Blaze knows how much of a daddy kink I have."

I chuckle again, and the rest look at each other, clearly thinking the end of the world is upon us. "I think that was deserving of burgers."

"I can't believe you laughed," Zander looks at me, shocked. "That was a swift kick while I was down. I'm trying to make her stop talking about my fucking father."

"You can't be ashamed of your past, Zan," Santos cuts in. "Selene fucked you and your daddy at the same time. That's like a milestone most don't get to hit."

"Thank you, baby." Selene nods.

"How about we ask Papi Loco to fuck her with you and see how you feel?" Zander growls, and I snort again.

"I wouldn't *consent* to that, fucker." Santos snarls, "if I remember correctly, you joined them? Right baby?"

"Mm-hmm." Selene is grinning as Zander rolls his eyes and heads to his car.

"Whatever," he mumbles.

Watching Selene moan and groan over a burger with ketchup dripping down her chin is causing havoc in my pants. I really should've made time to fuck her this morning because now I have something building up inside of me, and it's fucking consuming.

We dropped the women and children off at the hospital, not giving anyone an explanation, then leaving before we were questioned. It's the way we've been doing it for years and it's always worked, but they must be seeing the rise in forced trafficking, and yet, nothing is changing. It's so frustrating.

Selene stuffs the last piece into her mouth, moaning around it, and then licking her tongue along her chin, trying to reach the ketchup.

I scrape the chair back along the floor, making everyone look over at me, and storm off to the bathrooms. I'm pent up and about to explode. Between the frustration of not emptying my balls and the frustration with our justice system, I'm feeling slightly unhinged.

I lean against the counter and take a deep breath; I need to stay focused. I don't want to do this forever, stopping trafficking, shooting motherfuckers, running around, and avoiding being shot. I want to have a day to lie in bed, I want a quiet space, and I want to stop the craving for bloodshed.

The door opens and I roll my eyes shut. I can't even find peace in a fucking bathroom. I push off the counter, and then a soft, warm body pushes itself between me and the sink. I smell her before I look at her, knowing exactly who it is and who she belongs to. My hands find her waist and I drag her in closer, just wanting to feel her.

"Something's wrong," she whispers.

"Yeah, there's always something."

"I know we're a handful," she starts, and I finally look down into her blue eyes, "and I know you get the brunt of that, but we're grateful, Blaze. I hope you know how much we all appreciate you."

I don't answer her because right now, in this moment, I don't give a fucking shit how annoying they all are. I want to sink my dick inside of her. I begin to undo her pants, shoving them down her legs, and she doesn't question me, just kicks them aside. She drops her panties to the pile as well, and hops up on the counter, spreading her legs wide.

She's wet, practically dripping, and I drop my hands to the counter on either side of her, my forehead hitting hers with a moan.

"This is probably going to hurt," I grit out as I begin undoing my pants.

"I know," she widens those milky legs farther, "I'm counting on it."

My pants and boxers hit my knees, and I have my cock in my hand, stroking it and squeezing the pierced tip. I'm still considering getting the same piercings as that albino fucker had in Nevada, but I haven't had the chance yet.

I yank her to the edge, not even bothering to prepare her further. I need to fucking come and if I don't do it soon, I'm going to snap. I line myself up and slam it home, groaning while she screams. Her nails dig into my shoulders, the stinging bite sinking in beyond my shirt. I don't give her the time to adjust. I begin drilling into her tight, wet pussy at a punishing pace, watching as my dick gets coated with cream.

She begins to squirm, probably from being fucked to within an inch of her life, but I grip her hips, knowing there will be bruising, and hold her still. She whimpers with each one of my thrusts, but soon she begins to pant, and her little pussy begins to squeeze tighter as she nears her climax.

"Tell me what it was like to pull John's lungs from his body," she moans, and I look down at where we're joined. Her delicate flesh stretched to the point of pain, wrapped around my cock.

"Is that gonna help you get off?" I chuckle.

"Fuck yes," her hand snakes down between us and she begins to circle her clit, "I need details. Zander couldn't do it."

"Because he's a fucking pussy," I growl as I slam into hers.

"Please, Daddy," she moans, and I nearly explode. "Tell me."

I slow down to stave off my impending orgasm and look down into her big blues. "I sliced through the skin and muscle on his back." She moans so loud at my words. "Thick, warm blood sprayed out and coated my hands. He passed out before I even began hacking at his ribcage, breaking them open one by one, and revealing his bright red lungs. They felt like velvety thin sponges, quivering as I gripped them in my fingers."

"Oh fuck," she pants, her pussy clamping down. "Don't stop."

"I pressed into the soft organ and the blood pooled around my fingertips as I carefully lifted them out, such a vivid, red color. Then I settled them over the protruding rib bones, putting them on display."

That's when she fucking detonates all over my cock, and I watch in fascination, knowing this woman is my fucking equal in every sense. A warrior.

I follow soon after, filling her up with cum, and her pussy milking every last drop. Then I pull her closer, my cock still deep inside, and lean down to kiss her. It's slow, sensual, and fucking yanking on my cold heart.

"Is this where you tell me you love me?" She flutters her lashes as I pull out of her, tucking my wet cock back in my pants.

"Not today," I grin.

"Well, I'm not telling you either," she snaps and begins to put her pants back on, grumbling about my cum slipping from her pussy.

I will tell her, but it's not going to be in some dive diner's restroom.

# Selene

The throbbing between my legs is now a sharp ache as I walk behind Blaze back into the restaurant. He can really tear a pussy apart with that weapon he calls a cock. I sit at the table and squirm in my seat, trying to alleviate the pain.

"Someone got the big daddy dick down," Santos snickers.

"Jealous?" I grin at him as he drags my chair closer to his.

"Always." Then he moves closer to my ear, mocking a whisper loud enough for Blaze to hear. "One day I'll get that big daddy special, too."

"Like fuck you will," Blaze snarls, but his voice doesn't hold the same edge he had earlier. I grin, knowing I could not only milk him of his cum, but a bit of that grumpiness, too.

"Your phone keeps ringing." Zander nods to the burner I've had since Nevada. The one I stupidly left in the room while I went gallivanting my stupid self around with Henry's chauffeur. "It looks like a Nevada area code."

I yank it open, hoping to hear Aniyah's voice. "Hello?"

"Selly?"

I groan so loud right into the phone at the sound of my sister's voice, then I close the old-style flip and throw it back into Zander's lap. "Who gave her my number?" I screech as I look at each of them.

"None of us," Zander shrugs.

"Maybe your purple headed clit-licker did," Blaze says with a smug look on his face.

Oh. That makes sense.

"Shouldn't you talk to her?" Zander asks as he holds up my ringing phone, the same number flashing on the screen.

"No," Santos cuts in. "She doesn't have to until she's ready. Let's go home and figure out our next step."

By the time we get home, my phone has rung a total of sixteen times, and with each shrill noise, my anger rises.

"What if it's something important?" Zander asks as I stomp

through the front door, ready to toss the phone in the toilet.

"She has a whole MC she can turn to," Santos snarls, completely understanding me in this situation.

"What if it's something she needs a sister for?" Zander counters.

"Then maybe the fucking cunt should've found her, no?" Santos once again comes back with the exact sentiment I'm thinking.

Yes, I forgave her for not trying to find me hard enough, and for giving up too soon. But that doesn't mean I'm ready to slip back ten years and forget everything that happened. I need time and she's not giving it to me.

"She left a voicemail," Zander calls to my retreating back. "At least listen to it."

I slam my room door and sit on my bed, silencing the seventeenth phone call. Once it's finished ringing, I open the phone and call my voicemail, settling in to hear what the fuck she wants.

"Hey, Selly, it's me Jan, your sister." I snort because *duh*. "Loqi got a lead on where his sister might be, and I understand Santos isn't interested in a relationship right now, but I wanted to let you guys know, since she's his sister, too. She was taken like I was, and they think she's somewhere in Vegas. I was also hoping to find out a bit more about John Dempster, since it seems like he was the one who bought her. I spoke to Aniyah, and she told me as much as she could, but she said you were investigating him. Could you please call me back?"

I know Santos is pissed, and rightfully so, but I don't think he knows about his missing sister. I really believe he would want to help, especially because she's innocent in all that's going on between the rest of his family. I run out of my room and slide into the kitchen. They're all sitting there, trying to figure out the next step in tracking down the fat-assed, no teeth having, Mack Delaney.

"She does need something." I hold up my phone.

"I knew it," Zander nods.

"Loqi's little sister was taken a few years back, and she was sold to John Dempster." I look at Santos and watch as different emotions flint over his face.

"Little sister?" he finally says as he rises to his feet. "What little sister?" I can see the confusion making him start to lose his cool.

"I think we need to call Loqi," I say quietly. "We'll put it on speakerphone, and I can do the talking."

We gather around the table, and I plant my ass in Santos' lap, knowing he'll need me to keep himself under control. Darius grabs my hand and squeezes it, knowing exactly what it is I'm doing. We put my phone in the center of the table and listen to the ringing, all of our hearts clogging up our throats.

"Hey, Reaper," Loqi's voice fills the room. "Do you need help killing someone?"

I have a smart remark ready on the tip of my tongue, but Santos cuts me off. "Tell me about her."

"Is that you, Santos?" He gets a grunt in response and then continues, "Our *hermana* was sweet, nothing like you and me. She was always trying to help people, and even when she was acting like a brat, she was still kind."

"What happened to her?" Santos asks, his voice low and filled with emotion.

"Papi and I took her to see a movie being filmed in Vegas. Her favorite actor was there, and we made a mini vacation out of it. We got VIP treatment onset, and that's where we lost her. No one could find her; it was like she was gone without a trace. We emptied trailers and movie sets. She was gone. We interrogated everyone there that day, and after two years, someone has finally come forward. She was the makeup artist on set, and she said she saw a young girl being forced into a large, white van. When she questioned a producer onset, she was told the girl was a troublesome actress being carted off to rehab."

"For sure that was our sister?" Santos asks.

"We believe so. The producer's name at the time was John Dempster."

A chill snakes down my spine and I know without a doubt, Santos' little sister fell victim to John and his skin operation.

"But," Loqi continues, "John's dead, thanks to you guys. I won't be able to interrogate him. But we can go to his house and see what we can find. It's been closed and processed by the police in Vegas. Papi has paid for us to get in there for a day and see what we can find."

"Keep us updated if you find anything," I lean forward. "We'll come there if you need us."

"Thank you, Reaper." He sounds grateful. "And *hermano*," he says to Santos. "I'm not our papi. You and I should have a talk."

"Yeah," Santos grunts.

"Okay, I will be in touch." Then he hangs up the phone as I turn to Santos.

"Are you okay?" I ask him, resting my hand on his cheek. I wish we could go back to the version of Santos who woke up this morning.

"I went through most of my life thinking I just had my mami, and then when she died, I believed I was truly alone. Papi left us when I was nine, and Mami said it was because he didn't know how to be a husband or a father. Then she got really sick. She had a rare heart disease, and there was no cure, but I believe it was a broken heart. I was put in a foster home and even though the caregivers weren't bad, there were just so many of us. Darius showed up a few months later, and we became unruly, running the streets and pushing drugs."

"Out of control," Darius hums his agreement.

"We began taking care of the prostitutes, ya know? Making sure they got to their locations safely, and then back to their blocks again. We charged a small fee, but soon enough, we had a bunch of them requesting the service."

"You were pimps," Zander snorts, and Darius hoots.

"Still are, little bitch," he sneers at Zander.

"Go on." I nudge Santos.

"A few of our girls went missing, and both of us," he points at Darius, "felt like shit. It was our job to keep them safe. We followed the trail to a house party and became acquainted with Los Diablos. We found out they dabbled in a bit of everything: drugs, weapons, and girls."

"That's where we met," Zander finishes it off.

"It's hard to comprehend I have any blood relations after this long. My brothers here were my only family, and now, there are others." Santos wraps his arms around my waist, tugging me in closer, "what if they don't like me, like Papi?"

"I'll stab each of them," I promise, while kissing the top of his head. "No one, not even blood relatives, has the option of hurting you, and Papi Loco will find that out firsthand."

That piece of shit has a fucking date with my knife.

# Zander

We don't hear anything back from Loqi until a few days later, and our inside Diablo Pepe has also been a bit quiet. There are no upcoming shipments for Los Diablos, and I can see all the guys—including Selene—beginning to bite at the bit, needing something to calm our desires for blood.

That's why when the phone rings and we see Loqi's name, we all scramble over each other to get to it. I grab the little flip phone and open it, pressing it to my ear.

"Hello?"

"Which one is this?" Loqi asks, his voice filled with humor.

"The best looking one," I retort, and the rest of the guys in the room groan, all too well acquainted with how much I love myself.

I put him on speaker just as he says, "You're not my brother."

"That's right!" Santos hoots, and I roll my eyes.

"What do you have for us?" Selene shoves me aside and sits in front of the phone.

"I have a few names we found here." He continues, "he had a ledger."

"They all have fucking ledgers," Selene spits. "Your father's is still back in that Vegas apartment. We need to get back there and get my shit."

"What's in the ledger?" Santos asks.

"Tons of names, but we narrowed it down to three on the day she went missing, one being extremely familiar. I have an Earl Jr. —"

"Dead," Selene interrupts. "He's wrapped up in a tarp and buried in the desert." When I look at her in question, she shrugs, "Earl had to die."

"I watched her kill him," Blaze interjects and grabs his cock in his pants. "So fucking hot."

"Names," Darius cuts us all off.

"Okay, so we can scratch out Earl. Next one is Eugene Haynes. He bought about ten of the eighteen girls taken that day."

"He's dead, too," Selene cuts in, and I groan. "What? He was a bad man, but he had a nice castle for a home, horses, and paintings, and his staff called him King. I wanted to be Queen, but he was too furry, like a donkey."

"Yeah," Loqi snorts into the phone. "We knew he was dead. There are photos of him with a bloody scythe on his forehead."

"It was the only spot clear of fur," Selene nods.

"If he bought our sister, we need to know what happened to all the staff in his home," Loqi inquires. "So, we're looking into that."

Selene's face brightens, and I can see her squirming with excitement. "Loqi! There were a few young girls when I was there. I do know one was arrested in suspicion for murder. Look into that!"

"Thank you, I will." Then he chuckles, "The third name will interest us both, but won't be a surprise. Mack Delaney."

"He's the one who grabbed Selene," I inform him. "He's here in New York, still selling girls. We've been fucking with his shipments. You can leave him to us for now."

"Sounds good," Loqi agrees. "Let us know if you need backup. Selene, thank you for the heads up. We're going to check out the girl who was arrested."

"Let us know," Selene says as we hang up the phone.

We're all quiet as we mull over everything we've just been told. Mack Delaney has been in the skin business for over thirty years, and his end is coming near. I never knew he was this big or running this wide of a distribution. I always thought he was small compared to my father, but I was clearly wrong. He was always the big-timer.

"Let's try to get a hold of Pepe," I say. "We need some movement on Mack. We can't lose sight of him now."

"Agreed," Blaze nods.

"I'd really like to know where the fat fuck is staying," I growl. "I would like to have constant surveillance on him."

"If we find him, there's no surveillance," Selene growls. "My knife is slamming into his forehead."

Santos groans and reaches for her, making her straddle his waist. "Keep saying shit like that, baby," he moans as he slips his fingers up under my t-shirt she's wearing—the only thing she's wearing. "Fuck, and you're so wet."

Blaze growls in frustration again, but it's not as heated as usual. He's probably realizing there's no stopping them. This is just the way they are.

"We need to know who else he's dealing with, and if there's someone above him. We want to end this once and for all," I explain.

"I don't want to do this for the rest of my life," Blaze says, and everyone stops what they're doing to look at him. "I want to fucking relax."

I feel that. I want it too.

"Okay, Daddy," Selene whispers. "Let's do it the right way and take out as many as we can. Then we'll go on vacation."

"To where?" Blaze raises a brow.

"I say Vegas." She grins and gyrates her hips on Santos' hand. "I wanna visit Aniyah."

"I'm not too particularly keen on seeing that woman again." Blaze rolls his eyes, and I understand why. He and the purple-haired prostitute have a history.

"She's a friend," Selene tosses back. "And I'll see her if I want to."

That's the last of the conversation because Santos stands up and throws Selene over his shoulder. "Come, Darius," he grins. "I'm craving your dick and her blood."

Santos stomps his way down the hallway with Darius taking up their rear.

"You know, you're going to have to tell her what you did with Aniyah, eventually," I say to Blaze, and he shrugs.

"Maybe."

"It might one day spill from the prostitute's mouth, and you know damn well Selene will lose her shit."

"Maybe," he says again, this time with a sinister grin. "I do like when she loses her shit."

We're all so fucked up.

# Santos

My fingers flex against Selene's waist as I force her back onto the bed, my body pressing down on hers as I devour her mouth in a searing kiss. She whimpers as my fingers tighten against her skin, the small bite of pain urging her on.

The sound of Darius stripping behind me makes my cock harden more, and I pull back from Selene to watch him, his heated gaze already on mine. While I'm distracted, Selene takes advantage and flips us over, straddling my hips with a dark grin. She pulls her shirt over her head, grinding on me as Darius crawls onto the bed with a smirk.

"You going to get naked? Or do I rip the fabric from your body with your knife?" he murmurs, causing me to fly into action. Selene squeals as I buck her off, yanking my clothes off in record time. Darius tears what's left of Selene's clothes off, swallowing her curse as he kisses the hell out of her.

I love being with both of them. No jealousy or rules, just pure sex and acceptance.

I grab the back of Darius' neck and yank him toward me, loving the groan of approval as he kisses me almost aggressively. A battle of tongue and teeth. He bites my lip, a hiss leaving me at the sting left behind, the taste of copper spreading across my tongue as I lick the tender skin.

"You want me to bleed, *amante*?" I grin, not giving a shit if there's blood in my teeth. He has no idea how good it felt when he called me his lover that day. He is more than my anchor, and the warmth in my chest has been a constant lately whenever I look at him. The same warmth I get when I look at Selene.

His eyes blaze in need. As I reach for Selene, pulling her to me and plastering her back to my front, biting her neck sharply. "Touch her, D."

Darius does as he's told, moving forward to press her between us, snaking his hand down her front to toy with her clit. She arches against him, dropping her head back on my shoulder with a breathy moan. "Stop playing around. Fuck me."

I give Darius a glance, silently communicating with him to grab the shackles that are laying on the floor. She thinks I've forgotten about our little deal, silly woman.

The moment he climbs from the bed and the shackles clink, she stiffens in my arms and growls. "Don't even fucking think about it."

I run my tongue down her slender neck, my arms tightening around her as she tries to pull away. "You're such a sore loser, baby girl. May I remind you this was your idea?"

She snarls, thrashing against me as I restrain her, while Darius threads the shackles through the headboard and grins at me. "C'mon, bring her here."

She fights me, just like I was hoping. My dick is so hard it's painful. We manage to get her wrists secured, and Darius chuckles, waving the key in her face to taunt her. "Be a good girl, and I'll let you go."

"I'm going to kill the fucking pair of you!" she snaps, not bothering to yank on the shackles. She knows she isn't going anywhere until we let her.

I run my eyes over her naked body, leaning over to grab my knife from the bedside drawers to place it beside me. "You ready for me to make you bleed? You're going to look like a work of art against the bedsheets," I murmur, her eyes flashing with annoyance, but her body arches slightly in need. Our girl is desperate to bleed on my blade. I could sense it a mile away.

"You're in trouble when you let me go, *estupido*. You'll be bleeding too," she snarks, glaring at Darius. "I can't believe you're in on this."

"In on it? He's the one who grabbed the shackles from the floor," I chuckle, dodging her foot as she tries to kick me. I get on my knees and dip my head, burying my tongue in her dripping cunt, wanting to taste her more than anything. She moans, the shackles clinking as she tries to touch me, letting out a frustrated growl when she can't.

I startle as something wet touches my ass, relaxing as Darius' hand slides around my front to fist my length. If he wants to lick what was left of my soul out of my ass, I'm not going to stop him. It feels fucking good, for starters.

Selene watches us hungrily, wriggling when I slow down my attack on her pussy.

"Dammit, Santos! Eat me like you're going to starve to death if you don't, or let Darius do it!" she snaps, causing a wicked grin to spread across my face. My girl wants it rough? Then that's what she's going to get.

I suck her clit into my mouth and bite firmly, a surprised scream leaving her from the sudden pain. Darius groans, sending vibrations straight up my fucking ass and making me jump. Selene chuckles, eyeing me with amusement. "That feel good?"

I lift my head, pushing two fingers inside her without warning, her wet heat surrounding them as she clenches. "You're talking too much. D, how about you shut her up for me?"

"But I was…" Darius starts, but I cut him off.

"Do it. I promise not to cut her while your dick's down her pretty throat. I'd hate for her to bite it off."

"I might bite it off anyway," Selene grumbles, jerking against her shackles as I pull my fingers out to lightly slap her pussy.

"You bite it off, and I'll fuck your tight cunt with the sharp end of my blade," I threaten playfully, waiting for Darius to straddle her chest and jam his dick into her mouth, giving me five minutes of silence.

I thrust my fingers into her pussy again, leaning forward to bite Darius' butt. He flinches in surprise, choking Selene in the process, but after a second, he relaxes, letting me do whatever I want to him. I lift up on my knees, getting closer to shove my tongue in his ass, making it nice and wet before sliding a finger up and down his crack, easing it inside slowly.

"Fuck, do you want me to cum in minutes?" Darius grunts, moving in and out of Selene's plush lips, pulling back enough to sink over my finger more. I add a second finger, working both his ass and her pussy with ease, loving the sounds coming from them.

Selene clenches around me, her muffled moans becoming a cry as she comes hard, and my dick becomes jealous of my fingers. I pull away from them both, needing to be inside her right the fuck now.

I practically shove Darius off her, making him chuckle as I align myself with Selene's pussy, and slam inside, her loud moan music to my ears. I grab my knife and slow my thrusts, running the cool metal gently across her throat without marking her, loving how her eyes flash with heat. I press harder, the blade lightly slicing across her pretty throat and leaving a small red trail of blood behind.

Leaning forward, I lick across her skin, tasting the devilish, metallic honey and closing my eyes to savor it. She always tastes like Heaven in a sinful shell.

"Cut her here," Darius murmurs softly, running his fingers across her belly. "Make her bleed for me." Well, I can't exactly say no to that.

I do as he asks, watching her eyes as they stare into mine, the breath practically leaving her body as the bite of my blade cuts into her flesh.

Darius leans forwards, coating his fingers in her sticky blood before turning to me with a smirk. "You going to let me in, babe?"

I go to move back to let him have a moment with her, but his free hand stops me. "I meant *into* you."

"You want to fuck me, D?" I ask in a low voice, groaning when he nods. Selene looks ready to combust at the sound of me being nailed.

"Please, please let him fuck you," she begs, gasping when I smash my lips to hers and thrust harder into her while Darius moves in behind me. He uses his fingers to stretch me, grabbing more blood from our girl as he needs it, finally coating his dick in some and pressing firmly against my ass. He doesn't warn me, knowing I don't need it, slowly easing into me until he's almost all the way in, slamming the rest inside at the last minute.

I jerk forward, growling into Selene's mouth as he withdraws and does it again, slowly getting faster until he's fucking me into Selene almost painfully. I welcome the burn, letting it drive my hunger to inflict pleasurable pain, wrapping a hand around Selene's throat and feeling the drying blood under my fingertips.

"Oh, fuck," Darius grunts, leaning over me more as if he can't get close enough, something stirring inside me. I feel like I'm going to explode, and not out of my dick. I'd be lost without both of them, and I don't even think before I blurt out what I'm feeling.

"I love you."

Darius slows, while Selene's eyes widen a fraction before they soften. I stop moving, watching her with uncertainty. Did I just fuck everything up?

When she doesn't say anything, I glance over my shoulder and meet Darius' eyes, keeping my voice steady despite the fear seeping into me. Nothing scares me, but this? I'm fucking terrified. "I love you both."

He gives me a grin, dropping his lips to my shoulder, his words calming me. "I love you too, San."

Selene still hasn't said anything, and I turn my attention back to her and swallow the lump in my throat. It's like she's staring into my damn soul, a soft smile finally taking over her face. "You love me?"

"So much. I'd turn the town red for someone even looking at you sideways," I promise, scowling at the shackles. I want her hands on me. Sensing my thoughts, Darius pulls away from me and grabs the keys, unlocking the bounds on her wrists. She instantly throws herself at me, devouring my mouth as her hands run across my back, keeping me close.

"I love you too. You too, D," she breathes, the tightness in my chest vanishing and making room for the warmth I always feel when they're close. I drop onto my back, hauling her on top of me and sinking back inside her with ease, resting my hands on her waist with a smirk. "Prove it. Fuck the crazy right out of me."

"We could be here a while," she teases, reaching over to stroke Darius' length, his eyes darkening.

"I love you crazy fuckers, too," he growls, moving closer to kiss her hard, her moans filling his mouth as I thrust up inside her firmly. He finally pulls back and looks down at me, running his gaze over my sweaty abs and down to where I'm connected to our girl, his voice low. "You're both fucking perfect." Then he dips down to kiss me, his hand running along stomach until his fingers reach Selene's clit, making her gasp.

I've never cared about anyone like this. Selene and Darius are everything to me, keeping me steady when I want to explode. While Blaze and Zander were the brothers, I never knew I needed. We are family, and nothing will get in the way of that.

If it does? I'll set the fucking world on fire and watch it burn.

# Darius

I thought telling someone I loved them would feel different. There's no worry or confusion, just peace of mind as the words come from my mouth. Santos was worried about our reactions, but nothing felt so fucking right in my entire life.

I rub Selene's clit until she's screaming, grinding down on Santos until her body turns to jelly, but I'm not about to let her rest.

I hand her Santos' blade, loving how his eyes darken at knowing what I'm asking.

"Cut him."

Her eyes flare as his grip tightens on her waist, keeping their pace slow as she grips the knife and leans forward. "You want me to mark you as mine, baby?"

"Fuck yes, make me bleed so D can use it as lube, and then everyone will know who I belong to," he answers firmly, removing a hand from her waist to point at his chest, right where his heart is. "Right here."

He hisses as she carves into his skin, his eyes firmly on her as she works, the bloody S appearing vibrant against his tanned flesh. We never thought we'd find a woman who understood our need for blood and violence in the bedroom, wanting both of us for who we are. We hit the fucking jackpot.

Blaze and Zander probably wouldn't appreciate her brand being on them, but I love it. She's claiming us in ways no other women would appreciate as she does, and that causes something primal to burn inside me.

When she's done, she swipes her finger through the sticky liquid and pops it into her mouth, moaning as her eyes flutter closed. That snaps my control.

I grab her throat and turn her face to mine, forcing my tongue into her mouth to taste him, blindly rubbing my fingers against Santos' chest to gather the oozing liquid. I waste no time in coating my dick with it, not being gentle as I push myself inside her from behind, her scream of discomfort filling the room as I shove her chest down onto his, spreading his blood between them.

I fist her hair, making sure she doesn't move as I plow inside her tight ass, my balls rubbing against Santos' and urging me on as he starts to move in tandem with me. We work as one, chasing our pleasure while feeding each other's need for pain, the sound of flesh slapping and our grunts and moans bouncing off the walls like music.

The moment Selene clenches around us, Santos comes with a growl, his hand grabbing my thigh tight in his grip as if needing my touch to keep him from floating away. Selene's gasping for air as she comes down, lying there completely spent as I slam into her a few more times before following after them, my muscles bunching as I let go.

I slump over her back to catch my breath, reaching a hand out to run my fingers through Santos' black hair, my lips trailing across Selene's back to soothe her. I've never been the type to give a fuck about someone's comfort after sex, but it has always been different with these two. I want to comfort them, keeping their demons at bay while we enjoy the afterglow, not wanting to pull away from them.

"I need to pee," Selene mumbles, making me chuckle as I force myself to pull back, admiring the smeared blood that coats her ass and across her cheeks. I glance down to find blood mixing with my sweat on my groin and abs, calming something inside me.

Santos grumbles as Selene climbs off him, standing on shaky legs as she heads to the bathroom, giving us a moment alone. Santos glances at me, grabbing my hand and tugging me on top of him to kiss my neck. "I actually think my dick's gone to sleep."

I chuckle, running my hand down his body to find his dick soft, giving it a few gentle strokes. "Want me to wake it back up?"

"I've reached my limit. I'm spent," he groans. "You really love me? More than just friends?"

"I think we've been past the point of friendship for a long time, *amante*," I point out, a smile taking over his face and almost blinding me.

"This love thing's even better than the killing thing. To celebrate, let's go and murder some cunts."

My man sure knows how to flirt.

# Chapter Five

## *Zander*

I'm used to Santos and Darius' weird quirks, but it startles me to find Selene leaving the bathroom. Blood smeared all over her. We all know they like to bring knives to the bedroom, but I'm worried they really hurt her this time.

"Jesus fucking Christ. Let me look at you," I scowl, marching over to her and taking her face in my hand, tilting her head to the side to inspect the small cut along her throat. That's a stupid place to play with luck. If it had been just a bit too deep, she could have bled out with no hope of saving her.

She takes my hand and gives it a squeeze, her eyes calm. "I'm fine, Zan. Most of this is Santos'." That surprises me. They don't make a habit of cutting themselves, not that I know of, anyway.

"Should I check on him, too? Fuck, turn around."

She huffs but does as she was told, obviously too tired to argue. Blood covers her butt cheeks, and my eyes widen. "You're bleeding out your fucking ass."

"No, I'm not. It's Santos' blood there, too," she chuckles lightly, glancing at me with amusement as I cringe. They had a fucking great time, apparently.

"You need to clean up before Blaze sees you. C'mon," I sigh, dragging her into the bedroom to find Darius and Santos snuggled up together, blood all over them too. "You fucking crazy bastards."

Santos grins like the psychopath he is, but Darius shrugs. "You're being dramatic."

"Dramatic? Have you looked at yourselves? Is that a fucking S on your chest?" I snap as I notice the angry wound on Santos' chest, making Selene beam.

"I marked him!"

"I can see that. All of you get cleaned up. And Santos?" I growl, waiting for him to give me an innocent look to prove he's listening. "If you ever cut her throat again, I'll kill you. I don't give a shit what kind of kinks you share with each other, but that is downright stupid. What if you'd gone too deep?"

"I went really deep. Pretty sure my dick hit the back of her tonsils from her pussy," he cackles, pushing Darius off him to stand, my eyes catching on Darius' blood covered dick. I shake my head, deciding they are all bat-shit crazy. I mean, we know it, but this cements it.

"I'm going to clean Selene up. Then you fuckers can meet us in the kitchen."

Santos grumbles his annoyance, but I ignore him as I grab Selene's clothes from the floor and drag her back across the hallway to the bathroom, locking us inside and ushering her into the shower. I strip down and climb in with her, grabbing the soap and lathering it over her body once the water heats.

She eyes me silently for a while before finally speaking. "I love them."

"I know. Doesn't mean you all need to cut each other to pieces every time you fuck," I grunt, a frown taking over her face.

"I know it's not your thing, but I like it. I wouldn't let them if I didn't want it, you know that. They'd never kill me," she answers, making me snort.

"Not on purpose, but you know they both get carried away, especially Santos. The thought of you bleeding out wrecks me, sweetheart. I don't like them risking it."

Her arms wrap around my middle as she presses her chest to mine, peering up at me with a small smile. "I promise I won't let them kill me. If they manage to, I'll come back and haunt you all. Sleep naked. I'll fuck you in your sleep."

I can't help the chuckle that leaves my lips, giving her a smirk. "That's creepy. You know you're starting to sound like Santos way too much, right? Little psychopath."

"Where the hell have you been? I've been like this from the start.

Face it, you like me crazy," she grins, standing on tip-toe to kiss me. She's lucky I love her because I know exactly where her naughty little mouth has been.

# Blaze

Selene's old school phone rings on the table and I see her sister's name flash on the neon green screen. She's been calling a lot and even though Selene is closed off, shutting her out, the girl keeps trying. I respect the tenacity.

I grab the phone from the table and flip it open. "Hello?"

"Um..." She clears her throat. "I think I have the wrong number."

"You have the right number." I lean back on the couch, crossing my ankle over my knee.

"Which one is this?"

"The sane one," I fire back.

"Zander?"

"Fucking seriously? You think he's sane?" I retort.

"Um, shit," she curses under her breath, probably afraid to fuck this up further. "I don't know any of you, really."

"It's not us you need to work on," I relax. "Start with your sister."

"I'm trying," she exhales her frustration. "It's not working."

"Because you're not doing it right."

"Any advice?" I like that she's asking, it really shows she's invested.

"Actually, yes." I scrub at the scruff on my chin. "Your sister is not the average woman. She doesn't care about gifts or anything like that."

"Shit," she hisses.

"What did you send?"

"Flowers and a teddy bear. When we were growing up, she didn't have many toys, but she loved stuffed—"

"She's grown now," I cut her off. "She likes other things. She had to grow up fast and her interests have changed."

"Right." She sounds a bit defeated.

"She has a penchant for knives, large, serrated hunting types. We know she likes dicks; she has four of them."

She snorts on the line, "Lucky girl."

"But I think what she's craving the most is a family she thought she lost. She's tough, her skull even tougher, and it's not going to be easy. You have to somehow show her you're here to stay."

"I've been calling—"

"I know," I cut her off again. "Anyone can call someone. That shit's easy, but the hard part is proving you're sticking around."

"This is Blaze, right?"

"What makes you think that?" Curiosity killed the cat.

"You seemed the most serious of the group, or maybe the most mature."

"You're not wrong," I say with a shake of my head.

"So, I need to pull up my big girl panties and face my seriously intimidating sister," she says, her voice trembling with nerves.

"Bring a knife too. Make it a pretty one." I hang up the phone and place it on the table just as Zander comes into the room.

"Those three are going to fucking kill themselves one day," he huffs as he falls on the couch beside me.

"Who's suffering from blood loss?"

"All three of them could be at this point," he pinches the bridge of his nose. "I had fun with it in Nevada, but I couldn't do that often."

"Because you're you, and they're them. They're big boys, and Selene is a big girl. They can handle themselves." I flick his hand off his face. "Stop stressing, you're not their father."

"I know." He narrows his look onto my face. "What if something bad happens during one of their kinks?"

"We'll deal with it. But you can't judge them for what they like." I stand up. "Let's go see what we can find out from the new hookers on the street. I need to do something instead of waiting around for intel."

"Sounds good." He stands and stretches. "Make sure you're not sampling the product this time."

"Hey, if that's what it takes to get the job done, then so be it. Selene does the same."

"She will never open her legs for another person outside of the four of us again," he snarls.

"You guys spoke about it?"

"No." He gives me a confused look.

"It's her job," I shrug.

"It was her *technique* to find her sister, which she did, so she's done." He shoves by me, and I chuckle at his back.

"I think we should have a family meeting to discuss it. I really want to hear that conversation."

He shoots me a dirty look over his shoulder, and I chuckle again. No one tells our Little Reaper to do anything. I can't wait to watch as she hands Zander his balls.

# Selene

Santos and Darius are sleeping off our sexcapade, Zander and Blaze aren't home, and I'm bored to shit. On the plus side, my sister has finally fucked off with the phone calls. I don't like the way my stomach falls at the thought of her giving up. She's done that plenty already.

I lie on the couch, without a stitch of clothing on, and turn on a serial killer documentary on Netflix. All of these fuckers are seriously psychotic, and I don't know how the people around them didn't see it. Like hello? I'm clearly certifiable and *everyone* knows it. I watch the first episode and laugh as the cops fumble through crime scenes, their incompetence documented for all to see.

I just start to get into it when the doorbell rings, making me groan as I get up off the couch. Who the fuck would be here? I stride over and swing it open wide, only to find my Jesus humping buddy.

"What would Jesus do!" I yell, raising my hand in the air.

"Why don't you have any clothes on?" He stares at me wide eyed, but I don't miss his tremble of fear, which still strikes me as strange.

"When I first met you," I tweak the nipple that seems to have caught his attention, "you were tough, saying you wanted to kill me." Once the nipple is nice and hard, I move to the other, his eyes following the motion. "But now, you're acting like a little boy who has to spend one-on-one time with a priest."

"Because I had no idea who or what you were. I was recruited a week before, and when I saw you, I thought you were a helpless … person."

"You wanted to say 'woman'!" I point at his face with shock.

"It's not in the way you think." He holds up his hands, his eyes still darting from my tits and back to my face, little deviant. "The women in my family are strong, *mi abuelita* is the strongest. But none of them kill like you do." He almost sounds revenant, and that makes my pussy warm. "You killed everyone in the house that day."

"Not everyone," I bop his nose and hold the door open, "we still got time, though." I give him a wink and watch as he swallows, his eyes roaming down lower. "Come in. You must be here for more than to stare at my pretty pussy." My fingers spread it open for him, and he nearly chokes on air. "Or is that actually what you came for?"

"No! I have info on another shipment." His brow dots with sweat as he struggles to keep his eyes on mine. "You're injured. Was that from the fight at the warehouse?"

"Booo." I slap his face with the hand that was just toying with my pussy lips, then I run it down over his mouth. "I thought this was going to be a fun visit, and no, the blood from the cut was what my boyfriend used as lube to fuck my other boyfriend."

I move out of the way so he can come inside, and then I follow him to the kitchen as he sits at the table. I sit in the chair beside him, dragging it in closer, and giggling when he leans away from me.

Santos comes shuffling into the kitchen next, still half asleep, and his juicy cock swinging back and forth. "Did I hear the doorbell?"

"Son of Jesus is here with an update," I coo, and grin when Santos' eyes darken on my equally naked body.

"That's blasphemous," Pepe exclaims, then drops his face to his hands. "Why is everyone naked today?"

"Because we fucked like Adam and Eve," Santos deadpans, and I squeal with laughter.

"*Santa Maria,*" Pepe gives himself the sign of the cross. "I need to get out of this place."

"Why *are* you here, boy?" Santos turns with a tired grin. "Do you want to call me *Papi* and tell me your sins?"

"I know when the next shipment is coming in, and it's supposed to go to Nevada," Pepe groans, but that has me straightening in my seat.

"Nevada? Did you hear for whom?"

"No names, just an MC." Pepe looks between Santos and me, trying hard not to glance at our fun bits.

"It has to be for Papi and Loqi," Santos murmurs while I nod my head.

"When is the shipment leaving for Nevada?" I ask Pepe as I cross my legs and play footsies with his pant leg. "I also need the address."

"Tomorrow night." He digs into his pocket and pulls out a piece of paper, handing it to me. "The container is already there."

"All right," I nod, "you can go." I snap my fingers, and Pepe jumps from his seat, running for the front door. "Do you think he's a virgin?" I ask Santos.

"Why do you care, baby girl?" He leans on the table, his swinging cock slowly growing hard. "Do you want to play with him?"

"A little," I grin. "I wouldn't mind bleeding him dry and then fucking you over his Christian body. A gift from God, no doubt."

He snickers as he leans in, kissing me sweetly on the forehead. "What are we doing about this shipment?"

"Do you want to take a trip to the MC?" I grin at him. "I need to grab my stuff from that apartment."

He looks caught between a yes and a no, and I know it's because he's not ready to see his family yet, but he won't let me go alone.

"Maybe we can send Blaze with you." He smirks. "Darius, Zander, and I can try to pump little Pepe for more info."

I respect his wishes and give him an eager nod. Besides, I haven't had my fill of Daddy's big cock yet.

"Is this a good idea?" Darius asks from his spot beside Santos. They're holding hands, and I can't help but feel giddy inside at the sight of it. "What if it's not the Afilados who's picking up? There are tons of MCs in Nevada."

"I'll be with her." Blaze shrugs. "This would be the best time to see if there is another MC selling skin. We could put Afilados on to them."

"My mind is set," I stand, "I already purchased our plane tickets with the *new* Mr. Walton's credit card, and we need to catch that flight in two hours."

Zander groans at my admission.

"You were just going to leave again?" Darius' eyes narrow on me.

"No, *amante*," Santos squeezes his hand, "she sat here and told us her plans. She's not leaving us."

To hear the trust Santos has in me burns my chest with love, and I step forward to curl up on his lap. "Thank you."

"Be careful," he says as he nuzzles my hair. "Make sure you check in with us."

I nod and find Darius looking at me with sadness. "I promise to come back. I love you, remember?"

He gives me a small smile, but I still see the worry in his blue depths. There's nothing I can do about the mistrust I've caused in him; all I can do is come back and show him I'm here to stay.

"What are we doing in the meantime?" he asks Zander.

"The three of us are going to cause some mayhem with the Diablos. Blaze and I tracked down some of their new hookers this evening. With the right amount of money, quite a few were talking."

"They have infiltrated into our town and have taken up four residences. Well, three now, since we figured out the one they were keeping Selene in," Blaze adds.

"So, wait," Santos stills underneath me, "are you saying we get to blow some shit up?"

"Yeah, man," Zander snickers.

Santos hoots, slapping Darius on the chest. "Kaboom, baby!"

Darius' eyes meet mine and I see the excitement brimming in them. "We haven't *kaboomed* anything in a long time." His grin slowly grows.

I'm chomping into the small packet of roasted peanuts in my lap, smacking my lips together, and clicking my tongue off the roof of my mouth, but I don't get a reaction from the stone man beside me. He continues to watch the boring movie on the small screen, which makes sense with how boring he's being, as well.

I wiggle around in my seat, but I can't seem to stay still. I'm fucking bored. It's a five-and-a-half-hour flight and we're only an hour in. I'm going to end up hauled off this plane in cuffs, because I'm about to threaten the thing with a bomb if something interesting doesn't happen soon.

"Fuck it," I stand, Blaze's eyes finally swinging my way, nothing but apathy in the dark irises, "I'm going to the bathroom. Ask the attendant for more nuts."

I shove his big legs out of the way, and he grunts with irritation as I block his screen. I saunter down the aisle, grinning maniacally at babies, and then winking at their daddies. The mothers all give me nasty looks, but that just makes it all the more fun.

I get to the small bathroom and lock myself inside, sitting on the tiny toilet. I don't need to piss or anything. I just needed a change of scenery before I killed someone. Preferably the boring asshole sitting next to me. I couldn't bring my pretty knife onto the plane and even though Blaze has promised me a new one, I want to carve my name into the walls right now.

The sound of the sliding door opening is the only warning I get as Blaze stuffs his big body into this small room with me.

"Wait." I stare at the door, stunned. "I locked that."

"I know how to unlock just about anything. Now get up."

"Couldn't you have waited your turn?" I huff at him as I stand, my skirt still up around my waist. I didn't wear panties because I was hoping for an intrusive pat down by one of the hot security chicks.

"You weren't even using the toilet." He points into the empty bowl.

"So?"

He drops his pants and maneuvers us around, sitting on the toilet seat. He leans back so his hard cock is practically poking me in the eye, and his balls are hanging outside.

"You asked for nuts." He motions to his saggy ass balls.

"Oh!" I grin. "We're joining the mile long club." I drop to my knees between his long legs.

"You mean high." He rolls his eyes.

"Well, it looks long to me," I retort as I grab the fucking monster and suck it deep down my throat.

"Fuck," he hisses when I drag my teeth along the velvet surface, and then tug on the piercing in the tip. "Make it quick," he growls. "I want to eat that asshole."

*Well, damn.*

I continue to stroke his cock as I bend my head and suck his balls into my mouth. His legs tense beside me as I suck on one and then the other. Once they've had enough attention, I move back to his cock, the head a deep purple and the shaft jerking. I work his length, the sounds of sucking and gagging filling the small room, and when his fingers grip my hair, I know he's close.

"Right there," he grunts, and slams himself down my throat, his hot cum spurting in thick, salty ropes. He groans out my name, loud enough for the plane to hear for sure, and then he's making me stand.

"Put your hands on the sink and bend over. I want your asshole right here." He points at his mouth.

"Yes, Daddy." I grin and do as he demands.

He spreads my cheeks wide, lands a quick, sharp slap to my pussy, then seals his mouth around my asshole, just like he promised. He licks the tight rim, and then shoves his tongue inside, thrusting in and out.

His large fingers begin to work my clit with rough, tight circles against the sensitive nub. Then he forcefully shoves three fingers inside my pussy while his tongue fucks my ass. I'm so wet, I can bet everyone outside of this door can hear the sounds my pussy is making alone, not even including the breathy moans and whimpers coming from my mouth.

Blaze is rough, unforgiving, and so fucking delicious.

"You need to come now," he growls as he bites into the tight ring of muscle at my ass.

"Make me, Daddy," I dare retort.

And just as I figured, he gets rougher as a form of punishment for my disobedience. His hand cracks loudly against my ass cheek and then he's back to fucking my asshole with his tongue. His fingers slip into my pussy juices to spread it over my clit, giving it a hard pinch.

I lose my breath on the intensity of my orgasm. My legs shake, and my mouth gapes open on a silent scream. It's too much, and Blaze doesn't let up, draining me of every spasm, claiming each one with his mouth. Then, just as quick as he started, he pushes me up, and stands, dragging his pants up.

"Hurry back out and shut the fuck up for the rest of the flight," he grips my face in his hand, devouring my mouth with his.

Then he slams open the door, not bothering to close it, and heads back to his seat. I look up and find a lineup of people, all looking equally shocked as I pull down my skirt to cover my ass.

"You won't be getting the same experience as me, but enjoy your nature's calls." I give them all a curtsy and rush back to my seat, a giggle escaping as people shoot me dirty looks.

I shove by Blaze who's once again engrossed in the screen as if nothing happened, and squeal when I find another three packs of nuts on my seat.

"Stuff your mouth and shut up," he growls, but I see his scar twist with a ghost of a smile.

"Oh, look! Just as shriveled as yours." I crack into a crunchy nut loudly.

"You better watch your mouth before I fill it again."

"Promise?"

## Darius

Santos is practically bouncing out of his fucking seat, glancing at Zander, and grinning every few minutes as we drive toward one of the houses the Diablos has claimed. His energy is seeping into me, excitement coursing through my body at knowing we're about to start taking back what's ours.

"Are we there yet?" Santos asks Zander for the millionth time in ten minutes, causing Zander's knuckles to crack on the steering wheel.

"For the love of God, no!" he growls, glancing at me in the rear-view mirror. "If you want to make him choke on your dick right now, I won't stop you."

"I'm pretty sure my balls are one-hundred-percent empty at this point in time," I reply dryly, making him grunt. Santos, on the other hand, smirks at me over his shoulder and winks.

"I bet I could find more in there. It's not the explosion I was chasing today, but I won't say no."

Zander rolls his eyes, but the corner of his lips lifts into a small smile. He secretly loves our relationship. Seeing Santos so happy and carefree after he'd been down for so long is like a breath of fresh air, one we all appreciate. He might not be built big like Blaze, but my man can pack a punch, just ask my fucking face.

"Focus on the task ahead, not my junk. I say we blow shit up and ask questions later," I answer, and Zander chuckles darkly.

"That's the plan. We know there's no innocents in there, so go crazy. Send them a message they can't ignore," he grins, and I swear Santos squeals like a girl.

"I don't have to hold back? I can take them to pound town with my fists and I won't get yelled at?" he beams.

"Pound town? That's probably not the best way to describe it," Zander snorts.

"Why not? They'll be completely fucked once I get my hands on them. Seems pound town is fitting, after all," he shrugs, turning his attention out the window to watch the scenery. Most people would think he's zoned out, but he likes assessing his surroundings. If things go south and we get split up, he remembers every dark corner to run to. He's probably thinking about jerking off to the image of setting the whole damn neighborhood on fire.

"The only rule I have is to not blow us up in the process. I haven't forgotten the last time I let you loose," Zander adds, giving him the side-eye. "You burned my goddamn eyebrows off."

"And you looked so pretty, like a damaged little fire beetle!" Santos exclaims without looking away from the window. Zander shakes his head and scoffs.

"That doesn't even make sense."

"Does anything make sense?"

"Not when it comes from your fucking mouth," Zander mutters, pulling over one street over from our target. The neighborhood is quiet, half the houses being abandoned over the years as gangs started taking over, so if anyone sees us walking down the street with arms full of explosives, they won't do shit.

Santos bails from the car like lightning, not wasting time as he starts grabbing his toys from the trunk, while Zander runs through the layout of the property one more time, as if Santos is listening. Once the crazy bastard gets in destruction mode, his ears are usually turned off.

We lock the car and walk to the next street, seeing the house instantly, noticing one man standing on the front porch smoking a cigarette.

"You think I could get a bullet between his eyes from here?" I mumble, earning a scowl from Zander.

"Play it smart, D. Just because you have a silencer, doesn't mean you have to start the party early."

"You're becoming boring like Blaze. Besides, you said no rules, so that's on you," I throw back before lifting my gun and lining up my shot. Zander sighs but doesn't say anything, knowing I'm right. He let us out to play without setting boundaries, not that Santos or I listen when there are rules involved, anyway.

I fire my shot, the bullet sailing through the air and hitting the guy straight in the eye, his body falling to the ground instantly.

"You missed," Zander informs me, making me chuckle.

"Doubt it. He went down. That's all I give a fuck about."

"Anyone inside could have heard his body hit the deck."

"Good, they can all come running outside and get riddled with bullets," I shrug, but Santos starts running toward the house, a deranged laugh leaving him.

"Leave some for me, baby cakes!"

Zander watches him run, turning to glance at me after a moment. "Baby cakes? Why does his sweet side freak me out so much? He's a psychopath, and it's weird."

I grin, loving all of it. "Leave my cutsie poopsie alone." Then I take off after Santos, leaving Zander behind to fake a gag.

I catch up with Santos, who instantly unloads his armful of explosives into mine, taking pieces as he needs them. "You think they know we're here yet?" I ask, amusement filling his eyes.

"Nope. But they're about to. Gimme that," he states, motioning to a bunch of wires. I frown, handing it over to him.

"Don't you need a power source? C'mon, San. I think you're losing your brain cells finally."

"Leave that to me. What happens when things are wired wrong?" he asks, humming to himself and reminding me of Selene, causing a smile to tug at my lips.

"Electricity is a dangerous thing. Either nothing happens, or a hell of a lot happens. Are you asking me because you don't know?"

He peeks through the closest window, answering quietly as he cracks it open when the coast is clear. "I was just making sure you knew, that's all."

He makes his way around the house, distributing everything from my arms around it, then we make our way back to the window he opened where he hauls himself up onto the ledge and climbs inside.

"San!" I whisper yell, but he ignores me, fucking around with something on the wall before coming back out.

"When I say run, run," he says casually before turning on the little device in his hand. "Maybe start moving now, so Zander knows to stay back. His fat ass can't run as fast these days."

I snigger but turn to see Zander leaning against the fence farther away, motioning for him to stay put. He gives me a look as if I'm crazy, already aware it's best to stay back. After the eyebrow incident, he doesn't trust Santos with explosives in the slightest.

Santos chuckles to himself, pressing a button before his eyes dart up to mine. "Oh, shit. I meant to say 'run' first."

I grab his hand and yank him behind me as I start to run, his loud psychotic cackle filling the air, seconds before the house blows, shaking the ground under our feet, the force of the explosion knocking us down.

He lands on top of me, mischief taking over his face. "You wanna fuck right here? You little devil!"

"Get off me!" I laugh, pushing him away just as Zander runs over to help us up. Shouts fill the house as smaller explosions sound, making me frown.

"Do they have a meth lab in there? What's that sound?"

Santos can't wipe the smirk off his face as he eyes me. "I possibly plugged a device into their power inside. It sends a current through the entire wiring system and slowly burns away inside the walls. There should be another big boom any minute now and…"

I stumble as the next big explosion hits, the shouts getting louder, and a handful of people spill from the house, their eyes instantly finding us.

"You pieces of shit!" someone yells, but Zander blows out a breath and fires a shot over my shoulder, taking him out.

"You couldn't put explosives near the front door? You could have blown the entire thing up without any hassle."

Santos frowns, cocking his head slightly. "Where's the fun in that? I like playing with them."

"Go play then, because they look pissed," he grumbles, eyeing the men left who seem to all be armed now that the confusion has worn off. Wonderful.

I follow Santos as the guys start running toward us, firing shots that miss us by a mile. "Fucking hell, who taught you to shoot? A blind man?" Santos calls loudly, aiming his own gun at one of them to take them out. I watch the man I love as he skips toward the mayhem, talking to himself about wannabe gangsters, and I can almost feel the eye roll behind me from Zander. There are only seven people total in the house, so it doesn't take long for us to clear it out and head back toward the car, our next target on our minds.

Fuck, I miss Selene.

*Santos*

I didn't enjoy the first house as much as I thought I would. The explosions were cool, and it felt like a scene out of an action movie, but my dick didn't get hard over it. Maybe we've been fucking too much after all and my mini-me has finally had enough.

I try to stop thinking about my comatose dick as we arrive at the Diablos next house, my mind made up on how to approach it already. I jump from the car and open the trunk, pulling out a machine gun I hid in the spare tire compartment, the fabric of the trunk covering it up.

Zander glares at me, motioning to the trunk with his hands. "Where the fuck's the spare tire gone? And where the fuck did you get that?"

"Found it," I grin. "Hidden with a bunch of other cool shit."

"Where did you find it?" he demands, glaring at Darius as if it's his fault. I shrug, but I can't help the smile on my face.

"You know where Blaze hides stuff, so I can't find them?"

"Yes," he grunts, groaning when I continue.

"Well, there. That's where I found it. I assume it was a surprise for my birthday and that's why it was hidden. I'll have to thank him later. I love it!"

"He hides that shit from you because it's meant to stay hidden. You should not be in control of this type of weapon," he snaps, putting his hands out. "Give it here."

"Finders keepers!" I declare, clutching it tighter and accidentally firing a bunch of shots into the air. "Whoops!"

"Dammit, you *loco* piece of shit!" Zander barks just as the front door of the house flies open and men run out to see what's happening. Darius is laughing so hard I'm pretty sure he's going to piss himself, not seeming to give a shit that bullets are quickly being fired our way.

Zander curses at our cover being blown, but I let out a whoop and run headfirst toward them, swinging my new kick-ass toy in their direction, and holding down the trigger. Bullets rain across the front yard, my dick getting hard at the glorious view. *That's more like it.*

"San!" Zander shouts. I turn to look at him, chuckling as Zander and Darius dive for cover, and I realize I forgot to take my finger off the trigger.

"My bad!" I holler, hearing Zander curse me out colorfully as he gets to his feet to glare at me.

"This is why you don't get those kinds of toys, asshole! It's not your dick, you can't just swing it everywhere!"

"I don't see why not. Look, weeeeeeee!" I exclaim as I turn to fire more shots at the remaining men who've been trying to hide from my outburst, spinning in a circle as I go, causing Darius and Zander to duck for cover again. Seeing me almost kill my own guys probably has them wondering just how crazy I am. I'm not crazy, I'm passionate about my job. I should add that to my resume.

"No one would hire you, you stupid fucker!" Zander bellows over the sound of the gunfire, making me pause to look at him.

"You can read minds?"

"You said it out loud, you idiot!"

"Oh, thank fuck. You scared me, brother," I exclaim as I let out a breath, feeling his eyes burning into me.

"I'll scare you in a minute! Give me that!" he shouts, darting over to me and snatching my baby, making me pout.

"You're no fun!"

"Aren't I? I wonder why the fuck that would be?!" he snaps, holding the weapon tighter as I reach for it. "Don't even bother! Get in the car!"

"Yes, Mr. Walton," I mutter as I go.

"I wish I'd gotten a receipt for you. Some days I want to return you," he growls, turning to Darius so the pair of them could make sure the house was clear. Darius rigs it and blows it to pieces, leaving nothing behind. The Diablos need to know whose town this is.

It's ours.

# Chapter Six

## Zander

Santos can pout at me all he likes; we are done for the day. We drive in silence all the way home, his eyes drifting to me every so often to sulk. I told Blaze ages ago we can't hide anything from Santos, but he seemed to think it would be fine. Turns out, he was wrong.

Darius glares at me for most of the drive, annoyed at me for upsetting his boyfriend. I don't give a fuck; Santos should never have an automatic weapon in his grip. Ever. And this is why. Both Darius and I could have easily been killed today, but I seem to be the only one who gives a fuck about that.

I usually don't mind when I pull the short straw to play babysitter, but I've been doing it a lot lately, and it's starting to burn me out. I love Santos and Darius. They are family, but fuck, they drain the energy right out of you.

Once back at home, Santos climbs out and slams the car door, making me snort. He can throw a tantrum if he really wants, but he isn't getting his toy back. Imagine if he had it in the house? Selene and Blaze would come home to Swiss Cheese Avenue in their living room.

Darius runs after him, taking his hand silently to let him know he's on his side, leaving me to clear out the trunk and stash the weapons. Fine by me. I don't want them anywhere near it.

I make quick work of it, heading into the house once I'm done to find Santos lying on the couch, making the most annoying sounds possible. It's like a child sulking, crossed with Selene's singing.

"For fuck's sake. Would you shut up?" I groan, but he just makes the noise louder, the wailing noise grating on my nerves. "Either you shut up or I shut you up. What's it going to be?"

He goes silent, and I think I've won until he sits up to let me sit, only to sprawl across my lap with a sly smile on his face. "How would you shut me up? A gag? A punch to the face? Your dick? I mean, I'm not opposed to any of those."

"Get off me."

"Get you off? All right. Dick treatment it is!" he states and acts like he's going to unzip my pants. I move fast, flipping him off me and pinning him under me with a snarl.

"Stop it! Is that all you think about? Dick and violence?"

His tongue runs across his lips before he speaks. "No."

"What else do you possibly think about?!"

"My baby girl's heavenly pussy on my face. I think about that a lot, actually."

"I'm close to losing it with you. I really am," I warn, but he just chuckles and leans up to kiss my cheek because he's a dick.

"I'm close to losing control too, Mr. Walton. I can't explain it. You just do it for me."

When I said I loved them, I didn't mean I wasn't considering killing them.

"Oh, I do love a gang bang," Darius drawls as he wanders in, plonking down on the other couch, where I should have sat in the first place.

"Keep your boyfriend off me before I beat his ass," I grit out, glaring at him when he laughs.

"Let him torment you. He's bored without Selene."

"He'll be bored when he's bedridden and I'm not here because I'll be in a cell for attempted murder," I hiss, his eyes narrowing.

"Fine. Come here, *amante*. I'll occupy you," Darius claims, patting his lap. Santos raises an eyebrow at me, telling me silently to get off him, then he switches to the couch with Darius, sprawling contently across his lap. The happy sigh he lets out simmers some of my temper, and I can't help but smile as Darius runs his fingers through Santos' dark hair to calm him.

"I'm sorry. You just drive me crazy sometimes," I mumble, and Darius snorts.

"Sometimes?"

"Regularly," I correct. "How about we all shower and have a lazy afternoon while we wait to hear from our girl and Blaze?"

"You want to shower with us? All right. I'll allow it," Santos jokes, and I let out an exasperated sigh.

"Lord, give me strength."

"You've been hanging around Pepe too much. You seem to be praying a lot lately," Darius teases.

"I like that little shit. He's my favorite pet I've ever had," Santos says absently as he stands to stretch, and I can't help but laugh.

"He's your pet?"

"Yep. I want to keep him," he decides, finalizing the subject. Pepe has no idea what he's in for if Santos has claimed him. I can't wait to see how that plays out.

# *Blaze*

"Are we there yet?" Selene asks me for what must be the millionth time. We only just got into the rental ten minutes ago. It's like having Santos here.

"Knock it off," I growl at her. "Call your sister and tell her where the rendezvous point is."

"Fuck her and the cunt she was shoved out of!"

I snort because fuck, she's a clever little shit. "We need the guns and the extra help."

We found out the MC meeting up for the shipment was not the Dientes. Pepe texted Selene while we were on the plane, and we received it when we got off. It's another MC called The Highway Knights. They're known for their brutality and constant turf wars with Dientes.

"I know." She huffs, "that's why I'm calling Papi."

I don't argue with her because I understand what she's feeling, and

I'm not going to push her to talk to a sister who gave up so easily on her. Especially when Selene never gave up, even when the odds were slim that Jan was even alive.

"*Hola, Reaper Pequena.*" Papi's voice purrs into the phone, and my teeth crack with irritation.

"*Hola, culo* eater," Selene retorts, and a startled laugh breaches my lips. Fucking little shit is on another level today. "We're in Nevada running a lead on a skin drop off today."

"We're not picking anything up today," he replies, his voice sounding suspicious.

"It's for The Highway Knights. We also learned they're your rivals. Wanna help me kill some people?"

"Yes, we fucking do!" I hear Loqi in the background, his hoots sounding eerily similar to Santos'.

"I guess we'll meet you there. Send us the location." Papi Loco snarls before hanging up.

"Santos got the best out of that asshole's saggy balls," she growls as she tosses her phone in the cupholder.

"That's not saying much," I grumble.

Selene declines her seat all the way back and begins to hike up her skirt.

"What the fuck are you doing?" I ask, trying to keep my eyes on the road and not the slow exposure of my favorite pussy.

"All this talk about saggy balls and Santos has me needing to get off," she groans as her fingers dip into her pink flesh. "Besides, it'll help keep me focused when I need to take fuckers out."

I try to ignore her tiny mewls. I even try to ignore when they grow into loud moans for Santos, but the scent of her arousal has me snapping, quickly cutting the car to the side of the road, making other motorists lay on their horns.

"Get out of the car," I snarl, and her head quickly turns to look at me.

"What?"

"Now, Selene, before I choke you to death, and fuck your warm pussy until it turns cold."

She slowly pulls her skirt down and opens the door, stepping out into the stifling Nevada heat. Fuck, I miss New York already. I'm out of the car soon after her, and we meet at the hood.

"Are you making me walk the rest of the way?" Her arms cross over her chest.

"No." I grab her hair and drag her into me, slamming my mouth to hers in a bruising kiss. We part, and I throw her on top of the hot metal of the hood.

Her hands hit the metal, and she hisses through the heat, but just like I thought, she endures the pain as I flip her skirt up. I undo my pants in record time and slam into her already prepared cunt. Horns honk as the cars pass, and I continue to punish this little brat until she comes all over my cock.

"Fuck, yes!" she screams as I feel her begin to tighten. My hand cracks down over her ass and I grab her hair, yanking her back to my chest.

"Stop with the disobedience, or I will redden your ass at each turn off on this highway. Am I understood?"

"Yes, Daddy," she whispers as I shove her back down.

"Now, have this pussy creaming all over my cock before I shoot at these honking fuckers."

She listens like the good girl I know she can be, and we come simultaneously, our moans getting eaten up by the surrounding traffic. I pull out of her, slap her ass one more time and do up my pants.

"Now your cum is going to be all over the seat," she snickers.

"It's a rental. What the fuck do I care?" I turn on my heel and snap my fingers at her. "Get in the car, put the fucking seatbelt on, and behave for the rest of the way."

"Okay, Daddy." She smirks as she walks bow-legged back to the passenger side door. I don't know what it is about her calling me *Daddy*, but I kind of want to drag her back to that hood and this time, fuck her asshole raw.

I pull back out into traffic, and grin when she does indeed put on her seatbelt, settling in for a nap. Finally, fucking peace and quiet.

"The last time I was fucked on the hood of a car, I had Zander's dick in my mouth and his daddy's in my pussy."

Well, as close to peace and quiet as I can get.

# Selene

I feel rough fingers brush against my cheek, and I sleepily look to my left, finding Blaze giving me a rare, soft look.

"Are we there yet?" I croak out, and his scar tugs on his mouth as he smiles.

"Yeah, baby." He looks out the windshield and then back to me. "No sign of the shipment, but I see some bikes rolling up. I just can't tell who they are from here."

I follow his gaze and see that he's parked us up on a cliff, overlooking the meeting spot down below. It's discreet and we can sneak up on them when we're ready. There are about ten bikes rolling in, and as they get closer, I see the Dientes logo on the helmets. You can't miss the large shark teeth they have designed around the visors.

Blaze taps his horn four times in quick succession, and I see the lead bike point up at us. "He has a passenger," Blaze mumbles. It's Papi's bike and I know who's there holding on to his waist.

"I see that." I can even hear the deep tenor as my voice changes. I'm working on my anger toward my sister. I'm slowly coming to the realization she's not me, and her need to find me was doused when she found our bloody, ransacked apartment. But the operative word is *slowly*. I'm not one to be forced into anything, and that includes a relationship with her.

"Ignore it and let's kill some fuckers, yeah?" I turn back to Blaze with a large grin, loving how he used my line.

"Hell, yes," I squeal and throw open the door when I hear the bikes' roar coming up behind us.

I lean against the trunk of the car, my arms crossed over my chest, and watch as they all kick down the stands, their bikes lined up in a perfect row with Papi in the center. I want to kill the old fucker for what he's done to Santos, but I won't take that away from my man. He may just want to do it himself.

They cut out the bikes and all of them stand one by one. As they take off the helmets, I start to recognize them. Kho and Kaine, Perc and Vico, Loqi, Papi Loco and my sister, Hook, and three other older men I wasn't introduced to. They must be Papi's men.

"Reaper!" Loqi exclaims as he strides forward. "We meet again!" I bump his fist with my own, and he gives Blaze a nod.

"Let's distribute weapons," Papi says as he drops a bag down on the sand. His hand goes up and each biker comes forward with bags of weapons.

"This must be how Santos feels when he sees guns," I squeal through the excitement. At the mention of his son's name, Papi's jaw locks, but he's smart enough to keep his mouth shut.

"Selene?" I turn to look at my sister as she timidly comes forward. "I have something for you."

"Is it a fuck?" I watch as her eyebrows come together, "because I can't seem to find my own." Blaze's elbow digs into my ribs, and I growl. "Sorry," I give her a fake smile, "what do you have for me, dear sister of the east?" I lean into Blaze. "Get it? Like the Wicked Witch of the East?"

He snorts again and nudges me with his shoulder. "Give her a chance, *Dorothy*."

"I figured since you had to fly out, you wouldn't have your pretty knife belt. So, I had you one made by our very own forger, Hammer." She holds out a pretty metal ornate belt and tucked into the buckle is a gorgeous knife with the words Reaper Incarnate engraved into the handle. The blade itself is black, but a large silver scythe is etched into the surface.

I stare at its obvious beauty, completely speechless.

"You've somehow found a way to shut her up," Blaze snarks as the guys laugh, but I can't move my eyes from my new toy. Even after all these years, after how much I've changed from the little sister she knew, it's like she still gets me at my core.

"I hope you like it," she says nervously.

"I do." My voice cracks, and my eyes begin to fill, surprising the fuck out of me. Am I really going to cry over a blade?

"I think it's more over the blade your sister got you. Which is very much in your tastes," Blaze says as he whistles at the design.

"I said that out loud?" I feel the first tear fall over my cheek. Thank fuck all the bikers are laughing and not paying attention to my weak moment. I'd hate to have to kill any of them.

"So, you like it?" Jan wrings her hands.

"Yes," I nod, and finally my heart sheds its icy exterior. "I like it so much. It's perfect." I step into her and pull her in for a tight hug, feeling the tension leave her body at once.

"I'm so sorry, Selly," she whispers into my neck.

"I know," I tell her as I give her a final squeeze. I release her, and for the first time, I feel lighter. "Let's focus on killing some assholes."

"I'm gonna stay up here and watch you guys," she chuckles. "I'm not a fighter. I just had to come see you."

The distant rumble of bikes sounds in the valley below, and everyone stops their chatter.

"This is it." Loqi grins as he bounces on the balls of his feet. He has a fully automatic machine gun strapped across his chest with multiple rounds of ammo, and once again, I'm struck with how similar he is to Santos.

"We don't do anything until the shipment shows up." Blaze steps forward. "Which should be at any moment. Then we piss on their parade."

"Like actually piss?" I look at him. "That's not fair. I don't have an extension hose like the rest of you." I pout.

Loqi bends over with laughter as Papi Loco fights to stop the grin crawling over his mouth and failing. He distributes the guns and I end up with a handgun I tuck into the waistband of my skirt. The bikes park down in the valley, and we count four bikes and a large cargo van.

"Should be any minute now," Blaze says. "Let's start creeping down closer."

"You stay here, Henny." Papi grabs my sister around the waist and kisses her breathlessly. "Stay safe."

"Okay, Papi," she murmurs as her hand settles against his cheek. "I love you."

Watching them makes my heart hurt. I miss my boys, and I can't wait to get them all back together again. As if sensing my thoughts, Blaze puts his phone in front of my face and I watch a video of Santos skipping into a group of Diablos and spinning while shooting a machine gun, his maniacal laughter pulling one from me as well.

"He's getting knocked the fuck out when I get home," Blaze mutters, a ghost of a smile coating his lips. "I hid that shit from him for that very reason."

The video ends as Zander screams, a bullet whizzing by his head, and I laugh again, loving every second of it and wishing I were there.

"Here comes the truck," Papi says, and we look down at the valley.

"Let's move." Blaze brushes by me to lead us closer.

"Selly," Jan grabs my hand as I move to follow Blaze, "please be careful."

"Can't promise that, but I promise to stay alive." I grin at her. "I get to kill Gingivitis if he's here." I call dibs on Mack.

"Fine," Blaze concedes as we make our way down the steep incline. "No shooting until the shipment is safely boarded into the van."

Everyone murmurs their assent, and we continue down. To my great disappointment, Mack is not present for this drop off, but that doesn't mean I won't have fun shooting holes into the rest of these scumbags. We watch the exchange happen and I snarl when I see a few young kids among the group, crying and being slapped around for it.

"I wish I'd kept Walton's strap-on," I growl. "I'd be fucking some assholes."

Loqi chokes on his laugh, and Papi slaps him on the back of the head with a stern warning to be quiet. Once the victims are all safely inside the van, I aim my gun and shoot the closest biker to me, watching as he drops like a sack of shit to the sand.

"Dientes!" One of them yells just as we come running out of hiding.

The valley becomes a battlefield as bullets rain down around us and shouts of distress and the cries of death become overwhelming. I take out four men before I turn and find Blaze mowing down three in a row. Without panties to rein it in, I flood my fucking thighs. My man is a hot motherfucker.

When we finally kill every last piece of shit, I look around us, letting out a whoop when I find we've had no casualties.

"That was like taking candy from a baby!" I holler.

"Only because they weren't prepared for us," Loqi calls out as he opens the van. "I need to see if my sister is here."

My heart hurts once again for him, knowing the feeling all too well, and seeing his desperation. When he steps out of the van, my stomach sinks with his long face. She's not here.

"Hook," Papi calls out. "Drive the van back to the compound. Henny will drive your bike back."

"On it, Boss." Hook heads for the driver's side of the van.

"Loqi, call the scrappers to come for these bikes."

"You got it." Loqi nods at his father and pulls out his phone.

"You two can come back to the compound. We'll get you some food and you can rest. We'll return your car to the rental, and you can take one of ours back, unless you want to leave that shiny new knife here." Papi nods to my waist.

"Hell no," I shake my head.

"Let's get out of here." Papi heads back up the hill.

The compound is buzzing with excitement when we get there, and soon enough a party is underway. I sit at the bar in front of Licker, who gives me a wide smile in return.

"Deadly Reaper!" he exclaims. "Welcome back!"

He drops a whiskey on ice in front of me, and I hum my approval at his memory.

"How was the shootout? Did you get any?"

"You know it." I grin, "Killed those motherfuckers dead."

Blaze snorts as he sits on the stool beside me. "That she did."

He gets a whiskey pushed in front of him, and I grin seeing he drinks what I do. He ignores my look with a roll of his eyes, and drinks in silence.

"I wanna get back," I tell him.

"Same." He nods. "We take a few hours to relax, and we can head out. It'll take a few days to get home."

Loqi appears to my left, and signals for Licker to grab him a beer.

"Still haven't found your sister?"

"No," he shakes his head sadly. "The police station won't release the info on the woman they have in custody yet. It's just a waiting game."

"What is her name?"

"Cara."

My glass pauses in its path to my mouth as the name washes over me. I know that name. I wrack my brain and when it hits me, my glass drops to the floor, shattering.

"Loqi." My voice is a coarse whisper as the people around me stop and stare at the commotion. "I know your sister."

## Santos

Zander is still pissy with me for my machine gun Merry-Go-Round incident, but at least he's stopped glaring at me. I had so much fun, I passed the fuck out with my head on Darius' lap half-way through the first movie.

I wake up to someone shaking my shoulder gently, fingers tracing up and down my spine, and the scent of Darius surrounding me.

"San? Wake up."

I groan, cracking my eyes open and blinking against the bright light from the TV, finding Darius peering down at me with a soft smile on his handsome face. "Why? I'm tired after all the fun I had today."

"I know, babe, but Zander wants to take out the other house now. It's dark. There are more people there than the last two, and we're hoping they've all congregated there, licking their wounds. Let's go cause some mayhem," he replies, chuckling when I bolt upright with excitement.

Zander walks in as he's shoving a gun down the back of his jeans, his eyes landing on mine immediately. "No machine guns hidden in my fucking car this time."

"I wouldn't have had to hide it if you weren't such a stick in the mud, Zan. Didn't you see how many motherfuckers I gunned down?" I frown.

"I did see. You almost gunned us down in the process. You use your handgun and your knife, got it? Pepe is in there, so don't start blowing shit up unless you want us to use him as collateral damage," he warns, my eyes going wide. I don't want my pet to die. I like him.

"I'll be good!" I promise, making him roll his eyes as he walks toward the door.

"Sure, you will. Let's go and get your pet then, shall we?" Don't have to tell me twice.

I get to my feet and follow Zander, letting Darius lock up as we head toward the car. I consider bringing fireworks to scare them, but I have a feeling Zander wouldn't find it as amusing as I would, so I leave them at home.

I miss Selene. She would have loved playing machine gun Merry-Go-Round with me, and she definitely would have found the fireworks hilarious. I hope whatever they're doing in Nevada is going smoothly. I worry about her sister fucking with her emotions, but my girl can handle herself.

"I'm setting rules this time," Zander says as we drive, dragging me back to reality.

"Why? We had so much fun last time without them!" I huff, earning a side glance in return.

"Did we?" he deadpans. "I don't recall enjoying that. We stick together, no splitting up to do dumb shit, and don't blow anything up until I say so. You don't want to hurt Pepe, do you?"

"I'd never hurt Pepe!"

"Stick to the rules, then. Stay by me. This is a stealth mission until I say otherwise. *Entiendes*?" he asks firmly, making me grin. Of course, I understand, but I like fucking with him.

"*No comprendo. Otra vez, por favor?*"

"I won't say it again! If you don't understand, I'll turn this car around and drop you at home! Did you need me to repeat myself, or do you fucking understand?" he snaps, and I roll my eyes at his dramatics.

"*Si*. You need a strong coffee or a tight pussy to bury your dick in. How long will our tight pussy be gone? I can't deal with you like this for too long," I sigh, but he ignores me and turns the conversation to Darius.

"We check around the house for guards, try to locate Pepe before they know we're there, then somehow get his holy ass out before the gunfire starts, all right? Keep an eye on Santos and don't let him do anything stupid."

Darius grins, giving me a wink. "If he steps out of line, I'll punish his ass."

"Am I getting a daddy kink like our girl and daddy Blaze? I wouldn't mind one of us bending the other over and…"

"You don't have a fucking daddy kink, you have a *piss Zander off* kink," Zander growls, giving me the evil-eye before turning his attention back to the road ahead. He has zero humor, I swear. Selene needs to come home and fuck the stick right out of his ass.

We drive the rest of the way in silence, and the moment we park, Zander presses the button to lock all the doors, stopping me from bailing out. "Hey!"

"Tell me the rules," he demands, and I flip him off.

"How does go fuck a donkey sound?"

"It sounds like you're going home?" he offers, making me scowl.

"No explosions, no machine gun, not letting my dick out, no stupidity, and do as I'm told," I state.

"Sounds like you're ready then," he nods and unlocks the doors.

"Sounds like a fucking downer of a party, and I'll die from boredom. If anyone shoots at me, I'll let them take me out. Has to be more fun than this," I grumble, climbing out to stand beside Darius, who ruffles my hair playfully.

"C'mon, once we don't have to be stealthy, we'll have some fun. Let's get Pepe out and paint the walls in blood, *amante*," he declares, and nothing sounds more damn romantic than that.

Zander grumbles about us being idiots, but he's smiling, so that's a start.

We head toward the house and sneak around the back, peering in windows to try and locate Pepe. We find him in one of the back rooms, talking to someone on the phone. I tap on the glass quietly, ignoring Zander's growl, and Pepe turns to look at us with wide eyes. Someone enters the room, and we duck, not wanting to be seen yet.

"What are you looking at?" The person asks, his footsteps coming toward the window. We crouch down farther, managing to stay hidden until the footsteps retreat.

"Nothing. I'm just paranoid after those other attacks," Pepe replies, finishing his conversation on the phone as the other man leaves.

I peek through the window again, huffing, when I realize he's left the room. "How do we get him out, then? I was going to drag him out the window."

"Why don't you try knocking on all the other windows and find him? Maybe one of the Diablos can help you," Zander deadpans.

"Well, that's a dumb idea. They'll know we're here then," I snort, making him roll his eyes. "Oh, you're being funny." Asshole.

We make our way around the house until finding an open window, and before Zander can tell me not to, I climb inside. I can hear his muttered curses, but Darius follows me, not wanting to miss out on any action.

Zander soon does the same, giving me a dirty look as we sneak through the house, coming to a halt when we find Pepe in the kitchen with some of the Diablos. The floorboards creak under our feet, drawing eyes to us instantly.

"Shit," Zander mutters, so I figure that's permission to end the stealth mission.

I dart into the room, throwing Pepe over my shoulder and turning toward the hallway. "I'd wondered where I left this! Pretend I'm not even here, guys!"

"That's not yours!" someone shouts, as I start running, speaking over my shoulder.

"Finders keepers!"

Footsteps pound through the house after me, gunfire sounding as Zander and Darius cover for me.

"Put me down!" Pepe screams, making me laugh.

"Like fuck, you slippery little sucker! I'm keeping you! Boss said I could!"

"You're going to get me killed!" he snaps, swatting at my butt. "Put me down!"

"Calm down, at least buy me dinner first before spanking me! What would Jesus say? You little minx!" I cackle, ignoring his protesting as I find a back door and run outside.

I put him back on his feet and motion to the car farther up the road. "Go get in the car and hide. I won't let them hurt you, but I want to go back and play with them."

Surprisingly, he does as he's told, leaving me to turn some Diablos into *Pinatas*.

*Best day ever.*

# *Darius*

Zander's cursing about Santos as we cover for him, taking out anyone who tries to chase after him. I know he'll be back in a second. He hates missing out on all the fun.

I back down the hallway, keeping my gun in front of me as I wait for any of the Diablos to follow, but I freeze as an arm wraps around my neck from behind. "Nice try."

Zander's farther up the hallway. But with the dim lights, he might miss and shoot me by accident instead. I stay still, but the man is suddenly ripped off me, and Santos jumps on his back, clinging on as he smacks my attacker in the head with his gun multiple times.

"Pinata! Pinata!" he shouts, and I have to smother a laugh at the sight. Zander comes up to me and nods to make sure I'm okay. Then he keeps an eye out while Santos has his fun. The guy's nuts, and I fucking love him for it.

"Get off me!" the man slurs, his brain being rattled around by the hits.

"The only person allowed to choke D is me! Keep your slimy hands to yourself, heathen!" he barks, jumping off his back before grabbing his knife from his pocket and fisting the man's hair, yanking his head back to expose his neck. "*¡Adiós, pendejo!*" then he stabs him in the throat, dragging the blade down sharply.

The man's gurgling for air, and blood spills, slowly choking him to death as he drowns, but Santos is done playing with him as he moves toward me, taking my face in his bloodied hands to inspect me. "Did he hurt you? I'll kill him again if you want?"

"Since when do you care if I'm hurt?" I tease because he's being softer than normal. He scowls, glaring at the dying man before meeting my gaze again.

"I care because the only person allowed to make you bleed is me."

"Can you two have your foreplay later?" Zander asks dryly as car tires squeal out front, signaling the arrival of more Diablos. "We have things to do."

Santos grins manically before kissing me hard, not looking back as he turns on his heel and runs toward the threat like a cat chasing a ball of yarn. Zander sighs, his expression tired, but he follows to make sure he doesn't get himself killed.

Shouts and screams sound as the men enter the house, and I keep an eye on the surroundings as Zander and Santos gun them down one by one, then I join them as more Diablos arrive. *How many of these fuckers are there?*

"Zan, duck!" I bark as someone runs for him, and he does as he's told quickly, giving me a clear shot to the man's skull. Zander gives me a thumbs up before charging across the room at someone, unloading two bullets and knocking them down instantly.

I find Santos drawing Tic-Tac-Toe on one of the body's faces with his blade, seeming deep in thought, ignoring the chaos around him as usual. He curses, somehow losing against himself, then he stands and puts three rounds in the man's face with annoyance. "Stupid game." Then he takes off to jump on someone's back as they try to sneak up on Zander, pretending he's a cowboy riding a bronc. "Yee-fucking-haw!"

Two Diablos make a break for it, deciding against messing with my psycho man, leaving three behind which we gun down pretty fast, leaving the house in silence. Well, other than Santos' panting from burning all that fucking energy.

"We good?" Zander asks as we check ourselves over for damage. "Good. Let's rig this place up and get out of here."

It doesn't take long to fill the house with explosives, and once we are half-way back to the car, I give Santos the button to blow the place to Kingdom Come. He enjoys it more than I do, so I figure he'll appreciate the gesture.

"Pepe?" Santos singsongs, jogging toward the car to peek in the windows, seeming satisfied to find the shaking man in the back seat. "Oh, good! Let's go, my pet looks hungry!"

Santos climbs into the back with Pepe, letting me sit up front. I'm surprised when Zander silently drops the keys into my hand, climbing into the passenger seat and shutting himself inside.

I don't question him as I slide in behind the steering wheel, starting the engine and driving off toward home, smirking as Santos babbles on to Pepe about all the fun he just had. The poor man is whispering prayers under his breath, wondering why God put such demons in his path.

Back at the house, Zander mumbles about needing a shower and takes off for some peace and quiet, leaving me to deal with Santos and Pepe.

"You should have seen me! I smashed his skull in!" Santos

exclaims, his hands waving around as he gives Pepe a play-by-play of the evening's events. Pepe silently sits on the couch, looking out of place as his new best friend keeps talking, and I figure I'll break the ice a little and get the fucker to relax. He doesn't seem to understand he is one of the safest people in the damn house right now with how much Santos likes him.

"You want a coffee? Or a beer? Santos needs to go shower all that blood off," I offer, and Pepe lets out a breath of relief as he nods.

"Coffee, please."

"Oh! And get those little cheesy puff snacks! They look like fingers!" Santos grins, giving me a kiss on his way past to the bathroom.

Once Pepe has a coffee in hand and the cheesy puffs on the coffee table in front of him, Pepe looks at me with a frown. "Have you heard from Selene and Blaze? I hope they're okay."

I shrug. "They'll call when they're ready. They're probably neck deep in body parts right now. They can handle themselves, trust me."

"She's scary," he admits. "She doesn't seem to have a filter, either."

"Our girl's one of a kind. You'll get used to her antics eventually," I smirk, sipping my coffee and watching him, trying to see what Santos sees in the little weirdo. We make small talk until Santos comes back, instantly sitting beside Pepe and stuffing his face with the cheesy puffs, sucking the flavor off his fingers in the process. It's hot, and it shouldn't be.

"You know, you have blood on your face," Santos says to me, stating the obvious.

"I'm aware. You put it there. Can you two play nice while I shower? If Zan comes back out, give him some space. He's fucking tired and has had enough of our shit today," I grunt, knowing he deserves a rest. It can be hard trying to be the sensible one out of all of us, and Santos especially is probably giving him grey hairs.

Santos drops an arm around Pepe's shoulders, making him jump. "Me and Pepe will be fine! I'll put a movie on. You like slasher movies?"

I leave them to it, despite Pepe's panicked squeak, knowing they'll be fine.

I quickly rinse off the blood, scrubbing myself clean, and I'm not surprised to find Zander sitting on my bed waiting for me. He looks exhausted.

"You good?" I ask as I head toward my drawers and drop my towel, yanking some boxers on. He groans, dropping back on the bed.

"I'm so fucking tired, man. Santos is worse than a toddler, and you're not much better some days."

I find some sweats and put them on before sitting on the bed, looking down at him with a raised eyebrow. "Santos has a lot of energy, and he sees the world differently than you do. Let him be crazy and stop getting so uptight with him. You know why you're tired? Because you spend so much time and energy trying to control things, you can't. Let him have fun. We'll always get out alive. You saw him today; he was having a blast."

"I know, but earlier today was ridiculous. He could have shot us. I like spilling blood like the rest of you, you know that, but he's out of control," he replies tightly, scrubbing his face with his hands. "We can't rely on luck being on our side forever."

"Selene and Santos both like to handle things the same way. Let them. Stop stressing yourself out over things that don't matter. Selene and Blaze won't be gone for long, then we can fuck the hell out of her until we pass out. Things will be back to normal. Just hold out a little longer," I mumble, his hands lifting from his face to look at me.

"The fuck does normal look like? We've never been normal."

"It's our own normal. There will always be violence, sex, and frustration. It's who we are. You need to learn to roll with it, old man," I tease, sliding back from him as he swats at me.

"I miss them," he sighs, and I pat his shoulder as he sits up.

"Me, too. They'll call and fill us in soon. You want a coffee?" I offer as I stand, waiting for him to follow.

"Fuck, yeah. Where's Santos?"

"Playing with Pepe," I grin, chuckling as we walk into the living room to find Santos and Pepe on the couch, watching a horror movie and sharing the cheesy puffs.

I don't know what Zander is worried about. Things seem pretty normal to me.

# Chapter Seven

## Zander

The exhaustion is bone-fucking-deep. I'm tired of having to always be the one who makes sure we all stay alive, and more times than not, I'm left with these fuckers who enjoy flirting with death. I want to retire from blowing up houses, shooting down cunts, and saving little altar boys. Speaking of, I find our little altar boy relaxed on the couch beside Santos—of all people—and watching a bloody slasher movie.

I sit down across from them and take the offered beer from Darius, settling in for the night. I place my phone on the table between us, hoping to hear from Blaze or Selene soon, and begin to drink my beer.

I'm deep into the movie, the spray of blood, suspense of who the killer is, and females running for their lives, when the shrill ring of my phone interrupts us at a suspenseful part. Pepe shrieks like a cat in heat, tossing the bowl of cheesy puffs in the air, and Santos joins in, fear coating his features as he wraps his arms around the altar boy. Darius slides off the couch with roaring laughter, and I can feel my own bubbling up in my chest.

"Are you serious?" I glare at Santos, his arms still around a panting Pepe.

"Why is your ringtone set to *pig slaughter*?!" Santos roars as he releases his arms from around Pepe.

I answer the phone with a chuckle when I see it's Blaze and put it on speaker. "Brother."

"Tell me you all got out with your balls intact."

"Daddy Blaze is very concerned with our balls, even though he doesn't care to play with them," Santos explains to Pepe, and I laugh.

"Fuck's sake," Blaze growls, and I lose it again. "Will you all be quiet? We have some news. You'll want to pay attention, Santos."

The tone of Blaze's voice has us all sitting up straight. This isn't a check-in. "Go ahead," I tell him once I see we're all listening.

"Santos, we think we've located your sister. Her name is Cara. Selene believes she met her here in Nevada when she was on her *solo* mission." We hear a scoff in the background, clearly coming from our girl. "We were going to stop off at the apartment she had here for rental before the lease is up to grab her things, and maybe get a bit more info. I need you guys to be prepared to fly out."

I glance over at Santos and find his face pale, a look of terror coating his eyes. He's only ever looked to us as his family, and now he's being bombarded with multiple siblings.

"Okay," I clear my throat. "Did everything go okay over there? Did you get the shipment sorted?"

"Yeah, we took out a few bikers from the rival MC to the Dientes. Thanks to Pepe for his intel."

"Pepe is here with us now. Looks like we're keeping the little fucker," I snicker.

"Great, maybe he can cleanse Santos' soul," Blaze retorts.

This would be the point where Santos would have a snarky come back, but he's sitting there with his hands in his lap, looking lost. Darius glances up at him, and hauls himself off the floor, shoving Pepe aside to sit by his man. He takes his hand, and Santos finally reacts, looking into Darius' face.

"I need to save my little sister," he whispers.

"Hey, Blaze?" I call down to the phone.

"Yeah?"

"I think we're going to hop in the car and start on our way to you. That way, we can bring some toys. Santos should be there." I keep my eyes on Santos.

"Sounds good," Blaze consents. "We should have more for you when you get here."

He hangs up the phone, and the room falls silent. Santos is staring down at his and Darius' joined hands, and Pepe is glancing between all of us.

"Let's go pack a few bags," I say as I get up to stretch. "Pepe, since all your stuff was destroyed, you can borrow some of my shit. We'll grab you more clothes on the way."

"Can we leave now?" Santos asks, his face one of complete torture.

I'm so fucking exhausted, my eyes are screaming for sleep, but I won't let him down. "Yeah."

"I'll take the first leg so you can get some sleep," Darius says as he passes by me, his hand landing on my shoulder.

"Thanks," my shoulders deflate.

I really wouldn't want us dying because I fell asleep at the wheel. I'm pretty sure all of our fates are sealed to Santos with bullets from his Merry-Go-Round.

# Selene

Being in this apartment again feels so surreal. I can't believe it was only a few short weeks ago I was chasing down leads and trying not to kill John Dempster prematurely. Blaze comes striding through the front door, and I scoff, "Maybe you should've taken the window." I thumb over my shoulder. "For old time's sake."

He chuckles as he falls onto the couch. "Or I can spray cum all over this table again, or better yet, go cut off another dick?"

"Gross." I shudder with a grin. I begin packing up my clothes and toiletries into the one duffle bag. We're waiting for Loqi to get back to us, and then we're going to devise a plan to free Cara. When Blaze told me the rest of my boys were on their way here, I felt immediate relief. I want Santos to have a part in saving his sister.

I go back out to the living room to see Blaze watching one of the three channels I had here. It's the local news station breaking that they found a woman's dead body. She was believed to have been a prostitute.

"What the fuck?" I mutter as I sit on the couch. Thoughts of Aniyah fill my mind with worry. She wasn't at the compound when we were there, and the guys said she left to go back home. Something about being homesick. "I need to go to the bar."

"Good Times," he mutters, and I nod. "Let's go then."

"Wait," I put my hand on his arm, "you can't be seen with me. I'm going to see what I can find out, and no one will talk to me if I'm with you."

"Does my Little Reaper want to go hunting?" He gives me a sly smirk.

"Mm hmm." I smile.

"And she's not going to need her daddy's help?" My thighs immediately clench at the deep tenor of his voice.

"No," I shake my head slowly, "but Daddy can watch."

The bar is filled when I walk in a few hours later, and I spot a frazzled-looking Colleen behind the counter. I shove a dude off my stool, and when he turns to fight me on it, I growl in his face. He has the right idea to turn away because I'm ready to stab a cunt.

"It's not nice to be a bully," a girl snickers from beside me.

"This is my seat," I say loudly and grin when Colleen's head snaps around to look at me.

"Selene?" She rushes over and grabs my hand. "Thank God you're all right."

"Sorry I haven't checked in; it's been a crazy couple of weeks."

"It's okay. Aniyah filled me in." Colleen smiles as her eyes roam over my face.

"She's been here?" Hope soars in my chest.

"A few days ago, we celebrated the demise of the guys who were taking the girls." She leans in. "But now we have another problem."

"I saw." I nod. "And you haven't heard from Aniyah?"

"No." Worry clouds her eyes. "I'm afraid she's been caught up in something. She was trying to become a caregiver to the girls on the streets, teaching them how to spot trouble. And now I'm afraid she might've found some."

"Tell me everything you know."

"She told me what you are." Her eyes widen when she leans in. "I'm so glad you're back."

"Not for long, though." I grin when she pours me a whiskey. "I live in New York."

"She said that, too. She looked a little sad about it."

"She had her chance." I shrug. "Now, tell me what the rumblings on the streets are."

"The girl found dead was a veteran on the streets. She knew the ins and outs, and this was screaming more than just a random kill. Her body was found mutilated, riddled with stab wounds."

"Sounds more like a passion killing," I muse.

"Yes. Almost like a scorned woman." She nods.

"Who could've possibly caught her husband straying?" I tap my chin. "What else?"

"Aniyah found out who her last few clients were, and I'm worried she's gotten herself in trouble."

"Who were the clients?" I lean forward.

"I don't know," she shakes her head, clearly frustrated with herself, "but I know she found out from a few girls who work the corner." She lists off the street names, and I quickly down my drink, then get up out of my seat.

"Wait, you're going now?"

"The longer I wait, the worse it could be. I'll try to come see you again, Colleen, but with so much going on, I can't promise it. I will send you word that I'm okay, though." I reach over the bar and hug my friend, committing her scent to memory. I will miss the fuck out of her.

"Be careful," she says, and I give her a salute as I head out the door.

He's following me, those familiar tingles on the back of my neck alerting me to the fact, and I can't believe I never figured out it was him the whole time. I grin, knowing he has my back as I walk down the darkened streets, whistling another nursery rhyme.

"Slow, slow, slow will be your death. I can't wait to hear your screams. Merrily, merrily, merrily, merrily, your blood will make me cream." *Fuck, I really did miss my calling.*

A group of girls are huddled together at the next intersection, and I hurry over to them, not liking the fear I'm sensing. They hear my heels as I approach and slowly break apart, looking at me suspiciously.

"What's happening?" I ask as I come up next to them.

"Who are you?" one asks, and I grin at her, happy she has some sense.

"My name is Selene, and I'm a hunter. I like the flesh of men who hurt working girls." I give them a wink. "I'm here to help."

I give them a few moments to absorb my words, and finally one of them says, "We were just approached by a man. He asked us to come back to his hotel room. He said he and his *wife* were looking for a bit of fun."

"What happened?"

"We declined. None of us are interested in playing with a married couple. We know the risks of what could go down if the wife becomes jealous." Another girl pipes in, "He became angry and called us filthy whores."

"Did he say which hotel?" I can feel the excitement creeping up on me. They nod and tell me the name, pointing just further up the street. "Do you three know a woman by the name of Aniyah?"

"She was just here!" The last girl says, "She's headed toward the hotel." She points ahead again, and I sigh with relief.

"Thank you." I give them a nod. "From now on, arm yourselves. Pepper spray, a switchblade. Fuck, get a Pitbull out here, but don't continue on these streets unarmed."

Once they all give me a nod, I rush by them and run up the street, hoping to run into Aniyah. I reach the hotel without sight of her and rush inside. There are two women at the desk, and both give me startled looks as I quickly approach.

"Did a woman come in here just now? Purple curly hair and hot as sin?"

"Yes," the first answers. "She just got on the elevator. She's headed to the tenth floor, room ten-fourteen."

"Thank you!" I call out as I run for the elevators. I am going to kill her when I find her. This shit is dangerous, and Aniyah is not trained to take out anyone.

Finally, the elevator door opens with a ding, and I scramble inside, slamming my finger to the number ten over and over until the door closes.

"Come on." I begin to pace as the fucking thing crawls up the floors, and then I curse when it stops not once, but fucking twice, before getting to the tenth floor. I squeeze my body out as the doors slowly open and run down the first corridor, hooking a right to another one that brings me to room ten-fourteen.

I stand there, listening for ten seconds, and when I hear nothing, I knock on the door. No footsteps, no noise, nothing. I knock again, a little louder, and my heart rushes up to my throat. "Fuck."

"No room service," a small voice calls out, and I grit my teeth at its familiar tone.

"Aniyah, you Purple-Headed People Eater," I snarl. "Open this fucking door."

"Selene?" I hear her gasp, and the door opens. She rushes me in a mass of purple curls, and I hold her tight, so fucking glad she's all right.

"What the fuck are you doing here?"

"I could ask you the same thing!" she says excitedly. "I couldn't stay at the MC's compound; I knew I needed to be here and help the girls." She leads me back into the room. "Luckily, I returned when I did. These two," she points to two passed-out people on the bed, "are hunting women and killing them."

It's indeed a woman and a man, and both are snoring loudly. "What's wrong with them?"

"I drugged their drinks." She shrugs. "I found out they were the ones who killed that poor young girl. Stabbed her over a hundred times, all because the husband wanted to fuck other girls, and the wife liked to kill them after." Her eyes tear up. "They're not from around here. They could have hundreds of victims, and no one would care about murdered prostitutes."

"Tell me," I cross my arm over my chest as I look at the passed-out couple, "what were you going to do next?"

"Stuff pillows over their faces." She nods.

Not bad.

"But now you're here," she claps.

"Indeed." I grin.

# Blaze

It's been ten minutes since Selene ran into this fucking hotel, and she has yet to contact me or come out. So, it looks like I need to get my ass in there and look for her. I'm going to redden *her* ass later for causing me worry.

I stride inside and see two girls standing at the desk. They each give me frightened looks, unabashedly staring at my scar.

"Blonde chick, just came in ten minutes ago." I tap the counter's surface. "Where did she go?"

"Room ten-fourteen," one of them blurts.

"Thanks." I nod and bypass the elevators. This place is old as shit. Those elevators are probably like molasses on a winter day.

I take the stairs—three at a time—and reach the tenth floor, barely winded. Luckily, where the stairwell is, room ten-fourteen is right across the hallway. I stride across and lift my leg, kicking in the door with one blow. One female screams, and I know it's not mine. I round the corner and find Selene standing beside the purple-haired hooker. Selene is looking at me with a grin as the other one is wrapped around her, clearly terrified.

"I was wondering how long it would take you." Selene grins at me. "You remember Aniyah?"

"Yeah," I decide to let it all out. "She sucked my dick once while I was here watching you. I was pissed you were with these guys, and she was offering."

Aniyah backs away from Selene, clearly scared for her life, and I wait for the shit storm to begin.

"I figured something happened." Selene waves me off. "You're both lucky I love you or else you'd be bleeding out. Let's not do it again, yeah?"

"Not a chance in Hell," I agree.

"I didn't know he knew you … he was a random…"

"Aniyah," Selene huffs. "I know. It's all good. Anyway, we got it from here." Selene points at the people lying on the bed, drugged out obviously. "You need to go see Colleen and tell her you're all right. She's worried."

"Okay," she nods and walks by us, giving me a wide berth. "Am I going to see you before you go?"

"We'll swing back by the bar." Selene smiles at her, and then the hooker disappears. "I can't believe you stuck my daddy dick down my friend's throat." She shakes her head. "I should cut it off."

"I was missing you," I shrug, "and you were out humping everything."

"I know." She walks up the side of the bed, grabbing the woman's bright orange hair in her fist. "This is the one who killed the girl. Stabbed her over a hundred times."

I whistle and look at the guy. "What about him?"

"He's fucking them and letting his wife take out her anger on them after," she snarls, dropping the frizzy head back to the pillow.

"How do you want to do this?"

"How can we wake them up from such a deep slumber?" She gives me a mischievous look. "I kinda want them awake when I begin the torture."

"I'll grab some ice." I head back out through the door that's hanging off its hinges and find the ice machine on this floor. I fill up a bucket and head back to the room.

I find Selene slapping the guy's face, and his groans sounding as he slowly starts to wake up.

"The bitch isn't responding," she growls, "but this one is."

I head into the bathroom and fill the bucket of ice up with some cold water, making sure it's filled. Then I head back out to the bed and carefully tip it over the woman's face, holding it in place. Finally, she stirs, and then she begins to sputter around the ice and water.

Selene's face becomes radiant with excitement, and my cock hardens, pushing painfully against its confines. I want this done quickly, and then I want to fuck the shit out of her. I lift the bucket off the frizzy orange head just as the guy opens his eyes, and they widen as he looks between Selene and me.

"What's going on?" he asks groggily.

"I'm the girl you ordered to diddle your little dick while your wife watches, remember?" Selene coos. "Let's see what we have here." She begins to undo his pants while the guy struggles to fully wake up.

"You don't look like a prostitute." The wife tries to sit up and fails. "Why am I being drowned?"

I snort at their stupidity. "You passed out on us before the fun began."

Finally, her eyes connect with mine and her mouth drops. "We only deal with women."

"Shame," I begin to undo my pants, "your husband promised me a turn inside your ass."

"What?" The husband begins to understand what's happening, but Selene's fist to his jaw shuts him up.

I pull out my hard cock, giving it a few long, leisurely strokes. Her face pales, and I chuckle as her mouth falls open. "Her husband must be small."

"Let's find out," Selene says excitedly as she yanks his pants open, reaching down inside. He's too afraid to do a single thing, still unsure of what's going on. "Found it!" Selene begins to pull him out and laughs. "He's like a hairless mole rat!"

A strangled laugh leaves my throat as she points down at the man's hard dick, definitely looking like a hairless mole rat.

"Your wife should be the one getting the dick while you watch," Selene tsks. "That's shameful. Now, let's watch her ass get laid with that pipe."

"No," the wife furiously shakes her head, her eyes never leaving my cock.

"Oh, come on!" Selene begs. "If I can take it, you can, too. It only feels like a burrowing beaver, digging his way to your bowels, for ten minutes, tops!"

I can't help it; I bellow out a laugh as the woman continues to beg me to not touch her.

"Well, you're no fun." Selene pouts, then pulls her fancy new knife out of her belt. "I guess I'll have to make my own fun."

She grabs the guy by his hair as I tuck myself back into my pants, and the woman's gaze finally leaves my crotch. He's struggling to get out of Selene's grip, but he's still sluggish from the drug. Selene looks up at his wife and tosses her a wink, "I heard you like to get stabby, well, so do I."

Then she quickly begins to stab the guy repeatedly in the neck and throat, the blood spraying all over his wife. She begins to scream when his head starts to come away from the body, and I wrap my hand around her mouth, forcing her to watch as Selene fully decapitates him. *Savage.* If I hadn't decided to keep her yet, I would've done it right at this moment.

"I love you." It flies out of my mouth before I can stop it, and Selene looks up at me with shock, still holding the guy's severed head.

"Really?" She stares at me, her eyes wide.

"Fucking completely. You own me."

She tosses the guy's head into his wife's lap as the wife's muffled screams sound against my palm. "I love you, too, Daddy." Her eyes fill up with tears. "So much."

I pull my hunting knife out of the holster around my waist and slice into the wife's throat, her blood spraying out in a beautiful arc across the bed. I drop her gargling body as Selene crawls up onto the mattress and slowly comes toward me on all fours. "Take that pipe back out. I want the beaver burrowing deep."

"Fuck," I groan at her words, my cock once again solid.

She begins to take me out, then slurps me down her throat, her hands full of blood, and her outfit completely saturated. "Let's make sure he's nice and wet."

She spits down my length, thoroughly soaking my cock, and then she flips around, pulling her skirt up over her ass. "Love me, Daddy."

I stare down at her asshole, pink and tight, and I spit down onto it, sticking one, then two fingers deep inside. Her moans are loud, and I'm about to combust just listening to her. I press the head of my cock to her hole, and begin to push in slowly, not wanting to hurt her—this time. But she has other ideas.

"Ram me," she pushes back. "I want to feel it for days."

*Fuck.*

I pick up the pace, but I'm not fucking ramming her. I love her. I want her holes intact for future pipe laying. Once I bottom out, her pants are loud, and she grabs the dead woman's frizzy, orange hair. "See bitch? That's how it's done."

I plow into her ass, knowing I won't last long. "Baby, play with your clit."

"Okay, Daddy," she coos, and I have to stop or else I will fill her ass with cum right now.

She furiously rubs her clit, her hips moving against my cock. Then she surprises me again when she grabs up the husband's bloody head, placing it in front of her on the bed. "Take notes into Hell with you. I expect a show when I arrive," she tells him, and I come so hard into her ass, with her following not too far behind me. I pull out, watching as my cum pools out of her hole and slips down to her pussy. "You're welcome," she tells the head, and seals it with a kiss to its mouth.

Yeah, I found my perfect match.

## Santos

I'm a ball of emotions, more than usual, and I know Darius is worried about how I'll react by the way he's glancing at me in the rear-view mirror. Going from no blood family to finding my father and brother really started pushing me over the edge, but now we were off to save a sister, too? I really need a fucking drink.

I sit in the back with Pepe, thinking it will give me some time to brood on everything, but Pepe seems adamant to pull me out of my own head for some reason after being on the road for a while. I guess my pet likes me after all. He doesn't really know what's going on with my family, but he must sense my inner turmoil.

"I'll pray for her," he says firmly, closing his eyes and whispering words under his breath in the quiet car, asking Jesus to look out for my sister and bring her home to me. I want to tease him for it, because I'm not a believer in prayers being answered, but the fact that he wants to makes me feel warm and fuzzy.

"Thanks," I mumble, surprising Darius with my grown-up approach. He's expecting me to make jokes.

Pepe finishes his prayer and looks over at me with a smile. "It's obvious you care about her."

"I don't even fucking know her," I grunt, but he shrugs casually.

"So? She's still your family. I think it's good you're going to help her. Will you bring her back with you and get to know her?" Good fucking question.

I have no idea what to do when I find her, but a part of me wants to have her in my life. Papi is one thing, but Loqi and Cara are another. They didn't know I existed, so I can't exactly hold a grudge against them. Doesn't mean I'm ready to face the reality that I have a family yet.

"She might hate me. Or run home to Papi Loco. I can't be around him right now. I just can't," I admit, chewing on my bottom lip in thought.

If she's a nice girl with a different upbringing, she might be terrified of the man I've become. If it were anyone else, I wouldn't give a shit about their thoughts about me, but the thought of my own sister despising me? It's starting to eat away at me like a flesh-eating poison.

"C'mon, who wouldn't like you and your murderous antics and scary bomb skills?" he laughs dryly, making me snort.

"Normal people?"

"I have a feeling if she shares the same blood as you, she will be anything but normal. Try not to think about it until we get there. Let's play I Spy," he suggests, making Zander scoff from the front passenger seat. His eyes are closed as he tries to nap, but he never misses anything.

"It's dark out."

"So? I spy with my little eye, something beginning with A," Pepe continues, not giving a shit when Zander growls about us being children. I grin, loving the idea of playing some games to pass the time, especially if it annoys Zander.

"A? All right, let me see," I hum, peering out the window into the darkness around us. I can't see shit, so I turn my attention back to the inside of the car, thinking hard. "Air Conditioner?"

"Nope!" he grins.

"Radio?"

Darius chuckles, not taking his eyes off the road. "That doesn't start with an A, San."

"Who gives a fuck? It has an A in it!" I throw back, making Pepe laugh.

"Keep guessing!"

I frown, deep in thought, trying to think of anything else in the car that starts with A. I like the challenge, and the way Pepe is practically bouncing in his seat tells me it's probably funny.

"You want a clue?" he finally asks, grinning when I nod. "It's grumpy."

"Zander? That doesn't start with A!" I exclaim, but he cracks up laughing, slapping his knee in his excitement.

"No, but asshole does!" he wheezes, and I can't stop the cackle that leaves me. Darius is sniggering, but Zander glares over his shoulder at us.

"Watch it, or our threat to help you meet Jesus early will be added to the calendar."

Pepe's in hysterics, feeding my amusement and causing us both to laugh until our stomachs hurt. The little weirdo has a sense of humor, good to know.

"My turn! I spy with my little eye, something beginning with W!" I grin.

"Window."

"God-fucking-dammit!" I snap. "How did you guess that so fast? You cheated!"

"How do you cheat at I Spy?" Zander groans, but Darius snorts.

"He can't cheat, babe. Do another one."

I give Pepe the evil-eye, trying to think of something harder. "Fine. Something beginning with C."

"Car?"

"No."

"Chassis?"

"You can't see that from inside the car!" I growl. "C is for *cheater.* Because you cheated!"

Darius and Pepe burst out laughing, and Zander jumps, glaring at us again. "Can you play the fucking silent game or something? I need some sleep, or I won't be held accountable for my actions when I lose my shit."

"What's the silent game?" I frown, his voice lowering with annoyance.

"It's when you all shut the fuck up and see who can go the longest without making a sound. It's my favorite fucking game in existence."

"That sounds boring. How will I irritate you if I'm quiet?" I question, making him growl and turn around to face the front, shuffling down in his seat to try and block us out.

"Hey! I have something fun to do!" Darius announces, drawing my attention. "Let's do car karaoke!"

Zander lets out a loud groan, cursing out Darius and his first-born child, but I sit up straight with glee. "Yes! Put on Zander's favorite song and we can sing along. What Does the Fox Say by Ylvis!"

"I fucking hate that song!" he barks, but Darius ignores him and finds the song, putting it up nice and loud.

"Sorry, can't hear you!" he says, giving me a wink in the mirror.

Despite the murderous glare from Zander, I think I sing it perfectly well. Pepe seems impressed, anyway.

# Darius

We pull into a hotel for a night and finally let Zander sleep, knowing he needs to rest. I felt like an ass for torturing him with terrible songs and games most of the trip, so he deserved his nap. Pepe had fallen asleep too, leaving Santos to stare at him as if trying to figure him out.

But today is a new day, and Zander is driving while Pepe and Santos watch YouTube videos on Santos' phone. I barely slept last night, worrying about Santos and how he'll react when he meets yet another one of his siblings.

I must've passed out because I'm awakened by Zander giving me a shake, "you've been out for twelve hours. Think you're good to drive?"

I sit up and quickly look into the backseat. Empty fast-food bags are scattered, and Pepe is sleeping, Santos though is not. He's looking out his window with a forlorn expression on his face.

"We have about ten more hours of driving," Zander says, "I just need a few hours and then I can take over for the last bit."

"No problem." I nod.

"We got you some food," he points to the bag at my feet, "it's probably cold, but we didn't want to wake you."

"Thanks," I give him a smile.

We switch seats, and I pull back out onto the road, snorting when Zander falls into a deep sleep almost at once. Santos falls asleep next, and I let out a breath of relief. He needs to rest.

Eight hours later, and both Zander and Pepe are still out, but Santos stirs awake.

"You good?" I ask, feeling grateful to Pepe for cheering him up so much. The last thing we need is Santos having an emotional melt down inside the small car space.

He glances up at me in the rear-view mirror, a frown on his face. "I don't know."

"You want to talk about it?"

"I don't know how I'm supposed to feel," he admits quietly.

"There's no wrong way to handle it. You're confused, which is okay. Are you prepared to see Papi and Loqi again? Loqi seems nice," I state, remembering the similarities between them.

"I don't like dealing with Loqi because of Papi. I'm not mad at Loqi, just confused by it all. I want to get to know him and my sister, I think. What if they hate me?"

His voice is tight, telling me he's starting to freak out a little. I sigh, reaching back to rub my hand on his leg. "They won't hate you. Loqi and you are similar. He's crazy, loves the chase as much as you do, and he's been blindsided like you about all of this. If you can get to know him without Papi Loco around, I think you two would hit it off."

"I always wanted a brother," he murmurs. "I know I have you guys, but as a kid, all I wanted was someone to play with. And my sister? What if she's nothing like us? What if..."

"Relax. For all you know, Cara is as crazy as you two. If you want to stick around and get to know them, I'll stay with you. If you need more time, we can come back another day," I promise, his eyes filling with defeat.

"Yeah?"

"Yeah, San. I've got you. Pepe seems fun," I smile, changing the subject. Santos' face lights up and he grins.

"I like him. He's funny."

I chuckle. "Yeah, he's all right. Selene and Blaze will scare him to death if he sticks around."

He gives me a horrified look. "What do you mean *if he sticks around*? I'm not letting him go anywhere." Didn't think he would.

"You know what I mean. I'm glad you've made a new friend."

"He's my best friend," he declares, scowling as if I'm insulting him.

"What about me?" I fake pout. "I thought I was your best friend?"

"You don't count. You got promoted to boyfriend. Best friends don't usually enjoy each other's dicks in their asses," he grins. "And I *really* like yours."

"I love hearing that." I smile, making him laugh.

"What? That I love your dick in my ass?"

"That too, but I like being called your boyfriend," I shrug, starting to feel like a little bitch. If Santos grins any wider, his face will crack.

"I like hearing it, too. Never thought I'd have a girlfriend or a boyfriend, let alone both. I can't wait to cut you both again. I want a big S on your chest like mine." He's such a romantic sometimes.

"You want some good news?" I ask lightly as I pull over. "We're here."

His eyes widen as he glances outside into the dark, the sun starting to rise in the distance. "Our girl's here?"

"Yep. I think…" I don't get to finish my sentence before he places his hands on the window and smacks his head against the glass in his excitement, trying to catch a glimpse of our blood queen. I chuckle, leaning over to shake Zander awake. "Brother, we're here."

"You drove the whole way?" he mumbles, half asleep, sitting up properly to glance around. "You were supposed to let me drive halfway."

"Yeah, but you needed the sleep. We kept you awake half the drive, so it was only fair," I reply, and he doesn't disagree with me.

We climb from the car and head toward the apartment, and the moment the door swings open, Santos barrels past Blaze and almost knocks Selene over with a hug. Pepe hangs back, unsure of our crazy girl and the big brute blocking the doorway.

"What's Bible boy doing here?" Blaze grunts, looking the man up and down with a frown. I go to speak, but Santos darts over and drops his arm around Pepe's shoulders.

"Leave my bestie alone! Pipi is staying with us!"

"It's Pepe," Pepe says dryly, making Santos grin.

"Yeah, I know."

Zander's hugging Selene tight, kissing the top of her head and whispering something dirty in her ear, no doubt. The nap must have done him some good.

"What do you mean, he's staying?" Blaze growls, not impressed by the decision.

Santos huffs, hating to explain himself. "He's staying with us permanently. He's my best friend and I don't care what you say. My pet stays with me."

"You banging him too?"

"Bite your tongue," I scowl, glaring at Pepe as if it were his fault. "Santos is mine."

"Ours," Selene teases, coming over to stand in front of me, wrapping her arms around my middle. "Missed you guys."

"Missed you, too. Pepe played games with Santos the entire drive," I smile, knowing Selene will soften at knowing he cares for Santos. She smiles brightly, bouncing on the balls of her feet.

"What games did you play?"

Zander snorts, firing off everything that's happened since we left the house. When he gets to the car karaoke, she squeals loudly. "Oh, my god! You played that without me?!"

"Sweetheart, no offense, but your voice is too much for that small car," Zander cringes, and she blows him a kiss.

"I guess you're right. It's too good for a car ride. Maybe I should see if a record label wants me?"

The look of horror on Blaze and Zander's faces is hysterical, and I can't help but laugh. "Yeah, babe. I have a feeling you'd be too big of a star for them, too. I think you should stick to murder and bouncing on our dicks with that tight pussy of yours."

"You're right. It would be hard to calendar all that in while on tour. I guess we'll never know if it was meant to be," she sighs, turning to Pepe and crossing her arms. "So, what are your intentions with my man?"

I think we're in for a long fucking day.

# Chapter Eight

## Zander

I can feel the tension wafting off Santos as he paces the small apartment. We have the phone on the table in front of us, and Papi Loco is telling us what they've found out about Cara. "She's being held in a small police station because she's only nineteen. They don't have enough evidence to convict her, but she also refuses to tell them who her family is. Our guy who works there can't be sure if she's *our* Cara, and I can't see why she wouldn't say who her family was if it even is her."

"Maybe she's forgotten?" Blaze asks as he leans forward.

"She was taken when she was twelve. It's only been seven years," Loqi pipes up. "She would remember us."

Selene tosses me a look from across the table and I can read it loud and clear. Maybe she doesn't want to remember.

"We're gunning down the place tomorrow night. We're thinking around two in the morning. They have a guard shift change at one and then there's only two cops in the building until six." Papi continues, "gives us enough time to pump the place full of bullets and get her out."

"Yeah, sounds good," Blaze cuts in. "We'll meet you there." Then he abruptly ends the call and looks at all of us. "There's no need to pump the place full of bullets, two cops?" he scoffs as he leans back.

"I think we need to get to her before they do," Selene chimes in. "She'll recognize me and if she's Santos' sister, there may be a reason she's not giving them Papi's information."

"Do you think my father hurt her?" Santos' voice is deadly calm, and I can see the vein in his neck pulsing.

"I'm not sure, but there has to be a reason she doesn't want them to know where or who she is." Selene stands and walks over to Santos. "We'll get to her first. Let's make our own plans and then we'll go from there."

Santos drags her in for a hug, but I can see the stiff tension all over his body. He's still struggling with accepting his blood family. Even so, I know he would never want to put his little sister back in harm's way.

"Is this really a good idea?" I'm whining like a bitch because I left the planning up to the others and I'm questioning every bit of it.

"I'm a hooker, Zan!" Selene exclaims. "It's going to work perfectly."

We're sitting outside of the small police station, waiting to see if the shift change will happen as Papi said, and then we're heading in there ourselves, an hour before the Dientes arrive. I'm not feeling comfortable going against the MC. They could take us out in one fell swoop, regardless of Santos' blood relation. It's not like Papi actually cares about him.

"You're worried about retaliation," Blaze states.

"Obviously!" I throw my hands up. "They have their way of dealing with shit! Why are we getting in their way? We're just asking to have ourselves executed in the fucking desert at this point."

"If she's my little sister," Santos finally pipes up. "I will go in and get her myself. Maybe she'll hate me for it, but I think Selene is right. She's holding back information for a reason."

It's the most sensible I've heard him in a while, and I turn my head to look at him in the backseat. He's been quiet and inside his head, so unlike the man I'm used to. Usually, he acts out in violent outbursts when his emotions overflow.

"I think you should be the first one she sees," Selene agrees.

"I'll come with you," Blaze adds, and we all look at him with a bit of shock.

Santos nods and I look to see Darius' reaction. He looks a bit relieved. "You and I will cover the front, with our new friend Pepe watching the car." I nod at Darius.

About ten minutes later, two new cops pull up and head inside, just like Papi said. Then in the next five minutes, three cops leave to go home. Looks like the shift change is complete.

"And the new cops were men!" Selene squeals. "It's like it was meant to be."

"What if they're gay?" Blaze asks her, his mouth tipping up into a grin.

"Then you would have to take one for the team," Selene fires back.

"The fuck I would," he growls as he gets out of the car.

"Santos," Pepe says. "I will pray for you and the safe retrieval of your sister. God will be watching you tonight."

"Hopefully, not all night," Selene cackles, and I can't stop the grin on my mouth.

"Thank you, Pepe," Santos says as he gets out of the car next.

"Is he okay?" I ask Darius. "I'm waiting for the explosion."

"I think he's nervous," Darius mutters and gets out of the car.

"Pepe, as soon as you see us coming for the car, you start it up and move to the backseat, got it?" Pepe nods, his eyes wide. "If you see any other cop cars coming up the street, you text me or Darius."

He nods again, and I get out of the car, following Darius to the front of the station where Santos and Blaze are leaning against the wall, their heads pulled together in quiet conversation. I watch as Selene fluffs her long, blonde hair, the ends touching just above her ass, and she yanks down on the leather mini she's wearing. Her legs go on for fucking days, and her strappy heeled shoes are hot. I'm going to ask her to leave those on later.

"Let's go give these cops a good time." Selene claps her hands.

"If you even think of opening your fucking legs to them, there will be mayhem, Reaper," Blaze growls, and Selene tips her head back and laughs. Not at all affected by him.

"He's saying that because he loves me," she coos and blows him a kiss.

I look at my boy with shock. "Did you tell her?"

"She decapitated this dude, and she was covered in blood. You'd have said it too." He crosses his arms over his chest.

Fucking right, I would.

# Selene

I haul open the doors of the station and saunter inside. Two cops sit with coffee cups and a box of pastries, both looking at me suspiciously. I look every bit the hooker tonight, and I am fucking hot. I stride up to the desk they're sitting at and hold out my wrists.

"I've been a naughty girl, y'all need to cuff me."

"Pardon?" His name tag says *Duey*.

"Yes, Deputy Duey. I have been sucking and fucking cocks all night, and I can't take another moment of it. I'm tired and I need a bed. This was the first place I thought of."

"Are you turning yourself in for prostitution?" the second one asks; his name is Darryl.

"Yes, Darryl. I need you two to lock me up because if I go anywhere else, cocks will sniff me out like bloodhounds."

They both give me a slow perusal and then look at each other.

"Don't even think about cavity searching me, my pussy allure will have you both chewing at the bit, and like I said, I'm too tired. Double penetration just cannot not happen tonight, D-Squared."

Deputy Duey stands abruptly from his seat, grabbing the cuffs from his belt, and opening them. His face is one of incredulity and he gives a startled look to his partner.

"Darryl, is this not the oddest shit to happen here?"

"Indeed." But Darryl isn't looking at his partner. No, his eyes are still all over my body. I can work with that.

"Darryl, is it?" I shimmy my ass onto his desk, scattering papers to the floor. "I think you're cute. Want to share a cell? I don't think Deputy Duey would mind."

"Are you soliciting an officer for sex?" Duey astonishes from behind me.

I look at him over my shoulder. "why? Would that get me into more trouble?"

"You're darn right it would!" Duey sputters, red-faced, and shocked.

"Well then, yes." I turn back to Darryl with a wink. "I think I am."

"That'll get you processed and in the cell for at least a night," Darryl winks right back.

"Processed?" My mouth curls up farther. "Are you teasing me with a good time?" Duey slaps a cuff to my right wrist, and I squeal, "I love a good pair of shackles. I have a set at home."

"I don't think she needs to be cuffed," Darryl snickers. "She brought herself here, after all. We do need to bring you to the processing room, though."

Darryl stands and motions for me to follow him as Duey removes the cuff. I walk behind Darryl, and Duey takes up my rear as they lead me into a back corridor and then into a room with a single table.

"Take a seat," Darryl says. "We're going to need to ask you a few questions."

I sit down, Darryl sits across from me and Duey to my right, this couldn't have worked out any more perfectly. Duey still has the fucking cuffs in his hands, so fucking eager to see me shackled, I get it, it's hot.

Just as he sits his ass on the chair, I reach over the table and slam his face down into the hard metal surface. I hear a crunch, and before Darryl can react, my knife is out of my belt and pressed to his throat.

"Silly pigs," I snicker. "Did you think you were safe against a little girl?"

The cuffs are laying on the table, abandoned by Duey as he moans over his broken nose. I grab them with my free hand and secure it around Darryl's wrist, looping it underneath the large metal pole down the center of the table.

"Give me your gun," I hold out my hand. When he doesn't move, I press the tip of my blade into his throat and watch as a bead of blood pools out. "The gun."

This time he does as he's told, and I take it from his outstretched arm, tucking it into my belt. "Good boy. Look, I'm not here to kill you. We're just springing someone free." I give him a saccharine smile. "Cooperate, and you'll be just fine."

He settles into his seat with a shrug, and I grab the other side of the cuffs, hauling him into the table. I grab one of Duey's wrists and secure them together. Now they're trapped at the table underneath the pole. They can move from side to side, but they can't get up at all.

"There we go." I fire off a text to Blaze. "Now, what do y'all wanna do for the next ten minutes? I know a few good nursery rhymes."

# Blaze

"She's got them occupied," I say to the others as I open the front door. "She says the keys for the cells are hung on a corkboard."

Santos is following quietly behind me, his nervous energy clogging the air around us. I'm not going to bug him about it or question him. This can't be easy. Besides, we need to be in and out before other cops or the MC show up.

I find the keys easily enough and I head down a corridor that I hope leads to the cells.

"Do you hear that?" I stop at the sound of screeching.

"That's our angel," Santos chirps in. "She's singing somewhere in here."

"Jesus," I mutter and keep going down the hall. "She'll kill those cops, make them deaf at the very least."

Santos hums along to whatever it is she's singing. I don't know how he can even decipher it, and we turn into a large space occupied with three different cells. Two appear empty while one has a small form curled up on the thin, narrow bed.

"Cara?" I call out, and a dark head pops up from the pillow. "Is your name Cara?"

She turns on the bed and sits up; her face obscured by her messy, matted hair. But even from here, I can see the resemblance in her face to Santos, and there's no doubt in my mind she's his sister.

"Who are you?" She calls out.

"My name is Blaze—"

"I'm your brother." Santos steps forward, quickly coming out of his stupor when he sees her. "My name is Santos."

"I don't have a brother named Santos," she shakes her head,

confusion heavy in her deep brown eyes. Eyes so similar to her brother's standing next to me.

"That's because our dick-of-a father left me and my mom when I was young."

Her eyes narrow as she looks him over closely, standing from the bed and coming closer to the bars. "You have Papi's eyes," she says quietly.

"So do you." Santos nods. "And Loqi, too."

"I don't want to go back with Papi and Loqi," she whispers, and I come up closer to her.

"Why not?"

"They sold me." Her mouth begins to tremble. "The man they sold me to, told me. I was sold because Papi never wanted a little girl."

"If that were true," I say softly. "They wouldn't have been trying so hard to find you."

"Regardless," Santos growls. "They failed to take care of her."

"You're really my brother?" Her hand wraps around a bar.

Santos wraps his hand around hers and swallows. "Yeah, let's get you out of here, and if you don't want to go back with those assholes, you can come with me."

"Really?" Her eyes brighten, and I swallow my groan. Another one in the fucking house. My home is turning into a zoo of strays.

I unlock the door and open it; the young girl flies out and into Santos' arms. Too trusting, that's what probably got her into this mess to begin with.

"Let's get out of here," I tell them and lead them out the way we came in.

Selene meets us in the hallway, and when Cara lays eyes on her, she gasps, "You're the prostitute who killed Eugene!"

"Sorry you got in shit for that," Selene grimaces. "I did tell you to run."

"I know," Cara huffs, "but I was looking for more money. I knew that hairy dog had more stashed around the place!"

"I wish I knew who you were then," Selene shrugs. "I could've helped more."

"It's okay," Cara waves her off and slips under her brother's arm,

"I am starving, and I need a shower. How did you guys get me out?"

"Sounded like our girl here sang the guards into a deep sleep with her lullabies," Santos says.

"You heard me?" Selene's eyes brighten, and I grumble as I brush by them. I don't want to be here in case she starts off again.

"You sounded like an angel," Santos tells her.

"Is this your wife?" I hear Cara ask, but they're silenced when we all hear the sound of rumbling bikes.

"Fuck," I growl, and head out the door.

I see about four bikes pull up and Papi is at the head, Loqi to his right. They kick down their stands and take off their helmets.

"Why are you coming out of the fucking station?" Papi bellows.

"Watch your fucking mouth, old man, before I fill it with my fucking knife." I stride forward. Guns are cocked and aimed at me, but I don't give a fuck. I know how this cunt treats his oldest son, and I won't hesitate to take him out, even if I go down in the process.

Loqi holds up his hand. "Stop. What happened? Did you guys get Cara?"

"Yeah, she's inside with her *brother*. She has quite the story about her father and brother *selling* her."

"What?!" Papi jumps off his bike and rushes me until we are standing toe to toe and nose to nose. "Move aside, asshole. I want my daughter."

My hand itches to grab my knife and stab it through his eye, but I stay still, letting his hot breath hit my mouth. I don't move my eyes from his, I don't back down.

"Aw, look Cara, big, bad boys are out here fighting." Selene's voice hits my back. "All we need is a pool of mud and some popcorn."

Papi looks over my shoulder, and his body softens when he sees his daughter. "Cara." His voice cracks and I can hear the genuine emotion. Judging by his reaction alone, I don't think he sold his own daughter, but that'll be up to him to convince her.

"Cara!" Loqi jumps off his bike. "It's really you."

I step aside so Cara can have a clear view of her father. If she wants to go to him, who are we to stand in her way? Cara looks between the two of them, her brother and father, and when Loqi begins to get closer to her, she holds up her hand.

"No," she says firmly. "I don't want to go back with you guys."

"What?" Loqi lets out a strangled sound as Papi scoffs.

"You can't mean that."

"I do. You both sold me!" she screams as Santos' arms wrap around her.

"No, baby," Papi shakes his head, "we would never."

"How did it happen?" Cara cries out. "How did I end up here? And you're only here seven years later? SEVEN!"

"Come back to the compound where we can check you out." Papi's voice is pained.

"I'll only go if Santos goes." Her little body curls into Santos' side, and I watch as my brother glares down at his father.

"She needs medical attention," Papi says, trying to convince Santos. "I know I treated you terribly, and we have time to figure that out, but we have to do what's best for her."

"Just to get checked out, then we're leaving," Santos snarls.

"Cara," Loqi stands beside his father, "please rethink this. You should be home with your family."

"Santos is my family," she says and looks up at her brother. "Can I ride with you? I never want to be on a motorcycle again."

"Yeah," Santos says as he leads her to the car.

"We'll come to your fucking compound. Your fucking doctor can check her out, but when it's time for us to leave, you will let us," I grit out to both Papi and Loqi. "If either of you tries anything, I'll blow your shit to the fucking sky."

"Kaboom," Selene whispers, her hands spreading out over her head.

I watch as Zander, Selene, and Darius walk back to the car and I turn to look at the men next to me. "Don't start a war you can't win."

# Santos

I'm going to kill someone, many someones, if Cara's out of my sight much longer. She reluctantly let me go to get checked out, and the look of confusion and betrayal on her face is eating me alive. If Papi and Loqi had sold her like she claims, I'll kill them.

"Breathe," Darius murmurs beside me as I lean against the bar in the MC's compound, his fingers brushing my arm lightly to relax me. I meet his eyes and nod, but my jaw is so tight it's starting to hurt from clenching my teeth. I know I haven't known Cara for more than five-fucking-minutes, but the need to protect her is waging a war inside me, the confusion from earlier being completely taken over by pure rage.

"You look like you need a beer or six," Licker chuckles as he moves up to us on the other side of the bar, not waiting for a response before pushing two beers in our direction. Selene is talking to her sister, Zander and Blaze, standing close by in case she explodes. Selene isn't smiling, but she isn't stabbing her either, so that's good.

"Thanks, Licker. How have you been?" Darius asks lightly, not taking his eyes off me. Giving me alcohol while my emotions are so messy probably isn't the best idea. I don't need to get on the bar and reenact my pirate incident from the last time I lost the plot. I doubt we'll get out alive, but fucking hell, it's tempting.

Licker doesn't seem fazed by my grumpy attitude; he simply leans on the bar and grins at us. "I've been good. Maybe you should take your man into the bathroom and fuck that look right off his face. Man's going to chip a fucking tooth soon." He isn't wrong. My teeth are aching, but I grind down on them harder, giving him a dirty look.

"Mind your business."

"Oh, testy today, Santos? C'mon, I'm just playing with you. Drink your beer. Cara won't be long," he states with a softer smile. "She's stronger than she looks."

"Of course, she's fucking strong! Who wouldn't be after that piece of shit..." Darius slaps a hand over my mouth, his other hand resting on my waist, and giving it a firm squeeze.

"Let's go sit down, hmm? Thanks for the beer, Licker," he says before letting me go to grab our drinks, leading me toward a table in the back. I sit down heavily, glaring at him as he sits beside me.

"I want to kill him. He..."

"I know. If Papi did do it, I'm one-hundred percent starting a war by your side. We can't take on the entire MC without facts though, all right? I'm channeling my inner Zander right now. We need to do this with a clear head," he cuts in with a low voice, running his hand along my thigh and leaving it there. "I promise. Whoever hurt her will fucking pay."

That eases some of my anger, and by the time Zander and Blaze join us, I'm not so fucking murderous. Still a little stabby, but I'm less likely to go for a main artery.

"You two behaving?" Blaze grunts as he sits opposite me.

"Always," I snort. "Selene and Jan okay?"

Blaze glances at them as they chat away, now at the bar with drinks in their hands. Selene has the tiniest smile on her face, and it settles me to know she's starting to let her sister in. I'm jealous she can forgive her already, wondering if I could ever be the same way with Loqi. Especially because it isn't exactly his fault our father is a piece of shit.

"They're talking about knives, so she's in her element. Figured it was safe to give them some space," he shrugs. Zander looks at me seriously, concern swimming in his eyes.

"We're more worried about you. You look ready to gun the place down, and we can't afford…"

"I know, Zan. I'm cooling down, don't worry," I scowl, placing my hand on Darius' under the table, linking our fingers and giving it a gentle squeeze. I need his comfort and calming words, otherwise I'm likely to detonate and take everyone else with me.

He squeezes back, not giving a shit as he leans closer and presses a kiss on my shoulder. "Yeah. We were just talking about playing this smart."

"Well, fuck my ass and call me Susan. You two are learning," Zander deadpans. "It's about fucking time."

I'm way too tired and emotional for his teasing, so I keep my mouth shut and glare at him, ignoring his chuckle.

We sip our drinks silently for a while, but I bristle when Papi Loco joins us, his eyes firmly on me. "We need to talk, boy."

"You need to turn your ass around and leave me alone," I snap. "I have nothing to fucking say to you."

"Hear me out. I'm an asshole, I get it. We need to talk, and I'll drag you if I have to," he grunts, causing Darius to tense beside me.

"You can try, old man. I'll flatten you," I bite back, but I stand and shuffle past Darius, not wanting a brawl to break out. We're severely outnumbered in here. I'm not completely stupid.

He smirks, almost looking proud of my answer as he motions for me to follow him, and Darius grabs my hand, giving me an unsure look. "You want me to come, too?"

Papi Loco mutters something about us being pansies, but I give Darius a tight smile. "I'm good. This won't take long. Then we can grab Cara and get the fuck out of here."

I follow Papi into his office, not bothering to sit. I don't want him to think I'm going to sit around chatting for hours. He gives me a look, but he doesn't say anything as he sits behind his desk, eyeing me seriously.

"You're not taking Cara with you. She belongs here with her family."

I clench my jaw, glaring at him. "She doesn't want to be anywhere near you, asshole. Besides, I am her fucking family."

"She doesn't even know you."

"Who's fucking fault is that, *Papi*?" I snarl. "You running off and abandoning me was one thing, but not letting me know I had a brother or a sister? That's another. How does it feel to know two out of three of your kids hate you right now? I'm glad you left because you're the worst father anyone could ask for."

His palms slam down on the desk in front of him, his eyes blazing with anger. "Don't fucking speak to me like that!"

"Why not? You don't deserve my respect!" I shout. "You fucking abandoned me! You sold your own fucking daughter! You…"

"I didn't fucking sell her! I love that girl more than you could ever know!" he bellows, and he's lucky I don't stab his stupid fucking face.

"Of course, I don't know how you could love your own kid. You never loved me, so why would I know any different? If she says you sold her, then I believe her. It's about time someone stood by her side."

He glowers at me for a moment before calming himself, sudden sadness washing over him. "Cara was—still is—my baby girl. We have spent years looking for her. Whatever she's been told is a lie. We've spent our lives saving women from the clutches of that kind of evil, so why the *fuck* would I do it to my own daughter? My own flesh and blood?" he asks firmly, waiting for me to respond. He has a point, not that I admit it. They seem adamant to protect women from slavery and the sex trafficking ring, so it doesn't make sense to do it to his own kid.

If he did, I doubt Loqi was involved. I saw the relief on his face when we walked out of the station with Cara. No one can fake that kind of happiness. Well, maybe Papi could, but Loqi has been genuinely worried about her.

When I stay quiet, Papi stands, moving across the room to stand in front of me. "I know you won't believe a single thing that comes out of my mouth, but I'd never hurt Cara like that. I was devastated when she vanished. Loqi and I have been trying to find her from the moment it happened. You don't have to like me. Hell, I don't blame you if you don't, but I swear to you someone else took my baby girl and sold her."

"Until Cara says otherwise, I'm not changing my opinion on it. Right now, she's the only family I care about. The only blood family who exists to me. You'll be smart to drop it. Let me go to her before I lose my shit, and your men find you splattered from one wall to the other," I hiss in a low voice, his eyes narrowing.

"You're too much like your Papi, Santos."

"When you find him, tell him I said *hey*," I snark, turning on my heel and leaving the room, just as Cara walks out of one of the back rooms. She practically runs toward me, throwing her arms around me and clinging on as if I'm the only person alive who can keep her safe.

I hug her tight, keeping an arm around her as we walk toward where Darius and the others are all sitting, relief obvious on Darius' face to see me in one piece.

I sit down, putting Cara between Darius and me to keep her protected from both sides, and she gives me an appreciative smile. "So. You want to explain why I didn't know you existed? The resemblance between you and Loqi is kinda freaky."

"Like I said, Papi's a piece of shit and bailed on me and Ma when I was a kid. Didn't see him again until we got caught up in the sex trafficking shit."

Her eyes go wide in horror, and I rush to correct her thoughts. "Shit, not like that. Selene has been looking for her sister for years. She followed a trail out here, and when we got called out to join her, we found her sister."

"Where is she?" she asks softly, making me scowl. Selene, on the other hand, joins us with a teasing smile on her face, telling me she's about to be rude.

"Under Papi. Turns out, my sister likes old man dick." Jesus Christ.

"Where's Pepe?" My eyes widen as I fly to my feet.

Blaze rolls his eyes and motions toward the bar. "He's fine. He's been talking to Licker for the past ten minutes. He's been hiding in the car like a little bitch since we got here, though."

Cara's watching me with confusion, her brows pulling down. "Who's Pepe?"

"The guy who prayed for you all day and night, then again when we got you in the car," Zander snorts.

"The weird guy who kept mumbling under his breath the entire trip?"

"He's not weird!" I growl. "Leave my pet alone, Zan. I'll fight you."

"Shaking in my boots, brother," he chuckles. "I suppose the little Bible boy isn't that bad."

Darius grins, reaching over Cara to grab my hand and tug me back into the seat. "No one's going to hurt him, babe. You really need to work on your breathing exercises. It can't be healthy to be so high-strung all the time."

Cara's eyebrows almost fly off her face when I blow him a kiss. "Yes, baby cakes. You're right. Want to help me with that later? I find I focus a lot better when you're naked, though."

"Yeah, on this dick," he grins, sitting back in his seat, narrowing his eyes on Cara, who's appearing stunned. "What? You have a problem with queers like your Papi?"

"Wait, what? No! You two are together? Aren't you with the crazy blonde lady?" she sputters as she turns to me. I chuckle nervously, suddenly feeling terrified of her hating me.

"Uh, yeah. I'm with both of them, and all four of us are with Selene."

"That's so fucking cool!" she exclaims, jumping up and down in her seat, all anxiety seeping out of me as a smile hits my face.

"Yeah?"

"I would love to find someone after everything I've been through. I will say I was luckier than most. I wasn't a sex slave, and I've remained, you know," she leans in, "untouched, Mr. Haynes just liked to see me strip now and then, but the other girls," Her face grows sad, "they had to do things."

After knowing what she's been through, I don't want another man touching my sister. She will remain pure until the day she dies, and then we'll bury her with the nuns at the cathedral in New York.

As if sensing my thoughts, she groans. "Not you too! Papi and Loqi always said I couldn't have a boyfriend!"

"That's because men suck," I reply tightly, her eyes narrowing to slits and looking a hell of a lot like Papi.

"You're dating a man."

Darius chuckles, amusement filling his eyes. "Yeah, and trust me, I suck real good."

Everyone bursts out laughing, but Cara gives me a dirty look.

"You're lucky I like you already, or you'd get a fork to the eye, and I'd yank it right out of your socket to make you choke on it."

Well, what do you know? Turns out she is just like Loqi and me, after all. The rest of my panic melts away after that, knowing I have nothing to worry about.

## *Darius*

Watching Santos and Cara is awesome. They tease each other relentlessly, and by the time Pepe joins us—apparently deciding Licker is too scary to keep as company—Santos makes him sit down and tells him all about his cool sister. It's kind of cute if I'm being honest. He looks so fucking happy.

Pepe keeps glancing at Cara, not sure about her as she discusses how long they can torture a person before they die, and I have to bite back a grin. It's hilarious. Even Blaze seems to be amused by the whole thing.

Loqi wanders over, looking lost, his eyes on his sister. "Cara? Can…"

"No. Fuck off," she hisses. "I'm not talking to you. You and Papi sold me to those pieces of shit. They told me so. I hate you."

Pain fills his eyes as his shoulders droop, but surprise takes over his face when Santos points to the chair close by. "Don't stand around. Sit down or fuck off."

Cara looks ready to protest, but Santos drops a protective arm around her shoulders, his voice gentle. "Let him sit. I don't think he had anything to do with it. Papi can go fuck himself, though." That surprises the rest of us. Santos must have done some fucking deep soul searching to come to that conclusion and be okay with Loqi's presence.

Loqi grabs the chair and drags it closer, sitting without a word, not wanting to be sent away. Selene starts a conversation with him about the sex trafficking ring and how we're going to deal with it, and after a while the two of them are deep in discussion, easing the tension around the table. Zander gives me a *what the fuck* look, but I shrug. If Santos is giving Loqi an olive branch, I'll roll with it. It has to be better than the alternative of them killing each other.

After a while, we're all talking about it, and Cara is loudly voicing her opinion on the situation, causing both Loqi and Santos to fume at the thought of their sister going through anything like that. I keep my eye on Loqi, trying to catch even the smallest sign his love for her is full of shit, but I find nothing. He's pissed that she'd been taken, and we can all see what it means to him to have her back. Speaking of which.

"So, when do you guys want to head out?" I ask, and Loqi's eyes dart to mine.

"You're going to leave already?"

I shrug, but Selene sighs. "Yeah, we have shit to do. Besides, Santos doesn't need to be around Papi any longer than necessary. It's asking for trouble we don't need right now."

Loqi's eyes go to Cara next, pleading silently for her to stay, but she curls up against Santos and smiles sweetly at Selene. "I can't wait to see where you all live. Do you have a big house? Do you all share a bed? Oh, ew! Am I going to hear you fucking all the time? Please tell me I have my own room!"

Selene sniggers. "You'll probably see it if you aren't careful. We like to walk around naked, just a heads up."

Cara fakes a gag, but I chuckle lightly. "Don't worry. You can have my room. I usually bunk in with Santos, anyway. That way, you get your own space, and your eyes won't burn from the debauchery."

Santos' eyes soften, and he gives me a smile, grateful I've accepted his sister so fast. Of course I have, it's his sister. I'll do anything for him, so she gets the same treatment by default. She's my family now too, whether she knows it or not.

She turns and hugs me, surprising the shit out of me. "Thank you. I'm sure it's nice, but I really don't want to see your poo covered peen after it's been in my brother. I'm fucked up, but that's crossing a line."

Zander chokes on the drink he's sipping, and Blaze scowls. "Great, just what I need. Another one of you."

Selene giggles, reaching across the table and taking Cara's hand in an unusual show of acceptance. "It might be cool to have a girl around. Do you like knife throwing? I have targets set up at home for practice. Maybe we could find some moving targets and have a girl's day?"

Cara moans. Literally moans at the thought of throwing knives at a human being.

"Can you ditch these guys and be my girl instead? You're kind of perfect, even if you're a little scary."

Selene cackles, giving Blaze a wink over her shoulder. "Hear that? You guys are fired."

"Like fuck, you cheeky wench. Speak like that again and I'll spank you until you remember who owns you," he growls, her eyes filling with heat.

"Yes, Daddy." Good lord. Why does that make my dick hard when it isn't even aimed at me?

Cara laughs, but it dies down when Papi approaches, a no-nonsense look on his face.

"I don't want you leaving the compound. You belong here. We've looked for you for years, Cara. We…"

"I don't want to hear it. I'm leaving with Santos, and that's final. You can't make me stay, I dare you to try," she spits, looking ready to lunge over Santos and claw her dad's eyes out.

Pepe's eyes are wide, waiting for the shit show to go down, but Papi scowls and gives Santos a filthy look. "If anything happens to her, I'm taking my pound of flesh from you. You got that?"

"You mean something like what happened when you were watching her?" he answers dryly. "Don't worry, I actually give a fuck about my family. Well, some of them."

I'm sure Papi is going to explode, but he simply grinds his teeth together and stalks off, slamming his office door behind him.

Loqi hesitates as we all stand, getting to his feet and saying goodbye, but he turns to Santos and gives him a nod. "Keep her safe?"

"I will. We'll be in touch," Santos replies, seeming conflicted before offering his hand to shake. The move surprises me, and everyone else is silently waiting for Loqi's response. Relieved sighs go around the table as Loqi shakes his hand and gives him a small smile.

"Yeah, we will. I have a feeling we won't be waiting too long to run into each other again." He isn't wrong. I have a feeling we'll be running into each other again soon, too.

# Chapter Nine

## *Blaze*

Santos, Darius, Pepe, and Cara are taking a flight back to New York so as not to put Cara through the stress of a long drive. Two days of steady driving in a packed vehicle is stress enough, but with all of these fools, it would be torture.

Zander, Selene, and I are taking the car back home. But before we leave Nevada, Selene wants to pop in to see Aniyah and Colleen. I could go the rest of my life without seeing the purple-haired hooker again, but I don't want to cause a fight with Selene. I'm just happy she didn't take my balls when she found out what happened.

"Aniyah?" Zander snickers from the backseat. "That should be interesting, huh, Blaze?"

"Selene knows, asshole." I give him a look in the rear-view.

"I can't hold him to a different standard than I hold myself," Selene says. "But now things are different." She turns in the passenger seat and looks at Zander, "the five of us are in this together and if I even catch a wayward glance at another female, I'll begin taking trophies, starting with your ballsac."

"Jesus." I squirm in my seat and then a startled laugh escapes me when I see the look of complete horror on Zan's face.

"Glad we understand each other," Selene claps and turns back around.

I pull up to the bar and we all get out, stretching our legs. "We'll stay at the apartment tonight and then get back on the road tomorrow."

"Sounds good," Zander nods. "Now, let's go get a few beers. We deserve it." He strides for the door, and Selene goes to follow, but I grab her long, blonde hair and yank her back to my chest.

"You will not be putting your mouth anywhere on that purple hooker either, or I'll start collecting trophies," I press my mouth to her grin, "starting with your pretty little clit."

"I hear you, Daddy," she whispers and licks the scar on my lip.

I release her as she giggles and jogs to the front door. I look up at the sign *Good Times* and groan, I fucking hate doing people shit.

I get inside and find Selene at the bar sitting beside Aniyah, both of them speaking to the bartender and laughing. I find Zander at the old-fashioned jukebox, his face a mask of confusion. I head his way, not really wanting to be around the women, and come to stand beside him.

"It looks like you're trying to figure out how to put your little dick into a pussy hole."

"Will you fuck off?" he snaps at me. "My dick is well above average, asshole."

I chuckle and lean against the jukebox. "What are you trying to figure out? It's not Rocket Science."

"I put my *little* quarter in the *slot,* but nothing's happening," I snort at his attitude and shove him aside.

"It's not digital fucker," I roll my eyes. "This green light means it's ready for you to pick your selections. You get five songs per quarter. Which ones do you want?"

He lists off a bunch of songs I don't know, and then we head to a booth, giving the girls space to fucking squeal and shit. As soon as we sit down, a waitress comes over and takes our order for a pitcher of beer. The selections Zander picked starts to play, and I groan into my hand.

"You love some Emo-sounding music, dude."

He's tapping his fingers to the beat and tosses me a smile. "It makes my dick hard."

"What the fuck?" I give him a raised brow. "You're sitting here with me, you sick cunt. You've been around Santos too much."

"Yes, I fucking have." He leans forward, anger in his tone. "It's time I have a vacation from babysitting."

"Stop fucking complaining, those are your brother-husbands now," I chuckle. "Till death do us all part, brother."

"Which will be sooner than we think, with Santos helicoptering a machine fucking gun."

"You survived." I shrug.

"You would've lost your shit and killed them all," he scoffs.

"Which is why you are the most suitable for the job." I grin at him. "Look, I know it's tough with them sometimes, and I'm hoping when we finally get our paws on Mack, things will calm down."

"I need them to calm down," he huffs as he drinks his beer.

I leave it at that because I'm no therapist and I'm tired of his whining. I watch Selene laughing at the bar and I check the time on my phone, wondering if it's nearing time to leave.

"Chicks can talk for hours," Zander gives me a knowing look. "We'll have to entice her to leave."

"I'm not making out with you." I glare at him.

"Was that a joke, *Daddy*?"

"Call me that one more time, and I'll beat you exactly how your actual daddy used to," I spit out.

"Damn," he whistles. "You're heartless. But no, I'm not in the mood to kiss your ugly face tonight." He leans across the table. "There are a few chicks at the table behind you. They're giving us the eye. How about I give a subtle wink and entice them over?"

"You're really not that attached to keeping your balls, huh?"

"Hey!" He holds his hands up in the air. "It's not our fault if they approach us, right?"

"Does Selene come off as a rational female to you? Are we with the same woman?"

"Look, you're either in, or a big, fishy pussy." He leans back with a smirk.

"Fishy pussy? Seriously?"

"PH all out of whack, pussy." He nods.

"Jesus, maybe you have been hanging around those silly assholes too long."

"What is that?" He sticks his nose up in the air, taking a long inhale. "Oh!" he waves it off, "just Blaze and his yeasty pussy."

"Are you done?"

He does indeed throw a wink at whatever chicks are sitting behind me, and then nods. "Yep."

I groan as I hear chairs scrape along the hardwood floor, knowing exactly what will evidently go down. Three girls appear at the end of the table, and when one attempts to sit in the chair beside me, I shove her off. Her ass hits the floor with a loud thump and draws the attention of those around us.

"I didn't ask you to come over here, sit somewhere else," I say as I drink my beer.

Zander is laughing as the chicks congregate around him, and it's then I feel a sinister energy. Like the moment before a thunderstorm shoots its bolt of lightning across the sky, or the thick, damp air before a downpour.

"You're about to die of blood loss." I smirk at Zander's wide eyes. He must feel it, too. "I hear it's a long and painful death to endure from the loss of your balls."

"What's this?" Selene comes up behind Zander, placing her hands on his shoulders. "Looks like a small gathering of chickens. What are y'all clucking about?"

"Not me." I gulp down the rest of my beer. "Chicken's not my thing. I've always been more impartial to *fish*."

"I know, Daddy." Selene smiles at me as she rubs Zander's shoulders. "I know."

"I think you *chicks* should skedaddle," I grin, feeling the shit storm that's about to ensue. They get up quickly, darting back to their table, and Selene continues to rub Zander's shoulders.

"Should we leave?" Her voice is too sweet, too laced with sugar.

"Yeah," I lift my nose in the air, "Can you smell that, Zan?"

His jaw is clenched, and his eyes are tight as he glares at me.

"I thought it was fish for a second there, but no, it's more like someone shit themselves." I get up out of my seat and head for the door, chuckling to myself when I hear a scuffle behind me.

"Selene, fuck," Zander growls, and once I'm outside, I look behind me. Selene has Zander in a pressure-point hold at the back of his neck, and his back is contorted with pain.

"What the fuck was that?" she screeches as she shoves him forward.

Zander's face nearly kisses the pavement before he rights himself, and swings around to ward off any incoming attacks.

"It was him." I point at him, and he throws me a shocked expression.

"You wanted to leave!"

"True," I nod as I rub at my chin, "but I was willing to wait it out."

"I don't make idle threats, Zander," she tsks as she walks to the car. "Those balls are mine."

My balls clench up tight at her threatening tone, and I follow close behind her, not wanting to miss a single second of the action.

## Zander

I'm dead.

I really thought my best friend and brother would have my fucking back, but I was wrong. He's a sellout and clearly dropped me for the psychotic female we're all in love with. Now, I just have to remind her I am in love with her.

Fuck, why did I have to push it?

"You drive, Blaze." Selene sings out. "I want to sit in the back with my favorite boy."

I stop in my tracks, a few feet from the car, and vehemently shake my head. Nope, I'm not getting in there.

"Either get in, or you're a big, fishy pussy," Blaze calls out, the fucker somehow finding his funny bone that's been lodged somewhere up his ass his whole life.

"Nope." I shake my head, getting dizzy from the constant motion. "Not until I know my balls are staying firmly attached."

"Seems like he wants to walk back." Selene rests her ass against the car. "That sounds sweet. A midnight stroll through the strip? Lots of alleyways to explore, and dark crevices to traverse."

"I'm not doing that either."

"I think he's scared." Blaze chuckles as Selene begins to saunter over to me. If I could run without looking like a complete pussy, I would.

"Are you scared, Zander?" Her head is tipped to the side, her eyes looking every bit as deranged as she is.

"Yes." I nod, deciding to go with the truth.

"Tell me why."

"Because you're looking like you want to kill me." I point out.

"You're right." She stops, folding her arms across her chest. "I want to kill you for provoking me and thinking there would be no consequences. Now, I really don't want to take your balls because I know you weren't going to do anything with those girls." I let out an audible breath of air. "But…" My head quickly snaps back up to look at her. "I can't let such bad behavior go unpunished, right Daddy?" She looks over her shoulder at a manic looking dickhead.

"Absolutely not."

"So, Zander, tell me, how should I punish you?" she asks so fucking sweetly.

"Smother me with your pussy." I nod. "I will die a happy man."

"See? That's good and all, but you're not supposed to enjoy the punishment."

"I think he needs an ass spanking," Blaze calls out. "You have a few toys left over from your fun with the purple hooker. Is there a whip?"

Her eyes alight with excitement, and I groan into my hands. Is it the worst punishment? No, I can take an ass whipping, I guess.

"I love ass play." Selene squeals. "So, Zander? Will you let me punish your ass?"

I nod, sulking.

"Say it," she demands. "Blaze needs to be my witness."

"Yes, punish my ass." I throw my hands up and stomp to the car like a petulant child. Blaze has no idea what's coming to him. There will be a time he needs me to take his side, and I will gleefully throw him to the fucking wolves.

"You look mad," he snickers as he gets behind the wheel.

"He's going to be even more so when he realizes he likes it later," Selene cackles as we drive to the apartment.

Of course, I'm not going to like it. I roll my eyes as we pull up to the apartment, but my girl is crazy and if I don't give her something, it's a very real possibility I will be missing my balls when I wake up.

Walking up to her apartment door feels like the longest trip of my life. I don't know why I'm so apprehensive. It's just a whipping. Fuck, my father did a hell of a lot worse. I guess what it boils down to is the fact that my girl is a certifiable lunatic. Hot, but still loony.

We get inside, and she tosses her trench to the couch. Blaze takes a seat beside it.

"Let me freshen up," she calls out as she walks to the bathroom. "I'll call you in when I'm done."

"Scared?" Blaze asks.

"Fuck you," I grumble.

"I warned you," he chuckles.

"You sold me out."

"Nah, she would've known right away what you were up to. Should've listened to me."

I don't answer as I sit on the other end of the couch and sulk, waiting for when I'm called to receive my punishment. It doesn't take long until I hear her call out our names from the bedroom, a slight giggle escaping her at the end.

*She loves me.* I remind myself as I get up off the couch, and a sore ass will be worth fucking her for after. I walk into the bedroom, Blaze hot on my tail, and find a naked Selene, stroking herself with a black leather riding whip. The small, flattened end slips through her wet folds, and I groan as my cock expands.

Yeah, I can handle that.

"Take your clothes off," she demands. "Both of you."

"You're not whipping me with that," Blaze grunts as he throws his shirt onto the floor.

"No, Daddy," she smiles. "But you can whip me."

He's the next to groan as we both follow her instruction, tossing our clothes to the side. Selene rolls off the bed and comes toward us, slapping the whip against her thigh.

"Bend over the bed, Zander."

I groan as I do what she says, waiting for the crack of the whip, but when I don't feel it, I look at her over my shoulder. She's standing there with a tube of lube and coating her finger.

"Ass play, Zander." She winks.

I stand up straight away, my ass cheeks clenching and my heart pounding.

"No." I shake my head. "No way."

"Please?" Her eyes widen innocently. "I want to be inside of you while Daddy is inside of me." Why my cock jerks at those words, I'll never know, but she catches it. "You'll like it," she nods, "and then all will be forgiven."

I look at the lube coating her fingers, and then her other hand tweaking her nipple, then groan.

"It never leaves this room." I point at both her and Blaze.

"We won't tell," Selene shakes her head, and looks up at Blaze, "right, Daddy?"

"I won't utter a fucking thing; not like I want to be an accessory to Zander losing his ass virginity."

Selene holds up a strap on, and I almost pass out. It's already coated in lube, glistening in the room's dim light.

"No," I shake my head and back away. "No way."

"Your cock says otherwise." Selene points down to the fucking traitor standing straight up between my legs. "It's a small one, Zander." She holds it out. "See?"

I close my eyes and let my mind relax. I'm still turned on because it's Selene, not some dude. It's my girl, her big bouncy tits, toned stomach, and tight, sweet pussy. *It's my girl.*

"Okay," I exhale. "Fine."

"Bend over the bed, Zan," Blaze demands. "I want to be inside my woman."

I walk back to the bed and bend back over; how bad can it be? I like a finger in the ass now and then when I'm getting head; it doesn't mean I want dick. Just like my girlfriend coating my ass with lube, completely normal.

"Step in here," I hear Blaze instruct, and I know they're putting on that strap-on.

I begin to sweat with apprehension. I hope Selene knows just how far I'll go for her and realizes this is only happening because I love her.

"Ready, baby?" Her soft fingers skim down my spine. "Open up for me."

I spread my legs wider and feel her step up between them, her fingers gripping the globes of my ass. I'm so fucking hard, pulsing as she spreads me farther. The blunt end of the dildo presses to my ass, and I nearly jump out of my skin when I feel the slight vibrations.

"Shh," Selene continues to dig her fingers into my ass cheeks. "That's for me," she moans. "It has a built-in vibrator for my clit. I thought it only right I get fucked in the ass right along with you."

I hear Blaze groan and relax, feeling her push into me slowly, the tight rim of muscle slowly stretching to accommodate her. It burns, and when I think I can handle it, it gets worse. Until it isn't. Once the burn subsides, I can feel the dildo rubbing against a part of me I've never had explored.

"Fuck, Zander," she groans, pushing my shoulders down farther to the bed. "You have such a pretty asshole."

That's a first.

This is all a first, but I'll admit, it's not a bad first.

"I really want to fuck you hard," she pants, the vibrator pressing into her harder as she works the cock into my ass. "Can I?"

"I can help you with that," I hear Blaze, then I feel Selene's chest hit my back.

"Daddy's gonna fuck me right into you," she whispers.

I don't know what about that sets me off, or why it makes my hand slip between me and the bed to grab my rock hard, aching cock. I begin to pump it as the cock in my ass begins to slam into me, hitting a spot with each thrust, making me see stars.

Selene is a panting, screaming mess behind me, her sweat coating my back, and Blaze is cursing about her tight asshole. The sensations become too much, too intense, and my balls tighten painfully to my body. This is it, the most explosive orgasm I've ever had. I can feel it.

"Zan," Blaze grunts. "What does it feel like?"

"Good," I groan as Selene slams in again.

"Describe it," Blaze demands.

"Fuck," I moan. "Forbidden, but so fucking good."

"Fuck," Blaze groans, the noise long and deep as he comes.

I'm not too far behind as I shoot my load all over the bed. Then our girl between us is screaming our names and grinding herself into the cock in my ass. Everything feels like it's too much, and when I look down at my cock, I find it still hard, covered in my cum.

I feel the second Blaze pulls out of Selene, it's like a pressure is lifted, and then she's next, slowly withdrawing out of my ass, the hole sensitive from her brutal fucking. I collapse onto the bed, my stomach hitting my cum, and yet, I can't move to save my life.

A sharp slap hits my ass cheek, and I peek an eye open.

"All is forgiven, baby," Selene giggles as she drops onto the bed.

"Bring that thing home with us," I tell her as I lose the war with my eyelids.

Yeah, I like my girlfriend owning my ass, literally.

# Selene

I just fucked my boyfriend in the ass, and now I can die. I've lived a completely fulfilled life. *Satan, come get your girl.*

"Why are your hands in a prayer position?" Blaze asks as he lies down beside me.

"Because that's what I'm doing. I'm praying."

He snorts and pulls me into his chest, his chin landing on the top of my head. "I love you," he mumbles, and my heart soars.

"I love you too, Daddy."

"But you love me more," Zander mutters sleepily behind us. "I let you fuck me in the ass."

Both Blaze and I chuckle, and I turn in Blaze's arms to face Zander, leaning over to kiss his sweaty cheek. "I love you so damn much," I whisper into his ear.

The next morning, we get on the road early, and I'm curled up in the backseat with Zander. He's been quiet, and I'm worried he's feeling embarrassed about what we did last night. I hope he doesn't think we're judging him, and if Blaze bothers him in any way, I will break his fucking neck. I'll send him off with a kiss first, of course.

"Tell me what you're thinking," I murmur.

"Just tired." He lets out a long breath. "I want to be home; I miss the guys."

"The ones you were complaining about needing a vacation from last night?" Blaze smiles in the rear-view.

"Yeah," Zander chuckles. "I guess being away from the assholes puts things into perspective."

"We're a family," I say into his chest. "There's never judgment, no matter how hard we razz on each other."

"I know," he says quietly. "I guess I'm slightly questioning my sexuality after last night, as well."

"What?" Blaze nearly takes us into oncoming traffic at Zander's omission and quickly rights the car. "What the fuck do you mean?"

"I was fucked in the ass, and I enjoyed it."

"By your woman," Blaze scoffs, shaking his head. "Lots of men love ass play."

"Love it with a dildo?"

"Sure," Blaze shrugs. "Why not?"

I'm shocked at Blaze's nonchalant attitude, and I feel my chest swell with pride. He's so accepting, even though he comes off as the most hard-assed.

"But—"

"No buts, Zan," he growls. "And what the fuck does it matter, anyway?"

"Yeah," I feel him start to relax. "Yeah, you're right."

He tips his head back and tucks me in closer to his side, his breathing beginning to level out. When he let me fuck him last night, I was shocked. I knew he would fight me on it and, in all honesty; I didn't think it would happen. I would have never forced it on him, but I had a feeling there was more to Zander than what meets the eye. My most straight-laced, level-headed, even-tempered boyfriend likes to get a little crazy in the bedroom. My eyes meet Blaze's in the rear-view and he gives me a smile, his dark brown eyes shining with love.

"You came in like a fucking blizzard, Little Reaper, cold and harsh.

You ripped through all of our defenses and settled inside our frigid hearts."

I'm rendered speechless, my heart beating so hard against my ribcage.

"Now look at us, completely vulnerable and absolutely at your mercy. You've healed something different in each of us, and we've come out stronger in the end."

"You each give me something different, too," I whisper as I look up into Zander's sleeping face. "I could never live without you, any of you."

I rest my head against Zander's chest and listen to the steady beat, the first heart to reveal it loved me. The first person to ever tell me they loved me outside of Jan.

"What's happening with Aniyah and Colleen?" Blaze asks.

"Aniyah is stubborn and wants to stay in Vegas. She wants to make sure no more girls fall victim to prowling men. As much as I understand the feeling, I can't help but worry about her. Colleen promised me to look out for her, since they'll be rooming together."

"At least there's someone watching her. She's a big girl. You can't tell her what to do." He shrugs.

"I know." I sigh. "I was getting some weird vibes from them, though."

"What vibes?"

"I think Aniyah and Colleen are together." I grin. "I think they're dating."

"Good," Blaze growls. "Keeps her away from my woman."

"There was a moment," I admit to him. "I wanted her. I wanted her to be with me."

"I know." He looks at me through the rear-view. "It worried me. I was afraid we were losing you."

"No matter how hard I tried to forget you guys, I couldn't. The four of you were always meant to be mine."

The connection I had with Aniyah was intense, but it burned out fast, and in the end, I knew it was nothing more than lust. And maybe I was trying to fill a deep settled loneliness by missing my guys.

My soul's mates are all their own brands of crazy and it just so compliments mine.

## *Darius*

The plane ride went smoothly, and Santos, Pepe, and Cara talked non-stop the entire way. I napped for most of it, taking the chance to regenerate myself. We've hardly had any sleep lately, so even five minutes of rest was bliss.

We take an Uber home, and our relaxing time period ends the moment we get there to find a note stuck to the front door with a knife in it. I march up to it, yanking the blade out, and I take the note in my hands, reading it with a scowl. I don't like being threatened, especially not on my own fucking property.

"We are watching you. Every move you make, everything you plan, and every time you fuck your whore. We see it all. Watch yourself. You won't be around much longer. Give us back, Pepe, he's ours. You take something from us, we'll take something from you. Bet your girl screams real pretty." I growl, turning to face Santos. "Who the fuck do these cunts think they are? Threatening our girl like that?"

Santos snatches the piece of paper and glowers, his eyes angrily running over it. "I'll kill them. No one touches my baby girl."

Cara eyes us silently, assessing us as we fume, but Pepe pales.

"They're going to kill me," he squeaks. "What if they're watching us right now?"

I grab the back of his neck, unlocking the door and shoving him inside. "Then we act like you're here by force. But don't think for a second we'd let them get to you. You're one of us now."

I let him go, and Santos instantly picks him up in a bear hug, jumping up and down. "I told you we weren't letting you go!"

Pepe chuckles, his eyes bright. His friendship with Santos is awesome, and I know it'll grow even more over time.

"I thought that was because you're crazy."

"That's a big part of it," I smirk. "San, put him down before you make him hurl."

He does as he's told, putting Pepe back on his feet before turning to me with a serious expression. "So, what do we do now?"

"We sweep the house, then call the others to let them know, but we need to keep our eyes peeled. They might try to attack us now that we're home, and not all of us are here. We don't go anywhere alone, got it? That means you too, Cara," I inform them, turning my attention to Santos' sister. "They might see you as the weakest link in our group, and if they find out you're family, they'll definitely try something."

She grins, the same way Santos does when someone threatens him. "They can try. I'll gut them like a fucking pig."

Pepe's watching her with wide eyes, but I see the flicker of interest. *Oh boy, things could get interesting around here.* Especially if he starts chasing her around like a lost puppy.

Santos doesn't notice. He's too busy beaming at his sister with pride. "Damn fucking straight. Let's practice your shooting skills later. I wanna see what you got."

"I'll slaughter you if you make it a competition," she answers. "I'm a pretty good shot. We all had to train to be a part of King Hayne's court."

"You're the coolest sister ever," he groans, her face lighting up at his praise.

"Yeah? You're a pretty cool brother, too."

I let them bicker about who's better at using different weapons while I check every room in the house for an intruder, then I sit on the couch and pull my phone out once it is clear. "Time to call Blaze. You two can continue this argument later."

Santos sits beside me, his hand resting on my thigh casually. "Selene's going to be pissed."

"We're all pissed. I can't believe they walked up to the door and stuck a note on it," I scowl. "I'll check the cameras in a minute, too. Make sure they didn't actually get in."

Santos is instantly on his feet, jogging up the hallway. "I'll check now. We need to check the place for bugs before we talk to the others. For all we know, they've planted bombs here." Shit, he's right. I must be tired if I didn't think of it first.

I follow him, leaving Pepe and Cara to occupy themselves while we investigate, relief rolling through me at seeing two guys leave the note on the door and that's it. At least we know we can talk freely.

Santos is muttering under his breath once we rejoin the other two on the couch and wait for Blaze to answer the phone.

"You're on speaker," he says the moment he answers, his voice gruff as always.

"Hey. We found a note on the front door when we got home," I say immediately.

"What kind of note? Are girl scouts doing their cookies again? Be more fucking specific," he barks with irritation.

"Diablos. They're watching us, and they want Pepe back," I grunt, reading the note out loud to them. They're quiet for a moment, before Selene talks.

"I'm going to fucking kill them. They can watch us fuck if they want, but they aren't joining in. Did they get inside?"

"No, they put the note on the door, then left. They didn't even try to get inside the house."

Pepe excuses himself, and we wave him off. I have no idea why the Diablos want him. He's a scaredy cat. If he's going to stick around, we need to toughen him up a little.

"We'll try to get there as fast as we can. Let us know if anyone starts snooping around, all right? I know you can look after yourselves, but you have Pepe and Cara to look out for, too," Zander warns, making me snort.

"Pretty sure Cara can look after herself, right Cara?" I ask and look up, finding her gone. Santos frowns, not realizing she left the room either, but we continue chatting on the phone for a while before deciding we needed to find her. "Hey, we'd better go. How far away are you?"

"We'll be home the day after tomorrow. Don't fuck on the couch," Blaze grumbles, making me chuckle.

"You won't know if we do."

"I'll fucking know," he snaps before hanging up, leaving us to track down Cara.

## Santos

My sister is silent and sneaky. I'll give her that. I didn't notice her leaving the room, which concerns me slightly. I can't relax like that or someone else might slip by me who isn't supposed to.

"Where the fuck did she go?" Darius asks as he stands, glancing around the room. "It's like she vanished into thin air."

"No idea. Maybe she went to lie down?"

"In a house she's never been in? C'mon, we haven't shown her around yet," he snorts, following me as we start searching. We don't have to look far, because we find her in the hallway, pressing Pepe against the wall as she kisses the hell out of him.

"Well, well, well, what do we have here?" Darius says with a grin, and Pepe pushes Cara back with a gasp, panicking at being caught out.

"We, uh…"

"What are your intentions with my sister?" I demand, eyeing them both. I'm angry at him touching her, but I'm also confused. They hardly know each other, and they couldn't be more opposite if they tried.

He gulps at the glare I send his way, darting his eyes between us and Cara. "I didn't… I wouldn't…"

"You're trying to fuck my little sister," I state, stepping closer. "I don't like that."

"No! I'd never do that!" he insists, my eyes narrowing with annoyance.

"Why the fuck not? Is she not good enough for you?"

Darius is smothering a laugh, but I can't help it. I don't like him touching her, but I don't like him not wanting her, either. I'm giving *myself* whiplash.

Cara leans back against the wall opposite Pepe, a grin on her face, but she leaves him to sputter more answers, enjoying this as much as Darius.

"No! She's perfect! I don't want to have sex until I'm married! It's nothing against her. She's really pretty, I swear!" The way Cara had him against the wall tells me she started it, but I'm not done interrogating him. It's starting to amuse me.

"Wait, you're going to marry my sister?!" I exclaim with a grin, happiness seeping into me.

"I'm not marrying anyone, I was just trying to get laid," Cara says dryly, but I ignore her and focus on Pepe.

"So? You're marrying her?"

"That's not what I meant!" he cries. "I just meant I wouldn't have sex with her unless I married her!"

Cara smirks, moving up to him and running her hand down his stomach, stopping just above his groin. "Sure, didn't seem like that a minute ago."

His panicked gaze meets mine, and I grin. "Oh, my God. We'll be brothers! Like, for real! Marry her, or else I'll kill you."

Darius loses it, laughing his ass off while Cara scowls at me. "I'm not getting married."

"You are now. Pepe said so!" I whine. "You can't take my brother away from me!"

"Can't I just fuck him? It's easier," she throws back, making me growl.

"No. My brother's not a piece of meat, Cara."

"He's not your brother. We're not married!"

"Whose fault is that? Pepe, I'm sorry. I don't know why she's saying these mean things!" I exclaim, grabbing him and pulling him in for a hug. He flinches back as his hard dick brushes my leg, and I smirk. "Is that for me or my sister?"

"I need to go and pray," he rushes out, running to his room and slamming the door, and Cara turns to me with a glare.

"Look what you did. Do you want me to stay a virgin forever?"

"I don't want to think about it. What's wrong with Pepe? He'd be the best husband. Oh! We can all live here and…" Darius grabs my shoulder, wheezing from all his laughter.

"Stop, you're killing me. They don't have to get married, San."

"Yes, they do, Jesus says so," I snort. "Isn't that right, Pepe?! Jesus says you have to marry her if you want to fuck her!"

Cara huffs, giving me the evil-eye. "You're not married, and you fuck all the time, apparently. Jesus claims homosexuality is a sin too, but you don't care about that."

"No, but I'm not into Jesus like Pepe is. He's gotta respect that shit," I grumble, crossing my arms tight over my chest. "Speaking of homosexual fucking, it's good to be home. D, let's fuck."

Cara scrunches up her nose. "I'll leave you guys to it, then. I'll bunk in with Pepe, I assume?"

"I'd better not hear any noises from that room unless I see a ring on your finger!" I holler, and she flips me off before sneaking into Pepe's room, leaving us in peace.

Darius grins, ruffling my hair. "Stop teasing them."

I slam his back against the wall and kiss him hard, my fingers biting into his skin as I hold on to his waist. He groans into my mouth, his hand running through my hair and firmly yanking on it. I hear Cara curse at us from inside the bedroom, and I grin. "Maybe we should take this elsewhere?"

Darius doesn't argue. He pushes me back, fumbling with my belt as I guide us toward our room blindly, not letting his lips go. The moment the door's shut, I pull back to yank my shirt off, kicking my jeans off as I go. Darius wastes no time getting naked for me, his eyes hungrily running over my body as he stares at me. "Fuck."

"What?" I demand, looking down at my body. "Something wrong?" I've never been the type to give a shit about people's opinions of me, but Darius and Selene have knocked that wall down, and my insecurities are at an all-time high.

"Nothing's wrong, *amante*. You're fucking perfect," he groans, grabbing my hand and tugging me toward the bed. We should be keeping an eye on the cameras for the Diablos, but that's the last thing on our minds.

He pushes me back so I'm sitting on the edge of the bed, dropping to his knees instantly. I wish our girl were here to watch this. I know she'd enjoy the show.

The moment his lips wrap around my dick and his eyes peer up at me, I curse, fisting his hair. I hold his head still as I thrust down his throat, somehow getting harder as he chokes on it. Saliva runs down my shaft and soaks my balls, the wet choking sounds urging me on as I slam into him. I already need to fucking come, so I force myself to let his head go and push him back. "Get on your fucking knees. This won't be gentle."

"It never is," he grins, his lips swollen. The moment his ass is in the air for me, I grab some lube to make sure I don't split him in half, smearing it over his tight hole and pressing two fingers inside. He drops his forehead onto the bed, murmuring my name as I force in a third.

"San, fuck me," he begs. "Stop teasing me."

"It'll hurt," I warn, but he looks at me over his shoulder, his eyes dark.

"I'm counting on it." *Fuck.*

I remove my fingers and align the tip of my dick with the tight hole, grinning sadistically at him. "You asked for it." Then I forced my way inside, the sound of his discomfort sending tingles to my balls. I don't give him time to adjust, I just pull out and slam back in again and again, his desperate cries and praise bouncing off the surrounding walls loud enough for the entire neighborhood to hear.

I hope they all know who he belongs to.

# Chapter Ten

## Darius

elicious pain. It's all I feel as Santos goes to town on me like he'll die if he doesn't, and I'm at his mercy in the best possible way. I'm biting the blanket so damn hard I'm sure my teeth will crack, but I don't stop him. I want him to hurt me because, this feeling? It's the best. Our relationship is built around pain and destruction, and every hard stroke he gives me feels like home.

"I already want to fucking come," Santos pants, his fingers digging into my waist as he holds tight. "So fucking good."

I've never cared about praise before, but something burns in my chest at hearing it from him. I want to please him and Selene all the fucking time, so knowing I drive them both so crazy is really good for my ego.

I reach underneath myself, finding his balls and giving them a firm squeeze, causing him to jolt. "Fuck, D."

I want him to fill me up, and I want him to come so hard he sees stars, so I slide my hand back farther, just managing to reach his ass, and push a finger inside the tight ring.

I don't understand half the shit he's cursing, but that means I'm doing something right, so I push in farther, stroking his tight walls as he continues to slam into me. He comes with a shout, his hands dropping to the mattress on either side of me as he presses himself as deep as he can, needing a minute to recover. His sweaty chest covers my back, and he lets out a chuckle. "Well, that escalated quickly."

My legs are shaking slightly from being in this position for so long, and the moment he pulls out of me, I flip him onto his back with a grin. "Hope you're not too sensitive."

"You going to top me, D?" he smirks, exhaustion filling his eyes.

"Yeah, I want to come so deep in you, you can taste it," I murmur, lying over him and grabbing the lube. "I'm slowing it down a little, though."

He seems confused but doesn't protest. It's rare we fuck at a slower pace, but sometimes it's what I crave. I prepare his ass before sliding inside, hooking his muscular legs over my shoulders. His eyes clench shut as I stoke deep, leaning over him more to press my lips to his. His mouth opens instantly, his tongue massaging mine. I'm surprised he's letting me go slow, to be honest, but he doesn't complain as I keep my thrusts slow and deep, our breaths mingling the closer I get to my release.

My balls are tight, but I hold on longer, savoring it as long as possible. I never know when he'll let me take it down a notch again.

"I love you," I practically whisper, his eyes flying open to look at me.

"I love you, too," he murmurs, running his fingers through my hair and giving me a content smile. I let go, grunting as my hot cum fills his ass, and by the time we pass out, he's curled up against my chest, snoring soundly without a care in the world.

# *Zander*

I groan with relief when I see the front gates of Blaze's house—our house—up ahead. Being in this car with a woman who can't sit still needs constant stimulation, and barely sleeps; and with a guy who's grumpy as all hell, has random screaming outbursts, and needs constant quiet has been exhausting. I want my bed so I can sleep for the next week straight. Unfortunately, that won't happen. With lingering Diablos about, and Mack still on the loose, I know I'll have my work cut out for me. Why the fuck would the Diablos threaten to take our woman again? When it was she who slaughtered them all to free herself the first time? It makes no sense.

All I can determine is they're trying to hit us in what they must think is our weakest point, and they'd be correct. We love her and we would do anything to make sure she stays safe. With that being said, she can also take care of herself, and it's a relief we don't have to coddle her.

It's time we find Mack, kill him, and eradicate all Diablos. This finale has been decades in the making, and I'm ready to finally watch Mack meet his maker.

"If my house is a fucking mess, I'm kicking you all out." Blaze growls as we pull through the gates.

"What? What do Selene and I have to do with any of it?"

"Don't bring pets home if you can't house train them," he snaps, and Selene falls across the backseat laughing.

"I can't wait to get my bestiality on," she continues to snort, and I see the ghost of a smile on Blaze's mouth.

She's out of the car before we've come to a full stop, and she's running up the stairs, busting through the front door.

"Mommy's home!" she screams, her words traveling all down the street. "Ready or not, come fuck me!"

"Why'd I think coming home would be easier?" I groan into my hands.

"Because you forgot this was your one and only vacation from the pets," Blaze snickers.

He gets out of the car, stretching his tall, muscular body, and shaking out those tree trunk legs. I don't even know how he got himself in here. He's so large. And he's large *everywhere*. I cringe when I remember him fucking Selene in the ass on the dancefloor at the MC building, which couldn't have felt as good as she was making it out to, I know now.

My cock begins to swell in my pants as I watch Blaze walk to the front door, thoughts of him fucking her in the ass still fresh in my mind. *No.* What am I hard for right now? The thought of my girlfriend getting rammed in the ass by a massive dick, or my best friend who owns said dick? Oh my God, am I becoming gay?

I stumble out of the car and slowly walk up to the door, giving my confused dick time to deflate. I get fucked in the ass one time by my girlfriend, and all of a sudden, my cock wants to harden to the thoughts of dicks in the ass.

As soon as I step over the threshold, I find Selene with her arms wrapped around Darius' neck, her eyes meeting mine over his shoulder.

"Maybe Zander will want to join us later," she gives me a wink as Santos grins. My cock pulses against my zipper, and I swallow down my apprehension. Join them how? Will one of them be doing to me what she did? My cock halts its pulsing as I imagine Santos plowing into me. Okay, so not a lot gay.

"I'm tired." I give her a half-assed smile, hoping she doesn't read too far into it.

"How about I come visit you after," she slips from Darius' arms and saunters over to me, pressing her body into mine, "I'll bring our little friend, too."

My cock springs to attention, throbbing and pressing painfully into my zipper. Okay, so maybe just a little gay. I can handle that.

"As fun as it is to listen to you four figure out your train car formation, we need to get this Diablo thing under control once and for all." Blaze brings his laptop to the table and sits. "We'll figure out the *rail* complications later."

Asshole.

Selene cackles as she grabs Santos' ass, leading him to the couch, and when she sits, she looks around. "Where's Cara and our little Pepe?"

"Making wedding plans." Santos grins.

"What?" Selene's eyes bulge from her head. "They want to get married?"

"I wouldn't say that," Darius chuckles as I take a seat beside him on the couch, "but Santos and I caught them kissing in the hallway. Pepe is adamant it was innocent because he doesn't believe in sex before marriage."

"And since he wants to fuck my sister, they're getting married." Santos tosses his hands up. "I can't wait to walk the little fucker down the aisle."

"Your sister?" Selene looks at him, shocked.

"No, my Pepe," he huffs, and I can't help but let loose a laugh.

"Can you guys shut the fuck up now?" Blaze snaps as his fingers fly over the keys of the laptop.

"I don't think Cara should be buying the cow without testing the quality of the milk first." Selene grumbles, and I laugh again.

"Listen up." Blaze turns the screen so we can all see it. "Mack has been MIA for a while now, and the Diablos were in hiding after the explosions, so what makes Pepe so fucking important to bring them out?"

We all fall quiet with thought. It is strange how much they're worried about a new member, and a seemingly useless one at that.

"Has he left since you've been back?" Blaze asks Santos.

"No, we won't let him because we're worried about the Diablos snatching him. But he's been frantic about his abuela, and he calls her every day. I promised he could go see her with one of us."

Blaze points at the screen of the laptop, and we all lean in. It's an article dating back seven years ago, detailing a huge sex trafficking bust. The next article shows the key witness, along with his mother and father, killed a few days before the trial, resulting in the prosecution having to drop the case.

"What does this mean?" Selene asks.

"I remember this," I say quietly. "It involved my father and Mack. They celebrated when the case was dropped."

"They were implicated in this bust?" Selene gasps.

"No," Blaze answers, "but there was a good chance they would've been."

"I remember this, too." Santos leans forward. "We were so fucking pissed. It's when we decided to take down Walton and Delaney ourselves."

"Do you remember the survivors of the 'home invasion'?" Blaze asks, quoting the home invasion part because everyone knew it was a hit.

"The younger brother and the grandfather, wasn't it?" Darius scrubs at his chin.

"Grandmother," Blaze corrects. "An *abuela*."

The information all clicks for us at the same moment, and we all gasp. "That was Pepe?" Santos exclaims.

"Only one way to find out for sure. But I would say yes, and how much do you wanna bet the Diablos forced him to join?" Blaze nods. "Call him down here."

"No need." Pepe walks into the room, and we all snap our heads around to watch him. "That is, in fact, me. And that's why I have been desperate to get home to my abuela. I'm afraid they'll grab her."

"Why didn't you tell us this?" I ask him.

"Because I see the way you guys operate, and I really didn't want to put my abuela and myself in any more danger. You guys have a few things wrong, though. I wasn't forced to join the Diablos. I did that on my own, with the help of my father." He sits on a chair and leans forward.

"The one who was murdered?" I ask him, slightly confused.

"No, he was the man who raised me. I'm talking about my biological father." His head drops into his hands as he exhales, "I guess it's story time."

"About time," Blaze snarls.

"My mother attended Columbia University; she was a little older than the other students because she had a baby—my brother—right out of high school. During her second year, they had a serial rapist on campus, and my mother fell victim to him. She knew exactly who it was and when she reported it, it was ignored."

"Who was the rapist?" Selene's eyes have narrowed, her jaw tightened, and I can see the bloodlust seeping through her body.

"Mack Delaney, he got off with the help of Henry Walton." We all stare at him with mixed expressions of pity and anger.

"I was conceived through that attack, but since my family is strict Catholic, my mother would not abort me. My father in everything but blood agreed, and that's how I came to be."

"Does Mack know who you are?" Blaze asks.

"Of course," he nods. "He's the one who found me, and when he offered to take me into his gang of sex traffickers, I agreed. I was going to compile as much information as I could on them to give to the police, and all the while, make Mack believe I was truly interested in being his son. Then you came along and even though you weren't the police, I had a feeling justice would be better served through you. That's why I agreed to help."

"So that's why you're so important." Selene scratches at her chin. "Looks like I need to start hunting some Diablos and try to smoke out Papa Mack."

"Don't call him that." Pepe shudders.

"Well, he can't be Daddy; we have one already." Selene points at Blaze.

# *Blaze*

"We can't bring your grandmother here," I tell Pepe. "The Diablos could very well be watching her house, and I doubt they'll hurt her, considering who your father is. We need the Diablos to believe you're our hostage to keep her safe." I turn to Selene. "Go hunting and spread the word we have a Diablo captive."

"Yes!" she wiggles in her seat, excitement taking over. "Let's reap some motherfuckers."

"Zander will accompany you. Looks like he needs the vacation time." I wink at his scowling face, "and I will train our newest pet in the art of defending himself." I grin at Pepe who looks on the brink of shitting himself.

"Oh, thank you, but I'm okay. I have God's protection on my side—"

"Let's go." I cut him off as I stand. "I don't have all day. Call your sister down, too," I tell Santos. "It wouldn't hurt for her to learn, as well."

I don't bother to listen to any other whining and bullshitting as I head off down to the basement and into our workout area. I'm tired from being cramped in that fucking car for two days, and even though sleep sounds like heaven, I need to make sure we're all prepared. This is it, the day me and the guys have been waiting for, taking down Mack Delaney and his empire of skin. He's been a slippery fucker over the years, and with Walton down, he's our last target.

I hear thundering on the stairs leading to the workout space and turn to see an excited looking Cara in yoga pants and a t-shirt.

"Let's kick some fucking ass!"

"It would've been good for you to have that mentality seven years ago when you were abducted," I point out.

"I was a kid."

"And?" I lift a brow.

"I always thought my brother and father would protect me, and now I know how wrong I was. I'm ready to learn, sensei." She folds her hands under her chin and bows.

Fuck, she really is like her brother.

"Where's your intended?" I smirk.

"We're not getting married." Her fists land on her hips. "I just wanted to get laid."

I snort at her admission just as a skulking Pepe slowly comes down the stairs. His head is down, and his shoulders slumped at the prospect of having to learn how to fight. Then, I watch with shock as Cara leaps out in front of him, punching him square on the forehead, making his head snap up, and swiftly kicking him in the dick, making him tumble down the rest of the stairs with a garbled cry.

"Was that good?" She bounces on the balls of her feet, waiting for my praise.

"Actually, yeah." I nod, and she squeals as she rushes over to me.

We watch as Pepe struggles to stand, his fist gripping his cock, and his face green. "I really don't want to do this."

"Oh, knock it off, you pussy." Cara grins at him. "Come play with me, and later I'll kiss all your boo-boos."

Pepe perks up at the prospect of getting his dick sucked and hobbles over to us.

"What would Jesus think of you right now?" I tsk at him with a grin.

"Jesus would bless him." Cara nods. "All men love a good dick sucking."

"Blasphemy!" Pepe exclaims.

I'm in for a long ass day with Santos junior and the altar boy.

## Selene

I missed walking these streets with my trench flowing around my calves and my knife tucked into my belt. This has been my life since I was fourteen, and I'm glad to be back. I'm heading toward a strip club which the Diablos frequent called The Temple. The owner, Carl, knows Blaze well, and he let him know about a few Diablos who happen to be there now.

I get to The Temple and quickly look over my shoulder, seeing

Zander not too far behind. He's not coming inside, but he'll meet up with me when I lure my prey from this place. I walk inside and look around. The ambiance is sultry with smoke obscuring features, and the dim lights giving off a romantic glow.

I find the bar to my left and head that way, sliding up onto a stool. A monster of a man comes forward and leans on the bar, giving me a slow once over. "You look like you should be up on stage, not down here with the rest of us scum."

"Thanks." I give him a wide grin. "I'll take a whiskey on the rocks, hold the roofie."

"That's it from our Queenie," the MC croons into the mic. "Up next we have Tiny!"

I turn in time to watch a voluptuous woman saunter onto the stage, her long, light-brown hair swaying behind her, hitting just above her ass. She's wearing a metal chain dress and nothing underneath, save for a g-string. She grabs onto the pole and hoists herself up, twirling around it in a gleaming swirl of metal on metal.

I hear the glass settle on the bar behind me, but I can't take my eyes off the feminine display in front of me.

"Tiny can work that pole like no other," the bartender comments behind me. "We did have a stunner here before. Her name was Tempest. You would've loved her, too."

"Is Carl around?" I finally drag my eyes from the beauty on the stage. "I'm here to see him."

"Are you sure you're not applying for a job?" He winks.

"No, I've come here to kill someone, and you're looking to get yourself added to the list."

He laughs heartily, and when I don't join in, he swallows thickly with a nod, disappearing into a door. *Idiot men.*

A well-groomed, middle-aged man comes out of the door with the bartender trailing behind him. He comes to stand in front of me, giving me a skeptical once over.

"You're here for the Diablos?"

I give him a nod and sip my drink. "Yes, point them out."

I get another look, but finally he discreetly points to my left. I turn my head and see two rough-looking guys sitting at a table, drooling over Tiny on the stage. I can't even fault them for it.

"Thanks," I nod. "Blaze said he would be by with payment."

I down the rest of my drink and slap a twenty on the bar. I keep my eyes on the two men I'll be dealing with, trying to keep my anticipation tempered, and make my way over to them. They're so engrossed in Tiny; they don't even notice I've slipped into a chair at their table until I've cleared my throat.

"Who are you?" one of them asks, completely taken off guard by my sudden appearance.

"My name is Candy, and the owner suggested I come over to keep you guys company." I undo my trench, showing the lace lingerie I'm wearing underneath.

"Carl?" The other looks toward the bar, raising his hand. "That guy is fucking bomb."

"What are your names?" I ask as I lean on the table.

"I'm Joe and this is Tommy," the first introduces us, and I run my finger along the rim of his glass.

"I hear you guys are real gangsters." I widen my eyes. "You don't understand how hot that makes me."

"Really?" Tommy leans forward. He's huskier than Joe, with black hair and dark eyes. He has a gorgeous smile and plush lips. He's a looker.

"Yes." I make my voice breathy, and let my fingers skim down over my chest, disappearing under the table, and between my legs.

"Sounds like she wants to have a party, Tommy." Joe leers across at me. He's not so pretty, actually, he looks a bit like a meth-head, skinny with greasy brown hair, and dull brown eyes.

"Can we?" I perk up. I look around while biting my lip. "It can't be in here; the things I want to do to you both are illegal." I give them a wink.

"Are you taking us back to your place?" Joe licks his thin lips.

"I don't think I can wait that long," I moan as I continue to play with myself. "I need your fat cocks in me now."

"Fuck," Joe stands abruptly, his chair tipping over. "Let's get out of here."

Tommy nods, standing quickly as well. "There's an alley to the side of this place. Real dark and private."

*Like stealing candy from a baby.*

"That's perfect," I nod as I stand, letting them have a full look at what I have on, including my fancy metal belt, then do up my trench.

"Fuck, you are so hot. I can't wait to destroy that pussy," Tommy mutters as he leads us out of the bar, Joe trailing behind us. All these men claiming they can destroy pussy are fucking pathetic. We can birth a whole ass human from that hole, there's no dick too big, bunch of fucking losers.

We get outside and quickly make a beeline for the alley, and they are right. It is dark and private. Only I know someone else is in here with us, and I want to give him a bit of a show before I have all my fun.

"Who's eating me first?" I throw open my trench and prop my foot against the wall behind me, spreading my legs wide. My lingerie is crotchless, and regardless of how dark it is, I know they can see my pussy right there for the taking.

Tommy drops to his knees first, his face coming in close as he groans loudly, "Fuck Joe, she smells so good."

"Hurry up, asshole," Joe sneers. "I want my turn." He undoes his pants and pulls out his dick. It's not bad for a skinny fuck lacking in nutrients. He begins to pump it in his hand, groaning as Tommy sinks his tongue into my folds.

He knows how to use his mouth, and I almost forget what I'm here to do as I drop my head to the brick behind me. I hear a soft throat clearing and know it's Zander. He's probably fuming. My head comes up, but it looks like both men are too absorbed with my pussy to have heard it.

I grab the handle of my knife and slip it from my belt, the metal scraping has Tommy pulling back from my pussy. He looks up just as I stab it into the side of his throat; the blood spraying onto me and Joe's dick, giving him some much-needed lube. Not that he appreciates it as he begins to scream, dropping his dick in the process. *What a waste.*

I pull my knife out and kick Tommy onto his back, his gurgling death noises masking Zander's footsteps as he comes up behind Joe, wrapping his arm around his neck.

"We need you to get a message back to your leader, Mack," he says as I clean my knife off onto Tommy's shirt. "Tell him the Reaper Incarnate is looking for him, and she has something that belongs to him."

I begin to hum as I swipe up some of Tommy's blood and begin to paint the scythe on his forehead. Fuck, I really missed this.

"Put your dick away, Joe," I tsk as I look up into his frightened face. "Do you think your meth-damaged brain can remember the message, or should we just kill you as well?"

"I got it," he stammers out as Zander shoves him forward.

"Hurry," I wave him off, "or else I may just chase you; I love to chase."

He runs off out of the alley just as I finish my finger painting, and I sit back on my hunches to admire the artwork.

"You were enjoying that a little too much," Zander growls.

"A lot actually," I agree, and look up at him. "I expect you to finish what he started." I stand and lean against the wall, using the same pose I did for Tommy.

"There's blood on the ground." He points to the growing puddle.

"And?" I pop a brow, and he rolls his eyes, falling to his knees. "Don't forget my ass. She's been wanting some love, too."

His eyes shine with a bit of anger mixed with a lot of lust as he grabs my waist and spins me around, my chest colliding with the rough brick. I grab the bottom of my trench, hanging it over my arm as my pussy clenches in anticipation. Then he surprises me by grabbing the crotchless portion of my lingerie and ripping a bigger hole up the back. He spreads my ass cheeks, and his tongue begins to work my asshole, sinking deep inside.

"Fuck," I moan. My forehead hits the brick. His fingers begin to work my clit, and then three sink into my pussy as he stands.

"That's a good idea," he says into my ear. "I'm going to fuck this tight ass."

I look over my shoulder and watch him spit into his palm, dragging it along his length. He spreads me back open and begins to sink into my ass, chuckling when I begin to cry out. It burns, and it's almost painful, but when he begins to finger-fuck my pussy at the same time, I feel the beginnings of an orgasm.

"You love your ass being fucked, huh?" he snickers into my ear.

"Yes," I nod and turn to look at him over my shoulder, "and that makes the both of us, baby Walton."

## *Santos*

My sister is a fast-fucking learner. She took on anything Blaze threw at her. But, Pepe? Not so much. He spent more time praying and picking himself up from the floor than inflicting damage. Pretty sure he was looking forward to Cara kissing his boo-boos better like she promised, because every time she laid him out like she was training for the UFC, he got this stupid smile on his face.

"You didn't even try to defend yourself!" Cara whines, kissing the bruise that's forming on his cheek.

"I wasn't going to hurt you," he scoffs. "I'm not like that."

"You're a little bitch."

"Confirmed," he nods, eyeing me warily as she keeps fussing over him. It's kind of cute, I can't lie.

"You know I'm going to hang a massive photo of your wedding day on my wall, right? You're so cute," I smirk, ignoring the filthy glance Cara gives me. I don't care if she doesn't want to get married. They need each other. Well, Pepe needs her to keep him safe. I can't be there all the time to watch him, but that's beside the point.

Pepe clears his throat, his eyes remaining on Cara. "I bet she'd look beautiful, too."

Cara grins, her expression softening as she looks at him. "You think?"

"I know you would. You're gorgeous," he shrugs like it's no big deal, a yelp coming from him as she knocks him back and kisses the hell out of him. Darius grins from the doorway, watching the scene unfold, but Blaze rolls his eyes like the grumpy fucker he is.

"Is it weird this is making my dick hard?" I ask, earning a scowl from Blaze.

"Yes, it's fucking weird. She's your sister."

"They're just so cute! Ugh, when will my baby girl be back? I need to sink myself in her so bad right now," I groan, rubbing my dick through my pants, stumbling when Blaze shoves me.

"You're disgusting. Go dick your boyfriend if you're horny."

"Right here?" I tease, moving to unzip my jeans, but Blaze grabs the front of my shirt and hauls me closer, his angry eyes burning into me.

"No. Keep your dick away. You'll poke someone's eye out with it otherwise," he growls, making me cackle.

"Says the man with the python in his pants! You're restraining the hulk behind that zipper!"

"You're lucky I'm not into guys, San. Because nothing would make me happier than shoving it down your throat and choking you until the light left your crazy fucking eyes," he sneers, letting me go with a scowl when I moan.

"Oh, please, Daddy. Choke me."

"You're one sick little fucker."

"I know you are, you said you are, so what am I?" I sing-song, his eyes flashing with irritation.

"Real mature."

"You love me."

"Someone fucking has to," he grunts as he leaves the room, giving Darius the side-eye. "Tag, you're it."

"We're playing tag?!" I beam, but Blaze keeps walking, throwing his answer over his broad shoulder.

"No. Darius is on Santos duty, that's all. I've had enough for one day." *Asshole*.

Pepe's blushing like mad when I finally look at him again, Cara still kissing his face and arms as if he'll die without the affection. Like I said, they're so cute. I can't wait to be an uncle.

"Santos! I'm not having kids any time soon!" Cara snaps, confusing me.

"I said that out loud?"

"Yes!"

"Oops! That conversation wasn't for you. Pretend you didn't hear it!" I reply, glancing up at Darius, who's chuckling at us. "I say we knock Selene up. I bet being a dad's cooler than being an uncle."

"I think that suggestion would get you killed," he grins. "But totally. I say we bet on who manages it first."

"I might put my money on Blaze. Her womb would be too scared to say no to him," I laugh, ordering Cara and Pepe to shower before Darius and I head out of the kitchen. Blaze looks relaxed, which doesn't happen often, and I can't help but taunt him some more.

I throw myself across his lap on the couch, wiggling my ass in the air. "I've been a bad boy, Daddy Blaze. Spank me."

"I'm close to shoving a gun up your ass and firing, San. Don't push me," he grunts, trying to shove me off, but I hold tight.

"Kinky! Which gun would you use? The big one? Oh! Where's my machine gun?!"

"You mean *my* machine gun?" he snorts. "You're not touching it again. Darius, get him the fuck off me before you lose him."

I smirk over my shoulder at Darius. "Don't worry, babe! I won't leave you for him, despite his good looks and obvious charm!"

Darius sniggers, but my eyes flash to the front door as Selene and Zander walk in. Blood splattered on both of them. Zander's knees are covered in blood, and by the way Selene's smiling right now, I know just what happened. Lucky bastard.

"Baby!" I shout as I scramble off Blaze's lap and dive at Selene, kissing her hard as I hold her body to mine. She smells like death and vengeance. Well, like blood, which is the same thing. My sexy little Reaper.

She grins, running her hands through my hair. "Hey, San. Have you been good for Daddy Blaze?"

"Stop fucking calling me that!" Blaze barks, but he kisses her cheek on his way past to grab a beer, apparently not too angry.

"I was *super* good!" I wink. "But now I'm fucking horny. I mean, look at you! You're a walking wet dream, baby girl."

She swoons, leaning into me, and giving me a light kiss. "You're always horny, but thanks."

"So, what now?" Darius asks, hauling Selene from my arms and dragging her to the couch. She looks so pretty on his lap.

"Now, we wait," Zander shrugs, sitting down and taking a beer from Blaze as he returns.

"I say you give us a play-by-play of what you two have been up to. I'm jealous, whatever it is. Did you fuck on their corpse? Oh! Did you fuck their asses, Zan? Next time can I watch? If that's a kink, I want it. Dead-body-ass-fucking show!"

"I didn't fuck anyone's ass." He rolls his eyes, then stops to grin at Selene. "Well, I didn't fuck the Diablos' asses, anyway."

I fucking love story time.

Where's my popcorn?

# Chapter Eleven

## *Zander*

It takes a few days, but we do receive a message from the Diablos, and it's one that comes from Mack himself. I know how he operates, and he knows that I do. He and my father were close, and I know every single one of his signature moves. So, when a car explodes just outside our gates, I know it's his message, and I know just what he's conveying.

"We have to hand Pepe over or be prepared." I tell them as we sit around the kitchen table. We just finished dealing with the cops and after a few hours of hard questions, they reluctantly left, not at all buying that we know nothing.

"For what?" Cara asks.

"War." I shrug.

"How would he get to us?" she asks.

"Every time we need to leave, they'll be waiting," Blaze intercepts. "I remember the time he used a drone to fly a bomb into someone's house."

"Yeah." I nod. "He's not as dumb as he looks."

"He won't be making the same mistakes twice. He won't capture hostages anymore," Darius joins in. "Selene got away and left a house of body parts for him to find."

"It'll be a  kill on sight order." I nod.

"Do we have enough time to do this last kill?" Selene grins, her eyes looking unhinged.

I shrug. It's going to happen, anyway.

Pepe told us about the guy who lives near the harbor. He brings in girls from Manhattan and hides them in cargo containers until Mack picks them up. These girls aren't junkies off the street or prostitutes. They're taken from elite prep schools or locked inside Ubers on their way to upscale parties. Selene wants to take him out to send another message to Mack. No more high-end virgin girls to auction off.

"This time I'm coming with you." Santos grins, and my stomach flips.

"Is that a good idea?" I ask. "No offense, but you both need to be supervised."

"We've killed together before." Selene winks at Santos.

"In the back of that limo," he nods, "I want a repeat."

I know what they're referring to, so I leave them to eye-fuck each other and grab Blaze's laptop. I hack into the city's traffic cams and bring up the one nearest to the harbor drop-off. We all know it well; we've watched these runs plenty of times when Henry thought we were there to help. It's the end of the month and around the time a drop off is done. Pepe also confirmed Mack was waiting for that container before making another trip to Nevada. The Highway Knights buy them to auction off to the MC members to do as they wish with them. Selene told us Jan spent a month at the Knight's compound, being abused constantly, and that's how Papi found her.

"Let's call Loqi and see if he's heard anything about a shipment for the Knights." I look at Santos.

"My brother probably has a mole in the Knight's compound. I know over the years my father has caught many of theirs in Dientes compound. It's how they operate. You can never be too sure if a prospect is a genuine person or a spy," Cara chimes in.

"Fine, I'll call the asshole." Santos pulls his phone from his pocket. Once he's dialed the number, he turns on the speaker and places it in the center of the table.

"Is Cara okay?" Loqi asks as soon as he picks up, causing his sister to roll her eyes.

"Of course I am," she sneers. "I'm being looked after properly."

"Okay," Loqi sounds a bit defeated. "That's good. I will try to get up there to see you soon. We've been a bit tied up here."

She shrugs, completely unaffected by her brother trying to make an effort and leans back in her chair, the silence hanging heavy around us.

"Hello?" Loqi calls into the phone, and Santos clears his throat.

"Hey."

"Santos, what's up, *hermano*?" Loqi asks.

I can see the slight change in Santos' demeanor with Loqi calling him brother. "We're closing in on Mack up here, but I was wondering, have you heard about any monthly shipments headed for the Knights?"

"Yeah, we have a guy in there who feeds us info. The shipment is already on its way. It'll be here in a few days. Why?"

"Fuck," I growl. "We need to intercept that transport."

"Those shipments are moved like armored trucks. There's no intercepting it. Why? Is there someone on it who you know?"

"No, we're trying to flush Mack out, and we figured the best way would be to fuck up his shipment before he got his hands on it."

"I see," Loqi hums. "We don't usually get involved in those until the girls have been discarded. It's too risky. But let me see what I can find out, and if we go forward on intercepting, be prepared for a bloodbath."

"Is there any other way to bathe?" Santos snickers, and his brother chuckles.

"Not in this life, *hermano*."

The phone call ends, and Selene huffs from her seat. "Does this mean I don't get to kill the guy at the harbor?"

"You can kill whoever you want." Santos grins at her.

"You're with me tonight." She snaps her fingers.

"Hopefully, it catches Mack's attention." I tap my fingers to my chin.

"I have his phone number." Pepe straightens. "Maybe you could send him a detailed video?"

I fucking knew this kid would come in handy. "Good idea."

I've pulled up everything I could find on Christos Alexopoulos. His parents immigrated here from Greece, bringing their small overseas shipping company with them. Over the years, it's expanded into a large corporation, with Christos at its head.

He's a model citizen—as most of them are—with his foundations and charities. Tonight, he's holding a charity gala at the Ritz Carlton to raise money for children with terminal cancer, and I've purchased two plates at twenty thousand a pop. It's all worth it to see the excitement on Selene's face, and not to mention how her body looks in a red silk cocktail gown. Her hair is swept up into an intricate updo, with pieces curling down around her face, and her makeup is subtle, but those lips shine a bright red.

"You're gorgeous," I breathe as I haul her into my body.

"I can't wear my belt." She pouts.

"That's why you have me with you." Santos comes to stand beside her, looking dapper in an all-black three-piece-suit. His black, curly hair is brushed back over his head and gleaming with gel.

Selene is soaking him in like he's a tall glass of water on the hottest day, her mouth hanging open. I have to agree with her. He's never looked this put-together.

"Doesn't he look handsome?" Darius comes up behind him and kisses his neck. He reaches beyond Santos and grabs Selene's arm, pulling her from me and into Santos.

"Yes." Selene smiles, finally finding her voice. "It's nice now and then, but I still love my boy rough around the edges." She kisses Santos softly, then kisses Darius over his shoulder.

"Let's run over the details before you three leave." I motion for us to sit on the couch.

Darius is their chauffeur tonight, and we've packed the rental with a few necessary things for tonight to go smoothly.

"We go in for dinner." Selene looks at Santos, who's rubbing his hands together.

"I can't wait for some filet mignon." He grins. "Extra bloody."

"I can't wait to kill this guy." Selene wiggles in her seat.

"At least his blood will be disguised by that dress." I grin. "Run through what will happen after dinner."

"I will find Christos and ask him to have a drink with me." Selene grins. "Maybe flirt a little, and then act drunk, letting it slip how badly I want to fuck him in my limo."

"I'll leave right after dinner, and wait for them in the limo," Santos adds.

"We'll knock him out and bring him back to his port at the harbor," Darius tags on.

"And then the real fun begins." Selene nods, her teeth gleaming a bright white against the red of her lips.

## Selene

Dinner is finished, and I'm still fucking starving. There were about a hundred different courses, and each plate had portions that wouldn't fill a toddler. These rich people are fucking ridiculous.

I watch as Santos leaves the banquet room, his tight ass bulging with each step. I have to find a way to get him into suit pants more often. Once he's out of sight, I get up out of my seat and head over to the small group of men enjoying crystal tumblers of amber liquid. They look important and they must be if Christos is in the center of them. Maybe he's trying to entice them to join his lucrative skin export business.

I saunter up and lean against the bar, waiting to be noticed. It doesn't take long because most men love tits and the color red.

"Johnny," a man calls out from the group beside me, I don't look to find out which one. "Get this beautiful lady a drink. We mustn't keep her waiting."

"Yes, sir." The bartender hurries over.

I look over my shoulder and find all four of the men looking at me with predatory smiles. I want to give them one of my own, but I swallow down the urge. Instead, I give them what I'm hoping looks like a timid uptick of my lips. "Thank you," I say softly.

"What can I get you, miss?" the bartender asks. I'd kill for a fucking whiskey, but I'm supposed to be a gentile lady.

"A glass of champagne, please," I answer softly, my voice barely above a whisper.

I feel the heat of a body moving in closely behind me, and I once again have to tamper down the urge to turn around and deck a bitch.

"Which company are you from?" I turn slowly at the sound of his voice and come face to face with Christos himself. He's handsome in an older gentlemanly way. He sort of reminds me of Henry Walton, only more refined.

"I'm here for a friend who couldn't make it this year." I bleed sadness into my tone, just as Zander told me to do.

Christos' blue eyes crinkle around the edges and curiosity shines from his dark olive complexion. He tips his head, and his dark hair slips a bit out of place. "Who might I ask is your friend?"

"Was." I drop my gaze from him, making sure to put a slight tremble in my bottom lip. "Henry Walton."

"Henry was your friend?" He sounds skeptical and he should. That old fucker didn't have friends, only whores and business associates.

"We were … um…" I look around for effect. "Intimate friends."

"Oh, I see." He nods and gives me a once-over. "It's sad what happened to him."

"I was told it was a break in," I sniff and let my eyes water, "but I can't believe it just doesn't add up."

I turn back to the bar and find my champagne glass, tipping it back and drinking it all down in one gulp. I sniff again and lift my hand to the bartender; I'm using my so-called grief to pretend to get myself drunk.

I look at Christos over my shoulder and find him studying my ass. "Sorry. I just get so worked up whenever I think about it."

"I understand." His eyes are darker now as he begins to see me in a different light. "How long did you *know* Henry?"

"Two years." I suck back the next glass and set it on the bar. "I shouldn't have done that." I stumble a bit and right myself with a hand to his chest. "I've never been able to hold my alcohol." I hold a hand to my stomach.

"Do you need me to call you a car?" He places his hand on my shoulder, the fingers gliding over my skin.

"My car is outside. But thank you, mister?"

"My name is Christos Alexopoulos." He smiles, and I let my eyes widen with false shock.

"Oh, my!" I hold my hand to my mouth. "I'm so sorry. I had no idea. I must look so foolish."

"On the contrary, Henry was a good friend of mine as well. How about I walk you to your car, miss?"

"Oh, I couldn't ask you to leave your own gala." I give him my best seductive eyes. "I may not let you return. My name is Selene."

"Is that right?" He grins, his hand slowly making its way down my arm. "I think I could disappear for an hour and make it back in time for my speech."

*Nope, the only speech you'll be making will be to my knife as I cut you open.*

I bite into my bottom lip and look him over slowly, letting my desire saturate the air around us. "Okay," I whisper.

He leads me out of the gala, leaving behind his snickering friends, and places his hand on my lower back.

"I see a tattoo peeking out above your dress." His fingers skate along the top of my shoulder blades. "What is it?"

"Let's get to my limo and I'll show you." I grin at him over my shoulder.

I can't wait to show him just what that tattoo means.

"What about your date? Did you come alone?" he asks as I take out my phone to text Darius.

"He came for the food; I haven't been able to replace Henry." I give him a sad, wide-eyed look.

He hums his reply, and the hand that's resting on my lower back slips down farther over my ass. We step out from the hotel entrance, and I see my limo idling there. I step down the first stair when Christos grips the nape of my neck in a tight hold.

"Did you think I was fucking stupid, whore?" The pure venom in his words tells me he didn't buy my act.

"You're hurting me," I whine. "What are you doing?"

"Henry never entertained anyone for longer than a few nights." He halts our descent down the stairs, his fingers biting into the column of my throat. "He was a very close friend of mine."

"Couldn't have been too close," I try to continue to play my part. "He was with me for two years." I hate that I didn't wear an outfit that matched my belt.

"Wave your driver off and come with me," he demands. I wave

Darius off, throwing a grin to his window, knowing he's watching me. He won't let me out of his sights.

"Where are you taking me?" My voice shakes, and I congratulate myself. Acting scared is not easy.

He leads me to a white limo parked in the lot, and taps on the roof, his hand still firmly around my neck. It's really starting to ache, and I'm about five seconds from jabbing him in the eyes. The driver gets out and comes around to open the door for us.

"You couldn't open your own door?" I sneer, unable to control myself.

He shoves me inside, and I fall across the seat, cursing when my six-inch heel twists my ankle in an awkward position. I reach down to undo the buckle as he gets in the seat beside me. The door shuts, and I settle back in my seat, not in the least bit worried.

"Where are you taking me?" I ask him. "Or are we doing this right here?"

He gives me a strange look. "I'm going to dispose of you."

"Why would you want to do that?" I huff. "I'm nothing but a simple whore."

He yanks me around so my back is to him and unzips my dress in the back. So, he wants to fuck, then dispose.

"Ah," he chuckles. "There it is. The Reaper Incarnate." My heart stills. "Did you think our circle doesn't know about you? We know you were the one who killed Henry. I saw the top of your scythe tattoo while you were at the bar."

Fuck.

"And?" I sneer over my shoulder. "You're not even the slightest bit afraid?"

"No!" he hollers out a laugh as the car pulls out into traffic. "I'll have you disposed of and back in time to make my speech. You're really that cocky to show up to this thing without backup?"

"I'm the Reaper Incarnate." I give him a large grin. "Why would I need backup? You heard about what happened to Henry, so why aren't you scared?"

His fist collides with my cheek, and I immediately see stars. "That wasn't nice," I tsk. "Where are we going?"

He ignores me as he types something on his phone, and I turn to look out the window. I hope Darius is following us, since he has the weapon stash. We head to the harbor, and I bite into my cheek to hold my scowl in place. He's falling into our trap, even though this isn't going as planned.

"Are you going to drown me?" I snicker.

"No, I'm going to slit your throat and leave you in a shipping container. Your body won't be discovered for months while you're out at sea."

"That's cool. I've always wanted to take a cruise." I smile sweetly.

"Oh, yeah?" He laughs, "While you're dead?"

"It's all an adventure, am I right? Life, death." I wave my hand over my head. "And I'll meet back up with my lover, Henry. I'll give him one final pegging while we wait at the gates of Hell."

He screws up his face in disgust.

"His son tends to like a good pegging, too," I say as we pull into the pier. "Must be something in the genes."

"You're working with Zander Walton?"

"Working? Oh no, he's my boyfriend." I wiggle my foot in my unbuckled shoe. "He helped me take down Henry, and you're just a stepping-stone on our way to Mack Delaney."

"Then why the fuck did he let you come here alone?" he asks as I cross my leg over my knee.

"Who says I'm alone?" At my words, he turns his head to look out of the window, and I grab my dangling shoe, striking the thin stiletto into his cheek. It sinks through the delicate flesh, and the car slams to a halt at the sound of Christos' screams.

I hear tires squealing behind us over Christos' squawking, and then gunfire. I grab the stiletto out of his cheek, and the blood begins to gush down over his suit.

"Oh no, how will you make a speech looking like the Bride of Chucky?" I put my bloody shoe back on and open the door, finding the driver's dead body lying on the asphalt. "Oh, look." I point to the body, "maybe we'll send him on a cruise instead?"

I get out of the limo and step over the body, turning to see two of my men striding toward me. This is like the part of an action movie where the good guys are walking in slow motion, guns in their hands, and sadistic grins on their faces. I practically moan at how gorgeous they are.

"Is my baby okay?" Santos gets to me first, hauling me into his chest.

"Yep." I look over my shoulder as Darius yanks Christos out of the limo. "That man promised me a cruise and I don't think he'll be able to keep up his end of the bargain." I pout up into Santos' face.

"We'll go on a fucking world cruise once we take out these motherfuckers." He grins down at me, and I swoon.

"Selene," Darius calls out as he holds onto a struggling Christos. "What did you jab through his face?"

"My heel." I lift my foot to show him the evidence. "Whose face has my shoe been stuck in?" I begin to sing along to the tune of a Shania Twain song as I walk toward Darius and Christos.

Santos chuckles behind me and hums along. I stand in front of the sack of shit and slap him hard on the cheek, my hand sticking to the blood there. Christos grunts through the pain, and Darius groans.

"Fuck, I just want to sink my cock so deep into you right now."

"Why don't you guys head out?" Santos stabs his finger through the hole in Christos' cheek, laughing when the man screams. "You two have yet to pound each other alone." He gives me a wink, "don't break him, I want my turn when I get back."

Darius groans again and pushes Christos into Santos' arms. "Make sure you put the scythe on him, baby," I kiss his cheek. "We're all the Reaper Incarnate now."

## Santos

My dick's so fucking hard right now, it hurts. Between being left to torture this piece of shit, and knowing Selene and Darius are off fucking each other's brains out, it's no wonder. They need some alone time, and let's face it, I don't need help to torture someone. I'm in my fucking element.

I drag Christos toward an empty shipping container, ignoring his grunts of protest. I always find it hilarious how these big, tough assholes show no mercy when abusing and trading women and children, but the moment they meet someone who can fight back? They cower and cry. Pussies.

"Let me go!" the pussy demands, his voice sharp but with a hint of fear. I take a deep breath in, reveling in the scent. "This all comes back to Mack. Go after him instead, you heathen!"

"Wait, you think I'm pissed at you over that? *Pfft*, I'm going to rip you apart for that awful excuse of a dinner. I'm feeling insulted, and I'm fucking starving. Sorry if it makes me a little moody," I grin, shoving him into the container and causing him to stumble, his body sprawling across the ground with a thud.

He scrambles to his feet and tries to lunge at me, but I shoot one of his kneecaps, dropping him back to the ground with a cry of pain. It's a shame Selene's not here. I would have bent her over his corpse when I finished and coated our skin in his blood to celebrate. Another time, I guess.

Christos is wailing like a baby, clasping his bloodied knee in his hands while tears track down his cheeks. Pathetic, really.

"You want me to stop?" I ask with fake confusion. "I bet all those women you kidnapped probably asked the same thing of you. Such a shame you didn't listen. An eye for an eye, and all that jazz."

I fire a shot into his other knee, stopping him from going too far if he tries to seize the opportunity. Two bad knees are better than one, in my eyes. His agonizing scream sends a shiver of pleasure down my spine. I smirk at him as I step closer, and he attempts to crawl away. "Uh, Uh. Where do you think you're going? Don't run off. I have to set up a little something for Mack, then we can get started!"

He's sniveling in the corner now, giving me time to turn and set my phone up against the opposite wall of the container. The lighting is awful, so I turn the phone light on, then turning my attention back to the little bitch I left on the floor. "So, in the words of my baby girl, do you want to play a game?"

"No! I'll cut Mack off! I'll never touch a woman again! Let me leave and I'll…"

I pull one of my blades from my belt, flicking it at him so it sinks into his shoulder with ease, his screams music to my ears. "Too little, too late. You should count yourself lucky it's not my girl in here with you. You've heard what she did to Henry, right? Or would you have preferred her methods over mine? I can call them to bring me a big dildo if you wish, no lube, of course," I murmur, stepping closer to yank my blade out of his flesh.

"No! Look, let's talk. Man to man. That little blonde cunt of yours just…"

I grab his throat and drag him to his feet, forcing him to stand on his damaged legs. "My little what? I didn't quite hear you. Now, I know you didn't just insult my baby girl. Would you like to repeat that?" I ask in a low voice, grinning when he cries out. I make him take his own weight, seconds before letting him go, and watch him crumble to the floor. Kneecaps are important when you want to stand, you know?

"Your crazy girlfriend must have gotten her facts wrong! I'm not even that involved in Mack's skin business!" he spits, anger filling his eyes.

I tut, my lips curving into a sadistic smirk. "But you admit you're involved? Besides, my girlfriend's not crazy, she's enthusiastic. You should see the way her pretty eyes light up when she kills someone. She…"

"But I…"

I sink another knife into him, not meeting his eyes. "Excuse me, Daddy's talking! Anyway, as I was saying before, I was so *rudely* interrupted. My girl's really enthusiastic about our cause. You see, this is personal to her. She's seriously fuckable when she gets wind of creeps like you. You don't even have to touch the women involved, but you're still involved. An accessory to the crime, if you may." Then I throw another knife at him, nailing him in the crotch. *Oops?*

He screams, his voice already rough. "What was that for?"

"I don't really like you, Christos. I also have a twitchy hand, so I have a tendency to throw things by accident. You know what? I have a fun game we can play. Take off your shoes."

"I can't, you psychopath! You blew out my knees!" he snaps. I shrug, reaching down to grasp his ankle firmly, bending his knee painfully to take his shoe off. His cries bounce off the confined walls, making me smile. I whistle, wanting to feel like my baby girl is beside me while I play. Her energy usually gets me going, and by the time I have both of his shoes off, I'm fired up and ready to go. Now the party's started.

I sit on the floor, tilting my head slightly as I pull pliers from my pocket. I'm more into stabbing people and calling it a day, but I want to change things up. I like being spontaneous.

I hold his ankle firmly in my hand, squeezing his big toenail between the tips of my pliers. "This little piggy went to market."

"No!" he screams, just as I yank and twist, ripping the toenail from the skin, blood flowing like art down his foot. I can't help but stare at it, the bright crimson drawing me in like a moth to a flame.

He tries to sit up and shove me away, but I pull one of the blades from him and plunge it into his unharmed shoulder. That should slow him down a little. I soak in his sounds of pain, going for the next toenail with a smile. "This little piggy stayed home. Silly piggy. That sounds boring."

He continues to scream through my nursery rhyme while I work. Starting over on his other foot. He's skin is covered in sweat, his feet bloodied, and his voice horse. This is only the warmup; I have no idea what he's crying about. I haven't even fucking started yet.

"Give me your hand," I ask nicely, scowling when he shakes his head. "Fine. But for the record, I tried to be nice."

I get to my feet and walk around him, grabbing his hand, flattening it on the cold ground. His fingers curl, trying to hide the nails, but I'm not going for those. I lift my foot and stomp down hard, hearing the magical sound of bones crunching from under the sole of my boot. He screams, blubbering and getting snot all over his face. It's disgusting.

I do it again, making sure to grind my foot in the process, drawing as much pain out as possible. I suddenly remember my sister, and anger takes over at knowing these pricks are the reason she was taken. I make quick work of his other hand, then I grab a knife and cut down the center of his shirt, exposing his chest and stomach.

"Please, stop! I'll tell you anything you want! Don't kill me!" Christos begs, halting my movements. I stare at him thoughtfully for a second, before grinning darkly.

"Don't you see? We already know everything. You're here as a message for Mack. He's next on our list, but you're just a little steppingstone in our path to get to him. You know, my sister was taken years ago. I didn't even know she existed, but I've found her and can't help but hold a grudge. She's family, and no one fucks with my family, *entiende*?" I move toward my phone, turning on the camera before squatting down beside the piece of shit. "Say hi to Mack."

When he stays quiet, I punch him swiftly in the ribs, pulling a groan from him. "I said, 'say hi to Mack.' I don't have all night, believe it or not."

"Mack! Help me!" he sobs, making me cackle.

"What, you think this is live? You'll be dead before he gets it. Right, Mack? You know the drill. Where should I start cutting? Maybe here?" I question myself out loud as I start dragging my knife through his flesh, ignoring his agony as I carve patterns. I start whistling again, getting lost in the sounds of pain and the smell of blood. I'm covered in it. I wish my baby girl were here so I could mark her body with my bloodied handprints, my knife leaving scars across her perfectly imperfect skin.

I snap out of it when Christos makes a wheezing noise, my eyes going wide. "Oops! I got a little carried away. Hold tight, I'm not done yet."

He doesn't answer me, his body weak from the blood loss, and I can't help myself as I stand and start kicking his ribs until blood flies from his lips. I've punctured something with his broken ribs, most likely his lung. The more he wheezes, the harder my dick gets. I can't wait to watch the light leave his eyes so I can get out of here and sink myself into my lovers.

I set to work, drawing Selene's famous scythe on his forehead, chuckling as I add, *The Reaper was here*, down his one arm that's not as bloody as the other. Now he looks good and ready to meet his maker.

"Hey, Mack?" I grin into the camera, holding it close to my face as Christos makes one final, wet choking sound behind me. "We're coming for you. Enjoy this little gift, courtesy of the Reaper Incarnate. If you keep hiding like a little bitch, I'll have to play with Pepe. You know, your son? I've taken quite a shine to him. I might even fuck the Jesus right out of him before letting him bleed out. We'll be seeing you soon," then I wink for the fun of it and show him the mess I made of Christos again before ending the video, grinning as I send it.

Of course, I'd never hurt my Pepe, but Mack doesn't know that.

I grab all my toys, wiping them off on Christos' shirt, then I leave him in the container for Mack to find. I head toward his car, whistling to myself as I go, looking forward to getting home to my family.

## *Darius*

I don't even get in the front door before Selene attacks my mouth with hers, almost making me trip. Her teeth nip at my lip sharply, while her hands yank at my shirt, demanding I take it off. Someone chuckles, drawing our attention as we stumble through the door, my shirt on the floor and my pants undone.

"Good night?" Zander smirks, eyeing Selene as she shamelessly pulls her dress off, not caring that we have an audience. Pepe sputters from the couch, and Cara scowls at him, muttering under her breath about getting a spoon and carving his eyes out.

"Yep, Santos will be back soon," I reply, Selene's lips crashing into mine again as she starts pushing me backwards toward the hallway.

"Wait, you left him alone?" Blaze barks, and Selene pulls back from me with a huff, her hands going to her hips.

"He's fine. He needs to let out some demons, and I needed to fuck Darius. What's the issue?"

"What if someone followed you? Or someone catches him? Stop thinking with your pussy!"

She stalks over to him and jabs a finger into his chest, glaring up at him with defiance. "Santos told us to head back, and we scoped out the place properly, double checking on our way out. Let him play."

"How about I fucking spank you?" he grits out, her eyes gleaming with heat.

"Later, Daddy. I have a date with Darius. You get in line."

He goes to argue with her, but I grab her hand and haul her toward the hallway, shutting us in my room and shoving her toward the bed. She looks perfect, laid out across my blankets, her hair fanning around her and making her look like the goddess she is.

I kick my pants off, my boxers flying with them, and then I'm on her. She moans into my mouth as I grind against her, my hands grabbing hers to yank them above her head, pushing her delicious tits up more. She mewls, the soft sound sending electricity down my spine. I pull back and leave her in nothing but her fuck-me heels, an idea popping into my head suddenly.

"Trust me?"

"With my life," she says at once, licking her lips in anticipation.

"I have a surprise for you," I smirk, climbing from the bed and rummaging in the closet until I find what I've been looking for. The metal chains clank as I pull them out, her eyes widening.

"I was looking for those!"

"Well, I wanted to hide them in case Blaze got any ideas of throwing them away. You look so pretty when you're tied up at my mercy," I growl, heading toward her and closing one of the metal cuffs around her wrist.

"I'm supposed to be in charge!" she whines, but she doesn't

attempt to pull her hands away, telling me she likes being dominated by me. It's strange not having Santos beside me, murmuring curses about her stunning body, and I know he'll barge in the moment he's home, so I have to work fast.

Once she's secure, I don't hesitate to push her thighs apart with my shoulders and go to town on her pussy with my mouth. I don't want to restrain her legs, loving how they clench around my head. If she suffocates me with her pussy, I'll die a happy man.

The chains rattle as she tries to touch me, an annoyed huff coming from her. Surprisingly, she doesn't voice it, letting me take full control from her, knowing I'll have her screaming for the heavens in no time.

I run a finger through her dampness as I suck at her clit, moving my finger down until it reaches her tight ass, her breath hitching a fraction as I toy with her. It doesn't take long for her to get impatient.

"Hurry up and fuck me!"

I chuckle, not changing pace until I'm suddenly pushing my finger into her ass, her back arching off the bed. "Oh, fuck!"

I push it in and out of her faster, my tongue worshipping her clit until her thighs tighten around my head, almost crushing my skull. She comes loudly, and I have to press my free arm across her stomach to keep her on the bed. I don't let up, my name sounding too good coming from her lips as she screams.

I finally ease off, letting her recover for a moment before I climb up her body and kiss her. The chains rattle again, making me grin as I stare into her eyes. "We're only just getting started, baby."

"I'd like my hands back now," she pants. "I want to touch you."

"Nope," I reply, popping the *P* and kissing down her neck, biting her hard. She groans loudly, her legs wrapping tight around my waist.

"Even if I say please instead of '*get fucked*'?"

"I'm not letting you go. Ever," I murmur, her eyes narrowing. It's fun winding her up, and it gets my dick hard. Obviously, I'll untie her when I am finished ravishing her, but not yet.

I lift one of her legs over my shoulder, aligning my painfully hard dick against her soaked pussy, not giving her any warning before slamming home. Her eyes squeeze shut as she screams, her fists bunching since she can't do anything else with them, and I growl.

"Eyes on me, baby."

They fly open, holding mine as I lean farther over her and piston hard into her, her tits bouncing against my chest, her hard nipples dragging across my skin. She feels like home, just like Santos, and I know I won't last long if I don't slow down.

"You look so perfect chained up," I groan, slowing enough to lean down and take one of her pert nipples in my mouth. She gasps, trying to pull her hands out of the metal cuffs by force, and I wonder if she'll break her hands trying to get to me. Knowing she'll hurt herself in order to touch me causes a primal growl to burn in my chest, and I slam into her as hard and deep as I can.

It sends her into a sudden climax, and she almost deafens me with her screams, urging me on as I fuck her through it. Her body's quivering under mine, completely spent, but I know she can still walk. We can't have that.

I pull out and flip her over, her wrists twisting awkwardly, and I lift her to her knees. My eyes roam over the reaper tattoo down her back, and I run my fingers over the dark ink, mesmerized by her beauty. She's turned all four of us into sappy pricks, and I have zero problems with that. Being alone with her makes me realize how serious this is. I mean, I've always been serious about her, but Santos isn't here to banter with. We aren't playing games. It's just Selene and I getting lost in each other, and it feels so fucking right.

I fist her long blonde hair, yanking her head back sharply as I sink myself into her pussy from behind, her arms straining from the chains. "Fuck, I love you."

She's quiet for a moment, but she answers when I start thrusting in and out.

"I love you too, D. So fucking much."

"Brace yourself," I warn. "This will be hard and fast."

She grunts a response, but I don't pay much attention. I keep her hair tight in my fist and fuck her hard, the headboard slamming against the wall, letting everyone know what we're doing. I'd be concerned about their hearing if they weren't already aware, but that isn't the point.

She's screaming my name within minutes, her body convulsing around me as I yank her back sharply by the hair, fucking into her and drawing her body back to mine, my sweaty chest plastered to her back. I reach around and tease her clit, wanting to pull one more orgasm from her before I bust myself.

"I can't!" she moans. "It's too much!"

"Fucking come for me!" I snap, hardly recognizing my own voice. When the fuck did I channel Blaze? Oh well, it works for me.

A low groan leaves her at my command, and when she finally clamps down on my dick again, I come, burying myself inside her, as deep as possible, my legs shaking from the intensity of it. We collapse in a heap, catching our breaths, and she rolls over to face me, her eyes soft.

"Hey, D?"

"Yeah, baby?"

Her eyes narrow and she gives the chains a tug, reminding me she's still tied up. "Unlock the shackles before I kill you."

"Since you asked so nicely," I grin, managing to unchain her and drop the metal in a heap on the floor. I pull her against my chest and press a kiss to her forehead. "Better?"

"I can't feel my hands," she snorts, nuzzling into me affectionately. "But yeah. Better."

I sit up and shuffle back against the headboard, hauling her in front of me. Her back sticks to my chest from the sweat, but I don't give a shit. I'll get messy with her any day.

I reach around and take her arm in my hands, massaging her soft skin to help the blood flow, a content sigh leaving her. I do the same for the other arm, leaving kisses across her shoulder as I dote on her.

"I like spending time with just you," I admit, her head tilting to the side to look at me.

"Me, too. We should try to do it more often. Just because you and Santos are together too, doesn't mean we have to always share. Next time, I'm tying you up," she grins, and my dick jerks in agreement. "You like the sound of that?"

"Chained to the bed with you riding me? Sounds like Heaven," I grin, my hands moving to her thighs to continue the massage. The little sighs coming from her warm my chest, and without thinking too much, I slide out from under her and roll her onto her stomach.

"What are you doing?" she mumbles, tired of our fun.

"Giving you a massage," I reply, thinking she'll argue. Instead, she melts into the mattress as my fingers work over her tight muscles, eventually putting her to sleep.

I curl up beside her, giving in to my tired body and sleeping too, only waking up when a hard body presses against my back, and cool liquid is rubbed over my asshole. I shift onto my stomach more, parting my legs and hearing Santos' groan, the scent of shampoo and soap filling my nose.

"I missed you guys tonight."

"We missed you, too," I murmur, glancing at Selene's sleeping form. Santos chuckles softly, his lips trailing along my neck.

"Seems like you wore her out. You're not too tired for me, are you?"

"Never. Fuck me."

He sinks into me, not seeming hurried, his lips brushing my ear as he speaks, "I love you, D."

"I love you too, *amante*."

## *Blaze*

I watch as Zander books seven first-class tickets to Vegas and tut. He gives me a look with his brow raised.

"What?"

"Do we really need first class?" I raise my brow right back.

"You tell me, brother." He leans back in his seat. "All seven of us crammed into coach. How many times will we have to pull Santos off of Selene? How many times will we have to keep watch over Cara and Pepe? Then who's going to stop you from dragging Selene to the bathroom?"

"No one is fucking stopping me, if that's what I want to do," I snap at him.

"Exactly." He shakes his head, looking weary. "At least we'll have a bit more privacy."

I don't have any other argument because he's right. All seven of us crammed in coach would be catastrophic.

"Did we get anything else back about the shipment?"

"Yeah, Loqi's guy inside the Knights compound said they're meeting up with Mack himself the day after tomorrow. That's why I booked the tickets for the first flight out tomorrow. We need to plan this perfectly, like Loqi said. This one is going to be tricky." His brows crease as worry takes over his features. "I don't want anything to happen to us."

"Nothing will happen," I scoff. "It's a miracle we've survived this long."

"I know," he exhales, "something feels off." His hand lands on his chest. "I don't like it."

Maybe this feeling he's getting is the same one that's been keeping me on edge. I feel like everything is about to explode and we're not getting out of this unscathed like all the other times.

Or maybe I'm becoming as big of a bitch as Zander, and I need to remember my balls are bigger than his.

We touch down in Nevada—surprisingly after a quiet flight— around mid-day, and the heat is already stifling. I hate this weather; I could never live in Nevada all-year-round. Selene, Santos, and Darius are stretching and yawning, waking up from their naps on the plane. It was a quiet flight because they slept the whole time, and I'm thankful they burned themselves out last night.

After we grab our bags, we find Loqi leaning against a blacked-out SUV with another one parked behind it. He looks tired, but when he sees his sister, he perks up. I chance a glance at Cara and watch as her features soften. As much as she went through, she can't completely blame Loqi. He was young as well, and really, a lot of kids disappear from their guardian's sight.

"Cara!" He steps forward, unsure of how she'll react to him.

"Hi Luis." She goes forward and wraps her arms around his waist.

"Who's Luis?" Zander asks, and Cara laughs as she pulls out of her brother's embrace.

"You really didn't think his name was Loqi, did you?"

"I never really cared," Zander shrugs. "What's Papi Loco's real name?"

"Santiago," Santos answers, and we all fall quiet. "Similar to mine."

"We don't have much time," Loqi says. "We need to plan this out and be prepared for every scenario."

We get into the SUVs and head to the compound. I'm not at all happy to see it again so soon, and I can't wait to be done with all this. We head inside and a few of the guys we've come accustomed to holler out our names. As fucked up as this place is, they really are like a large family. Not that I have room to talk. The five of us—now seven—are the same, just on a smaller scale.

We leave Cara and Pepe to sit at the bar with Licker and follow Loqi down the narrow corridor toward Papi's office. It's quiet, not one snicker from any of us, and I can't help the ominous feeling that washes over me. My feet are following behind Loqi, one step in front of the other without hesitation, but my instincts are screaming for me to stop and turn around. I look over my shoulder to find Selene gripping Santos' arm, her teeth worrying into her bottom lip. Zander is on her other side, that crease between his brows a constant feature, and Darius shuffling beside me, watching the back of Loqi's head like he wants to take a bite out of it.

Loqi doesn't bother to make us wait this time as he opens his father's office door. Inside are a few guys and sitting on Papi's lap is Henny.

"Selly!" She jumps up and rushes to Selene. They embrace and Selene's eyes close as she takes in a deep breath.

"Hey, Jan," she says quietly.

"I don't like this," Henny looks around the room. "I think we should find another way to take down Mack."

"He has a shipping container filled with girls, Jan," Selene cuts in. "Surely, you know what they're feeling."

Henny's shoulders deflate and she grabs her sister's hand. "This is going to be very dangerous, and I wish I could command you to stay here with me."

We all make our way around the large table, taking seats as Henny and Selene continue their hushed conversation.

"Son." Papi nods to Santos, who grumbles as he sits down. He's a long road away from forgiving his father.

"The Highway Knights are a ruthless group of animals," Loqi spits out. "The shipment we intercepted before was small, and they sent mostly prospects for the pickup. That's why we took them down so easily."

"Our bomb specialist, Boomer, is in their compound now, and he's been with them for the past two years," Papi Loco cuts in. "He's our eyes and ears to the internal going-on in that compound. Their monthly shipment of young girls is their most lucrative business."

The room falls quiet as everyone silently seethes. We've been fighting this stain on our home soil for years, but to know it's rampant all over the US is daunting. There's no way we can bring it all down on our own.

"We can make an impact," Darius says, cutting through the silence. "We know Mack is a big player in the distribution of these girls and we've taken out three of his well-known associates. We can do this, and we have to do this." He looks from Santos to Zander, then his eyes land on me. "We've been fighting this war for years. He's the last piece of the puzzle. We can't back down now."

"We're not backing down." Santos' fist hits the tabletop. "Not after what they did to the girls we love. Even if we all die tomorrow while killing him, it'll be worth it. We'll continue to kill him for eternity in Hell."

"I'm with you, brother." Loqi reaches his fist across the table, and Santos smashes his to it. "Let's go out in a blaze of glory."

I want to be on the same page as them. I want to feel what they're feeling, but I just can't settle this bubbling anxiety inside of me.

"I think Selene should stay here," Santos says, as he turns to look at our fuming woman. "I need you alive."

"Fuck you," she snaps at him. "You need me out there to keep your unpredictable ass alive. Without me, you'd have been dead the first night I met you."

I can see the tears building in her eyes, and Darius' chuckle draws our attention. "I think that was the moment he fell in love with you, when your blade cracked open that Diablo's skull."

"Without a doubt." Santos nods, his face still solemn.

"The drop off point is never the same place twice, but Boomer has found a way to be there, and he'll text us the location as soon as he has it. This gives us a disadvantage because we don't know the terrain, and we'll lose our spy inside their walls," Papi states.

"It'll be nice to have our boy back home, though," Hook chimes in, his one eye shining with anticipation.

"Agreed." Papi nods. "So, this is how it's going to go down, and listen closely because Boomer left us a few surprises."

# Chapter Twelve

## *Zander*

Three hours locked in that room, planning what could be our very last hit. Our final fight, and instead of being afraid, I feel elated. Something inside of me is so proud of what me and my brothers have become, and we wouldn't have gotten this far without Selene.

I was seventeen when I saw my father strangle my mother to death, then throw her body into the pool. I was petrified. Back then, I knew he was shady; I knew his company did some illegal shit, and the thought of confronting him scared me. So, when the cops showed up and proved they were on my father's payroll, helping him cover up his murder, I knew something had to be done. My mother's death certificate says drowning due to intoxication, and I can never change that, but I've worked hard to avenge her murder.

In a heated argument a few years later, he admitted to killing her, and all because she threatened to go to the cops about his business in our basement. He fed me the same threat time after time, thinking he was molding me into his protégé the whole time my brothers and I were planning his demise.

With Selene's help, we succeeded, but then uncovered a whole can of worms. This became our life's mission, but I can't wait to see it come to an end. I want to watch Mack bleed out at the hands of one of us, not caring who, just wanting to be able to see it with my own eyes.

We're lying in a room with two king-sized beds pushed together, care of Sunshine who I'm sure is warming up to us, even though she called us a warren of rabbits. We're quiet, and that's saying a lot since both Selene and Santos are here.

"Is this going to work?" Selene says, breaking the silence.

"It has to," Santos replies, his response sounding doomed.

"All for five and five for all," Selene whispers, and I don't know why that makes my throat clog with emotion.

"Always." Darius whispers back, "whether from here or beyond."

My vision blurs as I contemplate any of us *beyond*.

"Pepe has to come with us tomorrow," Santos cuts in. "Mack needs to see him. I need him to see how his son has chosen us over his father. But Cara needs to stay here."

"She won't be separated from him," Selene groans. "But yes, I agree."

"We'll have to tie her up somewhere." Blaze growls, "she has a mean left hook, and loves to go for the fucking balls."

Again, we fall into silence, something we've been doing for the last few days, and it's tinged with worry. I feel like our time is slowly drawing to a close, like sands in an hourglass, slowly tumbling until not a single grain is left.

"I love you guys," I blurt out, because I need them to know it. "Each one of you is as important as the next, and I can't imagine anyone else when I think of family."

"Family forever," Darius joins in.

"No matter where we are, we'll always be together." Selene sniffs, her hand slipping into mine.

"Fuck this." Blaze gets up with a snarl. "I'm not sitting here and listening to our fucking eulogies. I need a drink."

He storms out of the room, slamming the door behind him, and making the walls vibrate with the force. It's silent again. Not even the sound of our breathing penetrates the heavy fog, and I close my eyes to try and block out the worries of the unknown. My heart races as I try to imagine how tomorrow will go, and I'm worried the others will hear its pounding beat.

"I think Blaze has the right idea," Darius grunts as he rolls off our massive bed. "Let's go have a drink together tonight." He walks for the door; Santos follows close behind him.

Selene and I get up as well, and I grab her hand. I won't say it out loud, but it was almost as though Darius meant this would be the last time.

# Selene

The sun is starting to set on the surrounding desert, casting reds and oranges, making the sand a vision of fire. Like the land is gradually transforming into Hell around us, a fiery premonition of what could come in the next hour or so. We're all tense, worry radiating from our pores in thick waves, nearly suffocating us. None of us wants to die when we feel like we've just begun to live.

Kevlar covers our chests and back—more mine than the guys whose bulky chests span wider—and our bodies are looking much like weapon arsenals. Both Darius and Santos have tied red bandanas around their heads to stave off the sweat, but I giggle at how closely they resemble Rambo.

Zander has been pacing a trench into the sand as he's stuck in his head, trying to control every aspect, and Blaze is a ball of burning fury on the cusp of exploding. I'm sitting next to a quiet Pepe as we play Tic-Tac-Toe on the sand. He's pretty calm considering we're thrusting him into battle with his father, while he believes the father in the clouds is protecting him.

"How many times do you think Cara has bitten Henny?" Darius snickers.

"None," Pepe answers solemnly. "She'll just feel abandoned all over again."

"She has never been abandoned," Loqi snaps back.

"That's how you see it, not her, though." Pepe meets Loqi's eyes. "If you make it out of this, I need you to make it right with her, no matter how hard she fights it. She deserves a family."

I prepare for Loqi's retort, expecting it to be filled with venom, and instead he gives Pepe a nod, his eyes softening for the man who cares for his sister. The other Dientes are huddled in a group not too far away, waiting for signs of company. Boomer told us they're coming in with twenty of their best enforcers, men trained to kill with their bare hands, if need be, and he said they won't hesitate to take us out. No questions asked.

Not that we didn't already know that. Getting Mack and

eliminating him is now our priority, no matter the cost.

I feel the vibration first, a soft tremor dancing along my fingertips as I draw my X in the sand. The sensation skates up my arm and slices through my heart. My head pops up at the same moment as Pepe, only he jumps to his feet quicker.

"They're coming," he pants.

Everyone is still, listening for the distant sound of engines, looking for the dust to kick up, and releasing our bated breaths. No matter what we're feeling on the inside, it's fucking showtime. As soon as the rumbles grow louder, we all scramble to our designated spots, and I end up beside Blaze.

He grabs my chin, looking me deep in the eyes, then crashing his lips to mine in a bruising kiss. "I love you." His teeth nip at my lip. "Don't you dare get yourself killed. Do you understand me?"

"Yes, Daddy," I whisper as I try to swallow down the lump in my throat.

"Good girl." He kisses me again.

We hear a soft whistle, the signal for the large eighteen-wheeler hauling a shipping container of young girls. Then the loud rumble of bikes reverberates off the Sierra Nevada mountains surrounding us, ramping up my heart. I stiffen, worrying about my guys. Are they in their spots? Should I have insisted the five of us stay together?

"I can taste your anxiety, Little Reaper," Blaze whispers harshly. "Get yourself together, warrior."

"I'm scared," I whisper back as the sounds of the engines form one loud rumbling anthem.

"So am I," he whispers back, and I swallow down a sob.

"You're not allowed to die on me, either." I grab the back of his shirt in my fist.

He gives me a nod and hauls me farther down behind the boulder we were assigned to. Papi Loco has strategically placed us around the area, giving us maximum coverage and opening up more targets, but it also leaves us in pairs with not a lot of backup if we ourselves are targeted.

The dust is thick around us in obscuring plumes, and I can barely see my hand in front of my face. This is bad. How can I aim if I can't fucking see? Blaze curses, probably feeling the same way. This isn't our everyday climate; we're not used to shooting in this environment. We'll be forced to follow the Dientes lead.

The engines finally stop, and the dust still hangs dense in the air, filling my lungs. My throat becomes dry, and I feel the overwhelming urge to clear it. My eyes begin to water just as we hear the first few voices. They're talking about the females inside the container, guessing at what they might look like, and how their tight virgin cunts will feel later. The bile works its way up from my stomach, threatening to spill with my disgust.

"Hey!" someone calls out, and my heart lurches up into my throat. "Mack himself came with this one. It must be a special haul."

"We gotta make this quick, boys." I hear the walking dental nightmare himself. "I have people who need killing back home."

The asshole. I grit my teeth, loving how the sound of the fat cunt's voice is bringing in an all-consuming rage, tearing through my fear. My hand finds one of the guns strapped to my waist, and I grip the smooth handle in my palm.

"They have a bus with them," Blaze whispers. "The Knights. I bet that's where the girls will go."

"Yeah, when we bring them back to the Dientes compound," I snarl.

I hear the scrape of metal doors opening, and then the sudden onslaught of tears and screaming. My stomach twists as the men begin to hoot and holler, calling out to the young girls with obscenities.

"How much longer?"

"Papi said he wants the girls safely in the transport vehicle before we attack," Blaze reminds me.

"It's taking too long."

"Get yourself under control," he snaps.

I huff out my breath and roll my eyes, sticking my tongue out at the back of the bastard's head.

"You'll be punished for that later," he grumbles, and my mouth drops open.

"How did you see that?" I whisper.

"I know you." He shrugs. "They're moving them. Fuck, the girls are young. Maybe twelve to fifteen."

"Fuck," I growl.

I hear doors shut, and then Papi Loco's voice ringing through the air. "I heard this belongs to someone here?"

This is where he walks out with a gun to Pepe's head. This whole plan makes me nervous because I don't know how much Mack actually cares about his son, and I'll never forgive myself if something happens to Pepe.

"How the fuck did you get here, Joey?" Mack calls out.

"I was traded," Pepe calls, his rehearsed words sounding scared.

"I don't like this," I moan.

"Papi Loco, let my son go," Mack calls out, his words slurred from his lack of teeth. His tongue must feel like an unrestrained slippery eel.

"Can't do that, Mack," Papi calls back. "Not until you hand over that bus full of girls."

"Not in your fucking dreams!" another voice yells. "You fucking Dientes need to get the fuck out of here before someone dies."

A shot rings out, and I nearly jump to my feet. Blaze's hand on my shoulder is the only thing that's stopping me. Gunfire echoes around us, sounding like thunder as it claps off the mountains and flings back around our heads.

Blaze turns and gives me a wink, his grin tugging at his scar and making him look irresistible. Then he's gone, running into the fray. I jump to my feet and see the chaos in front of me. When I see a man running toward me, his leather cut showing a knight riding a motorcycle, I lift my gun and shoot him in the throat. He drops like a fat log of shit hitting toilet water.

I rush out, trying to dodge bullets, and looking for my guys. Red dust clouds the space around me as people run for cover, and bullets hit the ground at our feet. I find Pepe cowering in a fetal position where Papi Loco must've dropped him, and I grab the back of his shirt, dragging him with me behind a boulder. We find Santos there, changing the mag on his gun, his face red from the dust.

"You found him!" He grins widely when he sees Pepe. "Little fucker must've been burrowing to Hell when I went out to look for him."

"No," Pepe shakes his head. "I was praying for one of you crazy assholes to find me."

"Well, Jesus must really love you today!" Santos exclaims as a bullet hits the rock we're behind.

"Hey!" Santos stands up and lets loose a string of bullets. "Who the fuck you shooting at, assholes?"

"Get the fuck down here." I yank on his shirt.

He crouches back down and gives me a wink. "I got one."

"Where are the others?"

"I lost Darius," he points to his right. "He ran that way. Zander was over there, too."

"I lost Blaze."

"They'll be fine," he nods, "this is what we live for."

A biker runs behind Santos and stops, raising his gun. I see the Knight's emblem and don't hesitate to knock a bullet between his eyes.

"That's twice now." I smirk at him.

"I wouldn't have needed it if you weren't distracting me." He winks. *Asshole*.

"Let's find the others." Santos darts out from the rock, and I go to follow when I remember Pepe.

"Are you coming?" I ask him.

"No. I think I'll stay here." He looks shaken, his skin ashen. I get it. This isn't fun for him.

"Here's a gun." I hand him one of my spares. "Shoot anyone who tries to shoot you, understand?"

"I don't want to—"

"You were willing to kill me at one point," I remind him. "You can do it and Jesus will understand. We'll celebrate by taking you to a priest to be molested after."

He snorts and looks up at me with watery eyes. "I can't imagine not having you around, Selene. May God be with you and protect you today."

"God bless you and your nuts." I nod and scramble out from behind the boulder.

The gunfire is tapering off, and I see bodies littered along the sand. My heart slams into my ribcage as I try to squint through the dust, hoping not to recognize any of them.

I get to a large rock, finding Santos and Loqi. Loqi has a bad gunshot wound on his thigh and blood is shooting out like a fountain.

"They hit his artery," Santos grunts as he ties his bandana around Loqi's leg, trying to stop the worst of the blood loss. "Can you stay here with him while I try to find Darius?"

"Yeah." I cringe at the sight of Loqi's grey skin.

Santos runs out, and I hear a few more shots ring out as I crunch down lower.

"I've always wanted a brother," Loqi moans, his words slurred and slow.

"Well, you lucked out. You ended up with the best brother ever." My throat is tightening, and my eyes are burning as I watch him slowly die in front of me.

"Don't worry," he gives me a wink, so much like his brother. "I'm not afraid to die."

"Don't you dare fucking die," I growl and grab the front of his shirt. "You have a brother and sister who need you."

"Loqi!" I turn and find Papi Loco running toward us, his face and hands covered in blood. "Don't you even fucking think of it, boy."

"Hey, Dad," Loqi grins. "I got him. I shot Daniel in the head."

"Fuck, that's war for sure. Boomer!" he yells over his shoulder, and an older man rushes forward. "Take him to the bus. We need to get out of here."

"Who's Daniel?" I ask as Boomer throws Loqi over his shoulder and runs off.

"The Knight's President's only son and VP." He heaves out a tired breath. "They were best friends as kids."

"That's going to be messy." I nod.

"Hey, Walton Jr!" I hear Mack call out to Zander. "Bring me my boy, and maybe I'll let this one live."

I stand quickly and find Mack standing in the middle of the settling red dust with Blaze on his knees in front of him, holding a gun to his head. I lift my own gun, aiming for Mack's head, when a couple of Knights step out, holding up guns.

"You shoot me, and they've been ordered to kill him," Mack snickers.

"Little Reaper," Blaze calls out just as Santos makes it back to my side. "Don't hand Pepe over."

Mack slams the butt-end of his gun into Blaze's temple, making him grunt out in pain, and fall to the sand.

I dart forward with a scream, "You toothless son-of-a-bitch!"

Santos grabs my arm, yanking me back, when a warning shot is fired near my feet. That does it. Santos lifts his gun and shoots one of the Knight's, causing a second round of mayhem. I see Darius run forward to Mack and Blaze, his gun firing, and I shrug out of Santos' hold, needing to get to Blaze.

The next few moments are in slow motion. I watch as a Knight steps up in front of Blaze, aiming his gun at me, then Santos runs in front of me, shielding me from the bullet that's fired. I slam into his back, trying to shove him, when Darius jumps in front of the both of us, his body jolting in mid-air.

"Darius!" Santos screams, dropping to the ground beside his lover. I hear another shot ring out and watch as the Knight drops to the ground, then Zander runs over to us.

Blood is blooming on the back of Darius' shirt, and I know it's bad. He took a hit to the chest outside of the Kevlar vest. The scream that rips from my throat is fierce and animalistic, not at all sounding natural. I jump over the guys on the ground in front of me, and my feet hit the red sand in loud thumps which resonate through my chest. Mack lifts his gun, pointing it at me, a sadistic smile on his face as Blaze begins to get up.

"You have one shot, motherfucker!" I scream. "You better pray you kill me!"

My hand wraps around the hilt of my knife as I yank it out of the sheath, and Mack takes his shot. I skid to the side, and the bullet, which was destined for my chest, slams into my shoulder, jarring me back a few steps. My shoulder screams with fire as I laugh maniacally.

"You missed!" I continue to cackle as I jump on him, stabbing my knife through his eye. He falls back with a shout, his back hitting the sand, taking me with him. His gun skates across the ground as I yank my knife back out, glancing up when I hear a click.

Blaze is standing over us, the gun pointed down at Mack's head. "This has been a long time coming." Then he fires the shot into Mack's forehead.

I hear the cries behind me, knowing it's bad, too scared to turn around. Instead, I continue to stab my knife into Mack's head repeatedly, the blood spraying up all over my face.

"Selene," Blaze calls me, but I'm too lost in grief; in bloodlust; in complete rage.

Mack's face begins to resemble minced meat when Blaze drags me off of him. I turn quickly, finding Papi Loco and Hook rushing Darius to the bus. His vacated spot on the sand is completely saturated with blood. Santos turns his eyes on me, their darkened depths filled with pain. I shake my head; the movement making me stumble as the world tips around me.

I'll never forgive myself if Darius is dead.

My vision begins to blacken around the edges, and when I turn to see where Darius is, everything tips on its axis. The ground rushes up to meet me, and I feel arms wrap around my waist.

"Reaper, what the fuck happened?" Blaze growls, but it's hard to form words around the pain of my breaking heart.

"She's been hit!" Santos yells, running forward. "No! Blaze, she's been hit!"

Oh, yeah. I try to reach for my shoulder, but my arm doesn't comply, and my head falls forward. I no longer have the strength or the will to try. I want to be where Darius is.

"No, no, no." I hear Blaze chant just as the world turns dark around me.

# Darius

I don't even think about it before jumping in front of the bullet Santos is trying to save Selene from. I'd do it for any of them, needing them to finish what we started. I know this may be the end for me, but I'll die knowing the people I love are still alive.

The bullet hits my flesh, sending hot searing pain through my body, the desperate scream of my name filling my ears from Santos as I hit the ground hard. It's hard to breathe, telling me this is bad. I can't form words as my vision starts to dim. Selene's screaming somewhere, her pain burning into me. She'll be okay. My brothers will look after her.

I'm getting cold, but I feel hands on me as I choke on my blood.

"Don't you fucking die on me!" Santos cries, trying to apply pressure to the wound that's quickly sucking the life from me. I want to tell him I love him, that I'd do it all again to save him, but my mouth won't work, and the darkness starts seeping in.

"Stay with me, please. I fucking need you!"

I think it's Santos, but I'm not sure anymore. Everything's going fuzzy.

"I love you, don't leave me!" Definitely Santos.

I hear a gunshot just as I fight for air, someone's hand squeezing mine as everything goes black. As my life is taken from me, all I can think about is how my family has to be okay without me.

They have no other choice.

## Santos

I zone out the sound of young girls crying as we drive to get medical help. The bus is packed, but the only thing I see is the devastation to my family. Darius' skin is pale from the blood loss, his hand cold in mine as I will him to be okay. He's been my anchor for so long now, I can't face the world without him.

Selene's just as still, both of them covered in blood as it seeps into their clothes. Panic swirls inside me, knowing the odds of saving everyone are so low.

I glance over to watch Papi with Loqi, my brother's body looking more like a corpse. He can't die either. I've just fucking found him. I curse myself for spending so much time hating him, knowing I might not get the chance to get to know him.

I hate myself for fighting with Selene before coming into this, wishing she were awake so I could spill my heart to her. If she'd stayed back, she'd be okay, but that isn't her style. I can't be angry at her for that, because if someone told me to stay behind, I would have bitten their heads off.

"Come back to me," I whisper, giving both their hands a squeeze, hoping for a response. I don't get one, and my throat goes tight with emotion at knowing this is it. We aren't all going home together to celebrate our victory. Some of us are going home in a box.

I don't give a shit that I'm crying like a baby as I cling to them, taking a page out of Pepe's book and praying they'll come back to us. I choke on a sob, my grip tightening on their hands as someone wraps their arms around me. If they try to make me let go of them, I'll flip out.

Instead, they just hold me, Zander's voice reaching my ears. "I've got you." That just makes my tears fucking worse. I'm glad Zander and Blaze are all right, but losing Darius or Selene will kill me. They are the calm to my storm, my tether when I lose control, and they are my home.

"I can't lose them," I force out, leaning into him for comfort. He doesn't answer, telling me everything I need to know. He doesn't think we'll all make it either, and he's not going to sugar-coat it with lies for my sake.

Blaze sits close by, his face tight with pain as he stares at Selene, wearing his heart on his sleeve for once. He meets my gaze, his voice rough.

"If the Grim Reaper even tries to take them, I'll fight that fucker myself. He's not taking them anywhere, San. I won't fucking let him."

"You'll fight death?" I choke on a small laugh at the image of him standing off with the Devil, not letting our family be taken to the darkest depths of Hell.

"You bet your ass I will. I'll do anything for them," he grunts, his eyes going back to Selene, ending the conversation.

Once we arrive, Digs carts them away, and Zander has to hold me back from following. "Let him help them. We'll only get in the way."

"I need to stay with them!" I snap, but there's no anger in my words, only pain. He takes my hand, tugging me toward some chairs, pushing me gently into one and dropping an arm around my shoulders, Blaze dropping into the chair on my other side. He doesn't hug me, but his shoulder brushes against mine, showing me he's there for me. I know deep down, he's chasing comfort too, not used to being so out of control in a situation.

I never thought the grumpy bastard would soften for anyone, but as we sit here, I feel his fear and misery. His love for Selene is so strong it almost chokes me, and I wipe my cheeks as more tears spill.

"Santos."

I glance up, finding Papi in front of me, and I have no idea how long he's been standing there. I'm drowning in grief, the worry eating me alive at what comes next. Will they all die?

"Yeah?" I manage to croak out, surprised when he squats in front of me and takes my face in his hands.

"I'm sorry. For everything. I can see what they mean to you. I know I never understood your relationship with Darius, but I see it. I respect him so much for what he did for you. He's your family, which makes him mine."

I want to lash out, scream at him for saying shit like that when he has no right, but he leans forward and hugs me, the anger vanishing as he tries to hold me together while I break.

"I'm sorry about Loqi, he's a pretty cool brother," I mumble, pretending I don't hear him sniff back tears of his own.

"When we all get home, we'll celebrate. No one's dying today," he states firmly, leaning back to look at me with a stubborn look in his eyes.

"Promise?" I rasp, needing him to make it all okay. He doesn't say anything, his jaw tight, but the sound of a heart monitor flatlining draws each of our attention to the closed door, my heart leaping in my chest.

"No!" I scream, launching out of my chair, but Zander and Blaze hold me back, their hands tightening as I struggle. "Let me go!"

Papi stares at the door silently, as if his eyes can laser through the wood and will things to be all right. Nothing's all right, though. Not when one of them just died. I hear them trying to bring them back, charging up the shock paddles, and I need to see who it is. I keep fighting against my brothers, but it's no use. My body goes weak, and I slump against Zander, my tears soaking his shirt as he clings to me.

Am I saying goodbye to my brother? Or the two people I love more than anyone in the world?

# Epilogue

## Selene

I stare at my reflection in the mirror.

My hair is shining a light blonde, shimmering with whatever oil is in it. My makeup is subtle, my eyelids shimmering in the light beside the vanity. My hand glides down over the long, black dress made of the softest material that hugs every one of my curves like a dream. It's strapless, the front dipping down to create the deepest sweetheart neckline.

The door opens, and I turn my head to see Pepe step into the room, looking handsome in his suit. My shoulder aches from the sudden movement, and my hand comes up to press at the still healing wound. The feeling of the raised, puckered flesh threatens to pull me back under, but it's Pepe's words that draw my attention instead.

"I don't think that dress is appropriate for a wedding." He gives me a confused look.

"Do I look appropriate to you?" I retort.

"You look beautiful, regardless of what you're wearing." His face softens.

Pepe has blended into our family of misfits perfectly, and it helps that he's dating a groom's sister. He still drones on about Jesus, prays for us every day, and truly believes all of our souls are salvageable, making it his mission to ensure we all end up in Heaven together. As long as I end up with *all* of my guys, I don't care where I am.

"Thank you," I whisper as a bout of nerves wash over me.

"I printed off the certificate." He holds up a piece of paper. "In case any of these guys want to question the validity of today's ceremony."

Pepe took an online course to become an ordained minister so he could officiate this wedding. There's no one else who could do the job justice.

"We'll frame it later and hang it on the walls when we get home." I smile at him.

We're still here in the Dientes compound. Digs wouldn't let me leave until I was back on my feet, and to be honest, I wouldn't want anyone else looking after me. He's a compassionate man who only lives his life to save others.

He saved *me*.

It's beautiful here, with the mountains as a backdrop, and the sky always a bright blue. Perfect for a wedding. Shockingly, Papi Loco was so excited about the prospect of a wedding, he planned every detail and decorated the large open field. Flowers, fancy chairs, and the food. He did it all. He's been doing everything in his power to win over his oldest son, hoping for forgiveness. I think he may have succeeded after today.

Loqi steps into the room, his cane clicking against the hardwood flooring. "Damn, sis, you are fine!"

He's taken to calling me sis since he's had a second chance at life. I accept it because it makes Santos happy to see us getting along, especially when he's working on solidifying his relationship with his brother.

"That sounds like maybe you want to fuck your sister, *Luis*," I tut. "Incest is a crime here, no?"

"I'm willing to do at least ten years for it." He gives me a slow perusal.

"I'm going to head out," Pepe says as he shakes his head, clutching the crucifix around his neck. He may be one of us, but we still tend to shock him regularly.

"How can I convince you to marry me next?" Loqi asks, a twinkle in his eye.

"I'll consider it when you don't limp like a gimp anymore."

"Ouch." His hand lands over his chest. "I may always be gimpy, though. Doc says I need a lot of *physical* therapy."

I saunter over to him and pat his cheek. "Your hand has been such a good companion up to this point. Let's not ruin it now."

His head tips back on a laugh, so similar to his brother's, I can't help but laugh with him.

"Come on, gorgeous." He holds out his arm. "People are waiting on you."

The sun is setting, shooting reds of all shades across the sky, and the outline of the moon is already high above our heads. It's picturesque and perfect, just like today. I'm walking between two of my guys, our arms interlocked, and our hearts beating as one. The love between us has only grown the two months we've been here, and we are the strongest we've ever been.

We reach the end of the aisle and I take Santos' face in my hands, leaning forward to give him a sweet kiss. He quickly deepens it, making it nearly inappropriate, causing snickers to sound around us. He lets me go with a mischievous grin on his face as I slap his chest.

"Naughty boy," I whisper. "I'll be punishing you later."

"As long as I get the same punishment Zander did." He gives me a wink over Zander's audible groan.

I turn to my left, taking in my next man, his eyes looking down at me, filled to the brim with love and appreciation. Their blue shining brightly, filtering through to my very soul.

"Darius," I croak, my voice losing its strength. "Thank you for fighting for us … for me." I can feel the tears coursing down my cheeks, the accumulation of stress and worry for the life of my lover, dissipating as I look into his smiling face.

It has been a rough two months. There were a few times we thought we were losing him, but he pulled through, later telling us he only saw our faces while he fought. He had lost a lot of blood, but thankfully, Papi Loco's blood type is universal, and he helped save my man's life.

"There's nowhere else I'd rather be, angel." He leans down, capturing my trembling lips in his, and I vow—as I have been vowing every day—to love them all with my whole being because tomorrow is never guaranteed.

"Who gives these men to be wed?" Pepe's voice rings through our kiss.

I grab Santos' hand and then Darius' as I step back, linking them together. "I do."

Darius looks so handsome and *alive* as he stands there looking into Santos' eyes. The sight of them looking so in love and ready to take this next step chokes me up. Just as a sob pounds against my chest, Blaze's heat is at my back, his arm slipping around my waist.

"Come sit with me and Zander and let our boys get married, Little Reaper."

I begin to cry softly as Blaze leads me back to our seats, and Zander wraps an arm around me, dragging me into his body. "You big softy." He kisses my cheek with a snicker.

"Do not start." I point at him while wiping my tears.

"You'll get that ass beat again," Blaze mutters.

"Really?" Zander's eyes light up. "Did you bring it with you?"

I slap a hand to his chest as we watch Santos and Darius get married. There's not one dry eye in the place as they recite their vows. Even, as Santos reads out his, filled with threats of death if Darius ever decides to try to leave us again.

I've never been so proud of anything in my life.

## Zander

My arms are around my girl, and her blonde hair is illuminated by the twinkling lights around us. We're swaying to a slow song, and she's smiling as Darius and Santos dance in the moonlight. It's been a rough two months, and life really comes into perspective when you fear you're losing someone you love. All of us have been to Hell and back, and now, we're thankful for every day we have together.

When Santos came to us, professing his need to marry Darius, we were all shocked. I was surprised because Santos has never spoken about marriage. Then there was the worry they were breaking apart from Selene, from all of us. But they're not, they just want to solidify their individual relationship, and we all support them for it.

"Where will they go for their honeymoon?" I ask my beautiful girl, and she looks up at me with a scowl.

"In my pussy, that's where."

I choke on a laugh at the seriousness on her face, knowing none of us will be let out of her sight for a long while. We all feel the same about her. When she was shot, it scared the living shit out of me, and I saw everything I was living for slowly drain away. There's no me without her, and I promised her when she woke up the next day, she would have to deal with me for the rest of her life.

"I'm so thankful my father paid you to fuck him," I tell her, a smile dancing across my mouth.

"Me, too, baby Walton," she coos. "The dick on that man." She lets out a long sigh, her eyes taking on a dreamy look. I pinch her waist, and she breaks out into giggles. "I'm really glad, too, Zan. It was always meant to be." She finally looks up at me with love in her eyes.

"I love you," I tell her as I press a soft kiss to her lips.

"I love you, too." She grins, and I prepare myself for whatever it is she's thinking. "How soon is too soon to leave? I really want to sink a big dildo into your ass."

And there it is.

# $\mathcal{B}$laze

Nothing in this world will ever compare to what I feel for the annoying woman dancing in the arms of my best friend. I fought the pull I felt the first moment I laid eyes on her, and I did everything in my power to push her away, only to have her cling on tighter.

I never thought love was possible for us four, but especially not for me, having never felt it for myself. Then this Little Reaper comes along and rips my heart out of my chest, holding its bloody warmth in her hands. She owns it through and through.

Zander tips his head back and groans while Selene grins like a sadistic bitch, making me chuckle. I wonder what she said to him this time. Darius and Santos have been inseparable all night—for two months really—and I'm happy to witness their pure love as they sway together on the dance floor.

"Thank you for taking care of my little sister." Henny sits down next to me.

"It's a group effort." I shrug.

"She's lucky to have you all."

"Are you needing more than just Papi Loco?" I ask her with a knowing grin.

"What?" She looks around wide-eyed. "Don't say that. He'll gun us all down."

I chuckle as she keeps looking around for her crazy old man.

"Pepe!" We hear Cara squeal from the dance floor.

Pepe is down on one knee, holding a little black box, his arms shaking with nerves. We knew he was going to be doing this today because Santos basically threatened him if he didn't. Not that he needed much pushing. It's not hard to see how much they mean to each other.

"Cara, I believe God brought you into my life, and I want to make this official." He opens the box and Cara gasps. "Will you marry me?"

"Say yes, Cara!" Santos bellows, and everyone begins to laugh.

"Of course!" Cara squeals as Pepe slips the ring on her finger.

Papi Loco and Loqi rush them both onto the dance floor, forming a large group hug. It's been a rough go with them, but they're on the road to healing.

"Damn." Henny wipes the moisture from her eyes. "That's beautiful."

My Little Reaper comes running toward me, and drops herself in my lap, her arms circling my neck. "Did you see that, Daddy?" Her words sound husky and winded from excitement, causing my cock to swell against her ass.

"Yeah, baby." I smile at her.

"We're going to be planning another wedding," she squeals with excitement.

"We?" I snicker, and Henny joins in.

"More like Papi will," Henny corrects while Selene scoffs.

"Fine, we get another open bar!"

My face burrows into her neck and I drag my tongue across her skin, tasting her. She shivers in my arms, and I chuckle into her skin.

"How soon is too soon to leave?" I ask her, and she gasps.

"I want to know that, too!" she exclaims just as someone wheels out a large wedding cake, making us both groan.

"Still too soon, apparently," I growl, and she giggles.

"Come on, Daddy." She stands and yanks on my hand. "I'll spread some cake icing on my pussy and let you clean it out."

Henny groans in disgust behind us, but I don't give a fuck. Now, I want a piece of that cake.

# Santos

I don't think I've let go of Darius all fucking day. I let Selene dance with him, but I lingered on the side, not wanting to be too far away from him. Hell, I don't want to be away from any of them. Honeymoon? Family fucking vacation. No exceptions.

"If you hold me any tighter, I'm going to bust my stitches," Darius chuckles lightly as we slow dance, an edge of pain in his voice. I quickly ease my hold on him, giving him a sheepish smile.

"Sorry. I zoned out," I admit, glancing around the room to check in that the others are okay. He gives me an understanding look, leaning forward to kiss me.

"We're all right, *amante*. Not even the Devil can have me. I'm yours."

"That fucker nearly did get you," I growl quietly. "He won't be getting a second chance. If anyone even knocks on our door, I'm shooting first. I don't care if they're Girl Scouts selling cookies."

"You can't start shooting Girl Scouts. I doubt they're a threat," he teases, pressing closer to me as he urges me to keep dancing.

"That's what they want you to think. Then once you buy the cookies and put them in the kitchen, *BAM*, explosion. Do you know how many cookies Zander usually orders? That's a lot of explosives in our house," I snort, making him roll his eyes.

"I think you'll find that *you* are the one who orders a million cookies."

"Not anymore! I'm onto those little pig-tail braided assassins!" I declare, spotting Selene motioning to me with a handful of cake. I didn't even let Darius' hand go when we had to cut the cake. I was too worried the fucking thing was wired and ready to blow.

"C'mon, our baby girl's summoning us," I grin, tugging him after me to make sure he stays with me. As we approach, I notice the cheeky glint in her eyes, making me smirk. "What are you plotting, my little blood queen?"

She runs her finger through the icing, popping it into her mouth and sucking it off, pulling it out slowly. "As much as this wedding has been perfect, how about we sneak off for a while? I have some fun places to put this icing where you can eat it out from."

My dick stirs at the thought of her body covered in it, my tongue licking her clean while she screams.

"Done deal. I'll just let Papi know we're going. He can keep an eye on Cara."

"She'll be fine. She has Pepe," she whines, making me snort.

"I think he needs more training before he can do much. I'll be two seconds. Meet us in the bedroom," I chuckle.

"I'll grab Grumpy and Zan," she exclaims before turning and skipping off to find them, leaving us to track down Papi.

It doesn't take long. He's boasting about Cara's up-and-coming wedding to a bunch of his guys, Loqi standing beside them with the biggest grin on his face.

He meets my gaze and winks, amusement all over his face. "Your girl getting antsy?"

"What makes you say that?" Darius frowns, and Loqi laughs.

"Because she's practically piling up all the cake that's left onto a plate and I doubt cake makes her horny, but she looks ready to burst."

We glance back to find Selene with a massive plate of cake, her ass rubbing back on Zander, who's whispering in her ear with a devilish grin. She says something to Blaze, who ends up with his hand around her throat, his lips crashing into hers so hard she almost drops her mountain of cake.

I look back at Loqi with a shrug. "What? She loves orgasms and we love cake. It's a win-win situation. The best flavored cake is pussy flavored."

He cracks up, grabbing my shoulder and tugging me close for a hug. "You guys are hilarious. Enjoy your night. And San?"

"Yeah?"

"Congrats on your wedding. Thanks for the invite," he grins, turning to Darius and gently pulling him in for a hug, too. "Welcome to the family, brother."

Before I can reply, Papi pulls me in for a hug. "My boy! You sure you don't want to relocate to Nevada?" He's spent a lot of time over the past few days trying hard to convince us to move closer to them.

"Sorry, Papi. We can't handle the weather. Blaze is still grumbling about it. We'll visit, promise," I smile, patting him on the back as we pull apart.

"Make sure you bring the rest of the family with you. It will be a party every time you stop by," he beams, turning to Darius and shooing Loqi away from him. "I know I've said it already, but thank you for saving my boy. You always have a home in Nevada if you ever need one. If you have any issues, you call me. We've got your back."

Darius is grinning so hard I'm surprised his jaw doesn't snap.

"Thanks. It means a lot."

"And call me Papi! You're my son now, after all," he scolds, my heart warming at his words. We still have a little way to go on building trust since he'd abandoned me, but we're off to a really good start. He treats Darius like family, the same as Selene, Blaze, and Zander.

"Excuse me, I need to steal the grooms. There's been an... uh, incident in the cake department and they need to see to it right away," Selene says quickly as she grabs my hand, her breath fast. Papi grins, glancing over at Zander, who has icing all over his fucking suit.

"You'd better see to that right away. It sounds important," he states dryly.

"It is. I'll bring them back in the morning after it's dealt with," she nods innocently, dragging us across the room, Blaze and Zander following with the plate of cake.

Zander already has his shirt off, his pants undone as we enter the bedroom, but I hesitate when I eye Selene stripping Darius beside me. "Uh, is this a good idea? Darius…"

"Darius can lie back on the bed like a good boy and let nurse Selene look after him," she coos, peppering kisses across his bandage. "I'll be gentle, won't I, baby?"

Darius snorts, giving her a dirty look. "You better fucking not be gentle, or I'll flip you over and ram your ass until you bleed."

She moans, shoving his pants down and fisting his dick. "Don't threaten me with a good time." She steers him toward the bed, encouraging him to sit. "Seriously, though. You really need to take it easy. Just a little. Lie back."

He looks ready to argue with her, but I glare at him, making him do as he's told. Blaze makes quick work of stripping the beautiful black dress from Selene's body, his lips trailing across her back as she sighs and leans into him.

"I need to be inside you, right fucking now," Zander groans, completely naked as he pumps his dick in his hand. His eyes are heated as he watches Selene turn and kiss Blaze almost savagely.

"I have an idea, but Darius isn't allowed to do the work," I smirk, stripping off and moving toward the bed. Darius scowls.

"I don't like the sound of that."

"You will in a minute," I promise, grabbing some lube before lying back on the bed, slicking my dick up before reaching for him. "Come here."

He raises an eyebrow but moves closer, seeming confused. "How do you want me?"

"Sit on my dick and lay your back against my chest," I instruct, helping him get into position. I align myself with his tight hole, slowly pulling him down onto me until I'm fully seated inside him. He groans, dropping his head back as he gets used to it.

"Now what?"

"Now we lean back so Selene can ride you."

"We'll squash you, idiot."

"Doubt it. Blaze and Zander can fight over her ass," I chuckle, both of them turning to each other with a grin. Selene's eyes go wide as she takes a step back, shaking her head.

"Nope. Daddy is not putting his big dick in my ass right now."

"I hope you're ready to choke on it then, Little Reaper," Blaze smiles sadistically.

"This won't work. It's…"

"Shut up and ride me, baby," Darius cuts her off, motioning to his solid dick. "It won't fuck itself."

She huffs, glancing at the plate of cake that's now on the bedside table. "But the cake…" Before she can finish her sentence, Blaze grabs her and throws her down on the bed, grabbing a fistful of cake and rubbing it all over her pussy, not hesitating to dive into it face first, making a meal out of it.

She moans, grinding on his face, and smearing cake and icing all over him, but he doesn't give a fuck. I sit up more, keeping Darius against my chest as we watch Blaze eat her like a man starved. It's hot seeing my wedding cake on her naked body.

Zander chuckles, grabbing the plate and plonking down on the bed beside them. He silently smears icing on her breasts, leaning down to lick it off with a groan. "So fucking good."

There's cake everywhere by the time she screams her release, and I fucking love it.

Without warning, Blaze drops onto his back and hauls Selene against his chest, her sticky tits pressing against his pecs.

"But, oh, fuck!" she gasps as he forces himself into her pussy, not giving her time to adjust. He holds her hips firmly as he fucks up into her, determination on his face. Making her come has been the best game we've ever played.

I take the hint, nudging Darius to climb off. Now Blaze is in her pussy, no one will be able to drag him back out. He holds her tight to his chest, slowing his thrusts as Darius shuffles toward them. She looks ready to snap at him to lie back down, but he lubes up and eases into her ass, her protest dying on a strangled moan.

Darius is obviously hurting a little, but he ignores it as he starts moving in and out, fisting her hair and pulling her head back. Blaze instantly claims her lips, muffling the noises coming from her, and as Darius leans forwards a fraction and parts his thighs, I know what he wants.

I waste no time as I scramble behind him, making my way inside his tight hole again, trying to be gentle so I don't end up making him tense too much. I don't mind him hurting, but I don't want to risk his stitches. If they tear, we can end up with another emergency trip. I never want to be sitting in a waiting room for him ever again.

"Dammit, Santos. Fuck me!" he snaps over his shoulder, groaning as I pull back and slam in a little harder.

"Better?"

"Keep going, fucker," he grits out, not seeming satisfied until I'm fucking him as hard as I can. Selene's cursing as Blaze picks up the pace, him and Darius almost competing to get her off, and Zander chuckles as he steps closer, swatting Darius' hand away from her hair so he can fist it.

"Open wide. You're being a little loud."

She does as she's told, almost making me laugh. It's a rare sight, one that makes my dick harden even more. Darius grunts as she comes apart, her body shaking between him and Blaze as if she's been electrocuted, and Zander keeps her quiet as he fucks her mouth, his eyes flicking up to me.

I can't help myself as I smirk, cocking my head slightly as I slow my pace. "You want a ride next? I promise I'll blow your mind faster than that plastic you copped last time."

I expect him to get angry, but he just smirks back, pushing deeper into Selene's throat and making her gag. "The only one of you fuckers allowed near my ass is our girl. My ass is too good. You'll fall in love with me, and Darius would have to share."

"Like fuck," Darius snarls, slamming into Selene and coming hard, only giving it a second before pulling out and shoving me back. Zander laughs as Darius straddles me, sinking onto my dick as his mouth finds mine, but we know he's not really jealous. He doesn't have to compete with anyone for me, and he knows it.

I vaguely watch Zander slide into Selene's vacated ass, but my attention is quickly drawn back to the man on my lap, his lips on my neck as he grinds his hips, trying to get me deeper.

"You're going to hurt yourself," I warn, biting his shoulder sharply when he ignores me. "Darius."

"Let me," he begs, but my eyes dart to his bandage as he leans back, a small drop of blood seeping through. It's not bad, but it will get worse if he keeps going.

I flip us so he's below me, lifting one of his legs over my waist. "Just lie back and take it. I'm close."

He sighs, forgetting all about it as I start fucking him harder again, the sound of skin slapping together filling the room. Without Zander's dick in Selene's mouth, she's moaning and begging loudly, close to her next orgasm. The moment she screams their names, I'm a goner, coming hard inside Darius as I drop my forehead to his, our breaths becoming one.

"I love you so fucking much," I murmur, his eyes peering into mine as he smiles softly.

"I love you too. I've always got you."

"Promise?" I ask, needing him to say it. He's mine forever, despite the piece of paper that proves it, and if death ever tries to take him again, that bastard had better be taking the rest of us, too.

Blaze comes with a roar, Selene's not far behind. Seconds later, Zander does too, and the three of them collapse beside us in one sweaty, cum covered pile. Darius' hand runs through my hair, and he gives it a playful tug, leaning up to kiss me.

"I promise, husband."

# Darius

We spend the entire night fucking. Sometimes just Santos and I, other times Selene would join in with the others. I'm between Santos and Selene, her hand on my chest near my bandage. She's been worried about me, but sleep is finally starting to take its hold over her.

"I love you guys," she mumbles, yawning as she snuggles closer to me. Santos mumbles that he loves us all too as he drifts off, clinging to me as if someone will snatch me. They'd bring me back if they succeed. No one could manage me, let alone my family, coming for them. Santos has nothing to worry about.

"Love you too, Little Reaper," Blaze mumbles from her other side, a soft snore coming from Zander who's curled up at the bottom of the bed, passing out after fucking her one last time. I can't imagine a better wedding day, my heart full at knowing our family was all witness to my love for Santos. Maybe one day Selene will be ready to take that step with the rest of us, but we aren't in a hurry. We're happy, and that's all we care about. I've been worried Selene would feel hurt about us getting married without her, but she has been thrilled, making me realize nothing will ever get between any of us.

Selene starts snoring softly, and I place a kiss on her head. I can't even remember a time when she wasn't with us. She came in like a tornado and swept us off our feet.

She softens Blaze.

She matches mine and Santos' crazy.

She balances Zander.

And she makes our house into a home, soothing our demons a little at a time. Sure, she also encourages those demons to come out and play, but they have leashes now and we're in control of them, not the other way around.

I stare at her in the dark, not being able to help the smile on my lips. It's pretty funny how she was just someone we heard about once upon a time, hiding in the shadows. Her name whispered on people's lips in passing as she left a bloodied trail behind her.

But it's not just her they need to fear anymore, and even though we have brought down Mack and the others on our list, we know more will pop up, eventually. We will be ready to bring those fuckers down the moment they surface.

Without mercy, we will avenge those who have been silenced or can't save themselves. Those we slaughter will die knowing our name.

We are the Reaper Incarnate.

# The End

Not ready to let us go just yet? Continue reading for a snippet of our MM Bloody Vampire Novella Called, **Blood Discipline.**

## **Blurb**

### *Xavier*

Day in and day out.

Every minute like sand in an hourglass,

And each one identical to the next.

I teach the science of time,

Conveying a message of life wasted on a daily basis.

To a bunch of morons.

I didn't think my sands of time could get any worse,

Until Nicolas De Aragon wandered into my classroom.

### *Nico*

I found a class called Horology,

And when I learned it had nothing to do with sex,

I was disappointed.

The human race has bored me for millennia,

And I really thought I stumbled upon a gem.

Without a single lesson in blowjobs,

I began to feel the boredom creep back in.

Until Professor X opened his mouth to berate us all.

# Prologue

## *Nico*

The tip of my cigarette burns a bright red as I stare through the smoke with squinted eyes. Cornell University is a prestigious, ivy league institution, geared toward molding perfect upper-crust humans.

Surely the life skill of turning your nose up to the average middle class and lower is necessary to survive here in Ithaca, New York.

I'm always looking for something new to cure my boredom. Roaming the Earth for thousands of years gets boring after a while, and I'm officially bored out of my fucking mind. I'd have an impressive resume if I were to ever put one together.

I've studied every damn course in existence, I swear.

Students all walk onto campus together, moaning and groaning about their futures and lectures as if the next few years of discipline are the worst torture they can think of, their youth being ruined. Some eye me as they walk past, some with interest and some dismissing me instantly. I'm not a student, but I make it my mission to check out every university as I roll through each town, trying to find something to catch my attention.

It's been years with no luck, and I'm getting twitchy, which isn't good for anyone's health and safety.

I take another drag of my cigarette, my heightened hearing picking up on a passing conversation between two students, drawing my attention.

"Horology? That's a stupid name for studying clocks. How the hell is there an entire class on clocks?" one snorts. "You'll be bored out of your mind."

"Not just clocks. It's the science behind measuring time, idiot," his friend throws back. "It's interesting."

"You're such a nerd," he snickers as they continue to walk toward the building, their voices slowly fading. I chuckle to myself, the class name holding my attention for a few moments as I consider it. I've studied all kinds of scientific shit over the years, but never Horology.

If they hadn't mentioned the clocks and time, I would have assumed it was a class for whores. I don't need lessons on how to please or seduce someone. Even without the years of experience I've had, it's also built into me.

Vampires wouldn't exist without seduction and pleasure. It's our entire purpose, besides feeding.

I absently drop the rest of my cigarette on the ground and put it out with the toe of my shoe, walking toward the administrative building without a second thought. It will take me two seconds to get into that class, hopefully satisfying something inside me before I snap.

I push the heavy glass door open, my eyes landing on a petite woman with silky blonde hair. Last week I had someone like her for breakfast. I'm not interested in round two.

Maybe I'll indulge in a brunette next time?

Her eyes glance up at me, giving me a slow once-over as I approach the desk. "May I help you?"

I rest my elbows on the scratched, wood surface, raising an eyebrow. "I'm bored. I want to join your little Horology class."

"Oh," she frowns. "You're a few months late. Applications closed months ago and classes began at the start of last month. We have openings for next semester?"

I narrow my eyes, leaning closer to hold her gaze, dropping my voice as she becomes completely focused on me. "Put me in your Horology class. Now."

Her eyes glaze over, a relaxed smile tugging at her glossed lips. "Of course, sir. Name?" Mind control has been making my life a hell of a lot easier since I mastered it. I can get anything I want without argument. Like the fancy penthouse I don't pay a cent for. I don't understand why they want so much for it. There were nicer places in Greece for less. I didn't pay for that either, though. I stayed for free until someone decided to do a welfare check on the owner after they hadn't shown up to work for a week.

What? I'd been hungry.

"Nicolas De Aragon. You won't be needing my address or anything," I say lightly, waiting for her to type it into her computer system. "You'll organize my textbooks, yes?"

"Yes, Nicolas," she agrees quickly, waiting for more instruction.

"Actually, find me everything I'll be needing. I seem to have misplaced my pens and notebooks, too," I sigh. "Call me Nico."

"Of course."

I glance away, breaking the hold I have over her. "I'll be back tomorrow. I expect everything to be ready when I arrive."

She nods, confusion filling her eyes as I stroll out the door and head back to my car, chuckling to myself as I drive back to my penthouse.

Horology. Who even fucking named a course that?

# Acknowledgements
## C.A. Rene

Thank you to Rach for taking this journey with me and seeing it to the end. I love these characters and I love that we created them together.

To my family for putting up with my constant disappearing act and half paying attention moments, I love you.

To our betas: Jocelyn, Kristen, Lo, Jaime. You are all so awesome, thank you for all your help.

To our editor Lori, you are the bee's knees. Love you.

To all the readers who took a chance on psycho Selene and her unhinged boys, thank you!!

# Acknowledgements

## R.E. Bond

Thank you so much to everyone who gave this series a chance! We never expected our novella to turn into a series, so thank you for wanting more of Selene and her guys! Chrissy and I had so much fun writing it! I'm sad it's over, not just because I fell in love with these characters, but because writing with Chrissy has been fucking awesome.

I hardly knew Chrissy when she asked me to co-write in the Violent Tendencies anthology with her, and I possibly shit my pants a little, but I'm so glad I took the chance because I have definitely found my soulmate. Whether it's a co-write or my own writing, she is always there to support me and cheer me on. Love you Papi Peanut!!!! Xx

To everyone who shared, recommended, or promoted this series, thank you so much! We couldn't have done this without your support! Xx

Until the next time you pick up a book of mine, love you all bunches.

Rachael Xx

# About the Author

## C.A. Rene

C.A. Rene lives in Toronto, Canada with her family, where most of the year varies from chilly to frigid. Most days you'll find her wrapped in her many blankets in bed while reading or writing her next dark, twisted story.

Her stories boast of inclusivity and refusal to be conformed in any small box. Writing across genres is a hobby and drinking wine is a must… Or coffee … with a splash of Baileys.

# About the Author

## R.E. Bond

R.E. Bond is a dark romance author from Tasmania, Australia. She is obsessed with reverse harem books, especially if they have M/M! She collects paperbacks as a hobby, has read or written every day since she started high school, and constantly needs music in her daily life. She loves camping and rodeos in the summer, and not getting out of bed in the winter. Coffee and books are life, and curse words are just sentence enhancers.

# Also by R.E. Bond

## Watch Me Burn

**Pretty Lies**
**Twisted Fate**
**Beautiful Deceit**
**Ignite Me**
**Perfectly Jaded**
**Don't Fear the Reaper**
**Wrath of Rage**
**Sinner's Reign**

## From the ashes

**King of Carnage**

**Pretty Little Psycho**

## The Night Thieves

**No Honor Among Thieves**

**Thick As Thieves**

## Dreary Shadows

**Dreary Shadows Pt. 1**

**Dreary Shadows Pt. 2**

**Dreary Shadows Pt. 3**

**Dreary Shadows Pt. 4**

**Stardust**

# Also by C.A. Rene

## Whitsborough Chronicles

THROUGH THE PAIN

INTO DARKNESS

FINDING THE LIGHT

TO REDEMPTION

## Whitsborough Progenies

IVY'S VENOM

CARMELO'S MALICE

SAXON'S DISTORTION

GABRIEL'S DECEPTION

## Desecrated Duet

DESECRATED FLESH

DESECRATED ESSENCE

## Hail Mary Duet

BLUE 42

RED ZONE

## Sacrificial Lambs

SING ME A SONG

SONG OF TENEBRAE

A VERSE FOR CAELUM

A HARMONY OF PROCELLARUM

## Steel Dragons MC

DRAGON SLAYER

DRAGON STRIFE

DRAGON SCORCH

FIGHTING THE TIDE

# Stay Connected

## C.A. Rene

## R.E. Bond

### WWW.REBONDBOOKS.COM